Advise and Consent

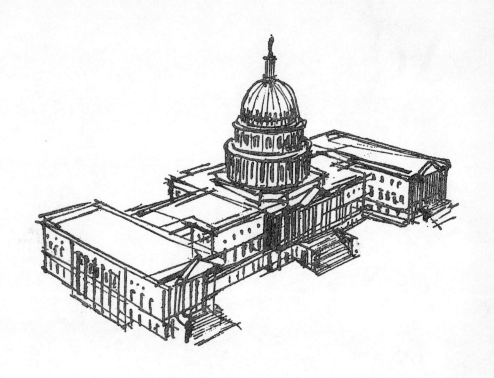

DRAWINGS BY ARTHUR SHILSTONE

Advise and Consent

BY ALLEN DRURY

DOUBLEDAY & COMPANY, INC., GARDEN CITY, NEW YORK

For
My Parents and Anne

and dedicated to
the distinguished and able gentlemen
without whose existence,
example and eccentricities
this book could have been neither
conceived nor written:
The Senate of the United States

Major Characters

Principal Members of the Senate

Robert Durham Munson of Michigan, Majority Leader of the Senate

Seabright B. Cooley of South Carolina, President Pro Tempore of the Senate

Brigham M. Anderson, senior Senator from Utah

Mabel Anderson, his wife

Pidge, his daughter

Orrin Knox, senior Senator from Illinois

Beth Knox, his wife

Hal Knox, his son

Stanley Danta of Connecticut, Majority Whip of the Senate

Crystal Danta, his daughter

Warren Strickland of Idaho, Minority Leader of the Senate

Thomas August of Minnesota, Chairman

Lafe Smith, junior Senator from Iowa

Arly Richardson, senior Senator from Arkansas

John Winthrop, senior Senator from Massachusetts

John DeWilton, senior Senator from Vermont

Harold Fry, senior Senator from West Virginia

Powell Hanson, junior Senator from North Dakota

Fred Van Ackerman, junior Senator from Wyoming

MEMBERS OF THE FOREIGN RELATIONS COMMITTEE

Principal Members of the Executive Branch

The President

Harley M. Hudson of Michigan, the Vice President

Howard Sheppard, the Secretary of State

Robert A. Leffingwell, Director of the Office of Defense Mobilization, nominee for Secretary of State

Member of the Judiciary

Mr. Justice Thomas Buckmaster Davis of the Supreme Court

Members of the Diplomatic Corps

Lord Claude Maudulayne, the British Ambassador

Lady Kitty Maudulayne, his wife

Raoul Barre, the French Ambassador
Celestine Barre, his wife
Krishna Khaleel, the Ambassador of India
Vasily Tashikov, the Ambassador of the U.S.S.R.

Others

Mrs. Phelps Harrison, "Dolly," a hostess
The Speaker of the House
The Rev. Carney Birch, Chaplain of the Senate
The Chairman of the National Committee
The President of General Motors
The President of the United Auto Workers
An Adviser to Presidents
A Cardinal
The Press

THE VICE PRESIDENT. A quorum is present. The pending business is the nomination of Robert A. Leffingwell to be Secretary of State. The question is, Will the Senate advise and consent to this nomination? The Yeas and Nays have been ordered, and the clerk will call the roll.

Congressional Record

Contents

One

Bob Munson's Book

When Bob Munson awoke in his apartment at the Sheraton-Park Hotel at seven thirty-one in the morning he had the feeling it would be a bad day. The impression was confirmed as soon as he got out of bed and brought in the Washington *Post and Times Herald*.

PRESIDENT NAMES LEFFINGWELL SECRETARY OF STATE, the headline said. What Bob Munson said, in a tired tone of voice, was, "Oh, God damn."

"As if I didn't have enough troubles," he added with growing vehemence to himself as he went in the bathroom and started getting dressed. "As if I didn't have enough to do, running his errands and steering his program. And he didn't even tell me." That was what hurt. "He didn't even tell me."

Thinking back to the White House conference of legislative leaders yesterday morning, Robert Durham Munson, who was senior United States Senator from the state of Michigan and Majority Leader of the United States Senate, couldn't remember so much as a single hint about Bob Leffingwell. In fact, hadn't there even been a denial that any appointment would be made just yet? Not a flat denial, of course, not an open denial, but an impression left, an idea conveyed, laced with smiles and ribboned with wisecracks. Something about, "We'll have to see about that, Bob. What's your hurry?" followed by a hearty reference to losing money at the races and a joke about Seab Cooley, who often did.

Seab Cooley. *That* old coot. The senior Senator from Michigan thought, and his thoughts were not loving, of the senior Senator from South Carolina. Seab Cooley was going to raise hell about Bob Leffingwell. Because of Seab Cooley the Administration was going to have a hard time. Because of Bob Leffingwell, the Administration was going to have a hard time. Why couldn't he have picked any one of ten thousand other outstanding Americans? Why the one most likely to cause trouble?

Pondering the mysterious ways of Presidents, with which he had had considerable contact in twenty-three years in the Senate, Bob Munson completed dressing and went to the telephone. In a moment the confident voice came over.

"He—*llo*, Bob! You got me out of bed, you son of a gun!"

"Mmmhmm," Bob Munson said. "That's a hell of an appointment."

"What's that?" the voice asked, losing a trace of its good cheer.

"You know what I mean. Bob Leffingwell."

"Oh, *Leff*ingwell," the voice said.

"Yes," said Bob Munson, "Leffingwell. Mr. President, why in hell——"

"Now, wait," the voice said. "Now, wait, Bob. Take it easy. You don't deny he's the best administrator we've got in government, do you?"

"No, but——"

"And you don't deny his general brains, character, and ability?"

"Oh, he's perfect," Senator Munson said. "But he isn't going to get through without a fight."

The voice dismissed that. "Oh well."

"Oh well, nothing," Bob Munson said. "You don't have to worry. You won't be up there on the Hill sweating it out."

"I'll be down here sweating it out," the voice retorted with some vigor. "It's my appointment. I'll take the rap for it."

"You take your rap when you announce the appointment. You don't have to take the day-by-day rap the way I do."

"You know, Bob," the voice said, "you sound awfully sorry for yourself. You break my heart, Senator. Please stop it."

"Just the same, I think you ought to give these things more thought."

"I've been thinking about Bob Leffingwell for that job for six months," the voice said.

"Oh, have you? It might have helped me lay a little groundwork if you'd told me about it."

"What do you need groundwork for? You know your opposition. Seab Cooley. We've had that problem before, haven't we?"

"Yes," Bob Munson said, "and it's licked us oftener than we've licked it."

The voice got its happy lilt, the one that went with the toss of the head. "I'd say honors are about even."

"Not this time. A lot of people don't like Leffingwell."

The voice chuckled. "A lot of people don't like me, either, and look where I am."

In spite of himself Bob Munson laughed.

"Damn it," he said, "you could charm the rattles off a snake. But you can't charm them off Seab Cooley."

The voice became slightly rueful.

"No," it admitted. "I found that out a long time ago. But I'm not worried as long as the matter is in your competent hands."

"Yeah," Senator Munson said.

"Now look, Bob," the voice said, getting the hard-boiled tone it acquired when the talk got down to the business of practical politics, "what's the situation up there, seriously?"

"The situation is," Bob Munson said, "that I'd never have let you make the appointment if you'd asked me first. I'd have raised hell."

The voice gave a triumphant little laugh.

"That's exactly why I didn't tell you, Bob," it said. "I knew you'd object, I knew you'd have a dozen excellent reasons why I shouldn't do it. I knew I'd better get myself committed first and ask questions afterwards. But seriously, in addition to Seab, who else have we got to worry about? What will they do on the other side of the aisle?"

A series of names and faces flashed across Bob Munson's mind—the Minority, good men and true, good friends and good enemies, and brothers in the bond.

"Well," he said, "they're split ten ways from Sunday, just like us."

"Just like us," the voice agreed with a laugh. "Then it's wide open and every man for himself, isn't it?"

"That's it," Bob Munson said. "And devil take Bob Leffingwell."

"Well, let me know what I can do from here. I want that nomination to go through."

"Oh, it will," Senator Munson said. "But it's going to take a little doing."

"I want it to go through," the voice said firmly.

"We'll see," Bob Munson said.

"Have a good time," the voice encouraged him.

"You know," Senator Munson said, "you're damned lucky to have me doing your dirty work."

"Oh, and vice versa," the voice said cheerfully. "And vice versa. Let me know how it goes."

"Right," Bob Munson said.

His next call was to Silver Spring, Maryland, just outside the District of Columbia. A maid answered. "Senator Munson to speak to Senator Strickland," he said; and after a moment, "Warren?"

The Minority Leader's voice came back with the lurking note of sardonic amusement it often held.

"Well, good morning, Bob," Warren Strickland said. "Aren't you up and about and beating the bushes a trifle early this morning?"

"You know my problem."

"Yes, I just heard it on the radio," Warren said. "How's Seab taking it?"

"I haven't talked to him yet, but it isn't hard to imagine."

"And the President is tickled pink, I suppose?"

"He seemed amused," Senator Munson said.

"You do have your burdens, Robert," said Senator Strickland. "What can I do to ease the load?"

"You can tell me how many votes there are going to be against him on your side of the aisle."

The senior Senator from Idaho thought for a moment.

"Somewhere between seventeen and twenty," he said.

Bob Munson groaned.

"That was about my estimate," he said, "but I was hoping I was wrong."

"No, I don't think so," Senator Strickland said. "That's giving him the benefit of the doubt. There could be four or five more. It's going to be tight, pal. Tight."

"Even with a President's right to have the people he wants in his Cabinet?"

"Even with that," Warren Strickland said. "You know Leffingwell. It's not a simple case."

"No," said Bob Munson with a sigh. "No, it's not. How do you stand?"

"Oh, I'm against him," Warren Strickland said cheerfully. "I'll be doing what I can to lick him. Seab and I, we'll be right in there pitching."

"I'll have to give the papers a statement charging an unprincipled, underhanded coalition against the people's interests, you know," Bob Munson said.

"Go ahead and charge, Robert. We've all survived that one before. How long do you think it will be before it comes to a vote?"

"I don't know yet," Bob Munson said. "I'll have to check with Tom August and find out when he wants to start hearings in Foreign Relations Committee. I'd guess a week for the hearings, maybe; say three weeks for the whole thing to be washed up."

"That's my guess too," Senator Strickland said. "Anything I can do, Bobby, just let me know."

"Yeah," Bob Munson said. "Go back and finish your breakfast."

"See you on the Hill," Warren Strickland said happily, and rang off.

The phone rang twice at the Westchester Apartments and was taken promptly from the hook. A girl's voice answered, and Bob Munson smiled.

"Hi, Crys," he said. "Is your dad there?"

Crystal Danta laughed.

"He's chewing the rug, Uncle Bob. Shall I stop him?"

"If you please," Bob Munson said. "Before you do, though, how are the wedding plans coming along?"

"Swimmingly," Crystal said. "Just swimmingly. I think Hal might like to back out, but after you get a man committed in the eyes of 180 million people, what can the poor sucker do?"

"He won't do anything if he knows what's good for him," Senator Munson said. "Anyway, Orrin Knox won't let him."

"Isn't *he* terrific?" Crystal said. "The brains I'm marrying into. Am I impressed!"

"The last time you were impressed was in the third grade," Bob Munson said.

Crystal Danta laughed happily. "It wasn't quite *that* early, Uncle Bob," she said. "I believe I see the distinguished and able Senator approaching, so I'd better yield. Take care of yourself."

"Why don't you come up to the Hill and have lunch with me?"

"One-ish?"

"One-ish."

"Right. I'll meet you in the Senators' dining room. Here's Dad."

"Stanley," Bob Munson said, "have you heard what I've heard?"

The calm voice of the Majority whip, never hurried, never upset, came firmly over the wire.

"I have heard, read, seen, smelled, tasted, digested, and otherwise been bludgeoned and assaulted with the news of the Leffingwell appointment, if that's what you mean. How does it look?"

"How does it look! You're the whip. You tell me."

The senior Senator from Connecticut chuckled.

"You sound as though you've already talked to our friend at the other end of Pennsylvania Avenue," he said.

"I have."

"How was he?"

"Happy," Bob Munson said. "Ecstatically happy."

"I am so glad," said Senator Danta gently. "And expecting us to do all the work as usual, I presume?"

"Who else?" Bob Munson said.

"Sometimes I wonder, Bob."

"What good does it do to wonder?" Bob Munson asked. "As long as he can get 423 electoral votes there's no point in wondering about anything."

"No," said Stanley Danta, "I suppose not. What do you want me to do?"

"The usual," Senator Munson said. "A little checking around. Suppose we do what we did on FEPC the last time—split the list right down the middle. You take Brigham Anderson to Maggie Hollingsworth and I'll take Reverdy Johnson to Al Whiteside. Give Brig special attention. I think the Power Commission business still rankles."

"I know it does," Stanley Danta said. "You didn't know this was coming, did you?"

"I did not."

"I guess nobody did," said Stanley Danta wryly, "but the man what dreamed it up."

"I doubt if he did two minutes before he sent the name up," Senator Munson said bitterly.

"Well, take it easy," Senator Danta said. "We were here before he came and we'll be here after he's gone."

"I'm not so sure," Bob Munson said dourly. "I'm not so sure. Any mind that can reduce the appointment of a United States Secretary of State to a parochial political problem of how to lick Seab Cooley has a lot of staying power . . . Well, I'll see you on the Hill. I just made a luncheon date with your daughter. Why don't you come along and maybe we can get Orrin Knox to join us. We can do a little spadework."

"On Orrin? Come, come, Bobby."

"Well, it's worth a try," said Bob Munson defensively. "I don't think Crystal will object."

"Oh, she'll love it," her father said. "She can't get over her father-in-law-to-be. She thinks he's wonderful."

"Don't we all," said Bob Munson without irony. "But difficult. Like a disgruntled mule after an all-night drunk."

"Orrin doesn't get drunk," Stanley Danta said, "but I know what you mean. His heels dig in. It makes it troublesome at times."

"Indeed it does," said Senator Munson feelingly. "If he hasn't gone off half-cocked with a statement to the press by midmorning, the way he usually does, I think it will be well worth talking to him. Half our side of the aisle is going with him whichever way he jumps, you know. Warren tells me there may be as many as twenty-five opposed on his side."

"Yes," Senator Danta said. "I'll see you at lunch."

"Good," Bob Munson said. "Keep in touch."

"That I'll do," said Stanley Danta.

The next number Senator Munson called was busy. He waited five minutes and tried again. A maid spoke softly from Arlington Ridge Road, five miles away across the Potomac on the Virginia side.

"Mr. Leffingwell's res'dence."

"Is Mr. Leffingwell there?" Bob Munson asked.

"Who's callin', please?"

"Senator Munson."

"Who?"

"Senator Munson."

"Oh." He heard a hand go over the receiver, a muffled conversation. The maid returned.

"I'm sorry Mr. Leffingwell not available. Mr. Leffingwell not here. He say he meet the press in his office at ten-thirty."

"Look," said Bob Munson sharply. "This isn't the press. This is Senator Munson. I heard Mr. Leffingwell's voice. Put him on."

"I'm sorry," the maid began again. "Mr. Leffingwell say he meet the press in his office——"

"You tell Mr. Leffingwell from me," he broke in icily, "that Senator Munson said he will certainly try to attend Mr. Leffingwell's press conference at ten-thirty."

"Yes, sir," the maid said.

"Thank you," Bob Munson said in a kindlier tone, for after all it wasn't the girl's fault; but his anger rose again after he hung up.

That was exactly the trouble with Bob Leffingwell, and it always had been. Supercilious, arrogant, holier-than-thou Righteous Rollo, trying to pretend he couldn't talk to the Majority Leader because it might prejudice his case before the Senate. One of the shrewdest politicians who ever hit Washington, wrapped in his snow-white armor above the battle—or so he managed to convince people.

Recalling the last big Leffingwell fight, when he had been appointed chairman of the Federal Power Commission in the previous Administration, Bob Munson remembered that even Brigham Anderson had gotten fed up. The matter had been in his hands as chairman of an Interstate and Foreign Commerce subcommittee, and toward the end the tensions of dealing with Sir Gawain, Purest of the Pure, had proved too much for even the mild-tempered senior Senator from Utah.

"Of course in a democratic government," he had remarked bitterly during the debate, "we deal with men as they are reputed to be, and not with men as they really are."

Bob Leffingwell as he was reputed to be, Senator Munson reflected, could mobilize at a conservative estimate seventy-five per cent of the Washington press corps on his side on any given issue. There were any number of writers, columnists, editorialists, bureau chiefs, and commentators who were ready and willing to go to bat for him at a moment's notice. Those who didn't know him well and believed in him as a matter of blind faith went along automatically; those who did know him well and had their doubts managed to convince themselves that not-so-good must be forgiven because quite-good often ensued. Certain phrases and attitudes, repeated day after day during his thirteen years in federal service— "a truly liberal mind . . . his profound and perceptive approach to the problems of government . . . America's ablest public servant, instinctively aflame with the cause of true liberty," and so on—had gradually produced a conditioning few reporters could resist. A protective screen of press adulation hung between him and large portions of the public. And since the opponents, though fewer in number, possessed circulations roughly equal in their millions to the circulations possessed by the proponents, of all men in government with the possible exception of the President himself, Robert A. Leffingwell was the most controversial.

The only difficulty with the state of mind which this induced in Mr. Leffingwell, Bob Munson thought, was that it had little application on the Hill. In that realistic place, where men are judged for what they are and reputations are ruthlessly reduced to size, it came down to a hard, practical matter of getting the votes. Bob Leffingwell could swing an amazing amount of weight by a careful and clever manipulation of public opinion, but Seab Cooley could swing almost as much by a careful and clever manipulation of the Senate. And although Leffingwell had twice slipped by his vindictive vigilance, on the third go-around Seab Cooley might be pretty well prepared.

Brought by this mental roundabout squarely up against the call he had been deliberately putting off to last, Bob Munson picked up the phone and gave the name. Two floors down and one wing over, an ancient hand picked up the receiver.

"Hello, Seab," he said hurriedly. "How are things?"

"Bob?" the thick old voice said. "Is this here Bob?"

"Yes, Seab," he said. "This is Bob."

"Well, sir," said Seabright B. Cooley. "I want to tell you. Yes, sir, I certainly do. You see where the President says he's going to appoint Mr. Robert—A.—Leffingwell? I'm against it! Yes, sir, I'm surely against it. I don't like that man. I don't like him mentally, morally, physically, or Constitutionally. No, sir!"

"Now, Seab," said Bob Munson. "Now Seab, don't fly off the handle."

"Fly off the handle!" the old voice roared. "Fly off the handle! Who's flying off the handle, Bob? Who's flying off the handle? You know what I'm going to do, Bob?"—and Senator Munson could see the crafty, crumpled old face becoming even craftier and more crumpled as the voice sank abruptly to a near-whisper—"I'm going to get that man. I'm going to get them both. Yes, sir, I surely am."

"I told the President you wouldn't like it," Bob Munson said.

"Not like it!" Seab Cooley roared. "Not like it! No, sir, I don't like it! I regard it as a direct, unmitigated, unwarranted, in-ex-cu-sable insult. He knows I don't like him! He knows I've fought him every chance I've had. He knows I despise him. Why does he do it, Bob? Why—does—he—do it?"

"As a matter of fact, Seab," said Bob Munson sharply, "I'm damned if I know why myself. But he has done it, and it's up to me to get the man confirmed and I want to know how much hell you're going to raise about it."

The old voice dropped to a sly whisper, and Senator Munson could visualize the slow and sleepy smile which crept across the pugnacious old mouth.

"I'm going to raise all the hell I can," said Seab Cooley, "and you know that's a mighty lot. You know that's a mighty lot, Bob."

"Yes, I know it's a mighty lot," Bob Munson said. "Why can't you just go easy, Seab? Why do you have to be so relentless?"

"Well, sir," Seab Cooley said, "well, sir, when that man denied something he had said to me and called me a liar to my face in open committee, I made up my mind then——"

"But, Seab," Bob Munson broke in. "That was thirteen years ago."

"I remember it like yesterday!" Seab Cooley roared. "I resent it, Bob. I resent his calling me a liar. I'm not a liar, Bob."

"He didn't call you a liar, anyway, Seab," Bob Munson began patiently. "What he said was——" The telephone erupted in his ear.

"He surely did!" Seab Cooley cried. "He surely did! Don't tell me what he said, Bob! Don't tell me. I remember every word. Every—single—word. And I'm not a liar! I'm not a liar, Bob! I resent it! I do, sir!"

"No, Seab," said Bob Munson, giving up. "You're not a liar. How many votes do you think you can round up against him?"

"One or two, Bob," said Seab Cooley softly. "One or two."

"Isn't there something I can do, Seab?"

Senator Cooley considered the offer for a moment, calculated its possible benefits, rejected it.

"No, sir, I don't rightly think so," he said. "I don't rightly think so, Bob.

I'm sorry to have to do it, Bob, but I can't help it. When any man calls me a liar, I resent it, Bob. I surely resent it."

"But, Seab——" Bob Munson protested.

"I resent it!" Seab Cooley roared, and slammed down the receiver.

"God Almighty," said Bob Munson with a sigh.

2

Like a city in dreams, the great white capital stretches along the placid river from Georgetown on the west to Anacostia on the east. It is a city of temporaries, a city of just-arriveds and only-visitings, built on the shifting sands of politics, filled with people passing through. They may stay fifty years, they may love, marry, settle down, build homes, raise families, and die beside the Potomac, but they usually feel, and frequently they will tell you, that they are just here for a little while. Someday soon they will be going home. They do go home, but it is only for visits, or for a brief span of staying-away; and once the visits or the brief spans are over ("It's so nice to get away from Washington, it's so inbred; so nice to get out in the country and find out what people are really thinking") they hurry back to their lodestone and their star, their self-hypnotized, self-mesmerized, self-enamored, self-propelling, wonderful city they cannot live away from or, once it has claimed them, live without. Washington takes them like a lover and they are lost. Some are big names, some are little, but once they succumb it makes no difference; they always return, spoiled for the Main Streets without which Washington could not live, knowing instinctively that this is the biggest Main Street of them all, the granddaddy and grandchild of Main Streets rolled into one. They come, they stay, they make their mark, writing big or little on their times, in the strange, fantastic, fascinating city that mirrors so faithfully their strange, fantastic, fascinating land in which there are few absolute wrongs or absolute rights, few all-blacks or all-whites, few dead-certain positives that won't be changed tomorrow; their wonderful, mixed-up, blundering, stumbling, hopeful land in which evil men do good things and good men do evil in a way of life and government so complex and delicately balanced that only Americans can understand it and often they are baffled.

In this bloodshot hour, when Bob Munson is assessing anew the endless problems of being Majority Leader and Washington around him is preparing with varying degrees of unenthusiasm to go to work, various things are happening to various people, all of whom sooner or later will be swept up, in ways they may not now suspect, in the political vortex created by the nomination of Robert A. Leffingwell.

At the Sheraton-Park Hotel the Senator himself completes his dressing and starts downstairs to breakfast, stopping on his way at the apartment of Victor Ennis of California to see whether he wants to share a cab later to the Hill. Vic and Hazel Ennis invite him in for coffee, which soon expands to breakfast, and before long Bob Munson has discovered that both Vic and his junior colleague, Raymond Robert Smith, a child of television out of M-G-M who progressed easily from Glamour Boy No. 3 to TV Commentator No. 1 and from there to the House and then to the Senate, will vote for Bob Leffingwell. They have already talked it over, Senator Ennis explains—Ray called from the Coast as soon as he got in last night from the Academy Awards dinner, "and of course you know Hollywood will be behind him, and Ray thinks he'd better be, and so do I." This is entirely aside from the merits of the nominee, but Bob Munson, who knows his two Californians thoroughly, is quite content to accept their votes without quibbling over motives, the first and most valuable lesson he learned in Washington and one he never forgets. Senator Ennis volunteers the information that he called Arly Richardson, just for the hell of it, and the Majority Leader asks quizzically:

"And what did that sardonic son of Arkansas have to say?"

"He said, 'I guess this will make Bobby sweat a little,'" Senator Ennis reports, and Senator Munson laughs.

"I think I'll put him down as doubtful, but probably leaning to Leffingwell," he says, and Victor Ennis nods.

"If you can ever expect Arly to stand hitched," he says, "that's where I'd hitch him."

And as Hazel comes in briskly with the firm intention of diverting the conversation from politics for at least ten minutes, they turn to her excellent meal and start talking baseball.

While the Ennises and the Majority Leader are thus occupied they do not know—although they would hardly be surprised if they did—that at this very moment, out Sixteenth Street in an apartment high in the Woodner, the Honorable Lafe W. Smith, junior Senator from the state of Iowa, is engaged in a most intimate form of activity with a young lady. This is the fourth time in eight hours that this has occurred, and Lafe Smith is getting a little tired of it. The young lady, however, a minor clerk on a House committee and new to the attractions of living in Her Nation's Capital, is still filled with a carefree enthusiasm, and so the Senator, somewhat against his better judgment, is doing his best to oblige. After the standard processes have produced the standard result, the young lady will shower, dress, and amid many tremulous farewells and mutual pledges will peek nervously out the door and then hurry away down the corridor, hoping she has not been seen. The Senator, who thinks he knows something the young lady does not know, which is that he will never see her again, will also shower, shave, examine himself critically in the mirror, be amazed as always at how his unlined and engagingly boyish visage manages to stand the gaff, and then will depart by cab for the Hill, where he is scheduled to meet two elderly constituents from Council Bluffs for breakfast. These kindly folk will be suitably impressed by his air of All-American Boy, and they will go away bemused and bedazzled by their

meeting, never dreaming that their All-American Boy, like many
another All-American Boy is one hell of a man with the old razzmatazz.

As this tender scene, so typical of life in the world's greatest democracy,
is unfolding at the Woodner, Walter F. Calloway, the junior Senator from
Utah, is also standing before the mirror in the bathroom of his house near
Chevy Chase Circle just inside the District-Maryland Line, muttering and
whistling through his teeth in his reedy voice just as he does on the floor
of the Senate. "It iss my opinion," he is saying (downstairs Emma Calloway, preparing the usual eggs and bacon, hears the faint droning buzz and
wonders tiredly what Walter is practicing this time), "that the confirmation of Mr. Leffingwell to thiss vitally important posst would seriously
endanger the welfare of the United Statess in thiss most critical time . . ."
None of Walter's colleagues would be surprised to hear this, and later
in the day, when he issues the statement to the press and takes the time
of the Senate to read it into the Congressional Record, they will shrug
and look at one another as much as to say, "What did you expect?" They
will be convinced then, prematurely as it turns out, that it is not among the
Walter Calloways of the Senate that the fate of Robert A. Leffingwell
will be decided, and they will promptly dismiss the opinion of the junior
Senator from Utah, who is likable as a person, mediocre as a legislator,
and generally ineffective as a United States Senator.

Also practicing, although unlike Walter Calloway not on his own superb
voice, is Powell Hanson, the junior Senator from North Dakota. Powell is
sitting in his study in Georgetown surrounded by Powell, Jr., twelve,
Ruth, seven, and Stanley, four, and he is practicing the violin, an instrument he played in high school and hadn't touched since until about six
months ago when Powell, Jr., began to play. Now by popular demand of
the younger generation, he has resumed it; and since he never manages
to get home from the Senate Office Building much before seven or eight,
and then only for a brief meal before either going out again socially or
locking himself up with legislation, it is only in the half hour before
breakfast that he can manage to really see the children. The violin was
Powell, Jr.'s own idea, which the Senator feels should be encouraged;
under the impetus of their joint scratching Ruth now thinks she may want
to start piano, and Stanley bangs a mean drum, purchased for his recent
birthday. Elizabeth Hanson, who gave up a promising future as a research
chemist to marry the young lawyer in whom she saw the same possibilities
he saw in himself, is quite content with the uproar created by the maestro
and his crew, even though it makes breakfast a rather catch-as-catch-can
meal. The price exacted by public office sometimes seems more to the
Hansons than they are willing to pay; but since they know perfectly well
that they will go right on paying it just as long as Powell can get re-elected,
they are doing what they can to protect their children and their home.
As long as the half hour is set aside as a special time, they feel, as long as

it comes regularly every day, it forms a small but unbreachable wall around the family; not much, but enough to do the trick.

Also living in Georgetown in houses of varying quaintness and antiquity whose price increases in direct proportion to their degree of charming inconvenience are some twenty-one Senators whom Bob Munson refers to for easy reference in his own mind as the "Georgetown Group." The quietest of these domiciles on this morning of Robert A. Leffingwell's nomination is probably that of the senior Senator from Kansas, Elizabeth Ames Adams, eating breakfast alone overlooking her tiny back garden; the noisiest is probably that of the junior Senator from Wisconsin, Kenneth Hackett, with his hurly-burly seven. Somewhere in between, in terms of decibels and general activity, come such homes as the gracious residence of John Able Winthrop of Massachusetts, the aunt-run ménage of Rowlett Clark of Alabama, and the parakeet and fish-filled home of ancient John J. McCafferty of Arkansas and his sole surviving sister, Jane.

Far from the Georgetown Group along their delightfully tree-shaded and quaintly impassable streets, certain other colleagues are also greeting the new day in their separate fashions. Twenty-two Senators are out of town, taking advantage of the lull which has come about during the debate on the pending bill to revise some of the more obscure regulations of the Federal Reserve Board. Some people, like Murfee Andrews of Kentucky, Rhett Jackson of North Carolina, Taylor Ryan of New York, and Julius Welch of Washington, can throw themselves into this sort of abstruse economic discussion with all the passion of Lafe Smith on the trail of a new conquest; but most of the Senate is quite willing to leave such topics to the experts, voting finally on the basis of the advice of whichever of the experts happens to be considered most reliable.

Consequently the experts, aware of their responsibility, are leaving no cliché unturned. All but Taylor Ryan, in fact, are already up and going busily over the economic theories they will hurl triumphantly at one another in a near-empty Senate chamber this afternoon. The small, chunky body of Murfee Andrews is already in imagination swiveling around scornfully as some scathing point sinks home in the unperturbed hide of Rhett Jackson, who in turn is contemplating the delicate sarcasms with which he will show up the ignorance of Murfee Andrews. Julius Welch, who has never gotten over having been a college president, is readying another of his typical fifty-five-minute lectures with the five little jokes and their necessary pauses to permit the conscientious titters to flutter over the classroom. Taylor Ryan, a man who likes his comfort, is still abed, but his mind is busy, and no one need think it isn't. He has no doubts whatever that he will be able to bull his way right through the flypaper arguments of Jay Welch and Murfee Andrews with the sort of "God damn it, let's be sensible about this" approach befitting a man who made his millions on the Stock Exchange and so knows exactly what he's talking about in a way these damned college professors never could.

Among the absentees, there are as many interests on this morning of the Leffingwell nomination as there are geographic locations.

In the great West, Royce Blair of Oregon, that ineffable combination of arrogance, pomposity, intelligence and good humor, is up very early preparing an address to the Portland Kiwanis Club luncheon on the topic, "The Crisis of Our Times." He has selected this title, with his small, private smile-to-himself, as being a sufficient tent to cover all the camels he wants to crowd under it; and the news of the nomination of Robert A. Leffingwell, provoking from him, as it did from the Majority Leader, a startled, "Oh, God damn!" provides the biggest camel of them all. Royce Blair does not like this nomination and Royce Blair, polishing sledge-hammer phrase after sledge-hammer phrase, is going to say so in terms that will take wings from the Portland Kiwanis Club and echo across the nation by nightfall. Already he has tried, in vain, to reach Tom August and tell him what to do, but the chairman of the Foreign Relations Committee, as usual in moments of crisis, is nowhere to be found.

Actually, by one of those happy coincidences which have characterized his turtle-like progress through three terms as Senator from Minnesota, Tom August at this moment just happens to be completely out of touch with almost everyone at a plantation in South Carolina. This is just as well from his point of view, because he knows that a lot of people are just as anxious as Royce Blair to tell him what to do and in his vague and gentle, otherworldly way, Tom August doesn't like to be told. So he is quite happy to be out of touch, and if his host should ask him to stay another day or two—there won't be a vote on the Federal Reserve bill until next week, so there's no rush—Tom August would be quite delighted to remain. The time for departure is nearing, however, and the Senator is beginning to perceive that the invitation will not be extended, and so with his usual philosophical and faintly resentful air of being buffeted unjustly by an unkind fate, he is getting ready to go back and face the music. His calm is not enhanced by the fact that for some strange reason known only to their host, his fellow house-guest and fellow voyager on the flight back to Washington is Harley M. Hudson, the Vice President of the United States. "What this country needs," Arly Richardson once remarked, "is a good five-cent Vice President," and Harley has never gotten over it. He has been fretting about the Leffingwell nomination ever since the news came over the radio, dropping all pretense that he had been informed of it in advance and professing freely a worry as deep as it is voluble. Harley always means well, but Tom August can't stand him when he gets in a fussing mood, and the prospect of six hundred miles of this is almost more than the soft-voiced and wistfully willful senior Senator from Minnesota thinks he can stand.

In Albuquerque at this moment the first Senator to give a comment to the press has been waylaid by reporters on his way to the plane for Washington. Hugh B. Root of New Mexico, chewing his cellophane-wrapped cigar and giving the whistling, wheezing, mushlike wail that passes for his particular version of the English language, is blurting something that the wire-service reporters hear as, "—mushn't shpend our time on sucsh shtupid—sucsh shtupid—mushn't—I'm opporshed—opposed—we shimply mushn't——" which they agree among them must mean, "The Senate must not spend its time and energies on such stupid nominations. I am unalterably opposed to the nomination of Robert A. Leffingwell to be Secretary of State." When they read this back to Hugh Root for confirmation he gestures with his dripping cigar, looks at them with sudden sharpness like an old badger unearthed in the sunlight, nods, waves, and clambers aboard, shaking his head indignantly. Then he takes the wings of the morning and is gone into the cold bright wind of the desert dawn.

In something of the same vein, though more quietly and cogently, the senior Senator from New Jersey, James H. La Rue, bravely fighting the palsy which always afflicts him, says in his quavering voice in St. Louis that "the Senate must and will reject the nomination of Mr. Leffingwell. Mr. Leffingwell's views on world affairs do not agree with those of many patriotic and intelligent Americans. It would not be safe to have him in the office of Secretary of State." It is not an opinion Bob Munson will like to hear about, but Jim La Rue, a good weather vane, has indicated the ground on which the nomination battle will really be fought. It is ground to which Seab Cooley will presently repair along with the rest, and it will make of the matter something much more serious than a thirteen-year grudge. It is ground which is already concerning not only the capital of the United States and its Senate but London, Paris, Moscow, and the whole wide world, which is now beginning to get the news. The fight to confirm Bob Leffingwell is not going to be a simple thing, as Jim La Rue, with customary prescience, foresees.

For seven Senators this fact is brought home with an extra impact, for they are dealing, or have just dealt, with areas where the Leffingwell nomination will create the most lively interest.

High above the Atlantic in a plane bringing home the American delegation to the Inter-Parliamentary Union meeting in Stockholm, the news coming smoothly over the radio brings much the same dismay to John DeWilton of Vermont as it has to Bob Munson and Royce Blair. Turning slowly about in the stately way which is his custom—"Johnny DeWilton," as Stanley Danta once put it, "doesn't bend, he sways"—the silver-topped human edifice which is the senior Senator from the Green Mountain State clears its throat and demands sharply of Alec Chabot, "Now, why in the hell do you suppose——"

The junior Senator from Louisiana shrugs and looks down at his impeccably kept hands and expensive suit, then darts a quick sidelong glance at Leo P. Richardson of Florida.

"Leo probably knows," he says, a trifle spitefully. "Leo knows everything about this Administration."

At this jibe Leo's round and earnest face squinches up in its usual preoccupied expression of intent concentration and he blurts out a short Anglo-Saxon word he does not customarily use. This indication of feeling is not lost on his seatmate, Marshall Seymour, the acerbic old hell raiser from Nebraska, who gives his dry chuckle and asks of nobody in particular, "Did somebody say there's going to be a hell of a fight? Because if nobody did, I will."

The junior Senator from Missouri, Henry H. Lytle, leans forward from the seat in back with the dutifully worried expression he always wears when he is considering matters affecting the fate of mankind and with one of his usual complete non sequiturs blurts out, "But what will the Israelis do?"

"Who gives a good God damn about the Israelis?" Johnny DeWilton snorts brusquely. "What will *I* do is what I'm worrying about."

In somewhat the same fashion, in the suite they are sharing at the Waldorf-Astoria in New York City, the two Senate nembers of the American delegation to the United Nations, Harold Fry of West Virginia and Clarence Wannamaker of Montana, are also getting the news. They are being apprised of it by the wife of the British Ambassador, who is in the hotel on a brief shopping visit to the city with the wife of the French Ambassador. Kitty Maudulayne and Celestine Barre, up bright and early to ready themselves for a descent on Fifth Avenue, have received the news on a daybreak telecast and Kitty has wasted no time in calling Senator Fry.

"Hal," she says excitedly as the sleepy Senator takes up the phone, "do you know what the President has done? He's appointed Bob Leffingwell Secretary of State! Aren't you excited?"

Hal Fry gives the slow and delightful grin that splits his fascinatingly ugly face, and chuckles into the receiver.

"Kitty dear," he says kindly, "I'm not excited, but just listen to Clarence."

He reaches out a foot to the other bed and kicks Senator Wannamaker, who rolls over and grunts.

"It's Kitty Maudulayne," Hal Fry says, "and she says the Old Man has appointed Bob Leffingwell Secretary of State."

There is a moment of silence, violently broken.

"*What?*" roars Clarence Wannamaker. "What the hell did you say?"

"Did you hear that, Kitty?" Hal Fry asks happily. "I told you he'd be excited."

"I do think it's thrilling," Lady Maudulayne says.

"What does Celestine think?" Senator Fry asks.

"She just smiles," Kitty replies.

"She would," says Senator Fry.

"Yes," says Lady Maudulayne.

At this point Clarence Wannamaker rears to a sitting position and begins some really scientific cursing. Hal Fry hangs up with best wishes to Lord

Maudulayne and Raoul Barre, after briefly considering and then rejecting as useless the idea of probing to find out what those two astute and self-possessed allies think about the Leffingwell nomination. They will all be at the party at Dolly's in Rock Creek Park tonight, he reflects, and perhaps there will be some inkling there. More than one crisis has been solved at Vagaries, that great white house amid the dark green trees, and possibly this one will be too, although he rather doubts it. He remembers as he pushes away the phone and lapses back for another half hour's sleep that the Indian Ambassador, Krishna Khaleel, will be there too. Much more to the point than Henry Lytle with his querulous wonder about "What will the Israelis do?" the senior Senator from West Virginia wonders what "K.K." and the Asians will do. Given the state of the world, the answer to that may really be of some consequence.

Also in the fabled city with the topless towers as it roars awake with an animal vigor Washington will never know are its senior Senator, Irving Steinman, quietly breakfasting in his apartment on East Eighty-second Street, and the junior Senator from Wyoming, Fred Van Ackerman, sleeping peacefully at the Roosevelt in the rosy afterglow of a mammoth rally of the Committee on Making Further Offers for a Russian Truce (COMFORT) in Madison Square Garden.

Farther north, in Franconia, the news comes to Courtney Robinson, symbol of that smaller but bothersome Senate group the Majority Leader privately classifies as Problems, as he stands before the mirror in the downstairs hall knotting his string tie around his high, old-fashioned collar. "Courtney isn't much," Blair Sykes of Texas is fond of pointing out about the senior Senator from New Hampshire, "but by God, he sure does look like a Senator!" This fact, Courtney's major contribution to his times, is the result of care, not accident; and now as he knots the tie just so, settles the collar just so, puts on the long gray swallow-tailed coat, shrugs into the sealskin overcoat with the velvet lapels, takes the big outsize hat and cane from the table, gives a pat to the dirty-yellow-gray locks at the nape of his neck, and carefully puts a hothouse rose in his buttonhole, there is no doubt that the day is going to see one more smashing production of Courtney Robinson, U.S.S. Across his mind there passes a momentary genuine annoyance with the President for having created such a mess as naming Bob Leffingwell to State is almost certainly going to be, but the thought is presently dismissed as he gives himself a last approving inspection and prepares to go in town for a little politickin'. He's speakin' to Rotary at noon, and mebbe they'll want to know what he thinks of the Leffin'well nomination. Doesn't think much of it, does Courtney Robinson; doesn't think much, period.

There are those who do, however, and in the Washington suburb of Spring Valley, in the comfortable home where the telephone has been ringing incessantly for the past half hour, the senior Senator from Illinois lifts the receiver once more and prepares to give the same answer he has already given to four other newsmen:

"I haven't reached a final decision on this matter and don't expect to until all the facts are in. At the moment, however, I am inclined to oppose the nomination."

But it is not another reporter who is calling Orrin Knox this time, it is the senior Senator from Utah. Brigham Anderson's voice, courteous and kind as always, is troubled and concerned, and Senator Knox can visualize exactly the worried look on his handsome young face.

"Orrin," Brig says in his direct way, "what do you plan to do about Bob Leffingwell?"

"I think I'll oppose him," says Orrin Knox, equally direct, his gray eyes getting their stubborn look and his gray head its argumentative angle. "How about you?"

"I don't know," Brigham Anderson replies, and there is real doubt in his voice. "I just don't know. In some ways I can be for him, but in other ways—well, you know the man."

"Yes," says Orrin Knox, and a tart asperity enters his tone. "I know the man, and I don't like him."

"You and Seab," Brigham Anderson says with a laugh.

"I trust my reasons are more fundamental than that," Orrin replies flatly. "I'm not at all sure he could be as firm as he ought to be in that job. I'm not sure he *wants* to be as firm as he ought to be—not that I'm prepared to say that to everybody yet, but you know what I mean."

"I do," Senator Anderson says. "And there's more to it, as far as I'm concerned. I've had reason to deal with him pretty closely on the Power Commission, you know, and I've never been convinced he's the great public servant the press says he is. I've got plenty of doubts."

"Of course you know what the press is going to do to us if we oppose him," Orrin Knox says.

"I guess we can stand it," Brigham Anderson says calmly, "if we know we're right."

"Which we're not entirely sure we are, at this moment," the Senator from Illinois retorts.

The Senator from Utah chuckles.

"I'll see you on the Hill," he says. "I wonder what Tom August is thinking right now?"

Orrin Knox snorts.

"Does he think?" he asks. "Good-by, Brig."

"Good-by, Orrin," Brigham Anderson says, and hangs up with a laugh, noting as he does so that the paper boy, a good-looking kid of fifteen, is only just now delivering the *Post* out front. For a moment the Senator considers a reprimand for this increasing tardiness; but the dark head turns suddenly toward the window, there is a wave and a smile, and Brig forgets the reprimand as he watches the straight back ride on down the

block. At the corner the head turns again, there is a final smile and wave
and the boy disappears. Brig starts out to get the paper just as Mabel
Anderson comes from the kitchen on her way to do the same; they meet
at the door and in the small domestic laughter of their near-collision
the ghost of a wartime summer goes back to rest, until the next time, in the
Senator's heart.

As of that moment similar telephone conversations on the nomination
are passing between many other friends in the Senate, and from none of
them, Bob Munson would be interested to know, is anything very constructive coming. Right now it is not entirely clear, even to those most
astute in judging such things, just how far the fight over Bob Leffingwell
is going to extend.

The President; the Senate; some labor and business leaders; the Barres
and the Maudulaynes, K.K. and the Indians, Vasily Tashikov in his closely
guarded embassy on Sixteenth Street, and all their respective governments; the chairman of the National Committee; the Speaker of the House;
that lively, cocktail-partying Associate Justice of the Supreme Court,
Thomas Buckmaster Davis; Dolly Harrison with her incessant parties at
Vagaries in Rock Creek Park; even a lonely young man nobody but one in
the Senate has ever heard of, far away in the Midwest—all will be swept
up and drawn into the endless ramifications of the nomination of Robert
A. Leffingwell to be Secretary of State.

But mostly, as they well know, it will be the ninety-nine men and one
woman who compose the United States Senate who will bear the burden;
and to each of them on this morning when a Presidential decision becomes
a world reality the news has come, is coming, or soon will come, with
exactly the same impact. For a brief moment amid the hubbub of morning
they are losing their identities to become imperceptibly, inexorably, for a
subtle second, institutions instead of people: the Senators of the United
States, each with a vote that will be recorded, when the day arrives, to
decide the fate of Robert A. Leffingwell and through him, to whatever
degree his activities may affect it, the destiny of their land and of the
world.

The split-second feeling of overwhelming responsibility strikes them
all, then is instantly superseded by thoughts and speculation about "the
situation"—how many votes Bob Leffingwell has, how many Seab Cooley
can muster, what Orrin Knox thinks, what Bob Munson is planning, who
will do what and why, all the web of interlocking interests and desires
and ambitions and arrangements that always lies behind the simple,
ultimate, final statement, "The Senate voted today——"

Underneath, the feeling of responsibility is still there. It will come back
overwhelmingly for them all on the afternoon or evening some weeks
hence—will it be two, or four, or twelve, or twenty? None knows; all
speculate—when a hush falls on the crowded chamber and the Chair

announces that the time has come for the Senate to decide whether it will advise and consent to the nomination of Robert A. Leffingwell.

It is the events between now and then, the bargains to be struck, the deals to be made, the jockeying for power and the maneuvering for position, which occupy them now. From Lafe Smith, staring wryly at his naked body in a mirror at the Woodner, to Hugh B. Root, airborne above the lonely plains and folded hills of Jim Bridger and the mountain men, each is aware that the Senate is about to engage in one of the battles of a lifetime; and each is wondering what it will mean for him in terms of power, reputation, advantage, political fortune, national responsibility, and integrity of soul.

3

"Oh, damn," Victor Ennis said as the elevator deposited them in the lobby of the Sheraton-Park. "There's Seab. Shall we look the other way?"

"No," said Bob Munson, "maybe he will." But of course he didn't, and they met at the door.

"Good morning, Senator," Seab said slowly to Victor Ennis. "Good morning to you, too, Bob."

"Good morning, Seab," Senator Munson said gravely. "I trust you breakfasted well."

"Poorly, Bob," Senator Cooley said. "Poorly. I kept seeing that man. I kept thinking about them both. I kept thinking, Bob. It made me mad."

"It's got us all a little concerned, Seab," Victor Ennis said heartily, "but I imagine we'll get it all worked out in time."

"I suppose you're for him," the Senator from South Carolina cried with sudden vehemence, stopping dead in his tracks in front of two bellboys and a wide-eyed young couple from Montana who were trying to get in. "I suppose you're all for him and nobody but poor old an-ti-quated Seabright B. Cooley is against him. I suppose that's how it is, Senators. I suppose I'll have to fight alone."

"I dare say it will be another of your magnificent, lonely battles, Seab," Bob Munson broke in dryly. "How about sharing a cab to the Hill?"

For a second the wizened old face glared at him without expression; then it changed abruptly and a little twinkle came into the heavy-lidded eyes.

"Why, that's the kindest thing you've said to me all morning, Bob," Seab Cooley said softly. "You're a kind fellow, Bob. I like you. One of God's noblemen, I always say when people ask me. That's what I say about Senator Munson, Bob."

"I tell them you're one of God's most amazing creations, too, Seab," Senator Munson said. "I tell them He really outdid Himself when He made you. I tell them we may not see your like again."

"I'll bet you say, 'Thank God for that, too,' Bob," Seab Cooley said.

"I'll bet you'll all be glad when poor old Seab Cooley is dead and you can get on that funeral train to South Carolina and stand by his grave and say, 'Thank God he's gone.' That's what I'll bet, Bob!"

"These people are trying to get by, Seab," Bob Munson said calmly. "Shall we let them?"

"That's all you think about, getting rid of me!" Senator Cooley cried bitterly. "Poor old Seab Cooley, seventy-five if he's a day, and they're all ganging up on me, ma'am. They're all ganging up on me! Now you pass right on through, and excuse me for blocking your way, ma'am. When you get home, you tell your folks you saw Senator Cooley of South Carolina and his enemies trying to lay him low. But you tell them it didn't work, ma'am. You tell them Senator Cooley is still here battling for the Republic. Yes, ma'am!"

"For *heaven's* sake, Seab," Bob Munson exclaimed, leaving Christ out of it, because the young lady from Montana was getting wide-eyed to the point of explosion, "will you come on and get in the cab?"

"Here's one now," Victor Ennis observed brightly. "Just in time."

"Just in time for what?" Senator Cooley asked ominously. "And take your hand off my arm, Bob. I'm not an old man, Bob. I can manage. You don't have to help me. I can manage very well, Bob. I don't have to be helped. I'm not senile, Bob, though you're all trying to drive me there as fast as you can."

"No, Seab," Bob Munson agreed patiently. "You're not senile, and I imagine you'll drive all of us crazy before we drive you anywhere. Except to the Capitol." He added to the driver, "Old Senate Office Building, if you will, please."

"Yes, sir," the driver said, and with Senator Ennis on one side, Senator Munson on the other, and Senator Cooley squeezed in unyieldingly in the middle, they set off on their fifteen-minute ride to the Hill, while behind them the bellboys smiled and the young couple from Montana told each other excitedly that their Washington visit had certainly begun with a bang.

Sitting on his side of the cab as it passed down the curving drive, made the short turn on Connecticut Avenue, and then angled right and plunged down past the Shoreham into Rock Creek Park, Bob Munson reminded himself as he had often before that he needn't have been Majority Leader and let himself in for all this if he hadn't wanted to. The paths of ambition lead to strange places sometimes, but in his case he could hardly claim that he hadn't known where they would take him. Grandfather Durham had been in the Senate from Massachusetts, and that was enough to decide *that*. A relatively undistinguished man who, to be frank about it, had accomplished very little in three terms, he had nonetheless imposed from his grave an obligation upon his likeliest male descendant to set his sights for Capitol Hill. By general family agreement, this meant the only son of the old man's only daughter; and after graduating from the

University of Michigan in the state where his parents had moved shortly before the First World War, he had gone on to Harvard Law School and then had come home dutifully to apply himself to the task of winning a seat in the United States Senate.

At the start, this did not appear to be a simple project, but in the first of the events which were ultimately to give him a certain sense of personal destiny—a modest one, which he never tried to push too far, but satisfactory enough, since it got him where he wanted to go nine times out of ten—he made a fortuitous connection with one of the leading law firms in Detroit and soon after discovered to his pleased surprise that he had been gifted with the ability to make quite a speech. Shortly after this revelation he happened quite by chance to be invited to address a group of auto workers, and since Grandfather Durham in any event was not a political fool and had transmitted some savvy down the line, his descendant perceived from their response and an astute study of changing economic conditions that this might be a sound foundation for the goal he hoped to achieve in Washington. He thus became one of the first to ally himself with the rising political power of labor, and because he was Bob Munson and not some other, he managed to do so without making himself its slave as well. Looking back, he was not always entirely sure how he had managed to do this and still retain his independence, and there were still occasions now and again when it was sometimes nip and tuck even at this late date. But on the whole he had managed to work out a very satisfactory accommodation which had seen him through his only failure, a close but unsuccessful race for the governorship at the age of thirty-four, two successful campaigns for the House, and four consecutive terms in the Senate. Along the way on his walk in the shadow of Grandfather Durham he had done all the things that people do in America to reach the Congress: made the speeches, shaken the hands, joined the clubs, formed the friendships, established the loyalties, created the ever-widening web of favor and counterfavor which forms the basis of so many lives that ultimately find their way into the close-packed pages of the Congressional Directory.

Also he had married well, to the daughter of one of the larger auto manufacturers, an interesting match from a political standpoint which was accepted pleasantly on all sides and which, because he was Bob Munson and somebody quite genuinely and universally liked, gave him a foot in each camp which neither held against him. There had been no children, and in the final ten years before her death, from cancer, a tragic event now six years in the past, they had found increasingly little to talk about; but there was no doubt that May had been a help to him all along the way. In the early days she had been his faithful companion at meetings, rallies, county fairs, and union conventions; after he won election to the Congress, she had turned her energies to the task of winning a steadily increasing standing in the life of the capital. She had loved Washington, as most people do who spend any time there, and aside from her activities in the Senate Ladies Club, to whose presidency she had aspired and presently risen, she had given any number of cocktail parties, dinners, and "conversations" at the big, old-fashioned place they used to own in Cleveland Park in Northwest Washington before her death. A "conversation" at the Munsons, usually held on a Sunday afternoon, drew its participants from politics, government, diplomacy, and the press with an astute and well-managed abandon that always guaranteed a good time; two Presidents and three Chief Justices had occasionally dropped in, and all in all the whole business had been a great success and a great assistance to the Senator in his gradual evolution from prominence, which so many have, to power, which is achieved by so few.

If over the years of this process he and his wife had become friendly strangers who happened to be devoted to the same ends, that was a condition not without precedent in the world in which they moved. Inexorably, perhaps inevitably, May had become like so many wives of famous men in Washington—not exactly loved by her husband, not exactly disliked, not exactly criticized, not exactly tolerated, but just someone who had been married a long, long time ago when the world was young and who was inextricably part of the show now with no way to get around it. Many a man in the capital showed just that air of rather tired sufferance Bob Munson developed in their closing years together; and for her part, May made the best of it, continuing her extensive visits to the state, her work on his campaigns, her entertaining in Washington, her bright, brisk way of going about things. She had loved him rather more than he had her, he suspected, even in the days when they were in love, and he still felt guilty at times that this had been so; but life is the way it is, and he had done his best for her. If she had perceived the absence of the added ingredient of genuine caring whose presence would have made her really happy, that was sad but not uncommon, and in material comforts and the position which went with being the wife of a United States Senator and one of the best of them, she had not been neglected. It was not a perfect bargain, but it held its own with the best that most people managed, and indeed there were many who never came near it; so the Senator did not feel too badly. He had never been unfaithful to her, and he knew she knew it, and since that was something that seemed to mean so much to women, maybe it had made up for the rest of it. He hoped so, anyway.

Thinking of his career in the Senate as the cab moved out of the park and shot along the drive toward Constitution Avenue beside the steel-bright morning river, he reflected with gratitude that it had gone steadily forward with a felicity Grandfather Durham had never matched. Because he was essentially a sunny person, whose life had been free of any insurmountable stresses or strains, he won friends quickly, easily, and for life, and in a body where so much depends upon personal likes and dislikes and the blunt appraisal of character, he soon became marked for bigger and better things. A single half-hour conversation with the chairman of the party conference had won him a seat on Foreign Relations over the heads of the ten others who entered the Senate the same year he did, and over some twenty other more senior heads as well; yet because he was so good-natured and such a work horse, so unaffectedly friendly and equable, the assignment was accepted with very little grumbling and the rancor was soon forgotten. A couple of years later the same good fortune took him off his second committee, Interstate and Foreign Commerce, and put him on Appropriations, thus giving him membership on the two most powerful committees in the Senate. In that same session the party whip died, and because Bob Munson had been dutiful in his attendance in the chamber, had cheerfully done all the little party errands asked of him, and also because his combination of good nature, diligence, and blustering, quick-dying, innocent temper had made him one of the two or three best-liked men in the Senate, he was given the job by a sort of majority concurrence that speedily obliterated the ambitions of one or two others who considered themselves better fitted. The Senate did not, and from that time he could date the dislike of Arly Richardson, who had really wanted the post. Nine years later, when the Majority Leadership finally fell open, Arly had made a definite campaign for it and Bob Munson had been faced with the necessity of beating him again. The Majority at that time had numbered fifty; Arly got his own vote and five others. The five others had forgiven and forgotten, but not Arly; in his sarcastic way, he wasn't the forgiving type.

With the Majority Leadership, there came to Senator Munson not only a much more direct responsibility for running the Senate, but in a curious sense which he never expressed to anyone except May, because it would have sounded precious and pretentious, an almost fatherly sense of responsibility for the country. Now there was somewhere at the back of his mind not only a constant mental map of his own enormous Michigan flung up northward over its carpet of woods and lakes, but of the whole United States as well; and soon his steadily increasing political travels and speaking engagements, taking him as they did back and forth into every section of the land, formed in his mind an underlay of vivid scraps and pieces of America: the soft velvet light of the desert at dusk, the primeval stretches of the Mississippi from La Crosse to St. Paul, a winding road through New England hills, the Shenandoah Valley in spring, the high cold plains of the Dakotas and Montana, the dreary swamps of the Carolinas along U.S. 301, the Columbia River Gorge, booming, bustling Florida, San Francisco, daughter of conquerors gleaming on her glittering hills above the beautiful Bay, New York seen against a cloud-filled sunset looking down the river from George Washington Bridge, fat Pennsylvania with her lush, well-kept farms, the flat cornlands of Kansas, Texas with an oil well in one hand and a highball in the other, and the rest. At any hour of day or night, brought by whatever impulse brings such things, there would flash into his perception some instantaneous sense of being in some certain place in America, the view, the surroundings, the feel of it; and with it would always come, renewed again and again to infinity, the same conviction that he was somehow personally responsible for the well-being of it all, that some overriding trust and obligation had been placed upon him to see that it was kept safe and its people protected.

And so, of course, there had been. There were many in the Senate who had that feeling, but upon the Majority Leader, if he was a good one, it rested more heavily than most. Especially was this so in a troubled time in which the great promise was being challenged and the great Republic which embodied it was being desperately threatened. In his lifetime he had seen America rise and rise and rise, some sort of golden legend to her own people, some sort of impossible fantasy to others to be hated or loved according to their own cupidity, envy, and greed, or lack of it; rise and rise and rise and rise—and then, in the sudden burst of Soviet science in the later fifties, the golden legend crumbled, overnight the fall began, the heart went out of it, a too complacent and uncaring people awoke to find themselves naked with the winds of the world howling around their ears, the impossible merry-go-round slowed down. Now the reaction was on, in a time of worry and confusion and uncertainty. Men walked the tight rope between brittle confidence and sudden fear, never knowing when reality would suddenly intrude and laughter fade and the dark abyss yawn open and remind them it was waiting there for a still unhumbled land.

He could not say, looking back, exactly where the blame was to be placed; except that he knew, as he had told an audience in San Francisco only last week, that "it lies on all of us." A universal guilt enshrouded the middle years of the twentieth century in America; and it attached to all who participated in those times. It attached to the fatuous, empty-headed liberals who had made it so easy for the Russians by yielding them so much; it attached to the embittered conservatives who had closed the doors on human love and frozen out all possibility of communication between peoples. It rested on the military, who had been too jealous of one another and too slow, and on the scientists, who had been too self-righteous and irresponsible and smug about shifting the implications of what they did onto someone else, and on the press, which had been too lazy and too compliant in the face of evils foreign and domestic, and on the politicians, who had been too self-interested and not true enough to the destiny of the land they had in keeping, and not least upon the ordinary citizen and his wife, who somehow didn't give quite enough of a damn about their country in spite of all their self-congratulatory airs about how patriotic they were. Nobody could stand forth now in America and say, "I am guiltless. I had no part in this. I did not help bring America down from her bright pinnacle." For that would be to deny that one had lived through those years, and only babies and little children could say that.

So now there was a time of uneasiness when everyone told everyone else dutifully that, "It is not our purpose to indulge in recriminations about the past," and tried to live up to it; and when all thinking men fretted and worried desperately about "how to catch up," and "how to get ahead"; and also, in the small hours of the night's cold terror, about what it would be like if America *couldn't* catch up, if history should have decided once and for all that America should never again be permitted to get ahead.

And already because of this, the smooth and supple voices of rationalization were beginning to be heard, the blandly clever voices of adjustment and accommodation and don't-make-a-federal-case-of-it and don't-take-it-too-hard and after-all-what-will-it-matter-in-a-hundred-years and maybe it-wouldn't-really-be-so-bad and I-guess-we-could-live-with-them-if-we-had-to. And for America it was a time of nip and tuck, and a darkening passageway with only God's good grace, if He cared to confer it again upon a people who sometimes didn't seem to deserve it any more, to see the country safely through.

God's good grace, Bob Munson told himself grimly, and a few good men. The President wasn't giving in, and he wasn't giving in, and there were quite a few others all through the country who weren't giving in; the majority, in fact, he believed. But people were only human, after all, and they were scared; and confronted with the possibility of a war with all the horrors it could now entail, they were not as resolute or as courageous as they once had been when they weren't so aware of what the consequences of resolution and courage could be. They liked to tell themselves they were brave, but they weren't; there was just enough of a feeling, just enough, to provide a very dangerous potential for an appeasement that would be fatal. Faced with an open challenge, an open attack, they would, if they had the time, rouse and fight back as they always had, no matter what the price, for America; but make the attack sufficiently intellectual, make the threat sufficiently subtle, give them time to think, let them mull it over and contemplate what would happen if they didn't go along, carry it to the conference table if you liked and be sure you gave them a way to save face as they retreated, and he would not, at this moment, vouch for what her people would allow to be done to America.

Through a combination of lapses, stupidities, overidealism, and misjudgments, each at the time seemingly sound and justified, each in its moment capable of a rationale that had brought a majority to approve it, the United States had gotten herself into a position vis-à-vis the Russians in which the issue was more and more rapidly narrowing down to a choice between fight and die now or compromise and die later. And out of that fearful peril only the most iron-willed and nobly dedicated and supremely unafraid men could lead the nation.

That was why so much was involved in the nomination of Robert A.

Leffingwell, and that was why it would, he knew, be a grim business in which men played for keeps before it was through. The fate of the Republic, in this instance, did indeed in large measure depend on what the Senate did; particularly since, for all his verve and vigor, the President of late had not looked entirely well to Bob Munson's practiced eye. He had hung back for a moment this last time as they left the oval office, and for a second had looked hard at the man behind the desk. The President had caught him at it, too; for a split second his face changed and a strange expression came over it. Almost as though he had wanted to tell him something, Bob Munson thought; something that he was afraid of, and thought might be mortal. It had shocked him, for he had never seen the President afraid of anything. Maybe he would tell him about it someday, he reflected; although, being a strange and unknowable man as all Presidents are strange and unknowable, he also might not. At any rate, a little cautionary thought had taken up its residence in the Majority Leader's mind; a certain silent, unexpressed factor in his thinking and planning. He knew it would not go away until the second term ended, or until the Lord resolved it, whichever it was to be.

This, which as far as he knew only he as yet suspected, lent an even greater gravity to the Leffingwell nomination. If the dark eventuality occurred and Harley Hudson succeeded to office, he would undoubtedly in his frantic insecurity keep Bob Leffingwell on, and Bob Leffingwell, Bob Munson knew, was strong enough to be Secretary of State and un-sworn President too. And thereby, if the President had misjudged him and the Senate confirmed the misjudgment, could hang quite a story; the sort of sad story that people sit upon the ground and tell, of great hopes crushed and great states lost forever.

Therefore there devolved upon him and upon his brethren on the Hill the responsibility of being absolutely sure about this man before they approved him. This meant that Seab, who was simply an obstruction under most circumstances, would be an obstruction pulling powerful support behind him in this case; and that he, who would push through a nomination in most cases as a matter of routine party loyalty, must in this instance be positive in his heart that he was doing the thing that should be done. It could not be decided lightly, and it would not be decided lightly. Too much hung upon it.

To the task, he reflected with some satisfaction as the grimness of his mood began to slacken, he brought a good equipment. In his deceptively amiable and easygoing way he was as strong a man as his times demanded. It had taken him some years to become so, and he could remember many times when through inexperience or uncertainty he had gone too far in one direction or the other, giving in too easily to someone when he should have stood firm or being too harsh with someone when he should have been gentle. But in time—and it took time, and much study of men's hearts and minds to be a good leader of the United States Senate—he had learned; and now he knew pretty well when to be soft, pretty well when to be tough, and pretty well when to refrain from those exaggerations of opinion and attitude which had too often destroyed bright careers in Washington. Not for him the endless, embittered, self-righteous twistings of a Paul Hendershot of Indiana, or the blind, unmoving, uncreative, unhappy conservatism of an Eldon P. Boyle of Wyoming. He stood where he stood, and he knew why he stood there; and thus his approach to the Leffingwell nomination would be what the circumstances made necessary for the good of the land. He was a mature man at fifty-seven, in a way that few men achieve maturity. It had taken him a while, and a good bit of living to get there, but he was unshakeable as a rock now, and everybody knew it.

Even Seab, he thought with amusement as the cab swung past the Washington Monument and the Bureau of Engraving, dashed across Fourteenth Street, and darted under the bridges over Independence Avenue that linked the north and south Agriculture Department buildings. Even Seab, staring straight ahead like a very formidable lump on a very formidable log.

"Isn't that so, Seab?" Bob Munson asked out loud. Seab grunted.

"I don't rightly know what you have in mind, Bob," he said slowly, "but I expect it's designed to make me look just a leetle bit ridiculous. Isn't what so, Bob?"

"Don't you know I'm unshakeable as a rock?" Bob Munson said.

"Who called you that, Bob?" Seab asked. "*Time* magazine? You ought to see what they call me, Bob. Unshakeable, sometimes, but a lot of other things, too. Not one of them as polite as 'rock,' Bob. Not one."

"I was just thinking it about myself, Seab," Senator Munson said. "I was sure you'd agree."

"If you're a rock, Bob," Senator Cooley said blandly, "you've met a sledge hammer. You know that, Bob, don't you?"

"Yes, Seab," said Bob Munson with a grin, "I know that."

"Yes, sir," Seab said; and after a moment, very softly to himself, "Yes, sir."

But withstanding sledge hammers, Bob Munson reflected as the cab passed the Botanical Gardens, made its lunge up the Hill past the New House Office Building, turned left, and started around Capitol Plaza toward the Senate office buildings, was what they paid him for. And he wouldn't want it any other way.

At the side entrance to the Old Senate Office Building on Delaware Avenue the cab stopped and its passengers got out. Senator Ennis, who, far from Russians and other matters he thought about as little as possible, had been lost throughout the journey in a tantalizing vision of the Jonathan Club beach at Santa Monica as it would be in another couple of months, came to with a start and reached for his purse. Senator Munson did the same. Senator Cooley forestalled them both.

"I'll get it, Senators," he said grandly, with his usual ironic little twinkle. "I come from a small state, you know, not like you big fellows who always use up all your expense funds. You know us in South Carolina, Bob; all we ever have to spend our money on is corn likker and lynching bees. You Yankees know that, Bob. I'll get it."

"Thank you, Seab," Bob Munson said; and, "Thank you, Seab," Victor Ennis echoed respectfully.

"My pleasure, Bob," Senator Cooley said graciously; "my pleasure, Senator." Then he grinned suddenly and waved toward the stone expanses of the office building before them.

"On your mark, get ready, get set, go, Bob," he said. "On your mark, get ready, get set, go."

4

On your mark, get ready, get set, go, was exactly it, Bob Munson reflected as he approached the familiar door with its picture of Lake Michigan and "Mr. Munson—Come In" at the end of the corridor on the second floor. He had soon found that his job, in which there were infinite problems and many rewards, could reasonably well be summed up in just some such jibe as Seab had uttered when they left the cab. When he became Majority Leader his day automatically expanded to sixteen, eighteen hours, the Capitol, which had dominated his thoughts for twelve years, became their absolute center, and he swiftly learned that his world began and ended in ninety-nine minds whose endless surprises he could never entirely anticipate. No sooner had he got somebody pegged in one place than he turned up somewhere else; his plans for steering legislation had to be constantly revised to accommodate the human material with which he had to work. Even such solid citizens as Stuart Schoenfeldt and Royce Blair were quite capable of jumping the reservation when issues got too close to home, and when it came to someone of the caliber of Courtney Robinson, for instance, all bets were off. Many a time he had discussed an issue earnestly with Courtney, been assured with the greatest sincerity that he was true-blue and steadfast, and then found as the roll call neared that the elocutions rapidly became elaborate to the point of obfuscation. Finally with great pain and reluctance he would be assured that there were "just too many reasons, just too many reasons," for the vote to be cast as he wished. Sometimes he did not even receive this courtesy, and it was only when the reading clerk called the names that he knew what would happen. Then Courtney would smile and wave graciously across the chamber, and later come over to apologize heartily for being a bad boy.

Fortunately for the orderly progress of the American government, this situation did not arise every time or with everybody. There was a bedrock he could count on, and he presently came to base his strategy upon it. He felt he had, on almost every issue, a bloc of approximately thirty sure votes; and to them it was usually not too difficult to add the nineteen or twenty more he needed for victory. Sometimes he hardly bothered to check, for many things went through more or less automatically. But on the big issues, such as defense, foreign aid, public power, the major appropriations, the major nominations, he always went automatically through the list, questioning, cajoling, sounding out, sometimes promising, sometimes warning, sometimes putting it on a basis he hated but one which occasionally proved effective when nothing else did—"Just as a favor to me." This was Seab's favorite gambit, and they sometimes met in battle array over the prostrate form of some poor wee, sleek, timorous, cowerin' beastie like Nelson Lloyd of Illinois or Henry Lytle of Missouri, desperately anxious to be friends with everybody and not offend either the powerful Majority Leader or his almost equally powerful opponent. Then it all had its humorous moments.

In the main, however, it was a serious business for the most part, and to a considerable degree a labor of love that had its own compensating satisfactions. He sometimes wondered, when he was arguing earnestly with someone as vapid as Walter Calloway of Utah or bargaining with someone as crafty as George Hines of Oregon, whether those who began it all had foreseen the down-to-earth applications of their monumental idea. Sometimes he would come out of the chamber and walk past the statue of Benjamin Franklin, who stood just off the floor at the foot of the stairs to the gallery, fingering his chin with a quizzical smile, and wonder if old Ben and the rest of them had ever had any idea, that steamy summer in Philadelphia, that their brain child would develop into as practical and bedrock a human process as it had. But then he would remember some of their discussions and decide that he probably knew why Ben was smiling. Dealing with prickly John Adams was probably no different from reasoning with prickly Orrin Knox, and certainly Arly Richardson in a pet could be no more difficult than Edmund Randolph.

Thus comforted by his wry imaginings of the past, he would reflect that this, in essence, was the American government: an ever-shifting, ever-changing, ever-new and ever-the-same bargaining between men's ideals and their ambitions; a very down-to-earth bargaining, in most cases, and yet a bargaining in which the ambitions, in ways that often seemed surprising and frequently were quite inadvertent, more often than not wound up serving the purposes of the ideals.

In this eternal bargaining there were five principal middlemen: the President of the United States, the Majority and Minority Leaders of the Senate, the Speaker of the House, and the House Minority Leader. Through these five changing-houses flowed the passions, the prejudices, and the purposes of the land, and on their particular skills in leading men depended that delicate balancing of dream and desire which moved the nation forward. At a time such as the present when all five were for all practical purposes equally adept, this made for a good deal of genuine progress in many matters. There had been times, as under the Roosevelts or Eisenhower, when one of the middlemen had either been strong beyond proportion or weak beyond proportion, when the balance was knocked out of kilter and the government either raced forward at a speed too fast to be comfortable or stalled at dead center and drifted helplessly through desperate crises without purpose, plan, or conviction at the heart of it. This was a penalty, and one that Ben and Company perhaps had not foreseen; but it was a penalty inseparable from freedom, and so far, despite great risks and perils, the country had survived them all. Whether it would under present circumstances was of course the question; and on that, it was too early to tell. All we can do, he told himself as he unlocked the door giving into his private office, took off his coat and hat, and prepared to buzz Mary to bring him the mail and start the day, is the best we can; aware that he was not alone in this, and that already, on the Hill, around town, and out in the country, others were already at work on the complex situation created by the nomination of Robert A. Leffingwell; some to help, some to hinder, but all, according to their lights, to do the best they could.

It wasn't that you objected to these little duties you had to perform, Lafe Smith told himself as he paid his cabbie, ran up the steps into the Senate side of the Capitol, and hurried down the poorly lighted hallway toward the Senate restaurant. You liked people, usually, or you weren't in this business. But the juxtaposition of breakfast with his upright constituents from Council Bluffs and a night with Little Miss Roll-me-over-and-do-it-again was one of those little ironies they didn't tell you about in the civics books. They told you about the machinery, but they never let on that human beings were what made it run; they talked grandly about a government of laws, not of men, concealing from the idealistic and the young the apparently too harsh fact that it is men who make and administer laws, and so in the last analysis it is the men who determine whether the laws shall function. They made it all so unreal, somehow; and it wasn't unreal at all; at least he didn't think it was. Certainly he didn't feel unreal, hadn't last night, and didn't now. It all hung together candidly in his pragmatic mind: Senators like it just as much as anybody, but that doesn't mean they're any less Senators for that. It was the sort of insight into the world that not very many of his colleagues knew he had. They all knew he had enough experience to have insight, but few were aware he had developed any.

However, he had, and those who realized it kept it in mind. That was why Bob Munson, for one, was so fond of him, totally unlike as their basic characters seemed to be; and that was why Lafe Smith was moving closer to the little group around Bob who generally called the tune for the Senate. And that was why, without even being asked, but just because he knew Bob would want to know, that he was about to make a quick, smooth, accurate, and reliable survey of what the Midwest thought about the nomination. Sometimes a single conversation could illuminate a whole region for you, if the people were representative and voluble enough; he knew his breakfast guests were. He had a good idea what their reaction would be: the Midwest wanted none of it. He wasn't so sure he did himself, as a matter of fact, though that would depend on Bob and a lot of other things.

Just ahead of him, white-haired, kindly, and a little nervous about this venture into the great world of government, he saw his company, and with the engaging, comfortable grin that put constituents and conquests equally at ease, he stepped forward, held out a hand to each of them, said, "I'm Lafe Smith, sorry to be late," and led them on into the restaurant.

At the press table in the restaurant as Lafe and his guests went by, Associated Press stopped in mid-coffee, looked up at United Press International and the New York *Times* and asked:

"What do you think he's going to do?"

"Him?" UPI said. "Whatever Bob tells him to do."

"I'm not so sure," the *Times* remarked. "I don't think this one is going to be so easy for Remarkable Robert."

"A presidential nomination?" AP snorted. "Why shouldn't it be?"

"But Bob Leffingwell," UPI said. "And the Russians. And Seab Cooley. And what have you."

"When Bob holds his press conference before the session we'll have to ask him if this nomination is an example of that bipartisan unity we've been hearing about so much," AP said. "I'll bet it is."

"I'll bet he won't tell us," UPI said. "He'll consider it a secret."

"Oh, well," AP said with a dry chuckle, "by noon he'll have it all sewed up anyway."

"That I doubt," said the *Times*.

Dolly's bedroom window, like most other windows in Vagaries, looked right out into the trees, and that was where Dolly was looking too. The morning papers were spread across the bed and Dolly—Mrs. Phelps Harrison, generally described as "one of Washington's most prominent hostesses"—was dreamily observing the first feathering green tips of spring along the branches. The sun was shining brightly, a crisp, fresh wind came in from the slightly opened window. It was a sparkling day out, and one of Washington's most prominent hostesses knew she ought to be up and doing.

Instead, she was lying here thinking that once again events had conspired to guarantee the success of a party at Vagaries.

Things couldn't, she reflected happily, have dovetailed more conveniently for her. When she had sent out the invitations she of course hadn't the remotest idea that the date would fall on the day the President finally decided to appoint a successor to Howie Sheppard as Secretary of State. It was simply fate and her favoring star, therefore, that the guest list should include not only Howie, but Bob Leffingwell as well; and not only those two, but Bob Munson, Tom August, most of the Foreign Relations Committee, Orrin Knox, half the Cabinet, Lord and Lady Maudulayne, Raoul and Celestine Barre, Krishna Khaleel, and even Vasily Tashikov, to say nothing of a wide scattering of other Administration, Hill, and diplomatic people. This was *the* party of the spring at Vagaries—in three years' time the society columns had become trained to the point where they automatically referred to it as "the Spring Party," without other identification—and it was always big. This time, though, she had an idea it was going to be positively sensational. Once again in a time of crisis, Vagaries might hold the key.

This, as she had congratulated herself so often before, simply confirmed again her great wisdom in deciding to settle in Washington in the first place. She had always had a lively interest in politics and world affairs, had fortunately been blessed with the native intelligence and shrewdness to give it point, and after the divorce when she was more or less at loose ends as to what to do next the idea had suddenly shot into her mind, "Why not go to Washington?" She and John used to visit there occasionally on business trips in the past, she had always liked and been thrilled by it, and now that she was adrift at forty-three with the family millions and no particular geographic ties, there was no reason why she shouldn't.

"I'm going to live in Washington," she had told everybody, and everybody had exclaimed; but not half so much as they did when they subsequently learned from press, radio, television, and newsreel just how overwhelmingly successful the move had proved itself to be.

Of course, that was the thing about Washington, really; you didn't have to be born to anything, you could just buy your way in. "Any bitch with a million bucks, a nice house, a good caterer, and the nerve of a grand larcenist can become a social success in Washington," people said cattily, and indeed it was entirely true. Dolly was no bitch, but the principle applied. First came the house—Vagaries, gleaming whitely, secretly yet hospitably among its great green trees on ten beautifully landscaped acres in the park, just happened to go up for sale less than a month after Dolly reached Washington and Dolly bought it outright at once—and then you began the routine. You got somebody you knew to introduce you to somebody *she* knew, and then you gave a small tea or two, and then a small cocktail party or even a small dinner, being careful to include the society editors of the *Star*, the *Post* and the *News* in one or more of them, and you were on your way. Then after the word had begun to get around a little, and you perhaps had been introduced to a Senator or two, and maybe a Cabinet officer and his wife or one of the military, you could sail right into it full steam ahead, set a date, send out invitations broadside to a couple of hundred prominent people, hire yourself the best decorator and caterer you could find, and sit back to await results. Since official Washington loves nothing as much as drinking somebody else's liquor and eating somebody else's food, the results were all you could hope for, and after that there were no problems. The quick-leaping friendships of stylishly dressed, scented, powdered, and bejeweled women screaming "Darling!" at one another, together with the amused tolerance of their amiable and almost always thirsty husbands, could quickly be parlayed into an endless round of party-going and party-giving that very soon took you to a social pinnacle limited only by your wealth and stamina. Before long you would find that *Time* and *Newsweek* were beginning to mention you in coy little asides in their news columns, and then would come the day when you picked up a magazine from the rack and found that all those carefully staged photographs at your last affair had finally resulted in a LIFE GOES TO A PARTY AT DOLLY HARRISON'S, and you could relax, at last, for you were finally, indubitably, beyond all peradventure of doubt and beyond all fear of challenge by mortal man—or, more importantly, woman —In.

After that, it was just a matter of continuing to lay out the food and the drinks and you could keep going indefinitely; especially if, like Dolly, you wanted to make it something a little deeper and more important, and so in time began to refine your guest lists to the point where they included not only the most important but also the most interesting people in Washington. Sometimes these were the same, but quite frequently they were not, and an astute realization of which was which and how often to mix them did much to give your hard-bought social standing a foundation as permanent as anything in the capital with its shifting official population could be permanent.

So it had been with Dolly, who along with her sister millionairesses was now one of the fixtures of the Washington scene. And, she told herself with considerable justification, quite possibly the best of them. Certainly her parties had a purpose—or at least they had since she had met Bob Munson. It was an event that had occurred last summer at Gossett Cook's place in Leesburg, and it had been an event that had changed her life a good deal already. She was determined that it should change it a great deal more before she was through.

Later in the morning she would have to call Bob and talk about the party and find out what she could do to help with the nomination. Because she was quite sure that once again, as on several occasions before, she and Vagaries were going to be a big help to Bob. This thought with all its ramifications and frustrations annoyed her as it always did, and with a sudden, "Oh, poof!" she hopped out of bed, rang for the maid, and prepared to go downstairs and begin checking over the preparations for the party.

At the White House the press secretary went through the first batch of wires for the day and found them running about two to one against Bob

Leffingwell. An impatient expression crossed his face. The Old Man wouldn't like it, and it would just make him more stubborn than ever. The press secretary sighed.

The trouble with the president of General Motors, in the opinion of Roy B. Mulholland, was that he thought he owned the Senators from Michigan, or at least the junior Senator from Michigan, namely Roy B. Mulholland. He didn't try to pressure Bob Munson very often, except indirectly through Roy, but he was always after Roy about something.

"Now, God damn it," he was saying vigorously over the line from Detroit, "we don't want a radical like that for Secretary of State. Now do we? Do we?"

"Bill," Senator Mulholland said with a trace of asperity, "I tell you I haven't made up my mind yet."

"Well, make it up, man," the president of General Motors said impatiently. "Make it up. Time waits for no man, you know. And you can tell Bob from me that we're going to be watching his actions on this very closely. Very closely indeed."

"Don't you always watch Bob's actions very closely, Bill?" Roy Mulholland asked. "I can't see as it makes much difference to him."

"Someday it will, by God," said the president of General Motors. "Someday it will. The day will come, even for Bob, you wait and see. And for anybody else who doesn't make the right decision for America."

"You like that phrase don't you, Bill?" Roy Mulholland said. "I've read it in at least three of your recent speeches."

"Now don't be smart-alecky like Bob, Roy," the president of General Motors ordered sternly. "Just make the right decision for America, and we'll be for you."

"I'll have to talk to Bob," Senator Mulholland said.

"He's more important to you than the voice of the people, eh?" said the president of General Motors tartly.

"In this instance," Roy Mulholland replied with equal tartness, "he is."

"Well, you tell him what I said," the president of General Motors reminded him. "You tell him we're watching him. And you too."

"I'll tell him, Bill," Senator Mulholland said, "and I'll be conscious of your piercing gaze. Give my love to Helen, and take care of yourself."

"Sometimes I wonder about you, Roy," the president of General Motors said in a disappointed tone. "Sometimes I do."

On the East River a couple of mournful tugs were arguing with uneasy persistence with the fog. Senator Fry looked out upon them through the vast glass expanses of the United Nations Delegates' dining room in a mood that nearly matched the weather. Already he was getting repercussions from the Leffingwell nomination. He had run into one of the members of the Saudi Arabian delegation in the hall just now, a billowing white vision of dark-eyed concern.

"Meestair Leffeen-gwell—" the Saudi had said abruptly. "Meestair Lefeen-gwell—— Does eet mean you are shaingeeng your poe-leecy een the Mheedle Heast?"

Hal Fry had suppressed an irreverent impulse to snap, "No, eet does hnotl" but had restrained himself. He had decided, rather, to give as good as he usually got from that sector.

"In the mysterious ways of Allah and the President of the United States, my friend," he had said calmly, "the inscrutable becomes the indubitable and the indubitable becomes the inscrutable."

"Yayess?" said the Saudi in polite puzzlement. "Yayesss?"

"Yes," said Hal Fry firmly, and walked on.

Nonetheless, it wasn't all quips and quiddities, by any means. It was going to raise hell in the Arab world, he could see that, to say nothing of a good many other places. And as for the Indians—well, he might ask K.K., but he knew that all he would get would be one of those typical Indian answers which go winding and winding off through the interstices of the English language until they finally go shimmering away altogether and there is nothing left but utter confusion and a polite smile. Still and all, he supposed he should find out if he could; and there was K.K. now, off on the other side of the room, and there was no time like the present. He picked up his coffee and made his way purposefully over. The Indian Ambassador looked up and flashed his gleaming smile.

"Senator Fry," he said in his rapid Brit'sh-In'ja way, "how good of you to grace my humble table with your honored presence."

"Good morning, K.K.," Hall Fry said amicably, "you can refrain from the flowers."

"How, please?" said Krishna Khaleel. "You are always joking me, Hal."

"Nothing," Senator Fry said gravely, "could be further from my mind. I meant we could dispense with the frills and get down to business. What position are you folks going to take on Bob Leffingwell?"

"Ahhh," said K.K. softly. "Bob Leffingwell."

"The same."

"He is an interesting man," the Indian Ambassador observed.

"Fascinating," Senator Fry agreed.

"Controversial, however," the Ambassador added.

"Most," conceded Senator Fry.

"But able," Krishna Khaleel hastened to remark.

"Among the best," Hal Fry admitted.

"It is a problem," K.K. said with a sigh.

"It *is* a problem," Senator Fry agreed cheerfully.

"Well," K.K. said abruptly. "You want to know what we think. We think this appointment could be one of great importance for the world, one which could do great good for the world. But we also think it could cause trouble in the world, and could precipitate difficulties in the world. Now then. It is a question, is it not, of whether it would cause good for the world, or whether it would cause bad for the world, and if the first, and indeed the second also, you understand, whether it would be the position of my government that the good it might cause would be sufficient to counterbalance the bad it might cause. It might, you see, cause both things in one man, you see. Such is the diversity of human nature. And one should not take too firm a position on the basis of human nature, for human nature, our friends in the West to the contrary, is always changing, is it not? And therefore sometimes it is better to ignore human nature and look at the long view of things. Although of course one cannot leave human nature out of account, for it too is important for the world. This is what we think of the nomination, since you ask me, Hal."

Senator Fry conceded defeat with a laugh.

"You damned Indians," he said genially, "are always using syntax as a weapon. Why don't you ever say what you mean, right out?"

"Half the troubles in this world, my friend," said Krishna Khaleel with sibilant explicitness, "are caused by people saying what they mean right out. You Americans always want to bring things to a head; you always want to make things come to an issue. But heads and issues are not good for the world, my friend. They make people take positions. Positions can be dangerous. Possibly positions are not good for the world. Or possibly they are, of course. Is it not so?"

"You lost me on the last curve, K.K.," Senator Fry said dryly. "I fell right out of the bus and I'm going to have to walk home. I'll tell Washington what you think."

"I shall tell Washington myself," Krishna Khaleel said firmly. "Is there not the party at Dolly's tonight? I shall be there."

"So shall I," said Hal Fry.

"A lovely woman, Dolly Harrison," the Indian Ambassador said thoughtfully. "A little too obvious about her feelings for the good Bob Munson, but very kind of heart, I think."

"She'll catch him yet," Senator Fry said with a chuckle.

"A consummation devoutly to be hoped," K.K. remarked; and added with a twinkle, "There, I have said something right out. Dolly and Bob—I am for it, I approve. The Indian Republic is for it, it approves. The world is for it, it approves. Is it not so?"

"It is so, O Akbar," said Hal Fry with a grin.

"In about another hour," Bob Munson said, "we're going to begin to get the reaction on Leffingwell from the country."

"You want to dictate a form letter?" Mary Hastings asked.

"How did you know?" Senator Munson said.

"I anticipate," Mary said. "Isn't that what you pay me for?"

"I pay you," said Bob Munson, surveying the dark-eyed, dark-haired, quick-witted forty-six-year-old intelligence that ran his office staff, "to be the best damned administrative assistant on the Hill. And so you are. Take a letter to whom it may concern—Joe Doaks, Susie Soaks, and all the folks——

" 'Dear So-and-So, With reference to your letter of present date, I want you to know how much I value your opinion on the President's nomination of Mr. Leffingwell to be Secretary of State. It is obviously an office of the greatest importance to all of us, and it is only through voluntary expressions of opinion from back home, such as yours, that we in the Senate can make up our minds about it.' Paragraph. 'As you know, in my position as Majority Leader, I am to some extent bound to follow the Administration view on most matters, but I consider this so vital that I am, for the time being, reserving final judgment on what I shall ultimately do. Your letter is one which will weigh heavily in my decision. It was most kind of you to write, and I appreciate it deeply. With warm regards,' etc. That isn't too evasive, is it?"

"No more than usual," Mary said.

"Well, damn it," Bob Munson said. "You know our problem. We can't commit ourselves too much in advance on something like this, there are too many factors involved. We've got to allow a little leeway, in case Seab turns up the fact that he was convicted for dope or white slavery or something. You know that."

"Yes," Mary said comfortably, "I know that, Senator. It's a good letter and about all you can say at the present moment, I should judge."

"Then don't give me back talk," Senator Munson said. "I can't take it, in my delicate condition of being pregnant with the hottest nomination in the present presidential term. Now let's get rid of whatever else there is. I've got to get on my horse and get out around the building."

Little warning bells rang on all the news-tickers in all the offices all over town that had them. "This is to advise," the teletype machine said impersonally, "that Robert A. Leffingwell will not repeat not hold his previously announced press conference at 10:30 A.M. today."

"This building," one of the Capitol guides was telling the day's first batch of tourists, listening attentively in the great rotunda, "stands on Capitol Hill 88 feet above the level of the Potomac River, on a site once occupied by a subtribe of the Algonquin Indians known as the Powhatans, whose council house was located at the foot of the hill. The building covers an area of 153,112 square feet, or approximately 3½ acres. Its length from north to south is 751 feet, four inches; its width, including approaches, is 350 feet. It has a floor area of 14 acres, and 435 rooms are devoted to offices, committees, and storage. There are 679 windows and 554 doorways. The cornerstone of the Capitol was laid on Sept. 18, 1793. The northern wing was completed in 1800, and in that small building the legislative and judicial branches of the government, as well as the courts of the District of Columbia, were housed in that year when the government moved here from Philadelphia. The southern section of the

Capitol was finished in 1811, the House of Representatives then occupying what is now known as Statuary Hall. At that time a wooden passageway connected the two wings. This was the situation when the Capitol was burned by the British on August 24, 1814, entering up the narrow, winding steps known as the British Stairway which you will see later in your tour.

"Restoration of the two wings was completed in 1817, and construction of the central portion was begun in 1818 and completed in 1829. Congress, which met in a special building erected on part of what is now the present Supreme Court grounds across Capitol Plaza, moved back into the Capitol in 1819.

"The building of the present Senate and House wings was begun on July 4, 1851. The House moved into its present chamber on Dec. 16, 1857, and the Senate occupied its present chamber on Jan. 4, 1859. The original low dome, which had been constructed of wood covered with copper, was replaced by the present dome of cast iron in 1865. There are two Senate Office Buildings and three House Office Buildings included in the Capitol grounds, which now cover an area of 131.1 acres. The statue on top of the Capitol which you saw as you approached the building is the Statue of Freedom, which stands with its back on downtown Washington. This is no reflection on our government, but is so turned because the East Front is the official front of the Capitol, the original builders having thought the District of Columbia would grow toward the east instead of the west.

"The Capitol dominates the city of Washington and is generally accepted throughout the world as the most familiar symbol of the Government of the United States, this great country of ours which is the world's greatest democracy and are we glad of it. Now if you will follow me——"

The Secretary of Agriculture, on his way out of the White House after seeing the President, met the Secretary of Defense on his way in. "Say," he began, "what do you think of——" The Secretary of Defense held up a cautionary hand. "Not me, boy," he said with a laugh. "I don't know nothin' 'bout nothin'."

When Brigham Anderson came past the press table shortly before ten, everybody was still there drinking coffee. Committees hadn't started yet, the day was still young, the daily budget of gossip not yet exhausted. Nobody was in much of a hurry to get to work, and the appearance of the senior Senator from Utah just went to prove that work, as often happened, might come to you if you sat at the proper crossroads and waited for it. So everybody said, "Hi, Brig," and invited him to sit down.

"If I dare, at this august table," Brigham Anderson said. "What's the topic before the house this morning?"

"As if you don't know," AP told him.

"What?" he said innocently. "The nomination?"

"Is there any other topic this morning, Senator?" the *Times* asked humorously.

"It's something, isn't it?" Brig said. "We're going to have a battle royal before we're through with this one."

"What are you going to do, Senator?" the Baltimore *Sun* asked bluntly.

"Yes, give us a lead for the afternoon papers," UPI suggested. "Senator Anderson condemns Leffingwell nomination. Says it's unpatriotic, un-American——"

"Attitude believed influenced by earlier fight with nominee on Power Commission," AP added.

"Now, wait a minute," Brigham Anderson said. "Curb these high-priced imaginations and slow down. Senator Anderson isn't condemning anything, yet."

"But he will?" AP asked quickly.

"Look," Brig said, "stop trying to get me in dutch, will you? I've got to sit on that committee and judge the nomination. I'm not ready to say anything at all about it yet. There are many aspects of it that I want to explore before I'll be ready to sound off on it."

"Can we quote you on that much?" asked the *Times;* Brigham Anderson hesitated.

"I guess so," he said slowly; "make it 'many aspects I want to explore before I am ready to take a position on it,' though. 'Sound off' is much too informal for a Senator, you know."

"And you're such a formal Senator," the *Times* noted with a smile.

"Hush," said Brigham Anderson. "Don't tell people. I'm always afraid they're going to bounce me out of the club any day for being so casual about it all. Why, I even fraternize with newspapermen, and you know what that does to a fellow's character and standing in the community . . . Actually, I'm much more interested right now in what kind of roses to plant this spring than I am in Bob Leffingwell."

"Assuming we can accept that persiflage at face value," AP said, "what kind of roses are you going to plant?"

"That's what I want you to tell me," Senator Anderson said. "I have room for about five alongside the house, and I can't decide what they should be. All white; all red; white, red, and yellow, red, white, and blue— you can see what a problem it is . . . But I've got to run. You let me know if you decide what I should do, will you?"

"You let *us* know when you decide what to do about Bob Leffingwell," the *Times* told him. The Senator flashed his engaging, boyish grin as he started toward the door, then came back and leaned confidentially over the table.

"As a matter of fact," he said in a half whisper, "I'm damned if I know," and left on their laughter.

"He's certainly a hell of a nice guy," UPI observed.

"Yes," AP agreed, "and he's going to play a hell of a big part in this one, too."

"Maybe," said the *Times* in a remark he was to remember and ponder over many times later, "a lot bigger part than he or any of us knows."

Across Capitol Plaza in the beautiful marble edifice that prompted Justice Sutherland to say that he felt as though he and his brethren were nine black beetles in the Temple of Karnak, Thomas Buckmaster Davis, Associate Justice of the Supreme Court of the United States, was busy on the telephone. The telephone was made for Washington, and Mr. Justice Davis was possibly its most devout disciple. Day in, day out, night in, night out, Tommy was on the phone, arguing, commenting, urging, suggesting, criticizing, lecturing, injecting his lively personality into the workings of government on every conceivable issue under the sun, regardless of whether anyone asked for, desired, or even listened to his opinion.

One of a long line of political Justices running from Jay to Frankfurter (with whose judicial opinions Tommy didn't always agree), Mr. Justice Davis was a born participant in practically everything. The Chief Justice had mildly reproved him about this once, noting that the ideal of American political theory was that the Court should be above politics. "When was the Court ever above politics?" Tommy had snapped, and the C.J. hadn't tried to argue very hard. "Well, people should *think* it is, anyway," he had said, rather lamely. "You make it so obvious it isn't." "It's a free country," said Mr. Justice Davis firmly.

There was illuminated in this brief exchange much about the relationship between the Court and the country, and more particularly, between Tommy and his colleagues. Tommy, it was true, had put his finger on something, and the C.J. with equal perspicacity, had done the same. Whatever the Court's awareness of the current political climate might be, and it was usually very good, there was a sort of agreed understanding among its members that they wouldn't admit it, publicly at any rate. Mr. Justice Davis gave a sort of tentative lip service to this, when he remembered about it, but most of the time he made no bones about his own avid involvement in any phase of politics that happened to interest him. This was all phases, and inevitably this brought considerable public criticism and a certain frigidity into his relations with his eight fellows. It was obvious every day when the clerk cried, "Oyez! Oyez! Oyez!" and the Justices emerged in their stately massed ballet from behind the red-velvet curtain that Mr. Justice Davis and his brethren were not entirely happy with one another.

Today, however, the Court was not meeting, nor were any conferences scheduled, and there was nothing to interfere with Tommy's favorite pastime. The Leffingwell nomination, he was aware, provided perhaps his greatest recent challenge, and he was rising to it with all the vigor at his command. At the moment he was arguing with the general director of the *Post*, who was giving him a bad time.

"But what other position *is* there for a liberal to take?" Tommy was demanding. "My dear boy, my dear boy; oh, my dear boy!"

"I'm still not sure we're ready to go all out," the general director of the *Post* remarked doggedly.

"But my dear boy," Tommy said, "suppose the Senate doesn't confirm him. Think what a black eye it will be for the liberal cause."

"Suppose the Senate confirms him and he does the wrong thing in foreign policy," the general director of the *Post* shot back. "Think what a black eye it will be for all of us."

"Surely you don't mistrust Bob Leffingwell!" Justice Davis said in a tone of shocked surprise. "After all he has done for the country, all these long, valiant years. Surely there couldn't possibly be a better choice."

"W-e-l-l," the director of the *Post* said slowly. "In many ways, you're right, of course. But so much more is involved in this——"

"Then why hesitate?" Tommy demanded triumphantly. "Isn't that all the more reason for being for him? Has he ever failed us? Hasn't he always been on the right side? Why, I can remember clear back under Roosevelt, he was one of America's greatest fighting liberals. And he's never changed one bit since; even when"—and the Justice's tone grew a little pointed—"even when *some others* wavered now and then, endorsing Eisenhower, and so on, Bob Leffingwell never did. Doesn't that entitle him to the support of all true liberals now?"

"Oh, I expect we'll be for him, all right," the director of the *Post* said hastily, "but it may be more gradual and not so immediate."

"It's got to be immediate," Tommy Davis said firmly. "It's got to be, my dear boy. Otherwise, *they* will get the jump on us. All the reactionary forces in the country are mobilizing right this minute to defeat this nomination. We've got to mobilize too. We've got to act fast. This is the latest battle in the unending war we liberals always have to fight. Will you fail us when the trumpets sound, my dear boy? Will your banner be trailing in the dust when ours goes gallantly ahead?"

"Very dramatic, I'm sure," the director of the *Post* responded. "But you do have a point. I'll have to talk it over down here and see what we decide. I will say yours isn't the only telephone call I've received along the same lines. It could be we'll come out strong for him tomorrow morning."

"I hope so, my dear boy, I hope so with all my heart," Justice Davis said. "Nothing would make me happier than to have you call back this afternoon and say it's all settled."

"W-e-l-l," the director of the *Post* said hesitantly. "Perhaps."

"Just to make an old liberal happy?" Tommy said wistfully. "Just so he will know that all the good company is together again and marching forward——"

"When the trumpets sound," the director of the *Post* finished for him. "All right, Mr. Justice. I'll call."

"Thanks so much, dear boy," Tommy said. "I know you won't fail us. It's so *important*."

"Indeed it is," said the director of the *Post* thoughtfully.

The *Star* and the *News* were thoughtful too. Their early editions, reaching the Capitol shortly after ten-thirty, sounded a note of cautious reserve on Robert Leffingwell. "We assume," the *Star* said, "that the President has excellent reasons for nominating Mr. Leffingwell to this all-important post, and indeed there is much in his public record to warrant this sort of confidence. Still, we hope the Senate will take its time and satisfy itself completely as to the nominee's qualifications. In this area, in this era, the country cannot afford a mistake." "We'd like to see this one given plenty of thought," the *News* said. "We've seen much to praise in Bob Leffingwell's record, and also plenty to criticize. We've done both, as we deemed necessary. Now we say to the Senate: take it easy and make sure you're right. Better safe than sorry, when we and the whole free world have so much at stake in this nomination."

The trouble with the president of the United Auto Workers, in the opinion of Bob Munson, was that he thought he owned the Senators from Michigan, or at least the senior Senator from Michigan, namely Bob Munson. He didn't try to pressure Roy Mulholland very often, except indirectly through Bob, but he was always after Bob about something.

"Now, God damn it," he was saying vigorously over the line from Detroit, "we want to get organized and get this nomination through as soon as possible. We want to help, Bob. We want you to let us know what we can do."

"John," Bob Munson said with a trace of asperity, "I think maybe this one is going to be difficult enough without stirring up a lot of old animosities to complicate matters."

"Rubbish, Bob," the president of the UAW said tersely. "Rubbish. We've got to beat these reactionary bastards at their own game. You're going to need all the assistance you can get, Bob, and we intend to help you. We want you to know that, Bob. Incidentally, what about that lily-livered pantywaist of a colleague of yours? What are they going to scare him into doing?"

"I haven't talked to Roy yet," Bob Munson said. "I imagine on this one he'll make up his own mind."

"Well," said the president of the UAW darkly, "you tell him we're going to be watching his actions on this one very closely. *Damn* closely."

"Aren't you always watching his actions very closely, John?" Bob Munson asked. "I can't see that it makes much difference to him."

"Well, someday it will, by God," said the president of the UAW belligerently. "Someday, by God, it will. He'll get it yet, you wait and see, even if he does have General Motors and half the fat cats in Michigan in his corner."

"Isn't it enough to own one Senator from Michigan, John?" Bob Munson asked. "Don't I satisfy you? Must you have a union label on us both?"

The president of the UAW uttered an expressive four-letter word.

"Who owns you?" he asked bitterly. "When did anybody ever own you? By God, Bob, you're the slipperiest character in seventeen counties. Every time we think we have you pegged you slide out from under us. I'll bet we can't even count on you on this one, even if you are Majority Leader."

"Oh, I wouldn't say that," Bob Munson said.

"We'll be watching you, Bob," the president of the UAW promised. "We'll be watching you, by God, and Roy too. Don't try any funny stuff on this. And we're going to help too, Bob, God damn it, so don't try to push us aside."

"You wait until you hear from me before you start anything," Bob Munson said angrily, and his tone suddenly hardened into one that would brook no nonsense. "I mean it, John. I don't want you messing this one up with any of your God-damned phoney-liberal headline-grabbing crusades. You stay out of this until I give you the word, do you understand me?"

"Well, all right, Bob," said the president of the UAW in a startled voice, "if that's the way you feel."

"That's the way I feel," Senator Munson said crisply, "and you keep your hands off this until I tell you. Good-by."

"Well, good-by, Bob," said the president of the UAW hurriedly, "if that's the way you feel."

"I really don't see why he didn't tell *me*," Harley Hudson was saying in an aggrieved way as the plane prepared to set down at National Airport. "Certainly I can be of some help to him in the Senate, even if he does act as though I can't. Don't you think I can, Tom?"

At this frank display of a rather woebegone approach to life, which the Vice President had kept fairly well bottled most of the way up from South Carolina but had finally expressed with embarrassing candor, the chairman of the Senate Foreign Relations Committee shook his head as though brushing away a persistent fly, or as though confronted with a problem for which there was no solution; as indeed there wasn't, for this one.

"I'm sure you can, Harley," Tom August said in his gentle, professorial voice. "I'm sure he will make use of you. After all, you know everybody."

"Of course I know everybody," Harley Hudson said, "and they listen to me, too. Not as much as they do to Bob Munson, of course, but I have some influence, don't I, Tom?"

"I believe you do," Senator August said reassuringly. "I do believe you do. I wouldn't worry about it, Harley; I'm sure you'll find when you get to your office that he wants to talk to you and enlist your help. After all, it would be very foolish of him not to, I should think."

"I should think so too," said the Vice President rather wistfully, "but sometimes he hasn't, you know. Why, I don't know half of what goes on, Tom. I wouldn't say that to everybody, you understand, but you're an old friend. It hurts me sometimes, it really does. Why, supposing anything should happen, Tom; I wouldn't even know how to begin."

"Now, hush, Harley," Senator August said abruptly, feeling as though this were entering a realm of self-revelation so devastating that he should at all costs head the Vice President off, "now, hush. Nothing's going to happen. Nothing *at all* is going to happen."

"I don't know," Harley Hudson said unhappily. "Lately I've been waking up at nights and worrying about it. You don't suppose it's a premonition, do you Tom?"

"No," Senator August said. "I wish you wouldn't worry so, Harley. Nothing's going to happen, and even if it did, I'm sure you'd do the right thing. We all know you would."

"I'd be scared to death," the Vice President said simply.

"You wouldn't have time to be scared," Senator August said.

"Oh yes, I would," said Harley Hudson. "Oh yes, I would."

"Well," Tom August said as the plane taxied to a stop, "I refuse to listen to you get yourself into a state about it any longer. He likes you, and he'll want your help, and so will we all. See, there's a White House car waiting for you, right now."

"I'll bet it isn't for me," the Vice President said in a lonely voice. "I'll bet it's for you."

And so it was. There was a young State Department officer with it, and he informed Senator August that the President wished to see him at once, and if the Senator didn't mind, could he come right along now——? After which, for he was a polite young man, he asked the Vice President if they could drop him anywhere.

"I have my own car waiting, thanks," Harley said stiffly. "You see?" he added to Tom August. "You see?"

"Hush," the Senator said, looking pleased and flattered in spite of himself. "I'll see you on the Hill, Harley."

"Give him my regards," the Vice President said, rallying his lacerated feelings for a parting shot, "tell him I said hello."

"I'll tell him he should make use of you in this," Senator August said, meaning to be kind but sounding smug instead.

"Oh, swell," Harley Hudson said bitterly. "Oh, fine and dandy. You do that, Tom. You do that very thing."

Shortly after eleven o'clock in his closely guarded Embassy on Sixteenth Street opposite the National Geographic, Vasily Tashikov framed a cable to Moscow on the Leffingwell nomination and sent it forward to the coding room for transmission. It was a shrewd if somewhat incomplete appraisal of the appointment, an assessment of its world and domestic political implications, and a suggestion for certain actions to be taken in the event of favorable action by the Senate. After it left his desk the Ambassador called home and reminded his wife that they were to attend the party at Mrs. Harrison's that night. She did not particularly want to go and neither did he, but they knew it was both a duty and an opportunity: a chance to spend an evening with people they despised, to whom they felt infinitely superior, and to whose destruction and that of their country the Ambassador and his lady were implacably and inescapably dedicated. He had received orders, given on a rising tide of confidence in victory, to be as brutal as he pleased in his diplomatic conversations, and Vasily Tashikov was looking forward with some satisfaction to doing just that.

At Her Majesty's Embassy out Massachusetts Avenue and at the French Embassy on Belmont Road, the nomination was also of some interest. Lord Maudulayne, pausing in a busy day to take a call from Kitty in New York, was advised that she had talked to Senator Fry, "and he sounds dreadfully amused about Bob Leffingwell." Senator Wannamaker, though, she reported, did not, and it was likely there would be quite a fuss in the Senate about it, she gathered. She would be flying in with Celestine Barre at four-thirty, and would he be good enough to call Raoul Barre at the French Embassy and tell him so? Both ladies wanted orchids for Dolly's party, so he could order hers at once, and don't forget to tell Raoul the same. She did think the whole Leffingwell thing was going to be exciting, and what attitude should she take officially if she happened to meet somebody she knew when she and Celestine went to the UN for lunch with the heads of the British and French delegations?

"Don't take any attitude," Claude Maudulayne said. "Let them guess. That's what I'm doing."

"Is that what you're *really* doing?" Lady Maudulayne wanted to know.

"That's what I'm really doing," her husband replied.

"Oh," she said thoughtfully. "Then I will too. It will be difficult, though, don't you think? He is *so* controversial, and everybody knows we will all be affected by his appointment, won't we?"

"I expect so," Lord Maudulayne said. "By all means be as blank as the sphinx if you see K.K."

"Pooh to K.K.," said Lady Maudulayne in a tone that left no doubt of her feelings about the Indian Ambassador. "That tiresome——"

"Ah, ah," Claude Maudulayne said reprovingly. "Ah, ah. Ties that bind, you know. Little brown brethren, dinner jackets in the jungle, we all went to Oxford and spent our hols together, and so on. The Commonwealth forever. One big, happy family, right?"

"One big happy my foot," Kitty Maudulayne said crisply. "Sometimes I think this whole thing is——"

"—is the best of a bad bargain and a bad bargain is all we can get in this happy era," her husband said with equal crispness, "so please don't say anything revolutionary to anybody."

"I'll try not to," Kitty promised. "Will you have a car meet us at the airport?"

"I think I can," Lord Maudulayne said. "Have a good time at the UN."

"I will," his wife said. "Don't forget to call Raoul."

"Immediately," Lord Maudulayne said.

And, as good as his word, which was generally recognized in Washington to be very good indeed, he put the call through as soon as Kitty hung up. After a couple of minutes with secretaries he achieved his objective and heard the pleasantly accented voice of the French Ambassador brighten with pleasure.

"My dear Claude!" it said. "To what do I owe this always happy event?"

"To wives," Lord Maudulayne said.

"Ah, those charming little ladies," Raoul Barre said fondly. "What have they done now, gotten themselves arrested for vagrancy in New York?"

Lord Maudulayne laughed.

"Nothing as drastic as that, old chap," he said. "Kitty was just on, and she wants to be very sure that I know, and you know, that she and Celestine want orchids for Dolly Harrison's party tonight."

"Ah, is that all," the French Ambassador said. "I was afraid it was something much more desperate and costly than that."

"She also wanted to know," Lord Maudulayne said, "what she should say to people who asked her what she thought about the Leffingwell nomination."

"Oh?" said Raoul Barre carefully.

"Yes," his colleague replied.

"And you said——?" Raoul suggested.

"Nothing," Lord Maudulayne said quickly. "I was blank as the Sphinx."

"I see," the French Ambassador observed.

"You do?" the British Ambassador asked.

"When did the Sphinx become British?" Raoul inquired.

"A temporary adherence," Lord Maudulayne said airily. "I'm sure I'll be as voluble as anything presently, but right now, no."

"No?" said Raoul Barre in a disappointed tone. "My dear Claude, I find myself in the same predicament as the lovely Kitty. What am *I* to tell people who ask me, if I cannot get guidance from the one who holds my poor country's hand and makes sure she proceeds in the paths of righteousness?"

"Hmm," Lord Maudulayne said. "I wonder if we deserve that?"

"On occasion," the French Ambassador said. "On occasion, as you well know, clever Albion. Actually, you will be glad to know that I too am sphinxlike. Not that anyone has asked me yet, but someone will before long. I am sure of it."

"Yes," said Lord Maudulayne. "I will. I am. What do you think?"

"Always unpredictable, always," Raoul Barre said with a mock sigh. "First the Sphinx and then the bulldoze. Well, I wonder if I should tell you."

"I think you should," Claude Maudulayne said. "I definitely think you should. Our hosts will be after us, you know; we can't escape them for long. By all means let's have a united front, old boy."

"The Americans!" said Raoul Barre with a real sigh this time. "They pin one down so. I shall tell them for the moment—not much. After all, the President must deem this man worthy to be our prophet on the road to greater salvation, or he would not have nominated him. I am sure he is quite as adept at combining sermons and sleight of hand as all the others have been lately."

"You sound bitter," Lord Maudulayne observed; his colleague snorted.

"I?" he said in an exaggerated tone. "*I?*"

"So you are doubtful, then?" the British Ambassador said.

"I am," the French Ambassador agreed. "Very. I do not know which way this American animal is going to jump, you know? He is scared and he is lazy; it is a fateful combination. And he cannot yet quite believe that this time he need not send to ask about the bell tolling, for this time it really could be tolling for him. He cannot grasp it yet; when he suddenly understands, what then? What will he do? That is what I wonder. It is what I wonder about Bob Leffingwell."

"There are others I would feel more comfortable with at a time like this," Lord Maudulayne agreed.

"Several," Raoul Barre said. "If my friends in the Senate ask me, I shall be polite—and reluctant. I shall indicate a doubt, perhaps, to those astute enough to see it, of whom there are a good many in that great body."

"That was my own idea," Claude Maudulayne said. "I just wanted to see if you agreed. I thought perhaps on this we had best see eye-to-eye."

"I believe so," Raoul Barre said. "I do believe so. After all these years of telling us that we all survive or go down together, they have finally created a situation in which it is true. We didn't want it to be that way, but they fought for us and aided us and told us what was best for backward peoples whose progress didn't match theirs and lectured at us and negotiated with us and prayed over us until it came true. Now we are stuck with them. If they go, we go. We all go. And that includes that deliberate dream of gentlemen in London and elsewhere who insist on staying asleep because the dream is so pleasant, your delightful Elizabeth's Commonwealth and Empire. What do you hear from the Indians?"

"K.K. is at UN," Lord Maudulayne said. "I hear nothing yet. I understand he will be at Dolly's. I may hear something then."

"I too shall offer an attentive ear to the exquisitely involved English of our distinguished colleague," Raoul Barre said dryly. "I do not know that I shall learn, but I shall listen."

"I too," Lord Maudulayne said. "Thanks for your time and your advice. We will see you at Dolly's. Don't forget Celestine's orchid."

"Immediately," said Raoul Barre.

"Darling," Dolly said when her call finally reached the Majority Leader in his second office on the gallery floor of the Senate wing, "I just wanted to see how you were feeling. I just wanted to know if there was anything I could do about Bob Leffingwell."

Bob Munson smiled.

"Not much," he said, "except be your usual charming self tonight and see that everybody mixes. We want a lot of mixing about Bob, the more mixing the better."

"How does it look so far?" Dolly asked.

Senator Munson grunted. "I've been so tied down by mail and calls in my other office I've hardly had time to find out. I wanted to get out around a little before the session began, but there were too many things to do. Most of Michigan picked this morning to call me, so I've been running errands."

"It's good for you. It keeps you humble to remember that you may be Majority Leader to us, but you're just an errandboy to them."

"Thanks," Bob Munson said. "I knew there must be some good purpose in it. What have you been doing?"

"Getting ready for the party. It seems to me I've been over everything fifty times, though I'm sure it was only twice."

"How many are you expecting this time," Senator Munson asked, "five hundred?"

"About three," Dolly said.

"Vagaries will be taxed to the limit," the Senator observed. "I hope every single one will be directly involved in the nomination."

"Not every one, but a good many. But do you know, the funniest thing? Louise Leffingwell called a little while ago and said they couldn't make it."

"God damn him anyway," Bob Munson said flatly. "What was the excuse?"

"Bob has a touch of virus, she said."

"He's just playing hard to get," Bob Munson said. "But maybe it's just as well, after all. His being there might serve to inhibit the conversation, and as it is we can say what we think. Except that a lot of us won't, of course."

"Isn't this going to be important diplomatically?" Dolly asked. "I mean, won't the allies be interested? Won't they try to influence it, even?"

"I expect they will," Bob Munson said. "I've got to talk to some of them tonight."

"They'll be here," Dolly said, "including K.K."

"Hal Fry saw him this morning at the UN," Senator Munson reported. "He called to tell me K.K. is also playing hard to get."

"Well, darling, Tashikov will be here and maybe he'll say what he thinks."

"Yeah," Bob Munson said dryly. "I'm sure of it."

"Bob," Dolly said seriously, "are you entirely happy about this?"

"It's my job to be happy about it," Senator Munson said. "How else can I feel?"

"I knew it. If Claude and Raoul are against him and K.K. quibbles and Tashikov smiles, I'm going to be scared."

"So am I," Bob Munson said, "assuming Tashikov would be so indiscreet as to smile, which I doubt. Anyway, we'll just have to see."

"Well, you let me know what I can do to help," Dolly said; then her tone changed. "How's your sense of the ridiculous?"

Bob Munson grinned. "I won't know till midnight, I suspect, and then if I've mislaid it somewhere I'll have to come through the back door in blackface, I suppose, to avoid comment."

"Why don't you make an honest woman of me and then you can forget comment?" Dolly asked.

"Oh, comment's all part of the game in my business," Senator Munson said.

"Now, darling," Dolly told him, "don't be like that. Just don't be like that. It isn't fair."

"I'm trying to be fair," Bob Munson said. "I said I'd wear blackface."

"Damn you anyway, darling," Dolly said lightly. "I'll see you tonight, and I don't care about your sense of the ridiculous after all. I'm sorry I asked."

"*I'm* not," Bob Munson said. "I would have been devastated if you hadn't."

"Oh, damn, damn, damn, *damn*," Dolly said. "I refuse to talk to you any longer."

"I'll see you tonight," Bob Munson said with a chuckle. "Somewhere among the three hundred."

"Well, don't try the back door," she told him. "It will be locked, blackface or no blackface."

"I love you too," Senator Munson said. "Don't slip on a french pastry."

"Go to hell," one of Washington's most prominent hostesses advised him. "Just go on and go."

And that, the Senator thought with amusement, was why life in Washington had become considerably more interesting recently. A couple of months ago when he had stayed overnight for the first time at Vagaries he had made some teasing comment about it all being rather ridiculous anyway, fifty-seven and forty-three, and Dolly had promptly given them their catchword.

"Darling," she had said firmly, "You know as well as I do that the first thing people have to forget is their sense of the ridiculous. Otherwise nobody could ever do *anything*."

Since then, Bob Munson reflected, the sense of the ridiculous had not intruded overmuch, even if its absence had not automatically produced an early rush for the altar and that "most fashionable Washington wedding of the year" that Dolly made no bones about wanting. He suspected it would come in due time, but he wasn't in any great hurry at the moment.

The two people connected with official Washington who had absolutely no thoughts whatsoever about the Leffingwell nomination this morning were walking down Connecticut Avenue window-shopping arm in arm.

"You know," Crystal Danta said, "I believe we can do the dining room in blue."

"Suppose I like black?" Hal Knox suggested. She laughed.

"That's what my father tells me about your father," she said. "Stubborn and contrary."

"That's just contrary," Orrin Knox's son said. "I haven't begun to be stubborn yet. You'll find out."

"I will, will I?" Crystal said speculatively. "I might tell you the Dantas have a long family tradition too. I wouldn't push my luck, if I were you."

"I have so much," Hal said.

"You do?" Crystal asked.

"I have you, haven't I?" he said with a grin.

"You," she said placidly, "are so sweet. Let's go into Sloan's and spend a million dollars."

"Good," Hal said. "I just happen to have it on me."

"Bob," Lafe Smith said earnestly, "I don't think the Midwest is going to go for this. I had breakfast with one of my county chairmen and the old boy was fierce. I've never seen him so upset."

"How do you feel about it?" Senator Munson asked. His visitor fidgeted a little in his chair.

"I want to stand by the President if I can, Bob," he said.

"Can you?" Bob Munson asked.

"Ask me in a week," Lafe said with his quick, appealing grin.

"I want to know sooner than that," Senator Munson said. "I'm counting on your help."

"I want to give it to you," Senator Smith assured him earnestly. "You can count on it, Bob. I'll be happy to run all the errands you want, you know that. Just give me a little time to make up my own mind, is all."

"I'm afraid that's the theme song I'm going to hear this afternoon all over the Senate," Bob Munson said.

"It's too important to jump at," Lafe Smith said thoughtfully. "Too much hangs on this, our whole world position and all. We can't have somebody in there who would sell all those little countries down the river just to appease the Russians, you know."

"You surprise me, Lafe," Bob Munson said with a tinge of irony that he promptly regretted, "I didn't know you cared."

"People misunderstand me," Lafe said, rather wistfully. "I do care. We live in a hell of an age, and I do care. You have to care, these days: there's always somebody screaming off stage."

Bob Munson shivered.

"God help us all," he said.

"I hope so," Lafe said, rising. "I'll see you later, Bob. I'll keep my ears open and let you know anything I hear."

"I appreciate that, Lafe," Bob Munson said. "I really do."

"Do you see what I see?" AP asked UPI as they cruised the corridors of the Old Senate Office Building in a rather aimless pre-session search for news.

"I wonder what that means?" UPI said.

"It means," said AP, "war."

"Seab and Orrin Knox?" UPI said skeptically. "Well, maybe. Shall we hang around and see?"

"Let's," AP said.

Halfway down the corridor, Orrin Knox was half-in-half-out of the doorway to his private office, looking impatient as he always did when anyone stopped him, no matter who or what the occasion. Despite the look, however, he was deep in obviously congenial conversation with the senior Senator from South Carolina, who had overtaken him on the third floor on his way back from a meeting of the Finance Committee. It had been a meeting in which Senator Knox had, as usual, lost his temper with the Secretary of the Treasury and had wound up twisting his body indignantly from side to side as he hit the table with the flat of his hand and made blunt remarks about the Secretary's general grasp of economic theory. The Secretary, as usual, had remained amiable, forthright, and unimpressed, and Orrin only now was beginning to regain his normal quick-triggered composure.

"I told him that three and one half per cent rate wouldn't work when he first announced it three months ago," he said indignantly. "I knew it wouldn't, it isn't logical, it isn't sensible, it's just a lot of economic hogwash. And it *isn't* working, either."

"He's a mighty stubborn man," Senator Cooley observed soothingly. "A mighty stubborn man, Orrin. I'm glad you told him what you thought."

"He knows what I think," Orrin Knox said impatiently. "He's always known what I think. He just laughs at me and goes his own way. I don't know what kind of economic shape we're going to be in when he gets through with us."

"Maybe he'll listen in time, Orrin. You just keep after him and don't give up. You're the best safeguard we have against all this economic tomfoolery, that's what I always believe. I don't know where we'd-be without you, Orrin. I truly don't."

"Well," Orrin Knox said with a grin and the sudden skeptical honesty that was one of his saving graces, "I dare say we'd survive. But, by gollies, he does make me mad sometimes."

"I'm a little mad myself this morning, Orrin," Seab Cooley said carefully. "It does seem as though the Administration just won't leave either of us alone. It's vindictive, that's what it is. Yes, sir. Plain vindictive."

"What, Bob Leffingwell?" Orrin Knox said with a smile. "Somehow I guessed you wouldn't be feeling good about it, Seab."

"No, sir," Seab Cooley said firmly. "No, sir, I don't."

"Want to come in for a minute and talk it over privately?" Orrin said. "I don't want to take your time, but our friends in the press are watching down the hall and big pitchers have big ears."

"Gladly," Seab Cooley said with alacrity. "Gladly, thank you, Orrin."

"Well," said UPI, "I guess that shows *us*."

"I guess it does," AP agreed with a chuckle. "Well, we'll just have to catch them over on the floor during the session."

"Let's stick," UPI said. "Nothing better to do for the next half hour."

"Right," AP said.

Inside the comfortable, brown-paneled office with its standard big senatorial desk and deep leather armchairs, the customary collection of framed certificates of election, honorary degrees, pictures of the President, Vice President, and fellow Senators cluttering the walls, and its view down the Mall to the Virginia hills beyond, Senator Knox gestured to a chair and settled back behind his desk.

"Now," he said, thoughtfully paring his fingernails as he talked, "how much help do you think you're going to get?"

"I haven't rightly begun counting yet," Senator Cooley said slowly, "but I expect a good deal, Orrin. Yes, I expect a good deal."

"I may support him, you know," Senator Knox remarked casually. Senator Cooley remained impassive.

"That's your privilege, Orrin," he said calmly. "That's surely your privilege."

"Or again, I may not," Senator Knox observed.

"That's your privilege too, Orrin," Seab Cooley said. "It surely is."

"I've got a lot of things to make up my mind about before I'll know. I don't think it's going to be enough to be against him just as a matter of personal spite."

Senator Cooley moved indignantly in his chair.

"I don't know anybody who's going to act on that basis, Senator," he said stiffly. "I truly don't. Who do you think would do a thing like that?"

"You would," Orrin Knox said bluntly, "and you know it perfectly well. But it isn't going to be good enough this time."

"Any man who calls me a liar——" Senator Cooley began angrily. Senator Knox held up a hand.

"It isn't good enough, Seab," he repeated. "We've all heard about that so often we can recite it by heart. It's got to be better than that."

"Where I come from," Senator Cooley said softly, "that's all you need to know about a man to decide what to do about him. He called me a liar, Orrin. Right smack dab to my face he called me——"

"I was there," Orrin Knox said calmly. "It isn't good enough. You can't decide a Cabinet nomination, particularly State, on the basis of a personal feud. At least, the Senate can't. Maybe you can, but the rest of us can't. There've got to be better grounds."

The crafty look his colleagues knew so well came over Senator Cooley's face, and with it his slow, sleepy smile.

"Maybe there are, Orrin," he said gently. "Maybe there are."

"Such as?" asked Orrin Knox.

"All in good time, Orrin," Seab said softly. "All in good time."

"You're bluffing, Seab," Senator Knox told him. "I've known you for twenty years, you old reprobate, and I know when you're bluffing."

Senator Cooley grinned.

"Be mighty hard to prove at this point, Orrin," he said amiably. "Be mighty hard, I think."

"Will it be hard later?" Senator Knox inquired.

"Maybe by that time," Senator Cooley said quietly, "it won't be a bluff, Orrin."

"Well," Orrin Knox said practically, "if you want anybody to go along with you, Seab, you're going to have to do better than that. We'll—they'll —want proof of things. Your word for it won't be good enough."

"You'll—they'll—have it, Orrin," Seab said dryly. "Of that you can be ab-so-lute-ly sure, Orrin."

"Well," said Orrin Knox, "I—they—we—will have to wait and see, Seab. In the meantime, you know I have doubts. Lots of doubts. Keep in touch with me on it, and we'll see how things go."

"I will, Orrin," Seab promised. "I surely will. And thank you."

"Thank you, Seab," Orrin Knox said. "See you on the floor."

"On the floor," Seab Cooley said, opening the door suddenly to disclose AP and UPI, who were standing by as close as they dared.

"Howdy, boys," he said amicably as he started down the hall, "how you all?"

"Senator," said AP, "did you and Senator Knox agree to oppose——"

"No comment, boys," Seab said bluffly, "no comment, no comment, no comment at all. No, sir, no comment a-tall." And he went padding away down the hall with his sloping, shuffling walk, still muttering absently to himself, "No, sir, no comment at all."

In the oval parking apron in front of the West Wing of the White House, Senator August, facing the ring of reporters and television cameras which greets all major visitors to the President, was insisting gently that he couldn't possibly tell his questioners about his talk with the Chief Executive.

"Did it concern the Leffingwell nomination?" CBS asked. Tom August gave his shy, modest, diffident smile, and replied in his almost inaudible voice,

"I think it would be a safe assumption that the subject came up."

"Senator," NBC said, "is it true that the President wants you to hold a committee meeting tomorrow morning and dispose of the whole thing by Monday?"

"My goodness, where do you boys pick up such rumors?" Senator August asked wonderingly.

"Is it true, Senator?" insisted UPI, unimpressed.

"I think it is quite obvious that the President wants the matter expedited as much as possible," Senator August said gently, "but I hardly think it would be possible to move that fast."

"Will you try?" AP demanded.

"Oh," Tom August smiled, "we always try."

"Senator," the *Times* said, "do you expect Senator Cooley to make a strong fight against the nomination?"

"Senator Cooley," Tom August said softly, "always makes a strong fight on everything he undertakes."

"Senator," the New York *Daily News* asked, "did the President give you a deadline date when he would like to have the nomination completed?"

"I think you will find," said Senator August in a tone of gentle reproof, "that the President is wise in the ways of Congress and knows how it reacts to arbitrary deadlines."

"Then he didn't set one?" The Newark *News* pressed.

"Oh," Tom August said gently, "I didn't say that."

"Then he did set one," UPI said.

"Oh, now," the chairman of the Foreign Relations Committee said with an air of wistful regret that he wasn't getting his message through, "I didn't say that, either."

"Thank you, Senator," said someone in a tone of crisp annoyance.

"Thank *you*," said Tom August politely.

From the oval office he had just left a call was going forward at the same moment to the Majority Leader.

"I had Tom August in," the confident voice was reporting. "He's out front now being very important about it all for the television cameras. I think he'll do what we want."

"What is that?" Senator Munson asked.

"A special meeting of the committee tomorrow morning, a pro forma appearance by Bob Leffingwell, a brief executive session afterwards, and a favorable report on the nomination to go to the Senate on Monday. Vote on confirmation late Monday afternoon."

"Where are you calling from?" Bob Munson asked curiously. "It can't be Washington, D.C."

"Why not?" the President asked, a trifle defensively. "What's wrong with that?"

"Only forty or fifty Senators are wrong with it, at this point," Bob Munson said. "You don't seem to realize the issue you've created, Mr. President. This isn't going to be solved over a weekend."

"You can buy off Seab, I tell you," the President said comfortably.

"In the first place," Senator Munson said, "I've tried and I can't, and in the second, it goes a lot deeper than Seab. A lot of people are genuinely worried about Bob Leffingwell as Secretary of State at a juncture like this."

"Do they assume I'm not worried about things at this juncture?" the President asked with a considerable degree of annoyance.

"I don't mean it that way," Senator Munson said, "but a lot of people aren't prepared to accept your judgment without arriving at their own. It's that kind of thing."

"Well, give them a week, then," the President suggested. "That ought to be long enough. Maybe you can tell Tom I said so."

"Oh, we'll try it your way first," Bob Munson said, "but just don't be surprised when it doesn't work." Then on a sudden nervy impulse he tried a long shot. "I can no more see that nomination clearing the committee in one day," he said, "than I can see Harley Hudson as President of the United States."

He knew the shot had gone home, for there was a sudden silence on the line. When the President spoke, it was coldly.

"That's an odd analogy," he observed. "What made you think of it?"

"I don't know," Senator Munson said blandly. "It just seemed to pop out."

"Well," the President said angrily, "you can pop it right back in again."

"Very well," the Senator said, "if you honestly think I should."

"I think so, Bob," the President said in a much more reasonable way; and then, in the first really impulsive move Senator Munson had ever known him to make he said tentatively, "Bob?"

"Yes, Mr. President?" Bob Munson said gravely.

"Sometime when you're free, come down and we'll talk."

"I would like to, Mr. President," Senator Munson said quietly, "if it would be any help."

"I think it would," the President said. "You bear everything alone, in this office, but once in a while you have to at least try to share it with somebody else."

"Alice won't do?" Senator Munson suggested.

"She isn't well herself," the President said, realized his slip, hesitated, but then went on, "and I wouldn't want to worry her needlessly."

"I'm sure it is needlessly, Mr. President," Senator Munson said, "but I will be down as soon as I can."

"You're a real friend, Bob," the President said with a revealing gratitude, "to a man who isn't permitted very many." Then his voice lightened. "It's in the Constitution somewhere. Having real friends is one of those reserved powers that aren't granted to the President."

"Well, glad to be of assistance," Bob Munson said in a businesslike tone. "We'll try to get the nomination through for you tomorrow and Monday, but be prepared to put a good face on it at your next press conference, because I really don't think we can act that fast."

"I appreciate whatever you can do, you know that, Bob," the President said. "I know it's in good hands. Try to keep Tom August in that rosy glow I put him into down here."

Bob Munson chuckled.

"I'll do my best," he promised.

Which, he thought as he said good-by, was a perfect example of what might be termed the Chairman's Law. There were ways and ways in which an Administration could take the Senate Foreign Relations Committee into camp, but perhaps the most effective was the *accorde intime* with the chairman. A gentleman whose normally healthy ego was almost invariably considerably inflated by his position as head of what was, in general, the most important committee of the Congress, he was usually easy prey for the whispered aside, the just-between-us confidences of the State Department and the White House. Take him up on the mountain and show him the vistas of the world, tell him about his own monumentally important contribution to it, consult him with well-publicized secrecy on projected moves in foreign policy, always include him when you entertained visiting foreign dignitaries, let him think you were deferring to his opinion while you did as you pleased, cozzen him regularly with the most blatant flattery, of which he was eager to believe every word, and nine times out of ten he was yours. With him, usually, went an indirect but effective control of the committee, for its customary disposition was to follow the chairman's lead and take his word for it in matters which could be clothed with a sufficient aura of portentuous mystery.

With this time-honored formula, tried and tested and found infallible in half a dozen recent Administrations, Tom August had been persuaded on numerous occasions to follow the President's wishes. If the formula was about to fail in this case, Senator Munson knew, it was because this case was of a nature the formula was not quite broad enough to cover.

Just before he left to go down to the floor for his regular pre-session talk with the press, at about the moment when he was really beginning to worry about the implications of their elliptical conversation on the President's health, two more calls came in for him. One was from Tom August's and Harley Hudson's recent host in South Carolina, dutifully fulfilling his historic role of adviser-to-everybody-about-everything, and the other was from the best-publicized cardinal in the hierarchy, dutifully fulfilling *his* role as the most egregious busybody in American politics. The Senator listened patiently to the adviser's sagely innocuous comments, unh-hunhed his way through several vapid moments with the Church's most ubiquitous prince, agreed heartily with them both that the Leffingwell nomination was certainly important, all right, and hung up with the fervent hope that he had satisfied them once and for all. He had troubles enough without being pestered by those two.

"In just a moment," the guide was telling his gallant band, by now a little wan and footsore, "you will enter the Senate of the United States and watch a session begin. You will see the Majority Leader, Senator Robert D. Munson of Michigan, holding his regular press conference at his desk, where he talks to reporters every day before the session, briefing them on what is going to happen during the afternoon. The Vice President of the United States, the Honorable Harley M. Hudson, will be in the chair as the session begins. The invocation will be delivered by the Reverend Carney Birch, Chaplain of the United States Senate. If you don't see very many Senators on the floor at first, this is because many of them are still attending committee meeting elsewhere in the Capitol or in the office buildings. Much of the most important work in the Senate is done in committees, which accounts for the fact that attendance may seem light at times. Also, Senators may be in their offices answering mail or performing other duties for their constituents. A quorum call may be demanded by any individual member, and when it is, you will hear a bell ring twice. This bell rings throughout the Senate side of the Capitol and in the office buildings and is used to call Senators to the floor to debate or vote on important matters. So don't be disappointed if you don't see very many Senators on the floor right away, because they are either in committee or attending to other matters for their constituents. Also, some of them may be eating lunch, which I'll bet you and I would like to do right now. Now if you will just file in quietly and take your seats where the gallery attendant tells you——"

5

Now in the moments before the Senate was about to begin the chamber resembled a sort of tan, marble-paneled fishbowl in which pageboys in their white shirts and black pants darted about like minnows distributing bills and copies of the legislative calendar to all the desks, whisking off stray specks of dust, shoving the spittoons carefully out of sight, checking the snuff boxes to make sure they were full, joking and calling to one another across the big brown room. A few clerks and secretaries drifted in, the parliamentarian and his assistant stood at one of the doors talking, the clerk of the Senate and the sergeant-at-arms stood talking at another, the first reporters waiting to see Bob Munson wandered into the well of the Senate and stood about exchanging chaff. At his desk on the majority side, Dave Grant, secretary to the Majority, busied himself with papers and made last-minute calls to senatorial offices advising the expected schedule of business for the day, and at his desk on the minority side Bert Hallam, secretary to the Minority, did the same. Above in the public galleries the tourists settled themselves in an excited, peering bustle, a few senatorial wives and special guests entered the family gallery to the Chair's left, a few dark-skinned individuals of indeterminate nationality took their places in the diplomatic gallery directly across from him, a few reporters came into the press gallery directly above and behind him. From his personal office across the Senators' lobby, behind the chamber, Harley Hudson peeped out quickly and then went in again, but not before several tourists had spotted him and exclaimed delightedly to one another. The press corps grew in front of Bob Munson's desk and in front of that of Warren Strickland of Idaho, the Minority Leader, directly across the center aisle. Paul Hendershot of Indiana, the first Senator to appear, came on the floor like some bright old peering bird and took his seat toward the back of the room; he was followed quickly by Cecil Hathaway of Delaware, John Baker of Kentucky, Bob Randall of New Jersey, and Powell Hanson of North Dakota. For a moment the four of them stopped to talk, a little knot of laughing, congenial men, then broke up and went to their respective desks. Murfee Andrews of Kentucky, loaded down with books and documents, came in prepared to do battle on the pending Federal Reserve bill; he was followed by his two principal antagonists, Taylor Ryan of New York and Julius Welch of Washington, looking fully as determined as he. It was ten minutes to noon on the day of the Leffing-well nomination and the Senate, with the exception of minor changes here and there, looked exactly as it had at ten minutes to noon in 1820, 1890, 1910, 1935, 1943, or any other time. As if by concerted agreement the Majority Leader entered down the center aisle, the Minority Leader entered from the side, and the press moved in on them both as they shook hands and gave one another friendly greeting while the tourists stared and twittered up above.

"How's the weather?" Warren Strickland murmured; Bob Munson grinned, pulled him close, and whispered in his ear, "Still cloudy and uncertain." The Minority Leader laughed and started to move across the aisle to his desk.

"Don't go away, Warren," AP said. "We've got things to ask you both."

"I don't know anything," Senator Strickland said with his quick ironic smile, coming back to lean against Bob Munson's desk. "You ask Bobby. He knows everything, that's his job."

"Bobby," Senator Munson announced firmly, "doesn't know anything either."

"Oh, come now, Senator," the Baltimore *Sun* said. "Surely you can do better than that. How soon are you going to get action on the nomination?"

"I believe Senator August will probably make an announcement as soon as his plans are firmed up," Bob Munson said.

"He didn't make any announcement at the White House," the New York *Herald Tribune* observed.

"Oh, was he at the White House?" Senator Munson asked.

"As if you didn't know," the Evening *Star* said amiably. Bob Munson smiled.

"Tom ought to be the one to say," he said. "It's his committee, after all."

"Is it, Senator?" the *Post* asked skeptically. "I thought you and the President ran it."

"Not quite," Senator Munson said. "Not quite. What else can we do for you boys?"

"You haven't done anything for us yet," AP advised him. "How many votes have you got, Bob? How many have you got, Warren? Let's be specific here."

"I think I have quite a few," Senator Munson said. "Warren thinks *he* has quite a few, and of course Seab Cooley thinks *he* has quite a few."

"Will yours stay hitched, though?" the *Times* asked. Warren Strickland gave the Majority Leader a poke in the arm.

"Not the way mine will," he said with a satisfied laugh.

Bob Munson laughed too, as noncommittally as possible.

"Leffingwell's in trouble then?" UPI said.

"My boy," said Bob Munson, "have you ever known Bob Leffingwell when he wasn't in trouble?" Everybody laughed and he added quickly: "Don't quote me on that."

"Seriously, Senator," said the Baltimore *Sun*, seriously, "how does it look to you right now?"

"It looks," said Bob Munson slowly, "like a terrific fight."

"Can we quote you?" the *Star* asked quickly.

"Yes," Senator Munson said thoughtfully. "Isn't that right, Warren?" Senator Strickland nodded and cleared his throat.

"From nearly all precedents of past presidential nominations for the Cabinet," he said carefully while the reporters scribbled hastily away, "Mr. Leffingwell will ultimately be confirmed. However, the issues involved here are so complex and the times in which we live are so serious, that there will undoubtedly be a most thorough Senate debate which could conceivably result in the defeat of this nomination."

"In other words," Bob Munson said with a twinkle, poking the Minority Leader in the arm in his turn, "like I said, a terrific fight."

"Right," Warren Strickland conceded with a smile, "but I knew they needed something more than one sentence from you to make a story."

"Not these boys," Bob Munson said jovially. "All they need is one word and they're off to the races with a two-column story."

"That's what's known as experience, Senator," the *Star* said, and at that moment the warning bell began to ring. Harley Hudson entered the chamber and took the Chair, Senator Strickland crossed to his desk and remained standing, Senator Munson and his other colleagues rose, the press sprinted off the floor, the room quieted down, and the session began as the Vice President banged his gavel. Carney Birch stepped forward and began the prayer, and Bob Munson realized with a start that as usual, everybody was trying to get into the act and not the least of these was Carney. This time it was even more flagrant than usual.

"Our Father," the Senate chaplain was droning in his snuffling way, "in these days of stress and strain when men are called upon to bear great burdens, give this Senate the strength and charity to ascertain of each who would serve his nation his true nature and purpose, lest through inadvertence and oversight there slip into seats of power those who would misguide and mislead this great people to whom You have given so much——"

The Reverend Carney Birch, Bob Munson reflected, was one of those ministers who go around slapping God on the back. A small, bulgy man with bad breath and an unctuous manner, he patronized both the Deity and his fellow men with serene assurance. "The Lord will do it for you!" Carney often promised, in a tone which indicated that he was both in a position to know and in a position to chastise the Lord if He didn't follow through. He was made further insufferable by the fact that he took with great seriousness the title, "the Hundred-and-First Senator," which had been conferred upon him many years ago in an unwise moment by a whimsical feature-writer for the Associated Press. This sobriquet Carney treasured, and he never missed an opportunity to live up to it, hanging around the floor for hours after the prayer was over, hobnobbing with great familiarity with people like Orrin Knox, who was too polite to object, and Blair Sykes, who didn't give a damn, breaking in on confidential conversations, running up from time to time to whisper in the Vice President's ear, and generally making himself beloved of all. But there was no getting rid of him: he was pastor of the church downtown to which Reverdy Johnson belonged, Reverdy had gotten him the chaplaincy twenty years ago, and every time anyone tried to oust him the *Star* and the *Post* would come forth with stern editorials beginning, "It is with great regret that we note that political partisanship is threatening the proper place of religion in the United States Senate." *That* always stopped *that*. So Carney stayed on, getting older and bulgier and more odorous and more obnoxious, one of those situations the Senate suffers with placid patience because it just isn't worth anybody's time to go through the fight necessary to get it straightened out.

Well-launched, he was repeating, reasserting and reinforcing his admonition to the Senate to watch its p's and q's about Bob Leffingwell, and to the Lord to help it out. "O Lord!" he cried, and, "O Lord!" Bob Munson thought with impatient annoyance, "why doesn't he shut up and let us get on with it?" Just then his eye caught that of Harley Hudson and before he stopped to think he had winked and Harley had winked back. The exchange brought his fellow Michigander squarely into his thoughts, and with him the President's health, and for a second the Senator looked full at the Vice President with a quizzical expression that brought an immediate reaction from Harley. A worried little grimace crossed his face, he struggled with it, but it was too much for him; his lips formed the silent question, "What's the matter?" above Carney's bobbing head. Bob Munson shook his head hurriedly in a small, hasty gesture and deliberately looked away, concentrating on the flag behind Harley's chair. Carney droned finally to a fervent conclusion and Senator Munson went smoothly into the routine of the day, asking unanimous consent that the reading of the journal of yesterday's proceedings be dispensed with and then suggesting the absence of a quorum.

"The absence of a quorum is suggested," Harley said in a tone that indicated he was still worried, "and the Clerk will call the roll."

Bob Munson sat down and began looking busily through his papers, but just as he had anticipated, he was aware that Harley was gesturing to Powell Hanson to take the Chair and was getting ready to come down from the dais to see him. A second later the Vice President slid into the seat beside him.

"What is it, Bob?" he whispered at once, and Senator Munson thought with a sigh that while the Vice President was wonderfully goodhearted and an awfully nice guy in many ways, he certainly had not been equipped by temperament or nature for either the role he had to play, or the role he might be called upon to play. Politics, he reflected as he had so many times, did some of the damnedest things sometimes; a rather guilty reflection, since he himself had had so much to do with it, in this particular instance.

"Nothing," Bob Munson said firmly. "Not a thing, Harley." But he had spoken without taking into account the fact that on one particular subject the Vice President, like all Vice Presidents, had developed a nervous instinct that was almost infallible.

"Is anything wrong with the President?" Harley asked tensely. Senator Munson dropped his papers and swung about in his chair to face him full on, a gesture that was not lost on the press gallery above.

"Nothing," he said in a savage whisper between his teeth, "is wrong with the President. Now stop acting like a damned fool and get back to the Chair where you belong."

"Well, I can't help but worry, Bob," Harley Hudson murmured apologetically. "I just can't help but worry."

"Take my word for it," Senator Munson said in the same deliberate tone, "there is no reason for you to worry." Then after these lies, necessary if Harley was not to go spinning right up through the ceiling out of sheer nervous tension, he decided instantaneously on the only diversion that would calm the Vice President down.

"I was talking to him about an hour ago," he went on quietly, turning back and relaxing in his chair, "and he said to tell you that he wants you to work very closely with me on the Leffingwell nomination. All that's wrong with him is that he feels you have been cold-shouldering him a little lately, and he's somewhat hurt about it, that's all."

"I?" Harley Hudson said in an audible cry of amazement which he promptly reduced to an agonized whisper. "I? Why, Bob, I've done my level best to co-operate with him in every way. You know that, Bob."

"Well, he gets ideas, you know," Bob Munson said soothingly. "There's so much pressure and tension in that office, sometimes a man overlooks his real friends a little. I'm sure it's just a passing thing, and the way to wash it out altogether is for you to pitch in with me and get this thing through as fast as we can. Then he'll know he was mistaken."

"Anything you say, Bob," the Vice President said humbly. "You know you can count on me all the way. You tell him so, too."

"He'll be pleased to hear it, Harley," Senator Munson said comfortably. "Now why don't you go back there and talk to Paul Hendershot? Calm the old boy down, put a good face on it—you know how to do it. Let me know what he says."

"Sure thing, Bob," Harley said in a relieved tone. "I'll go talk to him right now."

"Think up an excuse first," Bob Munson advised, "otherwise he'll be suspicious."

"Sure, Bob," Harley said. "I sure will." Bob Munson clapped him on the back as he rose.

"O.K., Harley," he said soothingly. "There'll be plenty to keep you occupied on this one."

"Good," the Vice President said fervently. "Good."

Senator Munson turned back to his desk with a sigh audible enough so that Warren Strickland stirred in his chair across the aisle. The Majority Leader looked at the Minority Leader and the Minority Leader winked. The Majority Leader grinned, shook his head, and winked back.

"Mr. Lytle!" the Clerk said in a tone full of reproof, for so far only eight Senators had answered the call and he was halfway down the list. "Mr. Mason! . . . Mr. McKee! . . . Mr. Monroe! . . ."

Remembering the national convention at which Harley had received the vice-presidential nomination—that convention from which so many subsequent tensions in the Senate had stemmed—Bob Munson reflected that the Vice President's story was in some ways so standard and in some ways so startling that it probably represented pretty much the mean of American politics. A wealthy businessman in Michigan who had never taken much interest in public affairs, he had suddenly been catapulted into the race for Governor when the original nominee had died in mid-campaign. Harley in his florid, jowling, graying style was a handsome and well-preserved fifty-three at the time, fortunately possessed of the ability to make a reasonably forceful and commanding speech. He had gone through the tensions of the campaign in good shape, had been elected by a large vote, had managed to perform his duties without visible stumbling, and a year later had been boomed for the Presidency by Bob Munson and Roy Mulholland, who had joined forces in a complicated cross-ruff by which they hoped to hold the delegation in line for the present incumbent of the White House, then only an amiable and rather enigmatic Governor of California. Orrin Knox had been the Governor's principal opponent, and for a while Harley, having sense enough to assess his own boom for what it was, had leaned very strongly toward Senator Knox in spite of his own Senators' pressure for the Governor. Like all timid men, when he decided to become stubborn he had been fearsomely so, and it had been touch-and-go right up to the night of the balloting as to who would control the Michigan delegation. In a final showdown Harley had won and they had thought they were going for Orrin Knox. At some point during the evening, however—and Bob Munson never knew exactly what happened, for neither of them would tell him—there had been some sort of friction between Harley and Orrin, and that had done it; Harley had cast Michigan's unanimous vote for the Governor. The minute his words were out, Senator Munson and Senator Mulholland had fought their way across the roaring hall to the California delegation and promptly gone to work. An hour later the news was out that Harley was the nominee's choice for Vice President, a job to which he had been re-elected four years later, not so much because he had done anything notable but just because he had not gotten in anybody's way, and so the President, not wanting to stir up any trouble in the new convention, had taken the customary easy way out and permitted him to run again.

This tale, no different in essentials from that of twenty men who had held the nation's second office, had just those elements of fantasy and cold-blooded practicality that seem to go into many and many an American political success. A shift here, a shift there, a change of timing somewhere else, a fluke that happened or a fluke that didn't, and Harley M. Hudson would not be Vice President of the United States. As it turned out, however, he was; no worse and no better than most selected by just the same process of fluke and no-fluke, but under present circumstances on a spot he half-sensed and wholly feared, in which he might presently be called upon to be considerably better than most, for his country's sake. Bob Munson sighed heavily again, and this time did not wink at Warren Strickland. He would have to hold Harley's hand as it had never been held before, if that happened. Indeed, the whole Congress would have to hold it, as best they could, if Harley was to make out in the way he would have to if he was to succeed.

"Mr. Parrish!" the clerk said, becoming steadily more aggrieved, for by now only about thirty Senators were on the floor, and a quorum was fifty-one, "Mr. Root! . . . Mr. Ryan! . . . Mr. Starr! . . . Mr. Sykes! . . ."

"That was a touching scene," Stanley Danta observed, sliding into the chair vacated by the Vice President, the chair that was actually Seab Cooley's as senior member and president pro tempore of the Senate. Seab had not yet come in to claim it this morning, and, "Where is he and what's he up to?" was not the least of the Majority Leader's worries at the moment.

"He's worried about the nomination," Bob Munson explained casually. Senator Danta smiled.

"He's worried, period. I hope you reassured him."

"Don't I always?" Senator Munson asked. "Half my time is spent re-assuring Harley. What do you hear?"

"I'll be a good second-generation Yankee and answer a question with a question," Senator Danta said. "What do *you* hear?"

"I haven't had time to hear much," Bob Munson confessed. "Michigan needed me this morning. I never got away from the office and made precious few calls."

"Well, I," said Stanley Danta, "have been a good boy. I've been checking, just the way you said. As of the moment I find five sure votes for Bob Leffingwell, sixteen doubtfuls, and seven opposed."

"Who's sure?" Bob Munson wanted to know. The sures, Stanley explained, were Murfee Andrews of Kentucky, Dick Althouse of Maryland, Cliff Boland of Mississippi, Powell Hanson of North Dakota—and Stanley Danta.

"That's a handsome nest egg to start with," Senator Munson remarked dryly. "What about Brig?"

"Brig," Stanley Danta said, "is being elusive. I think he suspects, no doubt with reason, that you have designs on him if this thing gets into a real hassle. And of course he knows it's going to."

"I haven't any designs on him," Bob Munson said. "I just want him in line, that's all. Of course if Tom August had to appoint a subcommittee to handle hearings, it would look good all around if Brig could chair it. But that's not 'designs.'"

"No?" Senator Danta smiled. "He can see you coming a mile away."

"Hmph," Senator Munson said.

"Mr. Wannamaker! . . ." the clerk said with an air of sadness as he came to the end with only forty Senators in the chamber, "Mr. Welch! . . . Mr. Whiteside! . . . Mr. Wilson!"

Senator Munson rose. He didn't know where all his distinguished colleagues were, but he knew they would drift in sooner or later.

"Mr. President," he said, "I ask unanimous consent that further proceedings under the quorum call be dispensed with."

"Without objection," said Powell Hanson in the Chair, "it is so ordered."

"Mr. President," Bob Munson said, "I move that the Senate proceed to the consideration of the pending business, Calendar No. 1453, Senate bill 1086, a bill to amend the Federal Reserve Act."

"Mr. President!" cried Murfee Andrews promptly from his side of the chamber, and, "Mr. President!" shouted Taylor Ryan loudly from his.

"The Senator from Kentucky," Powell said, recognizing one of his own, and Murfee Andrews with a triumphant smile at his opponent launched into what was obviously to be a lengthy speech. Senator Munson sat down.

"Have you seen Orrin?" he asked. "Your beautiful daughter is due here in another five minutes to have lunch with me, and I thought maybe he would like to join us. You too, if you like, of course."

"Thanks," Stanley smiled. "I think I can make it. No, I haven't seen Illinois's most indignant son. Nor, for that matter, have I seen South Carolina's. Do you suppose what I suppose?"

"Lord, I hope not," said Senator Munson emphatically. "I hope not! That's why I want to have lunch with him. Maybe I can head him off before Seab gets to him."

Senator Danta gestured toward the side door.

"Lo, he comes," he said, and indeed Orrin did, striding in with his bustling, purposeful air, a large briefcase in one hand, some books, some papers, a general manner of being able to solve the world's problems completely, at once, in the most practical and sensible way that they could possibly be solved. Bob Munson turned around and gestured to Tom Trummell of Indiana, sitting a couple of rows back. Senator Trummell came forward in his gravely ponderous and humorless way, but with a pleasant smile, and took the Majority Leader's chair. "Let's go," said Senator Munson to Senator Danta, and they beelined for Senator Knox.

"Well," AP said to UPI as the three Senators went past the press table on their way in to the Senators' private dining room, "I guess Orrin Knox must be putting his price pretty high."

"Apparently," UPI said, "he can name it."

Inside the small, dark, crowded room with its hustle and bustle of Senators, their families and/or constituents, they found Crystal Danta already seated at a table in the corner chatting with Bessie Adams of Kansas, who was just finishing. Bessie looked up and smiled in her pleasantly grandmotherly way that never missed a trick, and the slightest glint of amusement came into her eyes.

"Bob," she said, "Stanley—Orrin—what a distinguished gathering! I suppose you're going to talk about the wedding. That's what we've been talking about."

"If I know my daughter," Stanley Danta said with a smile, "and if

I know the senior Senator from Kansas, the talk has ranged farther afield than that." Senator Adams smiled blandly.

"We can't imagine what you mean, Stanley," she said. "It was mostly about the wedding, wasn't it, Crystal?"

"Mostly," Crystal agreed, "and anyway, the Senator didn't give me the slightest hint of how she intends to vote on the nomination."

"I didn't expect she would have," Senator Munson said. "I know Bessie." And his tone for a second sounded so forlorn that Elizabeth Ames Adams burst out laughing.

"Poor Bob," she said lightly. "Poor Bobby! He has so *many* problems, and I am one of them. But don't despair, Robert. Right and justice will triumph in the end."

"Thanks so much," Bob Munson said with a reluctant smile. "I wish I were sure of that."

"If you were more sure of what they *are*," Senator Adams told him suavely, "then you might be more sure of whether they *would*. But I must run along and get back up to the floor."

"Have you got an amendment to the Federal Reserve bill?" Orrin Knox asked with interest. Senator Adams shook her head.

"No, actually I've just got an editorial from the Topeka *Capital* on Bob Leffingwell that I want to put in the Record."

"That was fast work," Senator Danta said. "Did they wire it to you?"

"As a matter of fact," said Senator Adams, "they did. That's how important they think it is, out where I come from. Have a good lunch. I'll see you all later."

"So long, Bess," Bob Munson said. "Don't slip on any banana peels."

"Not before I vote on Bob Leffingwell," Senator Adams assured him pleasantly as she left.

"Hmph," Senator Munson said.

"I think it's very exciting," Crystal Danta observed with a wicked little chuckle as they sat down and prepared to order. Senator Munson looked at her sternly.

"I've spanked you before, young lady," he said, "and I might do it again."

"Right here?" Crystal asked. "Oh, Uncle Bob, *do*."

Orrin Knox laughed.

"That would be a sensation, wouldn't it?" he observed. "Yes, Uncle Bob, do."

"Order your lunch, everybody," Bob Munson directed them. "It's on me."

Around the room as they did so his practiced eye fell on Bessie's junior colleague, the careful and homespun Harold Kidd, eating with his wife; Donald W. Merrick of Colorado, looking as usual as though he hated the world— How do some people get elected? Bob Munson thought— Cecil Hathaway of Delaware, talking in his usual furious, shotgun fashion to George Keating of Nebraska, already well gone on his daily battle with the bottle; Charles W. McKee of North Dakota, handsome and vacant, with pudgy, pompous Bob Randall of New Jersey and white-haired, kindly Archibald Joslin of Vermont; Stonewall Jackson Phillips of Tennessee, looking competent and able and with that sort of closed-off efficiency that many young and ambitious men in politics develop, being courteous and attentive to peppery old Newell Albertson of West Virginia, who just happened to be chairman of Interstate Commerce Committee and violently opposed to an airlines bill that Stoney was quite anxious to have passed; Kenneth Hackett, lean and strange, talking to his self-possessed, noncommittal little colleague from Wisconsin, Magnus Hollingsworth; and portly, self-important Ben Mason of Rhode Island, hailing purse-lipped, eternally disapproving Walter Calloway of Utah to come join him and "these wonderful folks from Providence who've just dropped in to see me."

All of these perceptive gentlemen, Bob Munson saw, were quite as interested in observing him and his intriguing party as he was in observing them; and after collecting a number of sidewise glances that slid rapidly over his table and visibly registered surprise and interest, he turned deliberately to his menu and gave the waiter his order. As he did so Orrin Knox gave a chuckle at his side.

"Everybody certainly wonders why we're here, don't they?" he asked in a teasing tone. Bob Munson contemplated several strategies in a split second and chose the only one that worked with Orrin, complete honesty.

"Oh, they know," he said blandly. "And so do we, don't we?"

Senator Knox chuckled again.

"I dare say," he said. Stanley Danta chuckled too.

"Bob has a devious plot in mind, Orrin," he said cheerfully. "He just wants your vote."

"Not only that," Senator Munson said candidly. "I want your complete, one hundred per cent, all-out support."

"Have I always had yours?" Senator Knox asked quietly, and Bob Munson recognized with annoyance that there was that God-damned convention again.

"Most times," he said thoughtfully. "Yes, I think I can say most times." Then he looked Orrin straight in the eye. "Haven't you?" he asked bluntly.

Senator Knox laughed in an unamused way.

"When it suited your purpose, Bob," he said tartly. "When it suited."

"Isn't that how we all support each other?" Senator Munson asked calmly. "You're a realist, Orrin. That's the only way anything ever gets done in the American government—when it suits the purposes of enough people."

"Hmph," said Senator Knox. Then he remarked casually, "I suppose Seab is mustering the troops against him already."

"You ought to know," Senator Munson said quickly, a shot in the dark, but he could see it had gone home, for Senator Knox started a little, then broke into a laugh.

"I should," he admitted.

"I hope you didn't sign anything," Senator Danta said dryly.

"It was all verbal," Orrin Knox said with a grin. "He wanted something in blood, but I wouldn't give it to him."

"Well, that's good," Bob Munson said. "I guess there's still hope for our side, then."

"Some," Orrin Knox said seriously. "But I don't like it. If I support him it's going to be as an intellectual exercise and not because my heart is in it."

"Oh, well, if that's your only scruple," Bob Munson said comfortably, "you'll have lots of company there."

"Why," Senator Knox demanded in an exasperated tone, "*why* did he have to appoint someone who——"

"I know," Senator Munson said cheerfully. "It's a question to which we will never know the answer, I'm sure. Anyway, I take it you're in a position of benevolent neutrality at the moment."

Senator Knox snorted.

"A rather flowery way to put it," he said. Senator Danta smiled.

"Not neutral and not benevolent, eh, Orrin?" he said, and Senator Knox laughed.

"I wouldn't say that, either," he said.

"Well, what *I* would say," Crystal Danta broke in firmly, "is that that's enough business for now. I want to talk about me and Hal. We went shopping before lunch."

"I suppose you spent all his money," his father said.

"A good part of it," Crystal said cheerfully. "He might as well get used to it. We got some pretty things, though."

"I'm sure of it," Orrin Knox said with a smile.

"Well, we did. You'll see."

"There's Brig," Stanley Danta told Bob Munson. His daughter sighed.

"You see?" she said. "I try to brighten the day for Senators of the United States, and they go right back to business in spite of me."

"It's tough," her father agreed. "Ask him over, Bob."

The first shift was changing in the dining room, and people like determinedly homespun George R. Bowen of Iowa and squat, portly, toad-shaped Walter S. Turnbull of Louisiana, and their constituents, were beginning to replace Donald Merrick and Benjamin Mason, and their constituents. Senator Anderson, standing in the doorway, was obviously looking for a friendly face and company. Bob Munson raised a hand and waved and the Senator from Utah came over promptly in his pleasant, easy way to greet them all as they made room for him at the table.

"Crys," he said, "I'm delighted to see you. Everything all set for the big day?"

"Well, not quite," she said with a laugh. "After all, it's still three weeks off, and an awful lot can be done in three weeks, you know."

"Women," Brigham Anderson said. "How they do love to fuss. How's Hal bearing up?"

"At the moment," Crystal Danta said, "he acts as though he likes it. I imagine he may get skittish before the day arrives, though."

"I imagine," Senator Anderson said. Then he turned to the Majority Leader. "Well, Robert," he said, with just the slightest trace of challenge in his voice, "what vital information have you got to impart this afternoon?"

Bob Munson smiled.

"I'm more interested in what you have to impart," he said.

"Not a thing," Brig said pleasantly, hailing a waiter and ordering soup, coffee, and a piece of pie, "not a thing. The sovereign state of Utah is in good shape, and so is its senior Senator. I can't speak for its junior today."

Orrin Knox gave an abrupt laugh.

"He was in here a little while ago," he said, "looking as pickle-faced as usual."

"He compensates for my frivolity," Brigham Anderson said with his quick grin. "Stanley, are we going to get that atomic-power bill through next week?"

"Ask the Majority Leader," Senator Danta said. "I'm agreeable."

"I guess we can get to it soon," Senator Munson said.

"I suppose you'll want to get the decks cleared as soon as possible," Senator Anderson said. "I hear this Leffingwell business is going to be a rush job."

"What do you mean, a rush job?" Bob Munson said indignantly. "I'm not rushing anybody. Where did you hear that?"

"I ran into Tom August a while ago," Brig said. "I got the impression the word was out to ram it through on the double. Next Monday was what I gathered from his obscure murmurings, which seems like a real zippy schedule if you can do it, Bob."

Senator Munson looked pained.

"Tom always messes everything up," he said candidly. "Of course I think the President would like it to move, but I doubt if it can be done by next Monday. Certainly it can't if Tom goes around blabbing his plans to everybody."

"He tells me there'll be a special committee meeting tomorrow morning," Senator Anderson said. "Will you be in town, Orrin?"

Senator Knox frowned.

"I hadn't planned to be," he said. "I was going to Illinois for the weekend. But I guess I'll cancel that."

"I too," Brigham Anderson said. "I have to make a speech in New York tomorrow night and was planning to get up to the big city early. But I guess I'll catch a late plane, now."

"We thought it would be a good idea to get started on it," Bob Munson said defensively, "because chances are it will be somewhat lengthy."

"Somewhat," Brig said. "Have you talked to Seab?"

"Everybody has talked to Seab," Senator Munson said sourly. "He's going to perform on schedule."

"Then it will be more than somewhat," Senator Anderson said. "I hear you have plans for me too, Bob."

"Oh, hell," Senator Munson said disgustedly. "Can't Tom keep anything secret?"

"You know he can't," Orrin Knox said flatly. "He's the biggest fool in the Senate."

"Oh, don't be harsh," Stanley Danta said charitably. "He means well in his own odd way."

"I suppose," Orrin conceded, "but it's mighty odd, sometimes."

"I'm not sure I want to chair any subcommittee, Bob," Brigham Anderson said quietly. "In a way, I have a prejudice as strong as Seab's."

"That's one reason we want you to do it," Senator Munson said. "If you're in charge everybody will know it hasn't been stacked in his favor, and at the same time they'll know he's getting an absolutely fair and considerate hearing."

"That is true," Orrin Knox told him. "You have a wonderful reputation for fairness, Brig."

"Aw, shucks, Senators," Brigham Anderson said mockingly. "You make me feel all over funny. I still don't see why I have to get stuck with it, though."

"For just the reasons we've said," Bob Munson remarked. "It's practically inevitable."

Senator Anderson looked at him thoughtfully, and across his handsomely candid young face there came the intent, worried expression his colleagues knew so well in moments of stress.

"I have lots of qualms, Bob," he said soberly. "Not only national qualms, but personal qualms. Maybe it's a premonition, or something, but I feel I shouldn't get mixed up too directly in this."

"Somebody has to do the Senate's dirty jobs, Brig," Stanley Danta said quietly. "If there weren't a group of us who were willing, they'd never get done, would they?"

The senior Senator from Utah gave the senior Senator from Connecticut a quick smile and his worried expression eased.

"You're such a nice person, Stanley," he said. "You really are. Such a gentleman and such a fine one. How can I withstand pressure like that?"

"We'll all feel better about it, Brigham," Orrin Knox said.

"That does it," said Brig with a grin. "I'm lost. Crys, did you ever see such a snow job?"

"You're up against three old hands," Crystal told him, "and you haven't got a chance. I knew you were lost the minute you came in the doorway."

"You should have warned me," Brigham Anderson said.

"Oh, it's fun to watch," Crystal assured him. "I've been brought up on that sort of thing, remember. I wouldn't miss it for anything."

"Poor Hal," Senator Anderson said with a sigh. "A heartless woman awaits him."

"Very," Crystal Danta said softly with a smile. "Oh, so very."

Suddenly through the Senate side of the Capitol the two rings of the bell for a quorum began their insistent, repeated call, and Bob Munson looked at Stanley Danta in surprise.

"What do you suppose——?" He asked, and just then the slight, brisk figure of Dave Grant, secretary to the Majority, appeared at the door and came to the table with a harried look on his usually impassive face.

"Paul Hendershot is up," he told Bob Munson. "He's asked for a quorum and he says he's going to make a speech about Bob Leffingwell. You'd better get up there."

"So had we all," said Orrin Knox. "You go ahead, Bob. I'll get the check."

"Thanks, Orrin," Senator Munson said. "Sorry to rush, Crys, but you know how it is."

"I was born in a ballot box," Crystal Danta smiled. "I know."

The minute he stepped on the floor Bob Munson could sense that major events were under way, for as always when the Senate was about to get into a hot debate there was an electric tension in the air. Senator Hendershot was standing impassively at his desk, a slight scowl on his face, while the clerk droned again through the roll; around the chamber there was a kind of instinctive tightening-up and battening-down-the-hatches. Members were putting their papers aside and settling back, the pageboys were darting about again, bringing glasses of water to those who thought they might be impelled to speak; above in the public galleries the tourists were leaning forward eagerly, the press gallery was rapidly filling up. There was a general eddying-about all over the chamber, and this time the clerk was not having any trouble getting a quorum. Well over fifty Senators had come in already, Harley Hudson was back in the Chair, and the stage was set. Bob Munson just had time to reach his seat, say a hurried thank you to Senator Trummell and smile at Warren Strickland across the way when the Clerk concluded triumphantly:

"Mr. Wannamaker! Mr. Welch! Mr. Whiteside! Mr. Wilson!"

And the Vice President, after a hurried consultation with the Clerk, made it official.

"Sixty-eight Senators having answered to their names," he announced, "a quorum is present."

Senator Munson jumped up. "Mr. President!" he said, just as Paul Hendershot said the same. Paul looked distinctly annoyed, and Senator Munson hastened to reassure him.

"Mr. President," he said, "I just wanted to ask the distinguished Senator from Indiana how long he intends to speak, because for the benefit of other Senators, I desire to seek a unanimous-consent agreement on the pending Federal Reserve bill as soon as he concludes. Was the Senator planning to speak for fifteen minutes or so?"

At this there was a quick murmur of laughter and far over on the other side John Winthrop of Massachusetts snorted and remarked with audible sarcasm, "Nice try, Bobby!"

"I have no idea at all how long I intend to speak," Paul Hendershot said dryly, looking about the chamber in his peering, storklike way, "but I think I can assure the distinguished Majority Leader that it is apt to be slightly more than fifteen minutes. In fact," he added with one of his sudden bursts of indignation, "since the Senator asks, maybe it will be fifteen hours!"

"Attaboy, Paul," said Cecil Hathaway sotto voce, somewhere in the back. "You tell him, kid." Bob Munson smiled pleasantly.

"While I am sure we would all find fifteen hours of the Senator from Indiana edifying," he said, "he is normally so incisive, so cogent, and so expeditious that I still anticipate that fifteen minutes will be more like it. I was only asking the Senator."

"That's the trouble!" Paul Hendershot snapped, unappeased. "That's the way this whole shabby business is being handled. Rush, rush, rush, from the very first moment. I think—in fact, I am prepared to say it for a fact, that there is a deliberate, underhanded attempt to railroad this nomination through the Senate."

At this Bob Munson flushed angrily, and he was glad to see that Stanley Danta, Orrin Knox, and Lafe Smith were all on their feet, and that across the aisle Warren Strickland was rising deliberately to his.

"Now, see here!" he said with a touch of real anger in his voice. "I have not been party, nor has anyone I know, including the President, been party to any attempt to railroad through any nomination. I resent the remarks of the Senator from Indiana, Mr. President. I regard them as a deliberate, underhanded insult to me personally. I take them as a personal affront."

"That may be," Senator Hendershot said angrily, "that may be. I am sorry if the Senator takes my remarks personally. If he takes them personally, I apologize. But someone somewhere in some secret seat of power in some place in this government is trying to railroad this nomination through. It is not the distinguished Majority Leader. It is not the distinguished President of the United States. It is, perhaps, no one known to God or man. But someone is doing it, and the Senator knows it."

"Mr. President," Warren Strickland said quietly, forestalling a retort from Senator Munson, "Mr. President, it seems to me that just possibly, at this beginning of what promises to be a long and controversial episode, that Senators might refrain, at least at this stage of the game, from personal imputations and allegations. Not only is it against the rules of the Senate, but it is against the rules of common sense. We have to live with each other, and remarks such as those of the Senator from Indiana do not contribute to our living together in harmony. I regret that the distinguished Senator from Indiana has seen fit to indulge in such language so early in the debate over the nomination, and I am sure that upon reflection he will wish to modify his language in future. Courtesy and common sense would seem to make such a course advisable."

"I know what I think," Paul Hendershot said in a milder tone, "but if I have offended anyone, as I said, I apologize. Now, Mr. President," he went on, as the others resumed their seats, the tension lessened a little, and the Senate and galleries settled down again to listen, "what is behind this peculiar nomination as it comes up to us from the White House?"

Up at the Chair Senator Munson was in hurried conference with the Vice President.

"For Christ's sake," he whispered heatedly, "what did you say to Paul?"

"I didn't say anything to the old bastard," Harley whispered back with equal heat. "He started right in on me the minute I got to him. He said Seab had been talking to him about it, and he agreed with Seab, and he was going to say so. I asked him to wait until next week, and you saw how he obliged."

Bob Munson shook his head angrily.

"He's hopeless," he said. "Thanks anyway, Harley. Don't give up. There are plenty of others that need attention."

"I won't," the Vice President whispered. "You can count on me, Bob."

"Is there some sinister plot against the stability of this Republic?" Paul Hendershot was demanding, pacing back and forth behind his desk, as Bob Munson returned to his seat. "Is this some devious design by which we will be betrayed behind our backs by high officials presumably entrusted with our safety?"

At his side Senator Munson noted that the adjoining desk had finally been claimed by its rightful occupant. Seab was sitting with his legs stretched out, his hands folded across his ample stomach among the lodge and Phi Beta Kappa keys, his head forward in a half-drowsing way. But he wasn't asleep, Senator Munson saw; a little pleased smile was on his lips and he was humming "Dixie" quietly beneath his breath.

"Dum-de-dum-dum-dum-de-dum-de-dum-de-*dum-dum*," he was humming as Bob Munson leaned toward him fiercely.

"Well, I hope you're satisfied," he said in a savage whisper.

"Didn't think of Paul, did you, Bob?" Seab asked softly. "Didn't expect *him* to blow up, did you, now?"

"I'm not surprised," Senator Munson said. "I'm just surprised you're not in it. Since when did you hide behind somebody else to do your dirty work for you? One thing I thought you had, Seab, was the courage of your convictions."

"So I have, Bob," Senator Cooley said placidly. "So I have. I'll be talking in a minute."

"I hope so," Senator Munson told him, "because I want to answer."

"Are there not other patriotic men, better equipped to fill this great office, to whom we could accord confirmation more willingly?" Senator Hendershot demanded, and Senator Cooley rose slowly at his desk.

"Mr.–President," he said softly, and the room quieted down. "Will the Senator from Indiana yield for just a moment to me?"

"I am glad to yield to the distinguished and able Senator from South Carolina," Paul Hendershot said promptly.

"Can it be?" Senator Cooley asked softly and slowly. "Can–it–really–be, Senators, that this is the *only* man of all the millions in this great Republic, who is so distinguished and so able and so filled with his country's interests, that he must be named to this high post? Can it be that there is no–other–man? I find it hard to believe, Senators. I find it *mighty* hard to believe. Of course, now, I may be mistaken. It may be he is the–only–one. It may be there is no other among us who has the ability and the integrity and the patriotism and the concern for America of this man. But doesn't it seem a little strange to you, Senators, that he should be the–only–one?"

"Mr. President, will the Senator yield?" Lafe Smith asked crisply from his desk off to the side. Senator Cooley looked around slowly and a paternal smile came gently over his face.

"I am always delighted to yield," he said softly, "to our able and accomplished young colleague who always knows so much about what we all should do."

"That may be," Lafe snapped, flushing, "but if it is, it is immaterial. Does the Senator presume to think he knows more than the President does about what is needed for the office of Secretary of State at this critical juncture of our affairs? Does he think he knows better who the President can work with than does the President himself? I learned early when I came here of the omniscience of the distinguished president pro tempore of the Senate, with all his long decades of service, but I did not learn then nor have I learned since that he is infallible on all subjects under God's blue sky."

Senator Cooley smiled in his placid way.

"Now there, Senators," he said in a tone of wistful regret, "you have an example of the passions this man Leffingwell can arouse. Able young Senators, reared in the ways of their fathers, taught to be courteous at their mothers' knees, turn on their elders and rend them because of their passions over this disturbing man. It's disgraceful!" he roared suddenly, raising one hand high above his head and bringing it down in a great angry arc to strike his desk with a bone-jarring crack. "It's disgraceful that this man should upset the Senate so! Let us have done with him, Senators: Let us reject his nomination! Let us say to the President of the United States, give us a patriot! Give us a statesman! *Give us an American!*"

A spattering of applause broke from the galleries and Harley Hudson banged his gavel hastily.

"The galleries will be advised," he said sternly, "that they are here as guests of the Senate and as such they are not permitted to make demonstrations of any kind. The galleries will please observe the rules of the Senate."

"Mr. President," Bob Munson said icily, standing side by side with Seab but looking industriously at the Chair, "will the Senator from Indiana yield to me?"

"I yield," Paul Hendershot said.

"The Senator from South Carolina," Bob Munson said bitterly, turning his back on him and facing the Senate, "brings to bear all his famous eloquence and invective on Robert Leffingwell. It is not the first time that he has opposed Robert Leffingwell, and it will not be the last; but I venture to assert that his efforts on this occasion will meet with the same success with which they have met on other occasions. Colorful language and dramatic oratory, Mr. President, are not what the Senate needs on this occasion. This occasion is too serious for that. The Senate needs a sober and careful appraisal of this nominee to determine, in its own time and in its own high wisdom, whether he is fitted to fill the great office of Secretary of State of the United States to which the President has appointed him. The Senate is not in a mood for stunts, Mr. President. The matter is worthy of better than that from us."

At this the visitors in the galleries who hadn't applauded the first time broke into a rather hasty riffle of approval of their own, and again the Vice President started to gavel them to silence. Half a dozen Senators were on their feet shouting, "Mr. President!" however, so Harley thought better of it and hastily recognized Brigham Anderson.

For a moment, in one of those mutually appraising lulls that come in a heated debate, the senior Senator from Utah looked slowly around the chamber, aware of Henry Lytle sitting nervously on the edge of his chair nearby, of Archibald Joslin across the aisle looking upset in a dignified sort of way, of Johnny DeWilton, white-topped and stubborn, of George Keating watching blearily, and Nelson Lloyd listening intently, of the scattering of clerks, administrative assistants, and members of the House who had come in to stand along the walls as they so often did during major Senate clashes, of the tourists gawping and the press gallery scribbling furiously above, and the pulsating tension in the room. Then he looked directly at the Vice President and began to speak in a calm and level voice.

"Mr. President," he said slowly, "it is obvious already what all of us have known would be the case since we first heard of this nomination this morning. It has startled, and in some cases dismayed, the Senate. It has created already intense controversy and even bitterness. It has begun to divide us even before we have had a chance to unite on the only issue that should concern us here: can this man represent the United States in the councils of the world as we in the Senate wish it to be represented? The Senator from South Carolina asks if he is the only man who can do the job. That, I submit, is not the question. He is the only man before us, nominated by the President of the United States, to do the job. It is beside the point who else might do it; he is the only man selected to do it. It is up to us now to determine whether he can or not, on his own merits and in his own right. It is this question to which our energies should, indeed must, be directed now . . . Senators will recall that I have had occasion in the past to be critical of this nominee, indeed on one occasion to oppose and vote against him. It may be that I shall have occasion to do so again before this nomination is disposed of. The point now is that this nomination is not disposed of, that it has only begun to be disposed of; and that as of now, I do not know what I shall do on this nominee. Nor, I submit, does any honest Senator who is not blinded by prejudice or personal spleen know what he will do on this nominee. That is a secret the future holds, and I submit that we would be better advised now to leave it with the future, until this nomination has gone to committee and come out upon the floor in regular order for us to debate and vote upon."

"Mr. President!" several Senators said insistently as Brigham Anderson sat down, and Harley saw fit to recognize Orrin Knox. Paul Hendershot protested at once.

"Mr. President," he said in his acerbic way, "I believe I have the floor. I am not aware that the Senator from Illinois has asked me to yield to him, and I am not aware that I have yielded to him. I did not think I would have to instruct the Vice President in the rules of the Senate."

For once Harley looked really angry, and the Senate thought, with some delight, that for once it might see him provoked into angry retort. And for once, it was not disappointed.

"The Senator from Indiana," he said coldly, "is not equipped to instruct the Vice President in anything, let alone the rules of the Senate. The Senator from Indiana has the floor and may dispose of it as he pleases."

"Very well," Senator Hendershot said tartly, "then I yield to the Senator from Illinois."

"The Senator from Illinois," Harley said in the same cold voice, "is recognized by grace of the Senator from Indiana."

Amid a general titter, Orrin stood stolidly at his desk, absent-mindedly rearranging the papers upon it. When the titter died he looked up and far away, as though he were seeing things the Senate could not see. This trick of his always brought silence, and it did now.

"Mr. President," he said in his flat Midwestern tones, "I thank the Senator from Indiana for his courtesy, and I commend the Vice President upon his. It is not easy for the Vice President to preside over the Senate when passions are stirred as they are on this nomination. The Vice President at best does not have an easy job, and in my opinion he discharges it in a manner that should bring the commendation rather than the criticism of Senators who are privileged to work with him."

At this unexpected and startling compliment, uttered against a background of their differences at the convention, Orrin's shattered presidential hopes, his intermittent bitterness toward Harley since, and all the rest of it, there was an audible murmur which the Senator from Illinois ignored. The Vice President, looking first astounded, then greatly pleased, bowed his head slightly in acknowledgment. Senator Knox went on, in the same rather faraway manner.

"Mr. President," he said, "what is the issue here? It is not, as the senior Senator from South Carolina says, whether this man is the only man who can do the job; it is, as the senior Senator from Utah says, that he is the only man before us who has been selected to do the job. Like the Senator from Utah, I too am in doubt about this nomination; I too have opposed Mr. Leffingwell in the past, and I too may do so again in this instance. But I do not know at this minute whether I will or not, and I too submit that no Senator of integrity who really has the interests of his country at heart in this time of her deep trouble can know at this minute either. There is much involved here, Mr. President; much that has not yet even begun to be brought out. We have barely scratched the surface of this nomination and all its implications. I too," he said, his voice rising suddenly, his left arm shooting out before him with a paper still held tightly in his hand, his whole body twisting with the vigor of his utterance, "I too would like to take the easy way out, Mr. President. I too would like to demagogue. I too would like to say, 'This man did something to me once, and so I will oppose him forever!' I too would like to imply that there is 'some sinister plot against the Republic.' The point is, *I do not know,* and neither does anybody else. It is so much poppycock to say anybody knows. It is nonsense. It is demagoguery. I will have none of it. I will give him a fair hearing and I will make up my mind after the facts are in. Who among you"—and he turned slowly full around, searching from face to face while the Senate sat in absolute silence—"who among you is so petty, so uncharitable, and yes, so unpatriotic, that he will do otherwise in this hour of his country's need?"

After which, having proved that Seab was among his equals when it came to rafter-raising, he sat slowly down and returned to the impassive perusal of his papers while the galleries and Harley went once more through their little routine of impulsive applause and cautionary gavel banging.

"All right," Paul Hendershot said bitterly. "All right. Then I will ask the distinguished Senator from Minnesota a question, I will ask him this, if he will give me an answer: is it not true that the President of the United States called in the Senator from Minnesota this morning and asked him to rush this nomination through, perhaps by next Monday afternoon, if he could possibly do it? Is it not true that this plan was concurred in by the

Senator from Minnesota and the distinguished Majority Leader? I want to know the answer to that, Mr. President, and then I yield the floor."

Tom August got up slowly in his protesting, mole-like way, and looked around the chamber as if seeking solace and support. Apparently he thought he saw neither, for he gripped his desk so hard the press gallery could see his knuckles turn white, and when he spoke it was in his usual soft voice but with an unusual edge of angry resentment.

"Mr. President," he said softly, "I do not like the tone of the senior Senator from Indiana, nor did I, earlier, like the tone of the senior Senator from South Carolina. These are not tones normally heard in the Senate, Mr. President, and it seems to me there has been a strange loss of courtesy here this afternoon. It is not becoming to the Senate, and I as one member protest it. The Senator from Indiana asks if the President of the United States did not ask me to, as he puts it, 'rush this nomination through,' when we talked this morning. I am not privileged to divulge my conversations with the President of the United States, and even if I were, I doubt if I should divulge them to the Senator, that is the senior Senator, from Indiana. However, I say this only: the President of the United States very naturally wishes this nomination expedited as much as possible. I assured him that insofar as it lay in my power I would co-operate to this end, subject always to the wishes of the Senate. This, I venture to state, is nothing sinister; it is the natural request of a President and it is the natural rejoinder of a member of his own party who happens to be chairman of the great Committee on Foreign Relations." And with an asperity very rare to him, he added as he sat down, "I would suggest to the Senator from Indiana and the Senator from South Carolina that if they think they can make anything of that, they do so."

"Mr. President," Senator Hendershot began angrily, "Mr. President——" But Senator Cooley forestalled him.

"Mr.—President," he said in his slow, deliberate, opening manner, "again I beseech Senators to contemplate for a moment the spectacle we are making of ourselves here. Who is causing this bitterness and hatred and division among us? Robert—A.—Leffingwell. Who is disrupting the friendly and cordial flow of legislative interchange, so necessary to our country's welfare? Robert—A.—Leffingwell. Who is turning this Senate into a cockpit of angry emotions? Robert—A.—— No, Senator, no, Senator, I will not yield. I see my friend, the distinguished senior Senator from Michigan, the great Majority Leader of this Senate, who has sat beside me—or, rather, I should say, beside whom I have sat—for all these many years, Mr. President, in the greatest brotherhood and love and harmony—he is on his feet, Mr. President, seeking recognition, asking me to yield—still beside me, Mr. President, but oh, what a difference! Now he stands beside me in bitterness and hate, no longer my brother, no longer my companion in this great legislative body, Mr. President, his face contorted with passion, his tongue thickened with hate, and why, Mr. President?" He bent low

evasion. This time, however, the answer was surprisingly direct, considering the place and circumstances.

"Are we going to get that atomic sub contract for the Portsmouth Navy yard?" Charlie Abbott asked.

This, Bob Munson knew, was the sort of thing he was going to be running into repeatedly as the Leffingwell nomination progressed, and he might as well set his pattern right now, particularly since several Senators nearby had overheard the challenge and had quieted to listen for his answer to it.

"We'll have to wait and see, Charlie," he said crisply. "If you help us, we'll help you."

"You help first," Senator Abbott said pleasantly, but with a little tightening around his eyes.

"Run along, Charlie," Senator Munson said, starting to turn back to Lafe and Powell. "I haven't got time to play games today." Senator Abbott placed a hand tightly on his shoulder.

"God damn it," he said angrily, "my people need that contract. We have eight hundred unemployed in that town right now, and Portsmouth isn't any metropolis. That's a lot of people for a town that size, Bob. The Administration had better come through on this, or by God, there'll be trouble, not only out there"—he gestured toward the floor—"but up there at the polls. We could lose New Hampshire next year, Bob. It's changing fast and it's got troubles."

"Haven't we all," said Bob Munson dryly. Then he moderated his tone.

"See here, Charlie," he said, looking beyond him at Cecil Hathaway of Delaware and Ed Parrish of Nevada and Rhett Jackson of North Carolina, all of whom were listening intently, "the President is aware of your situation there, and he wants to do the best he can for you, and I think you'll find Portsmouth won't be forgotten. But it's not going to be remembered on any blackmail basis, I give you my word as Majority Leader on that. Now if you want to come in with us on Bob Leffingwell, wonderful, your support will be welcome and valuable. If you don't, we'll make out. It's up to you Charlie. I'll be hoping to hear from you favorably one of these days soon."

Senator Abbott looked at him for a long moment, and Senator Munson looked impassively back. The eyes of the Senator from New Hampshire fell first.

"O.K., Bob," he said, but coldly. "We'll have to see."

"I guess we will, Charlie," Bob Munson said, unmoved, as Charles Abbott walked away. Ed Parrish waved ironically from across the room.

"Another day, another dollar," he observed dryly; and Bob Munson, aware that here was one vote he could probably count on, laughed out loud.

"I hope so," he said. Senator Parrish smiled.

"I'm sure of it," he said. "Pride goeth before a surrender, particularly where Charlie's concerned."

"Of course," Cecil Hathaway remarked, "you may find all of us that difficult too, you know, Bobby."

Senator Munson smiled, but his reply was pointed.

"I trust you all heard the answer he got," he said, and Cecil Hathaway grinned.

"How could we help it," he asked, "when you were so careful to make sure we would?"

Bob Munson laughed.

"You're just too sharp, Ceece," he said. "I can't have any secrets around here."

"Not from us who know and love you," Ceece said jovially. "That's for sure."

"Tell me," Bob Munson said as the others turned away and he could concentrate again on his two younger colleagues, "what are you going to do, Powell?"

"I'm for him," Senator Hanson said promptly, his trim blond head nodding vigorously. "I always have been, as you know."

"Yes," Bob Munson said, "one man who's never had any doubts about Bob Leffingwell. You're a rarity, my boy."

"It's largely a matter of conviction," Powell Hanson said. "We see things pretty much alike, Bob and I, in spite of the fact that I, unlike him, am not engaged in any sinister plots against the Republic."

"What got into Paul?" Lafe asked, and Powell snorted.

"He's always been a damned isolationist," he said, "he's never changed."

"Apparently Indiana hasn't either," Bob Munson observed. "They keep sending him back."

"Yes, that's true," Powell said. "Something people forget, sometimes: if our people didn't like us, we wouldn't be here."

"A little truism that is overlooked by some of our higher and mightier publications now and then," Senator Munson agreed. "I'd like your help on this, Powell, if you're willing."

"Gladly," Senator Hanson said. "I'll do whatever I can, Bob."

"Let me know what you hear," Senator Munson said, rising. "I'm going over to the other cave and talk to Warren Strickland for a minute."

"Send for us if you need help," Cecil Hathaway called as he started out the door. Bob Munson laughed.

"I think my passport is still good," he said.

As he traversed the short distance from his own side across the center aisle past the main door to the Minority cloakroom, he noted that Taylor Ryan was now up and arguing bluntly with Jay Welch on the Federal Reserve bill while Murfee Andrews cast in waspish comments whenever he got the chance. Harley had left the Chair and disappeared somewhere, gracious gray Lloyd B. Cavanaugh of Rhode Island was sitting in for him, and in the Majority Leader's own chair Tom Trummell had given way to John J. McCafferty of Arkansas, a wispy little old man of eighty-three who always looked as though he would blow away in the next high wind but somehow clung to the well-riveted affections of the people of Arkansas in spite of it. Irving Steinman of New York was sitting in for Warren Strickland in the Minority Leader's chair, soberly signing correspondence and ignoring the debate as he did so. Elsewhere about the floor Senator Munson spotted Clement Johnson of Delaware, apple-cheeked and bright-eyed, chatting amiably with chunky little Leo P. Richardson of Florida, who was sitting on the edge of his chair and swinging his legs, which were just too short to reach the floor. Dick McIntyre of Idaho, small, dark and swarthy as befitted his Indian blood, was gesticulating violently to Raymond Robert Smith of California, tall, elegant, handsome, and faintly, just faintly, willowy; Lief Erickson of Minnesota, big, bluff and biting, was talking forcefully to Porter Owens of Montana, small, hostile-looking and obviously unimpressed; and Luis Valdez of New Mexico, young, earnest and bespectacled, was arguing suavely with Seab Cooley's dark-eyed, dark-visaged colleague from South Carolina, H. Harper Graham. In the galleries above the tourists were thinning out, only a corporal's guard of wire-service reporters manned the press gallery; the afternoon was wearing on. He pushed open the door of the Minority cloakroom and walked in to be greeted by the usual jocular ribbing that always greeted his rare appearances in that enemy enclave.

"Lock up the silver!" Allen Whiteside of Florida cried in his jolly, plum-pudding way. "We're being invaded!"

"Under which king, Bezonian?" demanded Verne Cramer of South Dakota lazily from a sofa where he was stretched out full length with a pillow under his head, "Speak or die."

"The wits they have in the Minority," Bob Munson said wonderingly. "Why is it they can never get control of the government?"

"It's our contention," said John Winthrop of Massachusetts in his dryly twinkling way, "that the nation prefers quality to quantity."

"That's no way to build post offices," Bob Munson observed.

"Or conduct a foreign policy either, hm, Bobby?" Winthrop of Massachusetts suggested. Senator Munson made a face.

"It must be nice to have all the fun and none of the responsibility," he said, and John Able Winthrop snorted.

"I never heard it put with such classic simplicity," he said. "I only wish you'd tell me how to vote, if it's as simple as all that."

"I could tell you," Bob Munson said, "but you wouldn't listen."

"I might," Winthrop of Massachusetts said. "I may. But not yet awhile. My Yankee ancestors caution me to go slow on this one." He clucked between his teeth in a parody of his Yankee ancestors and smiled blandly at the Majority Leader. "Yes siree bob, Bob," he said.

"You and your Yankee ancestors," Senator Munson said. "I wonder if your grandfather and mine had all these headaches when they sat in the Senate together from Massachusetts."

"First World War?" Senator Winthrop said. "I guess they did. Probably felt the end of the world had come then, too."

"I suppose," Bob Munson said. "Only this time it probably has. Where's Warren, Win? I thought I'd find him in here."

"He'll be back shortly. He got a call from the White House and decided to take it in his private office down the hall."

"The White House?" Senator Munson said. "The President's really working, isn't he?"

"Didn't he tell you he was going to call Warren?" John Winthrop asked in surprise. "I thought to hear Paul Hendershot talk that the two of you were in cahoots in some big plot to stampede us."

"When did anybody ever stampede the Senate?" Bob Munson asked, and his tone was sufficiently wistful so that Senator Winthrop laughed.

"You sound as though you wished it were possible, Bobby," he said. "What's the matter, is life getting complicated?"

"It wasn't so very at noon," Senator Munson admitted, "but it is now. Anybody made any estimates over here?"

"Just what Warren says he told you this morning," Senator Winthrop said. "It hasn't changed much since then."

"Maybe Seab has increased the tally some," Senator Munson suggested, making the sounding he had come over to make; Senator Winthrop showed an expression of distaste.

"Seab," he said, "is overdoing it already. I knew he would, but not this soon. That stuff goes big with the galleries, and you can see what the press is making of it"—and he held up the final edition of the Star with a banner headline reading SENATE IN BITTER ROW ON LEFFINGWELL—"but it doesn't go big here. At least not with the old hands who count."

"Well, I hope not," Senator Munson said thoughtfully, peering out through the glass of the doorway into the Senate chamber just in time to see Albert G. Cockrell of Ohio go sweeping by with his slickly handsome good looks, his covey of adoring aides, and his hot-pants yen for the White House, "I hope not."

"Anyway," Allen Whiteside spoke up with a chuckle from across the cloakroom, "you know the Minority can always be convinced by a sound and logical argument from you, Robert. It's like the dentist said to the salesgirl in Woody's lingerie department——"

Bob Munson held up a hand.

"Not today, Al," he said in a pleading tone. "I'm too weak to stand your little funnies. All I want is your lousy vote."

Senator Whiteside gave one of his total laughs that started at the top of his head and worked down gradually, with many secondary earthquakes and other seismological disturbances, through his ample paunch to the tip of his toes.

"Ho, ho, ho," he chortled like some cynical old Santa Claus who had been around for a long time, which he had, "do you now? And what will you give me for that?"

"I didn't come over here to bargain," Bob Munson said. "I just had to slap Charlie Abbott down about that sub contract and I'm not about to come over and bargain with the Minority when I won't bargain with my own side."

"You'll bargain, Bob," Allen Whiteside said shrewdly. "Not right now, but you'll bargain. The day's going to come, on this one."

"We'll see," Senator Munson said. "What are you reading, Verne?"

"The *Federalist*," Verne Cramer of South Dakota said in his lazy, half-mocking way. "I take a refresher course in it about once a year, right after I reread the unexpurgated *Arabian Nights*. What's on your mind?"

"Ha," Bob Munson said tersely. Senator Cramer laughed.

"Tell the Prez to call *me*," he suggested. "Maybe *I* can be had, with the right persuasion."

"Ha," Bob Munson said again, and looking once more through the glass into the chamber he finally saw Warren Strickland appear down the center aisle, tap Irving Steinman on the shoulder with a smile, and reclaim his seat at the Minority Leader's desk.

"Take care," Senator Munson advised the Minority cloakroom's inhabitants, and went down to take back his own seat from John J. McCafferty. The ancient junior Senator from Arkansas was asleep, which didn't matter because Taylor Ryan had the floor for an hour's time on the Federal Reserve bill and was droning along in his sleek Princetonian way. When Senator Munson touched Senator McCafferty on the arm the old man jumped and looked up with a sheepish smile.

"Sorry, Bob," he said apologetically, rising somewhat shakily to his feet. "Just dropped off. Taylor isn't—he doesn't—well, you know Taylor. I just dropped off."

"No harm done," Bob Munson said with a smile. "I would have too. By the way, where's Arly Richardson?"

"Haven't seen him all day," said Arly's colleague. "Probably cooking up hell someplace."

"For me," Bob Munson said, and the old man chuckled thinly.

"Wouldn't know, Bob," he said. "Wouldn't tell if I did know."

"Thanks, John," Senator Munson said. "Don't get caught pinching the waitresses."

Senator McCafferty looked startled, then laughed so violently Senator Munson thought he would fall down.

"Better that than some other ways, Bob," he said between chokes of laughter. "Better that than some others!"

"Bring me some of that goat-gland extract, will you?" Bob Munson requested. "I could use it."

But at this Senator McCafferty was completely overcome, and gesturing Bob Munson away with a gnarled and withered hand he went laughing and choking and wheezing and chuckling and staggering back to his desk at the side of the room while Senator Munson watched and marveled that he could make it without falling down.

The afternoon was drawing on apace, he noted, and he was beginning to get that restless, impatient feeling he usually did around 5 P.M. It ought to be time to quit pretty soon, and he was ready for it. He hunched his chair across the aisle to a place alongside Warren Strickland's and leaned against his arm confidentially.

"I hear you got the word," he said, and the Minority Leader smiled.

"I see you hear I got the word," he said blandly.

"Was there anything I should know?" Senator Munson asked. Senator Strickland looked even blander.

"Just a chat between old friends," he said, "on the parlous times in which we live."

"You told him how many votes you could deliver for him," Bob Munson suggested.

"I estimated how many votes I could deliver against him," Warren Strickland said. "He seemed startled but undismayed."

"That's my boy," Bob Munson said.

"I told him the Administration could probably make some headway on this side of the aisle," Senator Strickland said seriously. "Particularly if Seab keeps on performing."

"And Orrin doesn't join him," Bob Munson said glumly.

"Orrin?" Senator Strickland asked, surprised. "He certainly didn't sound much like it this afternoon."

"Orrin is a fair-minded man," Senator Munson said, "but he didn't commit himself to anything . . . Let's get out of here," he added abruptly. "It's almost five and we've all got to get ready for Dolly's."

"I'm game," Warren Strickland said, surveying the floor which now was empty of everyone save Taylor Ryan, Murfee Andrews, Julius Welch, and a handful of clerks and pageboys. "Taylor ought to be just about through."

And so, in five more minutes, he was, concluding with a spiteful flourish that threatened to provoke Murfee and Julius into lengthy rejoinders. Senator Munson, however, was on his feet in a flash asking for recognition, and Harley Hudson, back in the Chair for the concluding moments of the session, hurriedly gave it to him.

"Mr. President," Bob Munson said firmly, "I move that the Senate stand in recess until twelve noon on Monday next."

"Without objection," said Harley, banging his gavel, "it is so ordered," and at once the pageboys began leaping about the chamber, shoving papers into desks, banging desk covers, shouting and calling to one another again in the big tan fishbowl of a room as the last tourists left, the press gallery emptied out, and the Majority Leader and his few remaining colleagues moved slowly out the doors.

6

Night had come down on the District of Columbia, and with it clouds and a biting wind carrying promise of snow. The bright day Dolly had witnessed at 10 A.M. through her bedroom window had succumbed to the erratic climate of the nation's capital and the most chronically frustrated Weather Bureau in the world was already hedging its bets with the cautious prediction that there might possibly be a blizzard if, of course, it didn't clear. In private homes from Chevy Chase to Falls Church and from Westmoreland Circle to Forest Heights, department heads, agency employees, clerk-typists, secretaries, professional people, military folk, members of the press, lobbyists and what-have-you, and their wives were putting last-minute touches on the parties to which they had invited other department heads, agency employees, clerk-typists, secretaries, professional people, military folk, members of the press, lobbyists, and what-have-you, and their wives. Out among the embassies the Belgians, the Ceylonese, the Rumanians, and the Dutch were getting ready to entertain at lavishly decorated, lavishly catered receptions that would be attended by representatives of all the other embassies in town with which at the moment, they happened to be on speaking terms. In hundreds of giant apartment houses thousands of government girls were about to descend in thousands of self-operated elevators to meet thousands of government boys for a night on the town; and on Ninth Street and other drab haunts of Washington's incorrigibly small-town sin, little aimless groups of sailors, soldiers, airmen, and marines from nearby bases had just begun to wander about looking for wine, women, and a place in which to enjoy them. Under the swinging chandeliers in the great white portico at Vagaries the Cadillacs, the Chryslers, the Chevvies, and the Fords were driving up to discharge their chattering, self-important cargo, the men encased in tuxedoes like a stream of glistening beetles, the women gussied-up fit to kill.

Night had fallen on the capstone of Western civilization, and sex and society were on the move.

For Dolly, standing just inside the door as the first car drew up, this was always one of the most exciting moments in life. It was even more so in Washington, where one never knew who the accident of timing would bring to one's doorstep first. She played a little superstitious game with herself which usually proved out—the first arrival or two would set the tone of the evening, whether it was to be basically political, diplomatic, or just social. This time fate contrived the obvious by depositing both politics and diplomacy on the stoop at once: Bob Munson arrived in his tired old Buick just as Krishna Khaleel rode up with a flourish in the Indian Embassy's sleekest chauffeured Cadillac. Senator Munson turned his car over to one of the parking attendants as K.K. got grandly out, and after an effusive greeting they advanced together upon their hostess.

"Ah, you see?" the Ambassador cried gaily. "I was wise to come early, you see; I am the chaperone of our dear Dolly and her gallant Senator."

"I'm sure all sorts of terrible things would have happened if you hadn't been here, darling," Dolly said coolly, taking his hand and drawing him in. "We do appreciate it so."

"I don't," Bob Munson said. "I resent it, as would any red-blooded American youth."

"You," Dolly told him, "are undoubtedly Washington's most dazzling humorist."

"Ah, you Senators," K.K. said airily, moving on into the fern-decked hallway. "You and Hal Fry. All I get, all day long at the UN, is Hal making jokes. For me, at me, about me, but always jokes, jokes, jokes. If we had Senators in my country they would be less frivolous. They would realize life is a serious matter, for us poor Asians."

"We all sympathize with you, K.K.," Bob Munson said, "and of course we regret our own levity too. I know Hal just wants to lighten your heavy load for you with an innocent jest now and then. He can't help it if he isn't properly reverent."

"There you go," K.K. sighed. "Just like he is. I think you are laughing pleasantly with me and suddenly you bite. It is disconcerting, you know?"

"Dear old K.K.," Senator Munson said expansively, seizing him by the arm as Dolly turned away to greet the Secretary of the Navy, the Secretary of the Army, and an Assistant Secretary of State for something-or-other, and their wives, "do come in here someplace and let's talk it over privately."

The Indian Ambassador gave him a shrewd sidelong glance and smiled dryly.

"Yes, dear old Bob," he said, "I know you wish to talk privately, and you wish to talk about your problem, Mr. Leffingwell. But I have already discussed this unfortunate, for you, matter with dear old Hal, who I know was on the telephone to you five seconds after to tell you what I said, and I really fail to see why I should discuss it any further with dear old Bob."

"Have a drink," Senator Munson said, steering him toward a bar in one corner, "and don't be any more stubborn than you can help."

"Really," K.K. said in a different tone, and for a second Bob Munson was afraid he had gone too far, you always had to watch it with the Indians, they were always so alert to see an insult in everything and take umbrage at the slightest excuse, "really, Bob, I try not to be stubborn, I do indeed. It is simply my way of saying that there is really nothing I can say to you that would in any way make clearer my already clear exposition to your good colleague from West Virginia."

"He seemed to have a very firm grasp on what you meant," Senator Munson agreed, "but I'd like to hear it too. What do you want, scotch or bourbon?"

"Scotch and soda, please," K.K. said, and Bob Munson ordered it and a bourbon and water for himself.

"Now," he said against the glad greeting cries of Dolly, three generals, an admiral, the counselor of the Brazilian Embassy, and the Secretary of the Interior, and their assorted wives, "what have you folks got against Bob Leffingwell?"

The Indian Ambassador sighed, watching the rapidly-filling room with shrewd appraising eyes.

"That Hal," he said. "Why does he think we have anything against your able Mr. Leffingwell? I am afraid I must not have made myself clear to him after all. I wished to indicate merely that we were proceeding with caution, which of course is necessary in this distraught world in which we live. I did not wish to indicate distaste, although apparently that is the interpretation given you by your attractive colleague."

"Then you're for him," Bob Munson said quickly, and K.K. sighed again.

"Honestly," he said, going into one of his more petulant moods, "does nothing I say make sense to anyone? Mr. Leffingwell is a difficult and controversial man. In some ways he is excellent, but in some others, of course, not so excellent. In general I would say we are for him, except when it comes to those features of character and interest which, of course, might dispose us to be against him. On the whole, I think that is our position," he said thoughtfully; and then, with firmness, "Yes, I am sure of it. You may count upon it."

"Well, thanks so much, K.K.," Senator Munson said. "You know how helpful this is in our thinking about it. Because seriously, you know, if anyone has a really violent dislike for him, it would have some bearing on what the Senate does. We don't want to confirm someone who starts with a dozen enemies abroad to begin with; he'll make enough as he goes along without an initial handicap. So I'm glad you're not hostile."

"Oh no," K.K. said, and suddenly he laid a hand on the Majority Leader's arm and said sympathetically, "We do not wish to complicate your problem, dear old Bob. I shall talk about it to my colleagues, you know. Our paths will cross sometime during the evening somewhere in this delightful house. There will be some clarification of views, perhaps. There will perhaps be other clarifications as the days go by. Then we will know better where we all stand. If the Senate wishes then to know our opinion, strictly unofficially, of course, why, we will probably have one."

"Stated in English?" Senator Munson couldn't resist, and the Ambassador gave him a rather wintry smile.

"Since that is the language of our past, our present and, it would seem, our future," he said, "that is what it is most apt to be. And now I must circulate, dear Bob, and so must you. That is half our business, circulation, is it not?"

Senator Munson sighed in his turn.

"It is," he said. "Take care, K.K. See you later."

"*A rivederci*," the Indian Ambassador said with a pixyish expression and moved off toward a South American enclave that was beginning to form near one of the buffet tables. As he did so Bob Munson became aware of a reproving presence near at hand; large plump body, large dark face, large liquid eyes looking with wistful reproach: the Pakistani Ambassador. He sighed again, involuntarily, and cursed a small private curse at the burden of world leadership that made life at Washington parties a constant careful navigation between bruisable egos, vulnerable feelings, and quivering national prides. He did not, however, intend to talk to the Pakistanis yet a while, and so with a bright smile and a quick, "Good evening, Mr. Ambassador, don't leave before I get a chance to talk to you, it's important"—uttered with hearty haste before the Ambassador had a chance to do more than begin an uncertain half smile and start tentatively forward—he took his drink and moved slowly off through the growing crush toward Howard Sheppard, the outgoing Secretary of State, who had come in a moment before with his little gray wisp of a wife and now was standing near one of the bay windows with his usual drooping, uncertain, melancholy look. This was heightened by the inevitable he's-on-his-way-out atmosphere that was already beginning to surround him. This inexorable attrition of prestige, which could reduce a man's influence in Washington overnight, was now at work on the outgoing Secretary; the greetings he was receiving were just a little vague, a little absent-minded, a little oh-so-you're-still-here; the fervent cordiality of yesterday was giving way to the half-puzzled, half-forgetful greeting of tomorrow. Although his resignation for reasons of health had been announced weeks ago, he had been around so long as Secretaries of State go that it had not seemed really final until the President named a successor. Now he had, and Howard Sheppard was occupying that lonely position of men in Washington who yesterday were all-powerful but today are only men. His expression changed from wan to a little less wan when the Majority Leader approached.

"Bob," he said, putting a little more strength than usual into a normally languid handshake, "how nice to see you. Grace dear," he added to the slight little figure he had carried with him through law practice, the governorship of Ohio and seven uneasy years in Foggy Bottom, "you remember Senator Munson," and Grace said of course she did. Bob Munson felt he must say something to relieve the encircling gloom and offered the first thing that popped into his head.

"Well, Howie," he said expansively, "you must be glad to be getting out of this rat race." Then he remembered hastily that of course Howie wasn't and tried to make amends.

"We'll miss you," he said firmly. "Your hand on the helm has held us steady, Howard. We're going to miss it more than you know. I hope you're not going to be leaving Washington? Surely you'll stay close by and let us have your counsel from time to time?"

"I don't think," Secretary Sheppard said with a sudden flash of unexpected and uncharacteristic bitterness, "that *he* gives a damn whether I stay here or not. *He* hasn't taken my advice on anything in six months."

"Oh, now," Senator Munson said soothingly, "I'm sure you're mistaken, Howie. Why, he told me only this morning——"

"I don't care what he told you," Howie said morosely, taking a deep gulp of his Manhattan, "it was just words. Why do you think I'm quitting, Bob? This is strictly between us, you understand, but *he* wanted me to. I'm not sick, I'm sound as a dollar. But *he* said something about wanting to try a new approach with the Russians and maybe he should have a new face to do it. I've done everything I could to work out an accommodation with the Russians and I could have tried again, but *he* wouldn't have it and I couldn't refuse. I don't know what this means for the country."

"Continued good diplomacy, I hope, Howie," Senator Munson said.

"I hope," the Secretary said darkly.

"Well, I'm disappointed to know you feel this way, Howie," Bob Munson said, and he really was, because Howie still had quite a few friends in the Senate and some of them might listen to him, "because I was counting on you to help me with the nomination."

"Bob Leffingwell?" the Secretary asked in a tone so harsh that Grace murmured, "Now, dear," in a worried way. "I wouldn't help him for anything."

"I hope that won't be your final answer, Howie," Bob Munson said earnestly. "There's too much involved——"

"You're damned right there is," the Secretary said bluntly, "and I'm going to do everything I can to make sure the Senate doesn't make a mistake about it."

"I'm sure it won't," Senator Munson said, with a certain coldness coming into his voice, "if you appear before Foreign Relations as the opening witness and testify in his behalf."

"I'll never do that," Howie Sheppard said angrily and Bob Munson stared thoughtfully into his highball glass.

"I think you will, Howie," he said gently. "I think I will ask the President to ask you to, and I think he will, and I think you will. I don't want to get blood on Dolly's oriental rug," he said, and his voice dropped chattily to a confidential level, "but you're not a rich man, Howie, and you don't really want to leave diplomacy, and I know it as well as you do. The post of special ambassador to NATO is going to open up soon, as you know, and the President was asking me only the other day if the Senate would confirm you for it. I told him I thought we would. You're sixty-seven years old, Howie, and it would be a very pleasant way to spend your later years, a good salary, a good social life, enough association with our allies to keep your hand in. I want you to have it. I want the President to give it to you. I think I can promise he will, but he certainly won't if you're not up there tomorrow morning crying your little heart out for Bob Leffing-well. Which you will be, Howie. I'm sure you will be."

"I won't!" the Secretary said, so vehemently that the Chief of Staff of the Air Force, the Secretary of Agriculture and two members of the Dutch Embassy turned around to stare. "I'll be damned if I will!" he said in an abruptly lowered voice, with a half-hearted attempt to make his expression noncommittal.

"Think it over, Howie," Senator Munson said pleasantly, and Grace said, "Oh, dear."

"Why should the Administration treat me like this?" Howard Sheppard asked with muffled bitterness, turning toward the bay window as Bob Munson placed a brotherly hand on his shoulder. "Why is politics like this? I've done my best to serve my country, I've done everything I could to help him and please him. I've thought I was a friend of yours——"

"You are, Howie!" Bob Munson said in a shocked tone, "you are!"

"—and now I get this sort of treatment. Why does it have to be so brutal?"

"You were never brutal to anybody when you were Governor of Ohio and wanted something done, Howie?" Senator Munson asked softly. "You never laid it on the line to anybody as Secretary of State and told him he was up against something he couldn't defy and he'd better go along? You never did, Howie?"

"I don't see why it has to be like this," the Secretary insisted stubbornly, not answering. "I just don't see."

"It's a rough game, underneath the backslaps and the handshakes and the big noble speeches, Howie," Bob Munson said thoughtfully, "and we all discover it sooner or later. It's a cruel business, sometimes, when you're in the big time the way we are, because up here the country is involved and men play for keeps. Now you think it over and see if you can't get a good statement together for us tomorrow, O.K.?"

"I don't see," Howard Sheppard said bitterly. "I just don't see."

"Well," Bob Munson said bluntly, "you're still part of this Administration until we confirm him, so you'd just better have your cry and blow your nose and turn a bright face to the world and get back into this party and make it look good, Howie. And you needn't worry about the NATO job. It'll be there waiting for you, I give you my word on that."

"How can you be a party to it," Secretary Sheppard asked, without irony, "when you're such a kind person at heart?"

"Now you're getting maudlin," Senator Munson said. "Here comes

Henrik Kroll, just bubbling to see you, so you just bubble back, Howie, and I'll see you later."

And as the Danish Ambassador came forward, hand outstretched, a rosy smile on his rosy face, with his rosy little wife coming along as rosily at his side, the Majority Leader clapped Howard Sheppard heartily on the back, squeezed Grace's hand, and went on his way, observing as he did so that the Secretary of State after a moment's hesitation straightened his shoulders, smiled graciously if a little wobbly, and returned the ambassadorial greeting with a cordiality which, while not overwhelming, was adequate to the occasion. Bob Munson dismissed that particular matter from his mind and, noting that his hostess was looking a little tired, went forward to her side through the press of tuxedoes, dress uniforms, gowns, gossip and highball glasses.

"Hi," he said. "How are you bearing up?"

"All right," Dolly said. "What were you and Howie Sheppard talking about?"

"The price of wheat in China," he said lightly. "Nationalist China, that is. He's going to be our opening witness for Bob Leffingwell at the hearing tomorrow."

"Oh?" Dolly said. "That's nice."

"I thought so," Senator Munson said. "He didn't, at first, but I think he does now."

"Are you proud of it?" Dolly asked, and Bob Munson leaned close to her ear. "Sometimes I wonder," he said, "whether I was wise to give you the right to ask me questions like that."

"You'd be in a bad way if there wasn't anybody who could," Dolly said swiftly, and turned back to offer a cordial, "So nice to see you," to the Attorney General and his wife, looking as always small, neat and secretive. Just behind them there was a slight commotion and on a burst of cold air, a wave of perfume, and the little extra excitement that always accompanied their entrance no matter what the troubles of their ancient and indomitable land, the British Ambassador and his lady swept into view, accompanied by their colleagues from across the Channel.

"Dear Kitty!" Dolly said as they kissed, "Dear Celestine, dear Raoul, dear Claude. It is *so* nice to see you."

"It's starting to snow," Kitty announced excitedly. "Do you suppose we will all be able to get back home all right? Washington gets so *confused* when it snows."

"If you leave right now," Dolly said with a smile, "I'm sure you can make it."

"Not for hours," Lady Maudulayne said gaily. "Not for hours. Claude has too many people to see and I enjoy your parties too much. Isn't that right, Claude?"

"I think the latter reason is the more diplomatic," Lord Maudulayne said. "Don't let people know I'm here on business, Kitty. It destroys all my effectiveness."

"These British!" Raoul said dryly, while Celestine smiled and said nothing in her characteristic way. "Do they take nothing seriously?"

"Lord, I hope not!" Claude Maudulayne said with his abrupt laugh. "We'd all have shot ourselves long before this if we had. But here is Bob, too, how nice."

"Claude," Senator Munson said cordially, "Raoul, ladies, it's good to see you." Then he said to the men with calculated abruptness, "Why don't we let them gossip while we go talk about Bob Leffingwell?"

"Senator Munson," Raoul Barre observed, "manages to be subtle in the most unsubtle way."

"It usually works, too," Bob Munson said, and Lord Maudulayne chuckled.

"So it does," he said. "Well, lead us to the drinks first, and then we'll talk, eh, Raoul?"

"Indeed, he overwhelms us so we have no choice," the French Ambassador said amicably. "Farewell, ladies. Watch out for Dolly. She and the Senator have an *entente cordiale* that I believe extends to matters of state as well. She will be working on you as hard as he works on us."

"Anyone who can make Kitty and Celestine tell something they don't want to tell is pretty good," Dolly said with a laugh, "and I'm not. You needn't worry, Raoul."

"How nice we are all old friends," Raoul said, patting her cheek. "All these little lies serve only to draw us closer together."

"Run along with Bob," Dolly told him, "and have a good time."

"In your house," Raoul said with a bow, "always. Always."

There were now, Bob Munson noted as he linked one arm with Lord Maudulayne and the other with his colleague and steered them toward the nearest bar, approximately two hundred of Dolly's expected three in the house, and Vagaries was beginning to resound with their babble. Three orchestras were playing, one in the enormous living room, one in the great glassed-in sun porch and one in the ballroom upstairs, and there was a sort of loud, reverberating roar flooding the mansion, compounded of three different popular tunes going loudly at the same time, the thump of feet dancing, chandeliers tinkling, ice clinking, and everywhere amiable voices, getting increasingly loud and fuzzy, talking, talking, talking. He could sense already from the relaxed and easy tone of things that the party was very likely going to last until three, if not later, and as the two ambassadors got their drinks and he switched quietly to plain ginger ale he decided that much could be done about the nomination before it was over. At the door he saw Orrin and Beth Knox arriving with Brigham and Mabel Anderson, to be followed immediately by Lafe Smith, traveling alone, and Seab Cooley, arriving with Arly and Helen Richardson. Crystal Danta came in with Hal Knox, George and Helen Keating followed, and in a moment Tom and Anna August entered just ahead of the Ryans, the Welches, and the Andrews, who, their official differences on the Federal Reserve bill forgotten, arrived together in a merry group. Elsewhere in the room he could see Alexander and Mary Chabot of Louisiana talking animatedly to Allen and Evelyn Whiteside, and in the crush on the great winding staircase toward which he was leading his two companions he saw Winthrop of Massachusetts and his horsey, charming wife talking to Victor and Hazel Ennis, who looked hearty and a little tight, while behind them Fred Cahill of Missouri was struggling upwards with four drinks clutched desperately in his hands toward his wife and Luis and Concepción Valdez of New Mexico, who were hemmed in at the top of the stairs. The Senate was well represented already, and would be more so before long. He waved heartily to them all across the surging crowd and was about to take his captive diplomats up the stairs to Dolly's private study when he felt a nudge and looked around to find the Majority whip and their ebullient colleague from West Virginia beaming at his side.

"Where are you taking Claude and Raoul?" Hal Fry demanded, while Stanley Danta smiled pleasantly upon them. "And why can't we be invited?"

"I think it's a case of high-level rape, old boy," Lord Maudulayne said cheerfully. "We no sooner got in than we were told to come talk about Bob Leffingwell. Who wants to talk about Bob Leffingwell? Must we face these international crises day after day? Is there never a letup? Of course you're invited."

"The President was trying to reach you, Bob," Senator Danta said. "He said Howie Sheppard just phoned and said he was going to make the opening statement for Bob tomorrow morning."

"What a nice idea," Senator Munson said in a pleased tone. "That's very generous of Howie."

"Very," Stanley Danta said with just enough dryness in his voice so that Raoul Barre immediately looked as alert as a terrier. Senator Munson smiled expansively.

"If you see Howie around," he said, "you tell him how pleased I am, will you? He's a real member of the team and we won't forget it."

"Indeed I will," Stanley said impassively. "Are we interrupting something?"

"Not a bit of it," Bob Munson said. "Just a chat about things. Why don't you round up Orrin and Brig and maybe Tom August and drop up to the study pretty soon? Don't make it obvious, but when you can."

"No, no," Raoul Barre said quickly, "by all means don't make it obvious, Stanley. Only one hundred and seventy-seven people by conservative count are watching us at this very moment. Don't make it obvious."

"Nonsense," Senator Munson said firmly. "You French always exaggerate. As for you, Hal, why don't you see if you can find your UN pal from the

Mysterious East and bring him along too? I've talked to him once already, but more won't hurt."

"I'm glad Kitty isn't in on this," Claude Maudulayne murmured. "She despises K.K."

"A great statesman," Senator Fry said gravely. "A beacon light of Asia. At least I think that's what you called him in that Press Club speech, Claude."

Lord Maudulayne smiled blandly.

"You tend to your Republic," he advised, "and we'll tend to our Common-wealth. But do go get him, Hal. Nothing spices up a discussion like K.K.'s syntax."

"Brother, do I know it," Senator Fry said dryly. "I'll get him."

"I'll get the others," Senator Danta added.

"Good," Senator Munson said. "We'll see you up there in fifteen minutes."

"Right," Stanley said.

Looking back as he and the Ambassadors proceeded slowly through the crush up the great winding stairway, Bob Munson could see that there were indeed quite a few who watched them go, and upon them all he turned a cordial and noncommittal smile. Across the room he could see the Secretary of Defense talking earnestly to Charlie Dale, the missile boss, and just beyond he caught a glimpse of Justice Davis arguing vigorously with the editor of the *Star*. Nearby the director of the FBI was chatting genially with the Secretary of Commerce and his wife, and in a bay window to their left, surrounded by the Ambassador of Lebanon and several miscellaneous princes from Saudi Arabia the director of the Central Intelligence Agency and two of the primmer male members of his far-flung crew of motley misfits were passing the time of day. Dolly was looking refreshed and as though she had gotten a second wind from somewhere, and just before they turned the curve in the stairs and lost the room from view he saw Vasily Tashikov and his frumpy consort come in, causing a little stir among the guests. He would have to talk to Tashikov, too, but that was a sparring match that would have to wait until later; he could see from the Soviet Ambassador's quick start of recognition and little ironic smile as their eyes met and he observed the three of them that it would be a ticklish and probably unprofitable pro-ceeding. So he shrugged and waved and, chatting pleasantly with his com-panions, led them down the second floor hallway past the ballroom and the library to Dolly's study, where he closed the door firmly on the roar of the party, made sure the bar was well stocked, and then turned abruptly to his guests.

"Fellows," he said candidly, "what should I do?"

The Ambassadors looked startled, looked at one another, and laughed.

"You Americans," Raoul Barre said pleasantly, "what a race. Such a combination of indirection and candor. Sometimes you tell us nothing and next thing we know you have thrown yourselves upon our mercy. What are we ever to make of you?"

"It is puzzling, isn't it?" Bob Munson admitted with a grin. "Let's say our mutual aim should be enough understanding to get along and not enough to get in each others' hair."

"We haven't always been sure of that with Howie Sheppard, old boy," Claude Maudulayne observed. "Sometimes his aim has seemed to go much beyond that. Moralisms in one hand and missiles in the other, what? It has been a little disturbing at times."

"That's exactly it," Senator Munson said, seizing the opening. "I think that's probably why the President has wanted to make a change there for some time. I think he was beginning to get a little disturbed too."

"Oh, it was not health, then," Raoul said. "I did not think so, right along."

"No," Senator Munson said, "it was not health. It was a concession to our good friends in Europe, believe it or not. Sometimes we do take your opinions into account, Raoul."

"When we unite and make it impossible for you to ignore them, yes," the French Ambassador remarked. Senator Munson gave a little bow.

"So it appears," he said. "Our only hope on such occasions is that you know what you are doing and aren't getting us into something that may weaken the whole Western position and give our friends in Moscow an irrecoverable advantage. You're quite sure," he added tartly, "that this is never the case?"

"Even in your own country," Raoul Barre said calmly, "there is much sentiment for a new accommodation."

"There really is, you know," Lord Maudulayne offered casually. "I just got back from a speaking tour last week, you know, Seattle, San Francisco, L.A., Denver, Des Moines, Chicago, Philadelphia. The feeling was quite obvious all along."

"I know it is," Bob Munson admitted, "and I know you all will take advantage of it to pressure us as much as you can. I repeat, though, you're quite sure of what you're doing, you really know it's the wisest course?"

"Who knows what is wisest in this troubled age?" the French Ambassador asked with a moody shrug.

"Some people pretend to," Senator Munson said sharply. "Or so it seems to us."

"My dear chap," Claude Maudulayne said with an asperity of his own, "it is not that anybody pretends anything. It is simply that we are very old peoples who have been warring with one another for a very long time and we have developed certain instincts about what can and cannot be done over all these long centuries. I think our record stands well when it comes to the pinch."

"Oh, indeed," Bob Munson conceded, "except that you have so often waited until the pinch really pinched before you did anything about it."

"And that has not been your policy?" Raoul Barre asked shrewdly. "I do not recall America at the barricades leading us on so very often in advance of the pinch, as you put it."

"We've tried," Senator Munson said, a trifle bleakly. "Since the last war particularly, we've tried. We haven't your talent for leadership, maybe," he said to Claude, "or your talent for realism, maybe," he said to Raoul, "but we've tried. In our bumbling, blundering, well-meaning way, God knows we've tried. It isn't entirely our fault if somewhere along the way it's all seemed to go wrong."

"Good intentions," the French Ambassador said with a sigh. "How seldom they go hand in hand with reality."

"And now it's reality to give in to the Russians?" Senator Munson asked. "I cannot believe it."

"Not exactly, no," Lord Maudulayne said thoughtfully. "Not exactly. There again, to quote Raoul, you Americans. You oversimplify. You want it black and white. It isn't black and white."

"God knows," Senator Munson replied, "that anybody who has an active knowledge and experience of United States politics knows that things aren't black and white. But sometime, somehow, there has to come a time on nearly every issue when they are, when you're either for something or against it, when you're either with somebody or opposing him. That is what I think we have been searching for in international affairs ever since the war—that moment. And we don't feel you have helped us much to find it."

"Sometimes such moments are very small and very quick," Raoul Barre said softly. "Sometimes they come in a second's time, in some small aspect of events almost lost amid the general rush of things, here and gone before we hardly know it, only revealing later in their awful consequences how pivotal they were. Who knows if America's moment has not passed? Ours has," he finished, so bitterly that Lord Maudulayne made a movement of protest.

"Oh, not yet, old chap," he said firmly. "Not yet, if we can all stick together."

"Well, there we are again," Bob Munson said. "How, and for what goal? It seems to us right now that the goal seems to be complete surrender to the enemy."

"There you go," Claude Maudulayne said. "'The enemy.' With us, you see, enemies are not enemies until——"

"Until they are bombing your cities," Senator Munson said bitterly. "Yes, indeed. Well, not for us, thank you. We prefer to get them catalogued a little earlier than that."

"But what an inconsistent catalogue," Raoul Barre suggested gently, "and how temporary. Down with the Boche, up with the Boche, down with the Japs, up with the Japs, down with Russia . . . up with Russia? Who can say? With us, you see, once an enemy, always an enemy, no matter what the niceties later, which is why we have found it difficult to moralize our way from position to position with you. If you wish to use the Germans for your purposes, well and good, but do not tell us they are not Germans any more, because we know it is not so."

"And are the Russians any different?" Senator Munson demanded. "What makes them friends now?"

"Senator, Senator!" Claude Maudulayne protested. "They are not friends. They are never friends. They are an uncomfortably strong force at the moment which must be handled with care, not with bludgeons."

"Very well," Bob Munson said. "I give up. You should be happy with Bob Leffingwell, I take it. From these speeches of his lately, I would guess that he favors an accommodation sufficient to satisfy even you."

The British Ambassador looked at his colleague a trifle hopelessly and Raoul Barre shrugged.

"I do not know——" He began, but what he did not know was interrupted by a knock on the door.

"I'll get it," Senator Munson said, and Raoul took advantage of his doing so to murmur, "You see?" to Claude Maudulayne, who murmured, "Difficult," back. Hal Fry came in with his colleagues and Krishna Khaleel and a certain wary cordiality settled back over the room.

"There is some conspiracy here?" the Indian Ambassador asked with a jocular air which did not quite conceal his suspicion that there really was. "I am glad I have been considered worthy to be included."

"Nothing of the sort, old chap," Lord Maudulayne said comfortably. "Just a little talk away from all the hubbub. Bob Leffingwell and all that, you know."

"Ah," Krishna Khaleel said knowingly. "I might have guessed. Our dear old Bob never rests. He has a job to do, to get this man confirmed, and he will not rest until it is accomplished. Admirable, is it not, Mr. Ambassador?"

This form of address, which always surprised Claude Maudulayne a little considering the number of times he and his Commonwealth colleague had conferred on matters of mutual interest, almost provoked him to say something which he knew would be a very serious mistake. He almost suggested that K.K. relax; but he knew with a calm certainty that in his presence K.K. would never relax, that in the presence of the British it would be generations before any educated Indian could really relax, that there would always be this self-conscious, faintly hostile, faintly cringing relationship, and in spite of himself he felt a mild but satisfied contempt. Yes, he thought, you're top dogs now, aren't you, but there's one thing you'll never really have no matter how desperately you want it, and you know it, and that's our respect. And because he knew that K.K. knew pretty much what he was thinking he threw his arm around the Indian Ambassador's bony shoulders with an extra cordiality and informed him jovially, "Actually, we've been settling the problems of the world, K.K., and we need your help. Roaul and I have been trying to educate our American friend in the niceties of dealing with the Russians and he will have none of it. Now he has reinforcements and I suppose will have even less of it."

"I see," K.K. said, disengaging himself slowly but firmly, "perhaps then it is well I have come. It is most important for us what our friends of this great republic do in this matter, which is the only matter in the world, for that matter."

"Important for us too, Mr. Ambassador," Orrin Knox said crisply, mixing himself a whisky and soda and settling into a leather armchair. "We would like to know where you stand on it, if you don't mind telling us."

"Always so abrupt," Raoul murmured and flashed a smile at the Indian Ambassador which seemed to make him feel better about the whole thing. Senator Fry handed him a bourbon and water and he sat down in a rather gingerly way on the outsize sofa. Then he looked blandly around the circle and inquired gently, "But where is Mr. Tashikov?"

"Mr. Tashikov wasn't invited," Bob Munson said coldly. "He's somewhere downstairs if you want to talk to him later and tell him all about it."

"Oh, now," Tom August said in his soft, worried way, "I'm sure Mr. Khaleel wouldn't do anything like that. He was just inquiring, Bob."

"Of course, old boy," Claude Maudulayne said, growing heartier by the second in an attempt to stave off tension, "of course, now. He was just curious."

"I thought I would arrange a gathering of friends and talk about Bob Leffingwell a little," Senator Munson said in an easier tone. "I didn't realize it would turn into a full-scale debate on foreign policy or maybe I would have invited Tashikov too, K.K." Then his tone hardened again and he said impatiently, "However, that's just diversionary and we all know it, so why don't you answer Orrin's question?"

"I do not see," Krishna Khaleel said, turning visibly pale and speaking in a high, persistent voice, "why it would be improper to have Mr. Tashikov here. Certainly he is involved in this matter, no one more so. Why should he not be?"

"It wouldn't work and you know it, K.K.," Hal Fry said.

"I do not see——" K.K. began stubbornly again, and suddenly Bob Munson made an angry motion.

"Somebody go get him, for Christ's sake," he said angrily, "and stop this childish nonsense. Go get him, Brig. He's down there somewhere. Tell him we're deciding which of his cities to drop an H-bomb on and we want his advice."

For a second the Indian Ambassador looked genuinely alarmed, and both Raoul Barre and Claude Maudulayne made protesting gestures. Senator Knox remained expressionless, Senator August looked perturbed, and Senator Anderson and Senator Fry exchanged a quick glance. Senator Danta reached over calmly and jogged the Majority Leader's glass.

"Ginger ale," he said reprovingly. "I knew it, Bobby. Whenever you get on that stuff there's no holding you. Why don't you switch to bourbon and sober up?"

"I say," Lord Maudulayne said quickly, "I wondered what it was, right along."

"I had my suspicions too," Raoul Barre said, "but I didn't want to say anything."

"We try to keep it away from him," Hal Fry remarked, "but he finds it in spite of us."

At this the Majority Leader, after a moment's hesitation, laughed somewhat ruefully with the rest and held out his hand to the Indian Ambassador.

"I'm sorry, K.K.," he said. "I've had a long day. You're entirely right, of course. I don't think it will accomplish anything, but if you want him here, we'll have him."

Krishna Khaleel smiled with somewhat shaky benignity, looking, as did they all, considerably relieved.

"Dear old Bob," he said, shaking hands rather nervously. "I know you have had a difficult time with your restless brethren of the Senate, that great body. It is past. Like you, I doubt that our forbidding colleague will have much to offer us, but it is the position of my government, even in discussions among old friends, that the door should never be closed. We should always talk, you know, in the hope of avoiding—what you said."

"I suppose," Bob Munson said. "Run along, Brig."

"Whatever you say, Bob," Senator Anderson said. The roar of the party filled the room for a quick moment as he went out the door, and it was obvious that it was going very well. It was obvious, in fact, that it was a hum-dinging, rip-snorting, hell-raising sockdolager and then some. The door closed, silence returned and with it a little awkwardness that Orrin Knox sought dutifully at once to alleviate.

"Well, Claude," he said chattily, "I hear you had a very successful speaking tour."

"I enjoyed it very much," Lord Maudulayne said warmly. "It is always a pleasure to see this country."

"You went over very well in Chicago, they tell me," Orrin said. "Had them cheering in the streets, almost."

"Not quite," Claude said in a pleased tone, "but they were most hospitable."

"I do hope you will get to Minneapolis next time," Tom August remarked softly. "We have some very live-wire citizens out there. You, too, Mr. Barre and Mr. Khaleel. We would like to welcome you all to Minnesota."

"That is very generous," the French Ambassador said, "and I would like to go. Perhaps my colleague and I can go together—you know, an international trapeze act, as it were. See them leap through hoops of fire.

See them walk the tightrope of international diplomacy. Hurry, hurry!"

"You are always so witty, Mr. Ambassador," Krishna Khaleel said. "I could never compete with you on the public platform, it is obvious right here that I could not."

"Nonsense," Raoul said pleasantly. "You have no trouble at all being entertaining, K.K. It is a great gift. I am sure the Americans would love it."

"As always," the Indian Ambassador said dryly, "I am not sure how you mean the things you say, Mr. Ambassador, but in any event, if Bob would not warn them in advance——"

"I would," Senator Munson said, making a determined effort to regain his amiability. "I'd tell them hold onto your hats and guard your silver, this man is simply the most effective diplomat we have in Washington, so watch out."

"Flattery," K.K. said archly. "Flattery, always."

"Yes," Bob Munson said wryly, "and it gets me nowhere."

"Here they are," Stanley Danta said abruptly, and in spite of their firmest intentions he and his colleagues could not prevent a little wary tenseness from rising in them as Senator Anderson, talking easily and cordially, ushered the Soviet Ambassador in.

At once, as Bob Munson could see, there was a subtle but definite realignment in the room. He was pleased to note that Raoul Barre seemed almost imperceptibly to move a little closer to Lord Maudulayne and that the two of them, without stirring a muscle, seemed to move a little closer to him. A certain drawing together seemed to come over his own colleagues too, as they rose to greet the newcomer. Only K.K. remained in rather lonely isolation near the sofa and there, Bob Munson thought savagely, he could damned well remain, the snotty Hindu. But outwardly he smiled and walked forward with his hand outstretched.

"Mr. Ambassador," he said cordially, "so nice to see you."

"And I," Vasily Tashikov murmured, his little shrewd eyes under their heavy brows giving the entire gathering a split-second once-over. "It is not often I have the opportunity——"

"You're always welcome," Senator Munson said calmly. "Any time. I believe you know Senator Knox—Senator Danta—Senator August—Senator Fry. Mr. Khaleel, Mr. Barre, and Lord Maudulayne I am certain you know."

"Ah, yes," the Soviet Ambassador said, shaking hands with each with a quick downward motion and a tight little smile, "ah, yes. So distinguished a gathering must have some purpose in mind. Presumably it concerns my country. Yes?"

"Yes," Bob Munson said. "It also concerns the President's nomination of Mr. Leffingwell to be Secretary of State. You have heard of it, I assume, Mr. Ambassador."

"The world intrudes, even on Sixteenth Street," Tashikov said with a sudden sarcasm and a frigid little smile, and Hal Fry couldn't resist murmuring, "Good, we weren't sure." The Ambassador took him up on it at once.

"Oh, but it does, Mr. Senator," he said. "We hear many things there, of Cabinet appointments, of cultural triumphs, of economic achievements . . . of missile failures and troubles with allies. Is it not so?" And he looked with insolent directness at Lord Maudulayne and Raoul Barre.

"How quickly, Mr. Ambassador," the French Ambassador remarked, "you manage to make men hate you. It is a positive genius in your great country. Do they teach it you in school?"

"Possibly," the Indian Ambassador interjected in a nervous tone, "possibly we should all sit down and have a drink. Would you wish one, Mr. Ambassador?"

"I seem to be the official mixer," Hal Fry said calmly. "What will you have, Tashikov?"

"I think," the Soviet Ambassador said, finally breaking off the stare in which neither he nor the French Ambassador had yielded, "that I would like that favorite of our good friends the British, a whisky and soda."

"Done," Senator Fry said, moving toward the bar, and Brigham Anderson leaned forward in his frankest and most engaging manner.

"We were wondering, Mr. Ambassador," he said, "what your government thinks of Mr. Leffingwell and his appointment. It has created, as you are aware, some discussion in the Senate, and it seemed to us that possibly you might wish to express an opinion that would be helpful to us in our consideration of it."

An ironic expression came over the Soviet Ambassador's face, and he gave a quick, unamused laugh.

"Does it matter to you what the U.S.S.R. thinks?" he asked. "We were not aware it did, especially on a matter of such great import as a new Secretary of State. This is something on which I am sure the opinions of my distinguished colleagues are of much greater weight with you than mine."

"Yes, they are," Bob Munson agreed in a tone as cold as Tashikov's, "but the Indian Ambassador seemed to think we should listen to you. I was against it, myself, but he insisted."

"I only thought," K.K. said quickly, "I only thought that it would be courteous and a matter of international comity if the Ambassador's views should be sought out, that is all. After all, we cannot arrive at world peace if his great country is ignored in everything, is that not correct, Mr. Ambassador?"

"It has been tried," the Soviet Ambassador observed with a certain smugness, "but it has failed."

Senator Knox leaned forward with an impatient movement.

"Very well, Mr. Ambassador," he said, biting off his words in a way his Senate colleagues knew, "it is not ignored now. You have your chance.

We are asking. Does your government feel it can work with Mr. Leffing-well or does it not? That is a simple question."

"Is it?" Tashikov asked, looking again at Raoul Barre. "Are these distinguished North Atlantic allies in agreement with you about it? They do not look it."

"What do you think, Mr. Ambassador?" Orrin Knox repeated in a flat insistent tone, and Vasily Tashikov turned and looked him full in the face for a moment. Then he shrugged.

"I really do not believe it matters," he said. "I truly do not. You are opposed to us—he will oppose us. That too is a simple equation, Mr. Senator."

"Oh, I do think," Tom August ventured in his soft, hesitant way, "that we all perhaps are taking too stringent a view of it, Mr. Ambassador and my colleagues. I think we should try to find some common ground and try to discuss it calmly——"

"Common ground!" the Soviet Ambassador said sharply. "Common ground! America always talks about common ground and does everything she can to destroy it. What hypocrisy, this common ground. Yes, you will have common ground, on the day you all die. Then you will have common ground."

Into the little silence that followed Lord Maudulayne spoke deliberately in his driest, most arrogant, most patronizing, most slap-in-the-face manner.

"Oh, my dear chap," he said slowly, "are you threatening the West again? Don't you ever get tired of that little game? Frankly, I find it terrifically boring. We have heard it all so many, many, wearisome times. Hitler wished to give us common ground too. We gave it to him. Now do be a good chap and try to keep this on a sensible basis, what? My government has some doubts about Mr. Leffingwell. M. Barre's government has some doubts about Mr. Leffingwell; even Mr. Khaleel's government confesses to some doubts about Mr. Leffingwell. Does your government have no thoughts about Mr. Leffingwell?"

"Yes, you are so clever, you British," the Soviet Ambassador said slowly, "but you are committing suicide like the rest. We tell you and you do not wish to listen. So be it."

"Do you favor Mr. Leffingwell or do you not favor him, Mr. Ambassador?" Raoul Barre asked softly. "That truly is the only matter we are interested in here."

"And you too," Tashikov said in the same slow tone. "And you too."

"It is the position of my government," Krishna Khaleel announced firmly, "that nothing is to be gained, nothing whatever is to be gained, by these exchanges of threats and recriminations. It is our policy that there must always, you see, be a frank and friendly exchange of opinions, that it is imperative for all our peoples that we consult together in harmony, that only thus, you see, can we possibly hope to save the world from a most terrible——"

"K.K.," Bob Munson broke in as though he were talking to a little child, "can't you understand that they *don't want* to be friendly? They *don't want* harmony; they *don't want* things to be worked out in a peaceful way; they *don't want* all this maundering crap you're giving us. It's their terms or nothing, and it always has been, and not all the idealistic empty-minded fools in the world can change it."

"Oh, now," Senator August said hurriedly, "oh, now, Senator, I do believe that is a little unfair to Mr. Tashikov and his country."

"So do I," the Indian Ambassador said indignantly. "My government has seen no evidence that they do not want peace and are not working toward it."

"*What?*" Senator Fry said explosively. "What did you say?"

"We do not believe," K.K. said with a sort of serene and otherworldly assurance, "that anything is to be gained by mistrust of the Soviet Union. We do not see all these things you say about them. We regard them as our friends. So do we regard you as our friends. We wish our friends to be friendly. That is the position of my government."

"We are grateful," the Soviet Ambassador said formally, "for the friendship of the Republic of India and for its understanding of our work for world peace."

"You see?" Krishna Khaleel asked gently, "There is no hatred here. There is nothing but kindness for all peoples."

"He has just been threatening us with extinction," Raoul Barre said dryly. "That is all."

"Words, words, words," the Indian Ambassador said airily. "It is realities that count."

"More than four decades of dishonor," Lord Maudulayne said softly, "are reality enough for me."

"Dishonor, dishonor, dishonor!" Vasily Tashikov said angrily. "You think of nothing else, you British. Does honor build submarines and make missiles fly? Does honor launch a sputnik? No, it does not. What is honor and dishonor? Words, as he says; nothing but words. You will choke on words, you weaklings of the West. We offer you friendship and you despise us. We try for accommodations and you reject us. Will it be any different," he asked, suddenly dropping to a conversational tone, "when Mr. Leffingwell replaces Mr. Sheppard? We cannot see that it will."

"Supposing it should," Bob Munson said, knowing that he must suppress his feelings and concentrate on the main issue no matter how much he would like to tell the Ambassador off. "Supposing my government did wish to try another attempt at accommodation. What then?"

At once the Soviet Ambassador's face got its usual closed-off expression and he reverted to type, the Communist automaton hiding his motives behind his automation.

"That would have to be discussed on a higher level," he said in an emotionless tone. "I could not say what would happen."

"It would dispose you toward Mr. Leffingwell, however?" Orrin Knox suggested with a certain irony.

"That would have to be considered," Tashikov said, in a much milder voice.

"There, you see?" Krishna Khaleel cried triumphantly to Claude Maudulayne. "You see, Mr. Ambassador? It is as my government says. It is a matter of understanding and trust, it is a matter of seeing the other person's point of view, it is a matter of compromise and agreement. Where are all these bugaboos we were talking about? Where is this hatred? Already we have started to make a new move for peace!"

"Let's go down and have another drink, K.K.," Hal Fry suggested. "I think we've been serious enough for one evening. Right, Tashikov?"

"By all means," the Soviet Ambassador said, rising with a certain rigid expansiveness as though somebody had pushed the geniality-button. "It is a shame to spoil Mrs. Harrison's lovely party with such sober sentiments. I believe it will work out, Senators and gentlemen. I believe we have had a very profitable talk. I believe we understand one another. Thank you for inviting me, Mr. Senator."

"Thank you for coming, Mr. Ambassador," Bob Munson said, and they formally shook hands. "Just for the looks of it, suppose you and K.K. go along, Hal, and then you and the Ambassador, Brig. The rest of us can scatter casually. No point in getting everyone interested."

"No one, I am sure, is interested," Tashikov said with a slight smile as he and Senator Anderson started for the door. "Good evening, gentlemen."

"Now, you see?" Krishna Khaleel said happily after they had gone. "It was not so bad, was it, Bob? I shall tell my government of this. I shall tell them we have made a great new step toward peace, here at Dolly's, in this beautiful house at this wonderful party. What an event!"

"Let's go, Akbar," Senator Fry said, steering him out. "Peace, it's wonderful."

"Oh, yes," K.K. said with the flash of a shining smile, "oh, yes."

"I think there is only one thing to say in this triumphant hour," Raoul Barre suggested then, "and that is, how about another drink?"

"Yes," Bob Munson said, "and it won't be ginger ale this time, either."

"Good," Claude Maudulayne said cheerfully. "That's the ticket."

It was, as it turned out, one of the very best Spring Parties ever given at Vagaries. There had been three before it, and there were many after, but those who attended that night looked back upon it fondly as one of Dolly's greatest triumphs. It is true, of course, that a number of people, including two Cabinet officers, three four-star generals, half a dozen distinguished members of the press, and a whole clutch of prominent civil servants proved beyond all doubt that they could get just as drunk and just as mean and just as sloppy as, say, the president of the bank and the head of Rotary and the editor of the local paper at the country club dance back home; but on the whole it was a good crowd that enjoyed itself in a good way, liquid but happy. It was a party at which you could see, among other things, the tubby little Dean of the Washington Cathedral buttonholing the Vice President of the United States to give him an earful on how vital it was that the Senate confirm Bob Leffingwell; and the Chief Justice arguing vehemently with the Chairman of the Joint Chiefs of Staff on the same subject; and the counselor of the Embassy of Bolivia discussing it earnestly with the counselor of the Embassy of Ghana; and the wives of a hundred different officials, as interested and astute as their husbands, tossing it back and forth to one another in little gracefully catty and perceptive exchanges. It was a party at which the caterer's representative informed the hostess shortly after midnight that as of that hour her guests had consumed one hundred quarts of bourbon, fifty-seven quarts of scotch, two hundred cases of ginger ale and soda, five hundred pounds of ice, and approximately $5,000 worth of hors d'oeuvres, turkey, ham, chicken, celery, olives, salads, and *marrons glacés*.

It was a party, also, at which Lord Maudulayne, meeting Raoul Barre later during a pause in the dancing in the ballroom, remarked abruptly, "I did not like that," and the French Ambassador agreed soberly, "The change was too quick."

And at which Senator August, talking worriedly to Senator Danta, said, "You don't suppose he was really offended with us, do you?"

And Senator Fry, running into Senator Anderson soon after midnight, said, "By God, I'm not sure I like the way this is going," and Senator Anderson replied quietly, "I'm worried, Hal."

And Senator Knox, threading his way through the seated, eating couples on the great staircase, passed Senator Cooley and murmured, "Something to tell you tomorrow that may have some bearing."

And Krishna Khaleel, driving grandly off in his chauffeured limousine at 1 A.M. and heading straight for his Embassy, routed his secretary out of bed, and dictated an immediate cable to New Delhi hailing the start of a new rapprochement between Russia and the West.

And Vasily Tashikov, leaving with his lady a few moments after, went to his Embassy and told his government to prepare another *démarche* because the United States was softening again.

And Bob Munson, thinking of the implications of that talk in the study and all its ramifications and what they meant for his country and the world, suddenly said, "Oh, God damn it to hell!" in a loud voice that startled two admirals, a general, and the head of the National Science Foundation, all of whom had thought he was paying close attention to their rambling explanation of the latest missile failure.

And it was also the party at which the Majority Leader had a brief conversation with Lafe Smith which he remembered rather fondly later because it served to bring him closer to that rising young colleague, concerned nothing more earth-shaking or profound or terribly worrisome than Lafe's own private specialty, and served to precipitate a decision for later in the night which proved to be, as always, most enjoyable.

"You see that girl in green over there?" the Senator from Iowa asked him shortly after 2 A.M., appearing at his elbow from nowhere with a glass in his hand. "She's looking. I think I'll let her find me before the evening is over."

"Well, be careful," Senator Munson said. Senator Smith smiled.

"Oh, I will," he said. "Morals are a professional matter in Washington, you know, and I'm good at my profession."

"What do you get out of it, really?" Bob Munson asked curiously. "Anything you really give a damn about?"

Lafe Smith stopped smiling and gave him an oblique glance.

"No," he said soberly; and then, with a grin, "but you wouldn't want me to play with myself, would you?"

"Don't you ever want anything better?" Senator Munson asked, and a curious expression came into his young friend's eyes; haunted, Bob Munson thought.

"Of course I want something better, Bob," he said softly, "but it's too late for me. I've never had a chance. It started too early and it came too easy. People have been at me since I was eleven years old, all shapes, sizes, and sexes. I never had the opportunity to get started on the right track about sex. They all made it so simple for me. Everybody was so helpful. It's too late now."

"Maybe not," Bob Munson said gently.

"I think so," Lafe said, "though God knows why I'm telling you about it all of a sudden. Except that you're the great Earth Father of us all." His voice, already low, went abruptly lower. He smiled, but his voice remained serious. "*You* watch yourself with Dolly, buddy. There's beginning to be talk."

"Is there?" Senator Munson said. "Maybe I'll marry the girl and fool them all."

"I wish you would, Bob," Lafe Smith said seriously. "I'd like to see you settle down."

After which he had the grace to join in Bob Munson's delighted whoop of laughter before he clapped him on the back, murmured, "So goes the lemming once more to the sea," and began his casual, aimless, indirect and rather frighteningly determined stalk of the girl in green.

And so it was that still later, sometime around three, after the last guest had said a fuzzy good-by and begun the slow, ticklish drive home through the deepening snow, one of Washington's most prominent hostesses did leave her back door unlocked, after all, and she and the Majority Leader of the United States Senate did forget their sense of the ridiculous, and it was all very pleasant. And the snow came down quietly, softly, steadily, persistently on the wide deserted streets and lonely stone monuments and great gray buildings of the beautiful city of Bob Munson and Bob Leffingwell and Tom August and Stanley Danta and Brigham Anderson and Seab Cooley and Orrin Knox and Harley Hudson and the President and Vasily Tashikov and Raoul Barre and Claude Maudulayne and Krishna Khaleel and Tom Jefferson standing by the Tidal Basin and Old Abe enshrined forever in his temple by the Potomac.

7

Eight hours later, of course, everybody was back in business and the joint was jumping. Tom August had called the special Saturday meeting of the Foreign Relations Committee for 11 A.M., and when Bob Munson arrived at the door of the Caucus Room at ten forty-five it was to be greeted by the usual uproar of a major hearing in that fabled setting where so many of American history's most dramatic productions have been presented. All around the great marble room with its Corinthian pillars and its great windows on the east side opening on the sky there was the hectic turmoil of getting ready, the television technicians fussing with their machines off to one side, the news photographers taking their light readings at the witness chair, committee clerks moving in and out around the long committee table, an overflow audience filling every chair and standing along the walls and at the back, the news reporters moving in easily to take their seats at the long press tables amid many jokes and wisecracks and the customary exchanges of friends gathering for a job they have done many times before and know they will do many times again. How much of all their lives, Senator Munson thought, had been spent in the Senate Caucus Room; how many, many hours of testimony and investigation, high tragedy and tinpot comedy, frequently hectic and shabby, as America is hectic and shabby, but sometimes moving and noble, as America is moving and noble. The raw stuff of the government and the country came to the Caucus Room month in, month out, year in, year out, an unending pageant of idealism, veniality, astuteness, stupidity, selfishness, selflessness, failure, and achievement; and this time, he knew, the only difference was that extra excitement, that little edge of extra electric tension that came when participants and audience knew that something of really major import was under way.

The cop at the door waved him through with a cordial, "Good morning, Senator," and he started along the aisle past the press tables toward the committee table. The Providence *Journal* and the Dallas *News* hailed him at once, and immediately the wire services, the *Times*, the *Herald Tribune*, the *Star*, and the Chicago *Tribune* crowded around. He found himself holding an impromptu press conference before he knew it, a fact which he noted did not particularly please Tom August, already sitting rather forlornly in his chair at the center of the committee table. For some reason the press didn't seem to have much respect for Tom, and he was sure Tom didn't have the slightest inkling why.

"What's the truth of this, Senator?" the *Times* asked, holding out a copy of the *Herald Tribune* and pointing somewhat accusingly to a story at the top of the page. Under the headline SECRET CONCLAVE OKAYS LEFFINGWELL NOMINATION; RUSS, INDIANS, ALLIES GIVE GO-AHEAD ON NEW SECRETARY, it disclosed that something mighty fishy had gone on at Mrs. Phelps Harrison's party last night. The author of the story obviously didn't know exactly what, but by keeping his eyes open and his intuition untrammeled, by mixing a scrap of information with a hunk of conjecture and building twenty bricks with two pieces of straw, he had managed to come up with a good, sound, typical piece of informed Washington correspondence. The import was that "Russ, Indians, Allies" had given a ringing endorsement to Bob Leffingwell and therefore "it was believed" that this made his immediate confirmation by the Senate a foregone conclusion. Bob Munson glanced at it with a skeptical smile.

"Yes, I saw it," he said. "Very enterprising, I thought."

"Is it true, Senator?" the Baltimore *Sun* demanded. Senator Munson smiled.

"It's very interesting," he said.

"Well, we know you were at Mrs. Harrison's," the *Times* remarked, "and we know all the diplomatic crowd was too. It could have happened."

"So were several people from the New York *Times*," Senator Munson said blandly. "Don't *you* know whether it happened or not?"

"We're asking you, Bob," the AP said in a heavy-handed way, determined not to be diverted. The Majority Leader smiled again.

"I really couldn't say," he said. "I remember seeing one or two of the people mentioned there at the party, but that piece draws quite a few conclusions I wouldn't want to draw."

"That's all right," the Providence *Journal* assured him. "We can get it from the embassies."

"Let me know what you think it adds up to, if you do," Bob Munson said pleasantly and turned to greet Winthrop of Massachusetts, coming along the aisle in quick-humored dignity behind him.

"Win," he said, "tell these boys the real inside story of what went on at Dolly's, will you?"

"Lots of drinkin' and lots of talkin'," John Winthrop said with amiable crispness. "Don't know what kind of a story you can get out of that, boys."

"That's what I told 'em," Bob Munson said. "We'd better stop blocking the aisle."

"We'll ask the embassies," the Baltimore *Sun* called after them as they turned away and moved toward the committee table.

"Ask them," Bob Munson tossed back over his shoulder. "And be damned to you," he added under his breath. Senator Winthrop chuckled.

"Ah, ah, ah, Bobby," he said. "You didn't really think you could keep anything like that quiet, did you?"

"I thought we might try," the Majority Leader said as he took his seat next to the chairman and Senator Winthrop started to move along to the minority side.

"I suppose K.K. will spill the whole thing when they get to him," he added, "but at least they'll have to work for it. Good morning, Tom."

"Good morning, Bob," Senator August said in his gentle way. "I hope you're feeling better this morning."

"I wasn't aware I was feeling poorly," the Majority Leader said. The senior Senator from Minnesota gave him a sidelong glance.

"I meant, I hope your mood is better," he said. Senator Munson snorted.

"Perfectly fine," he said, "perfectly fine. I hope you didn't think I was too harsh with anybody."

Senator August shifted uneasily in his chair.

"I did think," he said in a tone of soft reproach, "that you were a little harsh with both Mr. Khaleel and Mr. Tashikov. I did feel it might tend to make things a little more difficult——"

"More difficult, hell," Bob Munson said shortly. "Sometimes I think that's the way we ought to talk to them all the time."

"Oh, now, Bob," Tom August said in a genuinely shocked tone, "I don't think that's a wise way to feel at all. I really don't. If they get the feeling that we mistrust them all the time and won't accept their word when they want to negotiate——"

"Thomas," Senator Munson said, "sometimes you amaze me. That's all I can say, you amaze me."

"But Bob——" Senator August protested. Senator Munson looked firm.

"I don't want to discuss it," he said aloofly. "I have troubles enough."

"But, Bob," Tom August said apologetically, "I only meant——"

"I know what you meant, Tom," the Majority Leader said, unyielding. "I know very well what you meant. Next thing I know, you'll be calling me a warmonger. I believe that's the jargon word, isn't it?"

"Oh, but, Bob," Tom August tried again, "I only meant that you should be a little more diplomatic with them. They don't understand our way of dealing sometimes and——"

"They understand that way a damned sight better than they do being wishy-washy, I can tell you that," Senator Munson said. "Anyway, we'll talk about it some other time. There comes Arly, and I suppose that means trouble."

"Oh, I hope not," Tom August said in an alarmed tone. "I have troubles enough."

"That's what I just said," Bob Munson reminded him. He could see that the long, lean, and sardonic senior Senator from Arkansas had been stopped by the press and had just uttered something that had positively killed them all. At that moment Arly's eye fell on the Majority Leader and with a happy wave he called across the twenty feet separating them, "Say, Bobby, I hear you had quite a row with Tashikov last night?"

Senator Munson waved back blandly.

"Thanks, pal," he said. "Don't believe everything you hear."

"Not in this town," Arly said, coming forward to take his seat on the majority side of the committee table while the press crowded up to listen and the photographers gathered around on the off-chance that this long standing and famous feud might produce some unexpected action. "Not in this town. They tell me it was pretty hot and heavy, though. The Indian Ambassador, too." He stretched out an arm and gave Bob Munson a clap on the back. "What were you doing, anyway, straightening things out with the whole UN?"

"Somebody has to put things in proper perspective," Bob Munson said, smiling in a noncommittal way at the eagerly attentive press. "God knows they're plenty confused."

Arly Richardson chuckled.

"Run along, boys," he advised with his lantern-jawed smile. "Run along. You can see he isn't going to confirm or deny. That's our Bob."

"That was pretty cute," The Majority Leader told him as the reporters went back to their tables. "Thanks so much, pal."

"I was just curious," Senator Richardson said blandly. "I heard all these things and I wanted to know, Robert. That's all."

"Yeah," Bob Munson said dryly. "Where were you yesterday? We missed you."

"I'll bet you did," Arly Richardson said. "I saw that you had quite a rumpus. Unfortunately I got tied up at the Federal Trade Commission. One of my constituents has gotten himself into a hassle with them and I had to be there to give him moral support. Nothing I could do, of course, but he felt better with me holding his hand."

"Do they ever realize how much they demand of us?" Bob Munson asked with a sigh. "Decide high policy, legislate for the good of the country, run the government, and play nursemaid to them too? How do they expect us to do any of it well?"

"They don't realize," Senator Richardson said with the wry knowledge of one who had held national office for twenty years. "All they realize is that if we don't want to do it there are plenty of people who will."

"You are so right," Senator Munson said. "Did you get it straightened out?"

"One of those damned things where the Commission decided to hold hearings," Arly said, "and you know what that means. It will probably take months."

"A damned shame," Bob Munson said sympathetically.

"But life," Senator Richardson said, and then added, with a capital, "Life . . . By the way," he remarked, as there came a little bustle at the door and Johnny DeWilton, looking stately and white-topped and every inch the United States Senator, came in with Verne Cramer, looking rather small and inconspicuous and just on the verge, as always, of saying something disrespectful and/or subversive to overpompous authority, "somebody was telling me that Bob Leffingwell wouldn't appear today. What's the matter?"

"I hadn't heard that," Bob Munson said ominously, "but he'd damned well better."

"Yes, he should," Senator Richardson said thoughtfully. "I have a few things to ask."

"Friendly, I hope," Bob Munson said, and Arly Richardson smiled in his sardonic way.

"I'll bet you hope," he said. "No, Bobby, I'm not so sure they will be friendly."

"I thought I could count on *you*, at least," Senator Munson said with a sardonic expression of his own, and Senator Richardson looked genuinely amused for a second.

"Maybe you can and maybe you can't," he said, "but in any event, there are some things I want to know from our great and distinguished nominee, and I intend to find out. Then maybe I'll be for him. I got a couple of strange complaints in my mail and telegrams this morning."

"Cranks," Bob Munson said.

"Maybe," Arly said. "Maybe not. One thing I do want to know, though, is what you actually did say to Tashikov and K.K."

"Nothing they didn't deserve," Senator Munson said shortly. "Good morning, Johnny. Hi, Verne."

"Good morning, Bob," Senator DeWilton said, stopping by his chair. "This is a hell of a situation."

"What's the matter?" Senator Munson asked. "Don't you like these little surprises from the White House?"

Senator DeWilton snorted and Verne Cramer put a friendly hand on Bob Munson's shoulder.

"You know Johnny," he said, "always getting upset. Now *I* thought it was double extra peachy, myself."

"It's good to know I can count on you," Senator Munson said, reaching back suddenly and poking him in the solar plexus. "Good boy!"

"God damn!" Verne Cramer said, doubling over on a burst of laughter. "Don't *do* that. What will the tourists think?"

"That's Bobby's way of smoothing your feelings and getting your vote," Arly Richardson offered. "It's supposed to make you think we're all big buddies and nobody's really going to get mad at anybody."

"Everybody's going to get mad at everybody this time," Senator DeWilton said abruptly. "Come on, Verne. Let's go sit down."

"Please do," Bob Munson said. "The chairman looks a little nervous."

"I'm not nervous," Tom August protested. "I just wonder where everybody is."

"They'll be here," Senator Cramer assured him. "Even Lafe is going to get out of bed to get here for this one."

"That depends on who he's in bed with," Arly Richardson said, and Tom August looked shocked and disapproving. At that moment the junior Senator from Iowa appeared at the door and, catching them all staring at him with quickened interest, flashed a big grin across the room, and hurried up to the committee table.

"No, I didn't," he announced in a conversational tone. "She was an absolute lemon, and I just didn't."

"Now *that*," Verne Cramer said, "if our friends in the press only knew, is news."

"I never knew you failed," Senator Richardson said, and Lafe Smith snorted.

"Lots of things people don't know about me, pal," he said crisply. "I hear Leffingwell isn't going to be here, Bob. One of the press boys just told me they got a note on the wire. He's got the virus, so he says."

"So he says," Senator Munson said tartly. "Well, Tom, I guess we'll just have to go ahead without him. Where's Howie?"

"He called at ten-thirty and said he'd be here on time," Senator August said. "I guess he'll have to be the only witness today."

"Well," Bob Munson said, turning his back on Arly Richardson and leaning close to Tom August's ear as the others took their regular seats along the table, "if you can manage it, Tom, I'd try to break it off after Howie appears, if I were you. It won't work, but make a stab at it, anyway."

"I know what to do," Senator August said with some impatience. "You don't have to tell me. After all, I'm the chairman."

"So you are, Tom," Bob Munson said soothingly, "so you are. I suppose you'll have some opening statement to make——"

"I have a letter from Bob Leffingwell to read," Tom August said, with an expression of what could only, for him, be called sly triumph.

"You knew all along!" the Majority Leader exclaimed with an admiring smile, and Senator August looked somewhat mollified.

"I trust I have some discretion," he said in a pleased tone.

"You certainly do, Tom," Bob Munson said approvingly. "I told the President he could trust you implicitly on this."

"I believe he can," Senator August said proudly.

"And on everything else, too," Bob Munson said, even more approvingly.

"Watch out, Tom," Arly Richardson said around Senator Munson's shoulder. "You're getting Snow Job No. 1 with all the trimmings."

"God damn it," Bob Munson said with real anger in his voice, "will you mind your own business? Tom and I are talking and we don't want you butting in. That's Brig's chair, anyway. Why don't you go where you belong?"

"That's right, Senator," Tom August said with dignity. "Please don't interrupt the Majority Leader and me."

"Well, all right, Senator," Arly Richardson said in a mocking tone, "my apologies, I'm sure, Senator," and he turned away and went to his own seat with a spiteful air.

"Well, well," murmured AP to UPI at the press table, "did you see that?"

"I don't blame Bob," UPI said. "I get damned sick and tired of Richardson myself. He isn't half as cute as he thinks he is."

"He's a born troublemaker," the Dallas News agreed. "Here comes Brig. Shall we grab him?"

"He ain't talkin'," AP said. "I've tried."

"Catch him when it's over," UPI advised. "He'll have something to say after the subcommittee's appointed."

"Hi, Bob," Senator Anderson said, taking his seat beside the Majority Leader. "Good morning, Tom. We seem to be playing to a full house."

"They think there are going to be fireworks," Bob Munson said, "but there aren't. Tom's going to see that everything runs like clockwork, aren't you, Tom?"

"I have hopes we can move expeditiously," Senator August said sedately, "as soon as the rest of the committee gets here."

"Orrin's on his way," Brigham Anderson said. "He was having coffee with Stanley Danta and George Hines in the cafeteria a minute ago."

"Here they are now," Senator Munson said, "and here's Warren Strickland and Ed Parrish. Now all we need is Howie."

"I'm sure he'll be here any minute," Senator August said, a trifle nervously. "At least I hope he will."

"Morning, Bobby," Senator Strickland said as he came by the Majority Leader's chair. "I'm sorry I had to leave early last night. Apparently things happened."

"I'll tell you about it," Bob Munson promised. "You didn't miss much."

"That's not the way I heard it," Senator Strickland said with a smile.

"Everybody hears too much in this town," Senator Munson said. "Good morning, Orrin and Stanley, George and Ed. How is everybody this morning?"

"I'm fine," Senator Knox said shortly. "Where's Leffingwell?"

"We're not sure yet," Senator Munson admitted. "He may not be here."

"What kind of a performance is that?" Orrin Knox began angrily, but just then Brigham Anderson broke in to call their attention to a sudden stir of excitement at the door.

"Here comes the honorable Secretary with a dozen outriders as usual," he said. "How does the State Department do it?"

And sure enough, in came Howard Sheppard in a dark blue pin-stripe suit whose cuffs and pants-legs appeared to be cut just a trifle too short for him; and in after him came ten assistants. Some were in their thirties, some were in their forties, some were in their fifties, but to them all there clung an ineffable effluvium of faintly seedy youthfulness. Some had pipes and some had briefcases and all had the same expression of secret purpose and superior knowledge; and each was clad in a dark blue pin-stripe suit whose cuffs and pants-legs appeared to be cut just a trifle too short for him.

The appearance of this familiar phalanx, the inevitable concomitant of all hearings on foreign policy, foreign aid, international catastrophe, and other matters of high import and earth-shaking significance, brought with it the customary spasm of activity among the photographers. "Mr. Chairman," they cried to Tom August, "will you pose with the Secretary, please?" And, "Mr. Secretary," they shouted to Howard Sheppard, "will you pose with the chairman, please?" There followed much posing and picture-taking and shouts of "One more, Mr. Chairman! Mr. Secretary, one more, please!" broken now and then by an occasional intense, "God damn it, get out of my way!" snarled in a savage tone by one of the congenial competitors to another. After ten minutes of this, during which the reporters at the press tables made their own contributions in tones loud enough to reach the milling entanglement, such as, "Christ, the damned photographers never do anything right," and "Why in the hell do they let them in here anyway?" the room gradually settled down again and it appeared that the hearing might at last be about to begin.

"Are we ready?" Tom August asked, peering down one side of the committee table and then the other as the photographers subsided, the press became attentive, the television cameras swung around to zero in on them and the audience quieted and settled itself. "I think we are." He banged his gavel sharply and the first formal step in the consideration of the Leffingwell nomination was under way.

"This hearing of the Senate Foreign Relations committee," he announced, while the official stenotype reporter clicked away busily at his little machine, "is being held to consider the President's nomination of Robert A. Leffingwell to be Secretary of State. The first, and it may be, the only, witness"—at this the press stirred and so did several members of the committee, including Orrin Knox—"will be the distinguished incumbent Secretary of State Howard Sheppard. Mr. Secretary, we are delighted to have you with us, and we deem it a significant indication of the high regard in which Mr. Leffingwell is held generally by the country that he should have an advocate of such great distinction."

At this, Bob Munson noted, Howie almost visibly preened himself. He was looking considerably better than he had last night, and the Senator decided that there must have been a family consultation ending in agreement that the NATO Ambassadorship wouldn't be such a bad form of retirement, after all.

"Mr. Chairman," the Secretary said gracefully, "nothing gladdens the heart of a witness from my department more than your friendly commendation."

"Except possibly," Lafe Smith whispered sacrilegiously behind his hand to Brigham Anderson, "the commendation of the chairman of the House Foreign Affairs Committee." Brigham Anderson grinned and agreed.

"And," Howard Sheppard went smoothly on, "nothing gives this witness more pleasure than his task today. It has been my privilege to know Mr. Leffingwell for approximately ten years, first when he was beginning his distinguished career of government service in the field of public power and I was governor of Ohio, at which time we had our first dealings on matters of interest to my state. Subsequently when I came to Washington——"

"Mr. Chairman," Arly Richardson interrupted suavely, "would the witness prefer to complete his statement, or would he be agreeable to having us question him as he goes along?"

"I would prefer, Mr. Chairman," the Secretary said, "to complete my opening remarks and then submit to questions, if that would be agreeable to you and to the members of the committee."

"I think that would be perfectly agreeable," Tom August said, and Senator Richardson remarked, "Perfectly," with a little dismissing wave of the hand.

"Subsequently," Howard Sheppard went on, "my work in the Administration has given me frequent opportunities to confer with Mr. Leffingwell, particularly on power matters of interest to this government and our NATO allies, on which we have both worked most closely, and I may say cordially, with the NATO governments."

Attaboy, Howie, Bob Munson thought, get 'em prepared for it. He gave the Secretary a wink which the Secretary blandly ignored.

"When it became obvious to me," Howie said, "that it would be best for my health that I begin to think about the possibility of retiring from government service, the President on several occasions asked me who I thought would be a suitable successor in this vitally important office of Secretary of State. Rather than suggest any single man, I deemed it my duty to present the President with several names. I am happy to say that Robert A. Leffingwell's was high among them."

He paused and started to reach about for a glass of water. In a movement so swift it almost defied the eye an arm in a dark blue pin-stripe sleeve placed it instantaneously in his hand.

"Therefore," the Secretary resumed, "I can only admit to a very real and genuine satisfaction that this nomination should now have been made. I can give you my judgment of Mr. Leffingwell in very few words: he is extremely intelligent, extremely able, and extraordinarily well equipped to fill the office to which he has been appointed. Knowing its problems and its difficulties as I do, I can say truthfully that I can think of a few who could handle them better. I am pleased with what the President has done. I am for this nomination."

"Thank you very much, Mr. Secretary," Tom August said. "I think perhaps before we go into questioning I should put in the record a brief biographical statement on Mr. Leffingwell prepared by the staff of the committee, if that would be agreeable?"

"By all means," Bob Munson said cordially, and there was a murmur of agreement from the committee except for Arly Richardson, who ostentatiously made a movement of protest and then dropped it.

"Well, sooner or later it has to be in, Senator," the chairman said sharply. "Can you think of any better time to do it?"

"Very well, Mr. Chairman," Arly said calmly. "Go right ahead. Go right ahead."

"I will," Tom August said shortly. "Mr. Leffingwell, now forty-seven years old, was born in Binghamton, New York, and attended elementary school and high school there. He attended the University of Michigan, graduating with a degree in public administration, and received his law degree from Harvard Law School. He taught public administration for four years at the University of Chicago and then was appointed to the Southwest Power Administration, becoming director of its public service division four years later. Five years after that he was appointed director of the Southwest Power Administration. Four years ago he was appointed chairman of the Federal Power Commission succeeding the late Governor Fred M. Robertson of my own state of Minnesota. He has been active in various international conferences in recent years, having served as head of the Advisory Committee on the Aswan Dam six years ago; as chairman of the International Hydroelectric and Power Conferences in Geneva four years ago and in Bombay two years ago; and as impartial arbiter, at the request of the two governments, in the recent water dispute between India and Pakistan. In addition, he was principal United States delegate to the United Nations Conference on Water, Power and Economic Development of Poorer Areas last year. This past December, at the request of the President, he left the Federal Power Commission to accept an interim appointment as Director of the Office of Defense Mobilization, the post he now holds. He married the former Louise Maxwell, and they have a son and a daughter. He is a member of Phi Beta Kappa, the American Bar Association, and the Metropolitan Club of Washington. He resides in Alexandria, Virginia. He lists his political affiliation as non-partisan . . . And now I think we may start the questioning in our customary fashion with Senator Munson for the majority and then alternate between the minority and the majority. Senator Munson?"

"First," Bob Munson said pleasantly, "I wish to welcome the Secretary and to say how much we appreciate, always have appreciated, and always will appreciate his sound counsel and sage advice. His relations with this committee have always been most cordial, and we can only hope that those of his successor will be half as good, for that will be very good indeed. We are happy to have you here, with your fine statement for this nominee, Mr. Secretary."

"Thank you, Senator Munson," Howie Sheppard said. "It is always a pleasure to be here. You are very kind."

"I shall be very brief, Mr. Chairman," Senator Munson said. "In your close relations with NATO, Mr. Secretary, which I know has always been a major and particular interest with you"—the Secretary nodded gravely—"was it your feeling that the NATO governments liked and trusted Mr. Leffingwell in some degree commensurate with their liking and trust for you, which we have all noted on many occasions?"

"Why all this emphasis on NATO?" Verne Cramer whispered to George Hines. "What the hell is that all about?"

"Some kind of pay-off," George Hines whispered back. "Wait and see."

"I should not wish to make comparisons, Senator," the Secretary said, "but I will say this, that I saw every evidence that the NATO powers have a high regard for Mr. Leffingwell."

"Yes," Bob Munson said. "And is it not true, based on your observation of him, that in other international dealings with other governments and peoples that he was well liked and did a good job for the United States?"

"That is my observation, Senator," Howie Sheppard said.

"I have no more questions, Mr. Chairman," Bob Munson said.

"Senator Strickland?" Tom August asked, and at his side the Minority Leader leaned forward with a pleasant smile.

"Like the distinguished Majority Leader," he said, "I too wish to commend the Secretary, to thank him for his appearance here, and to express my regret that his health is such that his counsel and guidance will soon be lost to us. Health," he added blandly, "is an uncertain thing in this uncertain Washington climate. We can only wish you a much-needed rest and a swift recovery that may permit your country to call on you again for service before too long." At this, for just a second, Howie Sheppard shot a look of quick alarm at Bob Munson, who looked quickly away. Senator Strickland went calmly on.

"My questions, too, will be very brief," he said. "Is it your impression that Mr. Leffingwell is loyal to the United States of America?"

There was a start of surprise among the committee and along the press tables, and the Secretary looked genuinely shocked.

"I have never had any indication whatsoever that he is not, Senator," he said firmly. "I am positive he is. I find the question surprising, to say the least."

"It is a question that many will ask," Warren Strickland said calmly. "I thought we had best get it out in the open right away."

"I am positive he is," the Secretary repeated.

"Yes," Senator Strickland said. "And you have never seen anything to indicate that he is not."

"Nothing," Howard Sheppard said. "Never."

"And you would trust him without reservation with the interests and the safety of the United States, fully confident that he would protect them as diligently and as forcefully as you have done?"

"I would," the Secretary said emphatically.

"That is all, Mr. Chairman," Warren Strickland said.

"Senator Anderson?" Tom August said, and the senior Senator from Utah reached for the microphone in front of him on the table and pulled it closer to him.

"I too wish to commend the Secretary——"

"I hope sometime," AP whispered to UPI, "that we will hear somebody tell some high official witness, 'You're a no-good bastard and we think your testimony stinks.' But of course we never will, even when we know they think it."

"—and congratulate him on his statement," Brigham Anderson said. "I am interested in the Secretary's impressions of how Mr. Leffingwell handles the people on his staff, if that would not be beyond the purview of questioning here. Does he strike you as a good administrator?"

"As nearly as I can judge," Secretary Sheppard said, "I think he is."

"One who is fair and decent and just to his subordinates?" Senator Anderson asked.

"So I believe," the Secretary said. "Insofar as I have had an opportunity to judge."

"The reason I ask," Brigham Anderson said pleasantly, "is that much can be told about a man by the way he treats those over whom he has authority. I believe you said your retirement was caused by reasons of health, Mr. Secretary."

"I did," Howie Sheppard said.

"You do not feel that you have in any way been shoved out of office to make room for Mr. Leffingwell?" Senator Anderson went on in the same pleasant tone. Howard Sheppard flushed.

"I do not," he said, a trifle loudly.

"Yes," Senator Anderson said, with the same senatorial "yes" of his colleagues, the "yes" that always carries with it the uncomfortable implication of polite and persistent unbelief. "And you gave the President of the United States, at his request, a list of names from whom he might pick a successor. Would you mind telling the committee what other names were on that list?"

"Oh, now, Mr. Chairman," Bob Munson broke in sharply. "I don't think the Senator has any right to ask a question like that. That is a privileged matter between the Secretary and the President, and it is none of the Senate's business. I really do not see that the Senator is in order with that question."

"He volunteered the information that he furnished such a list, Mr.

Chairman," Brigham Anderson said calmly. "He threw the subject open, I didn't. I think it is something the committee should know."

"I do not think it is," Tom August said with a gentle but determined firmness. "I agree with the Senator from Michigan that the matter is privileged between the President and the Secretary and no business of ours. It would only cause embarrassment to the Secretary and also, no doubt, to those on the list who were passed over. The Senator will proceed in order, if he so desires."

"Very well," Senator Anderson said offhandedly, while the press scribbled furiously and the Secretary looked relieved. "It remains, however, an interesting matter for speculation. What do you know about Mr. Leffingwell's views on Russia, Mr. Secretary?"

"I believe them to be those held by most Americans," Howard Sheppard said.

"Which are?" Senator Anderson asked.

"Well," the Secretary began, then stopped and started over again. "That the situation is serious and we must always be on the alert both against the possibility of surprise and against the possibility of being overly suspicious. We cannot relax our vigilance with them; neither, I believe, can we refuse to accept the possibility that they might ultimately wish to live with us in a peaceful world."

"A peaceful world on whose terms, Mr. Secretary?" Brigham Anderson asked, and the Secretary flushed.

"It would have to be on terms of mutual agreement, Senator," he said.

"You think that is an accurate reflection of the views of most Americans," Senator Anderson said, without other comment.

"As they have come to me in my office," Howard Sheppard said.

"You believe those are Mr. Leffingwell's views," the Senator said.

"Yes," the Secretary said.

"But you do not know," Brigham Anderson suggested.

"No," said Howard Sheppard.

"No further questions, Mr. Chairman," Senator Anderson said.

"What's got into Brig?" The *Times* whispered to the *Herald Tribune*, and the *Herald Tribune* responded, "Damned if I know."

"Senator Winthrop?" Tom August asked. John Able Winthrop smiled at the Secretary.

"No questions, Mr. Chairman," he said, "except to say that I too appreciate the Secretary's appearance, regret his departure, and pray that he may be right in his assessment of his successor."

"Hm," the Chicago *Tribune* murmured to the Washington *Post*, "that was a neat sideswipe." Senator Munson, who thought so too, leaned forward, looked down the table to the Senator from Massachusetts, and gave him an ironic little bow. Winthrop of Massachusetts bowed back, and the press tables snickered. Senator August rapped, a little querulously, for order.

"Senator Knox?" he said. Orrin opened his briefcase and took out some papers.

"Well, Mr. Chairman," he said brusquely, "this is all very nice, and I am sure the Secretary's appearances here are always valuable and always welcome, but I think it is really all rather superfluous. I think the committee would like to see Mr. Leffingwell, since he is the nominee here. I have no questions of this witness."

Tom August flushed and was about to reply when Arly Richardson spoke.

"I agree, Mr. Chairman," he said. "It is obvious that the Secretary, while his views are always welcome, is in no position to give us a really adequate appraisal of the nominee. I do not know about the rest of the committee, but I shall not be satisfied myself until this committee, or at least a duly constituted subcommittee of it, shall have had a chance to examine Mr. Leffingwell, either in public or executive session."

"If the committee please," Senator August began, in noticeable agitation, but before he could proceed further George Hines got into it from the other end of the table in his hearty, phony, fake-cordial way.

"Those are my sentiments exactly, Mr. Chairman," he said. "This seems like a strange proceeding to me. While I give all due credit to the Secretary —Howie, how are yah?—and am always glad to have his views, I feel we should have the nominee before us. This is no substitute for his own appearance, Mr. Chairman."

Tom August rapped his gavel sharply on the table and spoke in a rare tone of anger.

"If the committee please," he repeated, "I suggest that we proceed in the regular order with this witness, after which I have a letter from Mr. Leffingwell which I propose to read, and then a course of action which I propose to suggest to the committee."

"You have?" Bob Munson murmured in surprise at his elbow, and Senator August looked around for a second, startled. Then he went on.

"I assume," he said firmly, "that what we have just heard represents the questioning of Mr. Knox, Mr. Richardson, and Mr. Hines. That brings us to Mr. DeWilton. Senator?"

"Well, Mr. Chairman," Johnny DeWilton said tartly, "if this is the way this hearing is going to be conducted then I don't see why I should participate in it. It all seems highly irregular to me, I must say. What's in that letter?"

"Better read it to them, Tom," Senator Munson advised in a hurried whisper, and the senior Senator from Minnesota managed to look at one and the same time angered, upset, chagrined, worried, wistful, and saddened.

"It is obvious," he said, "that it is the pleasure of the committee that I read the letter, is that right?" There were vigorous nods from both sides of the table, and Verne Cramer said, loud enough to be heard, "Obvious isn't the word for it, Tom, boy." Senator August shuffled among the papers before him and then looked around in some dismay A committee clerk appeared at his elbow and handed him the letter, Howard Sheppard and his little band of brothers settled back to listen; Arly Richardson made a impatient movement.

"Who is the letter addressed to, Mr Chairman?" he asked.

"It is addressed to me," Senator August said

"I thought so," Arly said, and then, as Tom August hesitated, he added impatiently, "Go ahead, go ahead"

"The letter," Senator August said with dignity, "reads as follows 'Dear Mr. Chairman——

"'It is with real regret that I have to tell you that my scheduled appearance before the committee this morning must be delayed on doctor's orders. That old devil virus has me in his grip, and neither the ODM nor the Department of State apparently has sufficient strength to counteract his onslaughts this morning. My sincerest apologies to you and to the committee for this unexpected hitch in plans'"

"That's smooth enough," Brigham Anderson whispered to Stanley Danta, and the senior Senator from Connecticut observed dryly, "Oh, he is smooth enough."

"'I should like to take this opportunity, however, Mr. Chairman,'" Tom August read on, "'to express to you and to the committee, and for the public record, my feelings of awe and gratitude that the President should have given me this nomination. If the committee in its wisdom sees fit to approve it, and if the Senate in its turn confirms that decision, you have my deepest assurance that I will do everything humanly possible to discharge the high duties of Secretary of State as you and the President would wish me to do. You have my assurance also that in that office I will contribute, insofar as God gives me strength and wisdom to do, to the safe passage of our dear country through these perilous times which beset her. I have served her now, in one capacity and another, for thirteen years; it is my highest aim to serve her always, in whatever duty she may call upon me to perform, truly and honorably and as best I can.

"'If the committee should wish to hear me in person at some later time ["A safe assumption," Senator Cramer remarked to Senator Hines], then of course I am at your service. I would not presume to suggest to the committee its method of procedure ["That's nice of him," Orrin Knox remarked with audible tartness to Arly Richardson], but it would seem to me, as one citizen, that matters of such delicacy in international affairs are involved here, and that members of the committee might wish to question me so thoroughly on my views ["Yes, indeed," John Winthrop murmured] that it might perhaps be advisable to hear at least part of my testimony in executive session. I think we could all speak more freely, and certainly we should, on these subjects which concern us all so deeply.

"'With best wishes to you and the committee, and with assurance of my full co-operation, Mr. Chairman, I am, Yours sincerely, Robert A. Leffing-well.'"

As Senator August finished and the wire-service reporters jumped up to hurry downstairs to the press room on the floor below and send out their bulletins, Johnny DeWilton spoke up abruptly.

"Well, Mr. Chairman," he said, "I do not propose to let this nominee set the terms on which he will appear before the committee. That seems to me most irregular, Mr. Chairman. I resent his attempt to dictate to this committee."

"Mr. Chairman," Bob Munson said with equal vigor, "if the distinguished Senator from Vermont will yield, I resent *his* attempt to prejudge this nominee. It seems to me Mr. Leffingwell's suggestion is a most fair and reasonable one. It is in line with the suggestion a few moments ago of the senior Senator from Arkansas, Mr. Richardson, that the nominee be heard in executive session——"

"Public *or* executive, I said," Arly interjected.

"—and it seems to me that that is what we should do."

"I think I would be satisfied with such a course," Orrin Knox said, rather surprisingly, "provided we can be sure Mr. Leffingwell will be here as often as we need him, and will answer us as candidly as we may wish him to."

"I was about to suggest," Senator August said with a mild and wistful sarcasm, "before everyone else began talking, that the committee give serious consideration to hearing Mr. Leffingwell in closed session."

"God damn," UPI said to AP, "there goes our story."

"Wait a bit," AP suggested hurriedly.

"I am prepared to vouch for Mr. Leffingwell's willingness to be candid," the chairman went on, "and indeed you have heard his letter pledging exactly that. I think through the medium of executive hearings we can examine into his qualifications and his views without the distractions that might come about in a public hearing."

"If we can be assured of his co-operation, and assured of a thorough study, Mr. Chairman," Stanley Danta remarked, "then I would see no serious objection to the course you propose."

"Well, I do," Ed Parrish, normally one of the quietest of men, said suddenly from his seat near the foot of the minority side. "This matter concerns the whole United States, indeed the whole world. Why should it not be discussed in public session? What is there to hide? It strikes me, Mr. Chairman, as just one more of those situations where this Congress knocks itself out to protect the secrets of the Executive Branch from the Russians, only to find out when all is said and done that it is something the Russians already know and it is only the American people who have been kept in the dark. I don't like it, Mr. Chairman."

"Why don't we take a vote, Mr. Chairman?" Brigham Anderson suggested calmly. "It seems to me that would be the simplest and most direct and fairest way to proceed."

Senator August looked hesitant for a second and Bob Munson murmured, "Might as well, Tom. We've got ourselves in a box and that's the only way out." The chairman rapped his gavel and cleared his throat.

"Very well," he said, "I shall poll the committee. All those in favor of executive hearings on this nomination will say Aye, all those opposed No . . . Mr. Munson."

"Aye," Bob Munson said.

"Mr. Strickland."

"No," said Warren Strickland.

"Mr. Anderson."

"I pass for the moment, Mr. Chairman," Brig said, and there was a sudden heightening of tension in the room.

"Mr. Winthrop," Tom August said, and the senior Senator from Massachusetts, after a long moment's hesitation, said quietly, "Aye."

"Mr. Knox."

"Aye," Orrin said tersely.

"Mr. DeWilton."

"No, sir," Johnny DeWilton said firmly.

"Mr. Danta."

"Aye," said Stanley.

"Mr. Cramer."

"Aye," Verne Cramer said, and the second relay of wire-service reporters got up and stood poised to run downstairs to the teletypes with their second bulletin of the morning.

"Mr. Richardson," Tom August said and Arly spoke bluntly:

"No."

"Mr. Parrish."

"No," Ed Parrish said.

"Mr. Hines."

"I'm afraid not, No," George Hines responded.

"Mr. Smith," Tom said, and Lafe said, a little defiantly:

"I vote Aye."

"Is the Senator from Utah ready to vote?" Senator August asked, and Brigham Anderson leaned forward with one hand clasped tightly around his microphone.

"The Senator from Utah," he said slowly, "votes No."

Tom August paused, and there was silence in the Caucus Room.

"The committee," he said gently, "is tied six to six. The chairman votes Aye, the motion is carried, and the hearings on this nomination will be held in executive session. If there are no further questions, I think perhaps we can close this public hearing and recess the committee until Mon——"

It was then, as the reporters sprinted out and the audience let out a concerted gasp of exploded tension and somewhere a photographer struggling angrily for a picture of the committee wailed bitterly, "God *damn* it, get out of the way!" that there came a little stirring off to one side of the room and out from behind two high school girls and a Capitol cop there emerged a familiar figure, eyelids drooping, hair atangle, manner slow and subtly ironic.

"Mr.—Chairman," it said, and the room, a moment before alive with the shuffling of people getting ready to leave, abruptly quieted down again.

Oh, now, Seab, Bob Munson thought hurriedly. Now, Seab——

"Mr.—Chairman," Senator Cooley said thoughtfully. "Mr.—Chairman, I think I might have a little something to contribute. I do think I might."

Senator August hesitated and looked, a trifle wildly, at the Senator from Michigan. Bob Munson shrugged.

"What is the Senator's wish?" Tom August asked placatingly. "Would you like to testify, or just file a statement?"

"Oh, Mr. Chairman," Seab Cooley said softly. "Much more than that. Much—more—than—that. *I* would like to testify. *Others* would like to testify. I think *many* would like to testify. I would *like* many others to testify. Do you think it could be arranged, Mr. Chairman?"

"Why," Tom August said; and then, hastily, as he became aware of Arly Richardson and Brigham Anderson stirring down the table and Johnny DeWilton preparing to seek recognition, "Why. Why, yes, Senator, I suppose it could. Would you like to take the stand right now——"

"No, Mr. Chairman," Senator Cooley said. "No. Much as I would like to oblige you all, I have to meet some constituents for lunch, and then there's some Appropriations Committee business this afternoon, and I believe after that——"

"Very well, Senator." Tom August said hurriedly. "I think we can work out something next week that will be satisfactory to all concerned. But I am afraid the full committee may not be able to hear you, because the foreign-aid request is coming up from the White House tomorrow morning, and some of us are going to be tied up on that."

He hesitated, and Bob Munson told him sternly in the privacy of his own mind not to start truckling to the old man, because that would give him the advantage right off the bat; but Arly was stirring again, and Tom August hurried on.

"Would you mind if I named a subcommittee to hear you?" he asked. There was a movement from Seab and the chairman added hastily, "and any witnesses you may care to present?"

"That would be agreeable to me, Mr. Chairman," Seab said calmly, "if I might also sit as a member of the subcommittee to conduct certain cross-examinations after I testify."

"You have a right to request that courtesy, Senator," Tom August told him, and he was entirely correct in that, "and of course we will be glad to accord it to you."

"Then," Seab said, and for the first time the shrewd old eyes flickered briefly over the senior Senator from Michigan, "then I think that would all be mighty fine."

"Good," Senator August said, with so obvious a note of relief in his voice that the press tables snickered. "The Chair will appoint a subcommittee consisting of the senior Senator from Utah, Mr. Anderson, as chairman; the senior Senator from Illinois, Mr. Knox; the senior Senator from Arkansas, Mr. Richardson; the senior Senator from Massachusetts, Mr. Winthrop; and the senior Senator from Vermont, Mr. DeWilton, to hold such hearings on this nomination as may be necessary to ascertain the true sentiments of the Senate and the country. This hearing is now——"

"Mr. Chairman," Arly Richardson said sharply. "What does this do to our one-vote majority decision to hold closed hearings? Will the subcommittee hearings be public or closed?"

Tom August looked somewhat despairingly along both sides of the committee table and, finding little comfort anywhere, raised a hand that was beginning to tremble to his forehead.

"Under the circumstances," he said softly, "it seems likely that they will be open."

"We'd better make it official," Senator Richardson said quickly. "I move that the previous committee vote on the question of closed hearings on this nomination be vacated and that all hearings in this matter, whether in subcommittee or full committee, be open."

"All those in favor," said Tom August in an uneven voice, "say Aye."

"Aye," said the committee as one man, and Bob Munson shrugged and voted with the rest.

"This hearing," the chairman said in an aggrieved tone, "is now adjourned."

Orrin Knox made an impatient movement, scooped up his papers and plowed determinedly out through the crowd; Brigham Anderson hung back for a moment as the press came forward to ask his plans for the subcommittee; Howard Sheppard moved quietly out the door surrounded by his dark-blue-pin-stripe-suited entourage; and across the great Caucus Room the eyes of the senior Senator from South Carolina met the eyes of the senior Senator from Michigan head on.

You old bastard, Bob Munson thought bitterly. Just the trace of a grin crossed Seab's face, and in spite of himself Senator Munson grinned back. But you haven't won yet, you old coot, he thought; you haven't won yet, by God!

But he wasn't at all sure, really, and he knew Seab knew he wasn't.

Two

Seab Cooley's Book

1

On this Monday morning when Seab Cooley is about to begin his last
great battle against Bob Leffingwell and all the forces of detriment to the
country which the senior Senator from South Carolina firmly believes he
represents, the Senate, as on any average morning of any average session,
is hard at the committee work which forms so large a part of its activity.
In addition to the first meeting of the Foreign Relations subcommittee
on the Leffingwell nomination—promptly dubbed by the press, in customary fashion, "the Anderson subcommittee"—there are gatherings which
cover everything from space to the building of a dam in northern Wyoming. Each in its earnest, disputatious and searching way is advancing
the public business.

For Bessie Adams, chairman of the Defense Appropriations Subcommittee, and such hard-working colleagues as Alec Chabot of Louisiana
and Roy Mulholland of Michigan, the morning is centering around progress reports by the Air Force on the desperately slow and slowly desperate
attempt to pull ahead of the Russians. What the Senators hear is, as usual,
compounded in about equal parts of gain and frustration, and when they
emerge later it will be to tell the waiting reporters as little as possible
in tones as optimistic as they can manage. Their job, as Bessie often
says, is to maintain public hope while riding the hell out of the Defense
Department; and her uncharacteristic use of profanity lends her little
aphorism an extra impact with her colleagues, who grin and agree and
reflect that Bess, as usual, has put her finger on it. This shrewdness, which
is characteristic, makes of her that rarity, a woman in the United States
Senate who comes as close to achieving parity with her male colleagues
as a woman in the Senate ever gets.

Also meeting under the broad wing of Appropriations are the Subcommittee on the Post Office and the Subcommittee on Public Works,
both of which Seab would look in on ex officio in his capacity as chairman
of the full committee if he were not bound for the Leffingwell hearing.
Post Office is hearing testimony by the Postmaster General, a man whose
qualifications for running the public mails were decided decisively in
the last Presidential campaign when he contributed the surprising sum
of $150,000 to the President's cause. This was a handsome indication of

faith and loyalty from one of the nation's wealthiest hardware manu-facturers, and it did not go unnoticed at the White House, where it was presently rewarded with the Post Office Department. Now the maker of sleep-two sofas and friend of Presidents is outlining roseate plans to send airmail to California and other outlying points by intermediate-range ballistic missile, a project which has him starry-eyed, though it leaves the subcommittee somewhat skeptical. Robert Johnson of Connecticut wants to know what arrangements would be made with other countries if such service were expanded beyond the national borders. Would the Russians know, for instance, that an IRBM suddenly crossing the European frontier was on its way to the Moscow Central Post Office, or would they take a more abrupt and intolerant view of the matter? And in turn, how would we know, when the DEW Line reported an incoming greeting from over the pole, that it contained correspondence instead of cobalt? Victor Ennis of California says in his hearty and good-natured way that this is really kind of an absurd objection, Bob, and Marshall Seymour agrees with a little puckish needling of his own; but Senator Johnson, who thinks the Postmaster General's whole idea is silly, persists deadpan in his line of questioning while the hard-pressed hardware maker sweats and squirms in some discomfort on the witness stand.

Across the hall, in a mood of needling as persistent and sometimes not as good-natured, William H. Hamilton of Oklahoma, living up to his corridor reputation as "the worst spoilsman in the Senate," is raking the Army Corps of Engineers over the coals in the Subcommittee on Public Works. The subject is the annual rivers-and-harbors and flood-control bills, and Senator Hamilton is receiving staunch aid in his endeavors from George Hines of Oregon, who really ought to be attending the full Foreign Relations Committee to hear Secretary Sheppard testify on foreign aid. But George, who is quite as good a fighter for flood control and rivers-and-harbors as Bill Hamilton, has decided he can't afford to miss the opportunity to give the Engineers a little hell. In the same spirit dapper, ironically gracious Jack McLaughlin of Georgia has also decided to be on hand, along with busy, bustling little Dick McIntyre of Idaho and quiet-spoken, steady John H. Baker of Kentucky.

Confronted by these determined and forceful gentlemen, the Corps of Engineers is not in the least dismayed. Serene in the knowledge that they are proprietors of the lobby which is, year in and year out, the most ruthless, the most effective and the most untouchable on Capitol Hill, its high-ranking officers are going through this annual charade with un-perturbed suavity. In the comfortable Siamese-twin relationship which exists between the Corps and the Appropriations committees of the two houses, the Engineers know that when they reach to scratch their own backs they will also give solace to some solon, and that when Senator or Congressman in turn relieves his own itch he will in the process ease the Corps of Engineers. In close harmony and perfect accord they will spend the public monies together and both will be happy. When the bills reach the floor it will be found that there are handsome expenditures for Oklahoma, which Bill Hamilton represents; for Oregon, lucky birthplace of George Hines; for Georgia, personal satrapy of stylish Jack McLaughlin; for Idaho, home range not only of Dick McIntyre but of the Minority Leader as well, which means that it will be especially well remembered; for Kentucky, for which John Baker in his quiet way manages to extract a good many plums; and for the states of various other important people such as the Speaker of the House, the leading figures in his chamber, and the like. This will make everybody happy, not least the Engineers, for of course all these new funds and new projects will require new personnel to administer them, and so the always-swelling empire will continue its steady, inexorable growth. In the practical world of Washington the Corps and the Congress, it might be said, have each other firmly by a tender and important part of the anatomy; and in case either side should ever attempt to get out of line, a little squeeze is all that is necessary to restore a perfect understanding.

While this comfortable unity of view is being worked out in the Subcommittee on Public Works, the Banking and Currency Committee is considering another of its perennial bills to aid small business. Without small business, it sometimes seems, B. and C., as it is familiarly known, might well have closed up shop years ago. This of course has not happened, and today it is present in full strength, headed by Royce Blair of Oregon, whose harshly antagonistic speech to the Portland Kiwanis Club on the Leffingwell nomination has received, just as he knew it would, widespread national publicity. Widespread national publicity always makes Royce feel good, and today he is at his most expansive, beaming out from his big, round, curiously little-boy face and addressing everyone cordially in his full, round, pompously unctuous voice. This does not fool the Secretary of the Treasury, who has seen this smiling aspect before. But the Secretary, who is a stranger to his own office four days out of ten when Congress is in session, so popular a witness has he become, returns smile for smile.

Today he is agreeing with Royce and such other interested colleagues as Julius Welch, Murfee Andrews, and Taylor Ryan—all of whom can scarcely wait for the vote on the Federal Reserve bill this afternoon, so sure is each that he will triumph—that small business is certainly important to the economy, all right. (Sometimes, so various are the subjects upon which he is called to testify, the Secretary wonders if there is anything that isn't.) Agreement is not enough for Royce and his colleagues, however, and they are insisting that the Secretary give his endorsement to a bill to lower interest rates on loans to "certain selected classes of small businessmen." ("Little teeny-weeny businessmen," AP suggests to UPI when Royce enunciates this phrase in his rolling way.) The Secretary is not altogether sure he will. In fact, he is in process of deciding that he damned well won't. This will upset the committee no end, and so in sharp but amicable wrangling they will pass the morning and will eventually go ahead and pass the bill through the Senate just as they have intended all along. The Secretary will advise the President to veto it, the President, who has as kind a regard for the little teeny-weeny businessman as the next one, will disregard the advice, and a week after the bill becomes law Senator Blair and the Secretary will be out at Burning Tree playing golf together in the greatest of harmony with all differences forgotten until the next time.

The Finance Committee, as he is rather wearily aware, is also waiting to hear from the Secretary. Finance Committee wants to amend the Social Security Act, and of course the Secretary is an expert on that, too; and so presently, after the committee has spent most of the morning on minor witnesses from the Social Security Administration, the Secretary will be along, and they will have him for a few minutes that will reaffirm their proprietary interest in him too.

At the same time members of the Committee on the District of Columbia are considering a bill to build another bridge over the Potomac. There is always a bill to build another bridge over the Potomac, and the number of times these ephemeral spans have been launched across drawing boards and paraded before Congress and displayed to usually irate and always loudly outspoken citizens' organizations is almost beyond calculation. But the District Committee, charged under the Constitution with the management of the affairs of the voteless Federal City, patiently goes through the motions whenever required. This morning, with Magnus Hollingsworth of Wisconsin in the chair in his usual small, shrewd, purse-lipped fashion, it is giving the matter its usual intensive consideration. Just to show how seriously they take their duties and how important it all really is, such freshmen as bluffly vapid George Carroll Townsend of Maryland and worried Henry Lytle of Missouri are being as solemn as all get out about it, but Magnus Hollingsworth, as befits a veteran on the committee, is surreptitiously reading the funnies under the table edge and isn't paying attention at all. *He* knows that bridge isn't going to be built.

The Committee on Government Operations under Rhett Jackson of North Carolina is conducting one of its expeditions through the government procurement agencies, turning up as usual small, dark, loudly injured men from New York and Chicago who have been busily fleecing their country out of millions of dollars with the willing and well-paid compliance of several government inspectors who now wish they had taken up some other line of work or been more honest about the one they did decide to follow. It is too late now, however, and the committee is having a field day with their misjudgments. Senator Jackson, lean, hawk-featured and astute, is making the most of it, ably aided and assisted by such colleagues as razor-tongued Leif Erickson of Minnesota and patient, well-informed Lloyd B. Cavanaugh of Rhode Island. Right now all three of these gentlemen are bearing down on an inspector for the Army Quartermaster Corps, and the press is looking forward to some substantial sensations by noon.

Wool quotas, the Taylor Grazing Act, and the possibility of building a dam on the Big Horn are occupying the Interior and Insular Affairs Committee, and Fred Van Ackerman, forgetting for the time being his well-publicized campaign for a new approach to the Russians, is acting like the junior Senator from Wyoming for a change. He is opposed to both the proposed changes in the Grazing Act, violently unpopular among the big sheepmen in the state, and to the suggestion for the Big Horn dam. He is saying so at fiery length, treating the committee to a sample of his oratory almost as flamboyant as that with which he urged negotiations with Russia at a great rally of the Committee on Making Further Offers for a Russian Truce (COMFORT) at Madison Square Garden a couple of nights ago. Stanley Danta, sitting in for the chairman, is watching this performance with a kindly but appraising air and reflecting that it is probably pretty effective back home in Wyoming. He knows how effective it was at the COMFORT rally, for few recent public addresses have received quite such widespread national coverage as the dynamic young Senator's challenge to the Administration to fish or cut bait on this issue of imperative import to America and the world. With a fine careless rapture Senator Van Ackerman had cried, "Some say it means crawling to Moscow. I say I had rather crawl to Moscow than perish under a bomb!" Approximately 20,000 of his fellow Americans who felt the same way had made the rafters ring. Fred at the moment is applying the same free-swinging technique to the Taylor Grazing Act, and only the quietly deflating questions of Senator Danta—for some reason no other member of the committee is present, though Fred called them all last night to let them know that he would be testifying—are keeping the proceedings on a reasonably even keel.

In Judiciary Committee, on the other hand, attendance is high, for there, under the smooth chairmanship of glib Rob Cunningham of Arizona, the issue this morning is a bill to provide certain legal encouragements to defense-plant construction; and this is a subject on which Senators and certain influential constituents alike have powerful views. Equally high is the attendance in the Agriculture Committee, where the issue is the disposal of farm surpluses. The issue in Agriculture is almost always farm surpluses in one form or another, and all hearings on the subject have approximately the same features: the stern denunciation of the Secretary of Agriculture by the chairman and most of the committee, his amiable but stubbornly unyielding rejoinders, and finally the bitter climax of threats of retaliation and impeachment. The Secretary, who has gone through all this on both sides of the Capitol twenty times before, is not noticeably impressed by it today, and so the committee's annoyance is rising somewhat more rapidly than usual. The press is now betting that the threats of impeachment will begin somewhere around 11 A.M. instead of at noon as they usually do. This will give them the usual story on the subject, and later on in the chamber members of the committee will make their usual indignant speeches; and nothing will be done to the Secretary, nor will the Congress offer any sensible alternative of its own, nor will the earth stop giving its yields in ever greater amounts, nor will anything be done to solve the paradox of history's greatest producer of food, unable to find a use for its surpluses in a world where people starve.

Two other committees, in addition to the Anderson subcommittee and the full Foreign Relations Committee, where Howie Sheppard is about to have rather rough going on foreign aid, are meeting this morning: Armed Services, holding an executive session on space exploration, and Rules, going through one of its perennial sessions on the filibuster and Rule 22. Armed Services, like Bessie Adams's defense subcommittee, will not be too encouraged by what it hears, and its members will angrily demand answers to questions that are only partially answered. Rules, where Lacey Pollard of Texas is politely listening to the Dean of the Harvard Law School tell him why full discussion in the Senate is dangerous to the country, will presently recess subject to the call of the chair without doing anything about Rule 22. It will be quite a while before the chair calls again.

Thus proceeds the work of the Senate on a typical day on Capitol Hill. Inevitably, because it is the newest Congressional sensation, the major spotlight rests upon the Senate Foreign Relations subcommittee just getting under way in the Caucus Room. There is the day's, and perhaps the year's, biggest story on the Hill, and to it the senior Senator from South Carolina, as he trudges in his shuffling, sloping way down the corridor from his office, is bringing almost fifty years of craft, cunning and legislative know-how. He has a surprise or two in his pocket, has Seab, and the contemplation of all those years gives him a certain assurance that his battle may not be in vain. He knows, at any rate, that his opponents will be aware they have been in a fight; and if the result gives him no more satisfaction than that, he feels it will be well worth the struggle.

For even Seab, feudist that he is, carries in his heart a concept of the United States of America that he does not want to see damaged; and over and above the shrewdly calculated flamboyance of his long-standing vendetta with Bob Leffingwell there exists a purpose of more genuine and more worthy import. Mistaken he may be or mistaken he may be not, but at least underneath it all he is as sincere as he has ever been in all the long years that stretch out behind him as he moves slowly along with an occasional quick "How you all?" to those in the corridor who interrupt his deep concentration with bright good mornings.

What he is doing, though they cannot know it, is trying to decide in his own mind whether the project upon which he is now embarked will indeed be, as he would like to think it is, the final justification and culmination of all those years and choices and decisions and triumphs and acts which have gone into the making of that powerful, irascible, astutely implacable legend known as Seabright B. Cooley.

2

It had begun, like so many careers in American politics, with a speech. The story is a familiar one in the annals of the Congress: there was a high-school valedictory, and the hero delivered it with extraordinary fire and brilliance; or there was a debating contest, and the hero defeated ten other eager lads and carried off all honors; or the featured speaker at the county political rally dropped dead and the hero took his place with an impromptu oration that made strong men weep and maidens swoon; or casting about for a speaker at the annual Fourth of July picnic, somebody said, "Why not get young Seab Cooley? He's just back from law school and ought to know a thing or two." And they did, and there was awe and shouting and dancing in the streets.

"I told them," Seab would say now, looking back through sleepily narrowed eyes over fifty years, "that *they* were responsible for America. Yes, sir, I surely did. When all is said and done, I said, *you* are responsible for America, so don't pass the buck to anybody in Washington. It's your country, your vote, and your responsibility. So they quickly elected me to the House of Rep-re-sen-tat-ives and they've been passing the buck to me ever since. Yes, sir. Of course," he would add with a mischievous little chuckle, "of course when I worked so hard to get the invitation to make that speech I rather intended them to do exactly that. They thought it was all accident, but it wasn't. No, sir, they didn't know it, but it wasn't. Don't quote that, though. They're mostly all dead now, but I wouldn't want it to get out that my first venture into politics was a calculated thing. I don't like people to think I calculate. You don't think I calculate, do you, young man? Well, that's good, because I *never* calculate. No, sir."—the sleepy smile would become even sleepier—"no, *sir*."

Sometimes, trying to search back into the depths of time beyond that first hot, dusty day in Barnwell (he could still remember the intimation he received at the moment he arose to speak, that he was seeing the story of his life in a second, an endless procession of massed, attentive audiences and upturned, seeking faces) the interviewer or reporter, usually from *Time* or *Newsweek* or some other publication not disposed to be friendly to the Senator, would have the feeling that there was something being hidden, something concealed, for Seab would always turn aside those queries with a comfortable chuckle and a deliberate concentration on the chronological record. Sometimes he would give his earnest questioner the impression that he had lived from birth to twenty and from twenty-six, when he entered the House, to date; but that from twenty to twenty-six he had been somewhere else. It was not that he concealed the outlines of those years, but he never filled them in; and in the present era there was no longer any way, for there was actually no one still living known to his interviewers to help them, to find out what had happened then. Everybody agreed that somewhere in those years there must be "the key to Seab," but nobody ever found it; and part of the sly pleasure he took in concealing it was his knowledge that, terrible as it had been for him, the experience really was very common to the human race and nothing so very unusual when all was said and done. That, and the fact that it could still hurt him across all those decades of pomp and power since.

Outwardly, of course, the story was factual and complete and in many ways standard for that time and section. His father had been a country storekeeper, raising seven children by the gift of gab and the grace of God and enough hard work to keep a little food in the cupboard and the necessary minimum of clothing on their backs. Living on the edge of poverty had imposed on all the children the obligation to go to work young, and Seab, first child and first son of four, early began to help his father in the store. This, begun at nine, plus odd jobs for neighbors and other businessmen around Barnwell, had soon given him an ease with grownups and a familiarity with their world which rapidly sharpened an already highly active native intelligence to the point where he presently came to be regarded as one of the most promising youths around the countryside. His grades in school bore this out, for he had no trouble at all in leading his class consistently through grammar school and the first two years in high school. Then his father died, and there was no solution to the problem this posed except to drop school and take over the store to support his mother and the family. A year after this, driven to an almost frantic restlessness by the certainty that he had abilities far beyond storekeeping and the knowledge that he was not making use of them, he answered a high-school-by-mail advertisement and by dint of rising religiously at five every morning and studying until eight when he opened the store, and then studying again from immediately after supper until 11 P.M., he managed to complete his high-school course and received an accredited diploma in a year and a half. By then his next oldest brother was fifteen and able to take an increasingly active part in running the store (he kept at it all his life, and when he had died three years ago Cooley Stores, Inc., in which the Senator still held a sizeable share of stock, had branches in fifteen cities in the Carolinas, six in Georgia, and four in Alabama), and Seab began to think seriously about college.

Along about that time came his first association with the Cashtons, still operating Roselands ten miles out of Barnwell on the five hundred acres left after the war's debts and ravages had been paid off. Colonel Tom Cashton, who had been in the store a thousand times before, came in one day in 1908 and remarked, during a casual purchase of corn, that he had long had his eye on Seabright and he thought Seabright should be encouraged to go to college. Seabright, much pleased by this, said he had the same idea but no money to do it with, and Colonel Cashton, like many another southerner of means obsessed with the idea that the South's bright young men should be fostered and pushed ahead if the country was to come back eventually to parity with the North, offered as naturally as passing the time of day to finance the venture. He was nearing sixty, he had no sons, neither Amy nor Cornelia showed much interest in an education over and beyond that of any gracious and well-placed southern lady, and thanks to the colonel's luck and shrewd management, and that of his mother before him, Roselands had come back rather sensationally from the bitter night when General Kilpatrick had invited the tight-lipped, white-faced, dry-eyed ladies of Barnwell to come dance with his officers while his men set the countryside alight with their houses. He had the money, and he felt he should do something constructive with it for the South, and Seabright seemed the most obvious thank-offering at hand.

After some hesitation, for he did not wish to become too obligated to anyone, the seventeen-year-old storekeeper accepted the offer and went off to the University of South Carolina after his first visit to Roselands, an uncomfortable evening for which he had taken ten hard-earned dollars and bought himself a new suit, and prior to which he had lain awake nights for a week worrying how he would act. As it turned out he acted very well, with an earnest if somewhat stiff dignity at which Amy, just turning fifteen, had poked a little mischievous fun, but which Cornelia seemed to think was quite all right. The colonel too seemed to approve and assured Seab he had no misgivings about their bargain. All he wanted, Colonel Cashton said, was for Seabright to do his best and come home with a degree and do his part for Barnwell, Carolina, and the South. Seab had promised with all the fervor of youth and deep gratitude to do exactly that, and had ridden his horse off into the night with their final waves and good wishes from among the great white columns sounding sweetly in his ears. To this day he could see them smiling and calling and waving still.

There had followed four good years, indeed excellent years, at the university. The colonel's largesse, while not ample, was sufficient, and with the diligence, persistence, and intense application to detail that were to characterize him all his life, he had devoted himself to justifying the colonel's belief in him. In his own mind he had decided at that time that what the South needed most was education, and he pointed his studies toward becoming a teacher; to go home, bring learning where it was needed, lead the young, perhaps in his way do as the colonel had done with him and find a protégé or protégés to carry on the work and go on to do great things, seemed to him the best use he could make of his talents. Because he was good-looking, sociable, likeable, and gregarious, and had also an intelligence which soon carried him to the top of the campus world, this objective began to gather about it, almost without his knowing it, a broader aspect and implication. By his junior year, when he was on the football team, about to become chairman of the debating society, president of the junior class, and the inevitable choice to become president of the student body in the following year, his roommate finally voiced the obvious and suggested that he go into law and then into politics. This idea, which like many other ideas that would be mentioned to him later, already had come to life in his own thoughts, appealed to him powerfully and he said so with candor. But some reluctance holding him back, his obligation to the colonel, his feeling that the colonel might not approve of this course, kept him true to teaching and after a successful year as head of the student body during which he built with contacts and popular policies the foundation of his subsequent political career— forming along the way close friendships with the scions of some half-dozen of Charleston's leading families, without which his political ventures, while as successful, might not have been as comfortably easy as they turned out to be—he got his teaching certificate and went home to Barnwell.

There he found his brother in good health, the store doing well, his mother and family getting along in modest but steadily rising economic comfort, and the Barnwell school, by one of those happy happenstances that often characterized his later career, needing a new superintendent. To this post, with the help of Colonel Cashton and his friends, who comprised most of the leading men of the community, he was appointed at the age of twenty-one and moved into charge of three classrooms, two ancient maiden-lady teachers, and a grand total of forty-three pupils in eight grades.

For two years this kept him busy; but during this time the idea of going into politics became steadily more insistent and the suggestions of those who visualized him in such a setting steadily more pressing. The Congressman from the district was in his mid-seventies, there was the presumption that he would either die or retire before long, and there seemed a good chance the job presently would be there for the taking. There was some opposition, some other ambitious men of more mature years who indicated they might be interested, but he was confident he could beat them if he really went after it. There was still the colonel, however, and his almost superstitious gratitude and obligation; and it was not until he had been teaching for almost a year and a half, and only after six more increasingly intimate visits to Roselands, that suddenly one night the colonel made it as simple as he had made college by looking at him shrewdly over a late brandy and asking bluntly, "Why don't you go into politics?" Quite surprisingly to the colonel, for neither he nor anyone around with the exception of Seab's mother and possibly one other had any conception of the depths of emotion that lay in the school superintendent's heart, tears had welled up in his eyes and he had been unable to speak for several silent moments while the colonel looked tactfully at a china closet full of dried flowers and there managed to conceal an answering emotion of his own.

When Seab could finally speak, he said simply that this was his greatest dream and ambition and that he would give anything in the world if he could do it. But, he said honestly, he felt he was just a little young for it right then, and he felt he should go to law school first. Under the circumstances existing in the district, he went on candidly, he thought there would be just the right lapse of time in which to do it if he began in the coming fall. The colonel again offered financial help, but by then the store was doing well enough, and a second was about to be opened, so that Seab was able to refuse with heartfelt gratitude and thanks. He would, however, he said, appreciate it if the colonel could keep an eye on things for him otherwise while he was away. The colonel chuckled and said he would see to it that the incumbent Congressman ran again, which would have the effect of foreclosing anyone else's ambitions for the time being; the Congressman didn't really want to, the colonel said, but under the circumstances he would be persuaded. Seab thanked him deeply again and went off, this time to Harvard and the great world which he would never leave again.

At Harvard the story was much the same as it had been at the university: many friends, great personal popularity, intensive application, outstanding grades. By the time he came back to Barnwell from his second educational venture there were a good many people in the world who thought that Seabright B. Cooley was a young man with a great and worthy future. Happily for his political plans, a great many of them were concentrated in his home town and its neighboring areas.

From that point forward nothing stood in the way. There was an annual Fourth of July picnic and when its chairman asked about for suggestions for a speaker Colonel Cashton looked up lazily and asked, "Why not get young Seab Cooley? He's just back from law school and ought to know a thing or two." The immediate reaction was that of course this was the obvious choice and how could anybody have overlooked it. The invitation was offered, was quickly accepted, and after writing and rewriting and practicing day and night for three weeks, Barnwell's most promising young man stepped to the lectern and delivered an address so polished and effective that ever after, despite many later speeches on the same occasion to virtually the same audience, "Seab's Fourth of July speech" always meant just one thing, that first ringing, challenging, idealistic, and overpowering onslaught upon their minds and emotions in which man and destiny came together on an afternoon when the temperature stood at 101 and the trumpets of the future sounded among the moss-hung oaks.

Two weeks later the incumbent Congressman announced his retirement in a statement filled with gratitude to his fellow citizens for their long support and many kindnesses, concluding with the suggestion that they give their support to that rising young star of the Carolinas whose future was filled with such bright promise of great things for them and for his country, Seabright B. Cooley. A committee headed by the colonel waited on Seab the next morning, and with a dignified candor that endeared him even further to them, he dispensed with modest coyness and false reluctance and said that he would indeed like to be their Congressman, that he would indeed accept their call, and that they could consider him as of that moment their candidate.

There followed a short, intensive campaign in which he had only token opposition but during which he visited every town and hamlet in the district and personally shook the hands of all but a scattered few of its residents. In November he was given an overwhelming vote of confidence, and in March of 1913 he took his seat in the Congress with the idealism of his own victory strengthened and uplifted by that of the professor from Princeton who moved on the same day into the White House.

For the duration of the Wilson years, four terms to which he was elected by steadily growing majorities, he remained in the House, faithfully supporting the President on every issue, a vigorous and increasingly respected battler for purposes in which he believed absolutely. Something of the stamp of Wilson remained on him forever; to the romantic aura of the South's lost crusade, so much a part of him and all the South's representatives in Congress, there was added the gallant memory of another lost crusade: the War to End War and all its brave idealism that not all the bitter compromises and shabby deceits of subsequent decades could ever quite erase from the hearts of those who had been through it. Even today the years tied themselves together along that slender thread, and it was not hard for him to recall the spirit in which he had fought those early battles, and to go forward in that spirit to do battle again.

Not that this was always apparent to his colleagues or the country, of course, for it was not easy for his critics to accord to a man possessed of such vigorous passions and monumental stubbornness as he proved to have, anything but the most standard of motives. Seab, they early said, was out for what he could get for South Carolina, the South, and himself, in that order, and there was nothing he would not do to attain an objective once he had set it for himself. In the House he served on the Post Office and Civil Service Committee in the days when postmasterships were the bedrock of patronage, and he never forgot the ways in which men could be manipulated by appeals to their self-interest and to the interests of their voters back home. When he moved to the Senate, an event which came easily because the man he challenged had been living a little high on the hog in Washington and Seab made the most of it—and also because the old friends in Barnwell and the old friends in Charleston combined to launch a statewide organization that swept all before it—he was lucky enough to be assigned to the Appropriations Committee, and there he found his analysis of other men to be borne out to even greater degree.

There were some men who would make any bargain to get a needed appropriation for their states; these he early conquered. There were others who needed more subtle appeals, and because he possessed great intelligence, an instinct for the jugular, and a shrewd understanding of human nature, these too he eventually came to dominate. Very few remained immune to him. Appropriations, Finance, Post Office, and Civil Service were his first committees and were his committees still; and it was not accident that he should have passed up the chairmanships of the latter two, to which he succeeded in due time through the normal inroads of mortality and electoral attrition upon his colleagues, in favor of the chairmanship of Appropriations with all its power in the Senate and indeed throughout the government.

There followed the great years, during which "Seab Cooley runs the country" became a favorite saying in Washington. Not that he did, of course, in many fundamental respects; but in many others, it was not too wide of the mark. Using Appropriations for the weapon it can be in the hands of a determined man, sometimes sweet and subtle, sometimes harshly ruthless, he worked his will with many government departments and agencies and with many of his colleagues; a man to be feared and, many thought, mistrusted; yet a man who always, by his lights, was fiercely faithful to the causes and the friends in which he believed. To the simpler critics who dealt in black and white, the liberal journals, the great northern and eastern newspapers, he was an evil influence to be denounced and vilified and feared; but Seab, like every other human being in government or anywhere else, was not that simple, and indeed he was in many ways more complex than most. Because he was violent in his rages and monumental in his public passions, and because he staged his effects with a shrewdly calculated flamboyance that increased over the years as he grew surer of his power, he was easy to label. But his colleagues knew, as they always know, that the easy label very rarely fits a United States Senator, for his is an office that changes the simple to less simple and makes the complex infinitely more so.

Hurt at first by the labels, he soon decided that he could not escape them and so should bend them to his purposes. Steadily over the years, partly through the development of his native character, in greater part through a shrewd creation of his own legend, he built the picture of Seab Cooley that existed today: intelligent, industrious, persistent, tenacious, violent, passionate, vindictive, and tricky. Men did not take him lightly, and many a legislative battle he had won without a struggle simply because certain of his colleagues were actually afraid of him both politically and physically. There was still a lingering story, apocryphal but one he never bothered to kill because it suited his purposes, that he had once drawn a knife on a colleague on the Senate floor; it added to the awe in which he gradually came to be held as the years lengthened and South Carolina sent him back and back again until now he was in his seventh six-year term with a record of service unapproached by any other man but the late Kenneth McKellar of Tennessee. "Don't get Seab riled up," was a catch phrase around the Senate, and for many years it was a brave man who did. Some of course, such as Bob Munson, Orrin Knox, Stanley Danta, Arly Richardson, he had never been able to bluff, even though he had managed to beat them in open contest fairly often. It was only lately that he had begun to realize that perhaps the number of such men was growing, that perhaps he was no longer so strong as he once had been, that age was beginning to erode his position, that those who moved in awe of him just because he was Seab Cooley were dying off or being beaten by younger men who came fresh to the Senate and learned early that while Seab was a man to be wary of, he was also seventy-five years old and neither immortal nor infallible. Not yet had he really been toppled decisively from his throne, but he realized that there was a growing lack of respect for him among the younger members; Lafe Smith was such a one, Blair Sykes was another. There was a growing tendency, of which instinct and the increasingly jocular references of his older friends in the Senate made him increasingly aware, to poke a little fun at Seab, to make him the butt of little private jokes and sniping remarks that once no one would have dared to express, even privately, for fear they might get back and bring down his vindictive vengeance; there was even, as witness last Friday's exchange with Lafe, an occasional open clash on the Senate floor. And only a week ago there had been the acrid crack he had overheard Blair Sykes make when Paul Hendershot had been defending him in the cloakroom. "When he first came here in Wilson's Administration," Paul had said, "there wasn't a greater liberal than Seab Cooley." "Oh yes," Blair snapped impatiently, "I guess even Seab was young once." Well, so he had been; in the way Paul meant, and in another way too; not for long, but long enough to set the pattern for a life that had much to do with the destinies of the United States.

Smiling and waving and calling in the night from among the white columns of Roselands: to this day he could see them still, Amy and Cornelia and the colonel, long years gone to rest; the colonel during the First World War, his daughters during the Second; Roselands sold to rich Yankees in 1945 and now the center for a drinking, gambling, easy-moraled, industry-based crowd growing fat with Yankee money on the cheap labor of the South. He had only been there once since the new owners took over, and then it was for a visit almost as uncomfortable as the first he ever made there. He had been an object for them to examine, something for them to see, a contact they must make for the sake of their proliferating businesses: their United States Senator, Barnwell's brightest young man grown very old and just a little funny in his legend. He had been aware of a subtle ridicule, though he knew they would use him for all they could while he remained in office. He sensed that if they had their way this would not be for long, for he could perceive that they wanted a younger man, one not committed to the past, one who would be more flexible on racial matters and more adept at helping them impose a sort of reverse-quiet on the South by giving the spokesmen of its minority what they wanted while the Yankees made their money.

Well, it had not always been so at Roselands. He avoided it now and never even went down the back road that led along its well-kept fences; but it was not just because of the Yankees. They might think he was avoiding it because they were there, and if so, let them think it and be damned. Actually when he accepted their hospitality on that one occasion after the second war it had been his first visit to the plantation in almost fifteen years; and when they had asked in their casual way, "Have you been here before, Senator?" a curious little secret smile they could not fathom had crossed his face. He had not enlightened them. He had only said softly, "Oh, yes, ma'am, yes, indeed. But that was long ago. Yes, ma'am. That was very long, long ago, quite before you all lovely people were born, I think, it was so long ago."

He could never say exactly at what moment on that first visit he had fallen in love with Amy Cashton, but he could always remember the exalted state in which he had come away from Roselands. The world had been one thing when he rode up the winding lane on his old horse in his new suit; it was quite another when he rode down again. All the fantasies he had not had time or opportunity to indulge while he was running the store and studying nights for high school, all the enormous force of a heart that loved very seldom but when it did loved completely, found their outlet in a sudden overwhelming emotion for the laughing fifteen-year-old who mocked his careful dignity while the colonel shushed her mildly and Cornelia looked disapproving. He had not been able to respond very well, sitting there looking handsome and uneasy and abashed and rather like a mastiff harried by a terrier, and when he went away it was with the helpless conviction that however much he might want to see her again, she could not possibly want to see him. Two days later her maid came by the store and under pretext of buying some linen goods handed him a note telling him to meet her next afternoon at the old well house at the north back corner of Roselands. Next afternoon he turned the store over to his brother on some pretext of going down street to see a friend, hitched up his horse, and rode away into a golden world that lasted exactly three months; whereupon, although there were various later attempts to recreate it by a heart that found itself too late contrite, it ended forever.

For that much time, however, he discovered for himself the simple wonder of just being together with someone, the dreamlike state in which it does not matter what is said, what is done, when the mere state of being, as long as it is in the presence of the beloved, is enough. He could not recall much of what they said, talked about, did; mostly, he suspected, they sat by the well house and threw stones in the water; but around their secret hours such a golden haze enwrapped itself that it was as though all time and no time had come together in a moment of eternity that would last forever. Certainly it had for him, at any rate; and so, he knew, it had for her, even though she had chosen to destroy it because she was too young and too shallow then to understand the depths of the emotion she had aroused, or the qualities of the heart that had in absolute candor and absolutely without defenses offered itself to her.

Often and often he had gone over the course of those three months, during which they had met in such fashion eleven times. The elaborate secrecy, almost gamelike in its childish pretending, should have given him some warning, for a moment's reflection would have recalled that the colonel liked him, had given proof of it, and surely would not have minded him courting his daughter in straightforward fashion; but he was too bemused for reflection. Toward the end of their time together he had felt a sexual desire so great that he was afraid he might say or do something that would lose her forever; it was the measure of his innocence that he thought he was alone in this feeling. But he had been brought up by rigid standards, he had a romantic concept of what a lady thought and felt, and he feared more than anything in the world that he might violate it by some crudity or intimation of lust that would break the bounds of desperate self-control imposed upon him by upbringing and his own youthful imaginings. So it was that when she turned to him on that last day and first offered and then withdrew herself with a cruelly calculated deliberation that made a shattering mockery of his own emotions, instead of being angered as she wanted him to be into doing what had consumed him day and night, heart, mind, and body for weeks, he turned and fled in such tumult of being that it was hours before he finally got home and began the long, terrible, agonizing process of trying to put back together some semblance of a world that made sense.

His first conviction, for he was indeed an innocent then, was that the whole thing had been his doing, that it had been his exclusive idea, that he must have desperately shocked, offended, and horrified one who had trusted and cared for him and been his friend. It did not occur to him for many a long day after that this was not the case. So he began to apologize, writing crippled, agonized letters in which he abandoned all attempts to maintain the dignity of his own heart, taking on himself all blame, humbling himself endlessly, beseeching over and over again for lost happiness, addressing an Amy such as no Amy that ever existed except in his own mind; for of course if such an Amy had existed she would have been kind to him and answered, and of course there was no answer. He entered a period during which life became a dark valley that he walked through filled with shadowy figures that he talked to; while all the time sick, agonized, endless, futile conversations went on in his heart: I could have done such wonderful things for you. We could have been so happy together. If you would only let me show you how much you mean to me.

Help me, beloved; help me, dear love. All of this coincided with his first months in college, and it was not until later that he realized how very strong his own character must be, that he could have been going through all that and still have managed to matriculate, begin his courses, and start his campus life with an outward stability and ease that guaranteed it success. Looking back, he marveled that he had survived with sanity intact, so agonizing had the experience been; but in time he understood that having survived that he could survive anything. And the day came when he was even grateful that it had happened, for it had taught him things about himself and his own strength that he could never have learned any other way, and that, once learned, could never be shaken by anyone.

For several months after he entered the university he continued to write at regular intervals, but always without answer. Presently, at first in desperation but then in a more relaxed and pragmatic fashion, he turned to the easy sex of the town, and for a time that became the surest road back to sanity; he never regretted it or gave it a second thought, for he perceived instinctively that he needed it, indeed had to have it if he was to regain balance, and so went about it without compunction and without worry, violently though it flew in the face of his upbringing and earlier character. That was all in the past now and a grown man was being forged; he said good-by, a little late and without regrets, to the boy. "Seab does everything just a little larger than life," somebody was to remark of him once, years later. Nothing proved it more than the practical, realistic, matter-of-fact, and virtually emotionless way in which he went about getting himself over the transition from adolescence to maturity.

At the end of the school year he returned home, and inevitably was asked to Roselands again by the colonel. For a wild moment all the agonies returned, but nothing of this showed on the surface and he accepted with outward pleasure. Aside from a convulsion of heart and mind so great that he thought he would faint on the steps when he first saw her, his meeting with Amy passed off without incident; and before the evening ended he realized that while he would love her forever, and that it would in all probability keep him from marrying anyone else, he had come back armored and invincible with the invincibility of pain suffered too long, too unjustly, and too deep. But he was not to realize until several years later, when she finally decided she loved him, just how invincible he had become; for though it was still true that he would love her—or his dream of her, perhaps—forever, he found that in a curiously remote and removed sort of way he no longer cared enough to upset his life and go through the agony of subjecting himself to her again.

After that, the little bitter game was played out over the years as neatly and inevitably as might have been expected. Shortly before he went away to law school she offered herself to him again, and this time he took her savagely enough to satisfy his own ego; and then he walked out and didn't come back. There were appeals and apologizings and beseechings then, but they were on the other side and he did not respond; something was frozen away inside that never unthawed in the heat of their renewed association. Inevitably in time there came the spiteful marriage to someone she didn't love; and then, after twenty childless years and a union that satisfied appearances but never fooled either her sister or him, her husband died and she returned to Roselands, still trying to revive the past. There followed the long series of visits to the plantation over the years, the long talks with Cornelia, who had never married but had remained at home to carry on shrewdly and successfully after her father's death, with Amy always present but saying increasingly little. And in time, when another twenty years had passed so fast he hardly knew it, there came one night the frantic call from Cornelia about a heart attack, the hurried arrival, too late, at Roselands, and the burial in Barnwell beside the colonel and her mother; and then, three years later, the same sad journey for Cornelia, and then the tale was done. A long time ago, ma'am. Yes, ma'am, a very long, long time ago.

And now he was Seab the Irascible, Seab the Invincible, Seab the Holy Terror, the Scourge of the Senate; but not entirely—not entirely. Years after her death, one day in the Old Senate Office Building, he had seen far down the corridor a girl go swinging by, so much like her that before he knew it a strange animal sob welled up and broke from his lips. He looked around hastily, but the girl was far off, no one else was around, no one had heard him. After a moment he went on, smiling grimly to himself. What would they say, all his critics and enemies, if they could see an old man crying for his youth? They wouldn't believe it, because none of them believed that he had ever been young. But he had—he had. That was his little secret, for whatever good it did him now.

It had affected his public life in ways he sensed but could never be sure he understood in full. There had been iron in his soul before; maybe Amy had refined it into steel. There had been a youthful determination to win a fair break from the world and make his own way on even terms with others; maybe Amy had turned it into a ruthlessness bordering on vindictiveness. There had been an ambition that never rested; maybe Amy had driven it to the heights. Maybe after all it wasn't just Seab who had "run the government"; maybe Amy had helped to run it too. At any rate, he recognized it for what it was, the major personal experience of his life, and because to a considerable degree it did furnish "the key to Seab," it was something he never revealed to anyone. The lost years belonged to him, and he was not about to have them pawed over by strangers; to him and Amy and their golden world, so brief in time and so eternal in consequences.

It was perhaps no wonder, then, that he should have loomed large against the pageant of his times. The Wilsonian liberalism that never really died found itself muted and without much companionship in the foredoomed twenties; revived again under Franklin Roosevelt, it inspired a consistently progressive voting record that was not enough to blot out the apparent rapacity for patronage, power, and steadily rising appropriations for his native state and its sisters of the South. The character was too vivid and colorful, the facile, shallow attack too easy; writing about Seab Cooley was one of those things that the Washington press corps reserved for a dull day when there wasn't much news, because it was always easy to dream up something colorful about the Senator to fill up space.

Behind all this, in a mind that remained unfailingly alert and passionately dedicated to the country, he had watched with Bob Munson and Orrin and the other old hands while America rose higher and higher and then spiraled suddenly into tailspin with no one knowing the answer and no one sure of the future and no one certain that the tailspin would be ended and the course again made steady. Basically, although he had chosen to make a great public show of personal enmity for Bob Leffingwell, although it was true that he had never forgiven him for giving him the lie direct on that far-back day, his real dislike went to the fundamentals of what he conceived to be the sickness of the times. For he saw Bob Leffingwell, with all his graceful flirtings with this cause and that over the years, with all his clever skatings along the outskirts of the flabbily-principled and dangerously over-liberal fads of his era, as that perfect symbol of mid-twentieth-century America, the Equivocal Man. He could always find an excuse for being hospitable to this, he could always find a reason for not being too hostile to that; he seemed always, or so it appeared to Senator Cooley, to slide smoothly just between the sharp edges of clashing principles and there find a glib, soft, woozy area of gummy compromise and rationale that effectively blurred everything, enervated all issues, weakened firmness, and sapped resolve in a way that hamstrung his own country and made it easier for her enemies to move a few steps farther along the path they had set themselves. Seab was fully aware, Bob Munson might be interested to know, of all the implications of the Leffingwell nomination, and he knew full well the forces he hoped to mobilize behind his opposition to it. He had preferred for a little while to let the impression stand that he was fighting the nomination just as he had always fought it, as a matter of personal feud with the nominee; but his purposes went deeper than that. Bob Leffingwell, to Seab's mind, was one of the most dangerous men in America, and he felt with all the angry passion of all his angry years, that he had never engaged upon any project more vital to his country than his campaign to keep him out of the office of Secretary of State.

At this thought, as he turned down the final wing of corridor and approached the floodlighted entrance to the Caucus Room, a sudden black scowl came over his face, and it was this that the television cameras and the press photographers caught with quick delight as he entered.

It was one more proof that bolstered the legend, and he went on into the crowded, electric room without bothering to erase it with his customary slow smile and "How you all?" Let them send it out as it stood, if they liked; let them add to the legend of Seab the Terror. So much the better for the cause he was conducting now.

3

"I say, Big Chief," John Winthrop murmured, leaning toward Brigham Anderson at the committee table, "what says yon smoke signal appearing on the horizon?"

"Oh, God," Senator Anderson said with a grin. "It looks as though he's on the warpath already, doesn't it?"

"He doesn't look exactly cheerful," Senator Winthrop agreed, but as it turned out these forebodings were entirely unwarranted, for once inside the door an amiable change came over the senior Senator from South Carolina. A quick glance around the room informed him that it was fully as crowded as it had been on Saturday, the same full complement of press and television, the same jam-packed audience filling the spectators' seats and crowding along the walls and in the aisles; and his expression at once became bland. The blandness increased when his eye fell on the nominee, reading a New York *Times* calmly in the little section of chairs in back of the witness stand while he waited for the hearing to begin. Senator Cooley gave a cheerful wave to his colleagues at the table, changed course abruptly, and was on Bob Leffingwell before he knew it, hand outstretched and a slow, appraising smile on his face. For just a second—long enough to lose a little of his grip on his customary poise—the director of the ODM looked startled. Then he too rose and held out his hand, while press and photographers swarmed in on them and the tension in the room suddenly shot up in a burst of excited murmurings from the audience.

"Senator," Bob Leffingwell said with a fair attempt at cordiality while the flash bulbs popped and the cameras clicked and the crush of reporters crowded them closer together, "I'm delighted to see you."

"Well, now," Seab said softly, "that's mighty nice, Mr. Director. It is indeed. But I want you to know your pleasure isn't even close to mine. No, sir, it isn't even close. In fact, if I *hadn't* seen you here today, I would have been most e-gre-gious-ly disappointed, Mr. Director. Most egregiously."

"Well," Bob Leffingwell said rather lamely, "that's good. Shall we shake hands again? The photographers seem to want us to."

"I suspect," Seab said in a confidential way, with a wink and a grin and just loud enough so the reporters could hear, "that they just want to see us shake hands because they think we don't like each other. Do you suspect that's it?"

"Oh, I'm sure that isn't it," the nominee said and hated himself for adding a nervous little laugh. "But I suppose we'd better do it, or they won't be satisfied."

"I expect so," Senator Cooley said calmly, suiting the action to the word. "Is this what you all want?"

"That's it, Senator!" somebody cried approvingly. "Mr. Leffingwell!" somebody else cried, "can you stand a little closer, please? In a little closer, Senator!" And when they obliged, with Seab looking perfectly calm but the nominee beginning to look a little strained, somebody else called out in a tone as close to mockery as he dared, "Thank *you*, Mr. Secretary!" And for just a moment—which was what they were hoping for—Seab in spite of himself looked annoyed at the use of the title, a blaze of flash bulbs exploded in their faces, there were further cries of "Thank you, Senator!" and, more firmly now, "Thank you, Mr. Secretary!" and the picture-taking was over. The reporters were still hovering close, however, as Bob Leffingwell started to sit down, and the Senator decided to give them a little more for their money.

"I want to ask you about your virus, Mr. Director," he said, leaning over the nominee and placing a knotted brown hand on his shoulder. "I hope it's cleared up, I surely do."

"All gone, thank you, Senator," Bob Leffingwell said smiling up at him and looking a little more relaxed. "It went over the weekend and I'm feeling good as new now."

"That's good," Senator Cooley said softly. "That's good, Mr. Director. Because I suspect—I just suspect now"—and a slow grin crossed his face and he looked at the listening reporters with a sly twinkle in his eye—"I just suspect that before these hearings are over you may just need your strength. Yes, sir, I just suspect you may."

"I'm ready for it, Senator," Bob Leffingwell said, retaining his smile but speaking just a little more loudly than he intended; and Seab gave his shoulder a friendly squeeze before he let it go and started his slow progress toward the committee table.

"I hope so, Mr. Director," he said comfortably. "I hope so. Because *I'm* feeling mighty fine, I want you to know, Mr. Director. Yes, sir, I haven't felt better since—well, since the last time you and I were together at one of these little gatherings we both enjoy so much."

"I'll do my best, Senator," the nominee called after him in a suddenly firm tone, and Seab looked back with no further word but only a smile composed about equally of amusement and pity. Then one of the reporters offered the director of the Office of Defense Mobilization a cigarette, and he took it with outward composure but a revealing alacrity as he settled back with his newspaper again while Seab moved on to the committee table and the reporters scattered to their places.

"Round one to Seab, I gather," John Winthrop murmured.

"Apparently," Brigham Anderson said. "This is not going to be a pleasant experience for any of us, I can see that."

"Did you think it would be?" Senator Winthrop asked, and Senator Anderson smiled rather grimly.

"I had hoped we'd preserve the amenities," he said.

"Oh, we'll preserve the amenities, all right," Senator Winthrop said, "but the blood and guts are going to be running all over the place."

"If I can help it," Brigham Anderson said firmly, "there'll be as little of that as possible."

"Are you going to challenge Seab?" Senator Winthrop asked quizzically, and Senator Anderson gave him a direct look.

"I'm the chairman of this subcommittee," he said flatly. "You don't think I won't if I have to, do you?"

"I expect you will, Brig," John Winthrop said comfortably. "I just wanted to see if the starch was in you this morning. I didn't really think it wasn't."

"It's there," Senator Anderson said shortly. "Never worry about that . . . Well, Seab, did you get him sufficiently terrorized to start off with?"

"Why, now, Senator," Senator Cooley said blandly. "I don't know what you're talking about, I truly don't. Can't I exchange time of day with an old friend? Pretty pass if I can't, Mr. Chairman, I must say. Where do you want me to sit?"

"Sit right here by me, if you like," Brigham Anderson offered, but Seab rejected the suggestion with a little wave of the hand.

"That's Mr. Knox's seat," he observed with a twinkle, "and he might not like it. You know Orrin. Mighty touchy man, Orrin. No, I'll just find myself a place somewhere down the table, thank you."

"Suit yourself," Brig said. "Glad to have you."

"Yes, I know, Mr. Chairman," Senator Cooley said with the same little twinkle. "I surely do know how glad."

And after looking thoughtfully up and down the table he moved slowly on to take a seat far down at one end where he was separated from his colleagues in an isolated eminence that immediately seemed somehow ominous and forbidding. There he settled himself slowly into his chair and stared out at the audience with a deliberate lack of expression.

"Hmm," Brigham Anderson said. "Psychological warfare."

"All the tricks," Winthrop of Massachusetts said with a smile. "We're going to see them all before this is over."

"Here come my other little problems," Senator Anderson said, "so maybe we can begin."

At the door Senator DeWilton and Senator Richardson came in together, the senior Senator from Vermont looking, as always, faintly disgruntled, and Arly, as always, sardonic and rather spiteful. Brigham Anderson gave them a cordial wave and, noting that Orrin Knox was coming in just behind them with his usual briefcase full of papers, hunched his chair forward a little, and picked up the gavel. All three, however, went out of their way to detour by Bob Leffingwell and shake hands, while the photographers duly recorded their handclasps and the reporters faith-

fully jotted down their words in newsmen's shorthand in the hope they
might be as colorful as Seab's. They weren't. (DeW: Mr. Leff., har y?
Kn: Bob, gld see y, hope yr flg btr. Rich.: Gd mg, Bob. Sgoing be long,
tough summer. Leff. to each: Gd mg, Sar, sgood see y.) This rite per-
formed, his colleagues came along to the committee table and Brigham
Anderson hunched his chair forward just a little further, placed a hand
around the microphone in front of him, and lifted the gavel. The room
quieted down, the television lights went on, the press got ready; he rapped
sharply for order and began.

"This subcommittee of the Senate Foreign Relations Committee," he
said, "is meeting on authority of the full committee to hear such witnesses
and take such evidence on the nomination of Robert A. Leffingwell to be
Secretary of State as may be necessary to assist the Senate in appraising
this appointment. There is, first, a procedural matter to be decided, and
since we meet under terms of the resolution of the senior Senator from
Arkansas, adopted last Saturday, which requires that all our proceedings
must be held in public, we are foreclosed from settling it in customary
fashion in closed session prior to the public hearings. We will have to
decide the order of witnesses, and the Chair is ready to welcome any
discussion along this line that may suit members."

"God damn," whispered AP at the press table, "that's the way to speed
things along."

"Quiet," UPI retorted, "give the boy a chance. He's got four prima
donnas on his hands, and that ain't hay."

"He'll make it," the *Times* predicted. "Wait and see."

Bob Munson knew when the phone rang who it would be, and when
Mary buzzed and he picked up the receiver in his inner office he was not
disappointed. This morning, he noted, the President's voice sounded as
confident as ever, but there was a slight, an almost indefinable tiredness
running through it. This alarmed him and it must have shown in his own
voice, for as soon as he finished saying hello the President asked sharply,
"What's the matter? Aren't you feeling well?"

"I'm feeling fine," Senator Munson said. "How are you?"

"I'm fine," the President said heartily, and then the Senator sensed
him remembering that he had admitted differently a couple of days ago.
"I'm feeling all right," he amended. "I just thought I'd call and find out
how things are moving up there. How's the hearing going?"

"I haven't been in yet," Bob Munson said. "I'm going over pretty soon."

"Seab pulled a fast one Saturday, didn't he?" the President asked, not
without a trace of the admiration of one political craftsman for another.
"Had you all on the ropes, eh?"

"It wasn't quite that bad. But he got his way."

"How much longer is he going to?" the President asked.

"I expect most of the week," the Majority Leader said calmly. "Brace yourself. There's probably going to be bad news until this hearing is finished, I imagine; it's tailor-made for his talents."

"How does Brig feel about it?"

"He wasn't too happy about taking the chairmanship, but Orrin and I bowled him over with fulsome compliments and he reluctantly consented. He'll be fair about it, and he's the only man I know who can stand up to Seab if things really get rough."

"Can't Orrin?" the President asked.

"Orrin can," the Majority Leader agreed, "but on this one we'll let Orrin make up his own mind without being shoved, I think. It will be better that way."

"How do he and Brig feel about Bob Leffingwell?"

"Not so hot," Senator Munson said, "but willing to be convinced. I doubt if they'll really get in the way when all's said and done. After all it *is* a Cabinet job, and they're pretty loyal to you, on the whole."

"Even Orrin, who thinks he ought to be sitting where I'm sitting?" the President inquired with a certain dryness in his tone.

"Even Orrin," Bob Munson said firmly. "They're fair-minded men, both of them, and unless somebody comes up with something pretty dreadful, they'll go along."

"Well, that's good," the President said. "Do you want anybody else from down here to come up and testify?"

"I think not," the Majority Leader said. "I think the sooner we can wind it up the better; and that means the fewer witnesses the better. Witnesses just mean more time, and the longer it goes the more chance there is for somebody to throw a monkey wrench into it. I'd say everybody stay home down in your department and we'll worry along up here as best we can."

"That was my thought too," the President said. "What about helping you line up votes? Is there anything I can do down here, or anybody I can call who can call somebody else and put on the heat?"

"Not yet. We'll get to that, but let's just see how the hearing goes, for the moment. It may be it will be so smooth that nobody will need much pressure. Not that I really think so, you understand, but it's nice to dream."

The President laughed. "I'm glad your sense of humor is keeping up, anyway. Mine got a little out of joint over the weekend when I saw what Fred Van Ackerman had to say in New York. This mood in the country has me worried, Bob; too many people are getting ripe for another piece-meal surrender if it can just be tied up with pretty pink ribbons so it won't look like a surrender. And that two-bit little bastard knows it. I think he's dangerous."

"I know," Bob Munson said with a sigh. "People don't understand a war unless there's a gun going off someplace; they still don't see the other kind that doesn't make any noise but just goes on eating and eating the guts and the heart out of you until you collapse."

"That's it," the President agreed. "I wonder if I should go on the air again?"

"What would be the excuse? There's got to be one, or it looks forced and that takes away half the impact."

"Yes," the President said. "Well. I shall wait and I shall see, and maybe the opportunity will come soon. If it doesn't, I'll make my own opportunity, because it's got to be done. Too many people are beginning to listen to Fred and his likes."

"Of course you know he may be one of your strongest supporters on this nomination," Senator Munson said, and the President gave a snort of surprise.

"How's that?" he demanded.

"Fred and a lot of other people think Bob Leffingwell may be just the man for them," the Majority Leader said. "All the Fred Van Ackermans in this land want a new attempt made to get along with the Russians no matter what the cost, and it hasn't escaped them that you must intend to make one or you wouldn't be replacing Howie. And Bob's record is just equivocal enough on that subject so they think maybe he's it. No, you're apt to find Fred leading the parade for you, for all his speeches in Madison Square Garden and his big brave attacks on the Administration for being too rigid."

"Hmm," the President said; and then, in what appeared to be a sudden tangent, only Bob Munson knew it wasn't, "What do you think of Harley these days?"

"Harley," Senator Munson said slowly, "is an awfully decent, good-hearted, timid man who loves his country and will do whatever he has to do for her—if he has to do it."

"Yes," the President said, without other comment; and then returning to the nominee he said slowly, "I don't think Bob is an appeaser without principle, or I wouldn't have nominated him. I do need a new face, because it seems time to make another try and Howie is associated too much with nay-saying in too many minds all over the world. I'm not blaming him, he's faithfully executed the policy; but now the policy is going to shift a little—not change, though, Bob, and I want you to know you have my word on that, not change in any basic principle at all—and it just seems better for Howie to get out of the picture. What did he think of the NATO job?"

"He'll take it," Senator Munson said shortly.

"Well, that's good," the President said comfortably. "Then I can put him out to pasture with a clear conscience . . . How will the hearings be going by Thursday? Should I hold a press conference, or would it be better to skip it?"

"By Thursday," Senator Munson said, "it might be better to skip it, because just about then, I imagine, is when Seab will be displaying his full bag of tricks and Bob may not be looking too good just at that particular moment. It might be best if you didn't have to say anything about it right then. But what excuse will you give for skipping it? If there isn't one, they'll think it's health."

"Why will they think it's health?" the President demanded with some exasperation in his voice. "Do I really look as bad as all that?"

"You look fine," Senator Munson said calmly, "and I'm quite sure nobody thinks you aren't. But I still think it would be best to have an excuse."

"Oh, well," the President said airily, "I can call a meeting of the National Security Council. That's always a good cover-up for almost anything, you know, and there's always plenty that needs talking about. Yes, I think that's what I'll do. I'll tell Pete to announce it at his four o'clock briefing this afternoon. Also, there's another thing, anyway: the White House Correspondents' annual banquet is Thursday night, and that's as good an excuse as any for not meeting them. Say!" he said suddenly. "Maybe I can give them a surprise or two in my little talk at the banquet."

"Mr. President," Bob Munson said in a genuinely enthusiastic tone, "that's a real inspiration. They won't be expecting it, and——"

"That's right," the President said, his voice quickening as he picked up the idea and ran with it, "you know that little rigmarole they always go through about it's all off the record and 'There are no reporters present here tonight?' Well *tonight*, gentlemen—"and Senator Munson could visualize his head coming up with an air and the challenging gleam flashing into his eyes—"Well, tonight, gentlemen, I'm going to exercise a President's prerogative and change your rules, just temporarily. Tonight, gentlemen, there *are* reporters present, so get out your pencils and get set, because I have something to say. Certain crafty, petty men, operating behind the cloak of their ancient privilege in the United States Senate, are engaged in a massive conspiracy to—— Oh, ho, ho, Bob! *I'll* tell 'em!" And a laugh of pure relish that didn't sound tired at all any more came over the line to the Majority Leader's ear. He chuckled.

"That's perfect," he said. "Just perfect. And it ought to be timed just about right for the hearing, too."

"Tell *me* I'm losing my touch!" the President said scornfully.

"I didn't. I wouldn't dream of it. In the meantime, sit tight and we'll plug along up here and try not to let Bob have too hard a time."

"Good," the President said, back to business. "When are you coming to see me?"

"I'll see you at the banquet," Senator Munson said. "Maybe we can talk then."

"We'll plan on it. Thanks for everything, Robert."

"It's a pleasure. If it weren't I wouldn't be in this business."

Looking down the table from his outpost at the end of it, the senior Senator from South Carolina could observe with some satisfaction that his colleagues were just a little on edge as the hearing got under way.

Johnny DeWilton was fidgeting about in his chair, trying to find a comfortable base for his ample foundation; Orrin Knox was fiddling absentmindedly with his papers; Arly Richardson was looking restlessly about the room, and John Winthrop was showing his sure sign of tension, a slow and thoughtful rubbing of his right index finger up and down the bridge of his nose. Only the chairman, Seab perceived, looked at least outwardly calm, and the sight reminded him that Brig had always been one he could neither cow, browbeat, or intimidate. It had been so from the first day the Senator from Utah had come to the Senate, young and idealistic and eager to learn: it was so now seven years later when he was still young and idealistic and had learned a great deal. Polite and attentive and respectful and calm he had been when he first met Seab, and polite and attentive and respectful and calm he was toward him to this day. Browbeating and intimidation didn't work there, Seab knew, but politeness and a sort of cordial banter always did. The key to handling Brig, who was a gentleman, was to treat him as a gentleman. Senator Cooley decided that he would conduct himself circumspectly throughout as far as the chairman was concerned, and would play the rest by ear. So it was that he arrested his first impulse to speak when the chairman called for a discussion of procedure and waited calmly for the decision which might bring forth from him any one of several plans of action, depending upon what the decision was.

"My own thought," Senator Anderson said, "is that we should perhaps start with the senior Senator from South Carolina, Mr. Cooley, who has asked to be present with us and participate in our proceedings; then hear the nominee, Mr. Leffingwell; then hear such witnesses as the Senator from South Carolina may wish to present; and then recall the nominee to answer whatever material is then in the record that he or we may deem to require or"—and his tone became rather dry—"be worthy of, an answer. The Chair is, however, quite willing to entertain any amendments to that idea if anyone cares to offer them. Senator Knox?"

"Well, Mr. Chairman," Orrin said tartly, "nice as it is to hear the distinguished Senator from South Carolina, I am wondering if there is anyone in the room who has any doubts as to his sentiments in this matter? It is my feeling," he went on, as the press looked amused and a little murmur of laughter flickered across the audience, "that in the interests of expediting this matter, which I think nearly all of us want to do, we might, in a manner of speaking, consider that the opinions of the Senator from South Carolina have been read and placed in the record. Unless he has something of unusual interest to offer—which of course he may, Mr. Chairman, for we all know he is a tough and determined campaigner—it's my view that there isn't very much to be gained by a rehearsal of old grievances."

At this there was a slight spattering of applause from the audience and the chairman rapped sharply for order.

"The Chair will advise the audience," he said with some vigor, "that demonstrations of approval or disapproval are not permitted. This is a serious matter, so let's treat it as such. Senator Winthrop?"

"I'm inclined to agree with the Senator from Illinois," Winthrop of Massachusetts said. "Up in my country they have a sayin' that when you spill a bucket of"—he started to say "slops," then thought better of it— "of milk, there isn't much doubt what's in it. It seems to me, with all respects to my old and dear friend from South Carolina, that he's been spillin' the milk on this subject for quite a few years now."

Again there was a ripple of laughter, and Arly Richardson and John DeWilton said "Mr. Chairman!" as one.

"One vote for Orrin," UPI whispered. "Maybe this is the beginning of Seab's downfall," the New York *Herald Tribune* whispered back. "I'll believe it when I see it," AP snorted.

"I believe the regular order," Brigham Anderson observed calmly, "would be to recognize the Senator from Arkansas."

"Well, Mr. Chairman," Arly said in a tone that he made increasingly indignant as he went along, "I must say I fail to understand the logic or the courtesy of the Senators from Illinois and Massachusetts. I for one am sure the distinguished Senator from South Carolina has much to offer us in this matter, and I am a little shocked, I will say, Mr. Chairman, just a little shocked, at the cavalier way in which Senators would brush aside one of their fellow Senators in this manner. Senators should remember, Mr. Chairman, that what they do to someone today may be done to them tomorrow; this is one of the oldest rules of the Senate, Mr. Chairman, even though it is an unwritten one, and I think it should be remembered. I do hope my dear friends from Illinois and Massachusetts will reconsider what appears to be their decision on this and give our beloved friend from South Carolina a chance to have his say."

"I didn't say he couldn't have his say," Orrin Knox interjected bluntly. "If the Senator doesn't think the Senator from South Carolina will have his say no matter at what point he appears on the program, he just doesn't know the Senator from South Carolina, that's all."

"My statement stands, Mr. Chairman," Arly said straight ahead, not looking at Orrin Knox beside him.

"Let it stand," Orrin said shortly.

"Well, Senators," Brigham Anderson said matter-of-factly, "shall we get on with this? Senator DeWilton, I believe you wanted to be recognized?"

"Yes, I did," Johnny DeWilton said, his face flushed and his silvery hair quivering, looking rather like a cockatoo in a snit. "My sentiments are exactly those of the Senator from Arkansas, Mr. Chairman. Exactly. I fail to see why the Senator from South Carolina shouldn't be allowed to speak first and present his case. I want him to. That's my position, Mr. Chairman."

"Thank you, Senators," Senator Anderson said calmly. "Perhaps we should hear the sentiments of the gentleman in question." He leaned forward and looked down the table; his voice took on a friendly conversational tone. "Can you hear me, Seab?" he asked. Again there was laughter, and this time he did not rap quite so hard for order. Senator Cooley waved and gave a sleepy grin.

"I can hear you fine, Mr. Chairman," he said gently. "Just fine. Is there some matter you all want to question me about?"

"What would *you* like to do, Senator?" Brig asked with a smile. "Would you like to speak now, or forev—or speak later?"

"God, this is getting jolly," the Baltimore *Sun* remarked in some disgust to the New York *Times*. "Old Home Week," the *Times* agreed.

"Well, Mr. Chairman," Senator Cooley said softly, "if you all will recall, I am not a member of this subcommittee. I am here strictly on your sufferance, Mr. Chairman, and so I don't feel it would be proper for me to attempt in any way to influence you all. I wish to thank, however," he added thoughtfully, "my friends from Arkansas and Vermont for their great courtesy to an old man. It does my heart good, Mr. Chairman, it truly does, to find such courtesy still present in the Senate in these troubled days."

At this, as Seab knew full well he would, Orrin Knox made an indignant movement and started to say something, then changed his mind.

"Of course, Mr. Chairman," Senator Cooley suggested gently, "it could be put to a vote, I suppose, if you are in doubt."

"That's right, Mr. Chairman," Arly Richardson said quickly. "Let's have a vote."

Senator Anderson looked annoyed, which he was for having let himself fall so easily into so obvious a trap; and Seab knew from his expression that the vote was going to go the way he wanted it to, for as of that moment he had no witnesses, no prepared statement, and no real idea as yet of exactly how he would proceed.

"Very well," the chairman said in a tone of mild disgust, "let's have a motion and a vote."

"I move the senior Senator from South Carolina be heard first and be allowed to proceed in his own way," Senator Richardson said promptly.

And just as the Senator from South Carolina was sure they would, Senator Richardson and Senator DeWilton voted Aye, Senator Knox, Senator Winthrop, and Senator Anderson voted No, the motion was defeated, and he was relieved of an immediate appearance he was not prepared for and had no intention of making.

"All right," Brigham Anderson said firmly as the room broke into an excited buzz. "Mr. Leffingwell, will you come forward, please, give your name to the official reporter, and be sworn."

If only, Harley Hudson thought as he paced nervously up and down his office in the Old Senate Office Building and glanced outside resentfully at a gray and drizzly day teetering on the edge of spring, if only he could find out something definite about something from somebody. It wasn't that he wanted to know everything about everything, just a little about a little; but here he was, doing his best to co-operate with the President and the Majority Leader, trying to be as helpful as he could on the Leffingwell nomination, and all he got was crumbs, just crumbs. It was true that his first attempt at helping, his conversation with Paul Hendershot of Indiana, had turned out rather disastrously in the debate on Friday, but that wasn't his fault and they all knew it. Paul had just been in one of his moods, the ornery old bastard, and then, too, Harley suspected, Seab had probably put him up to it, anyway. Certainly it wasn't the Vice President's fault that his attempt at mollification and amelioration had gone awry; and he wasn't disposed to take the blame for it. But he hadn't heard a word since from the Majority Leader, and when he had run into him in the hall a little while ago Bob had only looked preoccupied and given him a very cursory greeting that hardly seemed adequate to their old friendship and long working alliance in politics. As for the President—well, Harley was very much tempted to call, but he was afraid that if he did he might get shunted off by some secretary and then the President wouldn't call back, and that would be too humiliating. He would just have to wait, he supposed rather forlornly, until the call came voluntarily from the other end. One heartbeat away from the Presidency, he thought bitterly, and for all practical purposes ten million miles away from the President. By God, it wasn't fair.

These musings, which were not much different from similar musings he had indulged in many times before, were, he realized beginning to make him feel tense and upset and he knew he shouldn't let himself get into that state. Not that he had anything to worry about concerning his own health—he wondered about the President, though; Bob had been so elusive about it on Friday, and Harley wondered nervously if there had been anything definite behind it—but after all, it *was* only one heartbeat, in truth, and he should keep calm about it, because if anything happened to that heartbeat and then anything happened to *his* heartbeat, the Speaker would succeed to the Presidency and Harley was damned if he was going to turn the country over to that crafty and self-satisfied gentleman. He might be worried about his own position, he might have feelings of inadequacy, he might be fearful of what would happen if the President died, but by God, he wasn't that fearful. The job was his, the Constitution said so, and nobody was going to take it away from him, by God.

Just at that moment the phone did ring and he jumped guiltily, for he had gone on instantly to reflect that of course the only one who could take it away from him in that eventuality was the Lord Himself and the phone call in its unexpected sharpness seemed almost like an admonitory reminder from on high that he had jolly well better remember the fact. But when he picked it up it was to hear one of his secretaries announcing calmly that the Secretary of State was in the outer office and would like to see him. "Show him in," he ordered and sat down hurriedly behind his mammoth desk, where he began reading thoughtfully through the only paper on it, a copy of the Senate Calendar of legislative business which he had read a thousand times before. When Howard Sheppard was ushered in he glanced up with a look of quick alertness that didn't fool the Secretary very much and rose with an air of expansive greeting.

"Well, Howie," he said, "this is a pleasant surprise. It's always good to see you."

"Mr. Vice President," Howie said formally, "you're looking well."

"I'm feeling well, Howie," the Vice President said comfortably. "I'd say you weren't looking so bad yourself. You must be beginning to anticipate that retirement a little." And then, like the Majority Leader, he realized that this was a delicate subject, flushed a little, and changed it abruptly.

"Sorry we missed you at Dolly's the other night," he said. "We went to La Salle du Bois beforehand and Ethel ate not wisely but too well, as you can do at that excellent place, and so we left earlier than we'd planned. I hear Bob Munson and the others got into quite a hassle with our ambassadorial friends. Were you there?"

"No," Howard Sheppard said rather sharply. "It's getting so nobody ever tells me anything any more."

"Well, now, Howie," the Vice President said comfortably, "I don't think there's any reason for you to feel that way. I'm sure it all developed very spontaneously and there probably wasn't time to invite you. I wasn't invited either, for that matter."

"Oh, well," the Secretary said with an off-hand moroseness. "But *I'm* the Secretary of State."

The Vice President looked decidedly miffed, and when he replied it was with a certain sharp enjoyment he would not otherwise have shown.

"Not for long, Howie," he said crisply. "Not for long." Then he added, as his annoyance grew with the full impact of the Secretary's casual dismissal, "What brings you to me this morning? I'm in sort of a hurry."

"It's the Russians and the Indians," Howie Sheppard said, oblivious to the effect of his previous remark—No wonder the President's firing him, Harley thought. He's certainly no diplomat!—and looking rather puzzled by the tidings he was bearing.

"What about them?" the Vice President inquired, his annoyance going rapidly as he thought he perceived a chance to be helpful. After all, Howie couldn't help his mood; it was tough to be ignored and fired. Nobody could fire *him*, he reflected complacently.

"They want to see you," the Secretary said.

"See *me?*" the Vice President asked blankly. "What on earth for?"

"I don't know," Howard Sheppard said. "All I know is that Vasily Tashikov came in to see me late Saturday afternoon and asked me to set up an appointment for him. At nine o'clock this morning Krishna Khaleel dropped by and asked the same thing. I didn't get the feeling they'd consulted each other about it. I think they both just got the same idea at the same time."

"What idea?" Harley Hudson asked sharply; the Secretary looked bland, and less puzzled.

"The idea to see you," he replied calmly.

"But why should they want to see me?" the Vice President asked.

"Your guess is as good as mine," Howard Sheppard told him suavely, and Harley decided he was a good diplomat, after all. He decided his own course should be complete frankness.

"Are they afraid the President is going to die?" he said bluntly. The Secretary started to look shocked and then thought better of it.

"That is always a human possibility," he said.

"My God, this town!" Harley Hudson said in a wondering tone. "The way an idea can travel, particularly if it's something somebody thinks is bad news for somebody! What on earth do they have to base that on?"

"No more than you do," the Secretary said.

"I haven't got anything," the Vice President said firmly.

"Not even a hunch?" the Secretary inquired dryly.

"Vice Presidents always have that hunch," Harley Hudson said, deciding that intimacy had gone far enough; an old friend like Tom August was one thing, Howie Sheppard on his way out was another. "I wouldn't be true to type if I didn't. The last time I saw him he looked fine."

"How long ago was that?" the Secretary asked.

"Last Wednesday," the Vice President answered promptly, and it was the truth, for there had been a National Girl Scouts' ceremony in the Rose Garden at the White House, and the girls had invited him to attend. A quick mental photograph flicked through his mind, the erratic day shifting between cold rain and weak sun, the President's thin hair whipping in the icy breeze, his look of genuine, fatherly pleasure, and just the faintest impression of—what? He could realize now why he had been vaguely worried ever since. It was nothing you could put your finger on; he just looked a little tireder than a President, even a busy President, ought to look. But that might be nothing at all that a vacation on the Keys couldn't cure, and he decided he had better do his best to counteract this racing rumor before it got entirely out of hand.

"He looked tired," he said, "and I imagine when you saw him last he looked tired too. He probably *is* tired. But he's been tired before and snapped back in no time, and I'm sure he will again. I think what he needs to do is get to Key West again, and I'm going to suggest it to him. Why don't you do the same, Howie, and maybe if we all do he'll listen and take our advice. Because I think he needs it, don't you?"

"I've told myself that was it," the Secretary agreed, "and I will suggest it when I see him again. In the meantime, what about Tashikov and K.K.?"

"Next week sometime," Harley Hudson said. "If we set it up too fast they'll think there's something in it, and after all, Howie, we don't really want them to, do we?"

The Secretary looked suddenly sober.

"No," he said, "we don't."

"You fix it up," the Vice President said. "Toward the end of the week sometime."

"Very well. How is the nomination going?"

"Hearings in the subcommittee this morning," Harley said. "We'll know better by the end of the week."

"I did my duty," Howie remarked in a cold tone, "so I'm out of it, thank God."

"The Administration appreciates that, Howie," the Vice President assured him. "We'll remember it."

"Hmph," the Secretary said, with no other comment, and rose to go.

"Don't say much to those two," he advised, and Harley Hudson smiled reassuringly as they shook hands.

"I'll be as discreet as you are, Howie," he said. The Secretary gave him a sharp look as he left which only increased the warmth of the Vice President's smile.

But after Howie was gone and the door had closed and he was alone in the room, a stricken look came suddenly upon his face.

"Oh, my God," he said in a helpless voice to nobody in particular. "Oh, my God."

Standing to take the oath in the glare of the television lights, his back straight, his right hand held up with no more than a normal quiver to it, his eyes looking candidly into those of the chairman, the focus of all their troubles appeared outwardly to be his usual calm, unhurried, businesslike, self-possessed self. Seab had managed to draw first blood, it was true, but the director of the ODM had a very fast recovery time, and when he took the stand he had already regained any composure he might have lost in the Senator's unexpected and pointedly challenging greeting. This lean-faced, dignified, graying, perceptive man exposed to his countrymen in the fateful moment when he moved to the ofttimes terrifying isolation of the congressional witness stand looked ready for anything. He also looked like what he was, a highly trained and highly competent public servant. It was easy in that moment to see why he held both the loyalty and the antagonism of so many, why so many were so passionately involved in his nomination, and why, among other reasons, the President of the United States had chosen him to be Secretary of State. He looked the part.

"Do you solemnly swear," Senator Anderson inquired formally, "that the statements you give to this subcommittee will be the truth, the whole truth, and nothing but the truth, so help you God?"

"I do," Bob Leffingwell said firmly.

"Please be seated," the chairman said, adding dryly, "If the photographers will kindly remove themselves to the sidelines now and leave the witness a clear channel, so he can see the subcommittee and vice versa, we will begin . . . The nominee's record and background are in the record of the full committee on Saturday, which will be incorporated with this record, so there is no need to have them again here. If the witness has any preliminary statement he wishes to make, we will be glad to hear it, and then we can go into the regular alternating order of interrogation— with other Senators, I think, free to interject any inquiries that may occur to them as we go along."

"Oh, oh," the Chicago *Tribune* murmured. "A free-for-all, eh?" "I don't quite get Brig's game yet," the Newark *News* responded. "Distraction through diversity?" the Washington *Post* suggested. "Harmony through hullabaloo," the Washington *Star* proposed.

"Mr. Leffingwell," Brig said politely, "is there anything you wish to say before cross-examination begins?"

The nominee leaned forward and with a slow, thoughtful gaze looked from face to face, including that of the senior Senator from South Carolina, while the room became quiet. It was a gaze returned with equal interest by the six men before him, and when it was finished he folded one hand upon the other and began to speak in a grave, well-modulated voice.

"Mr. Chairman," he said. "Senators: Senator Cooley: I have been thinking, since the word came to me last Thursday night of the President's decision to nominate me for the great office of Secretary of State, how I might best express to you my awareness both of the honor and the profound responsibility which it entails. And the words that have come to me are poor indeed. I might say that I am honored, yet this one might say if he were nominated for any job; I might say that I am humbled, yet that too is standard talk. I have concluded that the words available in the English language are at once too mundane and too sense-worn to do the office justice. As for honor, it honors me, but far more must I honor it. On that, the way is clear: I shall honor it by what I do, or I shall honor it not at all."

"Speaking of the English language——" The *Times* whispered. "He helped to write it," the Birmingham *News* whispered back.

"The responsibility?" Bob Leffingwell went smoothly on. "Greater, I think, than one man can adequately bear; which is why, Mr. Chairman, I shall make it my first duty to consult with your committee, and with its great sister committee in the House, on all broad aspects of policy and decision which may come before me. The constant aim of my predecessor, as it has been the constant aim of every farsighted Secretary of State, has been to work in the closest possible co-operation with the Congress; this will be my aim too. I shall not fail you in that, Mr. Chairman; on that you have my word.

"For the rest," he said, "the times will guide me. We are embarked, it seems to me, upon an era of great and far-reaching change throughout the world. To come to safe harbor in such an age requires all that mortal man can give, and beyond it, the guidance of Almighty God. That He will aid me in my labors I can only pray, and pray I will." He paused and then resumed in a deeper, more earnest tone, while the press took hurried notes, the subcommittee listened attentively, and only the busy whirr of the television cameras broke the silence in the big marble room.

"No man charged, as I will be charged to some substantial degree, with the guidance of this dear land and her protection amid the dark controversies and fateful conflicts which flare all across the globe in these desperate days, could do otherwise. God my solace and my strength, I will do my best to help her safely home."

And he leaned back slowly while the audience burst suddenly into loud and prolonged applause. Brigham Anderson let it run for a minute or two and then rapped sharply for order. When he got it he bowed slightly to the nominee and spoke in a tone of equal gravity.

"Those are sentiments which do you credit," he said, "and we are pleased to have them. Were nominations a matter of principles enunciated and hopes expressed, were the word sufficient and the deed of lesser import, many and many a hearing such as this could end at just this point with some such sentiment as you have just expressed."

"Brig knows English too," AP noted. "Many people on this Hill do, when they're pressed for it," UPI replied.

"Unfortunately, however," Senator Anderson went on, "in the case of a Cabinet officer, words and principles are not enough to take the place of deeds, even though, in your particular office, there have sometimes been men who tried to make the substitution. So we must regretfully move on to the more practical and, I am afraid, perhaps in some minds more pertinent, questions of what you think and what you have thought, and what you have done and what you will do. In short, we must now come to specifics. I say this not in deprecation of sentiments which you hold sincerely, and whose expression becomes you, and which of course we wish to have; but rather in recognition of the realities which confront us, here in the Senate of the United States . . . Senator Knox," he said calmly, having thus smoothly rearranged the mood, sapped it of its emotionalism, and brought it back down from the mountaintop to practicalities, "would you care to interrogate?"

"I would, Mr. Chairman," Orrin Knox said matter-of-factly in a tone which indicated he was about to do things to the mood himself. "Mr. Leffingwell, are you loyal to the United States?"

At this, as on Saturday when Warren Strickland had asked Howard Sheppard's opinion on the same subject, there was an audible gasp from the audience, for the senior Senator from Illinois had deliberately used a tone as shocking as ice water. For just a second the nominee looked nonplussed and angry; then he smiled, spread his hands palms up in a candid gesture as they lay before him on the table, and smiled directly at his questioner.

"Senator," he said quietly, the faintest hint of amusement in his voice in case Orrin Knox wished to find it amusing too, "if I were not, could it have escaped notice in all these long years of public service?"

Orrin, however, did not wish to find it amusing. He shook his gray head impatiently and cocked it at an argumentative angle.

"This is not a humorous matter, Mr. Leffingwell," he said sharply, "nor is that a responsive answer to my question. I didn't ask if anybody had discovered it if you weren't, I asked if you were."

Bob Leffingwell flushed slightly and then sat back with a time-gaining slowness, his shoulders relaxing against the chair.

"Senator," he said, "on the oath I swore in this room half an hour ago, I am."

Again there was applause, and this time Brigham Anderson banged the gavel in a way that showed he meant it.

"It is very obvious," he remarked, "that nearly everyone here is emotionally involved in this matter one way or another. However, one more demonstration of any kind for whatever reason and I shall direct the police to clear the room, public hearing or no public hearing. Is that clear?"

There was a little silence which indicated that it was, and after he had let it run long enough to emphasize his point, he said quietly, "Very well. Proceed, Senator Knox."

"The reason I ask, Mr. Chairman," Orrin Knox explained in a less challenging tone, "is because there have been complaints made to me, and doubts expressed, about some of Mr. Leffingwell's statements on our relations with the Soviet Union. Some complainants have gone so far as to indicate some doubt of his loyalty. I thought he should have an opportunity to answer these doubts directly. I do not share them myself."

"Thank you, Senator," Bob Leffingwell said gratefully. "I didn't think you did."

"No," Senator Knox said with a smile. "Of course we are not discussing the wisdom and judgment shown in some of the statements. That might be a different matter."

Bob Leffingwell, encouraged by the smile, smiled back, and the tension in the room alleviated a little.

"That is your privilege, Senator," he said. "I hope I've satisfied you at least part of the time, anyway."

Orrin smiled again, a trifle less cordially.

"That's as it may be," he said. "For instance, I have here a speech you made in Cleveland three weeks ago in which you said, and I quote, 'We must not bind ourselves arbitrarily to the outworn principles of the past when we find those principles standing in the way of affirmative action for peace.' What does that mean? If it means anything?"

The nominee smiled.

"Of course I must believe it means something, Senator, or I wouldn't have said it," he replied calmly. "What I meant to convey there was just about what I said—that we must not let the dead hand of the past lie upon our present efforts as we search for lasting peace. Or the lasting peace may escape us."

"Again, Mr. Leffingwell, you are not responsive," Orrin Knox said bluntly. "You mention outworn principles of the past. What did you have in mind?"

The nominee hesitated for a second and then leaned forward in a between-us fashion.

"Let me see if I can state it for you this way, Senator," he said slowly. "Under certain circumstances that may have existed in the past, the United States guided her actions by certain standards that had been proved to be valid for their time when those circumstances were found to exist. Now the circumstances may have changed and she may still be adhering to those standards although they no longer can be effectively or justifiably applied to the new circumstances which now confront us in which other standards may prove to be more beneficial than those of the past."

"Got it?" the Newark *News* whispered to the Houston *Chronicle.* "Got it," the Houston *Chronicle* whispered dryly back.

"But I want to know about those principles," Orrin Knox said. "What are they? Honesty is the best policy? A stitch in time saves nine? The shortest distance between two points is a straight line? Do unto others as you would have them do unto you? By their presents ye shall know them? What are they? Can't give us any clarification at all?"

"What I meant to express, Senator Knox," the nominee said patiently again, "was that there has been at times, it has seemed to me, too rigid an insistence by this government upon a quid pro quo with the Russians; perhaps too great an insistence that they should prove good faith before we would deal with them. If my choice of the word 'principles' was unfortunate, then I am sorry and I regret now that I used it. It was more a state of mind that I was driving at, perhaps, than an actual condition."

"That's what I'm driving at," Senator Knox informed him tartly. "*Your* state of mind. I think it's a very important state of mind if you're to be the new Secretary of State. I think it is very important to know what principles it is you adhere to and which you would discard. Now when you say 'principles——'" But at this moment there was a stir down the table and the Senator from South Carolina leaned forward.

"Mr. Chairman," he said softly, "if the Senator from Illinois will yield to me——"

"Gladly, Mr. Chairman," Senator Knox said promptly.

"—what I should like to know, Mr. Chairman," Seab went on, "if it isn't too much to ask our distinguished witness——"

"Not at all, Senator," Bob Leffingwell said crisply.

"—is how he came to be talking about that subject at all. I thought," Seab said, "that he was director of the ODM, Mr. Chairman. Was there anything in that speech, if I may rather irregularly question the Senator from Illinois, who has read it and I have not, was there anything in it that dealt with the subject of mobilization?"

"No, Senator," Orrin Knox said, "there was not. It was entirely devoted to foreign policy, and the entire tenor of it was summed up, I think the witness will agree with me, in the sentence I am asking him about."

"Not, of course, Mr. Chairman," Senator Cooley said with a slow grin, "that I think his ideas on mobilization are any good, either. But I do question just a little the propriety of the director of the ODM talking about general foreign policy. I do just a little. When did you say you knew you would be appointed Secretary of State, Mr. Witness?"

"The President called me about 8 P.M. last Thursday night and so informed me," Bob Leffingwell said.

"And somehow it got into the Friday morning newspapers, which go to press Thursday night, even though it was not announced at the White House until 10 A.M. on Friday," Seab observed gently. "How did that happen, Mr. Witness? Do you suppose the President called the newspapers himself and told them Thursday night? He's a busy man, Mr. Witness. Do you suppose he did that?"

"The press has ways of finding things out, Senator," the nominee said calmly.

"When men who desire to profit from publicity inform them, yes, sir," Seab Cooley said softly. "Yes, indeed they do, when men who want publicity inform them. But when you spoke in Cleveland three weeks ago you weren't Secretary of State, were you, Mr. Witness? Did you know then you would be Secretary of State?"

"No, sir," Bob Leffingwell said firmly. "I did not."

"But you wanted to be," Senator Cooley said, "and you were making speeches right along that would call attention to your desire to be, were you not?"

"Mr. Chairman," Bob Leffingwell said, speaking directly to Brigham Anderson, "in these times, what man among us is not called upon to speak on foreign policy and foreign events? How can one escape it? Am I to be attacked because I responded to an invitation made me by a reputable organization, the Chamber of Commerce of the state of Ohio? That was the topic they gave me, Mr. Chairman. I suppose I was to give them a discourse on stockpiling titanium?"

"I think," Brigham Anderson said, "that the witness's point is well taken, Senators. Suppose we return to the substance of what he said, if that is your interest, Senator Knox, and skip the whys and wherefores of how he came to say it."

"Very well, Mr. Chairman," Seab said politely, "if that is your desire. But in forty years' time, Mr. Chairman—no, sir, in almost fifty years' time—

I have seen many men angling for high office, Mr. Chairman, and this is how they do it, Mr. Chairman. They make speeches. They participate. They mingle into matters that do not concern them. They flaunt themselves, Mr. Chairman. That is how they do it. Yes, sir."

"Very well, Senator," Senator Anderson said. "Proceed if you wish, Senator Knox."

"This was, in truth, only one of a series of speeches you have been making in recent months, was it not, Mr. Witness?" Orrin said, deliberately adopting Seab's form of address, and Bob Leffingwell, who had started to relax, braced himself again.

"Yes, sir," he said.

"Christ," the Baltimore *Sun* snapped angrily, "so he made speeches. So what?" "Well, it's important," the Chicago *Tribune* countered. "Oh, hell," the *Sun* snapped back.

"I believe there have been some ten of them since the first of the year, have there not?" Senator Knox inquired.

"Yes, sir," the nominee said.

"And all have concerned foreign policy?"

"Yes, sir."

"And none has concerned the functions of your office?"

"No, sir."

"Well," Orrin said, "I shall not draw the conclusion from this that our colleague does, but I will say that these addresses furnish fertile fields for interrogation."

"Oh, that mine enemy would make a speech," Bob Leffingwell said with a little smile.

"And write a book, too," Orrin Knox said with an answering smile. "I understand they are being collected and published in book form."

"Yes," Bob Leffingwell said.

"For publication when?" Senator Knox inquired.

"A week from Wednesday," the nominee said.

"Under what title?" Orrin asked.

"*Do We Really Want Peace*" the nominee said. "With the subtitle, *A Program for America.*"

"Strangely challenging labels for a treatise on stockpiling," the Senator from Illinois remarked dryly. "However, to return to those principles, Mr. Leffingwell. Tell us about your principles, if you will. Just go ahead and expound on them for a minute or two. I know the country is interested, and so are we."

"Well, Mr. Chairman," the nominee said, leaning forward and folding his hands again one upon the other in a grave and earnest manner, "how does a man define his principles? By what he says about them, and by what he does about them. He defines them also, I think, by the consistency of what he says about them, and the consistency of what he does about them. In all my public life I have attempted to define them both by word and by deed, and I have attempted within the limits of human frailty to be as consistent as I could about them. I do not maintain that I have been perfect, for no man is that; I do maintain that, in general, I have done my best both to express them as forcefully as I could, and to live up to them as fully as I could. Allowing for a certain number of lapses—and who is so superior and above the customary needs and weaknesses of ordinary men that he can tell me he has never lapsed, and criticize me for lapsing?—I have done my best to uphold them. They are these:

"I believe that the United States of America, while imperfect in many ways, yet comes closer to achieving what might pass for perfection in an imperfect world than most; certainly I believe she tries harder than most, and means better than most, and has a more conscientious and, in general, I believe, a more humane and friendly purpose toward the world than most.

"I believe that I am fortunate, as all Americans are fortunate, that I have been born here and have been able to grow up here and live here in relative peace and well-being, free to think as I please and speak as I please and live as I please within the bounds of a stable society and a decent world.

"I believe there is incumbent upon me as an American, the charge of so living and so speaking and so acting that I may bear my citizenship proudly and be worthy of my heritage and do what I can to maintain and preserve it and pass it on undamaged and if possible increased and strengthened to those who will come after me.

"I believe that there rests upon the individual citizen the responsibility for America. I believe that each of us is America, and that together we are America, and that what we do is always and forever and in every way important to America. I believe I must never forget this. I do not think I ever have. I do not think I ever will. Those are my principles, Mr. Chairman."

As he finished, speaking quietly but firmly into the hush that had again descended upon the room, Brigham Anderson brought his gavel down sharply before the applause could start and said, "Senator Knox?" in a deliberately level tone.

"I admire your speeches, Mr. Leffingwell," Orrin Knox said with a certain coldness in his voice, "and I admit I asked for that one. I do not think, however, that they are helping you particularly with this committee. I would still like to know what the principles are which are outmoded and old-fashioned and out of date and tie us down when we search for peace. Is it wrong to ask the Russians to prove their good faith? Is it wrong," he said, unconsciously picking up Claude Maudulayne's phrase at Dolly's, "to be suspicious of more than four decades of dishonor? These are the things I want to know from you. Tell me."

"Of course it is not wrong to want to feel that those with whom you

deal are dealing in good faith," Bob Leffingwell said with a certain coldness of his own, "and I have never said that. I have felt that possibly we
were too suspicious, too quick to see bad motives, too hasty in attributing
desires and ambitions and evils that may not exist. I do not say they do not
exist. I say we may not know for sure that they do exist. I say we should
perhaps show a little Christian charity and once in a while assume that
they do not exist, and that there is a desire for peace which meets us, as
genuine as our own."

"On what basis, Mr. Witness?" Seab said flatly from his end of the
table. "Where's the proof? If a man lies to me and attacks me and is my
enemy for year after year after year, why should I assume he wishes to be
my friend? Oh, Mr. Chairman!" he said with a sudden harshness. "These
pious, hopeful men! Do you regard *me* as your friend, Mr. Witness? Should
I regard *you* as my friend? Is there any reason for *us* to trust one another?"

"Well, now, Mr. Chairman," John Winthrop said with a sudden quiet
anger of his own, "I think we can get along without that kind of questioning."

"I agree, Senator," Brigham Anderson said. "Senator will confine himself to the matters in hand, if you please, and proceed in order." Senator
Cooley gave him an impassive look and went on.

"I ask again, Mr. Chairman," he said calmly, "on what basis? On what
proof? Those are valid questions."

"Now they are," Senator Anderson agreed, "and I would like witness to
answer them if he will, please."

"Mr. Chairman," Bob Leffingwell said, "I do not know that I could
ever answer them in a fashion to suit the Senator from South Carolina, or
possibly even the Senator from Illinois. It is true that there is much in the
record to warrant suspicion of the Soviet Union; but we must not—I think
we must not allow that to obscure the greater objective of peace in the
world."

"In other words, they can do us dirt as much as they please but we
aren't to let it bother us, is that it, Mr. Leffingwell?" Orrin Knox suggested
dryly.

"Senator," the nominee said, "that is an oversimplification, but in the
most complete and highest sense, the answer, I think, would be yes. This
is an answer," he went on firmly as Senator Cooley, Senator DeWilton,
and Senator Richardson all stirred warningly, "which will be easily mis-
interpreted by those who wish to misinterpret. But I mean that we must
rise above our impatience, our mistrust, yes, even our feelings of vengefulness and retaliation, and greet them with a sincere desire for peace and a
candid willingness to see things as they see them."

"My God," Orrin Knox exploded suddenly, "what more would you have
us do? How many concessions do we have to make, how far do we have to
let them go before we have a right to ask that they try to meet *us* with a

sincere desire for peace, that they show *us* a candid willingness to see things as we see them? Must it always be a one-way street?"

"Senator," Bob Leffingwell asked quietly, "would you have us fight a preventive war?"

"Who in blazes," Senator Knox demanded in a tone that held a note of real distaste, "is talking about a preventive war?"

"That would seem to be the alternative," the nominee replied.

"There are people in this country and in this world," Orrin Knox said in a quieter tone, "who would attempt to persuade us that this is the only alternative, yes. They skip neatly over all the stages of honest negotiation, fair dealing, firmness of purpose, and unafraid adherence to principle— real principle, Mr. Leffingwell—that lie between. They cry surrender or they cry war; they try to prevent us from discussing the other possibilities that still exist, the only possibilities, it seems to me, of ever achieving that genuine peace they are always yapping about. They are usually people like yourself who either consciously or unconsciously prey upon the fears of their countrymen concerning the horrors of another war."

"I don't want war, Senator," Bob Leffingwell said simply.

"Do I?" Senator Knox demanded coldly, and for a long moment he held the witness's eyes with his own in a straight, unwavering stare. Bob Leffing-well was the first to look away, but when he did it was with an audible sigh, as though confronted with all the wayward wrongfulness of the world.

"Who can say what course means war and what means peace, Senator?" he asked. "I can only believe that my course is less likely to lead to it; you believe that yours has the same advantage. History may have to decide between us, each of us according to the other, as we must if the nation is not to be torn apart on these issues, the depth and sincerity of his belief."

Orrin Knox made an impatient gesture.

"I have no further questions of the witness at this time, Mr. Chairman," he said.

"I guess our boy showed him," the Washington *Post* whispered triumphantly at the press table. "Damned good stuff," *United Features* agreed. "I wonder," the *Herald Tribune* said thoughtfully.

There was a sleepy explosion at the other end of the line and Crystal Danta smiled in a satisfied way.

"I just thought I'd call to find out if you were sleeping well," she said pleasantly.

"Not as well as I will be in another week," Hal Knox replied promptly from the house in Spring Valley, and Crystal chuckled.

"That's a lewd remark," she observed.

"Prompted by a lewd woman," her fiancé told her. "Anyway, I was sleeping well until you woke me up."

"At eleven o'clock?" Crystal asked. "Isn't it about time you got up?"

"You forget," Hal said, "that I will soon be a married man with cares, responsibilities, and a job, and all this carefree life will be over."

"I haven't forgotten that at all," Crystal Danta assured him. "Particularly about your being a married man. Have you?"

"Right at this moment," her betrothed informed her candidly, "I'm remembering it with great strength and vigor."

"All right, now," she said, trying to sound severe but not succeeding too well. "That will do, young man. I didn't call up to listen to you being naughty."

"I'm not naughty," Hal said complacently. "I'm just a simple, passionate child of nature who right at this moment——well, anyway, if you weren't such a sweet old-fashioned girl you would long since have——"

"Yes, little boy," she interrupted. "No doubt. We'll see who's old-fashioned next week. How about lunch and some shopping?"

"Again?" Hal exclaimed. "We're in debt for thirty years to come as it is. All right. Where and when?"

"Pick me up at the apartment at twelve and maybe we can eat down on the waterfront," Crystal suggested.

"O.K.," Hal said. "Honestly, woman, I never knew you were so extravagant or I'd never have proposed in the first place."

"Want to reconsider?" Crystal asked, and he laughed.

"Not on your life," he said.

"Mr. Chairman," John Winthrop said in his level, clipped voice, smiling a little, "I shall try to be as brief as possible, because I know we want to move this along and I know that other Senators, like myself, have many demands on their time. In fact at this moment, Mr. Chairman, I am supposed to be present at three committee meetings, two subcommittees, an appointment with the chairman of the Interstate Commerce Commission, and a ceremony on the Capitol steps welcoming the senior class of Northampton High School to Washington, to say nothing of mail, phone calls, and miscellaneous constituents. All of which is typical of the situation with all of us on this Hill all the time. So I shall try to keep it short."

"Senator," Brigham Anderson told him gravely, "your devotion to duty does you great credit. Passing up committees, ignoring subcommittees, flaunting the chairman of the Interstate Commerce Commission, and missing phone calls from constituents is nothing. But when a man gives up the chance to be photographed on the Senate steps with the senior class of Northampton High School, he is making a sacrifice beyond compare."

"Those kids will be voting for you in another five years, John," Arly Richardson suggested into the general laughter that followed. "Maybe you'd better ask to be excused, and question the witness later."

"I don't know whether they will be voting for me or not," Senator Winthrop said, more soberly, "but maybe they're important in a much deeper way than that. The world they will be living in when they reach voting age is going to be determined in large part by the policies and actions of this witness, if we confirm him; so maybe I can serve them better by stayin' right here and askin' questions than I could if I went and had my picture taken."

"I think you're right, Senator," Bob Leffingwell volunteered with a smile.

"Good," Senator Winthrop said. "We start agreeing, anyway. How do you feel about all this pressure we're under from our allies for new efforts to snuggle up to the Kremlin?"

The nominee smiled again.

"I don't know whether I'd say 'snuggle up,' Senator," he said, "but I think there obviously is a great desire all over the world—including, I think, in our own country—that we make further attempts to reconcile our differences as soon as possible."

"And you aim to reflect that desire in your statements to the sub-committee here, and in the policies you plan to follow if the Senate confirms you?" John Winthrop asked.

Bob Leffingwell looked thoughtful for a moment and then answered with care.

"This is a delicate area, Senator," he said, "as we have already seen in the questioning so far, and I want to be very careful not to put myself in a false position by what I say. I do not, as the Senator from Illinois seems to think, wish to reach agreement on any terms whatsoever, regardless of whether it's convenient for us, or profitable for us, or not. But neither do I want to be so adamant that any possibility of agreement is killed before it starts."

"What terms do you think would be valid?" Senator Winthrop asked. The nominee hesitated and then his look became at once more candid and, curiously, more closed-off.

"There, Senator," he said, "you realize that we get into an area that must inevitably be one in which I cannot testify to any specific degree. It is a matter of agreement between the President and his Secretary of State, covered by the doctrine of Executive privilege, which must in most respects be confidential. What I might think were valid terms the President might consider unjustified, and naturally as his Secretary of State I would be bound to follow his views."

"Mr. Chairman," Senator Cooley said, and Senator Winthrop said promptly, "I yield to the Senator, if he intends to be brief."

Seab bowed ironically and leaned forward to stare along the table at the senior Senator from Massachusetts, who returned him stare for stare and then gave him a broad wink and grin.

"Oh, Mr. Chairman," Senator Cooley said with dignity, "now that is an unwarranted implication. The Senator knows I will be brief because I am always brief, Mr. Chairman; except when the fate of my country is concerned, and then I don't believe even the distinguished Senator from Massachusetts would want me to be *too* brief, Mr. Chairman."

"Proceed, Senator," Brigham Anderson said in an unimpressed voice, and Seab turned his slow and calculating gaze upon the nominee.

"Why are you afraid to tell us what terms you favor in talking to the Russians, Mr. Witness?" he asked quietly.

"I'm not afraid, Senator," Bob Leffingwell replied with equal quietness.

"Well, you won't tell us," Senator Cooley retorted. "Doesn't that mean you're afraid? Seems to me he's afraid, Mr. Chairman. If he isn't afraid, why can't he tell?"

"I've just attempted to explain, Senator——" Bob Leffingwell began, but Seab cut him off.

"We don't want lawyer's talk," he said with calculated rudeness. "We can get lawyer's talk in a court. We want to know what you propose to give away to the Russians when you sit down to negotiate for us, Mr. Witness. What is it you intend to give away?"

"I don't intend to give anything away, Senator," Bob Leffingwell said in a tone whose patience was belied by the way his feet tensed around the legs of his chair as he leaned forward.

"You won't tell us what your terms are," Senator Cooley observed. "It must be that you're ashamed to disclose them. It must be you plan to give something away. Yes, that must be it, Mr. Chairman. He must plan to give something away."

"Senator——" Bob Leffingwell began in a tone that for the first time showed real anger, but Senator Winthrop forestalled him.

"I reclaim the floor, Mr. Chairman," he said firmly. "This sort of thing is getting us nowhere."

"Well, now, Mr. Chairman," Seab Cooley said, beginning to let his famous temper show, "I resent the Senator's arbitrary attempt to silence questioning designed to show this witness' true intent to betray his country when he gets into the office of Secretary of State, Mr. Chairman."

"Do you make that as a formal charge, Senator?" Senator Anderson asked impassively.

Senator Cooley looked for a long moment at the press tables and then spoke with cold deliberation.

"I do, Mr. Chairman," he said.

"Mr. Chairman," Senator Winthrop said with a rare show of anger of his own, "I move that the entire colloquy of the Senator from South Carolina with the witness be stricken from the record."

"Mr. Chairman!" Seab said loudly. "That is most irregular, Mr. Chairman. That is never done to Senators. It would be the most gross insult to me personally, Mr. Chairman."

"He can give the witness the grossest insult," *Newsweek* whispered bitterly, "but you musn't insult him." "I hate the old son of a bitch," *Time* magazine said simply.

Senator Anderson rapped his gavel sharply and spoke in a firm tone.

"That motion is out of order," he said, "and the Chair will not entertain it. By the same token, neither will the Chair entertain further questioning of that nature from the Senator from South Carolina. The Chair if necessary will rule it out of order and put the ruling to a vote."

"Do so, Mr. Chairman," Senator Richardson said suddenly, with a certain ominous quietness. "Please do so."

For a long moment Senator Anderson hesitated while the tension grew apace in the crowded, silent room: and even as he hesitated, he knew he had lost, and Seab had won. But under the circumstances there was nothing for it but to proceed.

"Very well," he said, "I so rule and the committee may pass upon it. Senator Knox?"

"I'm not much of a one for curtailing Senators of the United States in the performance of their duty to get information," Orrin Knox observed dryly. "I vote No."

"Senator Winthrop?" Brig asked.

"Aye," John Winthrop said.

"Senator Richardson?"

"Why, of course not, Mr. Chairman," Arly said with a sardonic blandness. "You know that."

"Senator DeWilton?"

"No, indeed," John DeWilton said crisply.

"The Chair votes Aye," the chairman said, "and the ruling is overruled. The Chair will say, however, that he does not think the type of questioning indulged in by the Senator from South Carolina does him any credit, or the witness any damage, in the eyes of the country. But if that is the Senator's wish, he may continue in it. He has proved he has the votes."

"In other words they're going to let him slaughter Leffingwell," the Washington *Post* whispered angrily. The Chicago *Tribune* shrugged, not without satisfaction. "It's like Brig said, he's got the votes."

"Well, Mr. Chairman," Seab said gently, "I think that concludes my questioning for the time being. I thank the Senator from Massachusetts. I know neither he nor the Chair meant me any discourtesy. I thank all Senators." And he settled back, looking sleepy and content. Brigham Anderson shrugged.

"Let's get on," he said. "Any further questions, Senator Winthrop?"

"Yes, sir," John Winthrop said, and he smiled at the nominee. "You can see, Mr. Leffingwell," he said, "the effect you have upon this Senate. You get some little inkling here of the differences your nomination has created."

"I can only hope, Senator," Bob Leffingwell said simply, "that if a majority confirms me I may so conduct myself as to justify its confidence and persuade those who were in the minority that they were mistaken."

"Well," Senator Winthrop said, "the proof of that puddin' will be in the eatin'. I think," he said, picking his words carefully, "that it might tend to alleviate some of the reaction exemplified by the Senator from South Carolina if you would tell us just a little, in a general way, of the lines along which you think an understanding with the Soviet Union might be worked out. I am not asking in either the manner or the tone of the Senator from South Carolina, nor am I making the imputations he has, which I have just demonstrated my distaste for; I'm asking as one who is disposed to be friendly toward your nomination, and one who would like to see you emerge from these hearings with all doubts set at rest. We want to know, I think, at least in general, what we can expect if you are confirmed."

The nominee, who had been listening intently, gave the Senator from Massachusetts an earnest, level look as he concluded, and shook his head in an almost puzzled way.

"Senator," he said, "again I can only say that I do not know exactly how to answer your query. So much depends on what the President wants; on what the Russians want; on what our allies want; on what the circumstances may be at the moment of meeting—is it so unreasonable that I am unable to tell you what my terms would be, as you put it?"

Senator Winthrop gave him a long and thoughtful look and when he spoke it was in a tone in which there was a genuine regret.

"It is only unreasonable, Mr. Leffingwell," he said quietly, "when it is placed alongside the rest of your testimony. So far you have given us several fine statements of your personal belief; but you have refused to tell the Senator from Illinois the principles upon which you would expect to act, and you have refused to tell me the general terms that you would propose to seek from the Russians in the way of a decent settlement. You were, in a sense, unknown to us in this area when you took the stand, and you are unknown to us still, up to this point in your testimony. I regret that, Mr. Leffingwell, for I think instead of banishing doubts you have succeeded so far only in creating more. I hope you will be more candid with the subcommittee from now on, for I personally am not so sure now that I would want to vote for an unknown to be Secretary of State."

The nominee flushed deeply, but his voice disclosed nothing but a calm self-possession and certainty.

"I regret that you feel that way, Senator," he said. "I am attempting to be candid with the subcommittee and I shall continue to do so."

"I have no further questions of this witness at this time, Mr. Chairman," Senator Winthrop said and sat back with a grave expression on his face.

Down at the end of the table Senator Cooley leaned forward and spoke into the silence that followed.

"You see?" he said. "You cannot trust this man, Mr. Chairman. His purpose is to be evasive, and he is succeeding in it. Why is he being so evasive, Mr. Chairman? That is the question that should now be asked here. Why?"

Brigham Anderson sighed.

"All right, Senator," he said. "Senator Richardson, your witness."

And as Arly Richardson moved forward a little in his chair with a certain killer's gleam in his eye, the wire-service reporters left the press tables and started their hurried run downstairs to the press room to send in their new leads on the early morning stories. The Senator from South Carolina, knowing from long experience that it was time for this to happen, watched them go with a satisfaction which he did not permit to show in his face; for he knew what they were thinking, he knew the shrewd, automatic way in which the hearing so far was being sorted over in their clever minds as they leaped down the stairs; he knew that in the desperate necessity of competing for the attention of editors all over the country their leads would not be on what UPI referred to as "all that philosophical crap" as he went clattering down. Seab knew the lead would simply be, "Senator Seabright B. Cooley charged today that Robert A. Leffingwell will betray the United States in negotiations with Russia if he becomes Secretary of State." And knowing this, Seab was quite content.

Life has its own way of bringing about fantastic and illogical circumstances, and life in Washington sometimes brings about circumstances more fantastic and illogical than it does in most places. So it was that Mr. Justice Davis, thoughtfully reading over editorials and clippings on the Leffingwell nomination in his chambers at the Court; Fred Van Ackerman, junior Senator from Wyoming, testifying on the Taylor Grazing Act before Stanley Danta in the Interior and Insular Affairs Committee; and Ellabelle Proctor, the maid who came in three times a week at the Brigham Andersons', were at about this moment in the subcommittee's hearings linked together in one of those ironic little arrangements devised by fate far more often than logical human beings like to admit. It would be several days before any of the three would perceive this peculiar linkage —Ellabelle, it seems likely, never did realize it—but nonetheless events set in motion at that moment would tie them all one to the other; and in a way most ironic of all, this erratic, unexpected and casually inadvertent connection would turn out to have a most direct bearing on the career of a United States Senator, the future of the American Presidency, and the nomination of Robert A. Leffingwell.

None of this, of course, was apparent at this moment to Tommy Davis as he sat in a deep leather armchair before a window looking across the rainswept Capitol Plaza to the looming dome of the Capitol and read over the material his secretary, that alert young man from Princeton, had gathered together for him. Tommy, in fact, was far from any thoughts but the practical ones of how he might best advance the cause of Bob Leffingwell; and it was typical of the way things go in Washington that fate should even then, all unknown to him, be preparing him the way.

As of then, however, Mr. Justice Davis knew only that the editorial comment on his boy was, on balance, generally good. The Washington

Post had indeed, as he had hoped, come out four-square for the nominee in its Saturday morning edition, and an editorial of fervent affirmation had been accompanied by a brilliantly clever and savage cartoon. This combination of power was now spread before the Justice, and along with it were the following editorials of Sunday and today, each stressing, in a sort of dying fall, the worth of Bob Leffingwell and the imperative necessity for his confirmation. Almost every day from now on, Tommy felt confident, he could count on something, either editorial or cartoon or both, from the *Post;* and knowing the impact this journal had upon the breakfast tables of the nation's capital, he was well pleased with his evangelistic efforts in that sector in the nominee's behalf.

Also before him lay the Washington Evening *Star* and the Washington Daily *News,* and as he had expected, the *Star* was cautious but friendly while the *News* was friendly but cautious. In sum, the *Star* was for the nominee—"providing he can show, as we know he can, that he is fully devoted to the interests of his country abroad and has some specific solutions for the problems in that area which now confront her." The *News* (in an editorial entitled, "It's Up To You, Bob") was on the fence but leaning—"We're for him as head of the FPC and the ODM; we think we're probably going to be for him for Secretary of State. We'll be watching those hearings, as will all citizens, with an attentive ear and a watchful eye." Mr. Justice Davis, sure that both papers would come around and that the *Star* would then, with all the solidity of its traditional influence in the community, nicely complement the more high-flying *Post,* put the local papers aside and turned thoughtfully to those of a more national scope.

Of these, he noted that the New York *Times* had decided to endorse the nominee in a leader entitled, with all the simple yet dramatic effectiveness of the editorial page of that great institution, "A Nomination." The *Times'* thesis seemed to be that Mr. Leffingwell was a good public servant and the *Times* approved of good public servants. The New York *Herald Tribune,* slightly more informal, offered an endorsement entitled firmly, "What We Need"; Bob Leffingwell seemed to be it. The Chicago *Tribune,* taking a darker view of the matter, asked, "Can We Afford Another Do-Gooder?" while the *Christian Science Monitor* wondered soberly, "A Hope For The West?" and went on to discuss, not Bob Leffingwell, but a speech by the Secretary General of the United Nations calling for a more religious spirit in international dealings.

Of the periodicals before him, Mr. Justice Davis was pleased to note, the tenor was almost unanimously favorable to the nominee. *Time* had an account describing the general enthusiasm with which his appointment had been greeted in the capital; in 105 lines of laudation only one sentence—"Opposition, it seemed likely, would be confined to Spoilsman Cooley and one or two others"—indicated any possibility of conflict. *Newsweek,* while seeing a shade more cause for alarm, also concluded that generally clear sailing lay ahead. The nomination had come too late for deadline on *U. S. News and World Report*, which carried emblazoned on its cover the legend, WE CAN LICK THE TRAFFIC PROBLEM, backed up by one article, thirty-seven interviews with city managers and the sixty-three page text of a report by the President's special advisory committee on transportation. The Saturday Evening *Post*, with its usual luck, just happened to print an article, set in type three months ago, on "The Man Who Keeps An Eye on Metals." The *Saturday Review*, which had gone to press early but also seemed blessed with an equally remarkable luck, just happened to hit the target right on the nose with an editorial entitled, "Bob Leffingwell for State; A Proposal."

Recalling the weekend television programs, Mr. Justice Davis was equally comforted. Stanley Danta, appearing on "Face The Nation," had been reserved but friendly toward the nominee. Tom August on "Meet The Press" had been his usual elliptical, wandering self, but the sum total of it had been an endorsement. Powell Hanson had gone on "Youth Wants to Know" to tell youth what it wanted to know, which was that Bob Leffingwell was the greatest. "Person to Person," never an outfit to miss a bet, had violated tradition to devote its full half hour to a tour of the Leffingwell home in Alexandria; the nominee, showing no trace at all of the virus that had prevented his appearance before Foreign Relations earlier in the day, had been gracious and relaxed, his wife had been dignified and charming, and under the careful questionings of their host they had made a most effective impression upon their countrymen. "Omnibus" had also switched signals hurriedly and put on a twenty-minute review of "America's Foreign Policy" which included a good ten minutes of filmed excerpts from the nominee's recent speeches over the nation; and on "Today," "Tonight," and "High Noon" there had been flattering references, friendly quips, and staunch encouragement. All the vast publicity machine that always goes into concerted action for a liberal cause had gone to work for Bob Leffingwell; an operation so honed and smoothed and refined over the years that none of its proprietors even had to consult with one another. The instinct had been alerted, the bell had rung, the national salivations had come forth on schedule. Mr. Justice Davis was well pleased, and it was with a gay and defiant air that he looked across at the great dome looming against the gray sky and said half aloud, "So there. So *there*."

While Tommy Davis was thus congratulating himself on the course of events and pondering what else he might do to speed them forward, the junior Senator from Wyoming was reaching the end of his peroration on the Taylor Grazing Act in the Interior Committee. His views, stated with flamboyance and vigor, had not particularly impressed Stanley Danta, presiding in his quietly pleasant, even-tempered way in an otherwise almost empty committee room; and now as Fred Van Ackerman concluded and asked politely, "Are there any questions Mr. Chairman?" the senior

Senator from Connecticut gave his pleasant smile and shook his head.

"I don't believe so, Senator," he said, "and unless you have anything else to offer at this time, I think that will probably conclude the hearing for this morning. The committee will stand adjourned." And then as the official reporter began putting away his stenotype machine and the few persons in the audience began moving out of the room, he came around the table to where Senator Van Ackerman was gathering his papers together and put a hand on his shoulder.

"Walk down the hall with me, Fred," he suggested. "I want to hear about what you did in New York."

The junior Senator from Wyoming looked up with a characteristic quick motion of his head and smiled in a pleased way.

"Sure thing, Stan," he said, and Senator Danta, who despised the nickname, only looked the more friendly. "It was quite an evening."

"So I hear," Senator Danta said, slipping his arm through Fred Van Ackerman's and leading him out the door. "I heard," he added, as they walked slowly along together, "that you got quite an ovation."

"You didn't see it on television, then?" Senator Van Ackerman asked in a way that indicated he thought of course everybody had, and Stanley Danta smiled.

"I had to go to the Argentine Embassy to a party," he said, "so I wasn't in reach of a television set, I'm afraid. Tell me about it."

"Well, I tell you, Stan," Fred Van Ackerman said seriously, "you've no idea how hot people are for this idea of getting together with the Russians. I didn't realize it myself, really, until I began making these speeches a couple of months ago. It's taken hold like nobody's business. I've got twenty invitations to speak in the next six weeks, and more coming in every day."

"I remember it has been rather unexpected," Senator Danta said, his kindly face showing nothing of what he was thinking about it. "As I recall, you didn't really intend to speak on that subject at all the first time, did you?"

"No, sir," Fred Van Ackerman said, "I didn't. It just came out in the questioning and I sort of got carried away, I guess, and said something about how I would rather crawl to Moscow than die under a bomb, and by God, do you know, Stan, it brought down the house."

"So you tried it again the next time——" Senator Danta suggested; his young companion looked at him with a pleased smile.

"I tested it, Stan," he said. "I tried it out in just that way on three separate occasions after that, giving it a little more build-up each time, and before you know, within a week I was beginning to get anywhere from two hundred to three hundred letters a day about it."

"So you decided you had a good thing going——" Senator Danta suggested again in his pleasantly tactful, encouraging way.

"And I've kept at it, and it's been sensational," Senator Van Ackerman said in a rather bemused tone; "just sensational!"

"It takes you, Fred," Stanley Danta said in a tone he made admiring, "to find a good thing and stick with it."

"When I go after something," Senator Van Ackerman acknowledged, "I give it everything I've got."

"Indeed you do," Senator Danta agreed. "Indeed you do."

And indeed, he reflected, Fred Van Ackerman had, from the first moment he had arrived in the Senate a year ago. There had been about him even then a certain animal force that his colleagues could sense, an almost disturbing note of caged unbalance that might flare up at anything. Once he had thought Orrin Knox had shut him off too abruptly in a debate; there had been a strange whining snarl in his voice as he protested the indignity, giving the Senate a troubling sense of being in the presence of a spring on the point of unwinding altogether. Orrin had not apologized, but he had sat down with a puzzled expression on his face, for the misunderstanding had been minor and nothing to warrant Fred Van Ackerman's violence. And there had been other things, rumors and hints of double-dealings and dark underhandedness, verging on the criminal, in his surprise election at the age of thirty-three, a ruthless gambling spirit that kept breaking through. He wore a certain dark aspect, indefinable and somehow forbidding. No one yet had crossed him in any serious degree in the Senate, not knowing what this aspect might portend. His colleagues were still sizing him up; and now with this new interest of his in foreign affairs, it was beginning to appear that he might be going places. Just where, no one could say; but in recent days there had come the feeling that he was on his way. Senator Danta, like many another, was curious to find out the direction. The rally in New York seemed to furnish a possible clue, and he was determined to probe it as deeply as he could.

"I thought I'd drop in on the Leffingwell hearing," he said. "Want to come along?"

"That's a good idea," Fred said. "I'd love to."

"Tell me about COMFORT," Stanley said as they turned down the corridor toward the Caucus Room. "Where did that all begin?"

"I don't quite know," Senator Van Ackerman said thoughtfully, "except that it seemed to start up pretty soon after my first speech. There's a chapter in Chicago, you know, and one in San Francisco and one in Minneapolis, and of course in New York. I think it's big New York money, basically. I'm not connected with it directly; I've never even been approached except on this rally last Thursday night. Now I've got invitations from Chicago and San Francisco too, on the basis of that. It's the damnedest thing."

"But you certainly aren't going to turn down any chances?" Senator Danta suggested.

"Oh, hell, no," Fred Van Ackerman said with a quick grin. "Why, this might make me President, boy!"

And he grinned even more broadly to show he didn't mean it, which didn't fool Senator Danta, who knew with some alarm that deep in his heart he did. But he smiled in his friendly way and made the expected rejoinder.

"I'll bet it will," he said pleasantly. "I'll bet it will, at that," adding to himself, over my dead body. "You don't think the Russians are behind it, do you?" he asked innocently.

"I don't know," Fred Van Ackerman said slowly. "I don't really think so. I think it's mostly, as I say, big New York money. You know how they are about Causes, and this is just about the biggest Cause there is right now. Oh, if I thought it was a Commie outfit, Stan, I wouldn't have anything to do with it. I think it's just a genuine desire for peace. And if they want me to be their talker, why should I refuse? It gets me plenty of publicity," he concluded with satisfaction.

"It certainly does," Senator Danta conceded. "Well, here we are. Seems to be a crowd."

"You can sit at the committee table and I'll find a place somewhere," Fred said.

"Oh, no," Stanley Danta suggested casually, feeling in some obscure way that something important would come out of Fred's reaction to the hearing, "we'll find a couple of seats together."

As for Ellabelle Proctor at this moment, she wasn't thinking any philosophical thoughts about liberal causes or worrying about any yak-yak between a couple of Senators she never heard of. All she was doing was what Mabel Anderson, after a consultation with the Senator, had told her to do: clean the attic and get rid of his old Air Force uniforms, still kicking around, like those of many another veteran, in the attic. If she found anything in the pockets, Mabel said, she was to leave it in the study with the Senator's other papers; and having given these instructions the Senator's lady had taken Pidge, five years old and looking temporarily quite sedate and angelic in her little blue coat and little blue hat, and gone to visit Beth Knox while Ellabelle got on with her dusty work. Just now she had found something, a small brown manila envelope, and faithful to her instructions she was taking it downstairs to place it on the pile of legislative bills and other papers on the Senator's desk. After that she got herself a cup of coffee and went on about her work.

This was what Ellabelle Proctor did, perfectly logically from her point of view, however illogically it might seem to fit into the Big Picture in Washington, as Mr. Justice Davis read his papers and Senators Danta and Van Ackerman entered the Caucus Room.

"The Chair," the Chair said, "is glad to welcome Senator Danta, a member of the full committee, and Senator Van Ackerman. The Chair thinks it might be a good opportunity to take a ten-minute recess while they are being seated."

"I'm bursting," Arly Richardson confided candidly. "How did you know?"

"I didn't know," Brigham Anderson said, "but I think everybody is getting too heated about this and it might be good to have a break. Run along and hurry back. You're on next."

"Right," Senator Richardson said and arose with dignity to go to the nearest men's room. Senator DeWilton joined him and they went out talking soberly while Senators, audience, and press stood and stretched.

"Stanley," Brig said, "how are you this morning? Did you get over to the committee to hear Howie?"

"No, I didn't," Senator Danta said. "I had to preside at Interior and listen to Fred, here. Then we thought we'd come along and see your show."

"Hi, Fred," Senator Anderson said, shaking hands. "You had quite a show yourself in New York."

"I sure did," Senator Van Ackerman agreed expansively.

"I judge COMFORT is getting to be quite a force," Senator Anderson observed.

"Not as much as it likes to think it is," Fred Van Ackerman said. "But it's growing. I wonder why, just at this particular time? People haven't seemed to feel that way before—as organized about it, I mean. It kind of puzzles me, really."

"Maybe that's your doing, Fred," Stanley Danta suggested. "Maybe Man has met Movement. Maybe it's fate."

"I don't quite know what you mean by that," Senator Van Ackerman said, "but maybe you're right."

"It gives you quite a sounding board, anyway," Senator Anderson said. Senator Van Ackerman did not answer directly; instead his eyes swept the crowded room with an appraising look.

"I'm just wondering," he said, "if this thing would fit in with it."

Senator Danta started to speak and then thought better of it; his eyes flicked across those of Senator Anderson for just a second and when Senator Anderson spoke it was with a casual unconcern.

"Well, I don't know, Fred," he said. "It seems to me maybe this is rather beyond the scope of any movement such as that, which is probably only a temporary thing, anyway. You know how these things come and go."

"I'm not sure," Senator Van Ackerman said thoughtfully. "I just don't know. It could be this is just the sort of thing they'd want to support."

"No need for it," Senator Anderson said comfortably. "It's going through without any trouble."

"Is it?" Fred Van Ackerman said skeptically. "It hasn't looked that way so far."

"Well, don't let that fool you," Brigham Anderson said in the same relaxed tone. "You know how people talk around here and then when all's said and done the vote comes through on schedule. This'll be the same."

"Maybe," Senator Van Ackerman said doubtfully. "Do you think a speech from me would help?"

"Why don't you save it until the debate comes on the floor, Fred?" Senator Danta suggested easily. "There's the time to fire your ammunition if you think it's needed."

"Yeah," Fred Van Ackerman said. "I guess." And then in one of those quick apparent terminations of interest that his colleagues found characteristic and usually not very indicative of his true intentions, he·turned away. "Well, shall we sit down, Stan?" he asked.

"Take a seat at the table if you like," Senator Anderson suggested.

"Thanks," Stanley Danta said, "but I may have to leave again soon. I've got some things to do in the office before the session starts."

"Me too," Fred said. "We'll just sit along here in back and watch for a little while."

"Good," Brigham Anderson said. "Glad to have you . . . Well, John," he said, turning to the Senator from Massachusetts who had remained seated impassively beside him, "about as we expected, hm?"

"Yes," Senator Winthrop said. "I didn't realize we'd start having show-downs quite this soon, but aside from that everything's moving on sched-ule."

"I'm not so sure it's going the way I expected on the other side of the table, though," Senator Anderson said with a thoughtful glance at the nominee, chatting animatedly in the midst of a clustering circle of reporters. "You're right, and so is Orrin; and so is Seab, for that matter. He is being evasive. I wonder why."

"That's what Arly's going to ask," Senator Winthrop said dryly. "He's going to ask the Why."

"I may myself," Senator Anderson said, "if it isn't cleared up by the time it gets to me."

"It won't be," Senator Winthrop said in a tone even drier. "This is the day for noble sentiments. It isn't the day for getting to the guts of things."

"We've gotten to the guts of several things, I think," Senator Anderson said. "The public may not understand it, but it's all here."

"How much of that," John Winthrop wondered with a nod toward the eagerly listening, eagerly laughing reporters, "will they give the public?"

"Yes," Senator Anderson said thoughtfully. "I know."

"—and then," Bob Leffingwell was concluding his story, "I told him, 'Well, Senator, if that's the way you feel I guess we'll have to put it in the stockpile.'"

There was a flattering explosion of laughter from the press, and with it the nominee shot a quick look at the chairman; a quietly triumphant look that distinctly said: You see, I have them. And have them he did, for even at that moment the teletypes down in the press room were chattering with a counter-suggestion from the news editors in the wire-service bureaus downtown. SUGGEST LEFFINGWELL BELIEFS AMERICA BETTER LEAD THAN OLD COOLEY CHARGES, the messages read. The nominee was in good shape after all.

"The committee will be in order," Brigham Anderson said. "Senator Richardson?"

The phone rang twice at Vagaries and a maid answered. Mrs. Harrison was upstairs, she said, and might be asleep; would the Senator care to leave a message? He was about to when Dolly came on the line.

"I don't get it," she said as the downstairs phone clicked off. "*You're* calling *me*. How does that happen?"

"It happens sometimes," Bob Munson said amiably. "I'm just checking. I saw your picture in the *Post* this morning and the caption said you were at the Brazilian Embassy party last night with some man. Is this rumor true?"

"Don't tell me you care!" Dolly said, and the Senator chuckled.

"I'm passionately jealous," he confided, "especially of that particular gentleman."

"You'd be surprised," Dolly said.

"So would he, I'll bet," Bob Munson observed. "Anyway, I just thought I'd call and find out how you were."

"There's some other reason," Dolly suggested. "It can't be as simple as just plain, ordinary, friendly interest."

"It isn't plain and it isn't ordinary," Senator Munson said, "but it sure is friendly. I was going to ask if you wanted to do me a favor."

"Any time," Dolly said. "Any old time at all."

"I think you have a one-track mind," Bob Munson said. "This is a matter of great and solemn importance, vital to the future of the nation."

"I can't think of anything more vital to the future of the nation," Dolly said. "Where would we be a hundred years from now without it?"

"Woman," Bob Munson said, "be quiet and pay attention. I was wondering if you would like to come up and sit in on the Leffingwell hearing for me tomorrow and the rest of the week. I can't be there myself much and I need somebody who can give me a fill-in; also, I respect your judgment and I'd like to know what you think of it."

"You really respect my judgment?" Dolly said in a pleased tone.

"I really do," the Senator said.

"Well," she said, sounding entirely different, "that puts a whole new light on things. Nothing would please me more than to sit in on the Leffingwell hearings for you, darling. I don't care if it is all some elaborate political scheme of yours, as long as you genuinely want me to be a part of it."

"I suspect this may become a habit," Bob Munson said, "and I probably shouldn't encourage it if I want to keep my freedom. However, you come ahead and I'll arrange with Brig to have you seated along the back there, right behind the committee. Why don't you call Kitty and Celestine and see if they'd like to attend with you? I imagine Claude and Raoul would like to have their own observers on the spot, too."

"And I imagine," Dolly said, "that you would like me to tell that to Kitty and Celestine so that they will tell Claude and Raoul, who in turn will be impressed with how thoughtful and considerate you are, and—well, darling, I think I'll probably follow through on it, just as you want."

"I hope I'm not that transparent to everybody," Senator Munson said, and Dolly laughed in a proprietary way.

"I suspect you are," she said, "but that's one of the reasons we all love you so."

"Hmph," Bob Munson said. "What are you doing over the weekend?"

"A couple of parties, a couple of receptions—the gay, mad, Washington whirl," she said. "You know how it is. What did you have in mind?"

"The same thing you do," Senator Munson said. "I was thinking about Thursday night, which is the annual White House Correspondents banquet for the President. I may go back to the White House with him for a little while afterwards, but I ought to be free after that."

"We can always watch the late, late show," Dolly suggested dryly.

"Watch it, hell," Senator Munson said. "I want to be in it."

Dolly laughed.

"If Michigan could hear you now," she said.

"Michigan," Bob Munson said, "is as interested as anybody, I'm quite sure. I can expect you here tomorrow, then?"

"I'll be there," Dolly said. "I'll call the others right now."

"Fine," Senator Munson said. "You're really being a big help to me, you know."

"Any time, I said," Dolly reminded him.

For a long moment Senator Richardson looked appraisingly at the nominee and the nominee looked back. Then the Senator smiled in a way that looked more cordial than it actually was.

"Well, Mr. Leffingwell," he said, "there seems to be a feeling here that you aren't giving us quite what we're after. Maybe I won't have cause to feel that way, after you talk to me."

"I hope not, Senator," Bob Leffingwell said calmly. "I've always found you very fair in our dealings together."

"And I have always found you very capable," Arly responded. "So capable," he added slowly, "that I, like my colleagues, am finding it a little difficult to understand why it is so hard for you to be candid with this subcommittee."

"I'm doing my best, Senator," Bob Leffingwell said. "As clearly as the English language can convey it, I'm stating my position."

"But you haven't stated it in response to questions," Senator Richardson said. "It's been a somewhat more self-serving process. You've stated it as it has suited you, not as we have requested it. Like my colleagues, I wonder why. What sort of associations did you have, when you were in college, and when you were teaching at the University of Chicago, and later on. What sort do you have now?"

"That's several questions in one, Senator," the nominee said.

"Take them seriatim," Arly Richardson suggested. Bob Leffingwell looked both thoughtful and puzzled.

"My associations in college," he said. "Looking back to that distant time, I belonged to a fraternity; I went to class; I was on the tennis team; I helped edit the school paper; I went to a fair number of dances and social events; I was president of my senior class; I knew probably a thousand people on a more or less cordial basis, another thousand more casually. Associations? Approximately the same you had, I imagine, Senator, when you went to college."

"I have a telegram here," Senator Richardson said and paused as if to search for it, glancing sharply at the nominee, who remained impassive, "from someone who claims to have known you at the University of Chicago when you were a teacher there."

"I was a teacher there," Bob Leffingwell said, "and I am quite sure a great many people knew me. Who is it from?"

"Don't be impatient, Mr. Leffingwell," Arly Richardson said. "Let me proceed with this in my own way."

"I'm sorry," Bob Leffingwell said with a smile. "I thought possibly I might know him."

"His name isn't important," Senator Richardson said. "Gelb—Gelman—Gelman, that's it, Herbert Gelman. A student of yours. He says you had the reputation of running with a pretty shady crowd."

"Good God," the Baltimore *Sun* whispered angrily, "is nothing sacred? This man is going to be handling our foreign policy and dealing with other governments and he's tagged with 'running with a shady crowd.' Good God!" "This Hill can be a brutal place sometimes," the *Times* agreed. "You never know, though; maybe it *was* a shady crowd."

"Well, Senator," the nominee said with a trace of annoyance, "anybody can smear anybody with anything, of course, and if he wants to he can take advantage of a Senate hearing to do it."

"Are you accusing me of smearing you, Mr. Leffingwell?" Senator Richardson asked slowly, and the Washington *Post* hissed, "Say yes, God damn it!" But Bob Leffingwell chose not to.

"No, Senator," he said, "but it seems to me you are transmitting the unfounded allegations of someone else without checking."

"I'm checking them with you," Arly Richardson said bluntly. "There's nobody better to check with, is there?"

"All right, Senator," the nominee said coldly. "I did not 'run with a shady crowd.' Period."

"He goes on here," Senator Richardson said in a deliberately unimpressed tone, "to say that this group was generally supposed on the campus to be strongly left-wing and probably Communist."

"All that line of questioning is going to produce, Senator," Bob Leffingwell said in a tone equally unimpressed, "is a statement from the president and faculty of the University of Chicago testifying to my good character. I'll be glad to have it in the record if you wish."

"You sound pretty sure of that," Arly Richardson observed with interest. "Have you already arranged for it?"

"I've been told it's coming," the nominee replied, "and I can't conceive that this type of questioning will do anything but hasten it along."

"You're pretty sure of yourself, aren't you?" Senator Richardson asked, and Bob Leffingwell smiled.

"I feel," he said, with a smile that didn't quite remove all the arrogance, though he obviously thought it did, "that I am armored in the integrity of my own record."

"Well, well," Arly Richardson said. "Do you, now? Do you remember Herbert Gelman?"

"Frankly, I don't," Bob Leffingwell said. "I had, I imagine, some three hundred students, all told, during that year——"

"During what year, Mr. Leffingwell?" Senator Richardson asked. "I didn't mention any year."

Bob Leffingwell looked puzzled for a moment, then shook his head and smiled.

"I thought you did, Senator," he said. "My course only ran three quarters, it was completed in one academic year, students only took it for one year, I taught roughly three hundred students each year, and I assumed you meant the year that this fellow Gelb or Gelman, or whatever it is, took it."

"Gelman," Senator Richardson said. "Herbert Gelman. I am beginning to think," he said as the room became suddenly very quiet, "that we should all remember Herbert's name. G-e-l-m-a-n, Gelman."

"All right, Gelman," the nominee said. "I remember no Gelman."

"Well, he remembers you," Arly Richardson said.

"Now, see here," Bob Leffingwell said abruptly. "Just what are you getting at, Senator?"

"I haven't any plan," Arly said placidly. "Just whatever develops, Mr. Leffingwell. So you don't remember Gelman."

"No, sir," the nominee said, more calmly.

"Would you if you saw him?" Senator Richardson asked.

"Is he here?" Bob Leffingwell asked.

"Not to my knowledge," Arly said.

"Then how could I?" the nominee demanded.

"I just wondered," Senator Richardson said.

"I don't remember him," Bob Leffingwell said again. "Presumably he was at the university when I was, took my course, and indulged in campus gossip about people who were more prominent, and possibly more secure and better-adjusted to life in general and college life in particular, than he was. What else do we know about him, Senator?"

"That's all," Arly said, "unless you can tell us more."

"I don't know any more, Senator," Bob Leffingwell said frankly.

"Sure?" Arly Richardson asked.

"Sure," the nominee replied firmly. Arly shrugged.

"Very well," he said, "let's go back to your general philosophy. You've made it rather plain you don't want war."

"Who does?" Bob Leffingwell said shortly, and Senator Richardson smiled.

"That's right, who does?" he said. "You mean, I take it, war under any circumstances, is that right?"

"I can't conceive of a circumstance that would warrant it, Senator," the nominee said, and Senator Richardson looked thoughtful.

"Suppose a conference were held and it was demanded that we yield certain strategic positions?" he asked.

"We should, I suppose, reject any such demand," the nominee replied.

"But suppose we were confronted with the threat of immediate military retaliation if we did not," Arly went on, "and this is not beyond the realm of possibility these days, you know, Mr. Leffingwell. What then?"

"In that case, Senator," Bob Leffingwell said, "I assume it would be far past the point where anything could be done about it."

"Our only choice then would be what, Mr. Leffingwell?" Senator Richardson asked. "To give in, wouldn't it? To yield? To surrender? Anything else would be preventive war, wouldn't it?"

The nominee thought for a moment and then spread his hands wide before him again in that open, candid gesture.

"I suppose it would have to be considered so, Senator," he said.

"And you don't like preventive war," Senator Richardson said.

"No, sir," Bob Leffingwell said.

"And you wouldn't recommend it, as Secretary of State, because not only you but many another American, including a recent President of the United States, have formally announced to the world and our enemies that they never need fear force from us, because we will never use it until after we have given them the advantage of striking first, isn't that right?"

"I would never recommend it, no, sir," the nominee said firmly.

"So how would you get your country out of this not-so-hypothetical box in which I have placed her, Mr. Leffingwell? Can you tell us?"

"I would try to find some solution that would save the world from war, Senator," Bob Leffingwell said simply.

"Which, if we really believed the Russians meant war if we didn't yield, and if that was genuinely their intention, would be to surrender to their demands, would it not?" Senator Richardson asked. Bob Leffingwell smiled a little.

"I think you have me in a box too, Senator," he said. "I don't believe that the alternatives you state are the only ones." Senator Richardson leaned forward.

"Ah, then we're getting somewhere," he said, "because neither do I, nor does the Senator from Illinois, with whom you discussed something of this same point a few minutes ago. What alternative do you feel should be followed, then?"

"It might be necessary, under the conditions you state, Senator," the nominee said gravely, "to concede in some degree to those demands, providing there were some concessions on the other side. I think that might permit us to live with the situation."

"And keep our freedom?" Senator Richardson asked sharply.

"And keep our freedom," Bob Leffingwell said.

The Senator looked at him curiously.

"But where do we stop yielding?" he asked. "At what point do we say, 'No, it goes no further. This is where you stop and where we stand up for the things we believe in?' Do you have such a point in your own mind?"

Bob Leffingwell spread his hands again in that curious, candid gesture.

"All I can tell you," he said patiently, "is that it would have to depend on the situation as it then existed, Senator." Then his voice strengthened and he straightened in his chair. "But I tell you this, and I care not who challenges it: I will never recommend war to the President of the United States if I become his Secretary of State. Never!"

There was an excited burst of applause in the room and Brigham Anderson gaveled for order. Senator Richardson leaned forward again.

"You're so afraid of war that you'd give up anything to avoid it, wouldn't you?" he asked softly. "You wouldn't draw a line anywhere, would you? You'd just keep giving and giving and giving, until there wasn't anything left for us to give, wouldn't you?"

"Do you want war, Senator?" Bob Leffingwell asked. Senator Richardson snorted and slapped the table with the flat of his hand.

"By God, I do not," he said in a cold tone. "But I am not afraid of it if it should have to come in defense of the things we stand for. Let me make *you* a little speech, Mr. Leffingwell: I had rather go out of this world standing on my two hind legs like a man, fighting for the things I believe in, than yield and yield and crawl and crawl until nothing is left. Nor am I afraid of the consequences, which I grant you would be horrible beyond belief. But nobody ever achieved anything by running away, and I don't think we can achieve anything now by running away except the disappearance of the United States from the stage of history, quietly and neatly and without any muss or fuss, which is just the way the Russians want us to go. As for me, I had rather go ahead in the cause of what I believe in than scuttle and run for fear of something that might or might not happen."

"If it did happen, Senator," the nominee said quietly, "nothing would be left of the world."

"And if it did not, and we found that we had yielded ourselves beyond redemption simply because of the fear that it might, nothing would be left of us," Arly said with equal quietness. "So there we are. I have no further questions of the witness at this time, Mr. Chairman."

"I have one of you, though, Senator," Bob Leffingwell said with a smile as the room began to relax to normal.

"What's that?" Senator Richardson asked, and when the answer came a strange little expression came momentarily into his eyes.

"Have you tried to find Herbert Gelman?" Bob Leffingwell asked. "Not," he added with an easy smile, "that it matters one way or the other, but I'm curious."

"Yes," Arly Richardson said slowly, "I have. I called the president of the university and he had it checked for me, but he said they couldn't find any record of any such student in the past ten years and the records for four of five years before that had been destroyed in a fire. He said he personally was unable to remember any such name."

"As a matter of fact, then," the nominee said pleasantly, "we don't even know that he exists, do we? It could be just a figment of somebody's imagination, couldn't it; some crank who wants to embarrass me, which as you know often happens to people in the public eye."

"So far as I know," Arly Richardson said in the same slow way, "all there is of Herbert Gelman is on this piece of paper."

"Then don't you think, Senator," the nominee suggested with perfect courtesy, "that possibly I am due an apology for the implications made here?"

Senator Richardson looked at him steadily for what seemed a long time, and then he smiled too and spoke with equal courtesy.

"Perhaps you are," he said pleasantly. "But long experience on this Hill tells me that perhaps the record should stand as it is for the time being. If nothing further supports it on the day your nomination comes to the floor of the Senate I shall be glad to speak in your behalf and vote for you. Fair enough?"

Bob Leffingwell smiled again.

"If that is the extent of your concession, Senator," he said, "I guess I'll have to accept it as fair enough."

"Good," Senator Richardson said. "Then we understand each other."

"As you wish, Senator," Bob Leffingwell said with sudden indifference, and reached to light a cigarette as Arly sat back slowly in his chair. There was a stir and buzz in the room and in the midst of it Stanley Danta

observed that his young colleague, who had been watching intently without a word through Senator Richardson's entire questioning, was about to
comment.

"Why, hell," Fred Van Ackerman said, with an intensity made curiously
disturbing by the fact that he did not raise his voice above a half whisper,
"they're crucifying him, Stan, that's what they're doing, they're crucifying
him. This has got to be stopped. *This has got to be stopped.*"

"You're hurting my arm," Senator Danta said quietly, and Senator Van
Ackerman let go with an embarrassed laugh.

"I didn't even realize I had hold of it, Stan," he said. "Honest."

Below the city lay before them; the rain had stopped and a sharp
wind was driving the clouds apart; great shafts of sunlight slanted down.
Each in its accustomed place the Capitol, the White House, the Library
of Congress, the Court, the Washington, Lincoln, and Jefferson memorials,
the medieval spires of Georgetown University, and the bulk of the Washington Cathedral stood out. The river wound brown and muddy under
its bridges, stretching away south and east toward the Chesapeake Bay;
over the rolling countryside of Maryland and west along the Virginia
hills to the Blue Ridge and the Shenandoah the first light carpetings of
green were beginning to show; around the Tidal Basin the cherry trees
awaited the warming winds. Any day now—any minute, perhaps—spring
would arrive in sudden glory and the world would be a lovely place.

Looking down upon the great white city, the winding river, the kind
and gracious land stretching off into the hazy blue of the clearing horizons,
Krishna Khaleel sucked in his breath in a small, appreciative sound as
the plane climbed swiftly and moved into its course for New York.

"It is beautiful," he said, "It is a beautiful city and a beautiful land, Hal.
You should be proud."

"You can't know," Hal Fry said softly. "You can't know." But the Indian
Ambassador smiled.

"Oh, yes," he said. "I can know. I come from a bare brown land, but it
has its beauties, too, Hal, some of them equal to these. And it is mine,
which makes it beautiful beyond all other lands to me. Yes, I know."

"Why can we never——" Senator Fry began in a tone of angry frustration,
and stopped.

"—get along together?" Krishna Khaleel completed for him. "Why must
all this beauty in the world be so misused by the men who live in it?
Why do we live and work and strive, only to achieve no more than new
destructions of one another? It is a time to ask, with spring about to come;
though there will be no answer, I think, in spring. Or summer. Or winter.
Or fall."

"But we try," Hal Fry said bitterly. "We try. Why does it mean so
little? Why is it all so pointless?"

"Oh, it is not pointless," K.K. said, more lightly. "For instance, there were gains at Dolly's Friday night. And though we may feel some doubts at times, you and I at least are going back to the UN, drawn by some compulsion of hope as well as duty, I assume. At least I should hope it is hope, Hal."

"It is for us," Senator Fry said, frowning a little. "Some others, I doubt. As for Dolly's, I'm glad you thought gains were made. I'm not sure."

"A start," K.K. said, "a modest start. There was some indication from Bob, was there not, of a new inclination to make new approaches? Much, I presume, depends on what is happening down there"—and he gestured toward Capitol Hill, now far back and growing tinier by the second—"right now."

"I expect we'll confirm him," Senator Fry said. "It would be most unusual not to."

"I think you should," Krishna Khaleel said. "It is none of our business, really, but yet you all have asked our opinion, and of course it is our business, as it is all the world's, who is Secretary of State of the United States. Especially if he is to lead the way to a new arrangement with Russia."

"Don't jump too fast," Hal Fry said, "or too far. A new approach doesn't necessarily mean new negotiations, and new negotiations don't necessarily mean a new approach. Particularly when our good friends rush us into it with such overwhelming urgency that our hands are tied and we are automatically foreclosed from any real bargaining."

"But, Hal," the Indian Ambassador said. "We do not do that. It is simply that we all desire peace, and we think for all your faults, which, my dear friend, you must recognize you do have, you are probably most likely to achieve it for the world if we can but bring you to see the way."

"I feel we're losing hold of things," Senator Fry said, staring out the window as Maryland sped beneath. "I feel that somehow the United States isn't going to get anywhere unless it hangs onto the things that have always meant the United States. I feel you want us to give them up, if necessary, to win agreement; and I don't see how we can and still retain the inner conviction we need and have got to have if we are to survive and help the world survive. This is what troubles me."

"Possibly some of those things are not quite so—so applicable as they once were, Hal," K.K. said. "That is our only thought. *Do you know* what is best for the world? *Do you know* what is best for peace? *Do you know* what is best for yourselves, even? Sometimes we wonder."

"You have asked us so many questions like that in recent years," Senator Fry said, "that you have got us asking ourselves; and we have asked ourselves so much that sometimes I think we have forgotten how to do anything but question ourselves in one vast paralysis of self-doubt. There are times when men shouldn't ask questions, they should just go ahead and do what they know is right, or the chance is lost. But first our enemies,

and now our friends, have told us we must question ourselves on everything we do; we must sit around and debate with each other instead of
acting; and so while we have debated, others have acted, and often the
chance has gone. Or does that seem a too one-sided view to you?"

The Indian Ambassador too looked down thoughtfully upon the pleasant land as it rushed away, and shrugged.

"Who knows," he said, "whether those chances should have been taken
or whether history will say that it was best for you to miss them, and so
best that you should have asked and argued and talked and debated
instead of doing something rash and precipitate that might have changed
your course in a way that could not be modified? Perhaps it has saved
you from commitments that would have brought you down, and with you
the world."

"So what has it left us to be committed to?" Hal Fry asked moodily.
"Anything? That is the American problem right now, it seems to me: we
aren't committed, and we don't really care, about anything. Our enemies
and our friends together have succeeded in paralyzing us with self-doubt,
and under the tutelage of all of you we have become afraid to really care,
because to really care has become unfashionable and rather laughable;
and also, of course, because to really care would impose upon us the
necessity of acting in support of the things we really care for; and nobody
wants us to do that any more. We don't even want to do it ourselves . . .
So what purpose do we serve in the world any more, in your mind? Any?"

"Oh, Hal!" the Indian Ambassador exclaimed impatiently. "What purpose do you serve! Why do you say fantastic things like that?"

"Well," Senator Fry said, "it seems the only logical conclusion, doesn't
it?"

"It does not," Krishna Khaleel said firmly, "and you don't believe for
one moment that it does, either."

"Then what is it?" Hal Fry persisted; and after a moment his companion
laughed.

"Always joking," he said comfortably. "Dear old Hal. Tell me, do you
not think Mr. Leffingwell will have some answers that will reassure even
you, my dark, gloomy friend?"

Senator Fry gave him an appraising glance and suddenly he relaxed
and laughed too.

"Dear old Akbar," he said mockingly. "Always joking too, I suspect,
and somehow, I suspect, always at the expense of the United States of
America. To answer your question, all I can say is, I hope so."

"We hope so too," Krishna Khaleel said. "In fact, we are confident of it.
So all the dark worries and doubts are rather foolish, are they not?"

"We have a saying," Senator Fry said, "that it won't matter in a hundred
years."

"There, you see?" K.K. cried triumphantly. "Now you begin to regard it as we do!"

Below Maryland sped away, the flat gray roofs and white stone stoops of Baltimore, the pleasant enclave of Havre de Grace beside the Susquehanna, the kindly, gentle, greening land.

"Mr. Chairman," John DeWilton said, "I shall also try to be brief, if the witness will co-operate."

"Gladly, Senator," Bob Leffingwell replied with a smile. "This is six to one, you know; I'm as anxious to speed it along as you are!"

"I'd say the one has done pretty well so far," Senator DeWilton observed. The nominee laughed, against the comforting background of friendly laughter from the room.

"A little bloody, but unbowed, Senator," he said.

"I too," Johnny DeWilton said, quickly becoming all pink-faced, white-topped business, "would like to advert to your recent speeches. I believe you said in Des Moines two weeks ago that the Soviet Government, and I quote, 'now gives evidence of an earnest desire to negotiate in good faith.' I wonder if you could cite one specific piece of evidence to back up that assertion, Mr. Leffingwell."

The nominee smiled again and gave again his candid, ingratiating shrug and gesture with his opened hands.

"Senator," he said, and stopped to start anew with the thoughtful pause that lent so many of his words their little extra impact. "How shall I answer you? Of signed commitments and formal promises, no; there are none of these. Of an attitude of greater willingness and understanding, of a friendlier aspect toward the West and toward us in particular, yes, I think I do see signs. Certainly there is every evidence of their desire to negotiate with us; almost daily they urge it upon us; I think some candor must underlie such diligent appeals."

"You think so," Senator DeWilton said. "But again you cite a belief when you were asked for specifics. I still would like to know what basis we have for trusting them. They have urged negotiations before; we have met them and offered them much and they haven't conceded a thing. What is to be gained by another charade like that?"

"Well, Senator," Bob Leffingwell said, "as long as you have charades you don't have war."

The audience stirred with a little tentative applause and the Senator from Vermont looked up with annoyance.

"I say again, Mr. Leffingwell," he said, "that is no answer to my question. You are nominated here for perhaps the most important office next to that of the President himself, insofar as our foreign affairs are concerned, and we want from you some specific indications about things. If you are going to rush off and confer with the Russians in a rosy glow just because they say come hither, I'm very much afraid you're not going to either defend your country's interests *or* bring world peace any closer *or* prevent that war you had rather talk about than tell us what you think."

The nominee flushed and for a moment looked openly annoyed. But when he spoke it was in the same reasonable, patient tone.

"Senator," he said, "it *is,* if you like, a matter of belief; perhaps I might say a matter of faith. A faith that reasonable men prefer peace to destruc- tion; that they will greet one another in that spirit; that they will reason together and compromise their differences and work out agreements in the light of the overriding knowledge that if they fail the world goes. A man has to believe something, Senator, and that is what I believe. I cannot separate it from beliefs, for it goes beyond mere surface appearances and the dismal record of past misunderstandings. It urges a fresh start, a new leaf, a page upon which the finger of history has yet to trace its message. I call for a message of hope upon that page, Senator. I call for a future bright with hope, toward which we may move nobly and stead- fastly as becomes us."

Again there was a stirring of applause, and Senator DeWilton shook his head again in an annoyed way.

"You're a great man for words, Mr. Leffingwell," he said. "You seem to think they can absolve you from answering questions."

"My God," the Newark *News* whispered disgustedly. "What else does the old fool want from him?" "Seems to me he's answered very well," the Philadelphia *Inquirer* agreed.

"No, Senator," Bob Leffingwell said. "I don't think they can absolve me, as you put it, from anything. Nor have I attempted to evade questions or issues here. I think I have met them head on in every instance, and have answered them as fully and honestly as I know how."

The Senator from Vermont looked at him intently.

"All right," he said. "I'll try you once more, and then I'm through, Mr. Chairman. Can you give me one specific proof, Mr. Witness, that the Russians intend to negotiate with us in good faith if there is new attempt made, any more than they did at the last conference, or the one before that, or the one before that, or any other you care to name?"

The nominee smiled with a certain amiably helpless air.

"Senator," he said deprecatingly, "you cover so much ground. The last conference? I believe they said they would agree to consider the advisa- bility of working out a graduated disarmament. The one before that? My memory is that they pledged before the world their devotion to the principles of peace and justice for all peoples. I don't quite know what you expect of them, Senator."

"And those were what you call real concessions?" John DeWilton asked in a disbelieving tone.

"I do," Bob Leffingwell said. "In the light of their past record, Senator."

"You really do?" Senator DeWilton repeated in the same tone.

"I do," the nominee repeated firmly. Then he leaned forward earnestly.

"Oh, Senator," he said fervently. "Don't let us lose sight of the great objective in a mist of petty detail. Don't let us permit the angry past to betray the promise of the hopeful future. Mankind deserves so much more of us, Senator. Let us justify its hope and not cast it down in fruitless carping and the pointless tale of rehashed wrongs and imagined grievances."

"Well, I'll tell you, Mr. Leffingwell," John DeWilton said in an ironic tone, "If you were a Nazi, say, or a die-hard reactionary, or a labor-baiter or somebody else like that whom the press doesn't like and doesn't play up all over the country with a lot of hero worship the way it does you, you'd be charged with evasion and duplicity and double talk and every other kind of nasty thing that could be thought of to say about you. But since you're you, I dare say all this is being swallowed wholesale without a second thought as to what you're actually doing here. I suppose there are millions of people watching you right now who aren't getting it at all, just because they're so conditioned to think of you in terms of noble words and ringing phrases like you've put on display here. But I get it, Mr. Witness. I tell you you're avoiding the questions of this subcommittee, the legitimate questions to which the Senate of the United States has every right to have answers from the man it is asked to give the office of Secretary of State to. I don't know why you're doing it, but you're certainly doing it. And it's just about decided me to vote against you, I tell you that frankly."

There was an audible hiss from somewhere in the room, and for the first time Bob Leffingwell looked genuinely angry, a certain waspish, feline look that sat strangely upon his handsome, dignified face; and for a moment it appeared that he would voice his anger. Before he could, however, Seab Cooley spoke softly from down the table.

"My opinion, Mr. Chairman," he said slowly, "is that this witness doesn't know any more about the Russians than he does about Mr. Herbert Gelman. No, sir. He just doesn't know any more about them than he does about Mr. Herbert Gelman."

Then Bob Leffingwell did speak out, in a tone of rising anger.

"Mr. Chairman," he demanded, "how much longer am I to be subjected to this persecution? I have answered to the best of my ability every question put to me here, and I am accused of being evasive and engaging in double talk. I have expressed the hope and the aspirations of, I believe, the overwhelming majority of our countrymen, and I am told I am unfit to be their Secretary of State. And now I am subjected to petty harassment by the Senator from South Carolina, who hasn't had an original word to say on the subject of our differences in the past ten years. I demand of you how much longer I must tolerate this kind of pettifoggery?"

At this a loud burst of applause swept across the room, and Brigham Anderson banged the gavel repeatedly with a vigor that did not, however, stop it for well over a minute. As it began to die away, Seab had the last word.

"Yes, sir," he said impassively, as if to himself. "The Russians and Mr. Herbert Gelman. They're both mysteries to this man."

"Very well, Senator," Brigham Anderson said shortly. "I'd suggest we all calm down here. I can understand the witness' impatience in the face of a long and exhaustive interrogation; I can also, I must tell him candidly, understand something of the bafflement, disappointment, and annoyance with which many of his answers have been received by the subcommittee. But it is true, as the Senator from Vermont says, that millions of his countrymen are watching these proceedings; and they will make their judgment, as we must make ours in the immediate matter of his confirmation. The morning is getting on, there is a session of the Senate we all wish to attend at noon, I am the only member remaining to question, and I really will be brief. I would suggest again, therefore as I said, that we all calm down. Is that agreeable to you, Mr. Leffingwell?"

By the time he finished speaking the nominee had regained his self-possessed composure and was waiting to answer with a friendly smile on his lips and a friendly expression in his eyes.

"Quite, Mr. Chairman," he said. "I'm sorry if I let the accumulated tensions of the morning explode. Being a witness before a Congressional committee is not an easy task under the best of circumstances, and while I am genuinely grateful for your own kindness and fairness, Mr. Chairman, there have been moments, we all recognize, when these have not been the best of circumstances. However," he went on as the room rippled with appreciative laughter, "I think I can stand it for a while longer in good spirit, and will continue to do my best to be candid and honest with the subcommittee on these great matters which so vitally concern us all . . . Perhaps, Mr. Chairman," he added thoughtfully, "my views are in part directed by the overwhelming desire I have seemed to find everywhere I have spoken in recent weeks, for some accommodation with the Russians, some attempt to get along with them, some attempt to remove from the world this ominous cloud that hangs over us all. For the first time, I think, there is a real and genuine anxiety in this country, as there long has been in other countries, for such an accommodation." And quite without warning he suddenly switched his remarks in a new direction. "I believe your distinguished colleague whom I see sitting behind you there, Senator Van Ackerman, found this to be true in his great speech in New York last week," he said with a flattering smile.

Fred Van Ackerman looked startled and pleased, and replied in a loud and breezy and curiously defiant voice.

"I did," he said. "That's right. May I say, Mr. Chairman, the witness has been doing a magnificent job here, in the opinion of the junior Senator from Wyoming, and I am sure it is he and his like who will lead us out of our present situation to lasting peace."

"Thank you, Senator," Brigham Anderson said rather shortly. "We appreciate your comments, as I'm sure Mr. Leffingwell does too. Senator DeWil——"

"I do indeed," Bob Leffingwell interrupted smoothly. "It is Senators of the caliber of the distinguished junior Senator from Wyoming who will help me in that effort, I assure him."

"I appreciate that, Mr. Secretary," Fred Van Ackerman said. "I really appreciate it."

"Yes," Senator Anderson said. "Would the Senator care to join the subcommittee at the table?"

"No, thanks, Brig," Senator Van Ackerman said. "I'll just stay here and be an observer."

"The Chair had the impression you were becoming a participant, which is why he asked," Senator Anderson said, meaning to joke but unfortunately sounding a little sharper than he had intended. A strange expression came into Senator Van Ackerman's eyes.

"Why are you trying to choke me off, Brig?" he demanded in a loudly angry tone, and the tension in the room immediately shot up. Brigham Anderson swung half around in his chair to stare at him for a second.

"Not my intention, Fred," he said informally, and after a moment Senator Van Ackerman shrugged and seemed to lose interest at once.

"O.K.," he said. "Sorry."

"Senator DeWilton," the chairman said, turning back with a thoughtful expression.

"Well, Mr. Chairman," Johnny DeWilton said, "I'm through. I just want to say, though, that this strikes me as peculiar. The witness has explained everything except what I asked him to explain and he has been applauded for it repeatedly in spite of your ruling about demonstrations. Don't people really understand what is going on here?"

"They understand," the Detroit *News* whispered savagely, "that's why they're applauding Leffingwell, you stupid old fathead." "Johnny just doesn't get the picture," the St. Louis *Post-Dispatch* remarked.

"Everyone is free to judge for himself, Senator," Brigham Anderson said. "The Chair intends to question the witness briefly now, and then I think the subcommittee can stand in recess until ten o'clock tomorrow morning, at which time, Mr. Leffingwell, we shall turn you over to the tender mercies of the Senator from South Carolina."

The nominee laughed.

"I'll get a good night's rest, Mr. Chairman," he promised, and gave Senator Cooley a direct and confident glance. "After all," he added, buoyed by the knowledge that the crowd was with him fully, "if all he has to offer is a non-existent witness, I dare say I can survive him pretty well!"

A wave of appreciative laughter swept the room, and when all eyes swung to Seab it was observed that he was laughing too, in his sleepy, veiled-eyed way. This was taken to be a good omen by the nominee and his friends, a note of possible cordiality or at least a not too embittered animosity, and the atmosphere became more relaxed. Senator Anderson, who knew his man, was not fooled but reflected that the nominee was on his own and it wasn't his business to advise him. Instead he spoke in a reasoned tone as the laughter once again died away.

"I should just like to sum up your testimony this morning and put it in perspective, if I can, and see if you agree with my estimate of it," he said pleasantly. "First and foremost you are, I take it, opposed to war, particularly to what is generally termed preventive war, under any and all circumstances."

The nominee hesitated, then nodded.

"In essence that is correct, Senator," he said.

"And you are thereby on this record and in this public hearing which is literally being carried to the ends of the earth, including Moscow, renouncing war as an instrument of national policy of the United States under any and all circumstances."

"Except attack, Senator," Bob Leffingwell said. "I assumed that was understood. Except attack, of course."

"It wasn't quite," the chairman said, "at least not by me, and I am glad to have your clarification. And by attack you mean direct, open, overt military attack."

"I think that is the most reasonable definition, Senator," Bob Leffingwell said.

"And the safest," Brigham Anderson suggested.

"Yes, sir," the nominee said.

"If," the chairman added casually, "you don't wish to be called upon to take a definite stand at a point where a definite stand might conceivably ward off attack." The nominee shot him a suddenly sharpened glance.

"Or might conceivably precipitate world war, Senator," he said quickly. Senator Anderson nodded gravely, with a little smile.

"Granted," he said. "There is that possibility. You believe it to be a likelier possibility, in such a case, than the possibility that a firm stand would change Russia's policy and so not only prevent an overt attack but perhaps turn her efforts into a channel leading more directly toward peace."

"Such is my conviction, Senator," Bob Leffingwell replied.

"And you feel it advisable that the United States not cling too arbitrarily to some of her traditional principles of fair dealing and honest negotiation in her relations with the Russians, since that might prejudice an accommodation leading to peace," Brigham Anderson went on.

"I don't want her to abandon her principles, Senator," the nominee said. "I simply want her to apply them with more discretion."

"And you believe that by applying them 'with more discretion,' peace can be achieved," Senator Anderson said.

"I think it may be greatly advanced," Bob Leffingwell said.

"And you do not wish the United States to remember past betrayals and past refusals to co-operate and past bad faith, but to erase all that from her national memory and go forward in the hope that this time the Russians are at last prepared to deal with us honestly and in good faith?"

"I believe nothing is to be gained by rehearsing past grievances," the nominee said. "I believe there is hope in tomorrow."

"Yes," Brigham Anderson said. "And you do not care to state the terms on which you would negotiate for that tomorrow, because you believe they would have to be dictated by circumstances existing at the time of negotiation."

"Yes, sir," said Bob Leffingwell.

"And therefore you feel you have no choice but to keep this subcommittee and the country in the dark as to what your real intentions are in this matter so desperately vital to America," the chairman concluded. Bob Leffingwell gave him again that quick, sharp glance and smiled.

"Well, now, Senator," he said, "that is an oversimplification that perhaps does not do me justice."

"I'm sorry," Senator Anderson said. "If there is anything I want to do you, it is justice, Mr. Leffingwell. And I intend to. Let us say, then, that you deem it the better part of discretion in your approach to the office to which you aspire and have been appointed, not to tell your countrymen what you have in mind for their future?"

"If that is as fairly as you can state it, Mr. Chairman," the nominee said, "I suppose I must agree."

"I am simply reflecting the record, Mr. Leffingwell," Brigham Anderson said.

"I thought I had been clearer than that," Bob Leffingwell said.

"Again that is a matter of individual judgment," Senator Anderson said pleasantly. "I trust my own is clear."

"I think so, Senator," Bob Leffingwell said, his smile a little less comfortably confident than it had been.

"Good," Senator Anderson said. "I wouldn't want anyone to be in doubt on that, any more than I would want to deliberately misstate you. And if there is one thing to which you are passionately and completely and loyally devoted, it is the United States of America, is that right?"

"Yes, sir," the nominee said firmly.

"A devotion that you will find reflected, I think, in the Senate of the United States, which must pass upon your nomination, and whose members will as earnestly arrive at their own conclusion as how best to express it as you have arrived at yours," the chairman said quietly. "We can only pray, as our friends in England put it in their trials of state, that God may send us all a safe deliverance."

"I do so pray, Senator," Bob Leffingwell said soberly.

"The subcommittee will stand in recess until ten o'clock tomorrow morning," Brigham Anderson said.

Working their way through the milling crowd, out the great oaken doors of the Caucus Room and down the long marble corridor, the senior Senator from Connecticut and the junior Senator from Wyoming said nothing for the first few steps. Then Fred Van Ackerman said explosively, "By God, I hope we can get this over and get him confirmed damned fast. It's mighty important to world peace. I think he's a really great man."

Stanley Danta laughed in his pleasantly noncommittal way.

"If we can just keep Seab from getting too rambunctious in the next couple of days," he said.

His companion snorted and suddenly gave Senator Danta an insight into a very shrewd mind at work.

"Hell, that old has-been," he said scornfully. "He's a historic monument, that boy. You know where your real trouble is coming from, if it comes, don't you?"

"Tell me," Senator Danta said.

"It's coming from Brig," Fred Van Ackerman said. "Well, thanks for your patience in Interior Committee, Stan. See you on the floor."

"Right," Stanley Danta said and went on, considerably more thoughtful than he had been a moment ago.

But later in the Senate it appeared that Senator Van Ackerman's dismissal of the senior Senator from South Carolina might be a trifle hasty, for in his usual fashion Seab managed to precipitate several angry exchanges on the subject of Bob Leffingwell before, during, and after the concluding debate on the Federal Reserve bill in which Murfee Andrews emerged triumphant in the final voting over Taylor Ryan and Julius Welch. By the introduction of a comment here, a question there, once even a short, sharp exchange of his own with Tom August and Lafe Smith, he managed to keep the pot boiling; and during the lulls in the debate conferred quietly on the floor and in the cloakrooms with some twenty-five of his colleagues, getting from at least seventeen of them considerable indications of support. And when the session ran late with unexpected trivia—Jack McLaughlin of Georgia felt he had to speak for an hour on price supports for peanuts, Marshall Seymour of Nebraska was mad at the Federal Trade Commission for another hour and a half, and Newell Albertson of West Virginia spoke for three hours more on the necessity for a shake-up in the Bureau of Mines—he went downstairs for one of the potluck dinners put together by the Senate Restaurant for night sessions and spent it at a table with John Winthrop and John De-Wilton encouraging those gentlemen in their suspicions of the nominee. So it was not wasted effort, he reflected as the bell rang for adjournment at ten twenty-three and the great light in the Capitol dome that always burns above the town for a night session went out; but it was not until he had returned to his apartment in the Sheraton-Park and was beginning to think about bed that he had any real idea at all of how he would proceed on the morrow. Then a trembling finger touched his doorbell and as had been the case in many a bitter battle over five violent decades, luck once again proved to be with him and it all came clear.

4

"Pidge," Brigham Anderson said firmly, contemplating the small, defiant five-year-old figure seated before him at the breakfast table, "I want you to eat your oatmeal."

"But I don't want to eat my oatmeal," his daughter pointed out in a tone of reasonable logic.

"But I want you to," her father said.

"Why?" she demanded.

"So you can grow up to be a big girl," the Senator explained patiently.

"Won't I anyway?" Pidge asked.

"Not so fast," her father said.

"I don't want to be a big girl fast," Pidge said.

"Ellen," her father said in a tone that usually produced results, "please eat your oatmeal for me."

"I'll eat it for me," Pidge said with a sunny smile and proceeded to do so for at least ten seconds before she stopped.

"Why don't we have something else for breakfast?" she asked.

"Because Mommy wants you to have oatmeal," Brigham Anderson said.

"Do you have oatmeal too?" his daughter inquired.

"You know I have oatmeal," the Senator said.

"Does Mommy want you to have oatmeal too?" Pidge asked.

"Yes," the Senator said.

"Why?" Pidge asked.

"Just because she does," Brigham Anderson said.

"So you'll grow up to be a big boy?" his daughter asked.

"Yes," the Senator said.

His daughter gave a derisive crow.

"You're a big boy *already*," she pointed out in a scornful tone.

"Come on, now," Brigham Anderson said. "That's enough chitchat. Suppose you go on and eat some more. Otherwise Daddy is going to be very annoyed with you."

"Will you spank me?" Pidge inquired with interest.

"I may," the Senator said.

"*Will* you?" she demanded.

"Do you want me to?" her father asked. Pidge looked thoughtful.

"Not exactly," she said.

"All right, then, eat up." her father suggested.

"I guess I will, a little," she agreed.

"A lot," the Senator said.

"A little *first!*" his daughter exclaimed indignantly.

"And then a lot after that?" her father asked.

"I'll see," Pidge said thoughtfully.

"So will I see," the Senator said. "I'm going to stay right here and watch you until you do."

"You have to go to work," Pidge observed.

"Not until you eat all your breakfast," Brig said.

"You'll be late," his daughter told him.

"They'll wait for me," the Senator said.

"You're important, aren't you?" Pidge asked, impressed, and in spite of his best intentions Brigham Anderson laughed.

"Not very," he said.

"You aren't *really* mad at me, are you, Daddy?" Pidge said in a tone of happy discovery.

"No," the Senator said, "but I could be if you don't finish your breakfast."

"I'll bet you wouldn't be even then," his daughter said.

"You'd better not try me too far," the Senator said. "I can be fierce."

"You wouldn't really spank me, would you, Daddy?" Pidge asked.

"I do sometimes, don't I?" Brigham Anderson asked.

"When I'm naughty," Pidge agreed.

"Aren't you being naughty now?" the Senator asked.

"No!" she exclaimed firmly.

"You aren't eating your oatmeal," her father pointed out.

"Yes, I am," she said, and took several mouthfuls before she stopped again.

"Why isn't Mommy up?" she asked.

"She didn't feel like it just yet," Brigham Anderson said. "She wanted to sleep a little more."

"Is she all right?" Pidge inquired seriously.

"Yes, she's fine," the Senator said. "She just wanted to sleep a little more, so she asked me to feed you."

"What shall I do when you go?" his daughter asked.

"Then it will be all right for you to go and wake Mommy up," the Senator said.

"Is she mad at you?" Pidge asked.

"Nope," he said cheerfully. "How about three more mouthfuls, and then it will all be gone."

"I hope it can be fixed," his daughter remarked as she took another spoonful.

"You know what you are?" her father asked. "You're a precocious child."

"What's cocious?" she asked.

"You," he said. "Two more mouthfuls now."

"I'll bet she isn't really mad at you," his daughter said comfortably.

"I said she wasn't," the Senator pointed out. "One more mouthful."

"Daddy," Pidge said thoughtfully.

"What?"

"I really love you," she said.

"Well, that's good," he said, giving her a hug. "I love you too."

"Good," she said, hopping down briskly. "I think I'll go wake Mommy now."

"Fine," Brigham Anderson said. "Pidge!" he said reproachfully as she reached the door. "You didn't finish this last mouthful after all."

"You can have it, Daddy," she said graciously.

"But I have my own," he protested.

"You need more," she called back as she started up the stairs. "You're bigger."

Half an hour later, having hastily grabbed a pile of bills and papers from his desk and sprinted to the car, he was driving slowly along Constitution Avenue toward the Hill in the morning rush when he spied a familiar figure trudging briskly in the bright blue, rapidly warming day. He pulled over to the curb, opened the door, and gave several cheerful toots on the horn. Mr. Justice Davis hopped in with alacrity.

"I know I'm interrupting a pleasant walk," Brigham Anderson said. "But have a ride."

"This is good of you, dear boy," Tommy Davis said. "It really feels like spring today and I was enjoying it, but your company is always a pleasure, particularly these days when you're so involved in important matters."

"I am, rather," the Senator agreed as he threaded his way back into the main stream of traffic and moved along past the White House on the left and the Washington Monument on the right. "I could wish I wasn't, but I seem to have been chosen."

"I noticed from the papers this morning," the Justice said with satisfaction, "that things seemed to go very well yesterday."

"Is that what the papers said?" Senator Anderson inquired. "I saw the *Post* gave it the full treatment, but I haven't seen any others."

"Well, actually," Tommy Davis said, "I've only seen the *Post* and the New York *Times* myself. The *Times* ran the text of Bob's remarks just like the *Post* did."

" 'I Believe,' " Senator Anderson said in a quizzical voice. "Yes, I saw the *Post* had gone to town on it."

"But it was such a natural, my boy," the Justice said. "So spontaneous and so moving."

"And so off the subject," Brigham Anderson observed as they came alongside the National Gallery. "Can I leave you at the Court?"

"No, go on to the Senate," Tommy Davis said. "I'll walk over to the Court from there and get one more little breath of spring before I go in. I don't see how it was off the subject at all. I thought it was directly on it. Surely his beliefs in America indicate his fitness for the office."

"Well, I wouldn't want someone who didn't believe in America, that's for sure," the Senator said.

"Do you anticipate much trouble on the confirmation?" the Justice asked and gave him an intent look. Brigham Anderson shrugged.

"Some," he said.

"But of course you're going to be for him," Tommy Davis suggested. The Senator smiled.

"Stop pumping me, Tommy," he said. "You know what the Constitution says: three equal and co-ordinate branches, each in its own little niche. Don't try to invade the Legislative, now."

"My dear boy," Justice Davis said amiably. "I wouldn't dream of it. But naturally I am interested, because I am so pleased with his nomination and consider it so important for the country that it be confirmed speedily and by a large vote. And of course your wholehearted assistance would greatly advance this."

"I don't know," Senator Anderson said thoughtfully. "I'm not very happy with the way it went yesterday, myself. Fine sentiments, but a deliberate avoidance of specifics."

"For reasons he made perfectly clear and reasonable," Mr. Justice Davis said.

"Yes," Brigham Anderson said. "Well, I don't know."

"Surely you won't oppose him!" Tommy Davis said in a tone approaching dismay. Brigham Anderson smiled.

"I don't know," he repeated.

"Oh, dear," Justice Davis said in an aggrieved voice. "Oh, dear. I can sense you've already made up your mind to."

"Not really," Brig said. "We'll see."

"This worries me," Justice Davis said frankly. "Your opposition would really mean something. I wish there were some way to change your mind."

"That's hard to do once it really gets made up," the Senator said. "But don't worry about it too much, Tommy. It isn't yet."

"But it's getting there," the Justice suggested. Brig smiled.

"We'll see," he said again. They had reached the Hill and he passed alongside the Old Office Building, then swung back into one of the circular drives leading to the Capitol, and parked. After they got out the Justice stood for a moment as if reluctant to let him go.

"Well, my dear boy," he said, "I do hope perhaps you will find reason to moderate your view in the next few days. We need you in the liberal cause."

"Someday I'll come over to your chambers," Senator Anderson offered jestingly as he tucked his papers casually under his arm, "and you can give me a seminar in what a liberal is. You're one of the certified specimens of the breed, and you ought to know."

"I'll be glad to," Tommy said. "I do hope this will work out all right."

"He's getting a fair hearing," Senator Anderson said. "You will concede me that."

"Admirable," Tommy Davis said with conviction. "Do think hard, dear boy."

"None harder," Brigham Anderson said.

"And thanks very much for the ride," the Justice added.

"My pleasure," Brigham Anderson said, shook hands, and walked off toward the office building. Justice Davis stood for several moments watching thoughtfully as his stocky, compact figure grew smaller in the distance; then with a sigh he started to turn away and head across the green lawn of the Capitol Plaza to the Court. As he did so his eye was caught by a small brown manila envelope lying on the ground near the car. He thought it might be the Senator's and started to call after him; then thought it might not be and decided to take it along. He had a curious nature, did Mr. Justice Davis, and he could always run it over later in the day if it turned out to be Brig's.

The Caucus Room was crowded again, Seab noted as he entered it shortly before ten, and it was the same kind of crowd: earnest, rather frowzy young housewives, their earnest, rather unkempt young husbands, many students, some teachers, some Foreign Service types; all of these, he perceived, having the same rather uneasy, rather defiant, almost desperately emotional look about them. These were Bob Leffingwell's applauders, the eager laughers, occasionally the surreptitious and bitter hissers. Opposed to them was a scattering of middle-aged women, equally earnest, equally belligerent; their settled and prosperous husbands; a few professional people who might be lawyers or doctors; here and there, in both camps, a few genuine, wild-eyed fanatic types who had long since passed the point of no return on Bob Leffingwell and all other matters. Through the crowd ran a leaven of bright-eyed, pink-cheeked, freshly-scrubbed young servicemen from some nearby base, looking awed and baffled and puzzled by it all. Aside from these, Seab could see, it was a gathering that wanted blood, and he thought with a rather grim satisfaction that he had some for it.

None of this appeared on his face, however, as he moved into the room and found himself inevitably facing a circle of questioning newsmen.

"Senator," the Washington *Post* said, "what can you tell us about your questioning today? Do you think you can finish in one day?"

"Well, sir," Seab said comfortably, "you all know how much I want to oblige the Washington *Post*. Yes, sir, you know for sure. So if the Washington *Post* wants me to finish in one day, I'll surely try real hard. There isn't anything I wouldn't do for the Washington *Post*. Of course," he added dryly, "some may depend on the witness, you know. He may want more time."

"I doubt if he does, Senator," the *Post* replied with a smile, and Seab smiled too.

"I expect," he said gently, "the Washington *Post* knows a lot more about what the witness wants than I do."

"What do you plan to go into, Senator?" the Baltimore *Sun* inquired. "Your old feud with Mr. Leffingwell?"

"No, sir," Seab said. "No, sir."

"You mean you aren't going to mention that famous episode at all, Senator?" the Newark *News* asked with a wink. Senator Cooley winked back and decided that if they really wanted him to confuse the issue, he would do so; it might serve to put everybody off balance a little.

"Well, sir," he said slowly. "I might, you know; I just might. Just a little bit. Just a little." At this they all laughed knowingly, and he went on, knowing they would consider the reality the cover-up and the cover-up the reality. "Of course," he said, "there might be more serious things involved. Seems to me the country is involved; seems to me the whole world, maybe."

"You aren't really interested in that, are you, Senator?" the Providence *Journal* asked knowingly, and Seab grinned with contempt in his heart.

"Why should I feud with anybody?" he asked innocently. "Besides, I never feuded with him. We just didn't see"—and he gave his sleepy grin—"eye to eye."

"What specific things do you intend to question him about, Senator?" AP asked. Seab smiled.

"Specific things?" he asked. "I didn't know anybody was supposed to be specific around here. Specific? Seems to me we're freed from being specific by the witness's example."

"I thought he was specific enough," the Baltimore *Sun* said challengingly. Senator Cooley nodded.

"Enough for you, maybe," he said. "Some others didn't seem so happy. No, I expect, gentlemen, I shall just question the witness on a few little things that need clearing up. You must admit there were a few—little—things?"

"I didn't think so, Senator," the Jacksonville *Times-Union* said.

"You didn't think so," Seab repeated. "Well, sir, I did. Yes, sir. I surely did. Including," he added, looking deliberately sly, "certain things he's said in the past."

"About you, Senator?" the Los Angeles *Times* asked.

Seab grinned.

"You'll just have to wait and see," he said. "And now if you all will excuse me, I'll just pass on to the committee table."

"Just pass on," he heard somebody murmur, and with a sudden broad smile he turned back to them.

"Not yet, gentlemen," he said softly. "Not yet a while." And he looked at them until he stared them down, and then went on to the committee table.

He saw at once that it was considerably more crowded than it had been yesterday. The full committee wasn't meeting this morning, and several of its members had decided to drop in. Tom August was already seated off to one side, next to Seab's own chair; Lafe Smith and Verne Cramer were chatting amicably with some of the television boys at one of the water coolers; and close at hand, in the row of chairs just behind the committee he saw the Majority Leader chatting with Dolly Harrison, Kitty Maudulayne, and Celestine Barre. With a gracious little bow as he caught Kitty's eye he moved up to them.

"Well, ladies," he said in the courtly manner he could assume very well, "I must say this is a happy sight for these old eyes. Yes, indeed it is. It is indeed."

"Morning, Seab," Bob Munson said. "I decided that what this hearing needed was a touch of beauty, so I brought them along."

"That isn't why he chose us," Dolly said with a smile as Senator Cooley took her hand and gave it a paternal squeeze, and then proceeded to do the same with Kitty, who returned it warmly, and Celestine, who gave his hand a gentle pressure and smiled.

"Ma'am," Seab said with a little twinkle, "if he had searched the realms of Ind and Araby, he couldn't have made a better choice. No, ma'am."

"Ind and Araby, eh?" Bob Munson said with a chuckle. "What were you doing last night, reading Coleridge?"

Seab smiled.

"Oh, no," he said. "Not that, Bob; I was rather far from Coleridge last night, Bob. As," he added slowly, "you may get a chance to see."

"Oh, good!" Kitty exclaimed. "I was hoping you'd furnish us with something dramatic, Senator Cooley."

"What have you got up your sleeve, Seabright?" the Majority Leader asked in a tone in which banter could not quite conceal a rising concern; there was about the senior Senator from South Carolina a certain satisfied air that aroused a warning instinct in his colleague.

"Nothing much, Bob," Senator Cooley said amiably. "Nothing much at all. Ladies, I am mighty honored you're here. I hope you will find it most interesting. At least," he said, looking at the Majority Leader with heavy-lidded good fellowship, "I shall surely try to make it so. Yes, ladies, I shall surely try to make it so."

"We know we can count on you, Senator," Dolly said, and Lady Maudulayne said, "Oh my, yes!" Celestine Barre just smiled, and it was to her that Senator Cooley gave his final little bow as he turned away and went on to take his seat.

At the door the chairman and Arly Richardson came in together, followed closely by Orrin Knox, John Winthrop, and John DeWilton, and around them the press attempted to form its intercepting cordon. The subcommittee, however, did not seem to be in a mood for casual talk this morning, and its members came forward quickly to take their places. In the flurry of their entry Bob Leffingwell, who had entered just behind them, managed to reach the witness chair without being waylaid, waved to the press tables, lit a cigarette, and settled back patiently, looking refreshed and ready. Just as Senator Anderson gaveled for order Fred Van Ackerman came in quickly and sought a seat in back of the committee; a clerk sitting next to Dolly rose hastily and offered his chair and the junior Senator from Wyoming took it with a cursory nod.

"The subcommittee will be in order," Brigham Anderson said. "Under our arrangement with the distinguished Senator from South Carolina, he is now free to question the witness if he so—"

"Mr. Chairman," Bob Leffingwell said in a pleasantly firm voice. "Mr. Chairman."

"Does the witness wish to say something?" Senator Anderson asked, and the nominee leaned forward in his grave, judicious way.

"Yes, Mr. Chairman," he said slowly, "I do. I wish to say, Mr. Chairman, that while you and some other members of the subcommittee conducted themselves with decency and courtesy yesterday, I did feel that there were moments when I was not being fairly treated, and when it seemed to me that the approach of the subcommittee typified and symbolized the reasons why it is sometimes so difficult to get people of a certain character and education to enter government service. I am used to it, Mr. Chairman, but the example must be inhibiting to others whose services might be available to our country when she needs them, others who must be repelled and discouraged by procedures such as this."

"Attaboy, Bob," the Boston *Globe* whispered delightedly, "you tell 'em!" "I wondered when he was going to start fighting back," the Chicago *Sun-Times* said with satisfaction.

"This attitude," Bob Leffingwell went on, "which I think might fairly be characterized as anti-intellectualism, is, as I say, no surprise to one who has been its target on many occasions. But I wonder how it must seem to others."

There was a stirring in the subcommittee, but its members waited for the chairman to reply, and after a moment he did.

"If those are genuinely your views, Mr. Leffingwell," he said, "you are of course privileged to express them. I think, however," he went on, a slight frown on his earnest young face, "that you will be badly underestimating the Senate of the United States, and perhaps seriously overestimating the efficacy of your appeals to prejudice such as this, if you fail to understand the spirit in which many of the questions yesterday were asked. There *are* times, Mr. Leffingwell," he said dryly, "when Senators of the United States actually *are* concerned about their country; there *are* times when we actually do wish to find out the truth of things because it seems honestly important to the country's welfare. Anti-intellectualism is a good whipping-boy, and to tell the truth, Mr. Leffingwell, having been familiar with your tactics before Congressional committees in the past, I am somewhat surprised that you waited this long to resort to it. Having done so, I can only tell you it doesn't apply here. To put it on its most elemental level, the Senator from Illinois, the Senator from Arkansas, the Senator from South Carolina, and myself, Mr. Leffingwell, are all members of Phi Beta Kappa——"

"Johnny DeWilton and I are the only dumb bunnies in this crowd"—Senator Winthrop interjected suddenly with a chuckle that achieved its purpose, for the chairman laughed and relaxed and went on in a less didactic voice—"and we even read books," he said. "In other words, Mr. Leffingwell, nobody is anti-intellectual here. You have been appointed to a most important office, in which your views are of vital importance to your country; this is the forum where you must be judged for confirmation to that office, and you must concede us some right to try to find out what you think—and to be a little concerned when you seem to be deliberately withholding it from us."

The nominee, who had waited without expression until he finished, spoke in a cold voice.

"Nonetheless, Mr. Chairman," he said, "it seems to me that there is a deliberate conspiracy here to attack me for no other reason, really, than that I represent a segment of the population which seems to be generally unpopular on Capitol Hill."

"Mr. Leffingwell," Brigham Anderson said, "you're too shrewd a politician and too intelligent a man to make a phony charge like that. Why are you doing it? It isn't in character."

"It is my sincere conviction, Mr. Chairman," the nominee said, and because he was indeed too intelligent and too shrewd a politician, and because it really wasn't in character, Senator Anderson was suddenly aware that for some reason Bob Leffingwell felt that his back was to the wall and so was deliberately going on the offensive.

He gave no indication of this sudden instinctive knowledge, however, but only replied in a tone as cold as the nominee's own.

"Let me help you with your headline, Mr. Leffingwell," he said. "You are charging, I take it, that this subcommittee is attacking you as an intellectual and for no other reason, is that it?"

"I am," Bob Leffingwell said evenly.

"Leffingwell Charges Senate Out To Get Eggheads," Senator Anderson said dryly. "Very well, Senator Cooley, your witness."

"I don't see why Brig has to be so damned hostile to us," the *Post* whispered. "It isn't as though we've done anything to him." "Yet," the *Times* observed. "Anyway, boys," the *Herald Tribune* remarked, "the gloves are off and it's going to be blood from here on in." "Seab will be in his element, then," the Philadelphia *Inquirer* said. "Look at him," the Washington *Star* said. "This is going to be a major performance."

Down at his end of the table, where he had been sitting impassively after a brief greeting to Tom August, who as usual looked fretful and concerned about life, the senior Senator from South Carolina was deliberately putting some papers in order before him, deliberately lining up a pad of paper, some pencils, a glass of water. All this done, he looked slowly around the room until his eyes finally, in their apparently aimless wanderings, came to rest on those of the nominee, sitting patiently in his chair and watching the proceeding with a skeptical and amused expression he made no attempt to disguise. When their eyes met, Seab spoke in an amiable tone.

"You seem amused, Mr. Witness," he observed, "I'm glad you find something amusing. I thought a minute ago you were just a mite peeved with us. I'm glad you're feeling better now . . . Now, Mr. Witness," he said as Bob Leffingwell made no comment, but kept staring at him with the same quizzical expression, "tell us again about your teaching career. I find that mighty interesting, Mr. Witness."

"What do you want to know about it, Senator?" Bob Leffingwell asked with a casual air that indicated he was quite prepared for this line of questioning.

"You said it was administrative government you taught?" Seab asked.

"I didn't say, Senator," the nominee said, "but it was."

"Well, it was in your biography, then," Senator Cooley said. "What did that consist of, Mr. Witness?"

"Exactly what the biography said, Senator," Bob Leffingwell replied. "The forms of administrative government, the techniques of it, plus what I believed to be the best form and philosophy of it."

"Which you have demonstrated in the chairmanship of the Federal Power Commission and the ODM, is that right?"

"I have tried to," the nominee replied.

"Where did you live, Mr. Witness?" Seab asked, and Bob Leffingwell smiled.

"In Chicago." he said. "In a modest but pleasantly intellectual haunt near the university."

"Yes," Seab said. "What street?" Bob Leffingwell paused.

"Let me see, Senator," he said. "Fourteen years ago . . . Madison, I think."

"Were you married then, Mr. Witness?" Senator Cooley asked.

"No, I was not," Bob Leffingwell said.

"Madison Street," the Senator said. "What number on Madison Street?" The nominee frowned and thought.

"As I recall, 2726," he said, "but I may be off a few digits."

"It couldn't have been 2731, could it?" Seab asked, and the nominee shook his head firmly.

"No, Senator," he said. "I remember quite distinctly now I get to thinking about it, 2726."

"What's going on here?" the *Times* asked. "He's uncovered a Plot," the *Post-Dispatch* said with a grin.

"The address was 2726 Madison," Senator Cooley said thoughtfully. "It just couldn't have been 2731."

"No, sir," Bob Leffingwell said.

"No, sir," Seab said. "And what was your philosophy of administrative government, Mr. Witness?"

Bob Leffingwell laughed.

"Well, Senator," he said, "you don't want the course and I don't propose to give it here. In general, it can be gathered from the way I've conducted myself in Washington."

"On the liberal side," Seab suggested.

"I certainly hope so," the nominee replied, and there was a quick smattering of applause from the audience.

"All right," Brigham Anderson said. "Let's get on."

"It wasn't 2731 Carpenter, was it?" Seab asked, and the nominee looked annoyed.

"Senator," he said, "I don't know the purpose of these attempts at entrapment, but they don't appeal to me, I must say. Ask what you want to ask and I'll answer."

"Oh, now, Mr. Chairman," Seab said in a reproachful voice. "The witness seems to be getting impatient, Mr. Chairman. He seems to feel some pressure. Mr. Chairman, I wonder why."

"I'm not impatient and I'm not feeling pressure," Bob Leffingwell said, rather more loudly than he had intended. "But I don't intend to play cat and mouse games with the Senator from South Carolina."

At this the applause swelled up in a real burst, and Senator Anderson rapped sharply for order. When it came Seab looked his blandest and went on with a little shrug.

"Seems to me," he observed, "the witness is getting mighty upset about an address, Mr. Chairman. But he says he didn't live there, so I'll go on."

"These questions have some purpose pertinent to the inquiry, I assume, Senator," Brigham Anderson said, and Seab smiled.

"Oh, yes," he said. "Oh, yes."

"I'll bet they do," Bob Munson whispered to Lafe Smith, and Lafe grinned. "You'd better hope they don't, Bobby," he replied, and the Majority Leader nodded soberly. Behind him Dolly just then was startled to note that Senator Van Ackerman, who had been listening intently without a word, had suddenly risen with a certain catlike quiet and was now leaving the room.

"Mr. Witness," Seab said softly, "what did you do on Thursday nights?"

"Thursday nights?" Bob Leffingwell said with some amusement. He turned around and searched the front row of the audience until he found his wife, then turned back with a grin.

"Thursday nights were mostly occupied," he said, "in courting the young lady who eventually succumbed to my importunings and became Mrs. Leffingwell." There was a friendly laugh and applause from the audience. "Thursday nights and most other nights," Bob Leffingwell went on; and then he added smoothly, "If you know how it is, Senator."

Seab smiled in a sleepy way.

"Oh, yes," he said amicably. "I know how it is. Or rather, I used to know how it was, back before you were born, I expect. And that's all you did on Thursday nights?"

"Oh, occasionally a faculty meeting or some campus activity," Bob Leffingwell said. "But in the main, that was it."

"Who was Walker?" Seab asked abruptly, and for just a split second there was a slight hesitation in the nominee's manner. But he smiled and shrugged.

"Walker?" he said. "Walker who?"

"All I know is Walker," Seab told him.

"I had a cousin named Walker," Bob Leffingwell said thoughtfully, "who is dead now. I had a friend named Bill Walker, and there was a head of department before my time whose name was Sherman Walker. Other than that, I'm plumb out of Walkers, Senator."

"Who was James Morton?" Senator Cooley asked, and this time there was no hesitation at all.

"Who were Bill Jones and Bobby Smith and Susie Stone?" Bob Leffingwell asked. "I don't know. I don't know who James Morton was, either. That name I really don't recognize in any connection at all, Senator. By the way," he added in a suddenly icy voice, "just who was James Morton, and who was Walker, if you know, Senator?"

"Oh, Mr. Witness," Seab said slowly. "You're not asking the questions here. I'm asking the questions here."

"I hope to some point, Senator," John Winthrop said suddenly, and Seab turned upon him a slow and appraising glance.

"I thought you Yankees were patient people," he said with a smile. "Just listen. Maybe you will find out something."

"I hope so," Senator Winthrop said. "I haven't yet, except things the witness doesn't know."

"Says he doesn't know," Seab amended softly, and Bob Leffingwell leaned forward angrily.

"What are you trying to build up here, Senator?" he asked, "another of your little hate-feuds with me, or what?"

"That does it," the *Post* whispered gleefully. "Now listen to the old bastard." But Seab knew a better trick than that.

"Oh, Mr. Chairman," he said pleasantly, "is the witness still worried about that? Is he still worried because we once had differences? I assure him, Mr. Chairman, I've forgotten all about it. If I ever said anything to hurt him or bother him, Mr. Chairman, I apologize now. It's out of my mind, Mr. Chairman, it surely is."

"That's very handsome, Senator," Bob Leffingwell said coldly, "and I'll believe it when I see it."

"Are you implying I'm not telling you the truth, Mr. Witness?" Seab asked in a suddenly louder tone, and the *Herald Tribune* murmured, "Oh, oh, here we go."

Bob Leffingwell gave his interrogator a long look and spoke with deliberation.

"I am," he said, and everybody tensed with eager delight for the explosion to follow. But much to everybody's bafflement it did not. Instead Seab smiled sleepily and gave a little dismissing wave of his hand.

"The witness is still suspicious of me, Mr. Chairman," he said regretfully. "A most un-Christian attitude, which I shall not attempt to answer, Mr. Chairman. Time will show him the error of his ways, and right thinking will bring him to an ending of his bitter passions toward me, Mr. Chairman." Then he leaned forward suddenly.

"What does 'They'll understand in Dubuque' mean, Mr. Witness?"

Bob Leffingwell looked puzzled and then spread his hands before him in their candid, open gesture, and addressed himself directly to the Chair.

"Mr. Chairman," he said in an amused tone, "what sort of nonsense is this?"

"I don't know, I'm sure," Brigham Anderson said. "It hasn't been proved that it's nonsense, yet."

" 'They'll understand in Dubuque,' " Bob Leffingwell said and shook his head in a baffled way. "Well, I hope, Mr. Chairman, they'll understand *this* that's going on here today, in Dubuque."

"Maybe," the chairman said. "Senator Cooley, do you have any further questions of the witness?"

Seab looked long and thoughtfully at the nominee, who looked right back without a quiver. Then he turned half away in a slow, deliberate manner and half over his shoulder said, "No, sir, Mr. Chairman, I do not."

"Well," Verne Cramer murmured to Tom August, "there's a surprise." "A good omen, I trust," Senator August said hopefully.

"Then if there are no more questions," Brigham Anderson began in a businesslike way, "I think we can consider these hearings cl——"

"Mr. Chairman," Senator Cooley said softly, turning back. "Mr. Chairman."

The room suddenly became still, and the wire-service reporters who were preparing to run downstairs with their bulletins on the end of the hearings stopped and slowly sat down again.

"Mr. Chairman," Seab said slowly, "I have a witness of my own I should like to call if I may, Mr. Chairman."

"Very well, Senator," Brigham Anderson said impersonally. "That is your privilege and the subcommittee is ready to hear him."

"You don't suppose——" the *Herald Tribune* whispered excitedly with a look of wild surmise as on a peak in Darien.

"I'll bet it is," the *Times* said hurriedly.

"It couldn't be," the *Post-Dispatch* exclaimed.

"I'll bet it is," the *Times* repeated.

And so it was.

"Mr. Herbert Gelman, please," Senator Cooley said slowly. "Mr. Herbert Gelman, if you will come forward, please."

The room exploded into sound, the audience talking excitedly, the photographers rushing forward to get their pictures of the little man who was coming up from the rear of the room, the press standing at its tables to get a better view.

"God damn," Lafe Smith said to Bob Munson, "that tears it." The Majority Leader had time only to nod, for he was watching the nominee with great intentness.

So, for that matter, were a number of other people, including the entire subcommittee, Dolly Harrison and her guests, and a good many of the press. What they saw was a picture of calm puzzlement as the nominee swung around, as anyone would, with a baffled expression on his face and watched the small, nervous figure of the next witness approaching. Bob Leffingwell did not look annoyed, as well he might in the presence of someone who had already, in his telegram to Senator Richardson, attempted to destroy his character; instead he looked as steady and reasonable and interested and attentive as though it didn't really concern him at all. It was a look that made a very favorable impression on all but a very few who thought a trace of dislike might be a more human reaction.

"Mr. Leffingwell," Senator Anderson said above the wild turmoil of the cameramen, pushing and shoving in their attempts to photograph the new witness, "if you will just move your chair over and let the witness bring a chair up beside you, we can proceed."

"Very well, Mr. Chairman," Bob Leffingwell said indifferently, complying with the request and then lighting a cigarette with a steady hand.

The man whom Seab had thus materialized out of Arly Richardson's mysterious telegram and his fruitless check with the president of the University of Chicago was about five feet six, dark, stocky, perhaps forty years old; thinning hair, a neat gray suit, eyeglasses; an obvious intelligence, a diffident manner, the appearance of one who had spent much time in libraries. Observing these standard components, Verne Cramer could not resist nudging Tom August, and murmuring, "Well, well. An egghead." But Tom looked too worried to reply.

"Be sworn," Senator Anderson directed, rising to administer the oath. "Do you solemnly swear the testimony you are about to give this subcommittee is the truth, the whole truth, and nothing but the truth, so help you God?"

"I do," the witness said in a low voice with an obvious quaver.

"Give your name and address to the official reporter," the chairman said.

"Herbert Gelman, 2021 Grove Place Northeast, Washington, D.C.," the witness said almost inaudibly.

"Speak a little louder, Mr. Gelman," Brigham Anderson said, not unkindly. "We all want to hear you. What is your occupation?"

"I work for the Commerce Department," the witness said.

"In what capacity?" the chairman asked.

"I'm an analyst in the Bureau of International Economic Affairs," Herbert Gelman said.

"Do you have a family here?" the chairman went on.

"Yes, sir," the witness said. "Wife and two children."

"How long have you been employed by the government?" Senator Anderson asked.

"For the past ten years," the witness said.

"Always in Commerce?"

"No, sir," the witness said, and hesitated.

"Where else?" Brigham Anderson asked.

"The Federal Power Commission," Herbert Gelman said, and somebody at the press tables drew in his breath in a sound of explosive tension.

"In what capacity?" the chairman inquired.

"Until two years ago I was employed in an agency connected with the office of the chairman," the witness said, looking with an almost desperate intensity at Brigham Anderson.

"How closely connected?" Senator Anderson asked.

"A subsidiary agency," Herbert Gelman said.

"How subsidiary?" the chairman insisted.

"I wasn't directly in the chairman's office, if that's what you mean," Herbert Gelman said. Senator Anderson looked a little impatient.

"I don't mean anything," he said. "I'm just trying to find out what you mean. Did you know the chairman?"

"Yes," Herbert Gelman said.

"Intimately?"

The witness hesitated.

"No," he said finally.

"By sight," Senator Anderson suggested. The witness nodded.

"You'll have to answer verbally, Mr. Gelman," the Senator said. "The official reporter doesn't record nods. You knew him by sight."

"Yes, sir," Herbert Gelman said.

"Did he know you by sight?"

"Yes, sir," the witness said.

"By name?" Senator Anderson asked.

For the first time the witness turned his head and looked quickly at the nominee, seated patient, composed, and gravely interested at his side.

"Yes, sir," he said in a low voice.

"Under what circumstances did you leave the Federal Power Commission?" Senator Anderson asked.

Again the witness hesitated and the chairman went on.

"Unfriendly, were they?"

"Yes, sir," the witness said in a low voice. "I was accused of doing something dishonest."

"And had you?" Brigham Anderson asked.

"No, sir," the witness said.

"But the chairman, I take it, thought you had."

"Yes, sir."

"And you resented his action?" Brig said.

"Yes, sir," the witness said. "I thought he just wanted to get rid of me."

"Why?"

"Because of things I knew."

"Of the nature expressed in your telegram to Senator Richardson?" Senator Anderson asked.

"Yes, sir," the witness said.

"How did you get your new government employment after being discharged from another agency under those circumstances?" Senator Anderson asked.

"I believe the chairman arranged it for me," the witness said.

"Very well, Senator Cooley," Brigham Anderson said, "your witness."

"Mr. Chairman," Bob Leffingwell said quietly, "I assume I will have the opportunity to cross-examine this witness after direct examination is finished?"

"You certainly will," Brigham Anderson said. "Proceed, Senator Cooley."

"Good Christ, what do you make of *that?*" UPI demanded as the wire services went hurtling downstairs to file their bulletins. "Old story," AP said. "Discharged employee with a grudge." "Hope Bob can prove that," UPI said. "He will," AP said confidently. "I could see him sharpening those knives already."

"Mr. Gelman," Seab said, "I would like to establish first the circumstances under which you appear here today, sir. Your original intention was not to appear at all, is that right?"

"I didn't think I would, no, sir," the witness said.

"But you must have expected that after your telegram to Senator Richardson some attempt would be made to find you," Seab suggested.

"I guess so," Herbert Gelman said.

"So you really wanted to appear," Senator Cooley said.

The witness gave a small, rather shy smile.

"I did and I didn't," he said.

"Well, sir," Seab told him, "I think you really did. Yes, sir, I think so.

Because after you read the news reports relating that Senator Richardson had tried to find you and failed, you put in motion events designed to bring you here, didn't you?"

"Yes, sir," the witness said.

"What were they?" Senator Cooley asked.

"I came to your apartment at eleven o'clock last night." Herbert Gelman said.

"Entirely without any initiative on my part?" Seab asked.

"Yes, sir."

"Like others here, I didn't even know up to that moment that you existed, is that right?" Seab asked.

"Yes, sir," Herbert Gelman said.

"In fact you had to show me your driving license and your social security card to prove it," Seab said.

"Yes, sir," Herbert Gelman said with a little smile.

"And you told me your entire story and volunteered to appear here as my witness today?"

"Yes, sir."

"How did you come to pick me, Mr. Gelman?" Senator Cooley asked.

"You had the reputation of not liking Mr. Leffingwell," Herbert Gelman said, and the nominee himself led the laughter that momentarily broke the tension in the room.

"Yes, sir," Seab agreed with a little twinkle. "I have had that reputation, sure enough. So that was how it came about that I got to know you and you are here today. And why did you feel you must tell your story to this Senate, Mr. Gelman?"

"Because I don't think he should be Secretary of State," the witness said, shooting another quick glance at the nominee, who ignored it.

"Why not?" Seab asked. "Just because you think he discharged you unfairly from his agency and you want to get revenge on him, is that it, Mr. Gelman?"

"No, sir," the witness said with a sudden surprising show of indignation. "I don't think any man should be Secretary of State who is like Mr. Leffingwell."

Seab Cooley paused for a moment while along the committee table his colleagues leaned forward intently and silence held the room.

"What is Mr. Leffingwell like, Mr. Gelman?" he asked softly.

"I don't believe he is a loyal citizen of the United States," Herbert Gelman said.

"And you are, Mr. Gelman?" Seab asked bluntly.

"Yes, sir," the witness replied.

"How do we know that, sir?" Senator Cooley asked. "Just on your own say-so, is that how? Just because you say so?"

"I guess it comes down to that," the witness said quietly.

"Some of us, you know," Seab said, "may want more proof than that, Mr. Gelman."

"Ask me about what I told you," the witness suggested, "and maybe that will convince some people."

"Yes, sir," Senator Cooley said. "I just wanted you to know that it isn't always easy to convince people when it's a matter of matching your word against another man's, particularly a man so popular and with so many friends in Washington and in the press as Mr. Leffingwell has. I've tried to match my word against his sometimes, myself," he added with an amiable grin that again brought tension-lifting laughter to the room, "and I know."

"It's been about a draw, Senator," the nominee offered with a smile, and Seab smiled back.

"About," he said. "Where did you go to college, Mr. Gelman?"

"The University of Chicago," the witness said.

"Did you take any courses from Mr. Leffingwell?"

"I did."

"How many?"

"His administrative government course," Herbert Gelman said, "and the following year a seminar for graduate students."

"How many were in the seminar?" Senator Cooley asked.

"Ten," the witness said.

"Oh," Seab said with an air of sardonic surprise. "I thought there might have been three hundred. Did you get to know Mr. Leffingwell on a friendly basis in the seminar?"

"I did."

"Had he asked you, in fact, to take the seminar?"

"Yes, he did," Herbert Gelman said. "I had been one of his top students in the administrative government class the year before."

"You know Mr. Leffingwell says he doesn't know you and has never even heard of you," Senator Cooley said.

"He is lying," Herbert Gelman said quietly, and there was a startled gasp in the room.

"In fact, he knew you so well that he gave you top marks in one class and invited you to take another with him," Seab said.

"Yes, sir."

"What happened then?"

"He invited me to his rooming house on several occasions after the seminar, which was held in the evenings," the witness said. "We talked about government and politics mostly."

"What night of the week?" Seab asked.

"Thursday," Herbert Gelman said. Bob Leffingwell looked surprised and once again turned around to catch his wife's eye, grinned, and waved. She waved back, and a little comfortable stir of friendliness flickered through the audience.

"What happened then?" Seab asked.

"On the third occasion he suggested that he knew an informal group that liked to get together and chew the fat on these things and he wanted to know if I would like to go with him. He said it met at ten o'clock on Thursday nights after the seminar. I said yes, so we went."

"What was the address of his rooming house?" Senator Cooley asked.

"It was 2726 Madison Street," the witness said promptly.

"And where was the meeting held?"

"At 2731 Carpenter," Herbert Gelman said.

"Jesus," the *Herald Tribune* whispered. "This looks bad." "It's only the opening round," the *Post* assured him calmly. "Wait awhile."

"What was the meeting?" Senator Cooley asked.

"It was a campus Communist cell," the witness said quietly.

"You realize, Mr. Gelman," Brigham Anderson remarked, "that you may be jeopardizing your government employment with these statements."

"They're the truth," the witness said stubbornly. "I'd be jeopardizing it if I committed perjury too, wouldn't I?"

"You would," Senator Anderson said.

"All right," Herbert Gelman said.

"And the nominee, Mr. Leffingwell, nominated for this great office of Secretary of State, attended these Communist cell meetings with you," Seab resumed.

"He did," the witness said.

"Was he an active participant?"

"He was," Herbert Gelman said.

"What was his party name, so-called?" Senator Cooley asked.

"Walker," the witness said, and there was again a gasp from the audience.

"Was there anyone else of particular prominence in the cell?" Seab asked. The witness paused thoughtfully.

"I only saw him four or five times," he said. "He was wearing a beard then, so I probably wouldn't know him if I saw him now. His name was James Morton. I don't know what became of him."

"What was your password at these meetings, Mr. Gelman?" Senator Cooley asked.

" 'They'll understand in Dubuque,' " Herbert Gelman said.

"How did you arrive at that?"

"That came about," the witness explained, "because we had a saying sort of based on that old saying about *The New Yorker* magazine—you know, that it wasn't for the old lady in Dubuque. Our saying was that when the revolution came it would be sufficiently drastic so they'd even understand it in Dubuque. In time this got shortened to just, 'They'll understand in Dubuque.' I know it sounds kind of corny."

"Just corny enough," Seab told him softly, "so that it just might be true,

Mr. Gelman. And you actually said," he added in a disbelieving tone, "'when the revolution comes?'"

"I suppose that sounds silly now too," the witness said with an apologetic smile, "but we did. We meant it too, in those days."

"And those days," Seab said, "were after World War II when the Communist conspiracy against the free world was apparent to all thinking men."

"They were," Herbert Gelman said.

"Is there anything you wish to add, Mr. Gelman?" Seab asked.

"No, sir," Herbert Gelman said.

"You are aware of your oath to tell the truth," the Senator said.

"I am," the witness said.

"And you have told the truth in every particular?"

"In every particular," the witness replied.

"No further questions, Mr. Chairman," Seab said. "I release the witness to the subcommittee if you care to question him."

"Yes, Mr. Chairman," Arly Richardson said quickly. "I would like to interrogate a little."

"Go ahead, Senator," the chairman said.

"You sent me the telegram that I read into the record yesterday," Arly said.

"I did," Herbert Gelman said.

"Why didn't you come to me in person?" Arly demanded.

"He's just jealous," the Chicago *Daily News* whispered. "Wants to be in the act," the Des Moines *Register* agreed.

"Well, I——"

"Why didn't you come to me in person?" Senator Richardson repeated.

"I was reluctant, Senator," the witness said. "I wasn't really sure I wanted to do this, but I thought if you traced me through the university and found me, then I would have to."

"And this would have solved some moral problem in your own mind, Mr. Gelman," Arly said.

"I felt it would, yes, sir," the witness replied.

"What was that problem?" Senator Richardson asked.

"I didn't want to testify against a man who had been my friend," Herbert Gelman said in a low voice.

"Yet you called yourself deliberately to the attention of this subcommittee, so that you would sooner or later have to testify, isn't that right?"

"Yes, sir."

"That strikes me as a rather peculiar procedure, Mr. Gelman," Senator Richardson said.

"It might be for a strong man," Herbert Gelman said with his apologetic little smile, "but I'm afraid I'm not very strong, Senator."

"You appear to me to be quite strong enough to have done Mr. Leffingwell considerable damage here today," Arly Richardson said dryly. "And when you learned the university said it had no record, you decided then to go to the Senator from South Carolina. You realize, of course, Mr. Gelman, that you are making extraordinarily serious charges against a man who has filled public office under this government for thirteen years with generally high regard and respect from the country, don't you?"

"I do, sir," the witness replied.

"And you know he has been appointed to an office involving the most profound trust and honor, in which he will have the fate of this country in his hands in many international dealings?"

"That's why I'm here, sir," Herbert Gelman said quietly.

"*Why* are you here, Mr. Gelman?" Arly asked.

"For what I've done," the witness replied.

"And what was that?" Arly asked. "Did you start any riots? Did you touch off any bombs? Did you kill anybody for the cause?"

"No, sir," Herbert Gelman said.

"How many of you were there in this so-called cell?" Senator Richardson asked.

"Four," the witness said, and there was a skeptical titter from somewhere in the audience. "Mr. Leffingwell, myself, one other who is dead, and James Morton."

"That's not a very big group to overturn the government," Arly suggested.

"No, sir," Herbert Gelman said.

"And you didn't plot anything?"

"Not to my knowledge, no, sir," the witness said.

"In short, you just talked, didn't you?" Senator Richardson said.

"Yes, sir," the witness said.

"And that's all you did. A few ineffectual meetings fourteen years ago. Is that all?"

"I've felt badly about it, Senator," the witness said with a certain stubborn quietness.

"And you aren't just out to get Mr. Leffingwell because he got you fired from the FPC?" Orrin Knox asked.

"No, sir," Herbert Gelman said.

"You've forgiven him for that," Orrin said dryly. The witness smiled his little half smile.

"No, sir," he said.

"But revenge isn't a sufficient motive in your mind to warrant such grave charges as these?" Senator Knox inquired.

"No, sir."

"How do we know you're not crazy?" Senator DeWilton demanded suddenly from his end of the table, and the witness smiled again.

"Do I seem crazy?" he asked quietly.

"You're telling a crazy story," Johnny DeWilton said.

"Do I sound crazy?" Herbert Gelman asked.

"I don't know," Johnny DeWilton confessed. "I can't tell."

"I don't think you're telling us all you know, Mr. Gelman," Senator Winthrop said, and again the witness smiled.

"Maybe Mr. Leffingwell can bring it out when he questions me," he suggested.

"Are there any further questions by the subcommittee?" Senator Anderson asked. "If not, I think we will let Mr. Leffingwell cross-examine."

"Mr. Chairman," the nominee said quietly, "perhaps Senator DeWilton is in doubt, but I am not. This man is obviously insane, and while I certainly do intend to cross-examine, I would like to ask that it go over until tomorrow, when I shall have been able to gather together certain material I wish to use as a basis for questioning."

"You realize, of course, Mr. Leffingwell," Senator Anderson said, "that if you let his testimony stand overnight without challenge the press perforce will have to carry it without your rebuttal for nearly twenty-four hours before your side can be told."

"I realize, Mr. Chairman," the nominee said quietly, "but I am going to throw myself on the mercy and the sense of fair play of my countrymen and trust that they will withhold judgment until I have had a chance to develop my defense."

"The subcommittee is perfectly willing to have you cross-examine now," the chairman repeated, "or have you make any preliminary statement you care to make."

"I prefer to wait, Senator," Bob Leffingwell said.

"Very well," Brig said, "the subcommittee stands in recess until ten o'clock tomorrow morning."

The room exploded into an excited babble of sound as the audience began to leave and Herbert Gelman, looking neither to right nor left, darted hastily out like some small secretive animal while the nominee watched him go with an expression of half amusement, half contempt in his eyes.

"Well," Brigham Anderson said as Dolly and her guests came forward to the table, "some show, eh, Robert?"

"Yes," the Majority Leader said thoughtfully. "I wonder why he didn't want to cross-examine now."

"Think of the build-up in interest and tension in twenty-four hours," Senator Anderson said. "He knows what he's doing."

"My, it's exciting!" Kitty Maudulayne said. "Do you really think this little man is right? Do you really think Mr. Leffingwell is a Communist? Wouldn't that be exciting, you with a Communist for Secretary of State!"

"The thought," Brig said dryly, "makes me positively giddy. What do you think, Tom?"

"I don't know what to think," Senator August said in his gentle, worried way. "It certainly upsets things, doesn't it?"

"It certainly doesn't smooth them down," Bob Munson said. "But I never thought it would be easy."

"I can see I'd better get interested in this, now that Dubuque's been brought into it," Lafe Smith said with a grin.

"You're right on that," Bob Munson remarked to Seab as he came slowly along to join them. "It *is* just corny enough so that it might be true."

Seab smiled sleepily and made no answer, but instead bowed elaborately to the ladies.

"I hope you all weren't disappointed," he said.

"You gave us our money's worth, Senator," Dolly said. "We'll be back for the sequel tomorrow."

"Good," Senator Cooley said. "I just suspect—I just suspect it may be a leetle dramatic. Just a leetle."

"That's a safe prediction," Verne Cramer observed. "When egghead meets egghead it's no yolk, right, Robert?"

"You're a real funny man," the Majority Leader told him.

"Or," Senator Cramer said, "you can't make an omelet without breaking eggheads. How's that?"

"I think you're enjoying this," Brigham Anderson said in mock reproach, and Verne Cramer grinned.

"Something's got to give," he remarked. "I wonder who it's going to be?"

It was then, as they were standing in an amiably chatting group while the crowd shuffled out with many interested backward glances toward them, that Fred Van Ackerman came bursting in again in obvious excitement.

"Reconvene the committee!" he said breathlessly. "Reconvene it, God damn it!"

"What's the matter with you?" Senator Anderson demanded bluntly. "We quit five minutes ago."

"But I have proof," Senator Van Ackerman said, a sudden savage note coming into his voice. "Don't any of you *want* the proof, Senator?"

"Proof of what?" Lafe Smith asked shortly.

"Don't you *want* the proof when I *have* the proof?" Fred Van Ackerman demanded again with his strange, strangled, about-to-blow-up emphasis. "There isn't any 2731 Carpenter Street, Chicago. I called the city hall and checked. There's no building there. It's a vacant lot. I want you to reconvene the subcommittee, so I can nail that lie right now."

"Bob Leffingwell has asked us to go over," Brigham Anderson said calmly, "and we have. It's his wish."

"You don't want to help him," Fred Van Ackerman said sharply, a peculiar light in his eyes. "You're out to get him, aren't you, Brig? You're all out to get him, and you most of all. All right. All right. You just wait. You all just wait!"

And he turned abruptly on his heel and hurried out through the last curious spectators while behind him Kitty Maudulayne said, "My goodness, he's mad too!" and Verne Cramer said, "We dropped him on his head when he was two years old, but we've been hoping. Apparently we haven't hoped strong enough, have we, Brigham?"

"He isn't normal," Brigham Anderson said, shaking his head. "There's something all wrong inside somewhere."

"Well, watch out for him," Senator Munson advised soberly. "He plays rough."

"Let's all go to lunch together and forget about it," Verne Cramer suggested lightly. "Ladies?"

"I'd love to," Dolly said, slipping her arm through Senator Munson's.

"So would I!" Kitty exclaimed, and Celestine smiled.

"A quick one," Bob Munson said, "Because I think we've got to get to the floor pretty soon. I have an idea it's going to be a rather blowy afternoon in the Cave of the Winds."

"Yes," Brigham Anderson agreed; and on that understanding they all took the subway over to the Capitol and went along to the Senate restaurant for forty-five minutes of rather restless conviviality during which the ladies of the party found it difficult to hold the attention of their senatorial companions because the latter were all waiting uneasily for the commanding double ring of the quorum bell which they were quite sure would mean trouble.

Surprisingly, however, it did not come, and their automatic assumption that Fred Van Ackerman would go roaring to the floor and raise hell proved to be mistaken. Instead the Senate adjourned shortly after they finished lunch without anybody even mentioning the name Leffingwell; a fact the Majority Leader did not entirely like, for it seemed to him about time for some steam to be let off on the subject by some of his more vocal colleagues, and their careful quiet seemed more ominous than reassuring.

It soon became apparent as afternoon and evening wore on that this was not for lack of interest anywhere in the country, or, indeed, anywhere in the world. Raoul Barre called Lord Maudulayne to confess a certain misgiving; Krishna Khaleel, passing Hal Fry swiftly on the floor of the General Assembly at UN, pointed to the headline on the paper he was carrying, raised a quizzical eyebrow that might mean almost anything, and hurried on; on Sixteenth Street Vasily Tashikov in some puzzlement had one of his aides check some records in the vault in the basement and the aide came back in greater puzzlement to confess that he had drawn a blank; both the president of General Motors and the president of the United Auto Workers called Bob Munson in some agitation, as did the chairman of the National Committee downtown, and the Majority Leader had to spend a valuable forty-five minutes calming the three of them down; Seab received, by phone, personal visit, and corridor conversation, assurances from another round dozen of his colleagues that they were on his side in the light of the day's events; the *Star*, the *News*, and every other evening newspaper in the United States without exception bannered the Gelman testimony; the evening radio and television commentaries carried it completely if in rather gingerly fashion; loud voices in the Press Club bar argued violently with one another about it; it was noted in London, in Rome, in Paris, in Moscow, in Helsinki and Cape Town and Singapore and Sierra Leone and all the points between; and everywhere in the capital, everywhere in the country, and everywhere in the world that knowledgeable people gathered it was a major topic of conversation.

Of all these discussions sprung from the hearing around the globe, perhaps the most significant was the one which occurred toward midnight when the senior Senator from South Carolina took up the receiver and asked the Sheraton-Park switchboard to give him the apartment of the senior Senator from Michigan a quarter of a mile away in the other wing.

"Bob?" he said softly. "Is that you, Bob?"

"That's me, Seab," the Majority Leader said. "What are you going to tell me, that you're giving up your opposition to Leffingwell?"

"Now, I swear you're a marvel, Bob," Senator Cooley said amicably. "Your whole cause has collapsed and you're still able to make jokes. It makes you a great leader, Bob. Yes, sir, that's what makes you a great leader."

"I'm on my way to bed, Seab," Senator Munson said. "Is it anything that can keep until tomorrow?"

"No, sir," Seab said. "I just thought, Bob, that just maybe you might call the White House and tell him that it might just possibly be a good idea to withdraw this nomination, Bob. I think that's what you might tell him, Bob."

"Well, sir, Seab," Bob Munson said, "do you know something? I already called him, and do you know what he said?"

"What did he say, Bob?" Senator Cooley asked.

" 'Hell, no,' " the Majority Leader quoted crisply. "Good night, Seab."

"Good night, Bob," Seab said gently. "I hope you sleep well, Bob. Tomorrow may be a busy day."

5

And so it was. Busy for the two of them, riding again together in the early morning traffic from the hotel to the Hill, sparring warily but good-naturedly on the way; for press, television, and radio, arriving early in the galleries, gulping their coffee quickly in the restaurant, hurrying over to the Caucus Room to stake out their places of vantage; for Brigham Anderson and Orrin Knox and Arly Richardson and John Winthrop and Johnny DeWilton, leaving their respective homes early and making their separate ways as fast as possible to their offices to get mail and dictation out of the way before the burden of the hearing came upon them; for other members of Foreign Relations who had decided to be on hand today, and for Fred Van Ackerman who had decided the same, doing the same quick housekeeping duties in their offices; for Dolly and Kitty and Celestine, each choosing with quick skill the exactly right dress, the exactly right hat, the exactly right expression to wear for today's session; for the nominee, leaving his home in Virginia early after a restless night, driving in over the Fourteenth Street Bridge, turning right on Constitution and moving through the rush past Agriculture and the Botanical Gardens and up the Hill not far behind the Majority Leader and his shrewd old companion; for Herbert Gelman, coming in on the bus from Northeast, unseen and unseeing, unknown and unknowable; for the Capitol cops who had to be on duty at 7 A.M. to handle the crowd, and for the crowd itself which began arriving shortly thereafter and by nine forty-five when the doors opened was lined up four deep back from the doors, across the hall, and clear around the balcony of the front rotunda of the Old Office Building, well over a thousand more than could possibly get in.

This was in truth to be a busy day, for it was, and everyone knew it, the climactic episode in the committee-hearing stage of the Leffingwell nomination.

"Mr. Chairman," Arly Richardson said into the quivering silence that fell after Brigham Anderson gaveled the room to order, and the television cameras obediently peered around upon him like impassive black cows watching impersonally with little red eyes. "I have a brief statement I should like to make, and something to put in the record."

"Certainly, Senator," the chairman said. "Go right ahead."

"I have received this morning," Senator Richardson said, "an airmail special-delivery letter from the president of the University of Chicago. He tells me that there was found late yesterday afternoon a record of the student Herbert Gelman, who did attend the university as he says he did, and who did take the administrative government course from Mr. Leffingwell as he says he did. The letter states, however, that no record has been found of his ever having taken a seminar from Mr. Leffingwell. The letter concludes with an affirmation of continuing confidence in the nominee, and attached to it is a statement of endorsement signed by 346 members of the faculty of the University of Chicago. I ask that the letter and the statement of endorsement be placed in the record at this point."

There was a loud and prolonged clatter of applause which the chairman permitted to run its course. Then he spoke calmly.

"Without objection," he said, "it is so ordered. Mr. Leffingwell, I think if you will move your chair to the left-hand side of the witness table, as you face us, and Mr. Gelman, if you will move yours to the right-hand side, so that you face one another, that we can begin."

And after the nominee had done so, regarding Herbert Gelman with the same half-amused, half-contemptuous look as when he had seen him last, Herbert Gelman looking vaguely away, Senator Anderson spoke directly to the audience.

"The Chair," he said, "wishes to make very clear to the audience, who are reminded that they are here as guests of the subcommittee, that this morning there will be no more demonstrations of any kind. The Chair has been more than lenient in the past two days; but now we come to the nub of this matter, and I am not going to have it complicated by outbursts of emotion on either side. We are all under strain enough in this room without adding to it. So I will have your co-operation if—you—please." He paused and looked searchingly over the crowd, and the room was absolutely silent. Then he went on in a more conversational tone.

"Mr. Leffingwell," he said, "you have been the target of the most grave and serious charges made by this witness, Herbert Gelman; and because of their nature and the fact that, unless disproved, they cast the most damaging light upon your general integrity, if not indeed upon your personal loyalty to your country, the Chair thinks, if the subcommittee concurs, that you should be given the right to cross-examine without interruption or interference from us, just as though you were a member of the Senate and a member of the subcommittee. We of course reserve the right after you have finished to question both of you again if we deem necessary. The Chair will even go so far as to say that if you desire it in order to clear your name, the subcommittee will exercise its right of subpoena in your behalf to bring other witnesses before us. These are extraordinary courtesies, not without precedent though not often resorted to, but the Chair feels that in fairness, considering the nature of the attack and considering the nature of the office to which you have been nominated, and how important it is to all of us that you embark upon it, if you do, with your name and reputation in the clear, that they should be extended to you. Is that agreeable to the subcommittee?"

"Perfectly, Mr. Chairman," Orrin Knox said firmly, and John Winthrop said approvingly, "No one could ask for more." The nominee bowed gravely in agreement.

"Mr. Chairman," he said, "I appreciate your courtesy and that of the subcommittee more than I can say. This is, as you realize, perhaps *the* decisive moment of my life, up to now, and I am very grateful that you have seen fit to grant me such consideration to help me in it."

"You might point out, Mr. Chairman," Senator Knox said dryly, "that the motives, at least mine, anyway, are not entirely unmixed. Whatever develops here this morning, Mr. Leffingwell, I don't want anyone afterwards to ever be able to say that you did not receive fair treatment at the hands of the Senate of the United States." And he smiled, rather grimly, at the nominee.

"Do you wish to have counsel with you," Brigham Anderson asked, "or are you going to act as your own counsel?"

"I have no counsel," Bob Leffingwell said simply, "but the truth."

"We hope it stands you in good stead," Senator Anderson said. "Mr. Gelman, the subcommittee wishes you, too, to know that this final phase of this inquiry is not being undertaken in any spirit of hostility toward you. We are grateful that you have returned here voluntarily, without the necessity of subpoena, and we know you understand why we are adopting this particular course of procedure. Your charges against the nominee are of an extraordinary and hurtful nature, and it is only right that he should be given every opportunity to disprove them if he can. You are reminded that you, like Mr. Leffingwell, are under oath to tell the truth."

The witness gave his shy little half smile.

"I know that," he said in a low voice. "I told it yesterday and I am going to tell it today, too."

"The subcommittee commends both you and Mr. Leffingwell for your devotion to truth," Brigham Anderson said with a certain dryness in his voice, "and it hopes that out of your differing versions of it the real truth will be clear when this is over. Mr. Leffingwell, your witness."

For a moment, while the nominee opened a briefcase on the table before him and took out some papers, while he arranged some pencils and paper and the microphone and a glass of water, and while Herbert Gelman shifted once in his chair and then sat forward with an almost willfully dogged expression on his face, there came one of those friezelike instants of time which might, if there were Rembrandt to capture it, stand beside the "Night Watch" as a rendering more lifelike than life. "The Committee Hearing," it might be called, the chairman and his colleagues waiting intently, the audience tensed and silent, the press and television ready, the great marble room, filled to its utmost capacity, focused in a frightening fascination upon the two men seated at opposite ends of the witness table, the one so dignified, handsome, steady and sure, the other so wisplike, isolated and alone, yet filled with the fearful tensile strength of the righteous weak. Then someone coughed, the nominee leaned forward, the press tables stirred, the committee members shifted, there was an angry exclamation from somewhere among the television cameras, the moment broke, the picture moved and was lost.

"Mr. Gelman," the nominee said quietly, "do I know you?"

The question, unexpected in its indirection, brought a stirring of surprise from the subcommittee and the press, and from the witness a hesitant little laugh. But there was nothing hesitant about his answer.

"I believe you do," he said.

"You heard me testify that I did not," Bob Leffingwell said, and Herbert Gelman nodded slowly.

"And you believe I was deliberately lying," the nominee said.

"That was my impression," Herbert Gelman replied and the nominee frowned a little, glancing toward the subcommittee as he did so.

"I couldn't have been simply mistaken, could I?" he asked. "I couldn't have been puzzled, and not remembered you at first, and later had my memory refreshed by your testimony about the Power Commission, could I? It had to be a deliberate lie, in your mind, did it?"

"That was my impression," Herbert Gelman repeated stubbornly, and Bob Leffingwell looked him square in the eye.

"Why was that your impression, Mr. Gelman?" he asked.

"I could not believe that you would have forgotten such a thing," the witness said.

"What thing, Mr. Gelman?" Bob Leffingwell asked. "Playing cops and robbers with you in Chicago, or having you retired from the Federal Power Commission for reasons about which you were somewhat less than candid with the subcommittee yesterday?"

"You tell 'em, Bob," the Philadelphia *Inquirer* whispered with satisfaction. "Nail the bastard to the mast," the Newark *News* agreed with a chuckle.

Herbert Gelman's steady stare at the nominee widened a little, but he spoke in the same evenly stubborn tone of voice.

"Are you admitting you played cops and robbers with me in Chicago, Mr. Leffingwell?" he asked.

"We'll get to that, Mr. Gelman," the nominee promised. "We'll get to that in due time and in full, believe me. But first I want to know why you think I have lied to anyone in this matter of such gravity to the country, to say nothing of its gravity to me? You realize you have made a deliberate attempt here to destroy me, don't you, Mr. Gelman? Why, Mr. Gelman?"

The witness gave him an oblique glance and his face set in still more stubborn lines.

"How many questions are you asking me at the same time, Mr. Leffingwell?" he asked.

"Am I going too fast for a man in your mental condition?" the nominee inquired with a certain savage politeness. "Then I will take them in order. Why are you convinced that I have been lying here, Mr. Gelman? Answer that one and then we'll proceed to the others one by one."

"Just because I believe you are," the witness said doggedly.

"And just because you say you're convinced, you expect that to convince this subcommittee?" Bob Leffingwell demanded.

"I think some people may think I'm telling the truth," Herbert Gelman said quietly.

"And what is the truth, Mr. Gelman?" the nominee asked.

"What I said yesterday," the witness said.

"Very well, suppose we go to what you said yesterday," Bob Leffingwell said, turning to a blue-covered manuscript. "I have here a transcript of the proceedings yesterday——"

"I don't," Herbert Gelman interrupted. "Can I have one too?"

"You mean your story today would change from what it was yesterday if you didn't have a transcript to remind you?" the nominee demanded sharply, and the witness looked at him with an almost insolent blankness.

"Oh, no," he said. "I just thought if you had one it would be fair for me to have one too."

"Here," Orrin Knox said, sliding his copy across the table, "take mine."

"Thank you, Senator," Herbert Gelman said with a little smile.

"Now," Bob Leffingwell said, laying his copy aside unopened, "suppose we talk about your career at the University of Chicago. You have testified, and the university has now confirmed it, that you did attend during the time I was a teacher there. The university also confirms that you took my administrative government course. How many people would you say were in the two sections of that course each week?"

"About three hundred," Herbert Gelman said without hesitation, and there was a little stir of excitement in the audience.

"Does it seem strange to your mind that out of all those students I should not have been able at first to remember the name of one of them?" Bob Leffingwell asked.

"It wouldn't be strange if that had been our only contact," Herbert Gelman said quietly, and the nominee permitted himself to look a little annoyed.

"Well, Mr. Gelman," he said, "if you're going to come back every time with an answer like that, then we do have to bring it down simply to your word against mine, don't we? Because I am going to prove here that the facts refute everything you've said. If you're going to counteract every fact with an insistence that you're right and no one else is, then that's going to leave you in a rather sad position, isn't it?"

"Let's see the position I'm in when we're finished," Herbert Gelman said in the same soft, stubborn voice, and again there was a stirring through the audience.

"As you please, Mr. Gelman," Bob Leffingwell said indifferently. "We have now established, at least to my mind and I think to any fair mind judging this, that you were in a class of three hundred—which was only one of four different classes over four years, each containing approximately the same number of students, so that there were some twelve hundred, all told, over that period of time—and that it was entirely possible that I should not remember your name out of all those students. So now suppose we go on to the seminar. The university says you didn't take it. Are you still going to maintain you did?"

The witness looked at him with his closed-off, stubborn expression; some inner struggle was apparently going on, and when he spoke it was in an almost inaudible voice.

"No," he said, "I didn't take it."

There was a wave of excited murmurings over the room, and the first relay of wire-service reporters jumped up and raced downstairs to the press room with their bulletins. Behind the committee table Fred Van Ackerman drove his right fist into his left palm with an expression of triumph on his face, and at the table John DeWilton gave a disgusted snort. His colleagues, however impassively reserved judgment.

"Why did you say you took it, Mr. Gelman?" the nominee asked patiently. "Wasn't that a lie?"

"I started to take it," Herbert Gelman said doggedly, "because you asked me to. Then I got sick for a while and had to drop it. But we were still friends just the same, and we still did what I said yesterday."

"Yes," Bob Leffingwell said, looking thoughtfully through the papers before him, "you got sick. I believe you did get sick, Mr. Gelman. I, too," he said with a little bow to Arly Richardson, "have received an airmail special-delivery letter from the president of the University of Chicago. It contains the information, Mr. Gelman, that in your senior year you suffered a nervous breakdown, were under treatment in the university hospital for two months, and had to leave school, returning to complete your senior courses a year later. Is that true?"

"Yes," Herbert Gelman said almost inaudibly, "that's true."

"Speak up, Mr. Gelman," Bob Leffingwell said savagely. "Speak up loud and clear. You were loud enough yesterday when you were trying to destroy me. I want you to be just as noisy today while you're destroying yourself."

"Yes," Herbert Gelman said loudly, "that's true."

"That's good," Bob Leffingwell told him. "Now we can all hear. So you suffered a mental breakdown."

"It wasn't mental," Herbert Gelman said stubbornly. "It was just nerves."

"Well, you draw the distinction if you care to, Mr. Gelman," the nominee said contemptuously. "I'm sure we'll all listen. So how much credence are we supposed to put in the word of a mentally ill individual who was mentally ill at the time I was supposed to be conspiring with him to overthrow the government? Why should we believe *anything* you say?"

To this the witness did not reply, but instead stared at the nominee without expression until Bob Leffingwell went on.

"So you didn't take the seminar," he said. "You had a mental breakdown, and it's your word against mine about these little revolutionary get-togethers of ours. Where was it you said we held them, Mr. Gelman?"

"At 2731 Carpenter Street," Herbert Gelman said promptly. "On the second floor in that room on the left at the back."

"You have a great talent for specific detail that might lend credibility, Mr. Gelman," the nominee told him. "Perhaps it goes with a mind a little more—inventive, shall we say—than most. At 2731 Carpenter Street. You're quite sure of that."

"Pretty sure," Herbert Gelman said slowly. "Of course I might be mistaken in a digit or two——"

"Oh, no, Mr. Gelman," Bob Leffingwell said quickly. "Don't try to dodge, now, just because you can see what's coming. And don't ever admit the possibility of your being mistaken. Your whole case here rests on the fact that it's your word against mine, and that you, at least, never lie, are never wrong, and are never mistaken . . . Mr. Chairman, I wonder if the distinguished Senator from Wyoming, Mr. Van Ackerman, might be permitted to tell the subcommittee what he has told me about this magic address of 2731 Carpenter Street?"

"Certainly," Brigham Anderson said. "Fred?" Senator Van Ackerman stood up behind him and rested one hand on the chairman's shoulder in a friendly way as he spoke.

"Just the same thing I told you yesterday, Brig," he said easily, "only you didn't want it in the record at that particular point. There is no 2731 Carpenter Street. I called the city hall in Chicago yesterday morning and checked. It's a vacant lot. There's nothing there. There's no record of anything ever having been there. That's what I wanted you to make public yesterday, Brig, only you wouldn't."

"Is that all, Fred?" Senator Anderson asked impassively.

"That's all, Brig," Senator Van Ackerman said.

"Very well, Mr. Leffingwell," the chairman said. "Proceed."

"Well, by God," the Washington *Post* whispered excitedly as Fred Van Ackerman sat down again, "what's Brig up to, anyway?" "Maybe we'd better try to find out," the *Herald Tribune* suggested. "I think so," the Providence *Journal* agreed. But at the committee table, where experience had taught the lesson that it is always best to wait and watch and not jump too soon to conclusions, the chairman's colleagues were as impassive as he, as the nominee turned back to Herbert Gelman.

"I appreciate the concern of the Senator from Wyoming about the timing of this," Bob Leffingwell said smoothly, "and I am grateful for it, but I can also appreciate the decision of the Chair that these matters should be developed in their proper course in the record. The delay has done me no damage, I can assure the Senator from Wyoming, as long as we now have the truth made public, thanks to him. So, Mr. Gelman, no seminar, no meeting place. But you say there were meetings."

"There were meetings on Carpenter Street," Herbert Gelman said stubbornly. "It may have been 2733 or 2729, but it was on Carpenter Street."

"Well, Mr. Gelman," Bob Leffingwell said in a pitying voice, "if the facts cannot convince you, obviously nothing will. But suppose just for a moment, on a strictly hypothetical basis, we explore these alleged meetings a little bit further. According to your tale, there were actually only four people engaged in this great plot to overthrow the government——"

"I didn't say we were plotting to overthrow the government," Herbert Gelman interrupted.

"I stand corrected," Bob Leffingwell conceded sarcastically. "You didn't. There were four, at any rate, according to your story; yourself, myself, someone who is dead now, and someone named James Morton, who had a beard and you don't know who he was or where he came from or where he is now and you probably couldn't recognize him if you saw him again, correct?"

There was a little snicker from the audience, and Herbert Gelman if anything looked more stubborn.

"That's right," he said.

"And you have nothing to back this up except your own word, fortified by a record of mental breakdown and a series of exploded assertions," Bob Leffingwell said dryly.

"You," Herbert Gelman said slowly, "and me, and the one who died, as you know, and James Morton. That's all."

"And at these great sinister meetings, accepting for a moment the hypothetical—the very hypothetical—assumption that you could by the remotest chance be telling the truth," the nominee said, "what did you do, Mr. Gelman? Suppose I read from yesterday's transcript, page 975, Senator Richardson interrogating, and I quote:

SENATOR RICHARDSON: Why are you here, Mr. Gelman?

MR. GELMAN: For what I've done.

SENATOR RICHARDSON: And what was that? Did you start any riots? Did you touch off any bombs? Did you kill anybody for the cause?

MR. GELMAN: No, sir.

SENATOR RICHARDSON: How many of you were there in this so-called cell?

MR. GELMAN: Four. Mr. Leffingwell, myself, one other who is dead, and James Morton.

SENATOR RICHARDSON: That's not a very big group to overturn the government.

MR. GELMAN: No, sir.

SENATOR RICHARDSON: And you didn't plot anything?

MR. GELMAN: Not to my knowledge, no, sir.

SENATOR RICHARDSON: In short, you just talked, didn't you?

MR. GELMAN: Yes, sir.

SENATOR RICHARDSON: And that's all you did. A few ineffectual meetings fourteen years ago. Is that all?

MR. GELMAN: I've felt badly about it, Senator."

Bob Leffingwell closed the transcript. "And so you should feel badly about it, Mr. Gelman," he said softly, "coming here as you have to destroy a fellow being without facts, without proof, with nothing but the lurid imaginings of your own sick mind. You should indeed feel badly."

But once again, instead of speaking, the witness only looked at him with the same stubborn, dogged expression, and after a moment the nominee went on.

"So even if we accept this fantastic story of meetings, nothing was done at them except talk," he said. "So why were they held at all, Mr. Gelman, if we permit you for a moment to get away with the assertion that they were? What were they all about, anyway?"

"We believed," Herbert Gelman said quietly, "as you know, that we could work out a philosophy that would retain what we believed to be the best of the communist theory and apply it to this country. We knew by then what communism had turned into in Russia, and we didn't want that here. We thought we could develop a new communism. That was your phrase, you remember—'the new communism.'"

"You're a liar, Mr. Gelman," the nominee said quietly, and the witness shook his head.

"Oh, no," he said with equal quietness.

"But supposing all you say were true," Bob Leffingwell said in a tone of baffled wonderment as though he could not conceive how he happened to be involved in this fairy tale, "suppose the meetings were held and they discussed the new communism, whatever that is, and everything you say—it was still just talk, wasn't it?"

"Yes," Herbert Gelman said.

"Then why was it so important?" the nominee demanded in an exasperated voice. "What would it matter now? Why would it be significant of anything, if it all happened so long ago and meant so little?"

"The only reason it would be important or significant now," the witness said, and the room quieted down completely to hear him, "would be the way in which we react to it now. If we tell the truth about it, the way I am, that is one thing. If we lie about it, as—if we lie about it, then it casts a reflection on everything we have done and raises serious questions about what we may do in the future. That is why it is important, Bob."

At this sudden and startling use of the nickname, at which the nominee first paled and then flushed angrily, there was a sharp gasp from over the room, and as the full import of what the witness had said sunk in, it was followed by a mounting murmur of exclamation and excitement. At the committee table Orrin Knox leaned comfortably against the chairman's arm and murmured dryly behind his hand, "He should have quit when he was ahead." Brigham Anderson gave a grim little smile. "Let him do it his own way," he said. Then he rapped the gavel.

"The hearing will be in order," he said. "The Chair appreciates the audience's co-operation with his request earlier and hopes it will continue. Are you through, Mr. Leffingwell?"

The nominee, who had regained his composure without noticeable difficulty and was once more in command of the situation, smiled pleasantly.

"No, Mr. Chairman," he said, "not quite. We haven't established motive here, yet. We haven't discussed the Federal Power Commission."

"Yes, I think that would be interesting to the subcommittee," Senator Anderson agreed. "Proceed."

"Now, Mr. Gelman," Bob Leffingwell said, "and by the way, my name is Mr. Leffingwell, and I don't recall anything, nor have you been able to prove anything, that gives you the right to call me Bob—you said you worked at the FPC in an agency close to the chairman, as I recall. After all this testimony yesterday, I went back to my office and I checked with my own personnel people, and with the Civil Service Commission, and I find that, sure enough, you did work for two years for my commission. But isn't it true that this was as a minor clerk, not in 'an agency close to the chairman?' Isn't it true that you were never in my office, and that I never had any dealings with you at all until the unfortunate episode of your retirement from the Commission?"

"I was sure you knew I was there," Herbert Gelman said.

"That isn't responsive to what I asked you," the nominee said calmly.

"Because I was sure you had gotten me the job," Herbert Gelman added, as though he had not even heard the nominee's rejoinder.

"Are you about to have another mental breakdown, Mr. Gelman?" Bob Leffingwell asked curiously. "That would be three, wouldn't it? Maybe you ought to go to St. Elizabeth's for a while."

But again the witness gave him only that dogged, stubborn stare.

"In the two years since you left the Commission," the nominee went on, "many matters of course had come before me, and your case had entirely slipped my mind, so that yesterday when your name was mentioned to me it did not immediately ring a bell; particularly since it was mentioned to me in connection with the university, where of course, having dealt with you only as one student among many hundreds, I quite naturally had no recollection of it at all. But during your own testimony, when you mentioned the Commission, I did remember something of it; and after checking yesterday afternoon I now have all the facts in hand. The most important fact is the medical report we have on you. Not to prolong it unnecessarily, you had a second breakdown, didn't you, Mr. Gelman, and your resignation was requested as a result of that illness?"

"Good Christ," UPI murmured, "this guy's a mental basket-case." "I told you Bob would take care of him," AP responded.

"I did have another nervous breakdown," Herbert Gelman said, "but it wasn't a bad one. It was just overwork, the doctor said. I could have come back if you had let me."

"If I had let you?" Bob Leffingwell said in a tone of surprise. "Would you like me to read what our own medical report said about you, Mr. Gelman?"

"Then why did you get me another job, if you didn't know me and I was so crazy?" Herbert Gelman demanded with a sudden anger teetering on the edge of hysteria. "Why did you let me resign voluntarily and then get me lined up over in Commerce with the Bureau of International Economic Affairs? Why did you do that for me, if nothing I've said was true and I'm such a mess?"

Bob Leffingwell gave him a pitying look.

"Because I was sorry for you, Mr. Gelman," he said calmly. "You probably can't understand that, but it's true. It was just ordinary charity. You had done reasonably good work while you were in good health, the doctor did think you would recover with rest, and when you did there was still a feeling in the Commission that we perhaps shouldn't abandon you altogether."

"I had the impression it was your doing alone," the witness said more calmly. "I thought my boss in Commerce got in touch with me because you asked him to."

"Well, Mr. Gelman," Bob Leffingwell said in a kindly tone, "haven't we pretty well established here that your mind has occasionally gotten impressions that the facts just don't support? It's been a rather erratic mind in the past, apparently, in fact as recently as two years ago, and it seems a pretty fair presumption that it's erratic still. No, nobody got in touch with you at my suggestion. I believe a Civil Service bulletin did mention a couple of vacancies over in Commerce, I happened to see it when it came across my desk, I thought of you, or somebody in my office thought of you, and we passed the word along. But that's the extent of it. And please don't tell me I'm lying, Mr. Gelman. I don't think many people would believe you, any more."

For the last time the witness gave him that strange, intent, stubbornly dogged look.

"Just the same," he said, as though nothing at all had happened in the past hour and a half, "I'm telling the truth about those meetings. You've managed to cover up everything pretty well and confuse it all, but I still say you and I and James Morton and the boy who died held those meetings."

"I think you're lying, Mr. Gelman," Bob Leffingwell said calmly.

"I know you are," Herbert Gelman said defiantly, and the nominee shrugged.

"That's for the subcommittee and our countrymen to judge, Mr. Gelman," he said. "I forgive you for what you tried to do to me because you obviously aren't in a fit condition mentally to be responsible for your actions. I feel very sorry for you, because apparently neither in college nor government have you been able to come to terms with reality in a world that is obviously too difficult for you . . . Mr. Chairman, I have no further questions of the witness. I appreciate your courtesy."

There was a stirring and a relaxation in the room as the nominee turned his chair away from the witness and toward the subcommittee, as another relay of reporters ran downstairs to file new bulletins, as the audience stretched and began talking, as the television cameras wandered from face to face along the committee table and the still photographers scrambled to record such inevitable shots as Bob Leffingwell rubbing his ear, Herbert Gelman blowing his nose, Arly Richardson cleaning his glasses, Bob Munson talking to Lafe Smith, Tom August looking worried, Orrin

Knox pushing back his chair to turn and greet Dolly and her guests, Fred Van Ackerman glowering thoughtfully into space, Seab Cooley looking impassively out at the audience. For several minutes there was a general informality in the room during which some of the aching tension of the verbal duel just concluded was dissipated and blown away. When it seemed to him that this purpose had been sufficiently accomplished, Brigham Anderson rapped for order and the room quieted down again.

"Thank you, Mr. Leffingwell," he said, "Thank you, Mr. Gelman. Does anyone on the subcommittee have any further questions of either of these witnesses?" And when several of his colleagues responded, "No questions," he leaned forward to look down the table to the senior Senator from South Carolina.

"How about you, Seab?" he asked, and Senator Cooley gave his sleepy smile and little wave of the hand.

"No, thank you, Mr. Chairman," he said slowly. "I do wonder, however, whether it might be possible to get a complete copy of the transcript, including today's session, by later on this afternoon? I'd rather like to study it over, before you all decide what to do in this matter."

"So would I, Mr. Chairman," Orrin Knox said. "I trust you don't intend to vote on this today?"

"I should object to that too, Mr. Chairman," Arly Richardson said quickly. "I think we should take a little time on this, and in line with the suggestion of Senator Cooley, I think we should all be furnished with a complete transcript by this afternoon."

"That will be arranged, Senators," Brigham Anderson said. "And the Chair of course has no more desire to take precipitate action than anyone else here. Two stories, diametrically opposed, have been given us, together with other information bearing on the veracity of the witness—or," he added as Bob Leffingwell started to smile and then stopped—"witnesses. Perhaps a meeting to vote on the nomination tomorrow would be in order. Unless anyone has some further business to offer here today, we can probably consider these hearings concluded. Is that agreeable?"

"Mr. Chairman," Bob Leffingwell said, and there was something in his tone that brought the instant attention of the subcommittee and the room. "Mr. Chairman, I should like to make a concluding statement, if I may."

"You may," Senator Anderson told him, and the tension was suddenly back as taut as ever. Bob Leffingwell leaned forward slowly, folding his hands one upon the other, and when he began to speak it was in a grave and deliberate voice.

"So, Mr. Chairman," he said, "we come to the end of this extraordinary proceeding in which a witness of medically proven irresponsibility was allowed, without ever being examined or investigated or checked beforehand, to be brought before this subcommittee to be used in the most viciously unprincipled and underhanded way to smear and attack me. In thirteen years of government service, Mr. Chairman, I cannot recall an episode such as this, so evil, so inexcusable, so ill-befitting the dignity and the integrity of the Senate of the United States."

"Mr. Chairman," Orrin Knox said sharply, "it is not the business of this witness to be concerned with the dignity of this Senate, or to make such a spectacle as this."

"He has a right to have his say, Senator," Brigham Anderson said calmly. "Let him talk."

"That's right, Mr. Chairman," Seab Cooley said coldly from down the table. "Just let him talk. He's mighty good at talking. He's so good at talking he's maybe going to talk himself right out of the vote he was about to get here. Let him talk."

"That will do, Senator," Brigham Anderson said flatly. "Go on, Mr. Leffingwell. Tell us what else we've done. The whole world's listening."

"I repeat, Mr. Chairman," Bob Leffingwell said in the same measured tones, "an evil, inexcusable, underhanded, vicious, shabby attempt to smear me, destroy my personal character and destroy my usefulness to the President and to my country, so that I could not be confirmed for Secretary of State. I expected this sort of thing from the senior Senator from South Carolina, whose ability to damage good citizens and injure his own country has increased in direct geometric ratio to his lengthening years in this body, but I did not expect it of some other members of this subcommittee. I did not expect that they would give support, some directly and some indirectly, to his tactics. It has shocked and disappointed me, Mr. Chairman."

"By God, Bob, you tell 'em!" the Washington *Post* whispered exultantly, and the *Herald Trib*, scribbling too fast to do more than grin, grinned.

"Nor," the nominee went on, a certain acid iron coming into his tone, "did I ever expect to see such goings-on permitted by an instrumentality of the great Committee on Foreign Relations, particularly in the matter of a Secretary of State, a man who must go before the nations of the world to defend the interests of the United States. What is the position you have put me in here, Mr. Chairman? What will they say now, when I meet them in conference? Oh, yes, they will say, this is the man the Senate smeared. This is the man the highest legislative body in his country, yes, in many ways the greatest legislative body in the world, has attacked and slandered and attempted to destroy. That is what they will say, and how many years do you think it will be before I can meet them as an equal after this shameful, shabby episode? I ask you, Mr. Chairman, I ask you!"

Then while Orrin Knox flushed angrily and Johnny DeWilton seemed on the verge of blurting out some angry rejoinder, but Brigham Anderson, Arly Richardson, John Winthrop, and Seab Cooley all watched him with a certain coldly analytical attention and no other expression, his tone changed abruptly and he went on to his conclusion with his earlier quiet gravity.

"However, Mr. Chairman," he said, "there have been some courtesies here and I appreciate them. I also, of course, absolve members of the subcommittee of engaging in any premeditated conspiracy with the Senator from South Carolina. I am not even sure that I should blame him too severely, for as he said yesterday, he did not seek this man out, and apparently had no means of knowing that he was to be so miserably duped. And, of course, Mr. Chairman, win, lose, or draw my position with regard to my country remains what it was on Monday when this hearing began: I love her, I believe in her, I shall serve her to the very best of my ability in every way I can until the breath is no longer in me, and I swear you that as God is my witness."

And he sat back with an air as Brigham Anderson gave the gavel an admonitory rap and spoke in an impersonal tone.

"Are you through, Mr. Leffingwell?" he asked.

"I am," Bob Leffingwell said.

"Very well," Senator Anderson said impassively, "these hearings on the nomination of Robert A. Leffingwell to be Secretary of State are now concluded."

At once he was aware that Fred Van Ackerman was on his feet behind him vigorously leading the applause that broke and rolled and rolled again across the room while Bob Leffingwell bowed and smiled and waved a deprecatory hand, while the press crowded up and the television cameras swung back and forth across the milling audience. Under the protective roar of sound the junior Senator from Wyoming leaned forward and addressed his colleagues. "I'll see you bastards on the floor," he said with a tense and strangled violence in his voice. "We'll see about this. We'll just see!" And before they could answer he had forced his way around the committee table, elbowed Herbert Gelman harshly aside, and was out front being photographed with the nominee while the crowd continued to applaud and its excited babble filled the room.

"He's a really nice guy, that boy," John Winthrop commented, and Orrin Knox snorted, "He's a peach." "I have a good notion," Lafe Smith said thoughtfully, "to give him a punch in the nose." Tom August looked genuinely alarmed and Brigham Anderson grinned. "Go right ahead, buddy," he said. "Nothing would please the press more."

"Brig!" AP called, and Lafe smiled as a dozen reporters started toward the chairman.

"Here they come, pal," he said. "Your little problems. Tom, let's go have lunch."

"All right," Senator August said. "I do hope we can get through the afternoon without a bitter debate on this."

"We can't," Lafe said cheerfully, "so we'd better eat hearty. Come on, Seab. I'm not mad at you yet, today."

"I'll be over, I'll say to the Senator from Ioway," Seab said genially. "First, though, I want to hear what the chairman has to say to the press."

"So do I," the Majority Leader said. "Lafe, ask Stanley to sit in for me at the opening, will you? I'll be over just as soon as I get a bite, tell him."

"Right," Lafe said. "Tom and I will take the girls to lunch for you."

"Please do," Dolly said, and they walked out chatting animatedly together.

"Well, Brig," AP said, "what's the next step? When will the subcommittee vote?"

"I'll have to check with the members and see what their pleasure is," the chairman said, "but I would imagine tomorrow or Friday, probably."

"Why didn't you vote today, Brig?" the *Times* asked, and the chairman frowned thoughtfully.

"You heard Seab request some time to study the transcript," he said, "and several members of the subcommittee felt the same way about it. I know I did. It won't hurt if we go over for a day or two."

"What's left to be considered?" the Detroit *News* inquired. "It looks to me as though this whole Gelman business is pretty well exploded, isn't it? Obviously he's a mental case."

"Yes," Senator Anderson said thoughtfully. "Except that like a lot of mental cases, there are one or two points on which he seems awfully determined and positive. They may all be part of his general psychological pattern, or they may not. That's why I think we'd like to take a little time."

"You're going to have trouble with Fred Van Ackerman on that, you know," the *Herald Trib* observed. "He went out of here raving something about demanding immediate action when he gets over to the floor."

"The things Fred demands and the things Fred accomplishes are two different things," Orrin Knox broke in tartly. "I agree entirely with the chairman that there's no rush on this. We can decide tomorrow and nothing will be lost. I think we all want to go over that transcript."

"What do you think it all adds up to, Senator?" AP asked, and Orrin Knox looked skeptical.

"Nothing much, I expect," he said. "I wasn't convinced by Gelman, if that's what you mean, and Leffingwell didn't perform any differently than I thought he would. He's still too tricky for me, but he always has been and he's still done a pretty good job of it, and I expect he will here, too."

"How about you, Brig?" the Washington *Star* asked. "Are you satisfied too?"

The chairman gave him a direct look and his expression became more earnest and a little puzzled.

"Not entirely," he said. "But maybe after I read the transcript I will be. It helps to go over a thing and review it quietly out of the circus atmosphere you fellows create."

"*We* create," the Chicago *Tribune* demanded with a smile. "You can blame our friends the photographers and TV boys for that."

"You do your bit," Brigham Anderson said with an answering smile.

"The hearings are definitely closed for good, then, and we can expect a subcommittee vote sometime tomorrow or Friday," the Dallas *News* recapitulated. The chairman nodded. "And how about the full committee?" the *News* added.

"Of course that's up to Tom," Senator Anderson said, "but I wouldn't expect it to be very long delayed."

"Probably floor action by Friday, Brig?" AP asked, and the chairman smiled.

"Could be," he said.

"And you do expect confirmation, don't you?" the Providence *Journal* said.

"I'd consider it probable," Brigham Anderson said. "Now I'd advise you boys to hurry up and get a good lunch, because I have an idea it's going to be a lively session this afternoon."

And this time he was right.

6

It began right after the "morning hour," that handy parliamentary catchall which in the Senate naturally runs longer than an hour and furnishes the forum for the introduction of bills, insertions of material in the Congressional Record, and five-minute speeches which in the Senate naturally are often extended by unanimous consent beyond five minutes. Today's morning hour ran from noon to one thirty-six, and the minute it ended Fred Van Ackerman was on his feet demanding a quorum. The two bells rang commandingly through the two office buildings and the Senate side of the Capitol, and the minute Harley Hudson announced that sixty-five Senators had answered to their names, and a quorum was present, Senator Van Ackerman started talking. When the Majority Leader and the members of the subcommittee arrived in the chamber a few minutes later it was to find the Senate sitting in strained silence while Fred raved on against Carney Birch, who cowered like some small, malodorous wood animal in a seat beside George Hines. The whole thing presented a tableaux so out of keeping with the Senate that the Majority Leader, hurrying to take over his desk from Stanley Danta, stopped by Warren Strickland's for a moment before crossing the aisle.

"What in the hell is going on?" he demanded in an urgent whisper, and Senator Strickland gave him a sober look.

"I don't quite know," he said. "It just began a couple of minutes ago when Fred took after Carney."

"What in the Christ for?" Senator Munson demanded explosively, and Warren Strickland shrugged.

"Carney gave a prayer that Fred thought was anti-Leffingwell," he said.

"My God, are we getting that tense about it?" Bob Munson asked.

"Fred seems to be," the Minority Leader said.

"Now, Mr. President," the junior Senator from Wyoming was crying in his repetitive fashion, his voice rising and falling and seeming always just on the verge of complete frenzy, "it is not enough that this great man, this great public servant, yes, this man who may be able to show us the way to lasting peace, to lasting peace, Mr. President, is attacked and smeared—yes, Mr. President, attacked and smeared!—in the press and elsewhere. Now it must come to the floor of the Senate and we find the Senate chaplain, the Senate chaplain, Mr. President, joining in this chorus against him. Have the attacks not been vicious enough, Mr. President? Must they now enlist the Senate chaplain, yes, the Senate chaplain, Mr. President, in their conspiracies? I demand to know, Mr. President, yes, I demand to know, Mr. President. I demand to know!"

"Mr. President," Bob Munson said, moving to his own desk as Stanley Danta left it and moved over to his with a welcoming smile, "I hate to interrupt the Senator in mid-flight, but since he is in a demanding mood, I think it might be interesting for the benefit of all Senators, including those who came in after the quorum call and were not here for the opening, which I imagine is most of us, if we were to have the clerk read these fearfully offending remarks of the chaplain so that we may all judge them. It is not that I dispute," he added with the driest hint of mockery, "no, it is not that I dispute, Mr. President, the vivid and no doubt accurate reportage of the junior Senator from Wyoming, but I do think that for myself at least I would like to have the words themselves read back. Will the Senator yield for that purpose?"

Fred Van Ackerman shot him a dark and suspicious look and then suddenly decided to comply.

"Read it, Mr. President," he ordered. "Have him read it and we'll see."

While the official reporter riffled back through his shorthand notes, the Majority Leader leaned across the senior Senator from South Carolina, seated in placid inertness beside him, to Stanley and remarked with a grin, "I've always told Carney he'd put the Lord into politics just once too often. I guess this is it."

"Watch out for Fred," Senator Danta said seriously. "He's about to blow his top."

"You know, Bob," Seab remarked softly, "if I were you, you know what I'd do with that young man?"

"What's that, Seab?" the Majority Leader asked.

"I'd destroy him," Senator Cooley said, and he meant it absolutely. "Yes, sir, I'd destroy him before he gets any bigger. He means trouble, Bob; I've seen his kind come to this Senate before, and they always mean trouble, Bob. Destroy him, Bob, while you still can."

The Majority Leader knew he could, and the means flashed swiftly through his mind, keeping him off good committees, preventing his bills from ever coming to the floor for debate, floating rumors of contention and dislike in the press, attacking him obliquely in speeches around the

country, using all the little cruelties of parliamentary technique to razor a
man down to political nothingness inch by inch. It could be done, and
not with any great difficulty, either, at this stage of the game; but he only
shrugged and grinned.

"Of course, Seab," he said amiably, "he's on my side at this moment, you
know. Maybe that's why you want him destroyed."

"Just take my advice, Bob," Seab Cooley said gently. "Just take my
advice, or you are going to be mighty sorry someday."

"Yes," the Majority Leader said, suddenly serious. "I think you're
entirely right, Seab, but I've got to handle him carefully on this one,
because he *is* on my side."

"Suit yourself, Bob," Senator Cooley said indifferently, "but don't say
somebody didn't tell you." It was a conversation Bob Munson was to
look back upon bitterly only five days later and reflect how shrewd the
old fighter was still in his assessments of men.

"Is the reporter ready?" Harley asked, and the official reporter nodded
and began while the Senate listened attentively and Carney, aware that
he was in the process of gathering defenders, sat up straight beside Senator
Hines and looked as though he were beginning to enjoy it.

"TheSenateconvenedatnoon," the reporter read in a hasty monotone.
"TheReverendCarneyBirchChaplainoftheSenategavethefollowing——"

"Mr. President," Bob Munson interrupted patiently, "can the reporter
go a little slower, please? And we don't want the whole proceedings. Just
go to the prayer."

"*Lord,*" the reporter said carefully, unconsciously giving the word
Carney's proprietary emphasis, and there was a snicker from somewhere
on the Minority side, probably Verne Cramer. "*Lord,* who hath brought us
together in this great assemblage to decide the fates of men and our great
nation, give us the grace and the strength to study with care the things
we do, lest in the heat of haste and partisan passion we may make
decisions that would later cause us regret and perhaps send to high places
men whom we are not sure are worthy of our nation's trust. *Lord,* give us
the patience to study long and carefully such men, and if we satisfy ourselves truly of their merit, but only then, let us enable them to do our
nation's work. *Lord,* let us be humble and let us remember this. Amen."

"There, you see?" Fred Van Ackerman cried triumphantly. "If that isn't
an attack on Robert A. Leffingwell, Mr. President, I ask you, what is it,
Mr. President? I defy the Majority Leader, Mr. President, yes, I defy
him, Mr. President, to deny that that is an attack on Robert A. Leffingwell.
I defy him, Mr. President!"

"I get the idea, Mr. President," Senator Munson said. "The Senator
defies me. Well, I am not going to debate the chaplain's prayer with the
junior Senator from Wyoming, which I think would be a precedent
unique in a body which is never one to hesitate when it comes to establish-
ing unique precedents. Even for the Senate, Mr. President, I think debat-

ing the chaplain's prayer would be unusual. If the Senator wishes to make an issue of it, he can move to discharge the chaplain and get another chaplain. Does he wish to do so, Mr. President?"

"Oh, my goodness," Carney said feebly to George Hines, "he wouldn't really, would he?"

"You're safe, Carney," Senator Hines assured him. "Only you'd better watch your manners after this."

"Oh, I will," the chaplain said fervently. "Believe me, George, I *will*."

"Mr. President," Senator Van Ackerman said, more mildly, "I think the distinguished Majority Leader is trying to make a joke out of this now, and I'm not going to oblige him. Of course I'm not going to move to discharge the chaplain, Mr. President, even though," he added with deliberate cruelty, "I think we could find plenty who would be a whole lot better. I just say it's symptomatic of the way in which this whole matter has been handled this week by the subcommittee of the Senate Foreign Relations Committee. A great man has been crucified before that subcommittee, Mr. President. Members of the Senate have made a mockery of his sincere beliefs, they have attacked and villified him, they have permitted a man of proven mental unbalance to smear him and attempt to assassinate his character and reputation, and they have lent him their forum and sat by idly while he did it. It's been unfair, Mr. President, yes, I say it's been damnably unfair."

"Mr. President," Brigham Anderson said, "will the Senator yield to me?"

"Yes, I'll yield to the Senator from Utah, who has presided over this farce," Fred Van Ackerman said viciously, and there was a sudden tensing through the Senate and the crowded galleries at his tone. The Senator from Utah, however, looked at him calmly and spoke in a level and unhurried voice.

"The Senator knows," he said patiently, "that the nominee has been given every consideration before our subcommittee. The Senator is aware, because he was there, that the nominee, after the testimony of Herbert Gelman, was given the unusual opportunity to cross-examine him without let or hindrance by the subcommittee, and he also knows, for he was there, that the subcommittee extended to the nominee, had he cared to use it, its power of subpoena so that he might have brought other witnesses before us had he so desired. The Senator knows, for he was there, that the subcommittee interposed no barriers between the nominee and his right to say on the record whatever he wished to say concerning the proceedings, the charges against him, and the defense of his own character. These are the things the Senator knows, and I wonder, Mr. President, why he is attempting now to give the country, through the medium of the press which is busily transmitting his words at this moment, the impression that it has been otherwise. I would like to know," Brigham Anderson concluded quietly, "why he is dealing fast and loose with the truth in this matter."

"Mr. President," Fred Van Ackerman cried, and his voice sailed up suddenly into its almost pathological whine, "personal privilege! Point of personal privilege, Mr. President! The Senator is violating the rules of the Senate, Mr. President! He is accusing me of lying, Mr. President! I demand that his remarks be taken down and that he be directed to proceed in order!"

Half a dozen Senators were on their feet at this, among them Orrin Knox, the Majority Leader, and Powell Hanson, but Harley Hudson spoke in a tone of surprising bluntness which made clear that he didn't need anybody's help.

"The Chair will state," he said coldly, "that the Chair considers that the senior Senator from Utah has received ample provocation from the junior Senator from Wyoming for almost anything he cares to say about him. However, in conformity with the rules the Chair will suggest that the Senator from Utah moderate his language to some degree. And the Senate," he added firmly, "will be in order."

"Mr. President," Fred Van Ackerman cried angrily, "the Chair is favoring the senior Senator from Utah. The Chair is a party to this, Mr. President. It is a conspiracy, Mr. President, a conspiracy. Point of personal privilege, Mr. President!"

"What is it, Senator?" the Vice President asked in the same cold tone. "That the Chair is being unfair to him? Does the Senator wish to appeal to the Chair against the Chair? Is it his wish that the Chair rule upon the actions of the Chair? Is that the sort of nonsense this Senate is supposed to listen to this afternoon?"

"God damn," Senator Cramer whispered delightedly to John Winthrop. "What's gotten into Harley?"

"I don't know," Senator Winthrop said, "but whatever it is, I'm all for it."

To Stanley Danta, asking much the same question at the same moment, the Majority Leader gave only a quizzical look. He wasn't sure, but he rather suspected the Vice President had begun to come to grips with the possibilities of the future. He decided he would have to check this interesting idea when the opportunity arose.

In any event, Harley's unexpected bluntness had its effect on Senator Van Ackerman, who made one of his split-second switches and responded in a much milder tone.

"Mr. President," he said, "of course the junior Senator from Wyoming has no intention of getting into an argument with the distinguished occupant of the Chair about this. However, I think the facts speak for themselves, Mr. President. I am only sorry other Senators were not able to be present and witness this shameful, degrading spectacle——"

"Mr. President," Orrin Knox interrupted in a tone that brooked no denial, "the Senator knows that is absolute poppycock. He knows the nominee was given every opportunity to have his say and received the fairest of treatment from the subcommittee. Why is he indulging in this kind of nonsense?"

"I am not surprised, Mr. President," Fred Van Ackerman snapped, "no, I am not surprised, that the Senator from Illinois, who is one of the principal enemies of this great man who has been nominated to be Secretary of State should take that tack, Mr. President. It is what I would expect from him. It is just what I would expect from him. I repeat, Mr. President, this shameful, vindictive, evil spectacle was a mockery of justice, a travesty of senatorial procedure. I submit, Mr. President, that it was deliberately intended to destroy the nominee."

"Well, there's a new lead," AP whispered to UPI in the press gallery above, and UPI made a face. "I suppose so," he said, "but I wish it came from somebody but this madman." "Don't kick the devil," the Washington *Post* suggested, "when he's on your side." And they all got up, ran up the steep flight of stairs, through the swinging doors, and filed NEW LEAD LEFFINGWELL, with a few items of color on how Bob Munson looked and the expression on Fred Van Ackerman's face and what the Vice President had said tossed in for the continuing story, LEFFING-WELL RUNNING, on the wire.

Across the room Bessie Adams arose, looking neat, trim, and kindly in her usual black dress, her gray hair swept off face and up, her expression pleasant and alert; the sharpest grandmother in the country, they said about Bessie, and right now she looked it.

"Will the Senator yield to me?" she asked. "I have been reading the press stories most avidly, and following as much as possible of this on television, as I think most of us have, and the impression that has come through to me is one of most eminent fairness on the part of all members of the subcommittee; even from the senior Senator from South Carolina—most of the time. I am curious to know on what it is that the Senator from Wyoming bases his criticism. Possibly things were apparent to him, seated in the Caucus Room, which did not come over television; although I find," she added gently, "that this is usually not the case. Could the Senator enlighten me?"

"I will say to the distinguished Senator from Kansas," Senator Van Ackerman said sharply, "that I am sorry if she was not perceptive enough to grasp what was obvious to every intelligent observer in the room. I am telling the Senate what happened."

"Mr. President," Johnny DeWilton began indignantly, but Bessie, as always, was quite able to take care of herself.

"The Senator from Wyoming," she observed at her most grandmotherly, "has proven to us before that he possesses depths of perception and intuition which have not been conferred on those of us who are less fortunate. I for one, however, am constrained to tell the able Senator that much as I appreciate hearing about his particular view of the world,

I shall have to have proof more substantial than his unsupported personal word to convince me that Mr. Leffingwell was not treated fairly."

"Is the Senator saying I am a liar?" Fred Van Ackerman demanded ominously, and Senator Adams smiled sweetly.

"I am afraid the Record will just have to stand the way it is, Mr. President," she said. "The Senator's interpretations of it this afternoon are his problems, not mine. Of course," she added innocently, "if the Senator cares to make a point of order I can appeal it and the Senate can then have a vote on his veracity . . . I will say seriously," she went on placidly as Fred Van Ackerman looked furious but found no words for reply, "that I have had more than a few doubts about this nomination, Mr. President. However, on the basis of the hearings a good many of them have been set to rest, and it seems to me now that possibly Mr. Leffingwell's greatest handicap, if he has any, is the type of support he is getting from his friends." And with another kindly smile at Senator Van Ackerman she sat down while someone on the majority side murmured, "Good work, Bess!" quite audibly and the galleries snickered.

"Well, Mr. President," Fred Van Ackerman said angrily, "this is all very entertaining and amusing, I'm sure, and the Senator is welcome to take advantage of her sex if she wishes to do so to make attacks on other Senators——"

"Oh, come on!" Lafe Smith said disgustedly, and suddenly Fred Van Ackerman was transported out of himself into one of those frenzies his colleagues were coming to expect and be wary of.

"Yes!" he cried furiously, his face contorted, his voice suddenly getting its strange, unwholesome snarl, "Senators think this is a mighty clever, funny business here, don't they? They think it's all just ha-ha-ha and all so very jolly, don't they? Well, I'll tell you, Mr. President, the honor of the United States is involved here, yes, the future of the United States itself, may be, that's what's involved in the nomination of this great man to be Secretary of State, and what are Senators doing, Mr. President? What are they doing? They're sneering and making fun and joining in this attempt to smear and destroy him, and perhaps with him our best hope of peace, Mr. President. Of peace! That's what they're doing!"

He paused as suddenly as he had begun, while the Senate and the galleries waited silent and attentive. Some sort of internal struggle, very sharp, very short, very intense, seemed to take place; and when he resumed it was in a perfectly normal tone.

"Now, Mr. President," he said as reasonably as though he had never been disturbed at all, as though, curiously, he had already forgotten it and had no memory of it, "I ask Senators to consider what has happened so far on this nomination. Mr. Leffingwell was first subjected to a most severe and unrelenting cross-examination on his views by members of the subcommittee, and after it was finished the senior Senator from South Carolina was allowed to place on the stand a man who, it turned out, was a mental case, and he was allowed to fill the record and the newspapers and television and radio all over the globe, Mr. President, not just in America, with the most fantastic story. He said that at the University of Chicago he had been a student of Mr. Leffingwell's, which he was, and that Mr. Leffingwell had asked him to take a seminar with him, which Mr. Leffingwell did not, and that Mr. Leffingwell then invited him to attend a Communist cell meeting, which Mr. Leffingwell said he did not do, and the witness has no proof of it at all. Supposedly he attended these meetings with Mr. Leffingwell and some boy who is dead now and somebody else named James Morton, whom this witness says he couldn't identify if he saw him now because he wore a beard and he didn't see him very often. All of this Mr. Leffingwell denies, and the witness has no proof of it at all except his own word."

He paused and snapped his fingers impatiently for a glass of water, and a pageboy darted up to place one on his desk. He took a swallow and resumed in the same reasonable tone; Fred's spasm, his colleagues saw, was finished for the afternoon, though its strange unpleasant memory remained with them uneasily as he spoke. Even so, as Bob Munson could sense, he was beginning to make a little headway; toward what purpose, though, the Majority Leader as yet was unable to say.

"And what is his word worth, Mr. President?" Senator Van Ackerman went on. "Well, Mr. Leffingwell proved what it's worth. The man had a mental breakdown in college; he had another two years ago, at which time Mr. Leffingwell out of the kindness of his heart permitted him to resign without prejudice from the Federal Power Commission, where he was a minor clerk. Mr. Leffingwell later on, also as an act of kindness, steered him toward a job with his present employer, the Bureau of International Economic Affairs in the Department of Commerce. And in return for these kindnesses, this man has apparently become obsessed with the idea of getting revenge on Mr. Leffingwell, because he brought about his resignation from the FPC after his second mental breakdown. That's all there seems to be to it."

"Mr. President, will the Senator yield?" Powell Hanson asked, and Bob Munson began to get a little more actively worried about the trend of things.

"Isn't it true," the Senator from South Dakota asked, "that Mr. Leffingwell has categorically and completely denied any knowledge of, or connection with, or participation in, in any way whatsoever, any so-called Communist cell?"

"Why, of course," Fred Van Ackerman said shortly. "It's absolute nonsense."

"And all this man Gelman can offer is some tall tale about somebody who very conveniently happens to be dead, and somebody else named James Morton whom he very conveniently has lost track of and couldn't identify if he did see him?" Powell Hanson went on.

"That's right," Senator Van Ackerman said, and suddenly his voice filled with anger again, not wild this time, but righteous. "For this, Mr. President," he said, "for things as flimsy as this, our next Secretary of State is being crucified in the eyes of the world! I ask you, Mr. President, consider the effect this kind of thing must inevitably have upon him in the countries of the world where he must travel as our principal envoy. Shame on us, Senators, for permitting such goings on. Shame on us!"

"Mr. President," Orrin Knox said tartly, "if the Senator will yield, what would the Senator suggest we do about it?" But this proved to be the wrong question, for Fred Van Ackerman seized upon it instantly.

"I'll tell you, Senator," he said quickly, "what we can do about it. I'll tell you how we can make amends to him and at the same time wipe out the stigma of these shabby proceedings and prove to the world at one stroke that we're standing behind him one hundred per cent. We can discharge the Foreign Relations Committee from further consideration of his nomination and vote upon him right here and now. That's what we can do, right here and now. And," he concluded in a tone from which he made no attempt to exclude the triumph, for he knew he had caught them all flat-footed, "I do now so move."

At this suggestion, unorthodox, dramatic, and, as the older and more experienced heads could instantly see, exactly the sort of arbitrary move of which ideal headlines and ideal demagoguery are made, there was a stir all across the Senate and a number of Senators jumped up and began demanding recognition. Of these, Harley selected the Majority Leader, whose job it was to handle just such little problems as this, and Bob Munson prepared to speak with a certain grim humor about him. Even as he did so he had time to reflect how little opportunity one had to ever really delve very far beneath the surfaces of these 99 utterly independent and crotchety prima donnas, to find out, for instance, what kind of a family Fred Van Ackerman had come from, to find out how his mother could have loved him and how society had managed to restrain itself sufficiently to let him live long enough to attain the high estate and eminence of United States Senator.

"Mr. President," he said with the deliberate slowness that any good strategist uses when things have rushed to a peak of tension and time-gaining is the principal objective, "if I may be permitted first, before commenting directly on the motion of the Senator from Wyoming, to review briefly what happened in the subcommittee and place it, perhaps, in a little less heated perspective than he has done.

"It is true, to begin with, that members of the subcommittee subjected the nominee to a thorough and exhaustive examination of his personal views. Is it the function of a Senator to do less? Wouldn't you have subjected him to a searching cross-examination if you had been on the subcommittee? Of course you would, and who can sensibly criticize those who did, since they were acting not only as the instrument of the Foreign

Relations Committee but as your agents as well in the attempt to ascertain the truth?

"It is true that the senior Senator from South Carolina was allowed to cross-examine the nominee, and to bring before the subcommittee a witness against the nominee. Had your personal feelings and convictions been involved in this matter as his have been for so many years, would you not have requested the same privilege? And have expected the subcommittee to grant it to you, and made use of it in any way you deemed best in the pursuit of your objectives? Of course you would, and since the action of the senior Senator from South Carolina in this instance opened up a field of inquiry which inevitably had to be pursued in some form in view of many questions in the country concerning the nominee, who can justifiably criticize him for what he did? Whatever his motives, it served to explode a number of hints and rumors and allegations in a way that no other procedure, perhaps, could have exploded them.

"Which brings me to the treatment of the nominee. He was asked many sharp and pointed questions, yes, and members of the subcommittee rightly, in view of the enormous importance of the office for which he has been nominated, pulled no punches. But when the man Gelman had made his statements under examination by Senator Cooley, the subcommittee immediately asked Mr. Leffingwell to cross-examine, and the fact that the proceedings went over for twenty-four hours was his own decision, not the subcommittee's. And when he returned to the stand, the subcommittee granted him full rights to cross-examine without interference, and the chairman, the distinguished and able and most fair senior Senator from Utah, Mr. Anderson, even went so far as to offer him the use of the subcommittee's right of subpoena if he wished to use it to call further witnesses to the stand in his defense.

"So I do not think, Mr. President, that any fair review of the facts in the matter can come up with any honest conclusion except that the proceedings were fairly conducted, that the nominee was given every assistance in defending himself, and that the hearings marked a high point in the history of this Senate of which we can all be proud."

"Mr. President," Senator Van Ackerman demanded sharply, "will the Majority Leader yield?"

"I prefer not to until I am finished, Mr. President," Senator Munson said calmly. "The Senator has said quite a few things and made quite a few headlines here this afternoon, and I think it is time the rest of us had a chance to do some talking without interruption . . . Now as to the Senator's motion to discharge the Foreign Relations Committee from further consideration of this nomination and bring it immediately to the floor for a vote. It is of course his privilege to make such a motion——"

"Mr. President," Powell Hanson said, "will the Senator yield?"

"I shall be happy to," Bob Munson said graciously, and there was a little ripple of amusement.

"Will the Senator ask for the Yeas and Nays on that," Powell asked, "so that we may have a clear demonstration of the sentiments of the Senate at this time?"

At this standard form of request for a roll-call vote, which had to be supported by a show of hands from at least one-fifth of the Senators present, the Majority Leader hesitated. He was aware of a slight, a very slight movement of warning from the Senator from South Carolina beside him, so hidden that only years of friendship and familiarity permitted him to perceive it; and instinct told him that Seab was entirely right and it was an unwise thing to accede to. But he was aware also that Fred Van Ackerman had done some astute planning on this, underneath his flamboyant and inflammatory approach. An alliance with the much-respected Powell Hanson was a shrewd move; and since it was Powell who asked for the roll-call vote, Bob Munson knew that he was almost inevitably going to be forced to agree. So with only the slightest of split-second hesitation while all this went through his mind, he did.

"Certainly, Mr. President," he said agreeably. "That seems to me a perfectly justified request. I ask that the Yeas and Nays be ordered on the motion of the Senator from Wyoming."

There was a general show of hands, and the Vice President pronounced the traditional phraseology.

"Evidently a sufficient number," he said, "and the Yeas and Nays are ordered."

Now, Bob Munson knew, he must use the time between the ordering of the Yeas and Nays and the actual casting of the vote to insure that when the vote came it would go the way he wanted it to; and he proceeded to explain what that was as astutely as he knew how, aware that in the closely watching face of Kenneth Hackett of Wisconsin, for instance, the darkly intent visage of Seab's colleague, H. Harper Graham of South Carolina, the big, slumped yet attentive figure of L. B. Carter of Oklahoma, the vacantly handsome aspect of Albert G. Cockrell of Ohio, the shrewd appraisal of Stonewall Jackson Phillips of Tennessee, and all the rest, the issue would be decided. It was one of those decisive moments when a Senate debate can go either way; and he bent himself now to the task of seeing that it would go his way.

"Now, Mr. President," he said, "what are the merits of this motion and what are its demerits? Its merits, I think, can be summed up very simply. It would indeed be a dramatic affirmation before the world of our faith in this nominee and our support of him if we were to summarily vote him confirmation this afternoon, bypassing the regular procedures of the Senate to do so. It would also eliminate any chance of further argument about his nomination, which in the eyes of his supporters—of whom, I may say, I am one, both ex officio as Majority Leader and on the basis of the hearings—would be a good thing. Those are the two merits of this motion. They are not, it seems to me, sufficient to outweigh its demerits.

"The procedures of the Senate, slow as they are and cumbersome as they are in many instances, have gradually been established over all these long decades, which before long will approach two centuries, for one basic purpose: for the protection of the citizens of this Republic, for the protection of the states which compose it, and for the protection of Senators in the exercise of their duty to represent those citizens and those states. The whole story of the creation of the American Government is the story of the deliberate diffusion of power; the whole story of the life of the American Government is the story of the struggle between the deliberate diffusion of power, which in and of itself is perhaps the most brilliant device for the protection of liberty ever conceived by free men, and the deliberate concentration of power, which free men have often deemed necessary to preserve that liberty. If either diffusion or concentration were to win the battle once and for all, then I think freedom would finally be gone, and this great dream of liberty within discipline which is America would be ended forever. This continuing tension, this never-decided contest between diffusion and concentration of power is what makes this government the miracle of the ages that it is; and I for one would consider that day a sad and fearful day in which the decision went permanently to one or the other . . .

"In this, Senators, the procedures of this Senate play their part, a great part, which one comes to appreciate and value the more the longer he remains here. And so it is that every thinking citizen who really understands and really believes in his government will, when the final chips are down, defend them. They have been misused many times by men who would thwart the will of the majority; but they have been used far more often to advance the interests of all the people, and the proof of that lies in the state of being to which this most fortunate of lands has come through so many hard times and fearsome perils and so many dark, unhappy things . . .

"Mr. President," he said softly into the hush of the chamber, "I would wish that the motion of the Senator from Wyoming would be defeated; for it will not hurt us or Mr. Leffingwell if he must wait another day or two before assuming office. But it might hurt us all most grievously if it should become the habit here that the safeguards of our liberties, of which the regular slow and patient procedures of the Senate, for all their faults, are among the most supremely important, are to be tossed away whenever it suits us in the heat and passion of the passing moment."

And as he sat down solemnly there was a sudden surprising burst of applause from the Senate which was taken up vigorously by the galleries. Across the aisle Warren Strickland called over with a grin which Bob Munson answered, "This is the first time I ever knew a lecture on civics to get a hand from the public!" and then he rose in his turn and sought recognition.

"Mr. President," he said when Harley granted it, "I shall not attempt to match the eloquence of the distinguished Majority Leader, but I do wish to associate myself entirely with the burden of his remarks. It is true that I am inclined to be opposed to this nomination, but the issue now, as he so clearly states, is no longer the nomination; it is the way in which the Senate is to deal with the nomination; and that, as he also says, is infinitely more important in the long perspective of our history than any nomination. There are ways of doing things that conform to the pattern that constant testing and constant experience has shown to be good, and there are ways of doing things that abandon all this and rush off after the hasty, the ill-advised, the slick, and the expedient. Let us permit the subcommittee of the Foreign Relations Committee to make its recommendation to the full committee; let us permit the full committee to vote and then make its recommendation to us; and then let us vote, as we are in all probability going to vote, for this nominee in the customary way of our regular procedure. Nothing will be lost by this, whereas, as the Majority Leader says, much could be lost by the erosions of liberty to which another course might ultimately contribute."

"I love the Senate when it gets into one of these procedural fights," the *Herald Tribune* confided without irony to the *Times*. "It brings out the best in everybody." "Except Fred Van Ackerman," the *Times* observed dryly, and the *Trib* grinned as on the floor below the junior Senator from Wyoming was once more on his feet demanding recognition.

"Mr. President," Senator Van Ackerman said, "these are fine words. There are always fine words in the Senate when somebody wants to block something. I've stated the situation clearly here, I've stated what we can accomplish by adopting my motion. I don't see what is to be gained by delaying it any longer. A Secretary of State is involved here, Mr. President!" he cried in sudden anger. "Doesn't that *mean* anything to Senators? Aren't we *interested* in backing up our own man against the world? Don't we *care* about the way we send him forth to negotiate? What's the point in further talk?"

"Mr. President," Tom August said gently from his desk in the center of the majority side, "if the Senator will yield to me?"

"I shall be happy to yield the floor to the distinguished chairman of the Foreign Relations Committee," Fred Van Ackerman said, "and then I hope we can stop talking and vote."

"I thank the Senator," Tom said in his customary wistful way which sounded as though he were always mentally wringing his hands over the condition of mankind. "I shall not detain the Senate long, but I am going to take a position on this which may be somewhat surprising for the chairman of a committee——"

"I told you, Bob," Seab murmured, poking the Majority Leader's arm, and Senator Munson nodded. "The little bastard's pulled a fast one this time," he agreed.

"—and I should like to state my reasons," Senator August said. "I am going to support the motion of the Senator from Wyoming because I feel as he does that this nominee has been subjected to sufficient attack to damage him severely in the eyes of other nations unless we take some such dramatic action as the Senator proposes to indicate our support of him. Therefore I feel it is imperative that we do this, and even though it means bypassing my own committee, I feel this so deeply that I am prepared to join in the suggestion that we do so. I hope the Senate will so vote, Mr. President!"

Orrin Knox and Brigham Anderson were both on their feet as he concluded, and the Vice President recognized the Senator from Illinois first.

"Well, Mr. President," Orrin said indignantly, "if this is the emotional basis on which the Senator from Minnesota approaches all problems of foreign policy, God help us. The Majority Leader is entirely right, the Senators from Wyoming and Minnesota are entirely wrong, and it is beginning to appear that there must indeed be some conspiracy here as the distinguished Senator from Indiana, Mr. Hendershot, was suggesting the other day. Who is it who wishes this thing rushed through now, Mr. President? Is it the Majority Leader, who has stated with fine eloquence and perception the reasons why we have certain procedures in the Senate? No, it is the Senator from Wyoming, who proposes it. Whose leadership are we to follow, Mr. President? Which has shown itself more worthy of trust? I associate myself entirely with the Majority Leader in this, and I do so as one who also is pretty well convinced by now that Mr. Leffingwell should be confirmed. But not on this higgledy-piggledy, rush-rush-rush basis. It would look phony and it would be phony, and I have too much respect for the office of Secretary of State and the burdens its occupant must carry, I will say to Senator Van Ackerman, to be a party to it."

And he sat down with a contemptuous look at the Senator from Wyoming, who returned it with interest to the amusement of the galleries.

"Mr. President," Senator Anderson said, with a note in his voice which his colleagues knew meant a rare, genuine anger, "I would like to return to the matter of the treatment accorded Mr. Leffingwell, to point out that it was completely fair in every way, and to say that the desperate anxiety for an immediate confirmation which seems to be behind this motion raises the reasonable presumption, Mr. President, that Mr. Leffingwell's supporters must feel that if his case were further examined something might be found in it which would militate against a favorable consideration. I would hope that this is not the case, Mr. President, but the nominee has gone out of his way to seek favor with the junior Senator from Wyoming, and the Senator's motion, coming on the heels of it, raises some question as to how spontaneous the motion is . . . I may say, Mr. President, that I believe Mr. Leffingwell's record as it stands, aside from one or two minor equivocations, is worthy of confirmation; I expect I shall probably vote to confirm him. But like the Senator from Illinois,

I shall not vote on the basis of having it rammed down my throat. There is very little to be gained by this peculiar haste, and much to be lost, as the Majority Leader says. I am not convinced that the reasons behind it are valid."

And with a long, appraising look at the junior Senator from Wyoming, who was on his feet, his face twisted with anger, the senior Senator from Utah sat down.

"Mr. President!" Senator Van Ackerman cried, and once more the peculiar strangled snarl was in his voice, "that is typical of the attitude of the Senator from Utah throughout this whole proceeding. He has never liked the nominee and he doesn't like him now, and he's taken every chance he could get to smear him and attack him and make implications about him. Now he makes implications about me, Mr. President, yes, he implies there has been collusion about this. I swear to you, Mr. President, it was entirely my own idea and Mr. Leffingwell had nothing to do with it. This is just one more example of the unfair treatment he has received right along, Mr. President. I ask for a vote!"

"Give the baby his vote," Lafe Smith said, not trying very hard to keep his voice down, and what the Congressional Record always refers to in such moments of impatience and confusion as "(Several Senators)" cried, "Vote! Vote!"

"Seab," Bob Munson said hurriedly, as Fred Van Ackerman looked with angry insistence at the Vice President, "you don't want to say anything before we vote?" Senator Cooley gave him a slow and sleepy smile. "Bob," he said softly, "you know better than that. This is my day to keep quiet, Bob. Let's have our vote and see what happens." "I don't like the feel of it," the Majority Leader confided worriedly. "It's going to be too close."

But in a second he was on his feet all bland composure.

"Mr. President," he said, "I suggest the absence of a quorum, and then I ask for the Yeas and Nays as ordered."

And he sat down with an impassive and patient expression as the clerk went quickly through the roll while little bits of talk and gossip, quick conferrings, jokes and laughter and underneath it all a rising tension flickered across the surface of the Senate like St. Elmo's fire.

"Eighty-six Senators having answered to their names," the Vice President said, "a quorum is present, and the clerk will call the roll for the Yeas and Nays."

"Mr. Abbott!" the clerk said, and Charlie Abbott, because, Bob Munson knew, he thought he still might be able to work out a dicker on the Portsmouth Navy Yard if he had the time, voted "No!" in a firm voice.

"Mrs. Adams!" And Bessie too voted "No!" in a pleasantly decisive way.

There followed in rapid succession four Ayes and then the clerk came to Brigham Anderson, who voted No, followed by Tom August, who voted Aye.

On through the B's, Mr. Baker, Mr. Blair, Mr. Bliss, Mr. Boland, Mr. Bowen, Mr. Boyle, Mr. Brittain, with the Ayes gradually beginning to catch up and overtake the Nos; through the C's from Fred Cahill of Missouri to Frank Curtis of Maine, with Seab Cooley explosively crying "No!" while the tension mounted and the Nos again began to move up alongside the Ayes; Stanley Danta and John DeWilton, both voting No, Sam Eastwood of Colorado following with an Aye; Hal Fry, away at UN, not answering, H. Harper Graham of South Carolina voting No; through the H's, the J's, the K's, Jim La Rue of New Jersey leading off the L's in his quavery voice with a No; the M's, the O's, Ed Parrish of Nevada saying Aye; the Ayes thirty-two, the Nays thirty-five as Bob Munson and many another on the floor and in the press gallery kept score on the long white tally sheets; Arly Richardson saying a scornful No, his distant cousin, chubby little Leo P. Richardson of Florida countering with a firm "Aye!"; Courtney Robinson, Hugh Root, Taylor Ryan, all No; Stu Schoenfeldt of Pennsylvania, Aye; Raymond Robert Smith of California, over-dapper and over-elegant, Aye; the T's, the V's, with Luis Valdez of New Mexico saying No, and Fred Van Ackerman a defiant Aye; Julius Welch, Aye; Allen Whiteside of Florida, Aye, Herbert Wilson of Georgia, No, and a great expulsion of pent-in breath from the Senate and the press as a hasty tabulation showed the vote at forty Yeas, forty-one Nays. Again the tension as the clerk ran quickly through the absentees and five more answered their names; and again the explosion of excitement as another quick tabulation at the end disclosed what Harley announced a moment later after the clerk reported hurriedly to him.

"On this motion," the Vice President said, "the vote is forty-three to forty-three."

"Mr. President!" Fred Ackerman cried hastily, jumping to his feet to start the delaying tactic that always occurs on any close vote in the Senate when the purpose is to hold up the final announcement of the result until absent members can be rounded up, "am I recorded on this vote?"

"The Senator is recorded," Harley said, after checking solemnly with the clerk.

"How am I recorded, Mr. President?" Fred asked, and the Vice President checked again.

"The Senator is recorded as voting in the affirmative," he said, and Fred sat down. Immediately Ed Parrish went through the same procedure, and after him Sam Eastwood and then Allen Whiteside before Irving Steinman of New York finally hurried breathlessly onto the floor, still wearing the overcoat in which he had jumped into a cab to rush up from the Labor Department where he had been on a constituent's business.

"Mr. Steinman!" the clerk said in a reproachful voice, and Senator Steinman said "Aye!" in a firm voice that brought an even greater tension to the room, for now it was the opponents' turn to play the delaying game on behalf of Lloyd Cavanaugh of Rhode Island, whose plane, if it had been on schedule, had arrived at National Airport just about the time the clerk had called "Mr. Abbott!" And sure enough, after Brigham Anderson and Orrin Knox and two or three others had asked the Vice President to tell them how they were recorded, Senator Cavanaugh too rushed in breathlessly, still overcoated, to cast a hasty "No!"

"The vote," the Vice President announced, "is still tied at forty-four to forty-four." He paused and the Majority Leader told him with silent vehemence in his own mind, come on, Harley, make it good. And Harley, after a moment's enjoyment of the Senate's suspense, did.

"Under the rules of the Senate," he said formally, "a motion fails of passage on a tie vote, and therefore this motion is already defeated. Under the Constitution, however, the Vice President has the right to vote in case of a tie. Because he deems this decision sufficiently important to warrant an expression of opinion from him that may emphasize its gravity to the country, the Vice President will exercise his prerogative and vote No. The motion is not agreed to."

In the noisy aftermath of babble and talk and jokes and laughter, the junior Senator from Wyoming exchanged a look of open hostility with the senior Senator from Utah; the senior Senator from South Carolina, looking as sleepy and somnolent as before, gave one small chuckle and slapped the Majority Leader on the knee; the senior Senator from Illinois shook his head pityingly at the senior Senator from Minnesota, who pursed his lips and looked sadly disapproving; and the Majority Leader bowed with a grateful grin to the Vice President, who smiled with satisfaction in return. Above in the press galleries the reporters dashed out to send their new leads, filled with the drama of the afternoon and the exciting and intriguing fact that the upstart from Wyoming had come within an ace of overturning the Majority Leader and winning immediate consideration of the nomination. By that slim chance, though no one knew it then, LEFFINGWELL RUNNING had been extended considerably beyond the one or two days more envisaged by the opponents of the motion, and the door had been opened to events that otherwise would never have occurred. By so narrow a margin does the Senate on occasion decide the fate of causes and of men.

That evening there once again went across the nation and around the globe the exciting tale of Robert A. Leffingwell and his almost-victory. At their typewriters from Baltimore to Seattle the editorial writers for the morning papers went busily to work approving or condemning; on all the television newscasts the most favorable clips of the nominee and Fred Van Ackerman, accompanied by the most devastatingly unfavorable shots of the Majority Leader and Brigham Anderson that could be found, were displayed upon the little screen; the man who said, "This—is the news," said, "This—is the news," and the news was that a great man, momentarily hobbled by a blindly conservative opposition, would soon have a triumph that would give his nation under God a new birth of freedom and a new hope for peace; and everywhere the backers of Robert A. Leffingwell rejoiced, even as they cursed the Senate, in the all-but-certainty now that their man had only one small river left to cross before coming safely home.

But in the homes of the subcommittee the mood was more serious, for there men were at work going carefully over three days of transcript in preparation for their vote tomorrow. And on the second floor of the Old Senate Office Building in one of the last offices still alight as the hour neared ten, a similar mood held sway, for there the senior Senator from South Carolina, having dismissed his staff, was similarly engaged; and for the process he was mustering all the skill and experience he had ever known in one last supreme effort to work his will on Robert A. Leffingwell.

First, by a conscious effort that he had found effective many times before, he deliberately drained his mind, as much as was humanly possible, of every preconception, every emotion, every prejudice, every thought that had filled it on the subject heretofore.

Then he read through the transcript slowly and carefully from beginning to end, approaching it as though it were brand new and he a reader who knew nothing at all of what was involved, making a note or two from time to time on a large pad of lined Senate notepaper in his spidery old hand.

Then he laid the transcript aside and went patiently and slowly over his notes in the same open-minded, emotion-drained, first-reading way, methodically and deliberately tearing up each note as he finished considering it and dismissed it from his mind.

At the end of all this he had just one note remaining before him, and so he sat, his chin supported on the knuckles of his hands, staring down at that small piece of white paper in the little circle of light on the green blotter in the silent office in the great deserted building.

Thus Seab thought.

He thought for quite a long time.

And then suddenly the instinct which made him the fearfully shrewd old man he was came once more and for the last time in the Leffingwell matter to his assistance, and with it a flashing inspiration; and with a softly exultant little exclamation of triumph and certainty the brightest boy who ever grew up in Barnwell stopped thinking and started acting.

First he put through a phone call to a home over the District Line in Chevy Chase, Maryland, and asked a question so blunt and unexpected that its recipient gasped and admitted the answer before he had time to think of evasions.

And then Seab told him with a terrifying fury in his voice exactly what he should do if he wished to preserve his honor and serve his country well.

And then Seab hung up.

An hour later the phone rang at the Andersons' in Spring Valley and Brigham Anderson went to answer. A strangely muffled, strangely tired voice came over.

"I have something to say," it said, sounding far away and desolate.

"Who is this?" the Senator demanded sharply, and the voice seemed to gather itself together and make a great effort.

"There was a time when I was known as James Morton," it said.

Three

Brigham Anderson's Book

Now spring has come, suddenly, in a day, as it always comes to Washington. Over all the District, Maryland, and Virginia the winds are warm, the trees are abruptly green, the golden fountains of forsythia rise in every street; and the voice of the tourist is heard in the land. At this very moment on this brightly sparkling morning he is arising in his thousands in his myriad hotels, motels, and other temporary warrens and gathering himself together for another day of mass assault upon the noble monuments and busy offices of his government. There will be some of his kind who will make the excursion with friends or relatives; some who will take guided tours in sight-seeing buses; and still others who will start out on their own with cameras, dogged determination, and a rather hazy concept of what they will find. "Where does the President work?" some of them will ask when they go through the Capitol. "We've seen the Senate and the House, now can you tell us where we can see Congress?"

The first wave is here, tramping with weary tenacity through the Smithsonian and the zoo, paying their hasty camera-clicking tributes to Abe Lincoln in his temple ("Stand over there by his right foot, Kit,"), allowing half an hour for a quick run through the National Gallery of Art, hurrying one another along in a pushing, shoving, exclaiming line through Mount Vernon, the White House, and Lee House in Arlington, peeking in quickly at the massive red-draped chamber of the Supreme Court, viewing with suitable awe the blood-stained relics of the FBI, ascending the Washington Monument for a glimpse, all too brief, of the city, the river, the surrounding countryside, all the monuments and buildings, the great scheme of L'Enfant laid out before them with its broad avenues, its carpeting of tree tops everywhere, its veneer of world capital still not effacing a certain gracious, comfortable, small-town aspect that not all the problems nor all the tourists in Christendom can quite obscure.

The city has prepared itself for the onslaught by a sort of instinctive battening down of the hatches. "Just wait until the tourists come," people have been saying warningly to one another for weeks; or, "Well, I guess if we can't make it now we'd better wait until fall, because the tourists will be here in a little while and you know what a mess that is." Yet it is not done unkindly, nor is it entirely devoid of appreciation for the excitement of those who visit for the first time. There are enough who can remember their own first days here, when all the streets were golden and everyone who passed was ten feet tall and bound upon secret missions of high import. Although the streets have long since returned to asphalt and the unmoved eyes of experience now see that most of those who pass are not ten feet tall but just tired little government workers worrying about the mortgage, something of the aura lingers still; and so the visitors are patiently suffered and forgiven much.

Among those who really are, in a manner of speaking, ten feet tall, the sparkling morning is bringing with it both a heightened sense of being alive and a spreading interest, excitement, and in some cases dismay, as a result of Brigham Anderson's summary action of last night, announced in the Washington *Post*, the New York *Times* and all other morning papers across the land, echoed and restated and repeated and re-emphasized at regular intervals on every radio station. Interest in this is balanced about equally by interest in other news, coming out of Turkey suddenly and without warning as such news has been coming all too frequently in recent years, possessed of a significance no one can accurately assess but serving to fan through the world that stalking fear that is inspiring COMFORT and other manifestations of the mood of desperation gripping many in the West. MASSIVE NEW SOVIET LAUNCHING TRACKED, the papers say; TELLER, VON BRAUN FEAR MANNED MOON SHOOT; BASE COULD GIVE REDS TEMPORARY SPACE RULE; RESULTS MAY BE KNOWN IN WEEK; MOSCOW SILENT.

The reaction to this is partly a deepening of the constant worry that nags at all free men, partly a recurrence of that sort of tired oh-dear-what-now mood that comes upon them when confronted with the latest evil invention of the enemy. Possibly the news means nothing at all, based as it is on rumors, half hints, unconfirmed reports, and nervous guesses; or possibly it means terribly much. Unmanned satellites to the moon have been in orbit for some time, and the fantastic adaptability of the human mind has long since relegated them to the commonplace; manned satellites that could conceivably establish bases would be something else again. American preparations are nearing completion at Cape Canaveral, but Project Outward hasn't gone yet; is this one more race lost to the fleet and the crafty? Right now no one knows; and since the mind possesses also the ability to push back and shove away and place in some remote spot along with other to-be-thought-about-later things the possibility that bad news may be true, it is the news of Brigham Anderson that concerns Washington most directly now. Whatever the news from Ankara may mean, time will have to tell; there is little doubt in the capital that the news prompted by Brigham Anderson means a great deal right now.

Thus it is that he is the most immediate and pressing worry on top of all the other worries in the minds of those most concerned with the nomination of Robert A. Leffingwell. At the Sheraton-Park the senior

Senator from Michigan contemplates the news with profane dismay even as the senior Senator from South Carolina contemplates it with placid satisfaction; at the White House the President, pausing by his bedroom window to look down across the pleasant prospect of the Ellipse, the Washington Monument, the river, and green Virginia beyond, shakes his head in a puzzled way and determines upon an early call to the Majority Leader; at the UN Senator Fry and Krishna Khaleel, breakfasting together in the Delegates' dining room, discuss the event with equal bafflement on both sides; Lord Maudulayne, Raoul Barre, and Vasily Tashikov all decide to advise their governments at once on everything they can find out about it; on Arlington Ridge Road the phone rings unanswered in the nominee's home as the inevitable flood of calls comes in from the press; in the homes of the subcommittee, where the phones are answered, the reaction is approximately the same: a puzzled, "What the hell?" followed by "No comment" except in the case of Orrin Knox, who finally sums up the prevailing attitude for the *Times* by admitting that he was not consulted and then adding firmly, "However, I am quite sure that I speak for the subcommittee when I say that we have every confidence in Senator Anderson's judgment and are quite willing to abide by it." And in Spring Valley, where the phone is ringing too, Mabel Anderson patiently answers with the kind of lie that senatorial wives, aides, and assistants often have to tell: "No, I'm sorry, he's left for the office, possibly you can find him there." In the same way later in the day his office will say politely, "No, I'm sorry, he's not here. He had an appointment downtown. We don't know when he'll be back." The Senator wants to talk to certain people and he knows certain people will want to talk to him, and he does not intend to be interrupted by the necessary, understandable but distracting importunings of the press.

Actually at this moment, while the news of his action is spreading out along the news wires and over the airwaves to encircle the globe in company with the rumors from Ankara, Brigham Anderson is right outside in his own back yard studying the earth and doing his best not to think about anything but the felicities of the season. He still does not know what kind of roses to plant alongside the house, and his thoughts are divided about equally between his horticultural problem, the news from Ankara, and the twin problems posed by the telephone call from James Morton and his own instinctive and far-reaching action in response to it. It is significant of his attitude toward this last, four short days before it reaches a climax he could not now imagine, that at the moment, despite a feeling of deep trouble and unease about the rush of domestic events in which he knows he has become at least for the time being the central figure, it is the problem of the roses which briefly weighs the heavier.

But it is spring, the sun is bright, the winds are warm, and he is using his garden for the purpose men have gardens for: to relax, however briefly, to make appraisal and take stock, to get away for a few precious moments from the crushing responsibility which now has devolved upon him in the wake of the call last night. It seems safe to say that there is hardly a householder in the capital who is not at this moment turning about with pleasant anticipation in his mind the question of what to do with roses, whether it would be best this year to build the garden around dahlias, zinnias, or glads, whether to make the annual surrender to temptation and buy more azaleas and if so where to put them, what to do about the bare spots in the lawn and what preparations to make for the inevitable onslaught of crab grass later on. Momentarily one with them, even though beneath the surface of his mind dark questions and grave worries swirl, the Senator is occupied for the most part with the pleasant problems that go naturally and inevitably with spring. The other problems revolving around Robert A. Leffingwell he knows he will have to face soon enough as the day develops, so for this short half hour or so of wandering around the yard he is consciously making himself enjoy what spring has to offer.

When all this is said, however, it still must be confessed that even though he is applying himself to the task with great determination, the attempt is not entirely successful. He is an honest and a conscientious man and it is not possible for him to keep the world out for more than a minute or two at a time. Then it comes rushing back upon him as it must upon any responsible citizen. He too has seen the Turkish reports, and it seems to him all the more reason, if they should by any reach of the imagination be true—and indeed have the scientists not been saying since 1957 that they inevitably and very shortly would be true?—why he should have done what he did following the call from James Morton. Even more now, he feels, does the integrity and reliability of the nominee become an issue. Being right, however, is sometimes a rather fragile shield against the questionings of the world. He knows exactly the reaction his action must now be arousing in the minds of the Majority Leader and the Minority Leader, of Orrin Knox and Stanley Danta and all the other friends with whom he rates so high even though he knows they will stand by him patiently awaiting his reasons; he also understands the feelings that must be going through the mind of the nominee, who knows now that the past has presented its bill after all, just when he thought he had it safely canceled; and he is aware of the black, irresponsible yet fiercely clever anger that must be assailing the ruthless mind of Fred Van Ackerman, who will make trouble for him if he can over this, as a part of his own long-term ambitions. And with all these things passing through his thoughts, he is reminded with a sudden inexplicable feeling, coming out of nowhere and blighting the perfect day suddenly into shadow, of his own uneasy foreboding when it was first proposed to him that he take an active hand in the Leffingwell matter. He knew then, and he knows now, that it is bad business for him; he doesn't know why, yet, but he knows.

Nonetheless, he reflects with a sudden impatient kick at a gopher tunnel in the lawn, he is not about to back away from it, nor is he about to give in to any such feelings, which a split-second recapitulation convinces him are so much hogwash. He is a good public servant, doing what he knows to be a good job, filled with an honorable purpose and a high integrity; and he is not going to cut and run, he tells himself, just because events have now suddenly made him the focus of all the violent emotions, hopes, dreams, suspicions, dislikes, prejudices, ideals, and passions of the Leffing-well nomination. He has conducted the hearings with an impartial justice, he has done his level best to be fair to all concerned, and now he knows he has taken the only action an honest man could take. He knows it will bring down upon him all the organized, massive anger and criticism of those who are emotionally involved with the cause of the nominee, but he is not worried about his ability to defend it before his peers in the only forum that really matters now, the Senate of the United States.

At this thought, which fortifies him considerably as he reflects upon all the many friends he has in that body, the dark mood lifts a little and he tells himself with a quick impatience that he is a fine one to be driving himself into a stew with that kind of nonsense. He reminds himself with a swiftly rising optimism that he is after all a most highly thought-of, well-liked, and respected young man, with a wife who complements his career and a daughter he adores, an electorate with which after seven years he is still carrying on a mutual honeymoon, and a standing in the Senate which few can equal. And it is not just the present that lies bland and happy about him, for he faces a prospect such as few men in America are fortunate enough to contemplate.

At thirty-seven he is established in the Senate, secure in his state, one of the rising young men of the country, already accorded by his elders, as witness their insistence upon entrusting him with the delicate and demanding task of chairing the Leffingwell hearing, a confidence and respect very seldom given to men his age in the august body to which he belongs. Ahead lies a life of ever more satisfying and worthwhile public service, and nothing he can see before him on this bright golden day gives any indication to the contrary.

Only one immediate worry keeps coming back to nag him, and that is the thought that just possibly he had acted a little too hastily last night when, upon receipt of James Morton's call, he had telephoned the wire services and announced that the Leffingwell hearing would be re-opened at 10 A.M. tomorrow. This action was taken on his own and without consultation with anyone else on the subcommittee or anyone else in the Senate, and as such it was to some degree an uncharacteristic action, one of the few impulsive and uncareful moments in a life which has not known many. Underlying his attempt to enjoy the day is the uneasy thought that possibly he had moved too fast and may regret it. Yet such had been the desperate urgency of James Morton's call, and so deep its anguished intensity, that he had perforce been swept into the conviction that it was genuine; and when he had called the number back within ten minutes to check for sure, the man had displayed an even greater anxiety. This had strengthened his own general tendency to be essentially a lone wolf, and he had felt further that in this case there were party matters involved, the commitment of the President and the Majority Leader to the nominee, all the matters of party prestige and political standing now riding on the shoulders of Robert A. Leffingwell, which he felt imposed an obligation upon him not to divulge his reasons to the press or anyone else until he could have a chance to discuss them at the White House. Compounding this reaction also was his shock and surprise, for he had been coming around in his own mind to a point where he could actively support the nominee. Now all bets are off, and there is, indeed, the very strong probability that he will move into active opposition.

Nonetheless, he supposes, he might have taken the time to call Orrin Knox, at least; but Orrin, though his closest friend in the Senate, would have been just returning from a family party for Crystal and Hal, and Brig had decided not to bother him when his mind was filled with that pleasant occupation. This morning he is inclined to wish he had, for he knows Orrin would have agreed with him and he might feel easier in his own mind about it at this moment. There might not be the steady, insistent recurrence of the thought that he had committed an irrevocable act whose consequences might somehow, in some way, bear out his earlier forebodings about the Leffingwell matter and his own involvement in it.

Insistently, even so, he is reminded as he stands in his yard and studies the garden that the sky is blue, the sun is bright, the winds are warm, and spring is here. It is a lovely time of year in which to be alive, and the senior Senator from Utah, though understandably troubled by the world's ills and the problems attendant upon the nominee, is very glad he is.

2

Reflecting upon it soberly as his thoughts moved on in the sun-swept day, he came again, as he had so often, to the conclusion that his had been in the main a remarkably sun-swept life. It had known its problems and its trials, and it had not of course been free from all unhappiness and strain, but in general he had been much luckier than most at avoiding the more unpleasant aspects of human living. Often this had come about, not deliberately, but just because he was what he was, and so it was not something for which he took any particular credit. Both by religion and observation he had come to believe that luck or God or destiny or fate or whatever men chose to call it had much to do with human endeavor and the tides of life; and his own experience seemed to bear it out. He had been given much, and he had used it, on the whole, he thought, wisely; so his luck had held, and the end result had been a felicity that had touched the high peaks of a generally constructive life even as it had helped him across its few dark valleys.

This had been true in the beginning because he had been born into a prominent family in Salt Lake City, high in the councils of the Church, which had made for a major initial advantage; it had been true thereafter because of his own character and the uses he had made of it. Almost from the first, if his family could be believed, there had been about him a certain aura that drew people to him; "Brig's fatal charm," his oldest sister called it, and they had all been pleased when its effectiveness proved out far beyond the family's limits.

Even in earliest childhood there had been a quick alertness, an immediate response to others, a sunny friendliness that won the hearts of his elders even though it did not always entrance some of his more jealous contemporaries. He had known his share of troubles in the savage jungle where children grow up, but unlike those of so many others they were not brought upon him by any meanness or pettiness or over-aggressiveness on his part, and he found that his family background permitted him to survive them without serious damage. He was fourth in a household that included two older girls, one older boy, and two younger girls, and this in itself provided a fair proving ground. There was always somebody above to alternate between smothering him with affection and beating his head in, and there was always somebody below to whom he could accord the same type of running shock-treatment. A personality clearly self-reliant from the start was strengthened in self-reliance even more; and when he grew to an age to be running about and going out to play, he found himself able to cope with the mercurial tides of liking and disliking, playing together and not playing together, being in the group or out of the group at a moment's notice, having his toys stolen, being in fights, bearing the brunt of mean remarks and at the same time making a few, without much jolt to his nervous or emotional systems. He went through a lot of that at home and he was prepared for it; even though, he was quite sure now, his character from the first had been such that he could have surmounted its challenges quite successfully under any circumstances.

Physically he was solid and stocky from the first, which proved an invaluable asset both at home and around the neighborhood when the chips were down; and combining with it as he did a relatively placid and tolerant character, he had what he eventually came to realize was a close to unbeatable combination. He didn't go out of his way to push anybody else around; neither did he stand for it too long when anybody else tried to push him around. By the time he had gone through grammar school this was an established and accepted fact, and so in high school the way opened out for him without the necessity for proving himself that plagued the adolescence of so many. Even in Deseret people were human, kids most of all; but they didn't bother him. He went his way with a certain unshakeable self-possession, already marked by his teachers as mature and reliable far beyond his years, making the highest grades, participating incessantly in school activities, going out for all the sports available, becoming a football hero, and winding up in his senior year as captain of the team. He could also have foreshadowed his later career more actively than he did, had he so desired, for there were opportunities to run for student-body office and in his sophomore year he had been president of his class. But his closest friend on the team, whom he had grown up with since age three, wanted very badly to be student-body president, and Brig deferred to his ambitions—not because he had to, but just because he decided gravely in a mind that had its own areas of private contemplation, far more extensive and sometimes more moody than his teachers would ever have believed, that this was what his friend wanted and that if he was truly a friend to him he would help him have it. So he managed his campaign for him, which in the fashion that occurs at surprisingly many levels of American life, gave him an early taste of the practical side of politics. In his more philosophical moments after coming to Washington the thought would strike him how early it is, in schools, in clubs, in church classes, and kindergartens, that Americans become used to the idea of casting votes, electing officers, exercising political judgment, bowing to the will of the majority. This habit, he had an idea, had rather more to do with the general self-propelling elements in the American system, rather more to do with the profoundly stabilizing effect of the state of mind that this-is-the-way-it-is-done-because-this-is-the-way-we-have-always-done-it than the political scientists had yet realized or given proper emphasis to.

So he had deferred to his friend, who at that particular moment meant more to him in an innocent way than all the little girls eager to make life happy for the football team who meant a good deal to him right then in a less innocent way, and the election had come off a smashing success. Now his friend was president of a bank in Ogden and when they got together with their families they often talked with amusement of that first early trial run in which he had been campaign-manager for the successful candidate who subsequently, when the time came, repaid the compliment with great astuteness and skill as manager of Brig's races for the Senate.

Coming as he did from a household that had as its head an Apostle of the Church, he was under some family pressure to become a missionary and then make the Church his life's work, but this he resisted with a quiet determination that soon crumbled parental opposition. His older brother was going into the Church, he pointed out, and he thought that was enough; the world was moving on, even in Zion's pleasantly self-sufficient land, and he had dreams and ambitions beyond that. Basically, he supposed, although it was not until he had gone to the Coast to enter Stanford that he realized it, he really did want to enter public life; and on the beautiful campus of the Farm, where, as in all colleges, the emphasis on political activity sharply increases, he soon found himself actively engaged. At one point in his third year he was running for vice president of his fraternity, running for president of the junior class, and running for a position on the executive committee of the student government; and he made them all. Along with it he also kept up a grade average that was close to straight A, went out successfully for the football team, and continued his attention to the girls, if anything more numerous in college, who are anxious to be of assistance to anyone of any prominence in campus life.

Nowhere among them, however, did he find one that seemed to appeal to him so fundamentally that he felt he must have her for life or die. There were some he felt he must have, period, and those he usually did have, period; but there it ended, and he left school to go to war heart-whole and fancy free; or, at any rate, as free as he ever was in the quiet places of his heart where he faced himself.

To him the Farm gave what it gives to all who are lucky enough to do their most serious growing-up in that beautiful place: a certain common-sense approach to life, a certain equipment, much more important than anything noted in the grade averages, for decent, constructive citizenship; an undying love for San Francisco and the Peninsula; a realization that of all the springs on earth none is quite as sweet as the long, lingering, all-enveloping hypnosis of spring in the Santa Clara Valley; above all, a clear perspective and a far view, of men, of issues, and of life. He left it to go to battle with gratitude in his heart, for his time there had been well-spent and for the most part very happy, and he knew that he had made many friends and won a wide popularity that would always be a strength and comfort to him through the years.

Throughout his college life he continued to show to the world the same aspect he was always to show it: steady, earnest, tolerant, easygoing, filled with a friendly attitude toward humanity that humanity found flattering and always responded to. If he had his moody times, and there was a strain in him that prompted them more often than his friends could have imagined, he kept them to himself, and hardly anyone ever suspected they were there. Only once had one of his fraternity brothers, sitting across from him one night in some little bar south of Market Street and noting a fleeting expression of restless melancholy on his face, dared to take a long gamble and ask quietly, "It isn't easy, is it?" But this particular friend had problems Brigham Anderson suspected and didn't want to get involved with, problems he didn't think were his problems, so he turned it off with a grin and some noncommittal jest. For a while after that his fraternity brother looked at him with a little speculative expression in his eyes, but Brig was so matter-of-fact, so pleasant, and so straightforward about everything that after a time the speculation stopped and their

them all he had read the same message. All but one he had refused to answer, and with the same pleasant, straightforward, matter-of-fact elusiveness with which he always eased himself out of situations he did not wish to be in, he would gently extricate himself from all such episodes and go on his way with liking and friendship intact. Yet always he found he could count on it, wherever he went, and he knew that if that were really the answer for him he lacked no opportunities. With one exception, however, something always held him back; and in that case, he came to feel later, it was basically just the war and probably nothing very fundamental or long-lasting in his character. Yet such was his rigid and unsparing honesty with himself that he never tried to deny to his heart that it had, for a little while, been all-consuming.

Very late in the war, returned to Honolulu for two months' rest, he had been lying on the beach one afternoon when someone deliberately came over and lay down beside him on the sand. For the better part of an hour they lay there hardly moving, hardly looking at one another; to this day in unexpected moments he could hear again as though it were yesterday the crash of the waves and the exultant cries of the surf-riders, far out, on that fateful afternoon. Suddenly the whole surging loneliness of the war, his own tiredness and questioning of himself, the burden of so much agony everywhere in the world, the need for a little rest and a little peace without fighting any more with himself or anybody, had seemed unbearable, and like two children in a trance they had returned to the hotel together and from then on for nearly a month they were never apart for long. Any other time, any other place, he knew it would never have happened; but many things like that happened in war, he had observed, and no one noticed and no one cared. For four weeks he was happy, and he was unsparing enough in his honesty with himself to realize that it was a perfectly genuine happiness. Then for reasons which he could never analyze exactly, but which he became convinced later were probably sound, he became suspicious, and with suspicion came jealousy, and, for a time, an agony of heart such as he never hoped to undergo again. A savage, rending bitterness took the place of happiness; the beautiful island became a place of torment for them both. He asked to be returned to the front, the request was granted; against the windows and the sea as he left the hotel they saw one another for the last time, looked, and looked away. He knew then that they would never be together again, but he knew also that in all probability few things for either of them would ever again be as deep.

Very shortly thereafter the war ended and he returned to Salt Lake City, where he found his older sisters married, his older brother in the Church, the younger girls coming along, his parents, if possible, even more the unshakeable pillars of society than they had been. With his high school chum from Ogden he got away for a couple of weeks of camping in the Uintas and fishing along the Green, and then returned to his tidy little mountain capital to sit down and formulate more definitely the plan for his future he had developed during the war. It did not take him long to do so, and as a first step he went back to the Farm in the fall, this time to enter law school. Some instinct for what would be most appealing to the voters, some lingering feeling of his own against the East, prompted him to remain in his own general area for this final stage of his education; and, too, he had a feeling about the West that, like Antaeus, he should keep one foot on his own plot of ground. Western-born, western-reared and western-schooled, he knew, would be very attractive when the time came; and he felt better about it in his heart.

Coming back to an academic atmosphere after the war he found as difficult as many did, but he brought to it not only his many natural gifts of intelligence, determination, stability, and character, but a maturity that now had been refined and honed down to the point where he was ready to make the most of his final spell of schooling and also establish again that friendly link between himself and his immediate community from which flowed so much of his strength as a person and, later, as a vote-getter. The story was the same here as it had been everywhere: great popularity, great respect, almost universal liking. The time passed without disappointments and virtually without flaw. Once in his second year he got a letter from somewhere in the Midwest, forwarded from his home in Utah, an attempt to re-establish something he felt was completely gone, or at least gone for all the practical purposes of the life he had laid out for himself; he kept it for a day and a night, read it many times, thought of replying, started to jot down the address, and then changed his mind, finally tore it up completely and threw the fragments out of his car as he drove up the Bayshore to San Francisco the next afternoon. But it hurt still, and hurt badly; he was a little frightened to realize how much. For twenty-four hours he was not as sunny, open and friendly as usual, and this was noted by his friends; but exams were nearing, tension was high, and they put it down to that. Next day he was as outwardly serene as ever. He never heard again, even though there was a time after he first became nationally prominent when he was afraid he might hear, in some way that would be detrimental to him. But he never did, and as the years passed he came to feel that by a sort of tacit, long-distance understanding they had agreed with one another to let the dead past bury its dead.

He was president of the Law School in his senior year, edited the Review, began looking, more seriously and directly now, for a girl to love and marry and settle down with; failed to find her despite many candidates and opportunities which he accepted as calmly as he always had, and went home after three highly successful years to enter his father's law firm and begin the calculated process of making himself known from Logan to Kanab and from the Nevada border to the Colorado line. The cases his father handled, largely land, water, and range matters, gave him a steadily growing acquaintance over the state, and with it there presently began to come invitations to speak, at first about the war and his experiences and then, more seriously, about the problems confronting the country. It became apparent that within another two years a Senate seat would be open for the taking, and after another fishing trip with his high school chum from Ogden, during which they spent long hours at the campfire planning the campaign, he sharply increased his travels over the state, his speaking engagements at church suppers and social gatherings, service clubs, and professional groups. Because he was his father's son, many doors were automatically opened to him; because he was himself, he walked through them with ease, gathering friends and supporters everywhere as he went. One night in Provo he met a shy, plain girl who seemed to like him; in six months' time he was convinced he liked her too, and by the end of the year they were married in a ceremony that climaxed the social season and made his nomination virtually certain. He did his best sincerely to make Mabel Anderson happy, and for the most part felt that he succeeded. Sometimes old memories would return like a knife, but he was sure she never knew it, and he put them aside ruthlessly and concentrated on his home and his career. When the party held its nominating convention his only opposition was a former governor, an aging man unable to cope with Brig's splendid war record and earnestly handsome, youthful appeal. He won the nomination, won the election by a margin of 61,000 votes, which in Utah was sensational, and went to the United States Senate at thirty with a secret, almost superstitious determination to be a good man, a good Senator, and a good public servant. For seven years in an undeviating line he had pursued this purpose with a success the great majority of his fellows on both sides of the aisle were unfailingly quick and generous to acknowledge. A year ago he had won re-election as easily as though he owned the Senate seat; a few more years, he knew, and he would.

In the Senate he found his niche very quickly, because he was astute about his elders as he was about most men, and there as everywhere those who held the power were swiftly attracted by his courteously pleasant, respectful, and forthright ways. He was, as *Time* remarked shrewdly in a cover story when his colleague had died of a heart attack and he had become senior Senator at the age of thirty-four, "an old men's young man"; and to it he added many sound touches of his own. He was not a "mimeograph Senator," one of those frantic types who get themselves elected, usually quite young, and then spend their days sending handout after handout to the press gallery and making speech after speech in the Senate on every conceivable topic under the sun to the point where they are soon dismissed with a grin and a shrug. Such desperation for the limelight was not in him, and furthermore both instinct and a shrewd appraisal of the Senate told him that this was not the way to get along, or to achieve the position of influence and power he foresaw for himself. He had been in office seven months before he made his first Senate speech, and then it was on a reclamation matter on which he was thoroughly informed; the Senate listened attentively and gave him a good hand afterwards, as it does with maiden speeches, and so when he spoke again a week later on the growing threat of Soviet power his audience was receptive, ready to listen, and predisposed in his favor. This speech was a soundly reasoned, well-prepared and well-practiced exposition of the facts as he saw them, concluding with several specific suggestions of his own; its effect was exactly as he had planned. In the leadership and on the Foreign Relations Committee the thought got around that maybe it would be well to consider him when a vacancy arose. Seniority interfered with this for four years during which he cheerfully went about his tasks on the District and Commerce committees, but on the third occasion when a seat fell open Bob Munson, Orrin Knox, and Tom August were able to swing it for him, and the assignment was his. Soon after he was also given a seat on Interior to replace the traditional freshman bane of the District Committee, and so was set as he wished to be for the future. He had resigned his post on Commerce—where he had received his first rather trying taste of Robert A. Leffingwell when the latter was appointed chairman of the FPC—and had immediately made foreign policy his specialty. Now further attritions in seniority had put him fourth in line for the chairmanship, and he was generally considered one of the ablest and most promising members of the committee and the Senate.

In his first year, after his self-imposed seven months of being seen but not heard during which he had carefully studied the personalities of the men around him and thoroughly familiarized himself with the functioning of the Senate, he began to gravitate into that little group around the Majority and Minority leaders who had so much to do with making the machinery go: Orrin, Stanley Danta, John Winthrop, Seab, and a handful of others among whom he found quick acceptance. He and Lafe Smith, who had been elected two years earlier at the age of thirty-four, were the two youngest members of this group, and an easygoing friendship such as he had known so often in college and the war had sprung up rapidly between them. They generally hailed each other amiably as "buddy," and they were buddies, in a pleasantly non-obligational way that permitted them to work in tandem when it suited them and work at cross-purposes when that suited them, without any personal strain. He and Mabel and Lafe and Lafe's latest—there was always a latest, rarely the same latest as it had been the last time—often double-dated in a quiet, hometown sort of way, going to the Shoreham in good weather for dancing on the terrace, occasionally taking in a play at the National, once, before Pidge's birth, even taking a week-long cruise to Bermuda with the latest who seemed at the time most likely to become Mrs. Lafe. She didn't, but he and Mabel got a kick out of doing their best to bring it about. Lafe just grinned and wisecracked and stayed uncommitted with an independence

Brig could understand, even though he assured him sincerely that he was making a mistake and didn't know what he was missing.

Whether this was true or not, he was not always completely sure; but the storms were gradually dying in his heart, and he thought it was true most of the time. Certainly he did his best to make it true. Mabel was a thoroughly sweet and decent person, and he had no intention of letting his marriage become like so many he could see around him, a few islands of ease in a sea of tension. He devoted himself consciously to preventing this, and on the whole was quite happy with his bargain, fortified and strengthened as it was by time and circumstance and the public position in which he found himself which made a solid married life obligatory upon most ambitious men. How Lafe managed to be such a gay blade, coming from respectable Iowa, he could never understand until he happened to discuss the matter casually one day with a member of the Iowa delegation in the House. "What does the state think of all this chasing around?" he had asked humorously, and the Congressman shrugged. "They don't hear about it," he said, "and if they did, they wouldn't believe it." He sounded as though he really didn't, either. Obviously it was a matter of faith.

In addition to Lafe, he soon developed strong personal ties to the older members who had in effect adopted him, made him their protégé, and actively promoted his career. As Bob Munson once remarked to Stanley Danta, "We don't get material as good as that very often, we'd better make the most of it," and they did. Of them all he found himself most drawn to Orrin, who had an uncompromising honesty and a bluntly forthright way with the truth that immediately appealed to his young friend from Utah. Tart, tactless, impatient, fearless, and unimpressed, the senior Senator from Illinois wasted little time on fools; but on those he liked who were not fools he conferred a friendship of absolute loyalty and a deep warmth of affection that appeared surprisingly from beneath his shyly abrupt exterior. The twenty years that separated them were no barrier, and a very close relationship, almost father-son, was soon established. Happily it had extended to their wives. With Orrin and Beth he and Mabel had developed an in-and-out-of-the-house friendship that took them to Bethany Beach in nearby Delaware together for a couple of weeks and quite a few weekends each summer and generally made them members of the Knox family. It was Brig and Mabel, in fact, who had happened to bring Crystal Danta over one weekend when Stanley was away on a speaking trip and so had begun what Beth Knox referred to as "this joining of the ancient houses of Montague and Capulet," though the analogy wasn't very apt but just one of those dry and humorous things Beth would say. Both he and Mabel valued the Knoxes most highly, and of course in the Senate the friendship of the two men made for a strategic alliance that, added to all the other little strategic alliances that existed in the Senate, was frequently most profitable for them both. Neither ever asked the other to moderate his honest opinion in any degree, neither made much attempt to swing the other to his views; but in the majority of cases, they found, their views coincided, and when this wasn't so they went their separate ways in mutual respect and reformed their alliance the next time they saw eye to eye.

It was at Bethany with the Knoxes last Labor Day, in fact, that he had suddenly realized that he had found a happiness to equal or surpass any he had known. Pidge had been out at water-line shoveling busily in the sand; it was time for lunch and he had gone to bring her in. There had been some minor, muted disagreement with Mabel just before he had left the Knoxes' cottage and he was not in a very good mood; the waves had crashed, swimmers out in the sea had called to one another, a reminiscent melancholy had suddenly gripped his heart. Then he had reached his daughter, and with perfect love and trust and acceptance she had stood up and smiled at him. It had seemed to him then with a feeling close to revelation that in this tiny, sway-backed, ridiculous figure with her little behind sticking out in back and her little tummy sticking out in front, her blond hair caught up with a ribbon in a horsetail mop and her dark eyes filled with an amiable candor, all the love and hope of the world were concentrated. At that moment a surreptitious wave suddenly arrived at the rear of the ridiculous figure with surprising force, and the ridiculous figure sat down abruptly. There she remained for several seconds while a look of thoughtful concentration passed over her face. Then she looked up at her father with a sunny smile.

"I wetted the water," she explained.

Brigham Anderson gave a shout of laughter so completely happy that Mabel, coming contritely up the beach behind them, sighed with relief.

"The water wetted you, so you wetted the water," he said, scooping Pidge up onto his shoulder. "We'll pass a resolution and do something about it." And the three of them had started back in perfect harmony along the sand to the Knoxes' cottage.

It was that day, also, however, on which he had begun to realize most fully that the happiness he wanted would never come with Mabel, for all his conscientious efforts and her desperate attempts to match them, for she was one of those good people who are also in spite of all their earnest efforts basically dull. Perhaps if Pidge had come at once instead of five years after their marriage, perhaps if the bloom, laboring under handicaps Mabel would never understand, had not had time to go quite so fully off the rose before it was rekindled briefly by their daughter's birth, it might have been different; as it was, despite all his cares and attentions, they were no longer as close as they used to be, and he could not honestly say where the greater fault lay, though he was quite sure he had done everything mortally possible on his side. Of late there had been at times a gnawing boredom that he had not always quite concealed, though he never let it get out of hand. Nonetheless, Mabel knew, and there had been an increasing number of arguments about it, usually not very serious and turned off with a joke and a kiss and sometimes a small gift or a night out. The night before the morning Pidge had fussed so long over her oatmeal, however, the situation had suddenly become more serious for some reason neither of them could analyze. There had been a rather long argument over trivia, ending with Mabel in tears uttering the ancient cry of those who love more than they are loved, "Sometimes I don't think I know you at all!" At this her husband had given her a startled look she could not define from those level dark eyes she worshipped so much and in a faraway voice had said softly, "Maybe you don't." And then with a sudden contrition he had told her how much he loved her and done things she fiercely enjoyed to prove it, and they had gone to sleep at relative peace with one another. Later in the night, however, she had awakened to cry again, and the next morning she had slept late and then taken Pidge and gone over to the Knoxes' after telling Ellabelle to clean up the attic, and cried some more on Beth's shoulder. Since then they had re-established an outward harmony, and this morning in the bright spring day she had laughed and kissed him and sent him out to the garden in apparent high spirits, so things were easier again.

Searching his heart and mind with complete and unsparing honesty about it now, he knew with absolute certainty that the situation they were in could have happened, and indeed did happen, to many and many a marriage; it had nothing to do with ghosts from the past, though he never denied their importance to his life. He was a good father, a good if temporarily troubled husband, a good servant, a good Senator, and a good man; and central to all this, in a way he understood thoroughly in his own nature, was the episode in Honolulu.

Physically of course it was a closed book, for nothing ever again induced in him quite that combination of restlessness, uncertainty, impulse, and desire. It had come about after a long period of self-questioning, because of a unique set of circumstances that were never duplicated again, and he felt no need to try to recreate something that had flared once and was, he was quite sure, gone forever. Furthermore, there were ten thousand reasons of reputation, family, home, and career why it should not be revived, and so he steered deliberately clear of any such situations, which in Washington as everywhere were numerous, that even remotely seemed capable of leading to it. Furthermore, and this he knew honestly was also fundamental, it had meant something very important to him at the time, it couldn't be recaptured and he knew it, and that too was a major reason along with all the others of self-preservation, obligation to society, integrity, and self-denial.

If he had been possessed of a cowardly and self-protective mind he could have pretended to himself that this was not the case, but he was not the type to spare himself on anything and no more did he spare himself on that. Nor did he see any reason why he should, for in a way he came consciously to realize, what had started as a weakness became transmuted by a very strong character and a very decent heart into a profoundly important strength. As surely as Seab Cooley, surviving his own private hell in Barnwell half a century before, Brig knew when he emerged from his that it had been a proving ground. For all its pain, and for all that it was not exactly the sort of thing you would want to discuss in Salt Lake City, he did not regret that it had happened. There were things he had to find out about himself; the war, as it did for so many, furnished the crucible, and in it that episode had probably been the single most illuminating episode of all. He could not honestly say he was sorry; his only sorrow was that fate had ended it so hurtfully for them both instead of allowing the war to send them apart again as calmly and simply and inevitably as it had brought them together.

He was forthright enough to admit to himself that finding good in what many would consider evil might be all an elaborate rationalization, and yet if it was, both he and society profited from it, so what matter the label that was put upon it? Men, he had observed, believed about themselves what they had to believe to keep going; and matched against the general motley he did not think his method for coming to terms with himself was any worse than anyone else's. At least he felt that it was a positive reaction to something that otherwise could have been a constant drag upon his life, and so he did not quibble over the thought processes that permitted it. He had managed to emerge whole: he was grateful that it should be so, and wise enough not to question it.

Not, however, that anything changed the fact born in him that beneath the solid, easygoing, and likeable exterior there lived what was basically a highly independent and lone-wolf character: if anything, the years had strengthened the tendency to that. The self-reliance he had shown so early, the ability to smile and keep his counsel and go his own way had been steadily strengthened, in school, in war, in politics. One of those people, found so often in high official position, whose outward cordiality, responsiveness, and warmth persuade that they are giving much more of themselves than they actually are, he continued to remain essentially alone. He moved slowly and carefully, seeking few men's advice, usually withholding his own, weighing all the facts before taking action, acting decisively on his own independent conclusions, and considering himself answerable to practically nothing but his own conscience and the state of Utah. There was always that area of unreachability remaining inside where he worked things out in his own mind and formed his own judgments without much regard to those of others; it was this, though she did not realize it fully, that Mabel was up against in a more personal context. Fortunately, because his mind was astute and very well informed, this habit of independence usually brought him out on the right side of things in most cases, however much it might sometimes bother those who valued his support and sought to win it. Even to Orrin and Lafe he would on occasion show a frustratingly obdurate aloofness, sometimes on subjects on which they thought they were entitled as his two closest friends in the Senate to know his thinking. If he wished to let them have it, he did, and if he didn't, he didn't. Both had exploded at him at times for this, but he had only remained good-natured and uncommunicative, not telling them until he got good and ready.

It was this trait, perhaps, which more than any other accounted for his action last night when he had decided entirely on his own initiative to reopen the Leffingwell hearings. He might have consulted with Orrin, if Orrin had been available, but most probably he wouldn't have. He might, if he were someone else, explain his reasons to the subcommittee, the Majority Leader, and the press during the day today; but he was pretty sure he wouldn't. He had made the decision which seemed most valid to him, to make an announcement keeping the hearings alive if they should be needed, and then to refuse comment until he had been given an opportunity to talk to the man who had appointed Bob Leffingwell and find out what he intended to do. It might be that the whole thing could be ironed out in private conference, that the nomination could be withdrawn—the step he now felt imperative and the only one he would accept without an open fight—and another sent in before the truth could get out; and then in all probability it never would. Then it might all be smoothed over, with some embarrassment for the President, true, and with great disappointment and public reproach for the nominee; but that was politics, and politics, as Brigham Anderson had noted in seven years could sometimes be a most cruel and heartless business. Those who entered it took upon themselves always the possibility that it might someday turn without pity upon them. This the President knew; this the nominee knew; and so did he.

So he had made his decision alone shortly after midnight, not knowing what had prompted James Morton's call, for the man did not tell him, knowing only that it had come to him as chairman of the subcommittee bearing a responsibility to the Senate, the country, and his own integrity to do something about it. Given the character he had, he could have taken no other course. As he was, so he acted; a human tendency that in the average run of things produces nothing very drastic, even though in this case, time, place, and circumstance again combined against him to see to it that it did.

And even so, the sun was bright, the winds were warm, and spring was here. And even so, despite his recurring somber mood and despite the steadily-widening ramifications of the Leffingwell matter in the wake of his decision, he was glad to be alive and confident he could easily handle whatever, in this golden season, the future might divulge.

"What in the hell is going on up there?" the voice at the other end of the line demanded, and the Majority Leader could tell its owner was not in much mood for nonsense this morning. He decided to be equally vigorous.

"I'm damned if I know," he said crisply. "What does it look like?"

"Haven't you talked to him?" the President asked sharply, and Senator Munson let his voice become deliberately unhurried.

"No, I haven't," he said thoughtfully. "I've been thinking possibly he might get in touch with me, but he hasn't yet."

"This is a hell of a note," the President observed.

"It has its embarrassing aspects," Bob Munson agreed politely.

"Maybe I should call him myself," the President suggested.

"Oh, I don't think so," the Senator said firmly. "No, I don't think so at all. Have you ever gotten to know him very well?"

"Not particularly," the President said. "You know how it is in this job, everything gets formalized and everybody stands on ceremony; a few formal meetings, conferences, and so on are about all you get to see of anybody who doesn't work here. I gather it's a rather independent personality."

"That's hardly the word," Bob Munson said. "He's the original Cat That Walks Alone. But a hell of a nice guy, for all that. We're pretty well sold on Brig up here, as you know, so maybe you'd just better let us handle it our own way."

"Fred Van Ackerman isn't sold on him," the President said slowly, and the Majority Leader snorted.

"Fred isn't sold on anybody but Fred," he said shortly, "so don't get any illusions on that score. However, it's just as I told you, he's on your side for this trip, so let's don't be too impolite about him."

The President replied with a short and ancient Anglo-Saxon word that made his listener chuckle.

"Is this call being monitored?" he asked, and the President laughed.

"Better not be," he said, "the churches would be after me like lightning . . . Well. To get back to our problem. What do you intend to do about it?"

"I intend to let him work it out in his own way without too much prodding from me," Bob Munson said. "I'd suggest you do likewise. It's the only way to handle him."

"It puts me on one hell of a spot, you know," the President said soberly. "There's an awful lot riding on this nomination."

"Oh, I know." Senator Munson said. "Don't think I'm unaware of it. I have a certain investment in it myself, don't forget."

"You should have let it come to a vote yesterday and it would all have been over with," the President said. The Majority Leader laughed, rather humorlessly.

"Do you know what would have happened if I had?" he inquired.

"I'll tell you. If that nomination had been put to a vote yesterday afternoon it would have lost by four votes."

"You mean that lecture on the ancient rights and duties of the Senate wasn't just a spontaneous tribute?" the President asked dryly. "I thought you meant it."

"There's more than one reason for making a speech," Bob Munson said. "Of course I meant it. I meant every word of it. You downtown types just don't understand what the old place means to us who love it. Or what it means to the country, for that matter. But the speech also had its purpose. Most things I do have a purpose."

"Yes, Bobby," the President said. "Don't get on your high horse."

"Sometimes principles and purpose coincide," the Senator remarked. "You ought to know."

"It's helped me a thousand times," the President agreed amicably. "So you haven't got the votes yet, eh?"

"No, sir," the Majority Leader said. "Your little boy isn't out of the woods yet even if he was able to tag the opposition's witness with a bad case of mental heebie-jeebies."

"And now Brig thinks he knows something we don't know," the President said thoughtfully. "I wonder what it is?"

"Why don't you call in your man and ask him?" Senator Munson suggested bluntly. "Have *you* talked to *him?*"

"No," the President admitted.

"Don't you think you should?" Bob Munson demanded.

"I'm like you," the President said. "I'm waiting for him to call me."

"Isn't it a little more important than that?" Senator Munson inquired. "After all, this is a Secretary of State."

"Maybe we're both being too coy," the President said.

"I'm not," the Majority Leader said. "I know my man. Do you?"

"Well," the President said thoughtfully, and stopped. "I think so," he said, and stopped again. "Yes, I think so," he went on firmly after a moment, "on the basis of everything I have ever seen of him or know of him. I notice they didn't lay a glove on him up there. They gave him quite a grilling and he came through it with flying colors and his cause intact. What more do you want?"

"Is that all you want?" Senator Munson asked, and again there was a pause on the line. Then the President spoke firmly.

"What are we working ourselves into, anyway?" he demanded. "Just because one of your stubborn little charges gets a bee in his bonnet, we're letting it give us the shakes. The hearing brought up and answered all the charges, the record is clear; he already had the press with him and now I think he's got most of the country as well. He's come out of it in fine shape, and I really don't see what the problem is. Do you?"

"All I know," Bob Munson observed quietly, "is that Brig doesn't go off half-cocked. If he thinks he knows something, chances are he does know something. That's what's got me worried."

"Yes," the President said, and suddenly his tone hardened. "What will it take to buy him off?"

The Majority Leader gave an impatient exclamation.

"He can't be bought," he said. The President snorted.

"Everybody can be bought," he said shortly. Senator Munson laughed without humor.

"The hell you say," he remarked dryly. "Brig can't. Orrin can't. Seab can't. I can't. Oh, I can name you quite a few who can't. Think of something else."

"Are you with me or against me on this?" the President demanded sharply. "Which is it?"

"That depends," Bob Munson said deliberately. "What are you offering?" Then he went on in a more comfortable tone.

"I'm with you," he said. "The record reads all right, on the whole. I think he did a good job of handling himself, nothing really damaging is in there. Of course I'm with you. This'll work out, don't worry. I expect after he's had time to think about it for an hour or two Brig will call and tell me what it's all about. And then we'll talk it over and I'll smooth him down and we'll figure out some graceful way for him to cancel his announcement and the subcommittee can go ahead and vote tomorrow, and everything will be right back where it was and no real harm done."

"And if it doesn't work out that way?" the President asked quietly. "If there is something, and he won't drop it? What then?"

"Then if it's something valid, I assume you'll withdraw the nomination," Bob Munson said. The President gave an impatient exclamation in his turn.

"You know better than that, Bob Munson," he said. "You know much better than that. Barring a morals conviction or a murder rap or membership in the Communist Party, I'm committed to this man. The United States, in effect, is committed to this man, because I *am* the United States, in foreign policy. You've been here long enough to know what that kind of commitment means. If it comes to a showdown between my commitment and Brigham Anderson, something's going to give." Again his tone hardened and there came into it an iron the Majority Leader had rarely heard. "And it isn't going to be me," he concluded quietly.

"Suppose we all just calm down," Senator Munson suggested. "I don't even know what's on Brig's mind, yet. You're right, we're letting ourselves get too worked up about it. It can't be as serious as all that."

"If he can't be bought," the President said slowly, as though he hadn't been listening, "what can we use to threaten him?"

"Are you kidding?" Senator Munson asked sharply.

"I am not," the President said matter-of-factly. "I'm asking you as a practical proposition what we can use to threaten him with."

The Majority Leader started to reply in anger and then changed his mind.

"Nothing," he said pleasantly. "I can't think of a thing." And anticipating the President's rejoinder, he added quickly, so that their words came out together:

"There's always something."

"Well, there is," the President said quietly. "There always is. Somewhere, sometime, someplace, everybody has done some thing. All you have to do is find it."

This time it was the Majority Leader who paused, and when he spoke it was in a coldly withdrawn tone.

"I'm sorry," he said. "I don't play quite that rough."

At this the President sighed, and when he replied it was in a voice that suddenly sounded infinitely weary.

"Are you faced with the problem of leading this nation in an unending conflict with the Russians?" he asked. "Is it your charge, day in and day out, night in and night out, to be concerned always with the fear that if you don't do just the right thing they'll destroy the country that has entrusted you with all its hopes and all its future? Such a great country, Bob, meaning so well and hoping so much and trying so hard to do the right thing and being nibbled to death by friends and enemies alike, and you realize that if you fail—not somebody else, but *you*—that it may be lost forever—do you have any concept of what that means? Do you understand at all the lengths to which that can drive you sometimes?"

"I'm sorry, Mr. President," the Majority Leader said gravely.

"So am I," the President said in the same tired voice. "Talk to Brig and see what you can work out. I won't hurt him, even if I could. But try to make him see it a little bit from my standpoint, will you? Try to make him understand what's at stake here. If he's really stumbled onto something about Leffingwell that will really, honestly, genuinely damage the country, then of course I'll withdraw him and get somebody else. But if this is just some idealistic nonsense or something that isn't very important, I won't budge."

"I'll do my best," Bob Munson promised. "I only hope your idea of what is and isn't important coincides with his."

"Well," the President said, "my first duty is the country."

"So is ours," Senator Munson said. "Maybe you forget that."

"You see?" the President said, his tone suddenly becoming much lighter. "You did mean that speech after all, you old sentimentalist. You think that stuffy old Senate is the only thing that keeps America from going to pot, don't you?"

"It helps," the Majority Leader said in a relieved voice, and the President laughed.

"It's a good thing I wasn't at the Constitutional Convention," he said.

"Knowing what I know now, the Senate would never have gotten in."

Bob Munson chuckled.

"We sometimes think we could get along without the President, too," he said, "but I expect they knew what they were doing. It all seems to have hung together pretty well over the years. Am I still seeing you after the White House Correspondents' banquet tonight?"

"Oh, certainly," the President said. "I'm counting on it. I want you to come back to the house for a drink and a good talk. In fact, why don't you bring Brig? Assuming we're all friends again by tonight?"

"I'm sure we will be," Senator Munson said, "as soon as I can talk to him. Yes, I will."

"As a matter of fact," the President added casually, "bring Fred too. I feel I should study that specimen a little more thoroughly, too."

"Not together," Bob Munson said promptly.

"It's a real feud, is it?" the President asked with a chuckle. "Fred really means it?"

"More on his part than Brig's," Senator Munson said. "I don't think Brig quite knows what to make of it. There's some kind of jealousy there, I think; maybe Brig's got the respect and position in the Senate that Fred would like to have. And never will have, I might add."

"Well, all right," the President said in the same casual tone. "Some other time."

"Maybe you can get by without that speech attacking Seab, too," the Majority Leader suggested, and the President laughed.

"I don't know about that," he said. "If we're really four votes short, there's work to be done."

"I think I can round them up without too much of a strain," Bob Munson said. "I'd prefer to keep it harmonious, if we can."

"Always thinking about the next battle, aren't you, Bobby?" the President asked. "I suppose that's what makes you a good Majority Leader."

"I've found it helps," Senator Munson said.

"I'd appreciate a call as soon as you've talked to Brig," the President said.

"Sure thing," Bob Munson said. "Keep a stiff upper lip."

"I'll try," the President said cheerfully. "Not having a press conference today will help. Take it easy."

"Right," the Majority Leader said, and rang off. The interoffice buzzer sounded at once.

"Senator," Mary said, "Mr. Justice Davis waiting on the line."

"Yes, Tommy," Bob Munson said in some surprise. "This is an unexpected pleasure. I haven't heard from you in a coon's age. What's up?"

"How are you, Bob?" the Justice said in an uncharacteristically grave voice. "I was wondering——" He paused.

"Yes?" the Majority Leader said in some puzzlement. "What's the matter, Tommy?"

"This business about Brig," Justice Davis said slowly. "Could I come and talk to you about it?"

"Sure thing," Bob Munson said promptly, "except I don't know anything really."

There was a little silence and when the Justice spoke it was in a tone the Majority Leader couldn't quite analyze, both furtive and portentous.

"Maybe I do," he said. "Suppose I come over at four."

"That will be good, Tommy," Senator Munson said. "I'll see you then."

Now what the hell? he thought as he hung up. But the business of the day pressed upon him, events rushed forward, and there was no time to wonder about it now.

"You know," AP said thoughtfully, "I'd give quite a bit to know what Brig is up to."

"That's the understatement of the month," UPI remarked. "Who the hell wouldn't?"

"If the God damned Russians land on the moon, it isn't going to matter," The Wall Street *Journal* observed, and *Newsweek* gave a cheerful laugh.

"*I* think," he said, looking down the press table filled with the usual ten o'clock coffee crowd, "that what we ought to do is send Brig in a rocket to the moon after them and elect Bob Leffingwell to the Senate in his place. Then everybody would be happy."

"You get the damnedest ideas," the *Times* told him, "all good. When was the last time anybody tried his home?"

"We've been trying his home since 5 A.M. and we've got a man staked out at his office, too," AP said. "I'm here," he added with a grin, "to catch him if he comes into the restaurant."

"That's the first time I've ever heard a coffee break really justified," the Providence *Journal* observed, and the Kansas City *Star* smiled a trifle grimly.

"Listen," he said, "when that guy wants to hide out he's impossible to find. Did you cover that Leffingwell fight when Bob was appointed to the Power Commission? It was the same way then. No news, no comment, no Senator. I think he was hiding out on top of the Capitol dome at the time."

"Wonderful guy," the *Herald Trib* said without irony, "but he certainly does play it his own way, doesn't he?"

"What do you suppose this is really all about?" the Chicago *Tribune* wondered. "What does he know that everybody else doesn't know?"

"I don't get it either," the Newark *News* said. "Leffingwell shot Gelman off his horse, so what's left? This isn't quite in character for Brig somehow, it seems to me. He isn't tricky."

"Stubborn and independent," the *Times* agreed, "but not tricky. Did anybody reach Leffingwell?"

"Speaking of tricky people," the Chicago *Trib* said dryly. "I tried about ten minutes ago. The phone still isn't answering."

"And it won't be all day," UPI predicted. "Anybody staked out there? We are."

"So are we," AP said.

"He's gone to the ODM," the Wall Street *Journal* said, a trifle smugly. "We caught him there a little while ago. He ain't talkin'."

"What about the rest of the subcommittee?" CBS asked. "Are they?"

"That's probably our best target for today," NBC said. "Anybody want to go over to the office buildings and try to catch them?"

"In a minute," the Washington *Post* said. "Don't rush things."

"That was quite an editorial and cartoon you folks had this morning," the *Times* observed. "I guess Brig is a no-good bastard from now on, right?"

"For the time being," the *Post* said with a grin. "He can work his way back into our hearts if he chooses."

"Actually, that was my first reaction, too," *Time* magazine said. "Then I got to wondering. This guy isn't apt to shoot from the hip, you know. He's usually pretty sound."

"That's what bothers me," the *Herald Trib* said thoughtfully. "If it were anybody but Brig, I wouldn't be in any doubt."

"None of us seems to be in any doubt," the *Times* said dryly; "at least in the editorial columns."

"Well, why should we be?" the Newark *News* demanded. "They gave Bob the works and he came through it O.K., so what more do you want?"

"Is that all you want?" the *Times* asked. The *News* shrugged.

"What more is there?" he asked. "All we can do is go by the record. It looks O.K. for Bob as near as I can tell. Why aren't we justified in hitting Brig with everything we've got?"

"This is supposed to be an objective profession," the *Times* pointed out.

"When the world's going to hell in a hand basket and Leffingwell's one of the greatest hopes for saving it?" the Baltimore *Sun* demanded. "Why shouldn't we throw everything we can at anybody who gets in the way?"

"This does give us a hell of a black eye abroad," *Time* Magazine said thoughtfully.

"I see you've done your best," the Washington *Star* said, holding up the latest issue. The nominee was on the cover with the legend, "Robert A. Leffingwell: Toward the future nobly . . ." Inside was a skillful story deftly placing him on the right hand of the Lord and attributing to his opponents lineal descent from Lucifer.

"We're following suit," *Newsweek* said cheerfully. "Not quite that glowing, of course, but then you know us. The calm, reasoned approach, not these wild enthusiasms that afflict the competition."

"I'll bet Fred Van Ackerman is raving," the Providence *Journal* suggested, and everybody laughed.

"Either climbing the drapes or clawing the rug," the *Post* said. "Hard to tell which."

"He's for Leffingwell, though," the *Journal* said. "I suppose we'd better see him too."

"Here comes somebody who may know something," the *Herald Trib* said. "Senator, sit down and tell us what it's all about."

"I will," Lafe Smith said with a grin, "except you've got to buy me coffee. I don't buy my own when I'm giving a free interview."

"Fair enough," the *Times* said. "It's on us. What's got into your pal?"

"Well, frankly," Lafe said with a candid smile, "I'm damned if I know. You know as much as I do, and that's nothing. Maybe I'll find out later and you can check me then."

"He didn't talk to you last night, then," AP said. Lafe looked surprised.

"No, why should he?" he asked. "I'm not on the subcommittee."

"Well, you're a close friend and you're on the full committee," the Washington *Star* pointed out. "That might entitle you to some confidences."

"Brig isn't the confiding type," Senator Smith said, "as you well know. No, I haven't the slightest idea. I'll tell you one thing, though: the subcommittee trusts him and they'll go along with him until it suits him to explain himself. And so will the full committee."

"Even Tom August?" UPI asked. Lafe smiled.

"Maybe not Tom," he said, "but everybody else."

"Doesn't that seem extraordinary to you," the Baltimore *Sun* said, "that one man could occupy a position that powerful, that you'd all be satisfied to wait on his personal whim like that?"

"It isn't power, exactly, "the Senator from Iowa said, "and I doubt very much that it's a whim, either. It's respect, in the first instance, and for all we know it may be something damned serious, in the second. So why does everybody jump to conclusions the way they do? You, for instance?" he demanded of the *Post* with a scowl that was only half humorous.

"We want that man confirmed," the *Post* said simply.

"Hell, so do most people," Senator Smith said tartly, "but there's such a thing as fair play."

"Not when the fix is in," the Chicago *Tribune* said sarcastically, and the *Post* looked annoyed.

"There's no fix in," he said sharply. "We're just for him, that's all. So are we all, and why not? His public record is fine. The hearing record is O.K. He's come out of it stronger than ever. So why shouldn't we be?"

"That's your privilege," Lafe agreed, "just as it's your privilege to run that kind of an editorial and that kind of a cartoon if you really think Brig is a crackpot."

"Nobody thinks he's a crackpot, Lafe," AP said impatiently. "But he'd better have a damned good explanation, or he's going to get slaughtered."

"Nobody's waiting for his explanation," Lafe said bluntly. "The *Post* had an editorial. The *Times* had an editorial. The *Trib* had an editorial. *Time* and *Newsweek* are killing him in their cover stories. CBS murdered him on the morning news. NBC did likewise. They'll do the same thing again tonight. That's getting to be the trouble with you people, nowadays —you never reserve judgment any more. You always jump to conclusions and take it as a personal affront if somebody disagrees with you. Why in hell don't you hold your fire for ten minutes? You don't know what he's found."

"He could have said," the *Times* pointed out quietly. "If he weren't so damned independent, he could have said. Then we could judge it on its merits instead of making disagreement, of necessity, a personal attack on Brig. Isn't that true?"

Senator Smith gave him a long look.

"That's true," he admitted soberly. "That's very true. He's brought a lot of it on himself. But that's the kind of guy he is. Just because he's a lone wolf doesn't affect his judgment any. You tell me a nicer fellow or a better United States Senator and I'll concede your right to go after him without waiting to find out his reasons. O.K.? In fact," he added dryly, "don't bother to try to name a better. Here he comes right now, your little buddy. Fred!" he called as Senator Van Ackerman started through on his way to the inner diningroom. "Come on and sit down. We're having a hate-Brig session. I'm sure you have some ideas."

But the junior Senator from Wyoming did not choose to be amused. Instead he rested a hand on AP's shoulder and gave the junior Senator from Iowa an insolent stare.

"I'd expect you to be defending him," he said coldly, and Lafe Smith, who had spoken in a tone that was reasonably friendly, reacted at once.

"Against you, pal," he said with equal coldness, "any time."

"Listen to me, Lafe," Fred Van Ackerman said softly, while the press watched attentively and several tourists at nearby tables gave them startled looks, "I don't know what's gotten into high and mighty little Mr. Mysterious, but I can tell you it had damned well better be good or he's going to get run over by a steam roller. The country wants this nomination and it doesn't want anybody standing in the way, particularly somebody who thinks he's as damned good as Brig does. Why, hell! Who does he think he is, with all his high-flown, self-righteous pretensions, God Almighty? He isn't. He's just little Brigham Anderson from Salt Lake City, and he's trying to get in the way of history. It won't work."

Senator Smith smiled without amusement.

"I swear," he said, "you do live in a world of your own, Fred. These fellows don't approve of what Brig's doing on this, either, but at least they aren't psycopathic about it."

At this the press instinctively shifted a little, not knowing but what this would send Senator Van Ackermen into one of his rages, or perhaps even precipitate one of the few fist fights in senatorial history. But nothing so dramatic happened. Fred Van Ackerman only smiled in a rather remote sort of way.

"We'll get him," he promised quietly. "The country needs Leffingwell and it's going to have him. You can tell your buddy-buddy that if he doesn't get out of the way he's going to be sorry."

"He won't be the only one, Freddy boy," Senator Smith said pleasantly.

"I may have something for you boys later in the day," Fred Van Ackerman said, turning abruptly to the press. "Watch for it when the session opens."

And with a quick nod around the table he gave his colleague one more stare and went on into the diningroom.

"God, I despise that little bastard," Lafe Smith said quietly. "And that's what you prefer to Brig. Well, by God, you can have him. I want none of him."

"We don't prefer him to Brig," AP said reasonably. "We prefer Brig any time, when he's on the right side."

"You prefer him," Lafe said skeptically, "after what you did this morning."

"Oh, hell," AP said. "One day's editorials and one day's cartoons and one day's broadcasts. Anybody can stand a little riding from the press. That isn't anything."

"You can't kid me," Lafe said. "The pack's on the prowl, and you know it."

And though he decided it would be best to lighten the atmosphere by saying it with a laugh, and though they responded in kind, they all knew as the conversation ended and they broke up to go their several ways that it was entirely true.

"Mabel," the Majority Leader said, "this is Bob Munson. Are you hiding a United States Senator from me?"

"I'm helping to hide him," she admitted with a laugh. "Is it urgent?"

"That's what I want him to tell me," Senator Munson said. "I'm as baffled as everybody else. Except you, I imagine."

"Oh, no," she said quickly. "He never tells me anything. Hold on a minute. I'll get him."

And leaving Senator Munson to add that to one or two hints Orrin Knox had let drop in a worried way lately, and thus come to some swift conclusions about the present state of domestic tranquillity in the Anderson household, she went off the line. In a couple of minutes the senior Senator from Utah came on.

"Yes, Bob," he said pleasantly. "What can I do for you?"

"What can I do for you is more like it," Bob Munson said. "Is there anything I can do for you?"

Brigham Anderson laughed.

"Robert, Robert," he said. "No, I don't think so. I'm doing fine."

"No, you're not," the Majority Leader told him seriously. "The President called a little while ago. He wasn't pleased."

"That's strange," Brig said calmly. "I'm doing this for him."

"How do you figure that?" Senator Munson asked, and Senator Anderson made a mildly exasperated sound.

"Look," he said. "He's committed to Leffingwell, right?"

"Practically one hundred per cent," the Majority Leader said.

"And it would embarrass him no end if I came right out and told all I knew, wouldn't it?"

"That depends on what you know," Senator Munson said.

"Enough to warrant some serious thought being given to the whole situation," Brig said. "And so what have I done? Instead of issuing a statement about it to the press, all I've done is hold the hearings open, in case we should need them, and then keep my mouth shut until I can see him and talk it over. Is that such a crime?"

"A good many people seem to think so," Senator Munson said. "What is this mysterious knowledge of yours, anyway?"

"I'll tell you when I see him," Senator Anderson said.

"Hmph," Bob Munson observed. "Don't be so damned independent." Brig chuckled.

"Now, Bobby," he said. "Don't get in a huff. I'm handling this all right, I think. It makes me the lightning-rod for all the pressure for a little while, but that's all right. I can stand it."

"You can if you don't underestimate the pressures, and if you have a good explanation for it when the time comes," Senator Munson said.

"I have one," Senator Anderson remarked, rather grimly. "As for the pressures, I assume you mean these attacks in the press and radio and TV. That's just part of this business, it happens to everybody; it just happens to be my turn, at the moment. I'll ride it out all right."

"I hope so," Senator Munson said thoughtfully. "I hope it isn't any more damaging than that."

"Who else could damage me?" Brig asked. "The only other one I can think of is the President, and I don't think he could even if he wanted to. What could he do it with?"

"You'd know that better than I would," Bob Munson said, and though he thought his young colleague hesitated for an almost imperceptible second, it was with a note of skeptical scorn that he answered.

"Well, relax, Bob," he said dryly. "There aren't many skeletons in this closet. Furthermore, the President and I are going to find ourselves pretty much in agreement, I think, as soon as we can get together and talk it out. I think he'll be agreeable to doing what's necessary."

"And what's that?" Senator Munson asked. Senator Anderson replied without hesitation.

"Withdraw the nomination," he said, and there was a pause.

"Well," Bob Munson said after a moment. "You don't want much, do you?"

"Only what's right," Brig said calmly.

"I doubt very much if he'll be receptive to that idea," the Majority Leader said. "He read me a lecture on it a little while ago."

"Maybe he'll feel differently after I talk to him," Senator Anderson said.

Bob Munson made a skeptical sound. "That I doubt. He said unless you'd found Leffingwell guilty of a morals conviction or a murder rap or membership in the Communist Party, he wouldn't budge. You haven't found any of those, have you?"

"Not exactly," Senator Anderson said, and Senator Munson said, "Hmm."

"Serious enough to warrant withdrawal, you think," he remarked thoughtfully.

"I think so."

"Well, maybe I will, too, when you tell me what it is," Bob Munson suggested. His colleague laughed.

"Which will be when I see the President," he said with pleasant firmness.

"You're a stubborn cuss," Senator Munson told him.

"It's the way I am," Brig said in a tone that dismissed it. "I'd like you with me, Bob. When can we set it up?"

"I'm going back to the house with him after the White House Correspondents' banquet tonight for a drink and a chat. He thought you might like to come with me."

"Oh, he's already got it set up," Brig said with some surprise. The Majority Leader decided there was no point, with Brig, in beating around the bush.

"Yes, except that he expects that by that time you will have changed your mind, canceled further hearings, and come out with a statement to the effect that further study has convinced you the nominee should be speedily confirmed."

"Oh, he does," Senator Anderson said in an entirely different voice. "Oh, he does. Are those the conditions on which I'm to be allowed into the presence?"

"No, no," the Majority Leader said hastily. "Calm down. That only expresses the utmost limit of his fondest hopes. He'll be glad to see you in any event."

"No, he won't," Brigham Anderson said calmly. "So that's what's behind this call. You're supposed to head me off and then we can have a victory drink on it tonight. His victory. Well, that's not the basis on which I'm coming to see him, you can tell him for me. Any change in plans I may or may not make will be after I see him, not before. For Christ's sake," he added in an exasperated tone, "I'm only doing this to protect him. What in the hell's the matter with him, anyway?"

Bob Munson sighed.

"You're making this awfully difficult for everybody," he said, and in reply his young friend sounded completely serious.

"I'm sorry, Bob," he said soberly. "I don't mean to. It just seems to me this way is best, that's all. I've thought it all over, and that's my judgment on it. I'm trying to do what seems right to me. I can't help it if this is the way it comes out."

"All right," Senator Munson said, deciding to capitulate, at least for the time being. "All right, you do it your own way. We'll go ahead with it after dinner and you can talk the whole thing out with him."

"Maybe this will give us all a chance to re-examine our positions," Senator Anderson said. "Maybe we all need to."

"Maybe," Senator Munson said, not sounding very convinced of it. "You'll have some trouble avoiding questions at the dinner, I'm afraid."

"I doubt it," Brig said. "I'll just be pleasant and noncommittal, as usual."

"As usual," the Majority Leader said. "Suppose it comes out somewhere else during the day, whatever it is?"

"Well, then I'll just be justified in what I'm doing," Brig said. "Look, Bob. I'm only trying to play this by the rules. I'm only trying to protect my gallant leaders, the one in the White House and the one in the Senate. What's your problem, pal?"

"Someday," Senator Munson said thoughtfully, "you're going to go it alone just once too often, Brigham, and it's going to trip you up."

"Maybe," the Senator from Utah said calmly. "Maybe. But I don't think it will be this time."

"I hope not, for your sake," the Majority Leader said. "I'll tell the President you'll be coming along with me as planned tonight."

"Not quite as planned," Brig pointed out, "but I'll be there. Unless Fred Van Ackerman has led a lynch mob of COMFORT members out here and strung me up by that time."

"Maybe he will," Bob Munson said, not entirely in jest. "By the way," he added casually, "is Tommy Davis mad at you about anything?"

"Not that I know of," Senator Anderson said. "I gave him a ride to work the other morning and he seemed the same as ever. I'm sure he isn't happy about what I'm doing right now, he's such a Leffingwell partisan, but I can't think of anything personal. Why?"

"Nothing, I just wondered."

"You never 'just wonder,' Robert. What's on your mind?"

"That's all right," Bob Munson said airily. "You have your little secrets. I have mine."

"Bastard," Senator Anderson said affectionately, and the Majority Leader laughed.

"Come see us at the Capitol someday," he said.

"I'd rather you wouldn't advertise it," Senator Anderson said, "but I'll be in my office after lunch if you need me. And don't worry, Robert. I'm doing all right."

But after he had hung up and gone thoughtfully back out into the yard, there remained in his mind the uneasy feeling that perhaps he wasn't entirely. Despite his outward calm about the attacks of press and television, he had been somewhat dismayed by the extreme virulence which had greeted him with the dawn. He had realized that many people were emotionally involved with the cause of the nominee, but he had not realized quite the fanatacism that seemed capable of flaring from it at an instant's notice. He still, after seven years in office, retained some slight, idealistic belief that if you treated people in Washington and the great world of politics and the press fairly, they would accord you the same fairness; he was still shocked occasionally at the extremes of bitterness which often cropped out on what sometimes seemed the slightest of provocations. "You know," Stanley Danta had once remarked wryly, when his unexpected criticism of some proposal put forward by one of the more popular favorites had suddenly brought an avalanche of personal attack upon his own head, "I think I'll introduce a resolution to change the motto of the Republic from 'E pluribus unum' to 'It all depends upon whose ox is gored.' That would be more fitting, I think."

Senator Anderson had watched the process involve others, and now it was involving him; it was not pleasant, and basically, although he had meant it when he said it was just something to ride out and he was confident he could, there was a savagery about it that he found very disturbing. The debate over Bob Leffingwell was no longer—if it ever had been—a discussion on the merits; it was now simply a matter of personal attack and personal smear, with no holds barred and no weapons unused where weapons could be found. By doing what he thought was the right and honorable thing to protect the country, the President, and the party, he had apparently tipped over a witch's cauldron; and as he stood once more gazing thoughtfully about his yard, he wondered with a recurring sense of foreboding that threw into shadow the bright golden day whether he really could emerge without being genuinely and perhaps permanently scalded.

It was in this mood, which was not conducive to relaxed domestic conversation, that he looked up to see his wife and daughter emerging from the house to come toward him over the lawn. Pidge, dressed in bright blue blouse and jumper, looked her most angelic this morning, but he could see that Mabel, whose feelings were always close to the surface and ready to be rubbed raw, was as disturbed as he was. Because he was beginning to find lately that this state of mutual concern led too rapidly to argument, he knelt down and held out his arms, and Pidge with a glad cry hurled herself into them. As he stood up with her blond head and dark eyes alongside his, the sun playing upon them both, Mabel felt as though a giant hand had reached in and squeezed with implacable determination and great pain upon her heart, so touching and perfect a picture did they make together, and so certain was she that there was menace in the morning for them all.

And because she knew her husband would be annoyed when she said what she felt she must, it came out with a certain doggedly challenging air that she knew desperately even as she said it would prompt a defensive and probably hurtful rejoinder. But she couldn't stop, she felt she had to say it, and she did.

"I couldn't help overhearing some of that," she said in the direct, tactless way of people who aren't quite sure of themselves, when they feel they must come to grips with something unpleasant, "and I wondered if you were doing the right thing."

"Were you listening on the upstairs phone?" her husband asked pleasantly, and she felt like crying, "No, no!" But with considerable effort she managed a little smile and said, "Nope, I was working in the kitchen, remember?"

"Oh," Brig said in the same pleasant tone. "I do remember. Pidge, why don't you run on down and take a look at the goldfish and I'll come join you in a minute?"

His daughter, who was not the child of two intelligent people for nothing gave him a quick look, gave her mother another, and then turned away with a sunny smile.

"All right," she said. "Don't talk too long."

"We won't," Brig said, and for a moment he and Mabel were laughing at the same thing. It passed.

"Now," he said soberly, "what's the matter?"

"I'm worried for you," she said, trying hard to make it come out calmly. "Everybody seems so—so hostile toward what you've done, that it just worries me terribly. I just wondered if you really—really had to do it this way."

"My dearest," he said patiently, "you've known me now, for—how long is it now?—nine years. Nine years, almost ten. Don't I always do things the way I feel I have to do them? And don't I always think them over pretty carefully before I move? Of course I must feel I have to do it this way, or I wouldn't do it this way."

"You always have an answer," she said in a remote voice, while somewhere a cardinal called quickly to another and the warm capricious wind rustled the new leaves in the trees, "and it's always such a—such a *lonely* answer, somehow."

"Lonely?" he said in a puzzled voice. "How do you figure that?"

"I don't know," she said. "It just is. You always do what you think is right, and you don't care what other people think about it, and if they think you should do something different it doesn't matter to you, because you know you're right. And somehow it always seems awfully lonely to me."

He gave her a long look, and there was an emotion she could not fathom deep in the level eyes.

"I'm not lonely," he said. "Whatever in the world gave you that idea? I have you, and I have Pidge, and I have hundreds of friends in Washington and thousands out in the state, and more thousands of thousands I like to think, across the country. How could I possibly be lonely?"

"Well, maybe that isn't the right word for it," she said, "but—yes, yes, I think it is. You're always so sort of set apart from everybody, somehow." And she almost added, "even from me," but she knew she would cry if she did, so she hurried on. "You take these independent stands and up to now it hasn't mattered; but this time there seem to be all sorts of pressures involved and forces at work for Mr. Leffingwell that are bigger than anything you've ever tried to challenge before. I'm afraid they'll hurt you if they can."

"Please," he said gravely. "Please don't fail me now when it really does matter. You've been a politician's wife long enough to know that there comes a time sooner or later for everyone in politics when he just has to stand and take it, that's all. There just isn't any way out, sometimes. And now it's come for me. Sure, I could give in to the President, and to Bob; I could make another statement and close the hearings again and say hurrah for Leffingwell and join the mob and do it the easy way. Would you think better of me for that? I wouldn't think better of myself, I can tell you that."

"Couldn't Bob help you work it out so there wouldn't be any embarrassment about it?" she asked, aware off on the edge of her mind that somewhere a neighbor was running a power mower and somewhere children were shouting happily in the street.

"Yes, he'd like to," he said dryly. "I'm sure he'd like to. That's what the President told him to do, in fact."

"Why don't you talk to the President?" she suggested. "He seems like a nice man."

"Oh, Mabel," he said with a sudden real impatience in his voice. "The President is a nice man as long as it doesn't interfere with his concept of what he ought to be doing as President. Then he stops being a nice man. That's the way Presidents are."

"Then what will he do to you?" she asked, trying not to sound frightened. He shrugged.

"What can he do to me?" he asked. "I have my own responsibility as United States Senator, just as much as he does as President. I assume we'll talk it over after the banquet tonight and see what we can work out together."

"But if you insist on his withdrawing the nomination——" she began, and her husband smiled.

"You weren't working very hard in the kitchen, were you?" he said pleasantly, and her right hand went to her mouth to stop a cry of protest.

"Don't worry about it," he said, and she could see he was beginning the process of withdrawal that lately had proved so killing to her heart. "I'll manage. Apparently I'll have to manage alone, but I'll manage."

"Oh, that isn't fair," she said out of a sudden pain so deep she wasn't quite sure she could speak at all. "That isn't fair. You don't have to be alone unless you want to be."

His eyes widened suddenly, and because she feared he was on the very verge of saying, "Maybe I want to be," and that if he did they might never find one another again, she did cry out, a strange, harsh, awkwardly muffled sound in the bright spring day.

"I'm sorry," he said quietly. "Please don't worry about me, Mabel. I'm not alone. I have you and I love you, and everything's going to be all right. I think I'll go talk to Pidge for a while now. If the phone rings I'll be at home to Bob, the President, Orrin, or Lafe. Nobody else. Come out later and maybe we can decide what to plant in the back garden."

"I will," she said, very carefully and politely. "Yes, I will do that."

"Good," he said, and turned away to walk slowly along the lawn to where Pidge was busily poking in the water of the goldfish pond. The sun fell brightly on the two golden-headed figures she loved, and Mabel Anderson felt as though she might actually die right there in her own yard in Washington, D.C.

"It's just that I don't want you to be hurt," she whispered as her eyes filled with tears and she began to cry. "That's all. I just don't want you to be hurt."

There were times, Seab reflected, when he felt every bit of seventy-five, but this morning was not one of them. Today he felt somewhere around forty, or possibly even thirty-five, tip-top, in the pink, with everything going the way he wanted it to, firmly in control of the situation and thoroughly content with the pattern of events as it was developing in the wake of his call to the Assistant Secretary of Commerce for International Economic Affairs.

The inspiration to make that call and then to handle it as he had he regarded as among the shrewdest of all his long life, and he could not refrain from a certain feeling of profound self-satisfaction about it; a feeling he perforce had to keep to himself, for to disclose it would be to emerge as the man responsible for the new turn of events in the Leffing-well nomination, and this would automatically change the pattern, divert attention, turn the hue and cry back upon him, revive all the tired old animosities that always surrounded everything he did, and upset the delicate balance of the political developments now under way. For Seab Cooley to be the pivotal figure in such a striking change of course was one thing, for it would be immediately discounted and obscured by all the standard attacks; for Brigham Anderson to be the pivotal figure was quite another, because, for all that the nominee's supporters might turn upon him savagely, he simply could not be discredited and discounted in the way Seab could be. If Seab did it, it could be dismissed as part of the same old feud; if Brig did it, people had to stop, look, and listen. That was why Seab had arranged for Brig to do it, and made the arrangement with such deliberate care that not even Brig knew why Brig was doing it.

To arrive at the true identity of James Morton had not in and of itself been so great a feat, he felt, for all it took was an ability to approach the testimony of the witness Gelman afresh and take note of the points that seemed to be bothering him most; and the one that kept recurring, despite the nominee's scornful dismissals, was his dogged conviction that Bob Leffingwell in some way had been involved in getting him his new job in the Bureau of International Economic Affairs. This would seem to indicate some personal relationship or friendship or knowledge between the nominee and either the director of the Bureau or the man in over-all charge of it, the Assistant Secretary. And since a long memory reminded Seab that among other facts brought out about the Secretary at the time of his confirmation three years ago had been his age, which was roughly that of the nominee, and the fact that he had taught law at the University of Chicago for a time while building up his personal practice, all that remained was to have the gambler's instinct and the gambler's will to take a chance that in this case Herbert Gelman might be right, and to act upon it in a way that would permit of no evasions. This he had done, calling the Secretary's home and announcing in a tone of soft menace when he answered, "This is Senator Cooley, James Morton." The man had gasped and before he had found time to recover, Seab had gone on in a voice he made increasingly cold and frightening, "And now, Mr. James Morton, this is what I want you to do for me, if you will be so kind." And he had told him with great exactitude that he must call the chairman of the subcommittee and make a full confession and volunteer to testify, if the chairman so desired; and with a skillful combination of holding out the promise of future assistance in salvaging his career if he complied, and promising flatly to help destroy it utterly if he refused, he had extracted the assurance that James Morton would not disclose to the chairman the true origin of his call. Indeed, he had put it squarely on the basis of the man's own welfare. He really thought, Seab said gently, he really did think, that the chairman and the subcommittee and the Senate and the country would all be much more kindly disposed toward James Morton if they thought his coming forward had been prompted by true patriotism and love of country, and not because anyone had forced him to do it. Even in his shattered mental and emotional state at that moment James Morton had been able to see that; and he had promised with great fervor to do it just the way Senator Cooley suggested. And evidently he had, for if he had not, Seab was sure that he would have received a call right away from Senator Anderson to confirm it. Apparently desperation had given James Morton's call a sense of conviction and truth that had been sufficient to carry the day. And now the future was unfolding as the senior Senator from South Carolina wished.

What would come of it, he could not of course predict exactly, for one thing he had learned far back and very early was the futility of making exact predictions about either the Senate or the course of a political development. All you could do was assess the likeliest possibilities and build your plans upon that. The likeliest possibility in this case was the complete discrediting of the nominee, for Senator Anderson had already made it clear that the hearings would be reopened, and when they were Robert A. Leffingwell was not going to look very good. He was, in fact, going to look very bad; a proven liar, an evasive and unreliable man, a man to whom no thinking citizen would wish to entrust the country's foreign policies in a time of such dangerous international tension. The nominee, as Herbert Gelman had made very clear under Arly Richardson's prodding, had not done anything so very terrible, when all was said and done; he had just acted like a fool when he should have known better and then had made the mistake of lying about it. In the office of Secretary of State, however, this was not a trait his countrymen were inclined to look upon kindly or forgive. Now there would be no rationalizing it and no getting around it; he would be pinned down as neatly as a beetle on a piece of cork, and the President would inevitably have to withdraw the nomination, and would undoubtedly in the process be considerably damaged himself. This too the senior Senator from South Carolina thought he could manage to contemplate without dismay.

And all of this would come about because Seab Cooley had accurately judged two men: James Morton, whom he hardly knew at all, and Brigham Anderson, whom he knew quite well and had studied with considerable care. His instinct had told him that the man Washington knew under his right name would crumble when suddenly presented with the ghost of James Morton from the past; and his instinct had told him that Senator Anderson, confronted with equal suddenness with the same knowledge, would act as directly and forcefully as he had. The only point where Seab had not quite judged the chairman correctly lay in his belief that by now he would have told Bob Munson about it, that Orrin Knox and Lafe Smith would know, that the knowledge would be spreading already through the Senate and within a matter of hours or even minutes would be reaching the press and thus very shortly would hit the front pages and thereby create a situation that nothing could change. The one point where he misjudged his young colleague was that he believed him to be already committed, not only in his own mind and heart, but in the general knowledge of his friends and the Senate and the press which for all its partisanship would never hesitate to print the facts, however damaging to Leffing-

well, once the facts were openly at hand. Thus Seab believed the situation
to be already in the process of congealing, with no way out for anybody
but to move forward along the lines to which each was bound by character,
circumstance and overriding interest.

He was so convinced of this, in fact, that it was only the experience and
judgment of almost half a century that prompted him to consider the
alternative. It was possible he could just conceive of it, that Brigham might
not yet have told anyone about it, that the situation might still be fluid,
and that he might in some way yet yield to what Seab was sure would be
the angry and ruthless pressures of the White House that the matter be
dropped without a full disclosure. Senator Cooley could imagine no
pressures sufficiently great to persuade Senator Anderson to change his
course once he was fully set upon it, but there again long experience of
men and their motives told him he should keep at least one little door
open in his mind for that possibility. He was not a close friend of Brig's,
but like most of Brig's elders in the Senate he was very fond of him in
a fatherly sort of way, and he could not imagine anything in his past that
would make him subject to the sort of pressures that could be brought to
bear upon some men. Even so, he was a human being, and one thing
Seab had learned both in his own life and the many he had observed in
seventy-five years was that human beings occasionally act more human
than a prudent balancing of present need and future interest might make
advisable; and conceivably, just possibly, there might be a lever somewhere in Senator Anderson's past that the President might use, were it
ever to come to his hand.

In that case, Senator Cooley knew, he would simply use the lever he
himself possessed. Assuming Brig had not told his other colleagues, there
still was someone else who knew, a coproprietor of the secret, someone
else who could, by offering to expose the whole situation in the form of
a shabby and underhanded collusion between the White House and the
Senator from Utah, make a man stop and think twice if he wished to
save his own reputation. And from many things he had observed, Seab
knew that Brig was very sensitive about his own reputation. This admit-
tedly was a somewhat cold-blooded way to look at it, possibly a calculation
that might seem out of place in the heart of a man who really was genuinely
fond of his young colleague, but at this particular moment on this particular day Senator Cooley was much more interested in getting Bob
Leffingwell and the President than he was in protecting Brigham Anderson.

So he decided, as he prepared to leave his office and walk across to
the Capitol in the sparkling spring sunshine for an Appropriations Committee meeting, that he would just bide his time and see what happened.
Many things in politics come to him who waits, he had found, and as he
emerged blinking a little into the bright clear day he was waiting, bland
and sleepy-eyed and noncommittal and shrewd and monumentally in-
destructible as ever.

"—and therefore," the Majority Leader finished dictating, "much as I would like to attend your fine meeting in Hamtramck on Monday next, this new turn of events in the Leffingwell nomination makes it impossible for me to leave the Senate at this time. With all best wishes to you and your lively and progressive group, I am, etc."

He snapped off the machine and pushing it aside on the broad desk, swung his chair around to stare out the window, down across the Mall to the Washington Monument, the Lincoln Memorial, the lush green hills of Virginia beyond. It was certainly a beautiful day, and he had half a mind to play hooky; except that there were occasions when you damned well knew you had better not play hooky, and this was damned well one of them. Things were breaking too fast on this gorgeous spring morning, and there was no place for the Majority Leader of the United States Senate to be except right spang in the United States Senate.

Thinking with one layer of his mind as he had dictated—the political level that never went to sleep—he had pretty well decided upon his next move even as he conferred his regrets and blessings upon the good citizens of Hamtramck. In politics and the Senate, he was vividly aware, the shortest distance between two points is very often not a straight line. If you wish A to do something, for instance, you frequently are well advised to go to B, who knows him intimately, or even to C, who is an old pal of B, to start the wheels in motion. The matter of who asks who to do what often assumes a major importance; the whole future of a bill, the whole course of a committee action, the whole completion of a debate, can frequently be changed entirely by the personality of the man who sets it in motion; and while it might have seemed at first glance that he should have continued to hammer at his stubborn young colleague from Utah until he beat him around to the President's point of view, Senator Munson knew better than that. There were some with whom it could be done, but Brig was not one of them; and in any event Bob Munson was far too adept and far too capable and experienced a legislative operator to use such tactics on anyone as valuable, as close to him, and as strong and undisposed to yield to pressure as the senior Senator from Utah.

In the delicate region of who-asks-whom he had by now concluded that the man for him to talk to was Orrin Knox, who could be persuaded to talk to Lafe Smith, who in turn was young enough to meet Brig, as it were, on his own level, with the shared attitudes of a generation, memories of the war, sex, women, old friendship, reactions to their elders, and all the rest of it, to form a common meeting-ground. By this chain of personalities, the Majority Leader hoped, the subtle skein of events leading to a change in Senator Anderson's position and a re-establishment of the status quo ante could be brought about in a smooth and painless way that would leave few scars.

For the Majority Leader was aware from the President's tone that he was not, as he had said, about to abandon his commitment without a struggle; and it had been quite apparent from the iron in his voice the kind of struggle it would be. Occasionally in the past Bob Munson had seen the normally equable temper—equable as long as things were going his way—flare up; he had watched the force of that personality lash out at obstacles in its path, and he had known of actions taken with complete ruthlessness that had for all practical political and national purposes completely destroyed some of the men who had gotten in his way. Most Presidents who had an ounce of historical conception of the powers and responsibilities of their great office were bad business when crossed; and this one had considerably more than an ounce. He was not one to tangle with lightly; and the Majority Leader, still certain that the Senator from Utah had underestimated both the Chief Executive's present intentions and his basic general character, was anxious to ease him out of the situation before it reached a showdown where neither man would retreat. If that occurred, he would not vouch for what might happen to Senator Anderson; and he cared enough for him, both as friend and as a valuable Senator whose serious bruising in a battle with the White House would be a real blow to the Senate and the country, to want to do everything possible to head off any such clash, which at the least would be unpleasant and at the most might be tragic.

So it was with a serious heart that he lifted the phone and put through a call to Senator Knox's office, and after ascertaining that he was in, told his secretary to convey the information that he would be dropping by very shortly. He noticed that she sounded a little constrained, and a couple of minutes later as he turned the corner and started down the long corridor to Orrin's door he understood why. The area around the doorway was bathed in floodlight, three or four television cameras were at the ready, a large crowd of reporters was standing about, a few tourists were watching in an awestruck way on the outer fringes. It was quite obvious that some quarry had gone to ground inside, and it was also quite obvious that the next step in the Leffingwell matter had been taken out of the Majority Leader's hands without so much as a by-your-leave. Orrin in his blunt, pragmatic, impatient, and independent way, had obviously decided to move in.

There were some in the Senate toward whom the Majority Leader would have felt a considerable annoyance under such a circumstance, but Orrin was in a different category. Old friendship and complete personal trust, plus the fact that Orrin was Orrin and overlooked the subtler niceties not because he wanted to be nasty but just because he was too busy thinking about something else to pay any attention to them, prompted forgiveness. Whatever Orrin had decided to do, Bob Munson was quite ready to go along with it; and with complete calm and good nature he headed toward the inevitable onslaught of the press as he neared the door. "Here comes Bob," he heard the Washington *Star* announce, and instantly he was confronted by a circle of questioning faces and raised pencils.

"You know," he said comfortably, "you've no idea how happy it makes me to be greeted by all these bright morning faces. How do you manage to look so fresh and eager all the time?"

"I," said the Baltimore *Sun* dryly, "will have you know I was up half the night and then got up again at five to try to solve this little mystery."

"Poor you," Senator Munson said with a chuckle, "You should have gone into some other business."

"Now he tells us," AP said, and the Majority Leader laughed.

"Come on, now," he said. "You wouldn't be doing anything else and you know it."

"What's the purpose of this meeting, Senator?" the St. Louis *Post-Dispatch* inquired in a businesslike way, and Senator Munson shrugged.

"I assume Senator Knox has told you as much as he wants you to know," he said blandly.

"He hasn't told us anything," the *Herald Tribune* remarked in a tone of some reproach. Bob Munson smiled.

"That's what I mean," he said.

"Well, can't you tell us anything?" the Washington *Post* insisted. "There must be something we can be told."

"Who's arrived so far?" Senator Munson asked.

"Arly Richardson, John Winthrop, and Tom August are already in," the *Star* reported. "Johnny DeWilton is on his way, and I guess you complete the list, right?"

"I guess so," the Majority Leader said comfortably. "Won't you have fun speculating out here for the next hour and a half."

"Well, obviously you're going to decide whether to take the matter out of Brig's hands and go ahead with the nomination regardless," the *Post-Dispatch* said. Senator Munson raised a quizzical eyebrow.

"Oh?" he said. "Is that what we're going to do? Thanks for telling me, boys. I'll pass the word along to the others when I get inside."

"Well, what else would you be meeting for?" the Providence *Journal* demanded, and the Majority Leader adopted an air of mock gravity.

"Many important matters are now before the Senate," he pointed out solemnly. "Just because you're all excited about one little old bitty nomination doesn't mean that there isn't plenty else. Appropriations; a fishing treaty with Canada; whether or not to have a tax bill this year; foreign aid; reciprocal trade—oh, the subjects are endless. Just endless."

"Oh, now," UPI said amicably, "stop being cute. There's only one subject before this subcommittee, and that's Bob Leffingwell. Why else would Orrin Knox have called a subcommittee meeting, and why else would he want you and Tom August to be in on it?"

"You fellows are *so sharp*," Senator Munson said with equal amicability. "Just keep guessing, and the time out here will just fly by."

"What do you think of Brig's action, Senator?" the New York *Daily News* asked in a more serious tone, and the Majority Leader dropped the banter and replied seriously.

"I've talked to him," he said, "and I'm satisfied he has his reasons, and that they may be good ones. At least they seem sufficient to him to warrant the action he has taken. Therefore I for one am prepared to refrain from passing judgment until he makes his reasons clear."

"Has he asked to see the President?" CBS inquired.

"I'd say it's mutual," Senator Munson said with a grin. "They want to see each other."

"When?" the Washington *Post* demanded.

"I don't know yet," Senator Munson said.

"This morning?" the Newark *News* suggested, and Bob Munson smiled.

"It isn't definitely settled yet," he said.

"Supposing the subcommittee does decide to take it out of his hands," the Washington *Star* asked. "What then?"

"I can't conceive of it," Senator Munson said flatly. "It would be a most unusual demonstration of lack of faith in a member of the Senate."

"How about faith in Bob Leffingwell?" the Baltimore *Sun* inquired, and the Majority Leader grinned.

"There," he said, "you open up a whole new field of study. Now if you gentlemen will part your ranks like the Red Sea, little Moses will go on in."

"Will you have a statement for us when the meeting is over, Senator?" the Newark *News* asked.

"Orrin may," he said. "Or I may. Or we all may. Somebody will, so don't go away."

"Senator," the *Herald Trib* told him, "two thirds of our lives are spent waiting outside closed committee hearings. We won't go away."

"Well, make yourselves comfortable," Bob Munson advised. "Maybe you can spend your time thinking up some more nasty things to say about us for delaying the nomination. There must," he said with a grin that took some but not all the sting out of it, "be one or two left."

But as Senator DeWilton came along the corridor and they went on into Orrin's reception room together, he decided that there was little point in ragging the press. They were nice people, for the most part, very astute and very intelligent, and they were human like everybody else in Washington; so close to government, so much a part of politics, that it was almost impossible for them to refrain from developing strong opinions, and almost equally impossible for them to keep their opinions from showing. He was certain that none of them, confronted with the point-blank question, "Do you really want to hurt Brigham Anderson, or Bob Munson, or whoever?" would give an affirmative answer. It was just that their feelings got involved and they got swept along and one thing led to another and frequently, somehow, it all seemed to come out in a way that indirectly but forcefully promoted the causes and the people they believed in and did damage to those they did not. He knew this was a failing that afflicted everyone who got involved in Washington, and he was not going to set himself up to judge it. When they turned on you, as Brig had truly said, all you could do was ride it out. A week from now, with Bob Leffingwell confirmed and the bitter battle forgotten, they would be your friends again. It was just part of the game.

Inside the office with the door safely closed behind them, he smiled his greeting to the girls at the typewriters and piloted Johnny DeWilton by the arm on through the next office and into Orrin's private office in the room beyond. The senior Senator from Illinois got up at once and extended his hand in the inevitable senatorial handshake, that symbol of the club that occurs automatically whether Senators are seeing one another again after six months, six days, or six hours.

"I'm glad you could come, Bob," he said matter-of-factly. "I meant to call you about, but it slipped my mind until a minute ago and then Mary said you were on the way. Glad to see you, Johnny. Are there many reporters outside?"

"About thirty," Senator DeWilton said.

"Well," Orrin said tartly, "Tom thinks we should give them quite a story, but I'm against it."

The chairman of the Foreign Relations Committee gave the Majority Leader a rather reproachful look and spoke in his wistfully worried way.

"This meeting was Orrin's idea," he said, "and I thought since we were having it, maybe it would be best to reach some firm decision on the matter. That's all. I'm willing to be overruled if you feel it best, but we ought to do something, under the circumstances, it seems to me."

"What circumstances?" John Winthrop asked with a smile. "A little fussing in the press? Don't tell me that has you scared, Tom."

"It isn't only that," Senator August said defensively. "The President's all upset, too. He called me this morning."

"He called me, too," Arly Richardson said, "but I'm not scared."

"He's been a busy man," Senator Munson observed dryly. "Is there anybody here he didn't call?"

"He called us all, I expect," Senator Knox said. He smiled in a rather wintry way. "Didn't tell you he was going to, though, did he?"

"Nope," Bob Munson said cheerfully.

"He's a shifty man," Orrin said in a tone that dismissed him from further consideration. "Anyway, here we are. It was my idea. I thought we ought to get together and talk it over. It *is* causing quite a rumpus, and it seemed advisable to present a united front on it, if we can get one."

"I'm united," Senator Winthrop offered calmly. "I'm for Brig. Whatever," he added with a little chuckle, "Brig is for."

"So am I," Senator Knox said, "but I thought at least we should discuss it and maybe prepare a statement. If we agree. How about you, Arly?"

The senior Senator from Arkansas looked stubborn and Senator Munson could see he was about to be difficult.

"I'm not so sure," Arly said slowly. "It seems to me that whatever the trouble is, it was certainly presented to us in a way that put us all on the spot. What's the matter with Brig, anyway? Aren't we all entitled to be consulted on something like this? Why didn't he call us first?"

"Maybe there wasn't time," the Majority Leader suggested, and Senator Richardson looked skeptical.

"Hell," he said, "there was time enough on something like this."

"The first I knew about it," Tom August said reproachfully, "was when the New York *Times* called me at 1 A.M. and wanted to get my comment."

"Yes," Orrin Knox said, "I noticed you supported Brig."

"What else could I do at the moment?" Senator August asked. "I didn't know what he had in mind. It did seem to me, though, that as chairman of the full committee I might have been given the courtesy of an advance warning."

"And suppose he had given you one?" Senator Knox demanded. "Would you have stopped him?"

"That would depend on what it was," Tom August said. "I might have cautioned that he wait until this morning when we could all meet about it, rather than shoot from the hip right then."

"He'd be in better shape now," Senator Winthrop admitted.

"It looks to me almost like a shock reaction," Johnny DeWilton said. "He heard something, or somebody came to him with something, and he was so upset by it he acted without thinking."

Arly Richardson looked disbelieving.

"When did Brig ever act without thinking?" he asked.

"It happens," Orrin Knox said. "He's human."

"Yes," Senator Richardson said. "Well, I'd certainly like to hear from him right now before we announce anything. How about getting him on the phone, Orrin?"

"I've called him," the Majority Leader said calmly. "He won't tell us what it is until he's had a chance to see the President. And we've pretty definitely set it up that we'll see the President together at the White House tonight after the correspondents' banquet."

"Won't somebody see you leaving together?" John Winthrop asked.

"We won't leave together," Bob Munson said, "and anyway, it won't be much before midnight, and by that time very few people will be alert enough to notice we aren't around any longer."

"So we're stuck with the status quo until tomorrow," Arly said.

"We would have been anyway," Senator Winthrop pointed out. "We weren't planning to meet until tomorrow to vote on it. You didn't want it on the floor before Saturday, did you, Bob?"

The Majority Leader shook his head.

"As long as it's run this late in the week, I thought Saturday would be a good day for it," he said. "We could have a special Saturday session, meet early, and devote the whole day to it."

"Now that's really psychology, Bobby," Senator Richardson said dryly. "Push us right up against Sunday and let it discourage the talkers. You're mighty sharp."

"I try to be," Bob Munson said blandly. "Anyway, there's no point in talking to Brig until after he's seen the President."

"There's only one reason for that," Senator DeWilton observed. "He must think he can get the Old Man to withdraw the nomination."

"He does have some such idea," the Majority Leader admitted, and Senator August looked alarmed.

"Oh, my," he said. "I really don't think that's a wise move unless he knows something very, *very* bad about Mr. Leffingwell."

"He doesn't really think the President will stand still for that, does he?" Senator Richardson asked skeptically, and Senator Knox gave him an angry look.

"Why not?" he demanded. "If there's a legitimate reason, why not?"

"This town doesn't work that way, Orrin," Arly Richardson said. "You know that."

Orrin's jaw set and, as often happened, he said exactly what he was thinking.

"It would if I were running it," he said bluntly, and Senator Richardson couldn't resist the opportunity.

"But you're not, Orrin," he said gently. "You're not, you know, and some of us don't think you ever will."

"All right, fellows," Senator Munson said. "Let's get on with this without getting into presidential politics. We've got enough troubles as it is."

"I'll bet the President will smash him if he can," John DeWilton said with a frown, and Senator Richardson smiled.

"It's happened to better men," he remarked.

"There aren't any better," Senator Knox snapped. "Now are we going to agree on something or aren't we? I'm entirely for Brig. I can understand exactly why he did what he did, and if it's sufficiently damaging to Leffingwell, I can understand exactly why he wants the President to withdraw him. It's just the sort of thing I'd do myself. Maybe it isn't crafty enough for you, Arly, or for *him*"—and he made a scornful gesture with one outflung hand somewhere off in the sky in the general direction of downtown Washington—"but it's fine with me." And suddenly he whirled on the chairman of Foreign Relations, who was so startled he jumped. "How about you, Tom?" he demanded.

"If I did what I'd really like to do," Senator August said slowly, "I think I'd declare the subcommittee dissolved and then reappoint it with Brig off and myself as chairman."

"By God, that sounds like the White House talking," Senator DeWilton said explosively. "You'd never be clever enough to think of something like that by yourself, Tom. Is that what he told you to do?"

The Senator from Minnesota flushed but stood his ground.

"It doesn't matter where it came from," he said with an air of pained dignity. "It's just what I would do if I did what I'd really like to do."

"You'd have one hell of a fight on your hands if you did," Orrin Knox told him tersely. "I'd raise hell and so would Bob, I expect"—he looked at the Majority Leader for confirmation and Senator Munson nodded with a stern look at Senator August—"and so would a lot of people. What kind of a crackpot idea is that, anyway? I never heard of such a thing in all my years in the Senate."

"Oh, I don't know," Arly Richardson said casually. "There's nothing in the rules to prevent it. After all, Tom *is* the chairman, even though some of us always act as though he weren't. It's an interesting idea, Tom. You might have something there."

"God damn it," Senator Knox said angrily, "stop trying to make trouble and let's get on with this. They're out there waiting, right now."

"So they are," Arly said cheerfully. "Maybe they'll have their story, after all."

"Maybe we should have a vote, if we want to settle it," John Winthrop suggested, and Senator Richardson made an impatient movement.

"I'm not going to be bound by any vote," he said. "This whole proceeding is a violation of our decision to hold all meetings in open session."

"This isn't a formal meeting," Orrin said sharply. "How can it be when the chairman didn't call it and isn't here?"

"That's trimming it pretty close for blunt, honest, forthright Orrin Knox," Senator Richardson observed, and Orrin would have replied angrily if the Majority Leader hadn't forestalled him.

"Suppose we don't have any votes," he said, "or any big, dramatic clashes, Arly, if you don't mind. There are apparently going to be a lot of opportunities still to come in this nomination for that. If Tom really wanted to do what he suggests, he could. If you do, Tom, you'll have the backing of the White House. You'll have the opposition of most of the Senate, and we won't forget it. Which is most important to you in the long run, his support or ours?"

At this appeal to the ancient mores of the lodge, with its hint of penalties carried for years in the collective memory of the Senate, the senior Senator from Minnesota looked even more worried than usual and even, Bob Munson thought, a little pale.

"I'm willing to be bound by what you all agree," he said hastily. "I'm not making any objections. I think we should frame the language with some care, though."

"Such as?" Bob Munson asked encouragingly in quite a different tone.

"Well," Senator August said carefully, "let me see. How about, 'We have met this morning to discuss the decision of the chairman of the subcommittee, Senator Anderson, to reopen the hearings on the nomination of Robert A. Leffingwell to be Secretary of State. Although we have not been able to discuss the matter directly with the chairman——'"

"Strike that," Orrin Knox directed shortly. "'We are satisfied that his reasons for this action are sufficiently valid to warrant further study.'"

"Not so fast," Senator Winthrop said, writing it down on a pad of lined Senate note paper. "It's been forty years since I was a court reporter."

"All right," Senator August said meekly. "'We are satisfied that his reasons for this action are sufficiently valid——'"

"Strike 'sufficiently,'" Johnny DeWilton said. "'Are valid.'"

"'are valid,'" Tom August said obediently, "'and warrant further study. Accordingly——'"

"'Accordingly' nothing," Senator Knox said flatly. "Let it go at that. Read it back, Win."

"'We have met this morning to discuss the decision of the chairman of the subcommittee, Senator Anderson, to reopen the hearings on the nomination of Robert A. Leffingwell to be Secretary of State,'" Senator Winthrop read. "'We are satisfied that his reasons for this action are valid and warrant further study.' Period. Sounds a little abrupt," he observed. "Maybe Leffingwell deserves to be let down easy too, under the circumstances."

"I certainly want something in there to emphasize that we aren't prejudging him," Tom August said, and Arly Richardson nodded.

"Just for form," he said dryly.

"All right," Orrin said shortly. "'This in no way indicates that we have reached a final judgment one way or the other on Mr. Leffingwell.'"

"'Or on the wisdom of reopening the hearings,'" Arly added.

"I won't accept that," Bob Munson said calmly.

"'This is in no way a reflection upon Mr. Leffingwell,'" Tom August offered.

"How can it help but be anything else?" Senator Richardson demanded. "Let's don't be complete hypocrites about this. If we're backing our boy because he's our boy, let's say so. Especially if that's the best you can do for Leffingwell."

"I didn't realize you were such a partisan of his," Senator Munson observed.

"There's nothing in the record now to tell me why I shouldn't be," Arly pointed out. "I told him I'd support him if the record stood in his favor. I keep my promises."

"Very well," Orrin Knox said. "We'll combine my idea and yours. Add this, Win: 'This in no way indicates that we have reached a final judgment on Mr. Leffingwell, or on the wisdom of reopening the hearings.'"

"So we affirm our belief in the validity of Brig's action at the start and then turn right around and cast doubt on it at the end," the Majority Leader observed wryly.

"And by approving the validity of his action we imply we believe Leffingwell's at fault and then we turn right around and say we aren't judging whether he is or not," Senator DeWilton added.

"And all in three sentences," John Winthrop said with a chuckle. "Rarely has there been a finer or more outstanding example of the unequivocal and unflinching stand of this great body on anything."

"Write me out a clean copy," Orrin directed, "and then we'll all sign it and I'll read it to the reporters. Or do you want to, Tom?"

"Wouldn't that be more fitting?" Senator Munson suggested, and his colleagues nodded.

"Well, I intend to be there, anyway," Senator Knox said. "I think we all should be."

"That's so you won't try to slip anything over on us, Tom," Senator Richardson said, and the Majority Leader turned on him emphatically.

"We don't want you to, either, Arly," he said firmly. "This is a closed session, so let's keep it that way. I don't want to read about it in the Star an hour from now."

"Don't you?" Arly said blandly. "Well, we'll see."

"All right now," Orrin said, passing the paper to Senator August, "go ahead and sign, Tom, and then the rest of us will. You can too, if you want to, Bob."

"Sure, I'll bring up the rear," Senator Munson said agreeably. "It may be good for the President to know Brig isn't without friends."

"He may need them," John DeWilton observed.

"He may," John Winthrop agreed.

"All right, Tom, let's go," Senator Knox said impatiently, and taking the chairman of the Foreign Relations Committee firmly by the arm he steered him quickly through the door and out before the press and the tourists and the television cameras while the others trailed along to form a half circle behind them in the glaring lights.

"Senator August has a statement for you," Orrin announced. "Read it, Tom."

"Just a minute, Senator!" a technician called sharply, there was a muffled stir and flurry, and then he called, "Now!" the cameras began to roll and the chairman read in a soft voice:

"We have met this morning to discuss the decision of the chairman of the subcommittee, Senator Anderson, to reopen the hearings on the nomination of Robert A. Leffingwell to be Secretary of State.

"We are satisfied that his reasons for this action are valid and warrant further study.

"This in no way indicates that we have reached a final judgment on Mr. Leffingwell, or on the wisdom of reopening the hearings.

"This is signed by myself as chairman of the full committee, by the four members of the subcommittee here present, and by the Majority Leader."

He stopped and there was a moment's silence.

"Is that all?" somebody asked in a puzzled voice, and somebody else said in a tone of frank bafflement, "Now, what in the hell does that mean?"

This brought general laughter from everyone including the Senators, and after it was over CBS stepped forward.

"Senator," he said earnestly, "is this the unanimous position of the sub-committee and the leadership?"

Tom August looked shyly about and smiled in an apologetic way.

"I'm sorry," he said. "We agreed that we would stand on the statement and not answer any questions."

"You mean you're backing Senator Anderson, then," the Baltimore *Sun* suggested.

"Or are you?" the *Times* wanted to know.

"And you're criticizing Leffingwell," the *Herald Tribune* offered.

"Or are you?" the *Post* inquired.

Tom August shook his head again in his gentle, deprecating way.

"I'm sorry," he said, "no questions."

"That's all, boys," Orrin Knox said firmly. "Sorry we can't give you more at this time, but you've got all we intend to say right now. Bob, stick around for a minute, I want to talk to you."

And deliberately moving in front of his colleagues, he turned his back on the cameras and stood there until, after a moment, with more than a little audible grumbling, their interrogators gave up.

"Well," CBS said, "I guess that tells *us*."

"Tells us nothing," UPI said in an annoyed tone.

"Arly gave me the high sign," AP said. "Let's walk him down the hall."

And as Senator Winthrop, Senator DeWilton, and Senator August walked together down the hall in one direction, the reporters who sought without success to question them peeled away one by one like planes in formation and hurried down the other way after Senator Richardson, who was walking along slowly flanked by AP, UPI, and the *Times*.

Observing this progress as they stood together by the door while the cameramen packed their gear and the crowd dispersed, Orrin muttered, "Damned troublemaker," and the Majority Leader grinned.

"It never fails," he said. "He's no more sold on Leffingwell than the man in the moon, but this is a chance to embarrass you and me and Brig and a few other people, so he's not going to let it slip."

"Hmph," Orrin said in a disgusted tone. "Well, come on in, Bob, I want to really talk this over with you for a minute. I'm worried."

"So am I," Senator Munson confessed as they returned to the inner office and his host plopped down in his big leather chair and put his feet on the desk. "I don't like the way it's shaping up, frankly."

"That damned sneak at the White House," Senator Knox said tartly. "Imagine calling all of us separately without letting you know, and then trying to put Tom up to a crazy-fool stunt like that. What's wrong there, anyway? Is his poor health knocking him off base mentally?"

"What poor health is that?" Senator Munson asked, suddenly finding himself defending another of the Administration's many flanks.

"You know what I mean," Orrin said. "It's all over town. God help us if we have to have Harley."

"I don't follow you," Bob Munson said. "If he's so bad, what's wrong with Harley?"

"Oh, hell, nobody wants a President to die," Orrin said, "it causes too much of an upset in everything. Particularly at a time like this. I don't think Harley would be so bad, actually."

"He's terrified at the thought," Senator Munson said.

"Yes, I know," Senator Knox said. "But a lot of people are terrified of things they get over being terrified about when they actually have to do them. We could help him."

"We'd have to," the Majority Leader said. "However, I don't think all this activity down there indicates a dying man, would you say? He's just a little tired."

"Doesn't indicate a tired one, either," Orrin said with a grin. "But tell me, Bob, what's gotten into our young friend and what's going to come of it?"

"I don't know, exactly," Senator Munson said.

"I don't want him to get into a real row with the President," Senator Knox said.

"Neither do I," Bob Munson said, "but we can't head it off without his co-operation."

"Apparently it's kicked up hell at home, too," Orrin said thoughtfully. "Beth called a little while ago, and it seems Mabel had just called her, all upset. It isn't the first time in recent weeks."

"Mabel," Senator Munson said in a tired tone, "is a sweet girl, but she isn't the first who ever married a complex man and then spent the rest of her life wondering what he was all about. Brig is taking on the whole kit and caboodle of us, here. It seems to me she could be much more of a help to him by just standing by and supporting him and acting the way a wife ought to act instead of adding to his burdens by inflicting her own worries on him. But I suppose that's none of my business. Except as Brig is everybody's business, right now."

"Well, I suppose it isn't all one-sided," Senator Knox said. "You know how these things are. I think Beth told her more or less the same thing; although, as I say, it isn't the first time and I think Beth's beginning to lose patience a little herself. There's such a thing as carrying independence too far. Mabel keeps saying she can't figure him out."

"She never will," Senator Munson said flatly. "The only thing to do is accept and try to understand and stop fretting and try to be a wife in the classic sense, it seems to me."

"Women lead a hard life," Orrin observed, not without a touch of smugness. "Thank God we were born men, Robert. Well, what are we going to do about this?"

"What I would like," Senator Munson said, "is to get him to the White House this afternoon and see if we can't get it settled before the White House Correspondents' dinner. Otherwise the President like as not is going to take off after him in his little speech at the end of the evening. And that will just make it all the harder to work out when they finally get together."

"How do you propose to do that?" Senator Knox asked.

"There are two courses," Bob Munson said. "You and Lafe are both very close to him. Either you can talk to him or Lafe can."

"I would say Lafe," Senator Knox said promptly. "Not that he's any closer than I am, but I think age might be a factor in a situation as delicate as this one—they have the same general approach to things in that generation, you know, they see things more or less the same way. If they really started to argue Lafe could always talk about women, or something."

"And there isn't anything Lafe doesn't know about women," Bob Munson said with a grin. "Or something, either, I imagine. That was exactly my own view of it, but I wanted to clear it with you before I did anything. In fact, if you're agreeable, I think it might be better for you to call Lafe and put it up to him yourself. Tell him we're worried, as I'm sure he is too, and that we'd like Brig to see the President this afternoon. Maybe Lafe can take him some place to lunch where they won't be seen, and they can talk it over."

"Is there any place in Washington where you won't be seen?" Orrin asked dryly. "I've never found one. Not," he added quickly with a grin, "that I've ever really needed one, you understand, for any purpose. All right, then, I'll call Lafe. In the meantime, what are you going to do to head off the lunatic fringe, Freddy Van Ackerman and Arly and so on?"

"Oh, Arly's no problem," Senator Munson said. "After he's spilled his guts to the press he'll settle down and be all right for the long haul. Fred is something else again."

"Why don't you cut the session short today?" Orrin suggested. "I don't know of any particular business that needs to be done, do you?"

"I've been thinking I would," the Majority Leader said. "It would head off a lot of speeches. I'll talk to Warren and Harley."

"Warren will go along," Senator Knox said. "He understands the problem. Fine, I'll get in touch with Lafe right away, then."

"Good," Senator Munson said. "I'll talk to the others. We'll get our stubborn little boy to the White House before he knows it."

"Do you really think so?" Senator Knox asked skeptically.

"No," Senator Munson admitted with a rather rueful smile, "but we'll try."

Beside the fish pond with his daughter, he felt that there must be, somewhere in the golden day, some magic open sesame, some satisfactory answer to everything that would permit his heart to rest and Mabel's to understand it and enable them to preserve a reasonable harmony and peace together; but he was beginning to wonder if it were not slipping away. He had understood her mood but in the sheerest self-defense he had not been able to respond in kind. To do so would have been to become engulfed in what seemed to him a drowning emotionalism, and so to lose all control of a situation that was deteriorating fast enough without added stimulus. One of them had to keep calm, even if this meant that the other had to be hurt; and so it had been with a very honest pain but an inflexible determination not to abandon himself to an equal desperation that he had remained polite and self-possessed in the face of her unhappiness. He had meant only to be kind, in the truest sense, and thought he had been. It did not occur to him that it might have driven them further apart, for he was under such pressures both as a result of their difficulties and as a result of the nomination that he did not dare concede an inch to emotionalism for fear it might sweep him over the dam and away altogether.

Yet he understood fully the potentials for his marriage that there were in all the onrushing events of this deceptively bright and hopeful morning. He might not realize entirely just how much he himself was contributing to it, for it seemed to him that he was doing what was fair and best for them both, but he knew the abyss was waiting at their feet if they allowed events to push them but a little further toward it. And the thought appalled him, though she might not believe it, every bit as much as it did his wife.

He could not, now, imagine life unmarried, any more than he could conceive of divorce as a practical solution for two people who, when all was said and done, were used to one another, had a fair amount of love, were reasonable and intelligent and needed only time and patience to restore contentment. It would mean great unhappiness for them both, a tragic and perhaps permanent blow to their daughter, a loss of security and protective habit he could not possibly welcome now; and this was leaving aside political consequences, which were immense. Few states would stand for it, their own church state least of all. It would mean the end of all his career and all his hopes, all chance for service, all opportunity to do good, all possibility of justifying and fulfilling himself in public service. There were all the reasons in the world why he should work to preserve his marriage, none at all why he should not. Thus though he might have seemed temporarily unfeeling and hurtful, he was convinced that this was the best way to handle the growing tension between them. Certainly the alternative offered no lasting solutions, for sex was never an answer to anything for very long. Three days ago he had tried to handle it with a deliberate sexuality, as elemental and overwhelming as he knew how to make it, and he knew very well. The surcease had lasted only until the first new hint of outside pressure and then they were right back where they had been, and if anything a little worse. So this time he had tried a different approach, hoping it would prove more suited and more lasting. A little later if all went well, with the hysteria over and the moment's anguish passed, they could talk it over quietly and find their way back. He was certain this was the better way; or so, at least, he told himself.

Underlying the outward calm with which he had refused his wife's appeal and the apparent certainty with which he was holding to his course on the nomination, however, he was not entirely sure; some inner questioning, some insistent wondering, not the endless argument of alternatives that besets the weak but the really fundamental, scarifying self-doubt that only the strongest can endure, was eating at his heart in the wake of the Majority Leader's call and its emotional aftermath. Was he really doing the right and honorable thing on the nomination? Was he really being fair and decent to his wife? And would the Lord give him some sign, in the dancing sunlight and the perfect day, that he was still all right, that he was still a worth-while human being who had something of value to contribute to his country, his family and his people?

"You're thinking pretty hard, aren't you?" Pidge inquired thoughtfully from somewhere down around his feet, and forced by this to abandon a mood that he knew was only leading to a frustrating dead end that would do nobody any good, he laughed thankfully and bent to ruffle her hair.

"I was," he said, "but I'm not now. You've stopped me."

"Good," she said, and he chuckled.

"Yes, it is," he told her. "How did you know?"

"Daddy," she said politely, "what are you talking about?"

"I thought you knew," he said in mock reproach. "Don't you know everything?"

"I think one of these fishes is sick," she said matter-of-factly, changing a subject she had obviously decided she was getting nowhere with. "Why don't you take him out?"

"All right," he said, "go get me a stick and we'll throw him away."

"O.K.," she said cheerfully, and trotted over to the edge of the lawn, returning in a moment with a twig which she handed him gravely.

"This isn't a very big stick," he pointed out, "but we'll try it."

"You can reach in and get him if it doesn't work," she said, and her father laughed.

"I see I have a practical daughter," he said, flipping the fish out and then picking it up by the tail and hurling it off under the trees. "See, I did both."

"What will he do now?" she asked.

"That's a long story," he said. "Why don't I tell you some other time?"

"All right," she said. "He won't swim, though, will he?"

"No," he said, "he won't swim."

"Are you and Mommy friends?" she asked, and her father chuckled.

"You're a born politician, Pidge," he told her. "You always approach everything on a tangent, don't you?"

"Are you?" she insisted with a little frown, and he saw it was time to become serious.

"Yes," he said gravely, "we are."

"You were fussing," she said accusingly.

"Big people do fuss sometimes," he said. "It doesn't mean much."

"Even when you do it a lot?" she asked.

"Who says we do it a lot?" he demanded.

"You might," she said.

"Yes," he said firmly, "but we don't. And we aren't going to do it at all, any more."

"That's good," she said comfortably. "It's better if you don't."

"Yes, it is," he agreed. "I'm sorry we disturbed you."

"O.K.," she said equably, and then added in a perfect echo of her parents in moments of disciplinary stress, "I don't want to have to tell you again."

"Ho, ho!" Brig said, scooping her up on his shoulder, "don't you, now?"

"No," she said firmly, emphasizing her words by pounding on his head. "I want you to be good."

"Ouch!" he said. "Cut that out. All right, we'll be good. Here comes Mommy now, and you just watch how good we'll be. Pidge wants us to be good, Mommy."

"I should hope so," Mabel said with a rather tremulous smile, holding out her arms to Pidge. "I should hope so."

But instead of surrendering their daughter, her husband stepped into her arms with Pidge still on his shoulder and leaned down to kiss her cheek. "So," he said quietly, "we'll be good. Right?"

"I'll try," she said, with another smile that didn't look very sure of itself.

"Those are Ellen's orders," Brig said. "She thinks there's been enough fussing, she says."

"I'll try," Mabel repeated. "Will you?"

He kissed her again and holding Pidge carefully, let her slide slowly down the length of his body until she collapsed in a small heap on the ground at his feet.

"I will," he said.

"Is that a promise?" she asked in a half humorous way, and the level dark eyes looked straight into hers with the glance she could never withstand, no matter how she steeled herself against it.

"It's a promise," he said.

"Daddy," Pidge demanded from below, "I'm sitting on your foot. Play horsey."

"No, I won't play horsey," he said, setting her on her feet and giving her an affectionate swat. "You run along and get your ball and maybe I'll play ball with you."

"All right," she said, and went trotting off along the garden looking for it.

"I heard the news on the radio a little while ago," Mabel said, and he smiled.

"Am I still the villain of the piece?" he asked.

For a second worry returned to her eyes, and then she made a determined effort to banish it and look unconcerned.

"The subcommittee met," she said, and he looked surprised and suddenly intent.

"Oh, did they?" he said. "Orrin called it?"

"Yes," she said.

"What did they do?" he asked.

"They issued a statement that apparently rather puzzled everybody," she said, "but the main point seemed to be that they were standing by you."

"Well, then," he said in a relieved tone that surprised her, for it disclosed a depth of concern she had not known was there, "there's nothing to worry about, is there? I told you it was going to be all right."

"Yes," she admitted. "You told me."

"So you see," he said comfortably, "all those worries weren't necessary at all, were they?"

"I guess not," she said. "Lafe called, too."

"Oh?" he said. "Why didn't you call me?"

"Well, he said he wanted to take you to lunch somewhere quiet and get you away from it all for an hour or so, and I told him I thought that would be a good idea, and to come get you." She smiled again, a little uncertainly. "Was that all right?"

He grinned.

"That was fine," he said. "I wonder what he's got on his mind? Something Bob and Orrin put him up to, I'll bet."

"He didn't say," she said. "He said to tell you to be of good cheer, the troops are with you." And in spite of her best intentions her eyes, reddened from their quarrel and her talk with Beth, filled with tears again.

"Goodness," she said. "I'm certainly weepy today."

"Well, you've been worried," he said, "and I appreciate it. I really do." And he reached out and with one finger gently traced the outline of her right cheek from ear to chin.

"As long as *all* the troops are with me," he said softly, "I guess I can manage."

"They are," she said, blinking rapidly as she turned to watch their daughter advancing toward them over the lawn, holding her ball before her in both hands. "Especially us."

So he felt much better suddenly, for the Lord had given him a sign after all, he had love and he had friends and the day seemed to mean what it said when it held out hope.

"Before the press gets on the floor," the Majority Leader murmured casually, resting one hand on Senator Strickland's shoulder and looking thoughtfully up at the crowded galleries fifteen minutes before the opening, "I think I should tell you that I would like mighty much to adjourn this here old Senate in about five little old minutes flat. Would you be willing to go along with little old me on that?"

"I might," the Minority Leader said with a smile, "if the price is right. What's it all about?"

"We have a problem, as you know," Senator Munson said, "and I don't want to give anybody a chance to get up and sound off about it and make it worse before we can make it better."

"Particularly Fred," the Minority Leader suggested, and Bob Munson smiled.

"Particularly that case of overhypoed venom," he agreed. "I think we'll get along much better all around if we just quit in a hurry. Harley's agreeable. O.K.?"

"Well, let me see," Warren Strickland said in mock thought. "Sam Eastwood has his heart set on taking off after the Indian Bureau; Walter Calloway was going to attack the British; Harold Kidd thinks we ought to reduce excise taxes; and I believe Verne Cramer told me he wanted to say a few significant words about Algeria. And of course there is a certain amount of business pending—the Justice Department appropriation, for one thing. Will Seab let you get by with putting that over until next week?"

"I have some hopes," Bob Munson said, "that we will be long gone by the time both the distinguished Senator from South Carolina and the distinguished Senator from Wyoming reach the chamber."

"Have you talked to Brig?" Senator Strickland asked, and the Majority Leader nodded.

"Yes, I'm satisfied he has something on his mind," he said, "and we're trying to work it out. That's why I want to avoid aggravating everything here. Are you with me?"

The Minority Leader smiled.

"I'm against this nomination," he said, "but for you, Bobby"—he bowed slightly, with a little twinkle—"sure."

"Thanks, pal," the Majority Leader said hurriedly as the first reporters began to come on the floor for the pre-session briefing. "Collect when you want to."

"I will," Senator Strickland promised with a chuckle.

"Well, Bob," AP said, "anything to add to that clear, forthright statement we got earlier?"

"Not a thing," Senator Munson said blandly, "so why don't you run along?"

"What do you think, Senator?" UPI asked Warren Strickland. "Does it make sense to you?"

"Heavens," Warren Strickland said. "Washington stopped making sense to me about one month after I got here, and it never has since. Surely you old hands don't expect it to?"

"Are you going to protest the subcommittee's action?" the Houston *Post* asked, and the Minority Leader looked more serious.

"Certainly not," he said. "I'm quite content to await developments."

"There will probably be some on the floor today," the *Times* suggested, and the Minority Leader laughed.

"Oh, I think we'll get by without too much trouble," he said comfortably.

"What's coming up, Bob?" the *Herald Tribune* asked. Senator Munson looked thoughtfully through the papers on his desk.

"We have the Justice Department appropriation scheduled," he said, "and maybe one or two minor claims bills."

"Fairly short session, then," AP suggested.

"Fairly short," Bob Munson agreed.

"Think he'll go for that?" the *Post* inquired, gesturing toward the back of the chamber, and Senator Munson turned to see the junior Senator from Wyoming enter in a purposeful way.

"I think," he said impassively, "that we may be able to keep him within reasonable limits."

"We hope not, Senator," UPI told him. "Your loss would be our gain—in news, that is."

Senator Munson chuckled.

"Oh, we'll give you some news," he said. "It may not be what Fred expects, but you'll have some."

"What's this," the *Times* demanded, "have you got a letter from the White House to read?"

"Nothing so sensational," the Majority Leader said. "Wait and see."

"We will," AP promised as the bell sounded and they began to hurry off the floor. "We'll be right up there in the press gallery waiting."

The clock stood at noon and the Senate composed itself as the last of the reporters trailed out the door and Carney Birch stepped forward solemnly to give the prayer. There were perhaps fifteen Senators on the floor in addition to the two leaders; George Bowen of Iowa; Walter Turnbull of Louisiana; Clement Johnson of Delaware; and so on. They were going to be surprised, too, the Majority Leader reflected, but it couldn't be helped. This was the best way. He bowed his head dutifully.

"*Lord*," the Chaplain said, "grant us Thy blessings on these deliberations and make us truly worthy of the trust Thou hast placed in us. Amen."

"Is that all?" Bob Munson started to say, half aloud, and then caught himself with a wink at the Vice President, who winked back. The chaplain gave him a dignified look and disappeared into the back lobby. Carney obviously wasn't taking any more chances.

"Mr. President!" the Majority Leader and the Senator from Wyoming said together, and Harley said calmly, "The Senator from Michigan."

"Mr. President," Bob Munson said, "I move that the reading of yesterday's Journal be dispensed with."

"Without objection, it is so ordered," Harley said, and, "Mr. President!" the two Senators said again.

"The Senator from Michigan," the Vice President said, and Fred Van Ackerman gave him an indignant look.

"Mr. President," Senator Munson said, "I move that the Senate stand in recess until noon on Monday."

"What the hell?" Clement Johnson said audibly to Walter Turnbull, and, "Mr. President!" Senator Van Ackerman cried angrily, but before he could even complete the words Harley was saying calmly, "Without objection, it is so ordered." And with a bang of the gavel he rose and was out of his chair and on his way off the floor even as the galleries began to buzz with excitement and the few members present, looking at one another in considerable bafflement, gathered up their papers, and began to leave.

"Mr. President!" Fred Van Ackerman cried again to Harley's disappearing back in one last protesting wail, and then he dropped it and came forward angrily down the center aisle. Above the reporters in the press gallery were still watching intently, and he came forward into the well of the Senate until he was standing almost directly beneath them.

"Come down to the President's Room right away," he called. "I'm going to hold a press conference."

"And so what's on his little mind?" AP asked as they crowded out of the gallery and hurried to the elevator to go down to the floor.

"I'm damned if I know," UPI said, "but I imagine after Bob's little piece of legerdemain it may be newsworthy."

"Wasn't that neat?" the Herald Tribune remarked. "Zip, zip, zip. Now you see them, now you don't."

"I expect it will be a fairly short session, he says," the St. Louis Post-Dispatch observed. "And Warren Strickland right there acting as his water boy. Honest to Christ I wonder, sometimes."

"Oh, well," the Wall Street Journal said with a grin. "Furious Freddy will make up for it. He ought to be primed for bear."

And true enough, even as the elevator arrived and they crowded in to make the descent to the floor below, Senator Van Ackerman had turned back to the Majority and Minority Leaders and was making his views known to them.

"Pretty smart," he said scornfully. "Pretty smart, you two. Is that what you call acting responsibly?"

"We'll come to your press conference, Fred," Senator Strickland said pleasantly, "and you can tell us off before the whole wide world, if you like."

"You'd better," the junior Senator from Wyoming said grimly, "because I'm going to."

"Warren," Bob Munson said, offering his arm, "be my guest."

"With pleasure," the Minority Leader said, bowing low.

"Oh, hell," Senator Van Ackerman snapped. "Why don't you get up a minstrel act and be done with it?"

And turning on his heel he hurried away to the ornate, gold-painted, chandelier-hung, mirror-walled room off the Senate floor where Senators meet the press for interviews when the Senate is in session. There where Presidents up through Woodrow Wilson used to come on the last night of the session to sign bills, he found most of the reporters already gathered, seated in the big chairs and crowded on the sofas, leaning against the big green-baize table in the center of the room, standing in little gossiping groups. He waited for a moment until Senator Munson and Senator Strickland came casually along, and then began abruptly and without preamble.

"What you have just witnessed on the Senate floor," he said, "is typical of the atmosphere of secrecy and stealth which has surrounded the handling of this nomination from the first. You have seen the Majority and Minority Leaders deliberately mislead—yes, I say deliberately mislead, and I'm glad you're here, Bob and Warren, I take pleasure in saying it to your faces—the Senate and the country as to their intentions. You have seen something I can only describe as a conspiracy, yes, a conspiracy, between the Majority and Minority Leaders to suppress the facts in this matter and keep the truth from the country."

"Will you slow down, Fred," AP said wearily. "Some of us aren't shorthand reporters, you know."

"Sorry," Senator Van Ackerman said, and after a moment, with a quick glance at his two impassive elders, he went on at a slower clip.

"I charge," he said, "yes, I charge, that the senior Senator from Utah, the chairman of the subcommittee, is deliberately trying to put the nominee in a bad light and make the country think there is something evil about him, yes, something evil. He is deliberately trying to defeat the nomination by this phony act he has put on, this strange, peculiar secrecy and he is being aided and abetted, yes abetted and aided, by the senior Senator from Michigan and the distinguished Senator from Idaho. I say this is strange and peculiar, and that is what I think the conduct of the chairman of the subcommittee is in this matter, strange and peculiar."

"Do you think he is strange and peculiar too?" AP inquired in the same bored tone, and for a second the junior Senator from Wyoming looked at him with a gleam of real dislike in his eyes.

"I'm not making any imputations about the Senator from Utah," he snapped. "You can say that if you like, I won't."

"We can't unless you do," AP pointed out calmly. "We aren't editorial writers. Is that all you have to say?"

"No, it isn't," Senator Van Ackerman said angrily, and for a second it seemed he might explode into one of his rages. But he didn't, and his next words came more calmly.

"What I intended to do at today's session," he said, "before the Majority Leader and the Minority Leader decided to be so cute about it, was to move again, as I did yesterday, that the Foreign Relations Committee be discharged from further consideration of the nomination, and that it be brought up immediately for a vote. That was what I intended to do today, I will say to the Majority Leader, and now that he has blocked me I tell him that is what I intend to do on Monday."

"Do you have any reason to suppose that you will get enough votes to do it on the second try, Senator?" the Newark *News* inquired, and Fred Van Ackerman looked smug.

"I have received some assurances of support," he said. "I have reason to think I will have enough votes the next time. I will remind you I only lost on a tie vote yesterday. That gives me a good foundation to start with."

"You actually think you have enough votes to do it?" UPI asked with undisguised skepticism. "You actually think you've gained and the Majority Leader has lost?"

"I do," Fred Van Ackerman said firmly. "I certainly do."

"What do you think, Bob?" the *Times* asked, and the Majority Leader looked bland.

"This is Fred's press conference," he said. "Warren and I are only here by invitation. And," he added with a smile, "a cordial one it was, too, I can tell you. No, I haven't any comment. Do you, Warren?"

"No, indeed," the Minority Leader said, "except to say that in such close votes involving the traditions of the Senate, when attrition sets in it usually sets in against those who are trying to overturn the traditions rather than those who are upholding them. That is the lesson of history, but then," he said gently, "this is a newer and more dynamic age we are being ushered into by the distinguished junior Senator from Wyoming, and maybe he has surprises for us."

"You'll see," Senator Van Ackerman said coldly. "You'll see. Yes, as I said, a strange and peculiar business, and I shall do what I can to expose it and bring the nomination of this great man to be Secretary of State to an early vote. There is something sinister and evil here, yes, sinister and evil."

"I could name it," the *Times* murmured behind his hand to the *Herald Trib*, and the *Trib* murmured back, "Strange and peculiar, too. Senator," he said politely, "is that all?"

"No, it isn't," Fred Van Ackerman said. "I also want to announce that I have just heard from the national organizing committee of COMFORT in New York, and they have asked my assistance in arranging for a giant rally here this Saturday night in support of the nominee. I've checked the

National Guard Armory and find that it is available, and it has been reserved for the rally. Starting time is 8 P.M."

"Renting the Armory costs a small penny," the Denver *Post* remarked. "Who's putting up the dough, Senator?"

"I told you, the national organizing committee," Senator Van Ackerman said. "We expect to have cavalcades of cars converging here from as far away as Pittsburgh, Raleigh, and Cincinnati. It will be the biggest thing COMFORT'S ever done."

"Why?" the Washington *Star* asked bluntly. Fred Van Ackerman looked as though any idiot would understand.

"Because we feel it is needed," he said. "Because we feel that Bob Leffingwell needs our help. Because we feel the country wants him, and we're going to see to it that the country gets him."

"Will there be working space for the press?" AP asked practically, and Senator Van Ackerman smiled.

"We'll take care of you," he said. "You just come along out and see."

"We'll think about it, Senator," the Washington *Post* said thoughtfully.

"Good," Fred said. "Well, that's all, unless you want to ask me some questions."

"We get the picture, Fred," the *Star* told him, and for a second he looked around in a strangely insecure fashion.

"Fine," he said. Then his face hardened again as he turned to leave.

"You can be ready on Monday, Bob," he said. "Just be ready. You too, Warren."

"We'll be ready," the Majority Leader assured him as he left. "Now what do you suppose," he asked the press in a wondering tone, "that all adds up to?"

"Trouble for you, I'd say," AP suggested, and Senator Munson smiled.

"Oh, I don't think so," he said comfortably. "A vote he can't win and a rally of crackpots? I don't think so."

"Don't underestimate him, Bob," UPI suggested. Senator Munson allowed himself to look a little impatient.

"I don't underestimate him," he said, "but for Christ's sake, let's all try to keep our sanity on this, shall we? We're working it out with Brig, and I expect he'll be seeing the President before the afternoon is over, and then everything will be all right——"

"May we quote you on that, Senator?" the *Trib* interrupted, and Bob Munson waved a generous hand.

"Sure," he said. "Now run along."

"Let's get this straight," UPI said carefully. "You expect Senator Anderson to go to the White House this afternoon and that a satisfactory solution will be worked out then. Can we expect an announcement later?"

"Check with me around four," Bob Munson said, aware as he made the suggestion that there was something he was supposed to do at four, but it had slipped his mind for the moment, and anyway, it could probably be put off. "I think I'll have something for you then."

"Thank *you*, Mr. Senator!" the Washington *Post* said happily, and they rose in a body and took flight back to the elevator, up to the gallery, and to their typewriters where they began banging out their stories.

Left alone in the glittering gold room, the Minority Leader looked rather skeptically at the Majority Leader.

"That was going a little far just to top Fred Van Ackerman, wasn't it?" he asked. "How do you know Brig will agree to see him this afternoon?"

"We'll work it out," Senator Munson said comfortably. "Orrin's got Lafe working on him, and he'll come around . . . Damn, now I remember."

"Remember what?" Senator Strickland asked.

"I knew I had something at four," Bob Munson said. "Tommy Davis wanted to come over and see me about Brig, too. Well, it should all be settled by then, so that won't be any problem. He'll be pleased to be in on the press conference when it's announced."

"You're suddenly awfully confident of Brig," Warren Strickland said thoughtfully, "when you were so doubtful before. Why this sudden switch all of a sudden? Have you anything to go on?"

"Just the caliber of his opposition," Senator Munson said as they left the President's Room and started to walk down the stairs to the restaurant. "He's so far above what we've just seen that somehow I just feel in my bones that it will work out all right. He doesn't have anything to worry about, really, and neither do we. Aside from Fred, we're all reasonable men."

But in this, as they came up with Bob Randall of New Jersey and Jack McLaughlin of Georgia in the hall and formed an impromptu foursome for lunch, he perhaps was not entirely correct; for shortly after Fred Van Ackerman got back to his office and shortly after the news stories had gone out over the wire, a call came from the White House. He just wanted to congratulate Fred, the President said casually, on his support of the nomination, and why didn't he drop down sometime at his convenience and get better acquainted? Much flattered, the junior Senator from Wyoming promised that he would.

There was a clamor in the street, a stirring in the driveway, several cheerful honks on a rather loud horn, and in a clash and a clatter and a sleek red convertible with the top down the junior Senator from Iowa arrived with an air.

"Uncle Lafe!" Pidge cried, dropping the ball and trotting across the lawn as fast as she could go to leap into his outheld arms.

"How's my girl?" he asked, giving her a big kiss and then promptly putting an arm around Mabel and giving her one too. "I should say, how are my girls?"

"I swear," Brig said with amusement, surveying this happy scene, "from one to ninety, you get 'em all, don't you, pal? What is this fatal charm?"

"Good looks," Senator Smith said modestly. "Native intelligence. Innate gentility. Animal magnetism. SEX. They all enter in. How are you, buddy? You look a little peaked."

"I do?" Senator Anderson said in a tone of such concerned surprise that his colleague laughed.

"No, you don't," he said disarmingly. "You look fine for a man who's holding the whole world on his shoulders like Atlas. Doesn't he look fine, Mabel?"

"He always looks fine to me," Mabel said in a tone that made the Senator from Iowa look at her more closely.

"Now, see here," he said, tilting her chin and examining her eyes intently. "That's no way to act on a beautiful day like this."

"He has fatal charm, too," she said, gesturing toward her husband and starting to get watery again. "Oh, damn!" she added, vigorously dabbing at her eyes with a handkerchief. "Damn, damn!"

"My goodness!" Lafe said with a startled laugh. "That's strong language for you, lady. What's been going on here, anyway?"

"Nothing that kindly, wise old Uncle Lafe can't put to rights, I'm sure," Senator Anderson said. "Anyway, it's all over now."

"That's right," Mabel said, continuing to wipe her eyes rapidly. "I was just worried, but I'm not any more."

"She was just worried, boo hoo, but she, boo hoo, isn't, boo hoo, any more," Lafe said mockingly. "Boo hoo."

"Well, I can't *help* it if I'm weepy," Mabel protested, beginning to laugh, and in a second they were all laughing together, and blowing her nose vigorously and giving her eyes one last dab, she put the handkerchief away and seemed herself again.

"That's better," Lafe said. "You've got a hell of a nerve beating your wife, Senator. I guess it's time I came and took you away."

"I'll go quietly, Senator," Brig promised. "What did you have in mind?"

"*Women*," Lafe said fervently, and in the midst of their renewed laughter Pidge spoke up in a clear, thoughtful tone.

"Mommy," she said slowly, "Uncle Lafe's funny, isn't he?"

"I guess that tells you," Senator Anderson said with a chuckle, and Senator Smith looked dignified.

"Your daughter knows entirely too much," he said, suddenly raising her above his head, "for her age," he concluded, depositing her in an ecstatically squealing heap in her mother's arms. "How about Normandy Farms? I feel as though we were two-thirds of the way there already, you live so far out."

"Spring Valley isn't far," Mable objected.

"And anyway, it's fashionable," her husband added. "As all get out."

"You wanted to live here, too, because it was near the Knoxes," his wife reminded him, and he laughed.

"Let's get out of here before I start another family argument," he suggested. "Take care of yourself, you two," he said, kissing Mabel quickly and stooping to do the same to Pidge. "I expect I'll go along to the office after lunch. You can tell Bob and Orrin and the President, but don't tell anybody else."

"I won't," Mabel said. "Have a good time."

"We will," he said, and for a moment his eyes held hers with some expression she could not understand, one of the many she could not, and never had been able to, understand. "Be of good cheer," he quoted softly. "The troops are with me."

And he turned away toward the car as Lafe too gave her a farewell kiss. Abruptly she reached out and took his arm tightly.

"I'm worried for him," she said simply, like a little girl who can't pretend. "I'm afraid of what they'll do to him. Help him. He—he won't let me."

Lafe gave her a sharp look and frowned.

"Stop that," he said quietly. "You've got yourself all worked up over nothing. We'll take care of him. He has lots of things going for him, and not the least of them is you."

"I wish I could believe it," she said in a lonely voice, and he gave her hand a quick, impatient squeeze.

"Mabel," he said. "Stop it. You know the pitfalls in that kind of talk, so stop it. We're going to have a good lunch and get this thing all straightened out and he'll be a hero again by tomorrow morning. You wait and see." And he gave her hand another squeeze, more gently this time. "Now, relax," he said. " 'Bye, Pigeon." And he tousled Pidge's hair and gave her a hug.

"Hey!" Brig called from the car. "Stop smooching my women and come along. I'm hungry."

"Right," Lafe said. "Just have to keep in practice, is all. Take care, gals. I'll see you again soon."

And he gave them a wave, leaped in, turned on the ignition and started to back out with a dramatic roar; remembered suddenly that this was a street where children lived, slowed his pace so abruptly it almost drove his passenger into the back of the seat, and inched carefully out in a cautious crawl.

For a time after they turned onto River Road and headed at a leisurely pace toward Normandy Farms restaurant fifteen miles out from the Capitol in the rolling green Maryland countryside filled with the sights and sounds of spring, they were silent. It was the Senator from Utah who finally spoke.

"I wish she didn't take things so intensely," he said, staring out at the green fields, the white barns and fences, the Black Angus cattle dotted here and there among the trees and emerald grasses. "It makes her so vulnerable. I don't mean to hurt her, I try to do what seems best, but lately it always seems to be winding up in tears and trouble. Maybe you have the right idea, after all. Heart whole and fancy free, and so on. Maybe you're right."

"I don't know," his colleague said with a rather rueful grin. "I was thinking as I came through town on my way out, and do you know, it's getting so I can't travel ten blocks in Washington without passing three places where I've made love. It's a hell of a depressing thing when a town gets all filled up with memories of your one-night stands. I think I'll move out."

"Sure, sure," Brigham Anderson said skeptically. "I can see you moving out any time before the voters of Iowa ask you to. Well, then, maybe you don't have the right idea. Maybe you should get married, even if I'm not such a good example at the moment."

"You're a good example," Lafe said. "You're a fine example. Sweet girl for a wife, sweet girl for a daughter. What more do you want?"

"I don't know," Brig said, frowning at the gracious countryside going by. "Peace of mind and a heart at rest, I guess. Is that too much to ask for?"

"No, of course not," Lafe said soberly. "It's what all men ask for. Most get reconciled eventually to not finding it, though. Maybe that's your trouble. You haven't really accepted the bargain you made."

"What bargain?" Senator Anderson asked, but he could see his companion meant nothing more by it than a casual comment.

"Getting married," Lafe said. "Settling down. Being a pillar of society. Not catting around like me all the time."

"Is that how you find peace of mind and a heart at rest?" Brig couldn't resist asking, and his colleague smiled in a surprisingly bleak way.

"No, sir," he said. "I don't. That's why I still think you have the right idea and the ideal set up, not me. After all, what's sex, when you come right down to it? Right time, right place, right mood, right company, there's nothing more wonderful; but how often does that ideal combination of factors come about? Not very damned often, it seems to me on the basis of rather thorough study. And I imagine that's true even in marriage, right?"

"After a while," Senator Anderson said. "Except that marriage has a way of renewing itself from time to time. So if it's so all-fired stale for you what keeps you going?"

"Oh, you keep going through the motions," Lafe said, "hoping. And after all," he added with a sudden grin, "the motions aren't so unpleasant." Then he looked more serious. "But about you and Mabel——"

"Yes?" Brig asked.

"Are you sure it's——" Lafe began and then paused in a rare moment of hesitation.

"What?" his colleague asked. "All her fault, were you going to say?"

"How did you know what I was going to say?" Lafe asked with a smile. Brig shrugged.

"It's the standard thing to say in such cases, isn't it?" he said. "And this is quite a standard case, I'm sure."

"Look," Senator Smith said, skillfully navigating around a truck in the rolling, winding road as it plunged up and down through the spring-ripe hollows, "don't get bitter, boy. Mabel's a lovely girl and a fine, decent person. So are you. Trust wise, kindly old Uncle Lafe and don't get to brooding about it, O.K.? After all, you must have had plenty of time in the Pacific to find out what you wanted, didn't you? Unless it was dramatically different from ETO, that is. Over there, we never lacked opportunities!"

Brig laughed in a more lighthearted way.

"No, Daddy," he said. "We didn't lack opportunities in the Pacific, either."

"Then you surely tried what you wanted to try and did what you wanted to do and then came home and added it all up and decided you wanted to marry and settle down, didn't you?" Lafe said. "So what makes you question the bargain now?"

"You keep saying 'bargain,'" Brigham Anderson said rather sharply. "What makes you think it was a bargain?"

"Wasn't it?" Lafe asked with some surprise. "A bargain between desire and custom, dream and reality, wish and career, sex and society? We all make bargains in some way. You have to."

For a moment the Senator from Utah made no reply; and then he spoke in a curious, faraway, questioning tone.

"Do you?" he asked. "Do you really?"

"Look, buddy," Lafe said humorously, but even as he spoke some instinct told him he was making a mistake, that it wouldn't be received humorously, "just what *did* you do in the Pacific, anyway?"

He was aware as soon as the words were out that he had gone too far in some way he didn't understand, because suddenly his friend wasn't there any more; the wall that came down between Brig and the world when he wanted it to was suddenly in place. The level dark eyes looked calmly into his when he glanced up quickly from the road, but there was no communication, only a politely attentive friendliness that gave not an inch to anyone.

"Oh, come now," Brig said pleasantly. "This is getting awfully dramatic for a nice spring day. Let's talk about you for a change. I still think *you* ought to get married."

The Senator from Iowa smiled and let the moment go, even though he knew he would puzzle about it later until he understood it; and even without understanding it he knew in some instinctive way that right here in the midst of the clear golden day he had suddenly become afraid for Brigham Anderson. But as with any experienced politician none of this showed.

"Well, do you know," he said lightly, "this will come as a great shock to you, pal, but I'm seriously thinking about it."

"No!" Brig said in a much more responsive and delighted tone.

"Yes, sir," Lafe said, "I am. There's this little girl from Iowa who works for the Armed Services Committee over in the House, and I met her a couple of months ago, and one thing led to another——"

"It always does with you, doesn't it?" Brig said with a smile.

"Well, it did, yes," Senator Smith said, "specifically about a month ago at my place. Well, I thought that was that, but—it turned out it wasn't. There've been a couple of times since, and then last Friday night, I was quite sure I would never see her again after that. Intended not to, anyway. But do you know, the funniest thing happened? The next morning—that was the day the nomination broke—somebody on the Iowa State Society called and wanted to know if I knew of anyone to nominate to be queen of the society ball for the Cherry Blossom Festival, and before I really stopped to think I gave them her name, and last night they elected her, and now I'm supposed to crown her and be her partner at the ball, and—and, well," he said in a rather puzzled tone, as though he couldn't believe this was happening to him, "I'm beginning to suspect that maybe I won't be saying good-by to her after all."

"You're hooked, Senator," Brig said. Lafe shook his head in a baffled way.

"I'm beginning to think so," he said. "I find I get restless when she isn't around. I suppose that's a sure sign."

"It's one of them," Brig said. "Well, I think that's wonderful. I expect you'll settle down and never look at another woman, after all those thousands of bedrooms stretching out behind you into the past."

"I suppose," Senator Smith said, rather glumly. "What a hell of a depressing prospect!" He grinned. "Am I ready for it, that's the question? Maybe I need more preparation."

Brigham Anderson snorted.

"Preparation, my hat," he said. "Any more preparation and you wouldn't be able to stagger up to the altar. Mabel will be delighted. So am I."

"That's good," Lafe said. "You'll like her."

"Any girl you choose will be fine with me, son," Senator Anderson said in a kindly tone. "Anything you want to know, just ask me."

"Go to hell," said Senator Smith with dignity. "God, what a beautiful day."

"Yes, it is," Brig agreed. "Do you ever get the feeling at times like this that it's wonderful to be off alone miles away from the Senate with nobody knowing where you are or who you are or wanting you to do something for them, and all those problems and worries left behind? I certainly do."

"Oh, I do, too," Lafe said quickly. "I take this thing out about once a week, all by myself, head out into the country and just ramble for a couple of hours. It does wonders. It's a great job, United States Senator, and I wouldn't be anything else; but sometimes being one of one hundred people out of all this great nation, with all the terrific responsibilities we have and all the terrific pressures we're under—it gets kind of rugged, now and then. Particularly in days like these when it sometimes seems quite possible that if we fail it will all be wiped out and may never be re-established. It isn't easy."

"No," Senator Anderson said, "it isn't. It makes you wonder if you're worthy of it, sometimes. Or," he asked in a lighter tone, "am I just being too damned philosophical for words?"

"No, indeed," Senator Smith said amicably. "Not a bit. What are friends for, if you can't talk to them? I feel that way sometimes, too. I think, here I am, helling around all the time—what right have I got to say I know enough to help run the country? What right have I got to uphold all these fine principles and make speeches to my high-school classes when they come here about what a great heritage they have and how noble they should be? How noble am I, for Christ's sake? Not very. And what right have I got to set myself up to judge other men and their motives and take stands on things because I say they're right or wrong? What's right and what's wrong, and what does Lover Boy Smith know about it?"

"There, there," Brig said with a chuckle. "Don't let it get you down. But, of course," he added more seriously, "you're entirely right. It's a problem everybody faces everywhere. Who's perfect? Who's to judge? But somebody's got to, otherwise nothing would ever get done. About all you can do, I guess, is add up the good you do and the bad you do and strike a balance that does as much justice as possible to your own needs and the necessities of society, and then go ahead . . . At least," he said with a thoughtful frown and a recurrence of mood that shadowed the bright day suddenly, "that's what I tell myself."

"Well, one thing I think we can say for ourselves," Lafe remarked, giving him an intent appraisal for just a second, "at least we have the humility to admit we aren't perfect. And that we do judge from a real confusion of motives, sometimes, because somebody's got to judge in order to keep the country going and we're the ones who've been elected to do it, and so we do."

"We can have the humility to admit that to each other," Brigham Anderson said with a sudden smile. "I'm damned if I'm going to admit it to my opponent in Utah next time."

"You aren't going to have any opponent in Utah next time," Lafe said, in one of those remarks people remember later with wonder in entirely different contexts, and his companion laughed.

"I'd like to think I was in that solid," he said, "but I'm afraid I'm not . . . It does get tough sometimes, though. You wonder if you're being fair."

"Since you mention it," Senator Smith said quickly, and Brig laughed. "Yes?" he said dryly.

"I wasn't quite sure how I was going to," Lafe admitted with a grin, "but since you mention it—are you being fair about the nomination?"

The senior Senator from Utah was silent for several moments before replying, and his colleague was afraid that again he had pressed too hard on some sensitive nerve; but he reflected that Brig had indeed broached the subject, so he concentrated on his driving and waited patiently for the answer. It came in a thoughtful voice.

"Yes," he said slowly. "I think so. I really think I am. What I know—and I'm not going to tell you what I know, Lover Boy," he added with a quick flash of humor—"while it may not indicate any great crime, does go to the fundamentals of the man's character and whether he is reliable, whether he can be trusted, whether we really would be right to put him in that job at this particular time, or indeed any time."

"In other words, you're judging," Senator Smith said humorously, and a curious expression that wasn't humorous at all but dead serious and possibly even with a certain pain in it came into his companion's eyes.

"Yes, I am," he said with a little sigh. "And like you, I wonder who I am to judge. But damn it," he said angrily, suddenly doubling a fist and hitting the cowling of the dashboard, "you've got to judge. You can't sit still and allow yourself to be paralyzed by your own shortcomings, or by something you may have done sometime, or by some past mistake, or something. You've got to judge. You've been elected to judge, and you've got to; and you've got to do it on your own conception of what's best for the country, and if you really love the country you've got to stick with your judgment, no matter what." And he repeated slowly and deliberately as though he were arguing with himself, as his colleague could see he was, "No matter what."

Off on the left of the winding road in the sparkling sunshine there appeared the rambling contours of Normandy Farms set on a little rise among its trees and lawns, and Senator Smith decided it was a good thing they had come to it, for this was a good transition-point in the talk, with things left hanging that might not develop were they pursued consciously now but which might come of themselves later. Parking absolved him of any reply to Senator Anderson's last comment, and Brig himself broke the mood when he got out by turning back to survey the car with an air of exaggerated awe.

"I meant to mention this at the house," he said. "Very dashing. New, isn't it?"

"Yes," Lafe said with his engaging grin. "This is my sinning-in-the-nation's-capital car. I drive an old black Ford station wagon when I'm home in the state."

"What a cynic," Brig said in a more relaxed and untroubled tone. "I don't know why they never catch up with you."

"Because if truth were known, my friend," Lafe said crisply, "I am a damned good Senator. I take care of my people and I take care of the country insofar as I can. That's why they only catch up with me to vote for me. You know how that is. You're a damned good Senator yourself."

"Aw, shucks, you're so sweet," Senator Anderson said. "I think we may see someone we know. Isn't that a French Embassy car?"

"Oh, damn, I hope not," Senator Smith said. "I brought you 'way out here so we could have some privacy to talk this thing out."

"We won't join them," Brig said as they walked up the flagstone path and into the big, dark dining room. "Yes, there they are," he remarked as over in one corner Dolly Harrison and Lady Maudulayne waved frantically. "I guess we'd better say hello, anyway."

"Oh hell," Lafe said. "Now this will be all over town and everybody will know I've been deputized to bring you back onto the reservation. But here we go . . . Ladies," he said graciously. "See No Evil," he bowed to Dolly—"Hear No Evil"—he bowed to Kitty—"And Speak No Evil"—he bowed to Celestine, who smiled.

"Since we're in the presence of chastity and purity," Dolly said with a little twinkle, "it would of course be impossible to see, hear, speak, or even think of evil."

"Touché," Lafe admitted with a carefree grin. "Beautiful day, isn't it?"

"It's delightful," Kitty Maudulayne said, "and I'm going right back and tell Claude we saw you and we will all speculate as to what you're doing out here. Something to do with Mr. Leffingwell, we will all think."

"Well, what you all think might be right, you clever little diplomat, you," Lafe said with a chuckle, "but you'll just have to speculate, because we ain't agonna tell yah. Particularly this one. He isn't going to say anything."

"Oh, dear," Kitty said. "It would be so fascinating to find out all about it right out here in the country in this unexpected fashion."

"Yes, dear," Brigham Anderson said blandly, "but I've taken a twenty year vow of silence. Have a good lunch."

"You too," Dolly said, giving him an appraising look behind her cordial smile. He caught it and smiled impassively back.

"You can tell Bob, Lafe is doing his duty," he said. "I'm getting the treatment. It's designed to make me stop being a difficult boy and behave."

"I hope it does," Dolly said, and he could tell she really meant it. "Not," she added, "that I personally give a hoot about Bob Leffingwell, but we don't want you to get hurt."

There was in her voice something so quiet and so firm and so friendly that for a moment Senator Anderson was profoundly moved. But he tried not to show it, and thought he had succeeded.

"Everybody is so worried about me," he said lightly. "It's going to be all right. It'll all straighten out when I see the President. Eat hearty and forget about it. We'll see you later."

"You're coming to Crystal's reception at my place after the wedding," Dolly reminded them and they both nodded. "Good," she said, and as they turned away and went outside to find an isolated table on the lawn she looked thoughtfully at her companions.

"I don't think we're the only ones who are worried," she said.

Celestine looked up quickly.

"He is very worried," she said.

Out on the lawn, having found a table sufficiently remote and put in their order, the junior Senator from Iowa and the senior Senator from Utah looked at one another for a long moment and laughed.

"All right," Brigham Anderson said. "Out with it. Are you supposed to take me to the woodshed or feed me candy? What were the directions you received from the able Majority Leader and his distinguished friend from Illinois?"

"Damn," Senator Smith said, "that's the trouble with Washington. Everybody knows all the signals. You can't pull any surprises."

"Oh, you can," Senator Anderson said, "but not this time. I knew this was a put-up deal the minute Mabel told me you'd called. I didn't see what good it would do, but I like your company and it seemed a good chance to get away for a while in the spring weather. To say nothing of a free meal. On you."

"I'll come over for dinner some night soon and make up for it," Lafe promised. "I don't know that there's any reason to be coy about this. Bob would like for you to see the President as soon as possible, I think this afternoon rather than tonight—"

"He told me tonight when I talked to him earlier," Brig said quickly.

"I know," Lafe said, "but he's been thinking it over and feels the sooner the better. And of course he hopes you'll be willing to drop your opposition to Leffingwell so there won't be any head-on collision with the White House that might cause a lot of unpleasantness for you and the Senate and the President and everybody. It's that simple. I think Bob is right and I'm here to do what I can to bring you around. Fair enough?"

"Fair enough," Brig agreed.

"But since you're so sure you've got to judge, and you're so certain you're judging correctly, I suppose the execution of my mission isn't as simple as the statement of it, right?" Lafe added, looking down thoughtfully across the sun-swept fields and hoping this would restore the mood of the drive. It did.

"I can't go against what I feel is right in this situation," his friend remarked, rather desperately. "Surely you don't expect me to, Lafe?"

"Not if you're sure it's right, of course not," Senator Smith said. "You *are* sure, of course."

"You know from what I said earlier that I'm not sure," Brig said bluntly, "at least not in the sense of one hundred per cent, no-qualifications, no-doubts sure. Who the hell ever is, if he's honest? But I am sure in the sense that I have balanced all the factors as well as I can, and this is what I come up with. And you know me. Having arrived at that, how can I do anything else?"

"Yes," Lafe said with a frustrated little sigh. "I know you. As well as anybody can, that is."

"Oh, I'm not so difficult," Senator Anderson said quickly. "At least," he added, with a puzzled little frown, "I hope I'm not."

"You're O.K.," Lafe said reassuringly, for reassurance, underneath the confident manner, seemed to be what his friend needed most at the moment. "You're all right. You don't really think you could bring yourself to see the President this afternoon, then?"

"Well," Brig said slowly, "I want Bob with me, and I rather think, under all the circumstances, that I'd like to have Harley, too. And I doubt if it would be feasible to set that up on such short notice. And also, it would seem sort of—rushed, you know? As though I were being pressured into it. I don't like to be pressured into things, especially when he would think I was all ready to give in to him just because I came running when he whistled."

"This isn't a contest of wills between you and the President," Lafe said sharply, and his colleague gave him a quizzical look.

"Isn't it?" he said. "You know damned well it is, Lafe Smith, so who's kidding whom? I have excellent grounds, to my way of thinking, for wanting that nomination withdrawn. I'm not going to change my mind in ten minutes just because Papa says change it. And I don't intend to give him the advantage by hurrying to see him. There's some strategy involved on my side too, you know. It's reached a point where I can't afford to yield too easily."

"I don't think you intend to yield at all," Senator Smith said bluntly. Senator Anderson gave him an impassive glance.

"You can think that," he offered pleasantly, "if you like."

"Damn, you're a stubborn soul," Lafe said. "I still think you would be advised to see him as soon as possible even if you don't intend to yield. After all, this isn't an appointment for dogcatcher; an awful lot is riding on it, both here and overseas. I'm sure he'll see you just as soon as you care to come. Aren't you possibly being just a little stiff-necked about it not to go halfway in meeting him?"

The Senator from Utah frowned thoughtfully.

"Lafe," he said, "I'm thinking about it. I've been thinking about it all morning. Just don't pressure me, that's all. I would like to think I could go down there and talk to him as one American to another with the interests of the country at heart and work out a solution that would really be best for us all. But I don't know. Maybe I don't trust him enough."

"He's the President," Lafe said simply. "There are times when we've got to trust him."

"I don't go for that corny argument," Brigham Anderson said with a real sharpness in his voice. "He may be President, but I'm United States Senator and I have a responsibility just as deep as his, and so do you, running in a clear line to the Constitution, exactly like his. He doesn't need any by-your-leave from me to exercise his responsibility, and I don't need any by-your-leave from him to exercise mine. We're equally charged and equally responsible. I'm not his damned errand boy."

"O.K.," Senator Smith said calmly. "O.K., I won't say any more. I've done my best. Say," he said in a completely offhand manner, "that's a cute little trick at that table over there under the oak tree."

Senator Anderson gave him a quick look, and this time Lafe was quite sure there was a rare expression of pain in his eyes.

"And don't be like that, either," he said. "I'm thinking. I'll keep on thinking. I'll try to work it out in my own mind. Maybe by the time we get back I'll be ready to see him. But I've got to do it my own way."

"Sure you do, pal," Lafe said comfortably. "It's a terrific responsibility you're carrying, so just ignore me. Like so many people who consider themselves close to you, I just want to help you." He shook his head in a puzzled way. "If I only knew how," he said in a rather helpless voice.

"Oh, you do, for Christ's sake," Brigham Anderson said impatiently. "This ride, this talk, your friendship—it all helps. I'm grateful, believe me. Why," he said, and his tone became much easier and more humorous suddenly, "if it weren't for you, Senator, I just don't know how I'd get through the day. Honest to Pete."

"Sure, sure," Lafe said. "She really is cute, you know?"

"Yes," Brig said, studying her carefully, "she really is. Not as cute as the future Mrs. Smith, though."

"Well," Lafe said with a grin, "not as available, anyway."

And so the luncheon went pleasantly, they waved good-by happily to Dolly and company when they left, and the ride back through the bursting countryside was relaxed and comfortable, passing easily with small talk and nothing more about life, the nomination, or other profoundly philosophic matters until they drew up to a stop light on Wisconsin Avenue alongside a newsstand, carrying the late editions of the *Star* and the *News*. The Majority Leader had indeed topped Fred Van Ackerman.

"MUNSON SAYS ANDERSON TO SEE PRESIDENT TODAY," The *Star* said.

"BOB SAYS BRIG TO MEET MR. BIG," The *News* announced, more chattily.

"*That* does it," Lafe said humorously, and for just a second his companion looked annoyed. Then he laughed.

"Seems rather definite," he observed.

"Now, surely," Lafe said with a smile, "*surely* you aren't going to make a liar out of Bob. He means so well."

Brig smiled.

"He certainly does," he agreed, without further comment.

"Maybe I'll give him a call when I get in and tell him to set it up for this afternoon, then," Senator Smith suggested carefully, and Senator Anderson laughed.

"Are you sure that's safe?" he inquired. "I'm awfully stubborn, you know. Everybody says so. I might just get on my high horse again."

"I don't think you will," Senator Smith told him. "Or will you?"

"Keep guessing," Brig suggested cheerfully. "It's good for you."

But he sounded relaxed and he looked relaxed, as though he really had changed his mind and was comfortable about it, and so his colleague decided, as they went on to the Hill, that he would let himself be guided accordingly.

At the Delaware Avenue entrance to the Old Office Building he stopped the car, and the Senator from Utah started to get out and then turned back and held out his hand.

"Lafe," he said. "Thanks for lunch—thanks for everything. You're a good friend."

"I try to be," Senator Smith said. "It's one of my few virtues. As soon as this little girl I'm chasing catches me I'll let you know. I want you to be best man."

"I would love to," Brig said, sounding very pleased. "See you later."

"Right," the Senator from Iowa said.

Ten minutes later he was on the phone in his office telling the Majority Leader that the iron appeared to be hot and Bob had better strike it while it was.

"I'd suggest you tell the President to let you handle the details of setting it up, though," Lafe said. "I think he's coming around, but it needs your patient touch."

"Sure thing," Senator Munson said. "I'll explain the situation to him and I know he'll understand."

The President, however, had other ideas.

Back in his office, facing the accumulated calls, letters, and telegrams of the morning, the senior Senator from Utah felt as though he had been away for several days, so numerous were they and so long a process had he gone through in his thinking since the previous midnight when he had announced his decision to extend the hearings. It had been a rough fifteen hours, for all that they had seemed outwardly to affect him so little, and for all that it had been only Celestine, who in her silent way had recognized the full extent of the mental turmoil he had been going through. This was the biggest act of political defiance he had ever committed, the biggest single act of will he had ever displayed on the national scene, the first time he had ever stood out alone against the overwhelming weight of the White House, the party, the press, and a major portion of domestic and world opinion; and it was not an easy thing to do, however much an innate iron and strength of character had come to his assistance. He still had no great fear of the consequences, for he still felt he had a good case to make, and he still felt thoroughly capable of weathering whatever might come as a result of his actions; but this did not make it any easier to undergo, inside. Along with the stubbornness, the integrity of character, the impassive unyielding calm and tolerance there also went a very real sensitivity and a heart that could be bruised much more easily than the world knew. He didn't like to be going against popular opinion, he didn't enjoy being pilloried in the press, he didn't want to think he was giving trouble to his party and his friends. It did not make it more pleasant to feel that he was right in it, even though he managed to maintain for the most part an air that convinced most who saw him that he was armored in righteousness and undaunted in his convictions. He was, but he was paying for it.

Therefore it had been with a considerable feeling of relief that he had heard that Lafe would come to take him to lunch, for he knew at once what lay behind it, and he was grateful—so grateful that it surprised him a little, for he had not realized quite how much tension he was really under—that his friends should be taking care of him and trying to arrange a solution for him. The drive with his likable colleague, with his customary combination of philosophy, insight, good will toward the world and entertaining interest in sex, had relaxed and amused him as always, even though there had been moments of challenge to his own feelings that had not been too pleasant. But Lafe had a quality of innate kindness about him that was always comforting, particularly to his friends when they were troubled for one reason or another, and Brig had returned from their little excursion into the glowing countryside in a much happier frame of mind than he had started out. And, toward the end of it, he had finally begun to conclude that probably Bob and Orrin and Lafe were right, that probably he was being too stiff-necked, that probably he should meet the President halfway, give him his little triumph, if that was what he chose to consider it, of coming early to the White House, and try to get it worked out in as amicable and friendly a fashion as possible. He was convinced, for in general he approved of the President and conceived him to be a man of reasonableness and understanding, as concerned for the country's future as he was himself, that when they had a chance to talk it over the solution would not be difficult. He was even, in that moment of relaxation after his visit with Lafe, disposed to think that he might possibly yield on the point he deemed most fundamental and not insist on the withdrawal of the nomination—providing there could be some sort of confrontation with the nominee, some sort of satisfactory discussion in which all the cards could be put on the table and everybody could understand one another, and Bob Leffingwell could be put under a cautionary admonition he would not ignore in future.

Thus, by the time the phone rang and the interoffice buzzer sounded so that he knew it must be either one of his immediate friends or the White House, he was in a mood to be receptive to any reasonable approach. The President's first words sounded reasonable, and the chairman of the subcommittee embarked upon the conversation that was to be a major turning point in his life with a feeling of friendliness and accommodation that were quite genuine and sincere.

"Brigham Anderson?" the President asked cordially, and Brig said, "Yes, Mr. President, how are you?" with an equal cordiality. The President chuckled.

"Not as well as I was before you started creating problems for me, Brig," he said, but he said it with a jesting note in his voice, and Senator Anderson accepted it as such.

"I'm sorry, Mr. President," he said pleasantly. "I just did what I felt I had to do, under the circumstances."

"Of course you did," the President said encouragingly. "Of course you did. I'm glad to know we still have men in the Senate who have the guts to do what they believe to be right. We'd be in quite a fix if we didn't, wouldn't we?"

"I think so," Brig said simply. There was a little pause.

"Of course," the President said, with a shade less warmth in his voice, "it has posed really quite a major problem for me, you know."

"I'm sorry, Mr. President," Senator Anderson said, again in the same direct, simple way. This time the faintest note of irritation was evident in the response.

"What do you think we should do about it?" the President asked. The Senator from Utah laughed, rather shortly.

"What would you suggest?" he countered.

"I think we should talk it over," the President suggested, not bothering with much cordiality now but sounding very businesslike. "I'm sure we can work out something that will be satisfactory to you."

"That you wouldn't know until we had talked it over, I think," the Senator from Utah said, and there was another silence.

"Yes," the President said. "Well. What *do* you want, Senator? Is there anything we can do for you in the Administration, anything you need out West that we could arrange for you? Something in the reclamation field, maybe, or——"

"See here," Senator Anderson said sharply. "Mr. President. Is it your conception that I'm doing this just to place myself in a bargaining position with you? Do you really think that's all I have in mind?"

"Certainly not, Brigham," the President said quickly. "No, indeed. Bob tells me you're a man of great character and integrity, and I know from our brief contacts up to now that you are. I just thought that sometimes—

well, sometimes, if an understanding can be reached that will assist a man back home, it eases things a good deal, that's all."

"I don't know who you've been dealing with lately," Senator Anderson said in the same sharp tone, "but I don't belong in the same group. I don't need assistance back home, for one thing, and my integrity in this matter isn't up for barter, for another. So suppose we discuss it on some other basis, if you don't mind, Mr. President. This is a matter of conviction with me."

"Surely," the President said, sounding taken aback and a good deal more annoyed. "I apologize for any other implication. We're not going to pretend with one another that there aren't some who can be swayed by such considerations, but I'll accept your word that you're not one of them."

"You don't have to accept my word," Brig told him shortly. "Ask anybody."

"I wish I knew you better," the President confessed with a sudden injection of charm in his voice. "I'd tell you to stop being huffy with me and relax. But I don't know you that well, do I? So I must try to be very solemn with you."

"That might be better, Mr. President," Brig said in a voice that didn't give an inch. The President replied more coldly after a moment.

"Very well," he said. "Just tell me your problem, and we'll see what we can do about it."

"I'm not going to do it on the telephone," Senator Anderson said.

"Is it really that earth-shaking?" the President asked with a trace of sarcasm. "Or perhaps I should say, is it really that important?"

"Yes, sir," Brigham Anderson said, "it is."

"What would you like to do, then?" the President inquired. "Come down and see me?"

"I assume you feel, as I do, that that would be the sensible and constructive thing to do under the circumstances," the Senator said. "Or am I wrong in thinking you've had everybody up here working toward that end since early this morning?"

"I like the sound of you," the President told him in a fatherly voice. "You have a lot of spirit."

"So I've been told," Senator Anderson said dryly. "Is it agreeable that I come down?"

"Well, let me see," the President said thoughtfully. "Bob seemed to think it might be advisable for us to get together after the banquet tonight, but possibly—let me see . . . How about half an hour from now? Could you make it then?"

"Is that the time you have set aside for me?" Brig asked with an edge of sarcasm of his own. The President laughed, apparently free from care.

"Sure," he said amiably. "Come on down here, you firebrand, and we'll thrash it out."

"I doubt if I can make it in half an hour," Senator Anderson said. "I'll have to round up Bob and Harley——"

"Who said anything about Bob and Harley?" the President demanded with a sudden real annoyance in his voice. "This is a private talk between you and me to settle this. What have Bob and Harley got to do with it?"

"I'm sorry," Brigham Anderson said firmly. "I prefer to be accompanied by Bob and Harley."

"And I prefer to see you alone," the President snapped.

"Then we've reached an impasse already, haven't we, Mr. President?" Brig said politely. "Thank you for calling. I think we'd better go back to the original plan."

"I am asking you as President of the United States and the leader of your party to come down here alone and discuss this matter with me," the President said coldly.

"And I," Brigham Anderson said in a voice as cold as his, "am telling you as United States Senator from the state of Utah that I will not come down there unless I am accompanied by the Majority Leader and the Vice President of the United States. Who," he added with deliberate slowness, "conceivably may presently be a direct party at interest in this matter."

"Don't you trust me?" the President demanded angrily; and since he had asked the question of one of the few men in American politics with sufficient courage and integrity to give him an absolutely honest answer, that was what he got.

"No, sir," Senator Anderson said quietly. "Not entirely."

There was another silence, a long one this time, and when the President spoke again it was with a complete lack of emotion in his voice.

"I think you're entirely right in what you propose, Senator," he said. "I shall expect you and your friends at the White House after the banquet."

"My friends and I," Senator Anderson said with equal dispassion, "will be there."

"Very good," the President said and hung up without further word.

And so, Brig thought, he had made him mad and probably made it more difficult to reach agreement. But God damn it, he had perfectly good reasons for acting as he had and he wasn't anybody's damned lackey. This angry mood sustained him for at least five minutes as he turned back to his mail and began to scan the exhortations from across the country to do this, that, or the other on the Leffingwell nomination. But presently, being a fair and decent man, his native calm and tolerance returned and he reflected that after all, the President had his problems too and was of course as fully concerned as he was, and so soon he came back to the assumption that they were both reasonable men who could talk it over quietly, once they were face to face, and work out a solution together.

He did not understand then that in the short space of ten minutes he had made solution of their disagreement forever impossible; and looking back later when he finally did understand and fully realized all the terrible consequences it had brought upon him, he knew, so well did he know his own character, his own integrity, and his own high concept of duty to the country, that even so he could have done no differently than he had.

Nor, indeed, could Mr. Justice Davis, approaching the Majority Leader's office shortly before 4 P.M. with that combination of inner trepidation and defiant determination with which basically well-meaning men become involved in enterprises they know they shouldn't really be engaged in, but nonetheless feel impelled to. Tommy Davis, for all ordinary purposes one of the kindliest of men, wouldn't knowingly have hurt a fly; but he was walking forward down the long corridors of the Office Building now in the certain knowledge, which he tried his best not to think about, that he might well be about to hurt a fellow being, knowingly, a great deal. He told himself with a little shiver that it was only in obedience to the highest imperatives that he could even imagine such a thing—because so much depended upon Bob Leffingwell, because the crisis in the world was so acute, because speedy confirmation was so necessary if that crisis was to be helped toward a peaceful conclusion. These were the reasons, utterly genuine, utterly sincere, springing from the highest integrity and devotion to country, which were propelling the Justice, a citizen whose life and calling were dedicated to helping his fellow men, upon an errand that might well destroy a fellow man. The contemplation of so violent an affront to his own decency and kindly nature was causing a profound and desperately inward-arguing unhappiness as he walked along; and it was with a troubled expression he could not completely conceal that he came to Senator Munson's door and found it, to his surprise, surrounded by the press.

"Well, I'll be damned," AP said. "Look who's coming."

"What's he here for?" UPI wondered.

"Let's ask him," the Newark *News* said practically.

"Mr. Justice," the Washington *Star* inquired, "what brings you here, sir?"

"Why, boys," Tommy Davis said, rather more rapidly than usual, some of them thought, "I felt like dropping over to see my old friend Bob Munson, so here I am."

"Things rather quiet at the Court?" the Washington *Post* asked politely.

"We thought you were sitting this afternoon," the Baltimore *Sun* observed.

"We were," the Justice said, "Indeed we were. South Dakota rail case and a couple of appeals from the Third Circuit, as a matter of fact. But we quit shortly after three, so I came on over."

"If it isn't too inquisitive, Mr. Justice," the *Times* said, "could you tell us the purpose of your call?"

"Well, it is, you know," Justice Davis said with a quick and, they thought, rather nervous smile, "but I know you gentlemen of the press, that never deters you, in fact it's your business to be too inquisitive. If you weren't, you wouldn't get the news, would you?"

"That's right," the *Times* agreed. "Well?"

"Well what?" Tommy Davis said blankly.

"Well, what's the purpose," the *Times* said. The Justice blinked.

"Oh, my dear boy," he said. "I told you. I just wanted to chat with my old friend the Majority Leader——"

"About Bob Leffingwell?" the *Herald Tribune* suggested.

"Or Brigham Anderson?" the Philadelphia *Inquirer* proposed.

"About events," the Justice said brightly. "Just events. There have been events today, you know."

"Yes," the St. Louis *Post-Dispatch* agreed rather acidly. "What part are you playing in them?"

"Just a bystander," the Justice said hurriedly. "Just an interested bystander."

"Does your visit here," AP asked with heavy patience, "have anything to do with developments in the Leffingwell nomination?"

"Well, now," Tommy Davis said quickly. "Well, now, how could I tell you if it did? How could I discuss matters that might have a direct bearing——"

"In other words, it does," AP said.

"Well, yes," Justice Davis confessed. "But I can't tell you about it. Oh, I definitely can't tell you. And now if you'll excuse me, I must go in and see Senator Munson——"

"Are you the President's emissary?" the Providence *Journal* asked.

"Oh, good heavens, no," the Justice exclaimed. "He doesn't need any emissary to the Majority Leader. Let's just say I'm an interested citizen, that's all. Just an interested citizen who thinks he can help."

"Have you got something on Brigham Anderson?" UPI asked, strictly as a shot in the dark; but it went home in a way that instantly intrigued them all. The Justice looked very upset for a moment and then spoke with hasty firmness.

"Now if you will please excuse me," he said, "I really must go on in. I don't want to keep Bob waiting."

"Can we talk to you when you come out?" AP asked.

"Perhaps," Tommy Davis said hurriedly. "Perhaps. I'll have to discuss it with Bob."

"Now what," the Chicago *Tribune* wondered as he ducked quickly into the office, "is that all about? What's he doing here if Bob is about to announce that it's all settled?"

"I have a feeling," the Los Angeles *Times* said thoughtfully, "that there are things moving on the surface of the waters that we don't know about."

"Not yet," the Minneapolis *Star* observed rather grimly. "But we will."

And they relaxed in little gossiping, chatting groups to wait it out while Justice Davis gave his name to the girls in the office and was told to go right on in to see a man who happened to be, as he soon perceived, in a state of upset approximately as great as his.

The Majority Leader, in fact, was feeling at the moment like the canary that got caught in the badminton game. He had been proceeding through the afternoon in the relaxed mood that had followed Lafe's call, confident that things were finally beginning to jell, congratulating himself that his patient approach to the human tangle surrounding the nomination had started to pay off, when he had put in a call to the White House to be greeted by one of the severest tongue-lashings he had ever received. He had barely had time to say hello when the President launched into a scathing denunciation of Senator Anderson and the Majority Leader's tender treatment of him. It was not entirely clear from the conversation exactly which of Brig's many crimes had finally broken the camel's back, but there was no doubt something had. Stubborn, recalcitrant, smart-alecky, disrespectful, disloyal to the President, and a traitor to the party were among the epithets; and as for Senator Munson's own namby-pamby handling of one so willful, the adjectives were equally stringent. There had been a cold and bitter anger in that forceful voice, a determined vengefulness that had genuinely frightened the Majority Leader. He had never known the President to be so violent about anything, perhaps because in seven years there had been nothing comparable in its personal importance to him, nothing so directly associated with his own prestige, his own influence, his own concept of his position in history. He had said in so many words that he intended to destroy Brigham Anderson, and though the Majority Leader after several patient and agonizing moments had managed to calm him down to what seemed a more rational approach, he had left no doubt at all that he had passed the point of no return so far as the chairman of the subcommittee was concerned.

It had helped not at all to put in a call immediately after to the senior Senator from Utah and find there a reaction that, while quieter than the President's, was every bit as unyielding and adamantine. There had been an absolute refusal to consider the Majority Leader's appeals, and along with it, not an active anger like the President's, but a quiet disapproval that was baffling in the extreme. Although he had professed to be perfectly willing to meet the President after the banquet as planned, and though he had sounded genuinely willing to discuss the matter with the Chief Executive then, his whole basic unmoving attitude had soon provoked his exasperated colleague into words of anger and annoyance of his own. He too had used words like stubborn, unreasonable and recalcitrant, and without directly charging disloyalty to the party he had implied as much. The response had been just what he would have expected had he only been calm enough to stop and reflect, but by then he wasn't: there had been that inner withdrawal to some private fortress of his own that was Brig's standard answer to attack. With perfect politeness he had asked to be excused from further conversation and had hung up with the Majority Leader still in midsentence.

It was in the wake of these two most frustrating and angering episodes, with a growing impatience and a rising feeling that perhaps Brig should indeed be punished for a presumptuous young pup, that Senator Munson heard the not very welcome news that Mr. Justice Davis was on his doorstep and snapped, "Send him in!" in a tone that caused an immediate buzz of comment in the outer office.

"Well, Tommy," he said rather shortly, "what can I do for you?"

"What's the matter, Bob?" the Justice asked in some alarm. "Am I imposing on you? Shouldn't I have come?"

"No, indeed," the Majority Leader said shortly. "I didn't mean to sound abrupt. You're always welcome here."

"Are you upset about something?" Tommy asked in a worried tone. "Because if you are, I can come back some other time." And inside he said a fervent little prayer: please tell me to go away, I don't really want to do this. But Bob was Bob.

"Sit down, Tommy," he ordered, not unkindly, "and stop fidgeting. I'm just upset about this damned nomination. The whole thing appears to be blowing up again."

"Again?" Justice Davis asked. "Did you think it was settled?"

Senator Munson frowned, and because he was in a frustrated and bothered mood he let his visitor in on mechanics of the Senate he otherwise wouldn't have.

"After working all morning and through the day," he said, "Orrin and I thought we had it all fixed up. We had Lafe take him to lunch——"

"Who?" the Justice said. "Bob Leffingwell?"

"No, of course not," the Majority Leader said impatiently. "His high and mightiness, our young friend from Utah. Brig the Unbendable. Lafe had it all set up to have him go to the White House and talk to the President, and then the whole thing blew up. God damn it," he added, in a beleaguered voice.

"Did Brig back out?" the Justice asked.

"No, the President called him before I got a chance to talk to either one of them," Bob Munson said, "and apparently he got sharp, and Brig got stubborn, and the talk ended in a row, and now we're in a hell of a shape again."

"Won't he even see the President at all?" Tommy asked.

"Oh, he will, yes," Senator Munson said, "after the White House Correspondents' banquet tonight. But I have a feeling he isn't going to yield."

"What does he want the President to do?" Justice Davis inquired, and he actually turned a little pale when he heard the answer.

"He wants the President to withdraw the nomination." Senator Munson said. "Isn't that a hell of a note?"

"Oh, dear me," Tommy said unhappily, for he knew that this meant that he had no choice, he must do what he had come to do. "Oh, my, I wish he didn't want that."

"Well," the Majority Leader said abruptly. "I don't want to bore you with my problems. Unless you can help with them, of course. What did you mean this morning when you said you knew something about Brig that might be of assistance?" He smiled. "The President indicated earlier that he wouldn't be above a little blackmail. Have you got something he can use?"

But he could see that this remark, which was intended as no more than an ironic jest, had really upset the Justice, for he suddenly looked very strained and unhappy.

"I may have," he said in a barely audible voice, and Senator Munson leaned forward with a skeptical look.

"*What?*" he said. "Are you sure you're feeling all right, Tommy? The Court's docket hasn't been too heavy for you lately, or anything?"

"No," Justice Davis said, in the same low voice; and with a hand that noticeably trembled he drew a small manila envelope out of his breast pocket and laid it carefully on the desk blotter in front of Senator Munson.

"What's that?" the Majority Leader said, still in a mocking tone despite his caller's obvious confusion of feelings. "Evidence of crime and corruption?"

"It's something I found a couple of days ago," Tommy Davis said. "It fell out of the car."

"What do you mean, fell out of the car?" Senator Munson asked. "Whose car?"

"Brig's car," the Justice said carefully. "He gave me a ride."

"So you repaid it by stealing his private papers," the Majority Leader said cruelly, and he meant it to be cruel, for he had suddenly realized that Tommy Davis really did think he had something damaging, and all the instincts of a decent heart told him he didn't want to have anything to do with it; even as he knew, with a sort of sick anticipation, that he was going to.

"Don't," Justice Davis said as though he had received a blow. "Please don't. I don't want to hurt anybody. I've never hurt anybody in my life."

"Then why are you planning to hurt somebody now?" Bob Munson asked in the same cruel way. "Is this nomination really that important to you?"

"I'm not the only one who thinks it's important," the Justice said pleadingly. "The President does; you do; lots of people all over the country and all over the world do. What right has he got to stand in the way?"

"If he is standing in the way," Senator Munson said soberly, "it is because he is being true to his own integrity and his own concept of what is best for the country. Can you and I," he asked slowly, "say the same thing at this particular moment?"

At this Justice Davis became very still, and, if anything, paler. But he also began to look a little stubborn and a little resentful.

"I believe I am doing this for the country," he said. "I couldn't possibly do it otherwise, Bob. Don't you know me well enough to know that?"

The Majority Leader gave a sad and bitter smile.

"Nobody in this town," he said, "ever does anything except for the best of motives. I've never known a major issue yet in which all sides didn't claim, even as they slaughtered one another, that they were inspired by the noblest of reasons. Well, what is this—thing you have?"

The Justice reached over and pushed it an inch or two toward him.

"You open it," he said with a little shiver.

"Very well," the Majority Leader said impatiently, "I will." And although he dreaded he knew not what, he reached over quickly, picked it up, opened it, and shook the contents out into his hand. A photograph with an inscription scrawled in one corner stared up at him blandly from the past.

"Is this all?" he said bluntly after a moment. "Is this this great secret of yours? Is this what you stole from Brig?"

"Stop saying that," Justice Davis said as though each word were a physical pain. "Please stop saying I stole it. Please. I found it."

"And you kept it, and you brought it along, and now you want me to use it to blackmail one of the finest people who ever came to this Senate," Senator Munson said bitterly. "God help us."

"He hasn't any right to stand in the way," the Justice said doggedly. "He just hasn't, Bob. You want him out of the way, and the President wants him out of the way. Maybe this is the means."

"What?" the Majority Leader demanded savagely. "An old photograph that doesn't mean anything?"

"If somebody were to find out who the other fellow was," the Justice said carefully, "and get to him, it might be that something could be developed. There are detective agencies that do that sort of thing. It might be——"

"Yes, it might be," Senator Munson said in the same savage way, "or it might not be."

"I think it might be," Tommy Davis said.

"Do you," the Majority Leader said, and a strange, contemptuous smile passed across his face. "Just what do you think it means, Tommy?"

"Well, I don't know exactly——" The Justice began, but Bob Munson wasn't having any of that.

"Oh, yes, you do," he said cruelly. "Yes, you do, my fine, pious upholder of equal justice under law. Yes, you do, indeed."

"Well," Justice Davis said in a quietly stubborn tone. "So do you."

After this there was a little silence while the Justice stared at the Senator and the Senator stared at the photograph. Then Bob Munson spoke slowly.

"What I ought to do," he said, "is give this back to Brig. Better yet, I ought to tear it up so that he would never know that anyone else had ever seen it. That," he said carefully, "is what I ought to do."

"Yes, it is," Mr. Justice Davis said with a certain spiteful note coming into his voice. "But," he added softly, "you won't."

"There's nothing to stop me," the Majority Leader said. "I could do it right now."

"Go ahead," Tommy Davis said. "Go ahead, then. Let him get away with blocking the nomination. Let him defeat Bob Leffingwell. Let him destroy one more hope of peace. It doesn't matter," he said bitterly. "So many have been destroyed already."

"What do you want me to do with it, Tommy?" Senator Munson asked curiously. "What did you have in mind when you came here?"

"I thought you might give it to the President," the Justice said. Bob Munson laughed, a short, unhumorous sound.

"That would be fine," he said. "Oh, my, yes, that would be very fine. He's in a mood right now to destroy Brig, Tommy. This isn't tiddlywinks any more, you know. This is reaching the stage where everybody is beginning to play for keeps. Oh, my, yes, it would be just dandy to give it to the President. Oh, yes, yes, indeed."

"Then maybe you could let Brig know in some way that you have it but won't—use it, if he will go along," the Justice said hesitantly.

"Blackmail," Bob Munson said again. "How many civil rights cases have you passed upon, Tommy? How many noble declarations for the majority, how many ringing dissents for the minority, have you handed down over there? How often have you gone to bat for your fellow men? And where does blackmail fit into the picture?"

The Justice looked out the window with a strange far-off expression, as though he were staring down the years.

"Men do what they have to do," he said quietly. "I have to be true to what I believe to be best for the country. I think this nomination is. I think it has got to go through. I think Brig has got to get out of the way. If he won't get out of the way voluntarily, then he has got to be made to get out of the way. And I think this is a possible way to do it. That is what I think."

"There's a long way to go," Senator Munson said, "between an innocent-appearing photograph and what you're trying to fabricate from it, Tommy."

"The inscription isn't so innocent," the Justice said quickly.

"I'll admit it's equivocal, but it would take an awful lot of digging and an awful lot of luck to get any substantive proof. It was apparently taken during the war, and for all we know the boy may be dead now. As it stands, this is nothing."

"There are detective agencies," Justice Davis repeated stubbornly. "The name of the picture company is on the back, it's a big firm and it's still in business. I remember seeing it when I was in Honolulu last summer. It may have records running back, if they gave their right names. Somebody who wanted to could trace it . . . if he wanted to."

"Well," Senator Munson said, "I don't. Good Christ!" he exploded angrily. "What do you want to do to this man, anyway? End his career? Destroy his family? Ruin his life? Kill him?"

"I just want him to get out of the way," Justice Davis repeated doggedly. "That is all I want him to do. So does the President. So do you. Anyway," he said rather desperately, as though this might excuse everything, "we don't know that it could be traced. You could just tell him it might be."

The Majority Leader looked at the photograph again with an expression of bitter distaste, not for the two youths in uniform who looked candidly out of it with every appearance of an innocence that the inscription in some subtle, indirect way belied, but rather for what the picture was making men do just because it was in existence. Then he put it in its envelope and tossed it back across the desk.

"You take it, Tommy. Your mind seems to be suited to this sort of thing more than mine is."

"I don't want it," Justice Davis said hastily. "It doesn't belong to me. I've discharged my duty by giving it to you. What you do with it is something between you and the President."

"Have you said anything to him about this?" the Majority Leader demanded sharply, and the Justice shook his head.

"No, indeed," he said. "I thought I should talk to you first. This is a Senate matter."

Bob Munson shook his head with a helpless air.

"What a set of values," he said, "that you could think of such a nicety in such a connection."

Justice Davis flushed.

"If it eases your conscience to berate me, Bob," he said, "go ahead and do it. But just don't forget that the nomination is at stake here, and this is the way to make Brig get out of the way. It may be the only way. He's very stubborn."

Senator Munson sighed. "So he is. Well, you run along, Tommy. I'll think it over."

"Will you give it back to him or tear it up?" the Justice asked. The Majority Leader shrugged.

"I don't know yet," he said. "I'll have to think about it."

"Because if you should, you know," the Justice said defiantly, "probably then I would have to tell the President. And of course there's the press. They're outside waiting. What shall I tell them when I go out, Bob?"

"I don't think," Senator Munson said, "that you had better tell them anything, Tommy. I really don't. I think you've done enough damage to yourself after all these years of being honorable, so if I were you I'd just let it rest. You wanted to put the burden on me, and you have. Now just leave it alone."

"It's only because I believe the nomination should be confirmed," the Justice said with a sort of dogged, determined defensiveness. "Why did God let me find it if He didn't want me to use it to help the country?"

"Why does God do anything?" the Majority Leader demanded shortly. "You ask Him, I've given up trying to figure it out. Just one thing, Tommy," he added as the Justice rose. "I don't want you saying anything to the press about this now, and if I decide not to do anything with it I don't want you to say anything to anybody about it ever." His voice became both soft and filled with a genuine menace. "Is that clear?" he asked quietly.

Tommy Davis looked at him defiantly.

"You can't defend him," he said, rather shrilly. "You can't defend him if what we think is true, and you know it. You wouldn't dare, you just wouldn't dare. So don't try to bluff me, Bob."

"He's a decent and honorable man," Senator Munson said slowly as though he hadn't heard him at all, "who has paid his debt to society, if you're right and he had one to pay, a hundred times over."

"But you couldn't defend him if it came out," the Justice repeated, "and you know it."

The Majority Leader sighed.

"No," he agreed, "I couldn't defend him. Now why don't you run along, Tommy? You've done enough for one day."

"I will," the Justice said meekly. At the door he paused.

"Bob——" he said hesitantly. "Don't hurt him any more—any more than you feel is necessary to make him get out of the way. It needn't be anything drastic. My God," he said as though suddenly struck by the enormity of it all, "I don't want you to do anything that would really hurt him."

"I appreciate your charity and kindness, Tommy," Senator Munson said dryly, "and I'm sure Brig would appreciate it too, if he could only know. You'll understand and forgive me if I suggest that it's perhaps a little late in the day. Wait a minute until I get the press out of the way." And lifting the phone and pressing a buzzer, he told Mary to open the door and let the reporters into the outer office. When he was satisfied that they were all in he turned back to the Justice.

"Now, Tommy," he said, his voice suddenly becoming harsh, "you go out this door and beat it. Just get the hell back where you belong and don't stop to talk to anybody along the way."

"Will I be hearing from you, Bob?" the Justice asked, almost apologetically, and Senator Munson snorted.

"You may or you may not," he said. "Now, good-by. And don't call the President, either," he added.

"I may or I may not," Mr. Justice Davis said, not without a flare of spite provoked by the Majority Leader's tone. "Good luck."

"Thanks for nothing," Bob Munson said.

After the door had closed he remained seated at his desk for several minutes. He was surprised but not shocked that a Justice of the Supreme Court should be engaged in such an enterprise, for passions were running very high on the Leffingwell nomination, and a long life in politics, while it still left some small room for surprise, had virtually extinguished the capacity for shock. People did the damnedest things and quite often the damnedest people did the damnedest things. The same applied to his young colleague, though for him the Majority Leader felt a much more profound emotion tinged with a heavy sorrow. Once more he took the photograph out and studied it carefully, finally shaking his head in wonderment. "Brigham, Brigham, Brigham," he said with a sigh. *Tear it up now,* a voice of sanity and decency urged him; *Don't be too hasty,* another countered, *the nomination has got to go through.* "God damn it to hell!" he exclaimed bitterly, and with a sudden angry motion, as though if he did it very fast he wouldn't know he was doing it, he slipped the picture back in its envelope, put it in his coat pocket, and went out to see the press.

"I have no announcement to make," he said abruptly, before anyone could speak.

"Nothing at all?" AP said in a tone of disbelief.

"Nothing at all," Senator Munson said.

"But I thought you told us——" UPI began.

"I was mistaken," Senator Munson said.

"But Justice Davis said——" the Newark *News* protested.

"He was mistaken too," Senator Munson said.

"Can we see him?" the Philadelphia *Inquirer* asked.

"He's left," Senator Munson said. "Mary, bring those letters in and we'll get to work on them."

"Well, I'll be damned," the Providence *Journal* said as the Majority Leader turned his back upon them without ceremony and returned to his private office. "I thought we were going to get the end of this story this afternoon."

"I have a hunch," the *Times* remarked thoughtfully, "that this story is just beginning."

4

The radio was going on the nightstand while Pidge sat fascinated on her mother's bed and watched with an occasional comment as her father wandered in and out of the bathroom in bare feet and a pair of terry-cloth trunks, shaving and getting ready. One of the nation's most famous and colorful commentators was hard at work upon him at the moment, and the rich purple prose flowed out into the peaceful room with an air of intimate urgency that undoubtedly concealed from a good many millions of people the fact that its owner had spent most of the afternoon in the Press Club bar and had only blended together his on-the-spot coverage out of wire-service clips and one last martini just before airtime. But he was an old hand at the game, and it rolled:

"This day of dramatic behind-the-scenes maneuvering in the Leffingwell nomination is drawing to a close here in spring-drenched Washington with the deadlock between the White House and Senator Brigham Anderson of Utah apparently still unbroken. Not in years has there been a clash of wills as dramatic as that which is taking place between the President of the United States and the youthful Senator from the Far West. Senator Anderson's friends, including such powerful members of the Senate as the Majority Leader, Robert D. Munson of Michigan, and the senior Senator from Illinois, Orrin Knox, have spent most of the day attempting to bring about a face-to-face conference between their young colleague and the President; but the Senator, persistently refusing to disclose the reasons for his abrupt reopening of the hearings on the nomination, has so far refused.

"Since he has kept himself incommunicado from the press, Washington has been forced to speculate on what those reasons may be; and the speculation always comes up against the solid rock of the reputation and character of the nominee, Robert A. Leffingwell. It seems inconceivable to Washington tonight that Senator Anderson can really have in his possession any facts casting any serious reflection upon the monumental integrity of this man the President has chosen to be his principal assistant in foreign affairs. So speculation turns elsewhere. Can there be political advantage in it for the Senator? Is this an elaborate attempt to hold up the White House for some pet project out West? Does he have long-range ambitions for national office that are leading him to curry favor among reactionary elements which are opposed to the confirmation of the nominee? Or is it something as simple, and perhaps understandable, as that he wishes to focus the national spotlight upon a career which in seven long years, despite his youth and the apparent promise with which he came here, has been, if truth were known, relatively undistinguished? These are the things Washington is speculating about tonight. The speculation is not, as Senator Anderson apparently hoped it would be, What is wrong with Bob Leffingwell? Rather, it is, What is wrong with Brigham Anderson?"

"Yes, you son of a bitch," Brig said savagely, walking over and snapping off the machine, "that's the speculation, all right." Then he became aware of his daughter's wide-eyed surprise, gave a sudden laugh, and bounced the bed vigorously. "Isn't that the speculation?" he demanded, as she flew up and down in gurgling excitement. "*Isn't* it?" And leaning over with a fist planted firmly in the mattress on each side of her he suddenly ducked his head and pretended to dive into her tummy. "*Dadee!*" she squealed in ecstatic delight.

"What's all this unseemly noise that's going on in the bedroom?" Mabel asked from the doorway, and her husband looked up with a grin.

"I'm glad you came along," he said. "I have a young lady here who's quite a flirt. She was getting too much for me, as you can plainly see."

"As I can plainly see," Mabel smiled. "Looks to me as though nobody is doing any serious work at all."

"Daddy got mad at the man on the radio," Pidge offered, and her father bunted her again to the accompaniment of more loud squeals. Then he suddenly sat her upright and put a pillow on top of her head.

"Now you're a very stylish lady," he said.

"Daddy," Pidge said, "you're silly."

"So I am," he admitted, "in a few private circles where I am known and loved."

"What was the man saying?" Mabel asked, sitting down on the bed beside her daughter as he went back to the bathroom and started to mix up some lather.

"Don't tell her, Pidge," Brigham Anderson said. "It wasn't anything very original."

"I won't," Pidge said practically. "I don't remember."

"Well, that's as good a reason as any," Mabel agreed, and her husband chuckled.

"That's right," he said. "It wasn't anything Mommy would want to hear anyway. No different from what she's been hearing all day. It seems she's married to a bad, bad man who is doing awful, awful things to his country. She knows that already."

"No, I don't, either," Mabel said firmly. "I don't know that at all."

"Well, you're nice," he said, winking over the lather, "but that's what a lot of people think."

"What's happened to you in the last few minutes?" she asked curiously. "You seemed rather depressed when you got home, I thought."

"I *got* home," he said simply. "That's what happened."

And he gave her a warm look that was such a mixture of white-lathered Santa Claus and half-naked satyr that she suddenly burst out laughing as though all the cares of the day were rolling away, as indeed it seemed almost possible they might be.

"What's the matter?" he asked with a grin.

"Nothing," she said. "Just you. And me. And life."

"And me," Pidge reminded firmly, and her mother gave her a hug.

"And you," she agreed. "We're quite a sketch, all of us."

"I'm not," Pidge said. "I'm me."

"Sister," her father said with a chuckle, "there's no doubt of that. No, indeedy. As some young man is going to find out to his eternal fascination, bafflement, and enthrallment someday . . . As a matter of fact," he said as he finished shaving, "I talked to the President on the phone this afternoon."

"Oh?" Mabel said, and her fears suddenly came back stronger than ever. "How was he?"

"Pretty presidential," Brig said soberly. "Headmaster-to-boy-in-the-lower-form type of thing. 'I am asking you as President of the United States to come down here and discuss this with me,'" he quoted with an exaggerated emphasis.

"I hope you didn't antagonize him," Mabel said nervously, and a trace of impatience crossed her husband's face.

"'I am telling you as United States Senator from the state of Utah that I am not coming down there unless I am accompanied by my good friends the Majority Leader and the Vice President,'" he quoted, with a somewhat more emphatic emphasis.

"Oh, dear," she said, a real worry flooding her heart, spoiling the mood of their happy moments, shadowing the warm, familiar room. "Oh, dear, I wish you hadn't."

"Hadn't what?" he demanded sharply, coming into the room to get some socks and underwear from his bureau. "Hadn't what, for heaven sakes?" he demanded again as he returned to the bathroom and prepared to close the door. "I'm not a school child, Mabel. I have some rights and some prerogatives of my own. Anyway I'm going to see him at the house after the banquet. Lay out my dress shirt and cuff links while I'm showering, will you? I'll be out in a minute." And he closed the door to become engulfed in a roar of water.

"Mommy," Pidge said thoughtfully, "I wish Daddy would mind you."

At this, for which there was no very good answer, Mabel scooped her up with a half-laugh, half-sob, half some sort of sound she wasn't quite sure of, and gave her a hug.

"Help me fix Daddy's shirt and jewelry for him," she said. "He's got to get all dressed up and look handsome for the big party."

"I'll bet he will," Pidge said confidently, and her mother, although she felt as though she might start crying again if she didn't watch out, made her answer light.

"He sure will," she said. "He'll be the handsomest one there, I'll bet."

"He'll be the handsomest one there, I'll bet," Pidge repeated triumphantly.

And when a little later, shaved, showered, lotioned, and dressed in his tuxedo, he kissed them good-by and started across the lawn to the car, his wife felt with a pang of pride and pain and love and protectiveness like a knife that he very probably would be; for nature had favored him well, and tonight everything seemed to conspire to set it off. As he reached the car he turned back for a moment to wave, and the flat rays of the late afternoon sun, flooding through the trees and over the world, bathed his compact figure in a sudden glow, highlighted the sunburn in his cheeks, lent a ruddy tinge to his hair. She always remembered him as he looked at that moment, on that clear, gentle evening with a warm wind blowing, standing there in his white coat, black tie and black trousers, a smile on his lips, a confident look on his face, the level dark eyes carrying an expression of kindness and decency, his whole aspect steady and sure, his being caught and held in one of those rare moments of absolute physical perfection that come only fleetingly even to the most favored. That was how she always remembered him, later, that is, after enough time had passed so that she could stand remembering.

"I expect I'll be a little late," he called back casually. "You know how these things are."

"Good luck at the White House," she said.

"I'm scared," he said with a grin, "but I guess he won't eat me."

"Goodness, I hope not," she said, with a fairly good attempt at a laugh.

"Don't you worry," he said as he climbed in and turned on the ignition. "Little Jack is quite a giant killer."

"I hope so!" she replied with a laugh that sounded steadier, and a last wave as he drove away. "Oh, my darling," she said to herself as she watched him negotiate the corner smoothly and disappear from sight, "my beloved, my life, I hope so, oh, I hope so."

5

All across the great room with its deep scarlet carpets, its blue, starred walls and ceilings, its hundreds of white tables set with gleaming silver, its giant angular statues representing some awkward, self-conscious, mid-Forties concept of Humanity, the pride and pomp of America was assembling. The White House Correspondents' banquet for the President, along with the Gridiron Club a major socio-political event of the year for the press corps, was drawing its usual complement of Senators, Congressmen, Supreme Court Justices, Cabinet officers, high-ranking military, diplomats, and reporters. For all practical purposes, the Government of the United States was concentrated on that evening in the Statler, for anyone who was anyone in that government, anyone who was anyone diplomatically assigned to that government, anyone who was anyone in the business of recording the events of that government, was present. In from northwest, up from southeast, down from Bethesda and Chevy Chase and Silver Spring, out of Georgetown and across the river from Virginia they had flocked in their formal attire for this annual gathering, and now they were slowly beginning to fill up the ballroom amid a clatter of waiters rushing about banging dishes and silverware, a steadily rising babble of voices, greetings, laughter, and joking talk, and above it all the Navy Band softly playing "Velia" and "The Banks of the Wabash" and similar sentimental compositions on the platform at one end of the room. There was excitement in the air and it was rising steadily as more guests entered and the crowd grew. It was always an enjoyable affair, and tonight the nomination lent it a spice that promised to make it even more memorable than usual.

So they were coming to it from all over the world of Washington, Lord Maudulayne picking up Raoul Barre in a British Embassy limousine and stopping by also, although not without some mild acerbic protest from his colleague, for the Indian Ambassador, who had been invited to sit at the head table and couldn't help burbling about it most of the way down until he was quietly informed that both his companions had been invited too, after which he relapsed into an obviously miffed silence; Orrin Knox and Arly Richardson, sharing a cab in from Spring Valley, which gave Orrin a chance to fill Arly in on the plan for the White House conference, which he divulged, as soon as he reached the Statler, to his host, the *Arkansas Gazette;* Seab Cooley and Bob Munson, riding down together from their hotel through the soft breezes of Rock Creek Park, amiably telling one another lies about what they knew of the latest turn in the nomination; Harley Hudson, ordering his chauffeur to stop by Tom August's in the park near Dolly's so that the chairman of Foreign Relations could join him and arrive in style in the Vice President's limousine; the nominee being picked up by his host, a very happy AP staffer who had covered Defense Mobilization for a decade and had suddenly found the patient drudgery of years sensationally rewarded by the fact that his guest had overnight turned out to be not only the director of ODM but the Secretary of State-designate as well; the Chief Justice and five of his colleagues, including Mr. Justice Davis, who was baffling his host, the legal reporter for the *Times,* by remaining deep in a brown study which certainly bore no resemblance to his usual pleasant presence; the chairman of the Joint Chiefs of Staff, and the Joint Chiefs, the Secretary of Defense, the Secretary of the Treasury, the Secretary of Commerce, the Secretary of the Interior (Howie Sheppard, moved by an unhappy premonition that his days were numbered, had some weeks ago turned down the invitation of UPI's chief diplomatic correspondent at State), the Secretary of Labor, and the Secretary of Agriculture.

Now the head-table guests were beginning to come in with their hosts, walking along the dais looking for their seats, and suddenly somebody on the floor cried, "There's Leffingwell!" and there was a sudden burst of applause that rose and swelled through the glittering room until it almost drowned out the music. The nominee acknowledged it with a pleased smile, first bowing formally and then clasping both hands above his head in a prize fighter's salute. The applause rose and doubled, not dying until he reached his seat and sat down. During this, from different entrances to the room, the senior Senator from Utah, the senior Senator from Illinois and the senior Senator from South Carolina could be observed entering with their hosts; it was noticed that while Brigham Anderson did not join in the applause, neither did he display any particular emotion at all, that he only smiled in a calm, unworried way and turned to chat pleasantly with his host, AP, as soon as the sound died down; it was noticed that Orrin Knox and Seab Cooley exchanged a glance across the tables between them, that Orrin made a grimace he made no attempt to conceal and that Seab gave a dry little nod that might have meant many things. There was much interest in all this and much excited gossip all around as the Chief Justice and his colleagues, the Joint Chiefs, Lord Maudulayne, Raoul Barre, Krishna Khaleel, Vasily Tashikov, and the Ambassador from Libya also came in and found their places along the head table. Expectancy and excitement mounted, for there remained now only one more entry to be made, and no matter how often those present had witnessed it, there was always a stirring and an emotion and a thrill.

Abruptly there was a roll of drums and over it the two traditional challenging announcements by the trumpets, "Ta—ta-ta-ta-ta—*ta!* Ta—ta-ta-ta-ta—*ta!*" They got to their feet, the band swung into, "Hail to the Chief," and the President came in with the officers of the Association and made his way along to the center of the table, grinning and smiling at them all, waving first one arm and then the other, and finally, as he reached his seat, raising both arms together in his characteristic gesture that combined the best features of yell leader on Saturday afternoon and spiritual leader blessing his flock. He held this pose for several moments while they stamped and whistled and applauded, and then at the height of it he suddenly looked down the table to his left where Bob Leffingwell was standing applauding with the rest. With a vigorous gesture as the excitement rose he beckoned him forward, and when the nominee reached him he grabbed his right arm and raised their two hands together in a triumphant gesture while the cheers and whistles grew to a steady roar. When this had lasted just long enough, he lowered their arms, gave the nominee a hearty pat on the shoulder, and sat down with a happy grin and satisfied shake of his head.

"So much for me," Brig murmured to his host, but he had underestimated the President, for just at that moment men around him began calling loudly to attract his attention, pointing to the head table, and looking toward it he could see the President gesturing frantically. For a moment he hesitated, but he was helpless in the hands of a master showman, and there was no stopping this new scene in the drama. The President was half on his feet, reaching over for the microphone on the lectern at the center of the table. "BRIGHAM!" his voice boomed out. "BRIGHAM, COME UP HERE AND SAY HELLO TO ME, YOU SON OF A GUN!" And so after a moment, while the laughter and applause again mounted and rolled over the room and the spotlights in the control booth in the ceiling suddenly singled him out and accompanied his progress, the Senator from Utah slowly made his way to the head table.

"Brig, it's great to see you!" the President exclaimed, leaning over the table edge and shaking hands vigorously as the Senator stood beneath him reaching up and the flashbulbs flared and the cameras snapped and the photographers fell over one another in their zeal.

"Mr. President," Brig said with the exact degree of politeness necessary and no more, "I hope you have a good dinner."

"I'm looking forward to dessert, eh, Brigham?" the President said with a wink and a chuckle and a hearty laugh, and the angry expression that flashed across the Senator's face came and went so fast no camera caught it.

"I hope you don't find it indigestible!" he shot back sardonically as he turned away, and in response to some wild inspiration on the part of the conductor the band suddenly swung into the Stanford Fight Song and once again the room broke into an uproar of rather hazy, rather woozy, but oh, my, such delighted sound at the great big happy, glowing, wonderful excitement of it all.

With such dramatic beginnings, and coming as it fortuitously did at such a dramatic moment in the Leffingwell nomination, it was not surprising that this particular White House Correspondents' dinner should have gone down in history as one of the best ever. All the major characters in the drama were there in the great turbulent room filled with music and the uproar of eating, and whether they looked at one another or didn't, what they said, what they did, who they shook hands with, who they didn't shake hands with, whether they were relaxed and pleasant or ill-at-ease and nervous, was immediately noted by a thousand pairs of eyes, each belonging to someone who had access to newsprint. That heightened awareness, that extra alertness, that sending out of little perceptive antennae that characterizes every Washington social gathering, and particularly this one, was everywhere present; and although a number of distinguished gentlemen of the government and the press got very well oiled before the evening was over, as usual nothing much was missed by anybody.

Paramount in interest, of course, was the aspect of the President, for the racing rumors about his health that were currently traveling around town had made his physical appearance of extra interest to everyone. But so vigorous and dramatic had been his entry and his opening activities at the head table that only a few paused to note that he looked possibly a little grayer, perhaps a little tireder, than he should look, and that now and then he seemed to lapse into a rather blank look, with a certain slackness around jowls and eyes, that did not augur well. These moods of his seemed to pass so rapidly, and he appeared to be so animated and triumphant most of the time, that even those who saw these signs with some worry concluded presently that probably all he needed was a few days of rest in the sun. There were reports he would head for Key West as soon as the nomination was out of the way, and this was taken to mean that he would shortly be back in top form again.

It was carefully recorded that he seemed to make quite a point of dividing his nods and winks and waves between the nominee, seated down the head table at his left, and the chairman of the subcommittee, seated below and six tables away. These attentions invariably seemed to please Bob Leffingwell, who returned them with a pleased smile, and it was observed that Brigham Anderson, although beginning to look a little bored with the game after a while, nonetheless contrived to return the looks with an air of pleasant politeness that was completely correct. If it was nothing more, that was to be expected under the circumstances, and the President did not seem annoyed. At one point Senator Munson got up from his seat down the table at the President's right to come along and lean over his shoulder and chat for a moment. The newsmen nearby heard only banalities, and the two of them nodded together at Senator Anderson, who smiled back rather cautiously. Several tables away Orrin Knox made a tart comment to his host, who laughed and passed it around the table, and further away Seab Cooley, noting the continuing elaborate presidential performance, smiled to himself over some private joke that his fellows at the table were not privy to, and looked for a second rather grim. Only one odd little moment occurred, which was marked by quite a few, and that was when Senator Anderson left his table for a moment and started toward the head table, apparently intending to speak to Mr. Justice Davis. For a strange moment the Justice looked absolutely panic-stricken, and turning his back on the room with great haste he plunged deep into conversation with the Indian Ambassador, who appeared startled but obliging. After a second Senator Anderson turned back, looking puzzled and a little hurt; but he concluded after a moment that Tommy was just in one of his moods and decided with a certain amusement that he and K.K. were well-matched in that area and deserved one another. He soon forgot the episode.

As for the nominee, he played host all during dinner to a steady stream of well-wishers who came up from the floor to shake his hand and wish him well. Columnists, news analysts, bureau chiefs—the whole dazzling array was there, those who really deserved their fame, and those who had come from little towns to the nation's capital to master the portentous knack of representing great newspapers and dropping great names. He received them all with the same gracious air, looking dignified and steady and every inch the man who could be entrusted with the great office to which he had been appointed. Just to hedge their bets, for one never knew who had what on whom in Washington, a good many of these famous citizens also came by Brigham Anderson's table to extend the same courtesy, but it was obvious in most cases that this was something they felt they should do and not, as with the nominee, an indication of warm personal support and endorsement. If Brig received them a little sardonically though with impeccable courtesy, it could be understood under the circumstances.

So the dinner drew on and ended, the time came for entertainment.

Upon the stage vacated by the Navy Band two tired dancers, an aging ventriloquist, a shopworn babe with a big bust and a tiny voice, and a weather-beaten jazz trio took their turns; the program ended with a star from Hollywood who thought he was very funny but managed only intermittently to impart the same conviction to his audience. It was noted that the President seemed to be getting a little restive, to be fiddling a little with his cuffs and to be looking, now with a little more direct appraisal, at the impassive face of the senior Senator from Utah and the rock-like bulk of the senior Senator from South Carolina a few tables beyond. The correspondents became nervous at his nervousness, hoped the entertainment would end speedily, clapped with hearty relief when it did, and settled back as the president of the Correspondents' Association made his traditional introduction of the guest of honor.

"Tonight, gentlemen," he said, "as always at these affairs of ours, there are no reporters present. With that assurance and that caution, I present to you the President of the United States."

And once again they were all on their feet applauding vigorously as the President smiled and waved and embraced them all in his fatherly warmth. There was nothing fatherly, however, in the tone with which he began as they sat down again, and in no time flat the room was deathly still. To Bob Munson's dismay he was proceeding exactly as he had said he would.

"Mr. President," he began easily, "fellow members of the Association—the man says there are no reporters present. Well, tonight I'm going to exercise the privileges of the special gold membership card I got in this room just seven years ago tonight, and reverse his ruling. Tonight, gentlemen, there *are* reporters present, so get out your pencils and let's write ourselves a story."

There was a burst of excited sound, a babble of exclamations and comments, and a great many people did take out pencils or pens and begin scribbling on the backs of their programs as he stood confident and commanding above them and looked slowly over the room.

"You see before you," he said, "the President of the United States. You see down there at his left his nominee for Secretary of State. You see here at Table 8 and there at Table 15 the senior Senator from Utah and the senior Senator from South Carolina. And thereby"—and he cocked his head with a quizzical expression and everybody laughed in a sharp, explosive way that revealed the height of the tension in the room—"hangs the story. Now, the President of the United States thinks his nominee for Secretary of State is a good man and he wants him confirmed. But the senior Senator from South Carolina, for reasons—" and he drew his words out comically, so that they all laughed again—"with which we are all too, *too* familiar, doesn't think he's a good man and *he* doesn't want him confirmed. But up to late last night, the President thought—he had been assured of it by such well-informed sources as the Majority Leader of the Senate, and you all know what a good source *he* is"— Again he invited them to laugh, and they did so while Bob Munson permitted himself to look openly annoyed "—the President thought that the senior Senator from Utah liked the nominee too and also wanted him confirmed, just like the President did. Imagine my surprise," he said, and he said it with such a comical air that once again he got the response he wanted, "when I got up this morning and found that this wasn't so. Indeed, imagine my chagrin when the day drew on and I found it wasn't to *be* so. Imagine my feelings when I have come right up to this very moment, and it still isn't so. Well, gentlemen," he said, "and I must hurry this along, for I see the Senator from South Carolina is scowling, and you all know what an explosion that portends, and the Senator from Utah is looking disapproving, and you all know what a monumentally disapproving young man he can be—this is your story." His head came up in its challenging way and the fatherly eyes no longer looked fatherly but cold and strong and unyielding. "You can tell your readers that the President of the United States is standing by his nominee. You can tell them he hasn't heard anything to persuade him that he shouldn't. And you can say that he is going to fight with everything he's got to see that his nominee is confirmed." And he concluded with three words that startled Lafe Smith at Table 27, spacing them out with an unyielding emphasis: "No matter what!"

There was a spattering of applause which soon grew to a vigorous roar and in the midst of it the President once more looked down the table to the nominee and waved as the applause grew even more tumultuous.

"The Secret Service," the president of the Association said hurriedly into the din, "has asked that we all remain in our places until the President has left."

The drums rolled again, the trumpets blared, and the band broke once more into, "Hail to the Chief," as the President left, still waving and gesturing and smiling to them all.

"That was certainly a constructive move toward a peaceful solution," Orrin Knox snapped disgustedly, materializing at Seab's elbow, and the senior Senator from South Carolina smiled in a sleepy way. "He is an evil man," he said softly; "a strong evil man. But he hasn't won yet." "He thinks so," Orrin said tartly. All around them the correspondents and their guests were beginning to move out in the wake of the President's departure, many to go upstairs to the suites retained for the night by the major newspapers and magazines and rehash the events of the dinner over drinks. At Table 8 the senior Senator from Utah turned down an invitation to come up to the *Herald Tribune* suite, bade his host farewell, and began slowly working his way out through the crowd, moving parallel to the head table. So it was that the Majority Leader was able to intercept him near the door.

"Why don't you go out and wait for me at the corner of Fifteenth and K," he suggested. "I'll swing by in a minute and pick you up."

"I'm not going anywhere," Senator Anderson said indifferently. "Just home."

"Look," Senator Munson said desperately, "don't be like that, Brig. I told him not to do that, it was against my advice."

"Well, he did do it," Brig said quietly.

"All right, he did do it," the Majority Leader said, suddenly angry and not caring much that Claude Maudulayne and Raoul Barre had come along behind him and were listening with unabashed interest. "That doesn't change matters, it's still got to be talked out."

"Not by me," Brigham Anderson said tersely, waving to Tommy Davis, who was brushing hurriedly by and who again did not speak.

"Brigham," Bob Munson said, staring after the Justice, and his tone was a mixture of command and plea so peculiar that his young colleague stopped and stared full at him. "I am begging you for your own good not to be like this. You don't know—you just don't know——" He stopped lamely and then went on. "I will pick you up in ten minutes where I said. I beg of you to be there. Believe me, I am asking it as your friend. I am afraid of what may happen if you don't. Please, Brigham."

Senator Anderson looked at him thoughtfully for a moment.

"What's the matter, Bob?" he asked. "This isn't Russia, you know. I'm not going to be shot." But the Majority Leader was turning away with a strange expression of pain and worry and fear and anger all rolled into one.

"Please," he said as the two Ambassadors watched closely. "Please."

"All right," Brig called after him suddenly. "Don't forget to bring Harley."

"Harley's already left," Senator Munson said. "He went with the President."

And so, much to his surprise and some trepidation, he had. It was not unusual that this should have passed virtually unnoticed in the closing moments of the banquet, for the relationship between the White House and the heir apparent was so well known to Washington that even those few celebrants who had happened to perceive that the man the President was walking arm-in-arm to his car was actually the Vice President had refused to believe it. "Do you see wha' I see?" one had said to another; and the other, blinking carefully and looking twice, had dismissed it abruptly with, "'S'mirage!"

However, a mirage was exactly what it wasn't, even though Harley himself felt rather as though he were in the midst of one as he was escorted along to the sleek black Cadillac to the accompaniment of a running barrage of confidential comments on the people they met. "Hi, Bill!" the President would cry happily to some panjandrum of the press; "Damned bastard is out to get my scalp if he can," he would mutter to the

Vice President; "Harry, it's great to see you!" followed by, "Double-dealing son of a bitch!" in the Vice President's ear. This immediately established a feeling of intimacy and rapport of such hearty warmth that if Harley hadn't had a thousand and one snubs over the past seven years from his newly acquired buddy his head would have been quite turned by it. As it was he felt as though he were walking along a very thin edge of ice just above a crack in a glacier, and he thanked his lucky stars that he and Tom August had decided to have one gin-and-tonic apiece and then stick to tomato juice. He was bedazzled, but in his own slow, goodhearted, well-meaning way, he was not a fool; and so he was going along with the gag with a lively awareness that at any moment it might end abruptly and he might find himself sliding down the chasm into that outer darkness where the President usually preferred to keep him. This lent a certain understandable caution to his responses.

"How do you think it went?" his companion asked after they were safely ensconced in the car and, with one last smile and wave, had been swept grandly out onto the street in the center of a flying squad of six motorcycle cops with sirens blaring. "Do you think it showed them where I stand?"

"I don't really think," Harley said as they ran the red light on K Street and roared the three blocks to the main entrance to the White House grounds, "that anybody had any doubt, did they, Mr. President?"

"Well," the President said comfortably, "I thought just possibly Seab and our young friend from Utah needed a reminder. Tell me about Brig, Harley. Is he going to give me a lot of trouble tonight?"

"I don't know," the Vice President said cautiously.

"He insisted that you and Bob come along too," the President said with a chuckle, "so I guess he must expect he'll need friends. Do you like him?"

"Yes, I do," Harley said. "I like him very much."

"Got a lot of spirit," the President said thoughtfully as the cavalcade drew up under the great portico and the butler came forward quickly to open the door. "Out with you, Harley. Want to race me up the steps?"

This sudden, unexpected reference to an old joke involving Presidents and Vice Presidents so startled and shocked the Vice President that for a moment he looked completely aghast. This being exactly the reaction the President had hoped to produce, he gave a roar of laughter and pounded his companion on the back.

"Harley, you're a sketch!" he cried. "Here, give me your arm and help me up. I couldn't make it without your assistance, let alone race you. So you like young Anderson, eh?"

And still chortling he accompanied the Vice President up the steps while around them the watching Secret Service and house servants laughed and were amused and hardly noticed at all that he did indeed lean on Harley's arm, and very heavily, too. But Harley noticed, and it made his blood run cold.

"Yes, I do, Mr. President," he said again as they entered the main hallway and turned toward the elevator. "I really think Brig is one of the finest young men we have in government."

"The press didn't seem to like him much tonight," the Chief Executive said with some satisfaction.

"Oh, not on this," the Vice President agreed. "They're mostly for Leffingwell. But on everything else they like him fine, I think."

"Yes," the President said as they reached the second floor and proceeded toward his study. "Well. Maybe he won't recover from this, if he doesn't behave."

"I'm sure I don't know what he has in mind," Harley Hudson said. "He hasn't told me."

"Hasn't told anybody, apparently," the President said. "Here, take that big chair, Harley, and make yourself comfortable. Let me ring for a drink. What would you like?"

"I think just a little ginger ale," the Vice President said politely, and his host looked astounded.

"No!"

"Yes, I think so," Harley insisted in a rather defiant tone of voice.

"Well, I'll order the works," the President said, proceeding to do so, "and you can mix up whatever you like. I suppose Brig won't drink either and everything will be very grim. I thought we might just talk this over pleasantly like old friends."

"Like we always do," Harley couldn't resist saying quickly with an irony that was rare for him, and his host gave another roar of laughter.

"Touché," he said cheerfully. "Touché. Actually, Harley, I'd have you down here more often except that you're so valuable to me right up there where you are. Bob tells me you often give us invaluable support on these Administration measures. I always feel you're there when I need you. It's a comforting feeling to know I have a real friend up there. You have no idea how lonely you get down here, Harley."

This last remark, going rather farther in the heat of hyperbole than the President had intended and touching as it did very close to possibilities that were very lively in both their minds, brought a sudden awkward little silence that the President finally broke with a casual show of interest.

"How are things going with you these days, anyway?" he asked. "Legislative schedule pretty heavy right now, is it?"

"Well, you know how it is this time of year," the Vice President said politely, knowing very well that there wasn't a bill at the Capitol whose exact status at that moment the President didn't know. "We dawdle along for the first three or four months of the session and then it begins to pick up speed. I'd say it will be quite heavy from now on until adjournment."

"Do you find enough to do?" the President asked rather patronizingly. "Yourself, I mean? Maybe I could use you on some international projects if you'd like, NATO or UN, the Pan-American Union, that sort of thing."

"Oh, I find quite enough, thank you, Mr. President," Harley said with dignity. "Lately," he added casually on a sudden inspiration, "I find quite a bit of my time is taken up with talking to Ambassadors——"

"Ambassadors?" the President said sharply. "How's that?"

"Oh, they seem to want to see me," Harley said, suddenly finding that he was beginning to enjoy himself immensely. "Tashikov . . . Khaleel . . . The usual crowd," he concluded airily, and let some more ginger ale run into his glass with a satisfying fizzz! while the President looked at him closely.

"Why should they want to see you?" he demanded bluntly. The Vice President smiled.

"They don't tell me exactly," he said. "I just have to guess."

"Oh?" the President said dryly. "And what do you guess?"

"Oh, I really don't know," the Vice President said, wandering over to the window and feeling quite light-headed with his own daring. "What a beautiful view we get from here," he said, "over the Ellipse and the Washington Monument."

"I do get a nice view," the President agreed, stressing the pronoun.

"It must be pleasant working in here," Harley said thoughtfully. "I think I would use it a great deal if I were——"

"Well, yes," the President said quickly, not sounding amused at all, for this was a needling side of Harley he wasn't prepared for and he didn't like it. "Tell me," he said abruptly. "Are you going to help me beat some sense into this young whippersnapper tonight?"

"Why, I don't know, Mr. President," the Vice President said coolly out of a heady sense of having put his formidable superior temporarily on the run, "that depends on what he has to say."

"Well, Harley," the President said, suddenly deciding to revert to charm and intimacy, "I guess I can count on you when the chips are down, so I'm just going to refuse to worry about it. Did I ever show you my collection of coins? I have some beauties, you know. I once said inadvertently that I was mildly interested and people have been sending them to me ever since. Come over here for a minute." And he led him over to a glass-topped table and started to point out one or two prize specimens. He was well-launched when the butler knocked and announced the Majority Leader and the senior Senator from Utah. At once the whole atmosphere changed in some subtle, overpowering way as the President turned back to greet them. The charm was still there, but a noticeable reserve had come into it, ominous and boding no good for anyone who might get in the way. He also drew himself up a little, but it was probably only their imaginations: it didn't actually make him a whole foot taller.

Nonetheless, it was a moment when he consciously and very definitely set the mood for the discussion, and it was not a mood, they could all sense, that would brook much nonsense or suffer much opposition. He was leaving no doubt at all who he was: he was President of the United States and he intended for them to remember it.

"Brigham," he said, shaking hands gravely, "Bob, it was good of you to come. Please sit down. Harley and I were just looking at my coin collection—after Harley got through admiring my view and trying my desk on for size, that is," he added with a sudden grin that effectively put the Vice President off balance again.

"How *are* you feeling, Mr. President?" Senator Anderson asked quietly, and the knowledge that he was really asking and not just joining in a joke brought the President up short.

"I'm feeling very well," he said abruptly. "What would you like to drink?"

"I don't think I'll have anything, thanks," Brig said, and his host winked at the Vice President.

"Didn't I tell you, Harley?" he asked in a more relaxed and easygoing tone. "I predicted this young firebrand would be all sobriety and seriousness when he got here, and so he is."

"It seems a serious matter to me, Mr. President," Brigham Anderson said in the same quiet voice, and the Chief Executive started to make some sharp rejoinder and then thought better of it as the Majority Leader interposed smoothly.

"I'm sure it's serious to all of us, Brig," he said comfortably. "I think I'll have a scotch and soda if I may, Mr. President."

"Sure thing," the President said, fixing him one and then dropping into his chair and putting his feet up on the desk. "Now, then, Brigham, what's on your mind?"

The Senator from Utah studied him for a moment before replying politely but with complete firmness.

"I resent your tone, Mr. President," he said. "I feel you're patronizing me and I regard this as much too serious for that."

Bob Munson said, "For Christ's sake!" in an exaggeratedly exasperated voice, but the President did not flare up as he obviously expected and so the diversion proved unnecessary. Instead he returned Brig's look with interest for several seconds, studying him quietly before he spoke.

"Very well, Senator," he said finally, taking his feet off the desk, straightening up, and leaning forward, "you do it your way."

"First," Brigham Anderson said with a grim little smile, "I should say that your remarks at the banquet were hardly conducive to a friendly discussion of this business."

"That's right," the President agreed pleasantly, "but they were certainly conducive to a hell of a good press, and that's what I was after. And that," he added with satisfaction, "is what I got. Right?"

"Is that all you see in this, a good press?" Brig asked curiously. The President looked at him impassively.

"I see it as a problem in strategy," he said, "and as such, I have a feeling I'm ahead. How do you feel, Brigham?"

His young guest looked thoughtfully out the window for a moment, into the quiet night, past the lighted Monument to the lights of Virginia across the river. Then he got up abruptly and went over to the bar.

"I think I'll have a ginger ale," he explained and the President laughed in a friendly way.

"That's better," he said. "Put something in it. We're all friends here."

"No, I'll just have ginger ale," Brig said, and the Vice President spoke up suddenly.

"That's all I'm having, Brig," he said, rather loudly. "Good for you."

"Good for you, too, Harley," the President said dryly, and a dangerous little glint came swiftly into his eyes and went away again.

"Seriously, Brig," he said, "how else should I look at it? I don't know up to this moment any reason at all why I shouldn't feel the way I do. You haven't told me anything yet, have you?"

"All right," Senator Anderson said, sitting down again and cradling the ginger ale glass in his hands. "I will. I didn't take this action last night just for the hell of it, you know, or just because I'm a hardnosed, stubborn little bastard. I got a phone call."

"Good," the President said encouragingly. "Who was it from?"

"James Morton," the Senator from Utah said, and Harley gasped and upset his glass, the Majority Leader uttered a profane exclamation of surprise, and only the President appeared quite, quite calm. Around his eyes, however, little lines of strain were suddenly present and when he spoke he sounded tired.

"Who is he?" he asked, and when Brig gave him the name, he shook his head in what appeared to be bemused disbelief.

"Well, I'll be damned," he said slowly. "Who would have thought? Who put him up to it?" he asked shrewdly, and Brigham Anderson frowned.

"Apparently just his own conscience," he said. "I asked him, but he insisted he had just gotten to thinking about it and decided it was his patriotic duty to let me know. So, you see, I did have something to go on and I then did what seemed to be best under the circumstances, which was to hold the hearings open if we needed them and then clam up until I could talk to you. I really only wanted to help you and the party, Mr. President," he said with a rather helpless little laugh. "That's really all I had in mind, even though you've all been giving me hell all day long for it."

The President looked more kindly and spoke in a much more friendly and fatherly way.

"I'm sure you did, Brigham," he said. "I'm sure you did, and now that I understand it better, I want you to know how much I appreciate it. What a comedy of errors it has all been! All this needless criticism and antagonism and controversy, and all because you were trying to do the right thing." He shook his head wonderingly. "I guess that's Washington for you."

"It hasn't been so very pleasant, really," Senator Anderson said, sounding so young and rueful that Bob Munson reached out and gave his shoulder a friendly squeeze.

"Of course it hasn't," he said, "and we probably all ought to be shot. But why didn't you tell me, Brig? It would have saved so much trouble."

"You know me," Senator Anderson said simply. "I did what I thought was best in the best way I knew how. You must admit you all didn't help very much. Including you, Mr. President."

"I know," the President said apologetically. "Well, I'll just have to make it up to you somehow, Brigham. Maybe Bob and I can do some nice things for Utah one of these days—not as a bribe," he added with a hasty grin, "but just to make up for giving you a rough time . . . Well, now," he said thoughtfully, and they could see his mind clicking along swiftly, assessing the new situation and making plans, "that puts an entirely different light on it. Now that we know what the problem is, we can get to work and take care of it. What would you say if I took him out of Commerce and made him Ambassador to some place as far away as possible—Nepal, maybe? Or no, that would require confirmation by the Senate, wouldn't it? Maybe I could just send him on a special overseas mission for me for a while until it's all blown ov— What's the matter?" he demanded abruptly. "Doesn't that seem feasible to you?"

For a moment there was no reply, because all three of his guests were looking at him with varying degrees of dismay and disbelief. It was Brigham Anderson who finally spoke, and he sounded quite crushed and as though after climbing up a long hill he had suddenly found himself back down at the bottom with it to do all over again.

"You understand what I have told you, Mr. President," he said with almost painful slowness. "This man is James Morton. He is the man who met with Bob Leffingwell in a Communist cell in Chicago. The witness Gelman was telling the truth. There was a Communist cell and your nominee for Secretary of State was in it. He lied to the subcommittee about it. He lied to the whole world about it. Doesn't that suggest anything to you?"

The President studied him again thoughtfully for a second and then he smiled.

"It suggests to me exactly what I have been saying," he said, "that I should send him somewhere where he'll be out of the way for a while so we can go ahead and wind up the nomination and get Bob on the job. I'm glad you've told me about it, and now I'll take the necessary steps, so you won't need to worry about it any more. I'm sorry for the injustice I did you and I'll make it up to you. Is there anything more we should say about it?"

"Mr. President" Bob Munson said, sounding rather dazed. "Mr. President, I can't let you——"

"I'm not asking you, Bob," the President said softly. "I'm asking the man who has us in pawn. Well, what about it, Brig? Have you anything else to suggest?"

"I think——" Harley began, but the President looked suddenly genuinely angry, and the Vice President stopped.

"I repeat," he said in the same soft way, "I'm asking our young friend. What about it, Brigham?"

Senator Anderson gave him a bitter look and spoke in a bitter voice.

"You know what about it," he said with contempt. "You know what about it. You're just teasing me. You think you can play with me like a cat with a mouse. Well, you can't. There's just one honest thing to do under the circumstances and that's withdraw the nomination. *Withdraw it!* That's what you should do and stop playing your damned games with me." And he glared angrily at the President, who smiled back.

"Lots of spirit," he said. "Just lots. Calm down, Brigham. I just wanted to know where we stand."

"Mr. President," Senator Munson said bluntly, "I'm going to have to ask you to be more serious about this myself, or I'm going to be inclined to side with Brig if a real showdown comes. This isn't kid stuff, and I'd suggest we act accordingly."

"Would you, now?" the President said with a mock huffiness. "Well, you calm down too, Robert. Everybody calm down. I didn't really think any of you would go for it, but I just wanted to throw it out and see."

"So if we did, you wouldn't have to take the honorable course and withdraw Leffingwell," Senator Anderson said grimly. The President laughed.

"You youngsters do love to throw around the adjectives," he said. "Honorable. Dishonorable. Which is which, Brigham? Suppose you tell me . . . Now see here," he said with sudden force, leaning forward to emphasize his words. "Let me admit that it is quite possible that my nominee for Secretary of State is a liar, in this particular instance. But on the other hand, look at it this way. What are we up against, in this world? An extremely tough proposition, an extremely tricky adversary, an enemy that must be dealt with by every device available to the human mind. Here is a character that, on the record and on the face of it and at first blush, my angry young friend, appears to be unreliable and untrustworthy and dishonorable. Yet look at him for a moment from another point of view. Why has he shown these characteristics? Because he wants to protect a reputation carefully built over the years, a record of public service that I think we all agree has been forthright and honorable, whether one agrees with his social philosophies or not. Now. Is it not possible that a mind that self-protective, a mind that strong—yes, if you like, a mind that arrogant and unyielding—may be just exactly what we need in dealing with the Russians? Isn't it possible that exactly those qualities that have enabled him to go through a public hearing under the eyes of the whole world and deny his own past without ever turning a hair may be exactly the sort of qualities that would enable him to give the Russians blow for blow and match them iron for iron? Consider him that way and tell me how positive you are that you are right."

And he sat back in his chair and again put his feet on the desk, fiddling with a bronze letter-opener while his listeners did just as he had suggested and thought about his thesis. Finally Bob Munson sighed.

"Mr. President," he said, "you're the greatest man I've ever known for turning an argument inside out and making it say what it doesn't say. I think any ordinary mortal would have some difficulty in portraying duplicity as a strength, or even considering it as such, but you seem to have managed."

"Presidents aren't ordinary mortals," Brigham Anderson said shortly. "That's what he'll tell you."

"That's right," their host agreed, quite without egotism. "Ordinary mortals don't reach this chair. But let's don't get off on philosophizing about Presidents. Let's stick to Leffingwell. How do you answer my argument? We have a tough job to fill; we've got a tough mind to fill it. Whatever you think of his conduct before the subcommittee, the one thing you couldn't call it is weak, right? He was in there fighting every inch of the way, and he didn't yield one iota. Is that what we need to meet the Russians, or is it some wishy-washy old fuddy-duddy like Howie Sheppard, who has outlived his usefulness ten times over? You just bear in mind the fact that when you sit in this house you have to look at the whole wide world when you make your judgment on something, and then you tell me. I'm waiting."

And he swiveled around in his chair until he was staring out the window at the Monument, so that all they had was a view of the back of his head and the powerful set of his shoulders. At that moment the Monument floodlights went out and they all looked at their watches instinctively.

"Must be midnight," the President said in a casual tone. "I'm two minutes fast." He set it and continued staring out the window while the Vice President poured himself another ginger ale and the Senators from Michigan and Utah exchanged a quizzically hopeless look.

"Mr. President," Brig said finally. "I won't buy it. I just won't buy it."

"Won't buy it?" the President said, swiveling back. "Won't buy it? You have a better argument, perhaps? Look," he said vigorously. "I've been over that transcript with a fine-tooth comb, just like the rest of you, and if there was one thing Arly Richardson proved and the witness supported it was that this little den of iniquity in Chicago was basically rather innocent, correct? It was an error in judgment, a mistake that perhaps shouldn't have been allowed to occur; but it did occur. What is the man to do, destroy himself when he stands on the eve of his greatest public service, by admitting that it occurred? Which of us is so perfect he can judge? Are you, Brigham? You never did anything dishonorable yourself? You never did anything you might be ashamed of now, that might ruin your career if it could be proven against you now, even though it may be utterly immaterial in judging the kind of man you have become and the kind of public servant you are? Are you that perfect?" He stared at him challengingly, and there flashed through the Majority Leader's mind the sickening thought, *He knows.* "Are you that perfect?" he repeated. "Maybe so, but by God, I'm not. And I don't pretend I am, either, my self-righteous young friend."

"I don't mean to sound self-righteous," Brig said finally in a lonely voice. "I've thought of all the things you say. I know I'm not perfect. But somebody has to judge, in this world, and I've been elected to do it."

"We've all been elected to do it," the President told him bluntly, "and I most of all. My charter runs from Hawaii to Cape Cod and the Gulf to Alaska. Yours is bounded by the state of Utah. Are you saying your right to judge is superior to mine, or that your judgment is superior to mine?"

"No," Brig said with a sort of desperate quietness, "I'm not saying that. You're trapping me in words, now, and you're clever enough to do it, I expect. All I know is that you have named to conduct and in large measure influence our foreign policy in a time of great peril a man who is demonstrably untrustworthy and dishonest. There is proof of this available, and I happen to have it. I know you're a lot more your own Secretary of State than many Presidents have been, but there still are a lot of day-to-day things he'd be deciding that you wouldn't know about. How could we ever trust him? For the sake of the country I can't let you go through it. I must ask that this nomination be withdrawn."

"For the sake of the country," the President said with equal quietness, "I must say that this nomination will stand, and that it must be confirmed."

"Brig," Bob Munson said in a desperate last effort to placate, "are you quite sure the President doesn't have a point, and really a very valid one, considering all the circumstances?"

The Senator from Utah turned abruptly to the Vice President, sitting low in his chair as if hoping to stay out of it entirely; but as it turned out, he wasn't being craven.

"Harley," Brig said, "what do you think? Am I being too bullheaded? Is he right? Am I wrong?"

"You're right," said the Vice President with a firmness that surprised them. "I think you're entirely right." Then he sounded less positive. "On the other hand . . ." he began, and his voice trailed away.

"On the other hand," the President took him up on it quickly, "you can understand just as well as I can what I'm faced with, Harley. Suppose you were sitting here"—and he spoke with a sudden naked bitterness that startled and moved them all—"yes, let me state it in the terms all the ghouls in town are thinking of right now—suppose I died and you became President. You know very well that your whole approach to this would change. You can imagine pretty well, I expect, just what your position would be. It would be the same as mine, wouldn't it?"

"I——" Harley began, and stopped.

"Wouldn't it?" the President demanded, and the Vice President gave him a look compounded of reluctance and trepidation and understanding and something else that his host could hardly stand to see, sympathy.

"It probably would," the Vice President admitted in a low voice. "It probably would."

"All right, then," the President said. He looked very tired and the room was very still until he spoke again. It was in a voice that sounded defeated, and such is the nature of that office that Harley and Brig immediately felt that they must build up his confidence again, restore his spirit, help him to face things, since so much depended upon him and so greatly did they feel the necessity that he lead.

"I guess you've beaten me, Brigham," he confessed with a rueful smile. "I really haven't much of an argument, at that, and I really couldn't defend it before the country if you cared to disclose what you know. So I guess I've got to yield."

At this both the Vice President and the Senator from Utah looked pleased and overwhelmingly relieved, but the Majority Leader felt an ominous prickling of the hairs on the back of his neck. This wasn't the President he knew, and he felt a fearsome premonition as though he were watching a rattlesnake carefully disposing itself in position to strike. But there was nothing he could do about it, except determine with grim intensity that the President would never get from him confirmation of what he apparently thought he knew about the Senator from Utah.

"Well, Mr. President," Brig said in a tone of such quick acceptance and great relief that it revealed how much tension he had been under, "I want you to know that I think that's just fine. I really do. It's the only possible solution, it seems to me, that we could reach for the sake of the country. I'm awfully happy you agree, and I'm sure it can be done in a way that won't look like a retreat. Make him your special trouble shooter, if you like, or a roving ambassador or something, so he can still help you. But send somebody else up for State, and I promise you, I'll do everything I can to get his confirmation through right away. We all will, won't we, Bob?"

"Sure we will, Brig," Senator Munson said, feeling as though he were in a dream. "Of course."

"Do me one favor, Brigham," the President said. "This can't be done overnight, you know how that would look. Give me until Monday, will you? Make another announcement to the press—in fact, you can call them from here, why don't you? Tell them you've met with me and we've talked it over and have agreed on a solution—I'd appreciate it if you didn't tell them what it was, yet—and that accordingly you've decided to postpone reopening the hearings until Monday. That ought to be sufficient to do it. Then by Monday maybe I'll have been able to think of somebody else and have the name up there for you."

"Good," Brigham Anderson said, his voice becoming more happy by the moment, for his fears had proved groundless, the President could be trusted after all, he did have the country's interests at heart and he was worthy of Brig's basically quite idealistic concept of him. "That's what I'll do, and then we can rush it right through on Monday."

"Fine," the President said. "Call them right now," he suggested, offering one of the phones on his desk, and as Brig did so, first the wire services and then the morning papers, the *Times,* the *Herald Tribune,* the Washington *Post* and the Baltimore *Sun,* the President remained seated, looking subdued and even a little dazed, smiling from time to time in a rather beseeching way at the Vice President. He did not, however, meet the eyes of the Majority Leader, who got up suddenly in the midst of the telephoning and mixed himself a very heavy scotch and soda. He was quite sure he was going to need it.

"Well, Mr. President," Brig said as he concluded the calls, rising and holding out his hand, "I am awfully glad this has worked out as it has. I was sure we could reach agreement on it. I was sure you would do the right thing." A genuine emotion came suddenly into his voice. "It makes me proud to belong to the same party and to acknowledge you as leader," he said.

"Well, thank you, Brigham," the President said, seeming to revive both in spirits and in fatherliness. "Harley, I think your car followed us over from the hotel, didn't it? Maybe you can drop our young friend off in Spring Valley on your way home."

"The Statler," Brig said. "My car is over there."

"Yes, I can," the Vice President said, sounding rather puzzled at this sudden collapse of controversy. "It's all settled, then?" he asked, tentatively.

"Sewed up," the President said matter-of-factly. "Keep it under your hat, of course, you old gabble-mouth. Otherwise it will be all over town in ten minutes."

"Not from me," the Vice President said, looking a little starchy for a second, and the President poked him in the ribs.

"This man always believes everything I say," he said. The Majority Leader suddenly snorted right out loud.

"Don't we all?" he asked in a peculiar sarcastic tone.

"Stick around a bit, Bob," his host suggested easily. "I want to go over some of these names with you and see what we come up with."

"Must I?" Senator Munson asked in the same strange voice, and the President suddenly looked annoyed.

"Yes," he said coldly.

The Majority Leader shrugged. "As you say. Brig," he said, shaking hands fervently, "it was a great fight and you won it. Or did you?"

"I don't regard it as that," his young colleague said seriously. "It's much too important."

"Oh yes," Bob Munson said in a tone Senator Anderson couldn't fathom. "Oh my, yes."

"I'll talk to you in the morning," Brig said with a smile. "I think you've done a little too much celebrating tonight. Come on, Harley."

"Good night, Bob," the Vice President said. "Good night, Mr. President. I'm glad it worked out so smoothly."

"So am I, Harley," the President said pleasantly. "Come down again soon. I really mean it."

"I will," the Vice President promised, looking pleased. "I'll do that."

"Good," the President said, patting them both affectionately on the back as they went out the door. "I'll be looking forward to it. Sleep tight, Brigham. You come down, too."

"I will," Brig promised.

After they had left there was silence for a while, the President thoughtfully fiddling with his letter opener, the Majority Leader thoughtfully drinking.

Then the President spoke in a businesslike tone. "I think you'd better show me that picture. This was passed along to me at dinner." And he tossed over a folded piece of paper which Bob Munson slowly opened.

"Bob has a picture of Brig you ought to see," it said. "T.D."

The Majority Leader tore it across once and dropped it into one of the ash trays on the desk.

"God damn him," he said slowly. "And you for a treacherous and deceitful man."

"Well," the President said with a tight little smile, "I've been called that by experts, and I guess you're one of them. Now suppose you hand it over."

"I haven't got it," Bob Munson said. "I tore it up, just like that note."

"Oh no," the President said. "Oh no. You've got it, and the reason you've got it is that you've known subconsciously all along that you were going to give it to me. You know Brig and you knew we'd need it when all was said and done. So let's have it."

"You're a fearfully shrewd man," the Senator said, as though he were finally appreciating the fact in all its magnitude. "I wonder if you've been good for the country."

The President shrugged.

"I have to think so. I couldn't keep going otherwise. Which particular facet of our young friend's character does this picture illuminate?"

"An unfortunate one," the Majority Leader said, "and one I'm quite sure he put behind him a dozen years ago."

"Ah," the President said softly. "Just like Bob Leffingwell. No wonder he's so vindictive about it."

"He isn't vindictive, for Christ's sake," Senator Munson said angrily. "He's only doing what he thinks is best for the country."

"Who doesn't?" the President asked dryly. He looked gray, the Majority Leader thought, and very tired, but still with a force of personality that was ten times that of most men. "Well?"

"I want to exact one promise," Senator Munson said wearily. "Not that I believe your word is worth anything, but just for the record."

"You don't want me to hurt him," the President said thoughtfully. "Yet what other outcome is possible, obdurate as he is, and now that you are giving me the means?"

"It isn't necessary to hurt him," Bob Munson said desperately. "You wanted something to threaten him with. All right, threaten him, if you feel you have to. But I want you to let it stop there. It doesn't have to go any further than that. A threat will be enough, with this."

"What in the hell is it?" the President demanded in some exasperation. "You make it sound like the end of the world."

"It could be the end of his world," the Majority Leader said. "I want your word, Mr. President."

His host stared at him for a moment and in some insane way the Majority Leader felt they were the last two men on earth, so silent was the great historic house and so devoid of any indication of other life as the clock neared 1 A.M.

"For seven years," the President said softly, "I have had just one aim and one purpose—to serve my country. I have allowed nothing—*nothing*— to stand in the way of my concept of how best to do it. Nor will I now. I have just one loyalty, in this office, and it so far transcends anything you could conceive of—any of you could conceive of, except perhaps the other Presidents, and maybe not even some of them—that it just isn't even in the same universe, let alone the same world . . . No, I won't give you my word not to do something, when it may be the very thing I will have to do to protect the country. Now let me see the picture."

The Majority Leader felt for one wild second that he should turn and run, that he was so close to the absolute essence of the American Presidency, in the presence of a dedication so severe, so lonely, and so terrible, so utterly removed from the normal morality that holds society together, that he should flee from it before the revelation proved too shattering and some great and dreadful damage was done to Brig, to him, to the President, the country, and the world. But men do not often act on such impulses, which are immediately thwarted by reminders that this is the workaday world, after all, and here they are, after all, and such gestures would be completely irrational, after all, and what in the hell are they thinking about, after all; and so they do not do them. Instead with a bitter expression on his face he extracted the envelope from his pocket and tossed it on the President's desk with much the same desperate unhappiness that Mr. Justice Davis had initially felt when giving it to him.

There was a long silence while the President studied it, and somewhere down the hall outside a Seth Thomas clock went, "Bong!" once for one o'clock. The Majority Leader jumped, but his host gave no sign. At last he put the picture quietly back in its envelope, placed it neatly to one side on the blotter, and stood up.

"It's late, Bob," he said, "and tomorrow is another day. I'm quite tired, really; it's been a very long day for me and I'm stretched out to my limit, which seems to be getting more restricted all the time. Thank you for coming by, and thanks for all your help on the nomination. I'll be in touch with you. I've got to get to bed and get some sleep now or I won't be worth much in the morning."

"What will you do with it?" the Majority Leader asked in a low voice, and the President looked at him gravely.

"Who can say?" he said. "Certainly not I, at one o'clock in the morning."

"You never did intend to change your position on the nomination in the slightest, did you?" Bob Munson asked bitterly. His host held out his hands side by side, palms down, and looked at them for a moment, well-manicured, competent, strong, and not really trembling so very much more than was normal for his age.

"Never," he said quietly. "Good night, Bob. I appreciate your coming by."

"You try to keep the world the same by being polite," the Majority Leader said, "but you can't do it, it isn't the same. It won't ever be the same again."

"Get some sleep, Bob," the President said in a kindly voice, taking his arm and escorting him to the door. "Take the elevator down and I'll call a car and have them run you home."

"I don't want to go home," Senator Munson said as if to himself. "I want to go to Dolly's."

"Very well," the President said without surprise. "Tell the chauffeur and he'll take you."

"Thank you," the Majority Leader said elaborately. "Thank you for nothing, nothing at all."

"Give my best to Dolly, Bob," the President said impassively. "Good night."

And so the senior Senator from Utah felt very happy and very secure and as though all the cares of the world had rolled away, and off his shoulders, and would not come back. The Vice President, too, seemed much relieved by the outcome, explaining again on the brief run to the Statler that he could see the President's point of view but that he really felt at heart that it was best under the circumstances to withdraw Bob Leffingwell's name and get someone else. He was a little surprised, he said, that the President had yielded so easily, for it was his own im-

ADVISE AND CONSENT

pression that he possessed a much more tenacious character than that; but he agreed with Brig that the surrender apparently was genuine, that it was evidently based upon a real perception of what was best for the country in the wake of James Morton's appearance, and that the solution Brig had suggested seemed much the best. They agreed as they arrived at the hotel that this instant ability to change course and move forward along new lines dictated by patriotism and integrity was an example of what made the Chief Executive the great President he was, and Brig said again with a perfectly genuine sincerity as he bade the Vice President thanks and good night that he was proud to have him in the White House and leader of his party. When he reached home he tiptoed in and kissed Pidge, who turned over, mumbled something and went right back to sleep, and then went into the bedroom to find Mabel still awake. He looked so handsome and so relieved and so happy about the way the evening had gone that she too felt suddenly an equal happiness and relief, and they turned to one another eagerly without any complicating worries and then drifted off to sleep with a sense of peace they had not known together for some time.

And at Vagaries a White House limousine deposited the Majority Leader at the door and his hostess started to greet him with a jest about the lateness of the late, late show, only to have it die on her lips as she saw how very unhappy and tortured he looked. So without further word she drew him in and said no more about it until much later in the small hours of the morning when he finally told her what had happened and his fears concerning it, and she too felt afraid for him and for Brig and aware suddenly that no matter how complacent one might become about a man in the White House, no one ever really knew his full capabilities until the chips were down and then it was often too late.

And in his study the President, following through on the groundwork he had laid in a telephone call earlier in the day, pulled up the battered old portable typewriter on which he pecked out many of his speeches and taking a plain envelope, typed a name on it and started to insert the picture Senator Munson had given him. Then the thought striking him that while the addressee was shrewd, he should perhaps leave an implication that would amount to an order, he tore up the plain envelope with quick, decisive movements, took another bearing the simple legend, "The White House, Washington" in the upper left-hand corner, typed the name once again, once more inserted the picture and this time sealed the envelope. After that he walked all alone through the empty hallways of the great silent house to the servants' quarters, scared his valet out of seven years' growth by waking him from a sound sleep in the middle of the night, and told him to get dressed and deliver the message at once.

Back upstairs he took his usual good-night look across the Ellipse to the Monument rising dim and stately to the stars, made his usual last

check of the late news dispatches to see where the unhappy world was hurting this night, and went along to bed; aware as he did so that he had stayed up much too late and done much too much and that his heart was pounding painfully much too hard as a consequence.

6

"You certainly sound chipper," a familiar voice said behind him as he came whistling along the corridor in the Old Office Building, and he turned to find Orrin Knox bearing down upon him under a full head of steam, briefcase bulging, coat flapping, a look of purposeful determination on his face. For some reason on this particular morning—probably just because the world was back in place and all was well and everything was set to rights again—this spectacle, which he had seen so often, struck him as very amusing and he held out his hand with a welcoming grin.

"I am," he said happily. "Yes, I am."

"Why?" Senator Knox demanded bluntly. "Soft soap at the White House? You must have won, you look too smug to have lost. What did he tell you he was going to do?"

"I'm not in a position to tell you," Brig said amicably. "He's going to announce it as soon as the arrangements can be worked out."

"Certainly not withdraw the nomination," Orrin said positively. "If he told you that, I wouldn't believe him. Don't you believe him, either."

"Just between us, I think he was telling the truth," Senator Anderson said, and his companion made a scornful sound as they swung along the hall together.

"That two-bit liar?" he said. "Don't make me laugh."

"Well," Brig said mildly, "you have a more special reason than most of us to distrust him, of course."

"Oh, hell," Orrin said shortly. "If you mean the convention, that has nothing to do with it. I knew his quality long before that, when I first met him at the Governors' Conference, and seven years in the White House haven't changed it. Did you get anything in writing?"

"No, I didn't," Brig said, sounding amused. "Should I have?"

"Yes," Orrin said tersely. "Are you going to the Capitol?"

"Yes, Appropriations," Brig said. "I have to testify on a project we're interested in out home. Where are you heading?"

"Foreign Relations," Senator Knox said. "I think Howie is going to be up again testifying on the foreign-aid bill. Tom can't be there, and I'm afraid hardly anybody else will be, either. I happen to be free and I don't want poor Howie to feel entirely neglected."

"That's kind of you," Brig said with a grin. "My sentiments exactly. I'll drop in too, after I get through at Appropriations."

"Good," Orrin said as they emerged into the sunlight and started across Constitution Avenue to the Capitol. "I want to say one thing to you,

Brigham," he added, suddenly serious. "I know this man far better than you do. If anything goes wrong and he backs out on you, I want you to let me know about it and we'll fight it together. O.K.?"

"He won't back out," Brig said comfortably. "I think he's more honorable than you think he is."

"It doesn't have anything to do with honor," Orrin said shortly, "though I don't think he has any. It involves being President, and that goes deeper."

"I'm not worried," Brig said. "He promised in front of Bob and Harley."

"I wouldn't trust him," Senator Knox said stubbornly.

"You have to trust him sometimes," Brig said, in a mood rather far from yesterday morning's talk with Lafe.

"Well," Orrin Knox said shortly. "You remember what I say. If something goes wrong, you come to me. Hear?"

"'Hear?'" Brigham Anderson mimicked. "You've gotten to sound just like a Southerner. 'Hear?'"

"Well, I mean it," Orrin said firmly. "I have to be out in the state over the weekend on a speaking trip, but I'll be back on Monday, and I want you to let me know."

"Yes, Pa," Brig said with a smile. "I hear."

"All right," Orrin said. "My God, look at the tourists."

"They have a nice day for it," Brig said, and so they did. The sky was blue, the air was crisp, the sun was bright, a high-school band was playing in the distance on the House steps in the warm, searching wind, and at the foot of the Hill the Taft Carillon was observing the hour of 10 A.M. Near at hand in the ancient oaks of the Plaza and high on the Capitol dome a flock of crows bickered back and forth.

"Caw, caw!" said one on the dome in a disapproving tone.

"*Caw!*" replied another scornfully from the oaks.

Orrin smiled.

"And in the streets," he said in bum Shakespeare, "'tis said the crows do talk upon the Capitol. Isn't that a bad omen?"

His young colleague laughed in a completely relaxed and happy way. "Not today," he said. "There aren't any bad omens today."

But as they went on into the great building and parted to go to their respective committees, he ran into one, and it was not so pleasant. Fred Van Ackerman was coming out of the restaurant just as he went by, and when he saw the Senator from Utah he stopped and a peculiar expression of amusement, spite, triumph, and elaborate pity crossed his face.

"You poor bastard," he murmured, just loud enough so Brig could hear him.

"What in the hell is the matter with you, Fred?" Senator Anderson demanded in exasperation. "Aren't you ever pleasant? What's wrong now?"

"You're upsetting the tourists, Senator," Fred said sarcastically as he brushed by. "Let's be nice."

"Oh, run along," Brig said disgustedly.

"Sure thing, Brig," Senator Van Ackerman said with exaggerated politeness. "Anything you say."

Now what the hell, Brig thought as he turned away; what bug was
biting Freddy this time? There was no way of telling, however, and after a
moment he shook his head in a baffled way and pushed on through the
tourists who parted in some awe to let him through. It was true that the
Senator from Wyoming had looked pleased in some indefinable, secret,
sneaking sort of way; but the reasons for that could be as numerous as his
own twisted thoughts, and the Senator from Utah decided there was no
point in trying to figure it out. He shrugged and tried to forget it, though
it was hard to shake off entirely the unpleasant blight it had cast abruptly
upon the auspicious day.

In Appropriations, he was pleased to note, the mood was much more
friendly. Seab was presiding, flanked by Raymond Robert Smith of California, tall and dapper, and Alec Chabot of Louisiana, sleek and well-
groomed and looking as though he knew where the bodies were buried,
which he usually did. The hearing was being held in the small committee
room just off the hallway by the back elevator, and this inevitably lent a
certain enforced intimacy that made for a relaxed and casual atmosphere.
There weren't many spectators, but there was a sizeable delegation from
the press, attracted by word that he would be there. Arriving as he did a
little late, with the hearing already under way and the direct interview
barred by circumstances, he was immediately bombarded with notes when
he took his seat at one end of the press table and prepared to wait his
turn to testify. "Can you tell us anyg abt W.H. mtg?" AP wanted to know.
"Need soonest comment on report you and Prez agreed on new SecState,"
UPI advised him tersely. "Welcome back," the *Times* wrote. "Undstand
Leff out. Anytg to it?"

Up on the rim where the committee sat there was a little stir and the
chairman leaned forward and spoke with a gentle sarcasm.

"If you would like to take the stand right now, Senator," he said
softly, "maybe we could release you to your friends in the press early
enough for them to make the afternoon papers with their stories."

"I'm not going to tell them anything, Mr. Chairman," Brig said with a
grin, "so it's immaterial to me."

"Well, then," Seab said with a sleepy smile, "I suppose we might suggest
to them that they abandon this fruitless quest and let us perform our
duties in peace and quietude. I can't really believe—I just can't really
believe—that they are interested in an irrigation project in northern Utah.
Am I wrong, gentlemen?"

"We're interested in anything Brig is interested in, Mr. Chairman," AP
said amicably, and Senator Cooley smiled again.

"Well," he said, "you heard the Senator. It's no use. But of course you

all are welcome to inform yourselves on irrigation, if you like." And he subsided with a bland smile while the witness, an assistant director of the Bureau of Reclamation, completed his testimony. Then with elaborate courtesy he leaned forward again.

"Now, Senator," he said with a little twinkle, "if you will be so kind as to tell our good friends here what you think they ought to know about your project, the committee will be glad to hear it too."

"Thanks, Mr. Chairman," Brig said with a smile. "I won't be long."

And he wasn't, finishing in about ten minutes with a brief statement on why the project was necessary, what it would do for Utah, what it would contribute to the national welfare, and why it was imperative that it be done this year and not be delayed like some other less urgent, less deserving items in the Interior Department appropriation. Seab, who had promised him a week ago that he could have it, was suitably thoughtful and searching in his questions, Alec Chabot and Ray Smith went along with the routine, and in half an hour he was ready to leave after mutual expressions of gratitude, generosity, and esteem.

"I think, if it is agreeable to the committee," Seab said as Brig stood up and gathered together his papers, "that we can recess the hearings for the day."

"Fine with me, Mr. Chairman," Senator Chabot said promptly. "I'm supposed to be in three other places right this minute."

"I have to meet some constituents," Raymond Robert Smith said in his rather elaborate way that just skirted the edge of the overexclamatory. Senator Cooley smiled gently.

"If there is one thing I have learned in fairly long acquaintance with the United States Senate, Senator," he said, "it's to be kind to con-stit-u-ents. Yes, sir. Be very kind to con-stit-u-ents. Senator," he added to Brig, "if you would wait a minute, I'll walk along with you for a little bit, wherever you're going."

"Just down the hall to Foreign Relations," Brig said.

"That will be fine," Seab said, coming down from the dais and taking him by the arm. "Now, gentlemen," he remarked blandly to the reporters who were crowding around and obviously about to join the party, "you may follow but you may not eavesdrop. No, sir. You may follow, but you may not eavesdrop . . . You seem very relaxed this morning, Brigham, sir," he observed as they passed a group of tourists listening to a guide tell them all about Brumidi's paintings of wildlife in the hall. "I trust you had a very nice talk with our great man in the White House?"

"I can't tell you much about it, Seab," Senator Anderson said cheerfully, "except that I am quite content with the way things are going."

The senior Senator from South Carolina gave him a slow, shrewd, appraising look as they neared Foreign Relations and the press crowded close in an attempt to hear.

"Are you?" he asked challengingly. The senior Senator from Utah returned the look confidently.

"I am," he said.

"Well, then," Senator Cooley said with a little smile, "if you are content, I expect I should be content too."

"I think you'd be safe," Brig said, and Seab glanced at him quickly with an expression that looked curiously relieved.

"That's good, Brigham," he said. "I think we're both safe, and I think that's mighty fine, now. I really do. It eases me a lot. It surely does."

"Thanks, Seab," Senator Anderson said, starting into Foreign Relations. "Don't say a word," he said, gesturing with a grin toward the press.

"Oh no," Senator Cooley said with a sudden abrupt laugh, pushing his way through the reporters and shaking his head in response to all their questions. "Oh no. Oh no."

In Foreign Relations' inconvenient committee room, cramped and inadequate but full of tradition, Howie Sheppard and his phalanx—dressed today in a small, neat, discreet brown tartan plaid—were testifying before Orrin Knox, Lafe Smith, John DeWilton, George Hines, three wire-service reporters, six spectators, and five members of the committee staff. Senator Hines was giving him a rather hard time at the moment, asking questions obviously inimical to foreign aid and interspersing them with hearty references to "Howie," in his usual phony good-natured way. The Secretary of State was repelling this not unexpected attack with dignity as the senior Senator from Utah slid into a seat beside Lafe and gave Howie a smile of greeting across the big green-baize table. He thought the Secretary looked rather peculiar for just a second, but Lafe slumped comfortably against his arm and murmured, "Hail the conquering hero comes," behind his hand, and he forgot it.

"No comment," he whispered with a grin, and Lafe nodded knowingly and smiled.

"Well, then, Howie—Mr. Secretary," George Hines was saying unctuously, "if this program is to be continued indefinitely, shouldn't we have some general policy to make better use of it than we have in advancing the interests of the United States?"

"I assume that will be Mr. Leffingwell's problem, not mine," the Secretary replied, a trifle snappishly, and Senator Hines gave an elaborately surprised look at Senator Anderson and asked smoothly, "Mr. Leffingwell? Is it your impression the President is going to leave Mr. Leffingwell's name before the Senate?"

There was a sudden tensing among the reporters, and the little room became quite still. Howie Sheppard looked across the table at his questioner with a face virtually devoid of expression.

"That is my impression," he said.

"But I thought, Howie——" Senator Hines began in rather exaggerated amazement. The Secretary cut him off in midsentence.

"That is my impression," he said again flatly.

"When did you see the President last?" George Hines asked, and Orrin, who was presiding, moved restively in his seat.

"Shortly before I came up here this morning," the Secretary said.

"Did you discuss the matter?" George Hines inquired in a voice that suddenly was quite serious and intent.

"I am not privileged to discuss my private conversations with the President," the Secretary snapped.

"You did, then," George Hines told him. "And he gave you the impression he was contemplating no change."

The Secretary shrugged and, because he was on his way out, permitted himself a sudden candor that startled his audience.

"Who ever knows what the President is contemplating?" he asked.

"I think we've had enough on that subject, Senator," Orrin Knox said sharply.

"I think it's very interesting, Mr. Chairman," Senator Hines said, not at all abashed. "Apparently in spite of what we have been led to believe, the President doesn't have the slightest intention——"

"I don't know what you've been led to believe, Senator," Orrin said bluntly, "but it didn't come from the President, did it?"

"No," Senator Hines agreed blandly.

"And it didn't come from you, did it, Senator?" Orrin demanded, swinging suddenly on Brig, who smiled and only disclosed to Lafe, who had felt his arm grow tense against his as the questioning proceeded, that he was reacting to it much more than he showed.

"No, sir," he said calmly.

"Then I think we'd better get on with this and forget the rumors, George," Senator Knox suggested firmly, and after a moment George Hines grinned.

"Very well, Mr. Chairman," he said. "I just thought it was interesting, that's all."

"No doubt," Orrin said dryly. "Rumors are always more interesting than facts."

"If it is rumor," Senator Hines said, triumphantly having the last word.

After that there was of course no holding the press, who were determined to make Howie talk and surrounded him outside the door for that purpose when he was excused half an hour later. But he remained adamant, and after repeating politely several times for the hastily gathered television cameras that, "I have nothing to add to my testimony before the committee," he summoned his entourage and departed with an air of being bound on missions of high import, as perhaps he was. This left Brig, who had been corralled and asked to stand by, and presently he was standing in the glare of the lights while the tourists gathered and gawked in the hall and Orrin and Lafe, by a tacit agreement, stood impassively at his side.

"Roll 'em," somebody said, and CBS stepped forward with a bulldog air.

"Senator," he said, "you heard Secretary Sheppard's testimony that the President has decided to let Mr. Leffingwell's nomination stand——"

"I didn't hear any such thing," Brig said easily. "I heard an impression, but I didn't hear any fact. Did you?" he asked Orrin, and the senior Senator from Illinois shook his head and said firmly, "I did not."

"Well," CBS amended, somewhat lamely, "at least he left the implication that there might be some doubt about what the President is going to do."

"Did he?" Brig asked impassively.

"How does that conform with your understanding of the situation as expressed by the President last night?" CBS asked doggedly.

"Did you read my statement from the White House last night?" Brig asked.

"Yes, sir," CBS said.

"Did you understand it?" Senator Anderson asked.

"Yes, sir," CBS said, flushing a little.

"I have nothing to add to it," Brig said calmly. "Is that all?"

"Do you expect a statement soon from the President?" NBC asked. Brig hesitated for a moment as Lafe made a little warning movement at his side.

"I would expect he would make his position known in due course," Senator Anderson said.

"Do you expect it to be pleasing to you, Senator?" NBC inquired, and Brig smiled.

"I would expect it to be consistent with the President's usual patriotism and high concept of his office," he said smoothly. "Anything more?"

"Nope," CBS said. "Thank you, Senator."

"My pleasure," Brig said, not without acid.

But as they walked along back to the Office Building, taking, as Lafe said, "the overland route" rather than the subway because they wished to enjoy the beautiful day, he was more concerned than he wished to reveal, even to them. This did not fool them, however, and Orrin with a determined attempt at tact that was so far out of character it was funny talked of the aid bill and the legislative perils it faced this year, while Lafe was full of interest about the Interior appropriation. Just before they parted to go to their offices, with a promise to meet a little later for lunch in the Office Building cafeteria, Lafe asked casually, "By the way, what's with Furious Freddy?"

"What is?" Orrin asked.

"I don't know," Lafe said, "but he got paged out of the restaurant about nine-thirty to take a phone call and came back all excited about something —I mean, not just raving as usual, but really excited."

"Was it local?" Brig asked dryly, raising the topic they had been busily avoiding. "Maybe he got the true word from the White House."

"No, they said long distance," Lafe said.

"Oh, well, who ever knows about Fred?" Orrin asked, dismissing him. "And who gives a damn?"

"My sentiments exactly," Brig agreed with a grin. "See you at lunch."

Back in his office, however, going over his mail and checking on the day's routine, some little warning signal kept recurring in his mind. Fred's expression and his unprovoked nastiness earlier in the morning; Lafe's report of a long-distance phone call. What did they mean? What could they mean? Did they mean anything? And why should he suppose that they had anything to do with the nomination or with him? But he could not quite get the thought out of his mind, and it was still nagging uneasily, for no particular reason he could understand, as he went along half an hour later to lunch.

In the cafeteria the early editions of the *Star* and the *News* were already on the newsstand. LEFFINGWELL FATE UNCERTAIN, the *Star* said cautiously; "AGREEMENT" IN DOUBT . . . WHO WON? the *News* asked in large type on the front page, and in smaller type below, HINT WHITE HOUSE MAY REJECT SENATE DEMAND FOR LEFFING-WELL OUSTER. "It was expected," The *Star* story concluded, "that the question might be further clarified this afternoon at the regular four o'clock briefing of correspondents by the President's press secretary." Brig bought both papers and studied them thoughtfully as he stood in the slowly moving line, while at a nearby table AP, UPI the *Herald Tribune* and the Washington *Post* virtually stopped eating to study him. His expression was completely noncommittal, however, and so was his greeting when he came by with his tray a little later and went on to the back row of tables reserved for Senators. There he found that Orrin and Lafe had been joined by Dick Suvick of Alaska, which cramped conversation some, and so the meal passed in an equally noncommittal fashion. As soon as it was over he went back to his office, checked to find out if the Majority Leader was in, and, ignoring a rather odd reluctance he seemed to note in his voice, went on immediately to see him.

"Mary," he said, and this was the fourth or fifth—or was it the fifth or sixth, he was beginning to lose count—time today that he thought someone had looked at him with an unusual intentness, "is the big boss in?"

"Just a minute, Senator," she said politely. "I'll find out."

"I know he is," Brig said, starting toward the inner office. "I talked to him on the phone a minute ago, remember?"

"So you did," Mary said pleasantly, "but would you mind waiting just a minute?"

"I think I would," he said, suddenly annoyed, and with a rare expression of anger he strode on through the middle office and without bothering to knock opened Bob's door and went in. The Majority Leader was seated at his desk apparently doing nothing, for he looked up slowly when his young colleague entered and made no attempt to pretend that he was reading any of the letters piled high on the desk before him.

"Hello, Brig," he said. "I had an idea it was you. Sit down."

"I told you on the phone it would be," Senator Anderson said shortly; then his manner changed as the temporary annoyance passed. "How are you, Bob?" he asked, more equably. "I see you've got a lot of those, too."

"Oh yes," Senator Munson said.

"What do they want you to do?" Brig asked.

"Mostly confirm Leffingwell," Bob Munson said. His visitor smiled.

"So do mine," he said, "though most of Utah seems to be giving me a general endorsement for whatever I want to do. What have you heard from the President?"

"I haven't," Senator Munson said, and Brigham Anderson looked surprised.

"Somebody seems to have," he said. "The *News* and the *Star* seem to think he's backing out. Is he?"

"Oh no," the Majority Leader said with an odd little expression. "He isn't backing out. He's going through with it."

"Well, that's good," Brig said, feeling and sounding relieved. "I was beginning to get just a little bit worried. I believe him when he gives his word, and all that, but——"

"Did he give his word?" Senator Munson asked with a sort of mock surprise his young friend found puzzling.

"Yes," he said. "Didn't he? At least it was implicit in what he said, I thought."

"Yes, I suppose," Senator Munson said. "What are you worried about?"

"Well, the reports in the *Star* and the *News*," Brig said. "Plus the fact that Howie got very coy in Foreign Relations this morning and as much as said the President wouldn't withdraw the nomination. I'm afraid the press may have gotten the wrong impression, because I didn't feel I could argue with him and tell what I knew, so——"

"That's right, Brig," Bob Munson said, again with a sort of unhappy irony that Senator Anderson found baffling. "Don't tell what you know. That would upset his plans no end, if you did that."

"Well, I won't," Brig promised, "but I'd still like to be sure everything is going the way we planned and that there haven't been any slip-ups."

"It's going as planned," the Majority Leader said, again with a peculiar wryness, "and I don't imagine there will be any slip-ups."

"Did you decide on anybody last night?" Brig asked. "Not that I want to know until the name actually comes up, of course, but just so I'll be able to ignore all the newspaper talk and feel at ease about it. Did you?"

"Oh, Brig," Bob Munson said with a sudden mixture of impatience and what seemed, curiously, to be pain. "Why are you so decent and so——"

He stopped abruptly. "No, we didn't decide on a name last night," he said, sounding almost angry.

"I thought that's why he wanted you to stay," Brig said in a puzzled voice, and the Majority Leader smiled in a strange way. In fact, it suddenly seemed to Brig that everything he was doing and saying this afternoon was strange.

"So he said," Senator Munson said. And he repeated it slowly: "So he said."

"Do you suppose we should call him and—and talk it over?" Brig asked hesitantly, for he was not at all sure, now, what the matter was with Bob or whether he should try to figure it out. He was beginning to think he couldn't.

"I don't think so," the Majority Leader said shortly, not looking at him. "No."

"Bob," Brigham Anderson asked earnestly, "am I offending you in some way? Shall I leave?"

"No, you're not offending me," Senator Munson said, a trifle too loudly. "What makes you think that?"

"I don't know," Brig said, sounding baffled and unhappy. "You seem so sort of—strange today. What's the matter? Have I done something?"

Senator Munson stared intently at the letters before him for a long moment. He did not look up when he spoke.

"No," he said. "You're all right, Brig. It isn't your fault. I'm just—tired from last night, I guess. I don't mean to be unfriendly."

"Well, I hope not," Brig said, trying to restore the conversation to their usual bantering tone, though it didn't quite come off. "I should hate to think I had betrayed my gallant leader."

"You haven't betrayed me," Senator Munson said. "God, no," he added harshly, in a voice Brig couldn't interpret except that he knew it indicated he had really better go. Maybe it's Dolly, he thought; maybe they've had a fight. Maybe that's it.

"Well, thanks Bob," he said, somewhat awkwardly. "I just wanted to get your reassurance that things are still the same as they were last night."

"They haven't changed," Senator Munson said, again with a peculiar little laugh. "You can be sure of that."

"Well, good," Brig said, and he meant it. "If you should be talking to him, you can tell him they haven't changed here, either. I'm keeping my part of the bargain, tell him. He can count on me."

"Brigham," Bob Munson said harshly, "I really do think you had better go now. Please. I'll talk to you tomorrow. I'm not feeling very well today."

"Sure, Bob," Senator Anderson said. "I didn't mean to disturb you," he added apologetically.

"Oh, please," Bob Munson said in a voice that sounded very oddly almost as though he were going to cry. "Oh, please."

"All right, Bob," Brigham Anderson said hastily. "I'm going."

After this conversation, which was not exactly calculated to reassure even though it did tend to allay some of the misgivings about the White House that the press stories had aroused, he went back to his office quite bothered. He didn't know what Bob's problem was, but he had certainly sounded and acted as though he were terribly unhappy about something, and his young colleague, much as he wanted to help, didn't quite know how. If it was a falling out with Dolly, he couldn't, things like that had to be solved by the people concerned and outsiders never helped much; if it was something to do with the Senate, maybe Bob would let him know presently, and then he would be able to help. Apparently it did not concern the nomination, for Bob seemed to think that was moving along as planned, and for that Brig felt grateful and relieved, even though he felt now that it had been foolish of him to doubt the President's conduct even for a moment. It had been difficult not to, with Howie's peculiar reaction in the committee; the unpleasant little brush with Fred, who had made such a point of being Bob Leffingwell's noisiest champion; and then the press rumors, not based on too many specific facts but, he knew from experience, based on a pretty accurate assessment of the mood of the moment in Washington plus a logical projection of what it might lead to. Evidently in this case, in view of the Majority Leader's statements, the projection was mistaken, but that had not made it any less disturbing for a little while.

As he reached his office the thought occurred to him that even though Bob had seemed to recommend against it, it might be helpful all around to let the President know directly that he was still standing loyally by their agreement, and to tell him, also, that he wasn't letting himself be upset by the press reports—that, in short, he believed in him. Certainly that couldn't do any harm, and it might make the President feel better. But when he called the White House he was told the President was busy and so had to be content with a promise by his assistant that he would return the call later in the afternoon when he was free.

For approximately two hours after that he was busy in his office attending to the business of the constituency, answering letters, checking various projects with departments downtown, studying up on hearings and upcoming legislation, gradually relaxing from the worry he had felt about Bob as the result of their uneasy talk. Orrin called once, to say that he was sure his own skepticism earlier was probably unwarranted, and to offer the reassurance that all was well, something Brig knew he really didn't mean, but he was amused and touched by the consideration. The proprietor of "Meet the Press" called and asked him to appear on Sunday afternoon, and after a moment's thought he agreed, for surely everything would be in the clear by then. Lafe called twice, once to say much the same thing Orrin had, and once to repeat a joke he thought Brig might feel like laughing at; he did, and appreciated not only the joke but the friendship and concern behind it. Somewhere around three, struck by a sudden thought, he tried to reach Tommy Davis and kid him out of whatever had been troubling him last night, but the Justice's secretary, after an awkward hesitation, said he wasn't in. The President, apparently swamped with work, which was certainly understandable, had not called by four thirty, when the AP did.

"Senator," he said, "our White House man has just phoned me about the briefing they had down there at four. Somebody asked Pete whether the President was withdrawing the nomination and his answer was, 'No comment.' This has aroused a lot of speculation, as you can imagine, and I was wondering if you cared to comment yourself?"

"No, I don't see why I should," Brig said with a laugh. "If 'no comment' is good enough for Pete, it's good enough for me." Then just to make conversation and keep his refusal from sounding too ungracious, he asked, "Was that all they talked about at the briefing or was there some real news out of it?"

"Nothing much," AP said. "A few appointments, tomorrow's schedule, the usual odds and ends. Some assistant secretary has gone overseas on a special mission for the President—Commerce, I think—and they're still trying to firm up a date for the Queen to come over in the fall. It was pretty routine stuff, on the whole. We can't get anything out of you on the nomination, then?"

"That's right," Brigham Anderson said slowly in a voice his listener thought was suddenly quite peculiar, "you can't."

But even then, for he was a reliable young man who kept his promises, it did not really occur to him to believe that the President was not keeping his. There was a momentary shock, true enough, but it was swiftly succeeded by the reflection that after all, it might be entirely logical for James Morton to be sent away if the nomination were to be withdrawn, perhaps much more logical than that he should stay in Washington, a potential time bomb who might, under the impetus of emotion and the excitement of swiftly moving events, go off in some fashion that would reveal to the press that there was much more to the President's decision than met the eye. It was only when he tried to reach the Majority Leader again for confirmation of this assumption, and was told by Mary in what he could sense was a lie she did not enjoy that he was not in, that he began to feel an increasing uneasiness. Casting about for some way to alleviate it, he thought of calling Harley, and did so; but the Vice President wasn't any better informed than he was.

"I think you're entirely right in the way you've assessed it, Brig," he said, "and I could try to call him and confirm it for you if you want, but you know how it is. You could probably get through to him just as fast as I could, in spite of all that buddy-buddy talk last night."

"There *was* quite a lot of talk last night, wasn't there?" Senator Anderson observed somewhat ruefully. "I'm glad to hear you weren't taken in by it."

"Oh, he's charming, all right," the Vice President said, "and I still feel he was sincere about it. But you know how he is. You have to be careful."

"Yes," Brig said, "you have to be careful. Well, thank you, Harley. I guess there wouldn't be much point in trying to call him again."

"I'm sure everything is all right," the Vice President said. "He's just working it out in his own way."

"Maybe that's it," Brig said with an irony that was not lost on Harley, who became very fatherly and told him to stop worrying, everything would be fine.

"I wish I could think so," Brig said, sounding young and uncertain again, "but now I'm not entirely sure."

"I tell you what, Brigham," Harley said then. "If you feel by tomorrow that something has gone wrong and it isn't going the way we were given to understand, you call me and we'll get in the press and tell them the full story together."

The magnitude of this offer, with all its enormous political connotations and implications, left the Senator from Utah speechless for a moment. He spoke finally in a tone of deep gratitude.

"That's wonderful of you, Harley," he said, "but I couldn't ask you to do that. He would never forgive you."

"I don't care," the Vice President said, and he sounded as though he meant it, as though last night had been for him too a fundamental turning point of some sort. "I have a hunch I may be President myself before long. And even if I'm not, what can he do to me, anyway?"

"Well, I really do appreciate it, Harley," Senator Anderson said. "But we'll just have to wait and see what happens."

"I mean it," Harley said. "Don't get to feeling you don't have friends, because you do."

"Thanks, Harley," Brig said, touched by his tone. "That's very kind."

After he had hung up, however, kindness suddenly did not seem to be enough. There had been too many strange happenings during the day, too many odd little things, not big and dramatic but just sufficiently out of focus so that the sum total was somehow very disturbing. It was strange, he thought, the way the two days shaped up. Yesterday had begun as a day of imagined shadows and had ended at midnight in the sunlight, figuratively speaking, of victory. Today had begun in sunlight and was ending with shadows; and in some intangible, ominous way he was beginning to feel, as he concluded work for the day and left the office shortly after 6 P.M. that this time the shadows were real.

It was not until he reached home, however, that he realized how real. And then it was not until after he had been home for some time, for although he could sense at once that Mabel was under strain of some sort, he did not for some hours associate it directly with himself. Partly this was because his wife, by an effort whose magnitude he only understood later, managed to maintain a relatively calm outward aspect, and partly it was because the early part of the evening was dominated, as always by his daughter. Dinner was a pitched battle, for some one of those mysterious reasons unclear to parents, and he got all his own stubbornness thrown back at him in a way that was, characteristically, both charming and infuriating. At the end of it she suddenly climbed into his lap, threw her arms around his neck and said, "I forgive you, Daddy," in a tone of such gracious tolerance that he burst out laughing, and her mother taken out of her own preoccupations for a moment, laughed too.

"You've been naughty, so *you're* forgiving *me*," he said. "Well, Pidge, I think that's very kind of you."

"You like me, don't you, Daddy?" she inquired happily as he tossed her onto his shoulder and started up the stairs toward bath and bed.

"Don't tell anybody," he said, "but I do."

"That's nice," she said comfortably. Halfway up, he paused and turned back.

"Coming, Mommy?" he asked, and Mabel smiled in a forced way that told him that whatever he had to face when he came down again would not be pleasant.

"I'll wait here," she said. Then she added with a sudden open urgency that disturbed him deeply, "Don't be too long."

"We'll hurry it up," he promised. "I'll pop Pidge in and then I'll be down."

"Pop Pidge in," his daughter repeated, for the words had a satisfying sound. "Pop! Pidge! In!"

As he came back down, leaving her rosy and angelic, playing thoughtfully in bed with Pooh and Piglet, he was suddenly conscious that the house was very still. Through the open windows the last of the light was dying out; a power mower was going somewhere; kids shouted, a car passed in the quiet street. Peace lay on the world, except, he sensed, in his own house. He sighed and went into the living room, where he found Mabel with the television on, just loud enough so they could talk over it and still not have their voices heard beyond the room.

"Well," he said pleasantly, "have you had a good day?"

"Oh, pretty good," she said, with a small attempt at politeness to match his.

"What did you do?" he asked, picking up the *Star* and surveying its last-edition headlines: NOMINATION REMAINS MYSTERY; and, TRACKERS LOSE SOVIET SPACE SIGNALS. "Go over to Knoxes?"

"We went shopping with Beth this morning," she said, "but we've been home all afternoon."

"Did Pidge take her nap?" he said. "She seemed awfully lively tonight."

"She got about half an hour, I think," Mabel said, smiling faintly. "Then she decided that was enough."

"Just like her father," he said with a mock wryness. "Headstrong."

"Yes," she said, and a little silence developed and grew while he looked thoughtfully at the paper.

"Did I leave my slippers down here?" he asked finally, and she got up promptly, went to the hall closet, brought them back, and dropped them by his feet.

"Thanks," he said.

"That's all right," she said, and he became conscious that she was still standing close beside him. He took her hand and smiled up reassuringly.

"What's the matter?" he asked humorously. "What have I done this time?"

"I don't know," she said, pulling her hand away and looking as though she might cry. "I just don't know."

"Well," he said, "I certainly won't know either unless you tell me. What is it?"

"Some man called here a little while before you got home," she said, going back to her chair across the room.

"Who?" he asked. She shook her head with a strained, worried expression.

"He didn't say," she said.

"An anonymous caller," he said with a little flare of angry contempt for whoever it was. "That's always pleasant for a public man's family. Did he threaten you or Pidge?"

"No, it wasn't that," she said, and just then the television blurred and she went to adjust it.

"What did he want, then?" he asked, putting down the paper and reaching for the slippers.

"He didn't say," she said in the same worried tone.

"Well, what *did* he say?" he asked with some impatience, and if her answer struck him like a physical blow it was not surprising, for nothing at all could have prepared him for it.

"He said to ask you about what you did in Honolulu," she said.

For a second he had a horrible falling feeling as though he were spinning down and down into a fearful vortex with no way to stop. But by a great effort of will he managed to hold the universe still long enough to say with a fairly successful attempt at a laugh, "I haven't been in Honolulu since the war."

"That's what he said," Mabel told him. "Ask him what he did in Honolulu in the war."

"Well," he said, and he bent down to take off his shoes very carefully and deliberately, as though the exactitude with which he untied a shoestring might somehow put the world back together again, "I rested. I swam. I went surf riding. And I ate a lot. Did I ever tell you I put on ten pounds in that rest period?"

"Did you?" Mabel asked, and something about her tone made him look up with an odd, haggard expression on his face.

"Don't you believe me?" he asked, and he could see through a sort of gray cloud that was beginning to settle over everything that this was the wrong thing to say, that it was too defensive and would only make her worry more. But he was so completely shattered, as whoever had attacked him with vicious cruelty through his wife had evidently calculated he would be, that all the self-control of a lifetime was temporarily in ruins.

"I don't know," she said at last, sounding lost and afraid. "He sounded so—odd, as though he knew a secret"—she gave a little shudder "—a dirty secret. Who was it? What did he want? What did he mean by it? Why won't you tell me?"

"I don't know," he said desperately, as though reiteration would make it true. "I don't know. Maybe it had something to do with the nomination. I don't know."

"But I thought the nomination was all settled," she said in a voice that was half cry.

"I don't know," he repeated dully. "Maybe it isn't." He looked up with a stricken expression she had never seen.

"Please," he said beseechingly, as though he were three years old and the sky had fallen in. "Please." For now the day made sense.

But this change, so abrupt, so uncharacteristic, so utterly unexpected in one who had always seemed so strong and above any real need for her, so terrified her that she could hardly speak; and so instead of realizing that this was the moment to go to him, to accept and not ask questions, to give him the strength he had never asked from her but desperately needed now, and that if she did they might weather whatever it was and he would be hers forever, she gave a sudden cry and ran from the room.

How long he sat there alone he did not know, except that he knew out of some deep well of pain that it was a period in which he seemed to draw away irrevocably from humankind. Mabel he felt had abandoned him; Orrin and his other friends never even crossed his mind, so great was his inward agony. There was no one for him, he kept repeating to himself as he mechanically finished putting on his slippers and tried without success to turn back to the blur of newsprint that used to be the evening paper; no one.

He knew now with a sickening certainty that it was not only the nominee upon whom the past was rendering its bill, just as he knew instinctively that in some way he did not yet fully understand the agent responsible for it was the man who had assured him with smiles and good wishes at midnight that all was well.

In his pain and confusion and uncertainty, his first instinct was to call him immediately and make whatever sacrifice he wished in return for having himself and his family left alone. But when he walked as in a curious muffling fog to the downstairs phone and called the White House he was told that the President had gone to bed early with strict instructions that he not be disturbed except in the event of the greatest national emergency.

"I take it this is not that, Senator," the White House operator said crisply, and he managed a harsh half laugh.

"Oh no," he said as in a dream. "No, it isn't that."

7

"It seems to us," the *Times* said editorially next morning, "that the Leffingwell nomination has passed suddenly into a strange, hazy state in which motives are confused, decisions are unclear, and the future is in doubt. With all the world literally waiting upon the Senate, it is as though the principals had disappeared suddenly behind a screen.

"The Senator from Utah, Mr. Anderson, apparently the main road block at the moment to Mr. Leffingwell's speedy confirmation, is aloof and uncommunicative with the press. No one knows what he wants.

"The President of the United States, confronted with a mysterious but apparently severe challenge to his nominee for Secretary of State, is similarly uncommunicative. No one knows what he intends.

"Mr. Leffingwell, though recipient forty-eight hours ago of the most ringing public endorsement from his chief, has received no public encouragement since and is remaining discreetly incommunicado too.

"The incumbent Secretary of State goes about his remaining duties with an air of knowing where the bodies are buried, though they may be the wrong bodies and he may conceivably be looking in the wrong graveyard.

"In the Senate, all is confusion, with everybody puzzled and nobody sure of what is going on. Guesses are a dime a dozen and rumors that the President will withdraw Mr. Leffingwell, that he will not withdraw him, that at Senator Anderson's importuning he has agreed upon a substitute, that he has defied Senator Anderson and has refused to consider a substitute, are flooding through Washington and over the country. It is as though someone had reached up suddenly and yanked the lights on the capital's most dramatic political performance in years, leaving the actors to move about in darkness while the audience shuffles nervously and wonders whether it should hiss or applaud.

"We think it is time the lights went back on and the actors got on with the play. It has been eight days since the President submitted Mr. Leffingwell's name to the Senate. Searching hearings were held during which all sorts of embarrassing questions were asked and answered, we believe completely, by the nominee. But now suddenly everything seems to be at sixes and sevens. Rumor says this is because Senator Anderson has received information of a nature damaging to Mr. Leffingwell that was not disclosed at the hearings. If this is so, Senator Anderson owes it to the country, the Senate, the President, the nominee, and himself, to state what this new evidence is. If there is no new evidence, he owes it to all concerned to say so unequivocally.

"Similarly, the President should make a statement or take some action that will indicate where he stands in the matter. Despite his dramatic endorsement of Mr. Leffingwell at the White House Correspondents' banquet Thursday night, his silence now lends weight to growing speculation that for political reasons he is in the process of abandoning Mr. Leffingwell and seeking some other course.

"We could think of nothing more disastrous, to his own prestige, the success of his Administration, and the future of American foreign policy, than to allow this second-rate melodrama to continue. This is doubly true if the Russians, as seems possible, are actually on their way to the moon with a manned expedition. If Mr. Leffingwell is unfit—a contingency we cannot conceive of or accept—then it should be stated and he should be removed at once from further consideration for Secretary of State. If he is fit—and we heartily believe he is—he should be swiftly confirmed without further dilly-dallying.

"It is time, in other words, to fish or cut bait."

And so, he thought as he put the paper slowly down and began going with a tired determination through his mail, it was: time to come to grips with the President, time to come to grips with himself, time to decide once and for all what he was made of and what, in the face of all the pressures now bearing so fearfully down upon him, he would do.

For a while last night, after Mabel had left the room and he had felt so utterly alone, he had descended into the depths of an agonized despair and it had seemed to him that he might conceivably never recover, that the pressures would be too great and the burden too frightful and the difficulties too overwhelming to surmount. Fortunately the black mood had been too black to last; before long his native courage, stubbornness and tenacity had begun to reassert themselves. So someone knew, the one thing he had hoped no one in the world, particularly the world of Washington, would ever know, and in some way apparently connected with the nomination someone was making use of it. Was that enough to make him give in? If he had been able to reach the President when he tried, it might have been; he was glad now that he had failed, for the delay had given him the chance to recover. It had taken him quite a while, fighting all alone with the television babbling on senseless and unnoticed across the room, to decide that he would not give in that easily; it was almost midnight before he reached that conclusion. When he did it was final. He decided then with a fatalistic acceptance of the consequences that he knew he would not change, that his obligation to the country—the country, in whose name they all were acting, the country, which imposed upon them all a single high duty pursued through paths as many and various as the men who owed loyalty to it—was such that he could not abandon his position, no matter what the pressures were or might become.

The decision made, he had begun to appraise the situation in the light of political and social realities as he had come to understand them in his seven years in office. Although the calculated cruelty of attacking him through his wife had temporarily thrown him off balance, the more he thought about it the more he came to see that it was what might be expected of the type of mentality that would use such a weapon at all. Whether that mentality possessed much more than a shrewd guess to go on, he did not know; evidently it did possess a little more, for the reference had been specific enough for him to understand and the time and place had been exact. But whether there was real proof beyond that, he was unable to tell, and the only assumption he could make was that this was the limit of it, and that if he handled it with sufficient calmness and steadiness he might see it through and emerge relatively unscathed. It was the type of attack that most decent men rejected, no matter what lay behind it, and he thought his friends would. Furthermore, there was the self-protective nature of a political community, the instinctive drawing-together prompted by the feeling that an attack on one was an attack on all, and that what might be turned upon one today might, if allowed to succeed, be turned with impunity upon another tomorrow.

He had had occasion to note from time to time when personal scandals, some much more current and much less innocently connected with the tensions of wartime, had shaken the fabric of the higher echelons of Washington, that it was possible for such things to be smoothed over and hushed up and forgotten and everything to proceed as before. There was a sort of necessary workaday hypocrisy, as inescapable here as it was back home on a thousand Main Streets, that imposed its own adjustments on a society caught in the overriding need to keep things going. More often than the country suspected this enforced a combination of front-door idealism and backdoor acceptance of human realities that worked its own imperatives upon such situations. The government went on, people who knew the most startling things about one another met with bright un-blinking urbanity at Georgetown cocktail parties, Washington conversation rattled chattily along its appointed customary courses, and few echoes, or none, reached the country. So, with a little luck, it might be with him— looking at it from the most practical and cold-blooded standpoint.

Unfortunately for any really genuine peace of mind, or even adequate pretense of it, however, he was not, of course, a cold-blooded man. Rationalize it how he might, he could not escape the brutally appalling reality of what had happened last night: someone, with absolute ruthless-ness, appeared to be out to destroy him, and given the weapon he ap-parently possessed, might well succeed. For there was just one little qualification to be made about the self-protective nature of official Wash-ington society: anything could be forgiven in the capital if the troops were

with you and the right ox was being gored; but if the troops weren't with
you, if the White House, the press, and all the combinations of interest
and pressure surrounding a popular nominee were on your trail, if you had
chosen the wrong ox to go after and all its friends were in alliance against
you to protect it, then you had better look out, for there would be no
mercy shown you. And this, he knew, was his situation now.

Therefore there were certain things he might have to do, he felt, if he
were to hold out and survive it; assuming he could, which of course any
man who was not a coward had to assume. The first was to get in touch
with Orrin and tell him all he knew about the nominee and James Morton;
and quite possibly, for he thought their friendship could stand it, all there
was to know about himself. This last would not be easy, but it would be
honest and fair to Orrin, if he were to ask him to help; and he had an
idea Orrin would understand and forgive him and think the more of him
for his candor, for he was a man of fifty-eight and not an hysterical child.
Another thing would be to take Harley up on his offer, which he knew
had been entirely genuine, and which he was quite sure the Vice President
would not hesitate to validate if he should ask him. And a third would be
to make use of "Meet the Press" and any other means at hand to get across
to the public the truth about Robert A. Leffingwell.

These, however, were desperation counsels, and as his spirit and confidence and fighting stubbornness returned he felt that he wanted to wait
a little and see how things developed before yielding to them; for if it
should turn out not to be necessary, if the anonymous phone call had
been just a one-shot attempt to scare him that he would hear nothing
more from, then it would be foolish to provoke a public showdown. More
immediately and much more imperatively for the sake of peace in his
own house, he must reconcile the situation with his wife; and shortly after
midnight this became possible, for she came back in, red-eyed and
exhausted, accepted, or seemed to accept, his calm statement that the
call had been nothing but the evil mouthings of a crank, and clung to him
crying bitterly at her lack of faith in him and her leaving when he needed
her; too late to recapture the moment when she might have put their
marriage on a basis it had never known, but not too late for his purpose
of restoring their life together to some basis of rational stability from
which to repel any further attacks that might be made upon it in the
ugly turn of events that had now come about in the nomination.

Or so, at any rate, he thought; and though it did not re-establish any
real happiness, it re-established enough of the customary to bring the
day eventually to an end in a more or less normal manner. There was no
question of love, but there was a reasonable calm. Mabel took a sleeping
pill, sobbed quietly for a while, and drifted off. He took one too, which
did no good and only left him feeling even more logy in the morning
than he would have been otherwise. He slept only fitfully and his mind
raced most of the night; less and less panic-stricken, more and more

practical, increasingly confident it could cope with the situation, but never happy. He wondered if he would ever be really happy again.

Now he found as he tried to wade through the Saturday morning accumulation of mail, telephone calls, and telegrams that he was even tireder than he had thought. A sort of dull weariness, compounded of lack of sleep and terrific inner tension, seemed to be dragging him down, an all-pervading exhaustion that put chains on his mind and sapped his physical energies. This was not, he realized, a good condition for a man who must stand off the world and all the pressures he was under, but there was no help for it. He could not stay home this day, he had to keep going, he had to be on the job, he had to be ready on the firing line for whatever new attack might come. When it came shortly after eleven it was from an unexpected quarter, and he could not say afterwards that it had exactly been an attack. Rather, he supposed, both an encouragement and a warning; not really necessary in view of his own decision, but one which revealed to him that even if he wished to change course, it would not be without unpleasant consequences, not so drastic as those which might attend his present course but not so very enjoyable either. The buzzer sounded and he was informed that the senior Senator from South Carolina was in the outer office. He put aside his mail with a sigh and said to send him in.

"Seab," he said, rising and shaking hands, "make yourself at home. How are you?"

"Well, sir," his visitor said, slumping comfortably into one of the leather armchairs and surveying him with a sleepy smile that did not entirely conceal the thoroughness of his study, "I'm fine, Brigham. But I think—I just do think, now—that you look rather tired. Yes, sir, you do. Very tired. Did you stay up late?"

"Rather late," Senator Anderson agreed. "I slept very little last night."

"I thought possibly that was it," Senator Cooley said. "I wonder why, now? Surely you weren't having second thoughts about your talk at the White House. Surely you weren't disappointed by the appointment."

"It had to do with the nomination," Brig admitted. Seab smiled again.

"He wants you to back down, doesn't he?" he said. "He wants you to turn tail and be a coward and give in and let this evil man become Secretary of State. Two evil men together, running the country into the ground in the face of her enemies. Yes, sir. That's what he wants, isn't it?"

"That's what he wants, Seab," Brigham Anderson said shortly. The Senator from South Carolina looked at him sharply.

"Are you going to do it, Brigham?" he asked softly. "Are you going to do what that bad man wants?"

His young friend thought for several moments, staring out the window, his eyes, looking glazed from lack of sleep, wide with considerations whose nature Senator Cooley did not know but whose seriousness he could easily perceive.

"I don't think I will, Seab," he said finally. "No, I don't think I will."

"He's a mighty strong man," Seab pointed out thoughtfully. "Mighty fierce temper, he's got. He might do you a lot of damage if you persist in it, you know. He's broken other men, and he wouldn't hesitate with you, of that I am quite sure. Yes, sir, quite sure."

"I know it," Brigham Anderson said. "I'm aware of all that, Seab."

"And you're not afraid," Senator Cooley inquired gently. Senator Anderson stared again out the window and spoke in a remote voice that still held an unyielding iron in it.

"I was last night," he said. "Maybe I still am today. I don't know, Seab. But I don't care any more. I know what I've got to do and I intend to do it. However," he added, and his voice suddenly became more personal, "I may need help."

"I think you can get it from me, Brigham," Seab said softly. "Yes, sir, I really do think you can get it from me."

"Is that a promise?" Brig asked. Senator Cooley shrugged.

"I've said it," he noted. "What did he threaten you with last night, Brigham?"

"He didn't," Senator Anderson said. "I don't even know directly that he's involved in it. Some anonymous well-wisher called my wife."

"That I would expect," Senator Cooley said calmly. "There is no end to the duplicities of that man. But you think you can withstand it."

"I think, with help, I can withstand it," Brig said. "I may not be able to force him to withdraw the nomination, now, but I think I can beat it on the floor. If you are with me, and one or two others."

"There will be one or two others," Seab said softly. "Oh, yes, Brigham, there will be quite a few more than one or two others."

"And you will help me, no matter what charges may be made against me, and no matter what they say?" Brigham Anderson asked earnestly.

"Will the charges be true?" Senator Cooley asked calmly, and with a look that disclosed to him just how near the ragged edge his young friend was, Brig said in a low voice,

"They may be, Seab. They aren't nice, but they may be. After all," he added with a bitter dryness, "even I was human once."

"Do they have proof?" Seab asked. Senator Anderson stared down at his mail, and a sudden impulse for understanding, a sudden desire for friendship, prompted an answer more candid than he might otherwise have given.

"Not so far as I know now," he said. "I don't see how they could have. There's only one person in the world"—he stopped and then forced himself to go on—"only one person in the world who could furnish proof, and I don't think that—that person would. I don't even know if—if that person is still alive."

"Well, then," Seab said reassuringly, "I don't think you should worry, Brigham. I think you can weather it. I think we can all weather it together, and I think we can beat that man. Yes, sir, I really do, I think we can beat him thoroughly, completely, and with finality."

"I hope so, Seab," Senator Anderson said. "I hope so." He hesitated. "I want to say one thing more, though. If the—the charges are made, I shall of course deny them, and they'll be exaggerated enough, if they are made, so you can be sure that most of them will be false. But if they produce proof of even—of even one per cent of them, I want you to feel entirely free to abandon me. Because then," he said with a lonely desolation that touched and alarmed the Senator from South Carolina, "I won't be worth saving, anyway."

"Now, sir," Seab said firmly. "Now, sir, you stop that kind of talk, Brigham. I don't want to hear any more of it at all. No, sir, I do not. There isn't anything I haven't seen or heard about or known of, or maybe"—he gave a sleepy grin—"maybe, to hear what folks have said about me over all these years, done, and I am not about to be shocked or horrified or flabbergasted like some silly little stupid mincing schoolgirl. No, sir, I am not about to be any of those things. So you can count on me, Brigham. You can surely count on me. I mean it. I do mean it, now."

"Well, thank you, Seab," Brig said, and the Senator from South Carolina could see he was profoundly moved by it, and again he felt alarmed, for what attack could possibly have produced such depths of emotion in his normally steady young colleague? "You don't know how much I appreciate it. You just don't."

"Well," Seab said comfortably, turning to what he had come to say, "I want you to know I am very pleased that you are standing firm, Brigham, because it is exactly what I should expect of you. In fact," he added gently, "I should have been extremely perturbed—ex-treme-ly per-turbed —indeed, if I thought you would back down. It wouldn't be like you, Brigham. It would upset everything if you did. You have no idea how much it pleases me to have you insisting on standing firm."

"What would you do to me if I didn't, Seab?" Brig asked with a grim little smile, for he had not expected to get out of this conversation without some little quid pro quo. Senator Cooley smiled again.

"Oh, probably not much," he said casually. "Probably nowhere near as much as the President will try to do to you for standing firm. About all I could do, would be to charge that the two of you all had joined together in a conspiracy to cover it all up. That's really all. Of course," he said gently, "I could do quite a bit of talking about that. Quite a little bit."

"How could we have done that?" Senator Anderson asked curiously, and Seab chuckled.

"Well, sir," he said lazily, "you all could have cooked up this plan to send James Morton out of the country."

Brigham Anderson's eyes widened, and in spite of his tiredness and worry a little expression of ironic appreciation crossed his face.

"So it was you," he said, "I might have known. How did you ever hit on that?"

"Well, sir," Senator Cooley said, not without satisfaction, "I have learned a thing or two in this Senate over the years, indeed I have. But more than that, it was instinct. It really was. It just came to me, with a little study. You develop instinct if you stay here long enough. You'll have it eventually yourself, if you haven't already. It just takes time."

"If I stay here," Brig said slowly, and Seab smiled.

"You will be here many years, Brigham," he said confidently. "You're the kind of Senator who stays. Don't worry about that." He rose slowly to his feet and shook his coat into shape like a ponderous old dog. "I'm mighty glad we agree, because I wouldn't want to have to attack you. I would do it if I had to, but I wouldn't like it, because I am a friend of yours, Brigham. I really am. I hope you regard me so."

"I do, Seab," he said, and he meant it. "I do."

"Well, sir," Seab said, "I think that's mighty fine. We're together, and I'm proud of it, Brigham. Proud of it."

And with a smile and a nod and a firm, enveloping handshake, he went on his way, a friend and a supporter and also the one other man on Senator Anderson's side of the issue who knew about James Morton. If he were to let it ride, he was sure Harley and Bob would never say a word, but Seab most assuredly would. And so, he realized with a certainty that was both wry and deeply troubled, he was in checkmate. If he moved one way, the President was waiting, and he had already been given a taste of what that could mean. If he moved the other, Seab was waiting, and for all his friendship, which was genuine enough, the old man would not hesitate to act as ruthlessly as he knew how if Brig crossed him. Brig had no intention of crossing him, but just the same the thought was not too comforting in his present state of mind. He decided, after a few more futile attempts to concentrate on his mail, that if he was to get through the day with any sort of reasonable efficiency, he had better go over to the New Office Building, take a swim, and go up to the solarium and lie in the sun for a while until he felt more rested.

Walking through the Saturday-emptied corridors, he was pleased to find that hardly anyone was about, for this spared him the necessity of being bright and sociable when he felt like the devil. The same applied to the pool, which was deserted save for one attendant. He stripped, took a shower, methodically swam twenty laps, and crawled out. The atmosphere of a gymnasium, redolent of steam, disinfectant, sweat, and nakedness, made him think of things he didn't want to think of, in fact hadn't really thought of at all during the past twenty-four hours, even though they were of course central to what he was going through. With a peculiar mixture of melancholy and distaste he dried himself quickly, slipped into a pair of trunks, and went on to the solarium. He was both annoyed and relieved to discover that he was not to be alone there, for recumbent in the sun he saw the lean and craggy frame of Clement Johnson of Delaware alongside the mahogany bulk of Bill Kanaho of Hawaii. They were talking as he arrived, and for a moment he stopped in the door to listen, though he soon wished he hadn't.

"—why that was necessary, I can't see," Bill Kanaho was saying. "I suppose you've heard the gossip that's going around."

"About Brig?" Clement Johnson said with a nod. "Sounds damned sinister all right. Damned unspecific, too, it seems to me, the damned smear artists."

"Exactly," Senator Kanaho said with an air of contempt. "Do you believe it?"

"If I can understand what they're talking about," Senator Johnson said, "no, I do not. Do you?"

"No, indeed," Bill Kanaho said. "You can hear any damned thing about anybody in this town if you listen long enough. I'd give a lot to know where it started, though, and who started it. That would explain a good many things."

"The Press Club bar last night, I imagine," Clement Johnson said, "and somebody from the White House, I wouldn't be surprised."

"Or was it Freddy Van Ackerman?" Senator Kanaho suggested. "He hangs around there a lot, it's such a good place to start things going."

"Yes," Senator Johnson said. "Or was it both the White House *and* Freddy?" he added, and Brig came forward from the doorway.

"I think it was," he said easily, as his two colleagues started guiltily; but they were friends of his and no friends of either Senator Van Ackerman or the White House, so he smiled candidly. "I think they're both out to get me on this," he said as he stretched out a towel and lay down beside Bill Kanaho. "What do you think?"

"I think," the senior Senator from Hawaii said comfortably, "that I'm getting much too fat and flabby. The days when I was an Olympic swimmer and able to surfboard all day long off Waikiki and Kailua are gone forever, I'm afraid." He squeezed a roll of fat on his stomach and looked at it with a comical distaste.

"Too much fish and poi," Clement Johnson said.

"And a few other things, I'll bet," Brig said. Bill Kanaho grinned.

"That's right," he said. "You know how it is out there, don't you? Didn't you say you were in Honolulu during the war?"

"I don't remember saying it," Brig said with an outward calm.

"Oh," Senator Kanaho said in a puzzled voice. "Well, I heard it someplace."

"Probably the Press Club bar," Brig said dryly, and stretched his arms with an air of elaborate unconcern in the sun, though he knew very well that was quite likely exactly where it had come from, and felt suddenly sick inside.

"Maybe," Bill Kanaho said. "You can hear anything there. Well, tell us, Brig, what's going to come of all this, anyway?"

"Oh, I don't know," Brig said slowly. "What's your guess? It's probably as good as mine."

"I hope he's going to withdraw Leffingwell," Senator Johnson said. "It would simplify things greatly for the Senate."

"To say nothing of me," Senator Anderson said with a grim smile. Clement Johnson nodded.

"Yes," he agreed. A helicopter droned over against the bright blue sky, a white cloud drifted far above. Muffled by distance the noises of cars and buses arriving and leaving at the Capitol came faintly up. The wind had died and the sun was hot. Clement Johnson spoke again.

"What are you going to do if he doesn't, Brig?" he asked quietly.

"I think I'm going to fight it," Brig replied with equal quietness. Senator Kanaho grunted.

"May get hurt," he observed.

"I'm hurt already," Brig said. "My wife got an anonymous phone call last night."

"The hell you say!" Bill exclaimed, and Clement Johnson said, "The bastards!" indignantly. Brig shrugged.

"There are penalties as well as rewards in public life," he said with a savage irony. "Or so I tell my high-school kids when they come here."

"What was it about?" Bill Kanaho asked. "Or don't you want to say?"

"It was about the same thing you were talking about, I imagine," Brig said bluntly. His colleagues looked embarrassed.

"Don't pay any attention to that damned nonsense, boy," Senator Kanaho said. "I hope your wife didn't, for God's sake."

"It wasn't clear enough for her to understand," Brig said. "It got her very upset, however."

"*We* know there's nothing to it," Clement Johnson said, meaning to be helpful but embarrassing himself all over again at the way it sounded.

"Thanks," Brig said. "I know you feel that way and I appreciate it. But you're friends of mine. My enemies may not be so charitable."

"You haven't very many enemies, Brig," Senator Johnson said encouragingly. "Honest, you haven't."

"One is enough in this town," Brig said tersely, "if he sits in the White House." Senator Kanaho sighed.

"It's a tough situation," he admitted. "Speaking of your enemies, and I guess he is one, now I remember where I heard about you and Honolulu. What do you and Fred Van Ackerman have in common, anyway?"

"You know we have very damned little in common," Senator Anderson said. "Why?"

"Damnedest thing," Bill Kanaho said. "He called me about 3 A.M. last night—no, night before last—and wanted to know if Miller & Haslett was still operating. Must have been drunk I guess."

"Oh?" Brig said, and from somewhere far back down the years he was conscious of the first dismaying stirrings of a long-buried memory. "What's that?"

"One of our big photographic houses," Senator Kanaho said. "Freddy said he had been there once during the war and had his picture taken. He said he thought you once said you had too."

"Not together, I hope," Clement Johnson said with a laugh, and Brig laughed too, though it cost him quite a bit for now another piece of the puzzle was beginning to fall into place. There flashed into his mind his conversation with Mabel about throwing out his old uniforms; could the picture have rested forgotten in one of them all these years, when he had thought it long since destroyed? And if it had, then it must have been placed with his papers on the desk, and from there it must have gotten to—whom? Surely not—but he knew with a sickening suddennesss that it must be. No wonder the Justice had avoided him the last two days; no wonder his manner had been constrained with the constraint of a terribly burdened conscience. And what a burden it was, and how utterly alone it left the Senator from Utah feeling, that someone he had always considered a friend could betray him so completely. What was this nomination, that it could make decent men do such things to their fellows? The shock of this realization disturbed him even more than the thought of the photograph, though that was bad enough. He could remember little about it, except that he was sure that standing alone it didn't prove very much: a picture, a casual inscription, a couple of buddies in uniform who had decided to have their photograph taken together. But this was small comfort, for its very existence would lend substance to gossip; and it was only with a great effort that he made himself relax and continue the conversation as casually as he knew he must.

"No," he said, "I can't really think Fred and I were together. And is the company still in business?" he asked Bill Kanaho. The senior Senator from Hawaii nodded.

"Gone downhill some in recent years, as I told Fred," he said, "but it's still there." And for just a second he looked very quickly and shrewdly at his young colleague with the appraising, dispassionate curiosity of a thousand years of China and Japan and Malaysia and Polynesia that had come out of the far reaches of the Pacific to settle in the Islands and produce one day a Senator of the United States. "Can't imagine what Fred had in mind," he added comfortably as Brig shrugged and rolled over.

"I can't either," he said. "Too bad you didn't ask."

"Oh, why should I bother trying to find out what's in that queer little mind?" Senator Kanaho asked impatiently. "All it's good for is to make trouble."

"That's right," Senator Anderson said grimly, "and it's making quite a bit for me."

And even though they both urged him heartily not to let it upset him, and promised again their full support in whatever he wanted to do, he could feel their speculative eyes upon him half an hour later when he picked up his towel and went down again; and he realized then the cruel shrewdness of his adversaries. It was not the battling on the floor, the fair fight in open contest in the national forum where he held membership that would wear him down; it was the gossip, the speculation, the be-hind-the-hand talk and the sidelong glances, the anonymous phone calls and the dirty letters, if they should come—all the sneaking cruelties of really brutal political in-fighting. There were men in Washington right now to whom this process had been applied, and although they walked around as though they were alive they were dead inside. It was not a fate he wanted for himself, nor could he contemplate the possibility of it without a shudder . . . He wondered as he went slowly in a brown study back to his office what would come next to add to the pressures he was under, and how he would face it; for his talk with Bill and Clement, with all its intimations of vicious personal gossip that he now knew was run-ning through the town had quite effectively erased any relaxation he might have gotten from his swim. He was as tired and tense now as he had been before. He wondered desperately whether there was to be an end to it or whether it would just continue to wear him down until he broke under it. That, he gathered, was the intention.

In his office he was aware at once that something was out of the ordinary, for the two girls whose turn it was to take Saturday duty looked excited and upset as he came in.

"We didn't know where to put him, Senator," one of them told him hurriedly, "and we thought the press might come in and you wouldn't want them to see him here, so we took him right on into your office."

"That's good," he said automatically. "That was very smart. How long has he been here?"

"About fifteen minutes," the girl said. "He looks just like his pictures," she added earnestly.

"I should hope so," Brig said with a smile as the humor of this cryptic conversation began to strike him. "He doesn't have a gun, does he?"

The girl looked shocked.

"Oh my, no," she said. "Oh no, sir!"

"Fine," Brig said gravely. "I shall beard him single-handed." He went on into his private office, expecting to meet at least a crooner or a movie star. He was quite unprepared for the man who rose to greet him, and he took occasion to gain time by closing the door slowly and carefully behind him before he spoke.

"Hi, Bob," he said finally. "I'm sorry you had to wait. I hope the girls made you at home."

"They were very discreet," the nominee said with a little smile. "They hustled me right on in here as though I had just robbed the Riggs Bank. You have them very well trained."

"It wasn't my idea," he said, "but it was wise under the circumstances. Sit down, Bob. We won't be disturbed."

"I don't expect I'll take long," Bob Leffingwell said, "but I thought perhaps we should talk."

Senator Anderson looked at him thoughtfully.

"I expect we should," he agreed, "but there's one thing I want an honest answer to first. Are you here because the President sent you?"

The nominee looked puzzled.

"I am not," he said firmly. Brig continued to stare at him for a moment and then nodded.

"Very well," he said, relaxing a little in his chair, "I believe you."

"Why did you ask?" Bob Leffingwell inquired. "Or can't I be told?"

"There's been a pattern," Brig said slowly, "and I thought you might be part of it. I'm sure you know about it, at any rate."

"I know very little," the nominee said, and the Senator could see he meant it. "You saw everything there was to see at the banquet; he hasn't called me since, and I haven't called him. I went straight to my office yesterday and stayed there all day, took no calls from the press, and saw nobody outside my immediate staff. I came here this morning straight from home. So you see I couldn't possibly know what you're talking about."

"I believe you," Brig said again. He smiled for the first time, somewhat cautiously. "You're being very discreet yourself," he observed. Bob Leffingwell smiled too, offered him a cigarette, which he accepted, and lit one for himself.

"I decided the best thing for me to do was lie low," he said. "After all, I don't know what this is all about."

"Is that why you came to see me?" Senator Anderson said. "To find out?"

"That was part of it," Bob Leffingwell said. "And," he added thoughtfully, "because we are two rational men who seem to have gotten involved in an unpleasant situation and I thought possibly if we could talk it over privately away from outside pressures we might work out a solution that would make sense to us both. Does that seem so unreasonable?"

Brigham Anderson sighed.

"If you and I are rational about this," he said with a tired smile, "we're the last two men in the world who are."

"Well, I don't know about that," the nominee said, "but I did want to talk to you. I gather that you must know something very bad about me. It is very disturbing to me, I won't pretend it isn't." He frowned. "Disturbing to my wife too," he added. "Some crank called last night and got very vituperative over the telephone. You know how these things are, they always bring that element out."

"Oh yes," Brig said bitterly. "I know how these things are. Somebody called my wife last night too, only it wasn't just a crank. It was someone with a deliberate, calculated, cold-blooded plan to destroy me through her. That's why I asked if the President sent you. I thought it might all be part of the same scheme."

"No," Bob Leffingwell said. "Well. I'm sorry to hear that." He leaned forward curiously. "Tell me, Senator," he said. "Why are you opposing me?"

Brigham Anderson looked at him, handsome, gray, and distinguished, appearing to be quite tired—had he too been wakeful in the night? Probably—and decided there was no point in anything but candor.

"Because I got a call from James Morton," he said, not knowing what reaction this might produce in the self-possessed figure before him but feeling there was nothing to be gained from softening his words.

For whatever satisfaction it was to him, and in his strain and tiredness it wasn't so very much, he could see that the impact had been almost as great as the one he had suffered last night. His visitor paled and sat slowly back in his chair, his hands gripping its arms so hard the knuckles showed white. It was several minutes before he spoke and when he did it was in a voice that had become deeply weary.

"So you know," he said.

"Yes," Brig said, "I know. Do you think it justifies me in opposing you or do you not?"

The nominee sighed and relaxed a little in his chair.

"I suppose," he said, "looked at from your standpoint, it does."

"I know how it is looked at from your standpoint," Brig said dryly, and regretted it the moment he spoke, for he knew at once that it had cost him his advantage, but he was too tired to be careful and it just came out, "because the President explained it to me Thursday night."

He was aware that the room was very still and that Bob Leffingwell was leaning forward again slowly.

"Let me get this straight," he said carefully. "You told the President about this?"

"I felt he had a right to know," Brig said, for there was no point in evasion now.

"And what did he do?" the nominee asked, still in the same careful fashion.

"He told me he would withdraw your name," Senator Anderson said.

"In those words?" Bob Leffingwell said, and Brig knew his last chance of winning the battle was slipping fast away.

"Those were my words," he admitted. "He agreed to them. Or," he added bitterly, "I thought he did."

"And that was Thursday night," Bob Leffingwell said slowly. "Thursday night and this is Saturday afternoon." A growing excitement began to enter his voice. "So that's why he sent him abroad yesterday," he said.

"He's going to stand by me. He wanted him out of the way because he's going to stand by me."

"How do you know," Senator Anderson asked with a fair semblance of scorn, "when you haven't heard from him?"

"He's standing by me!" the nominee exclaimed triumphantly. "Of course he is! Then *why*," he demanded, his voice turned vigorous and cold with a rising anger, "should I be afraid of you?"

At this all the tiredness and strain of the past forty-eight hours, his feeling of being harried and hounded and boxed-in, the growing knowledge he was very likely fighting in a lost cause, suddenly created a reckless anger in the Senator from Utah, and he spoke with a fury as cold as the nominee's own.

"Because, by God," he said, "I'm going to beat you if it's the last thing I do. You're a liar and a cheat and a double-dealing son of a bitch, and you aren't fit to sweep up the Capitol, let alone be Secretary of State. I know what you are and I'm going to tell the whole wide world. Now get the hell out of my office. I'm sick of the sight of you."

His visitor stood up, and it was quite apparent that he was holding himself under control only with the greatest difficulty.

"Very well," he said, his voice shaking. "I'm going. I came here to try to reason this out, but you don't want to be reasonable. If you think you can beat me, try and be damned to you. You can't beat the President."

"Go out that door right there," Brig said coldly. "I wouldn't want the girls in the front office to see you and decide we'd been having a row."

"I will," Bob Leffingwell said unevenly. A sudden hard gleam came into his eyes.

"Where is Senator Van Ackerman's office?" he asked.

"There's a list on that card hanging on the door," Senator Anderson said shortly. "Look it up."

"All right, I will," the nominee said, his voice still uneven, and with a finger that trembled he traced down the list of names and suite numbers.

"Twelve thirty-one in the New Building," he said after a moment, and Brigham Anderson nodded.

"I hope you find him in," he said grimly.

"I hope I do," said the nominee.

After the door closed the senior Senator from Utah remained for a long time standing by his desk. He felt dull and sick and savagely regretful. He shouldn't have antagonized Bob Leffingwell when he had come to him voluntarily, he shouldn't have been so stupid as to abandon his advantage, he shouldn't have been so quick to anger, and no matter how tired and ill and unhappy he felt he shouldn't have allowed the pressures he was under to provoke him to the point of unseemly and uncharacteristic invective. He shouldn't, he shouldn't, he shouldn't. But he had, and if there had ever been any real hope that this unexpected confrontation might offer a way out, it was too late to salvage now. Presently he sat down again with a small, lonely sound of tiredness, pain, and frustration. He was beginning to feel strung tight as a wire. The tension was increasing, and there was no let-up in sight.

He sent one of the girls to the cafeteria for a couple of candy bars, ignoring her surprise that this was all he wanted for lunch, and got them down as best he could; knowing they weren't enough, but unable to stomach more in his taut and uneasy condition. Then he returned to his correspondence, knowing with a grimly ironic certainty that before long he would get two phone calls. He guessed that Fred Van Ackerman's would come in about half an hour and the President's in about an hour after that. He was 15 minutes early on Fred, but otherwise it went just about as he had expected. Their conversation was brief and to the point and neither of them wasted any time on false courtesies.

"Leffingwell is here," Fred said. "He says you won't give in."

"Does he?" Brig said, and added sardonically, "You're sure he's a trustworthy source."

"Don't get smart," Fred said with a trace of anger. "This is too serious for that. Do you know what I have?"

"I haven't the slightest idea," Senator Anderson said, trying to sound calm and aided by a cold distaste for his colleague.

"It doesn't look good," Senator Van Ackerman observed.

"Doesn't it?" Brig asked.

"Oh, stop it," Fred said impatiently. "You know damned well how it looks, because the way it looks is the truth."

"Is it?" Brig said.

"Yes, God damn it," Senator Van Ackerman said angrily. "I think you'd damn well better give in."

"Who are you kidding?" Brig demanded with a scorn he didn't feel, but contempt for Fred lent it substance.

"You don't think that's all I have, do you?" Fred inquired with the sort of phony menace he liked to throw into his questions when he faced a bothersome witness in committee.

"Why don't you play cops and robbers with somebody else, Fred?" Senator Anderson asked. "I'm not interested."

"God damn it," Senator Van Ackerman said. "Are you crazy? I have it, God damn it. I'm warning you for the last time."

"Warn away," Brig said. "I wouldn't deal with you if you were the most reliable man on earth, and nobody's ever called you that."

"I tell you what," Fred said with a jeering friendliness. "Suppose you just listen to my speech to the COMFORT rally tonight. It'll be interesting, Brig, boy. I'm going to tell them all about it."

"I'd watch that if I were you, Fred," Senator Anderson said sharply. "I have a lot of friends and there are laws against slander."

"In this town?" Senator Van Ackerman said. "Since when?"

"I'm warning you, Fred," Brig said quietly.

"Just be sure to watch," Fred said again.

"I will," Brig said, and added contemptuously, "If I thought you had the guts to match your mouth, I'd be worried."

"Just watch," Fred said. "Little Brigham may be surprised."

"Listen, Fred," Senator Anderson said. "I'm not scared, and I'm not quitting. Have you got that straight?"

"I've got it," Senator Van Ackerman said.

"Tell the man who took you off the leash," Brigham Anderson said. "He may want to know."

"God damn it," Fred said with furious anger, "if you think you can talk to me——"

But the senior Senator from Utah had hung up on his raving rejoinder, and that was that. Unwise again, in all probability; but a more placating tone would have made no difference, and a man, however driven, had to stand up to such as Fred Van Ackerman for the sake of his own self-respect, if he was a man.

Which left the President and a conversation he could well foresee. In the interval before it came he received two telegrams from home, one signed by his parents and his brother and sisters which said, WE ARE ALL WITH YOU AS ALWAYS. ALL LOVE, and one from his high-school chum in Ogden which said, WE'VE LICKED THEM BEFORE AND WE CAN DO IT AGAIN. LET ME KNOW WHAT I CAN DO FROM HERE. These made him feel better for a little while, and it occurred to him that it would also be nice to hear from Spring Valley as well. There was no answer at the house, however, and he decided that Mabel and Pidge were probably over at the Knoxes. He expected he could talk to them a little later if they were, for he had just about decided now that it was time to call Harley, and to try to reach Orrin, through Beth, wherever he was out in Illinois. Before he could proceed with this the buzzer sounded and when he lifted the phone the girl said, "Senator, it's the President!" in an excited voice.

"Yes, sir," he said crisply, and the response came back as he knew it would, light and airy and full of good will, for why should he be brutal when others were so skillfully being brutal for him?

"Brigham!" the President said. "How are you today, you earnest young man?"

An expression of distaste crossed the Senator's face, but he tried to make his reply as impassive as possible.

"I hope I am always that when serious matters are involved, Mr. President," he said, knowing he sounded stuffy but too tired and angry to care very much. The President chuckled as though he hadn't a care in the world.

"Oh, you are, you son of a gun," he said jovially, "indeed you are. I'm sorry I didn't return your call yesterday, but I got tied up in the afternoon with some Boy Scouts and a cancer group and the Sudanese Ambassador and a delegation from the Portland Rose Festival with a couple of plants for the Rose Garden——" He paused with a comic laugh. "More damned chicken feed attached to this job," he said candidly. "Anyway, I'm sorry I didn't manage to talk to you, and I hope you forgive me."

"It's quite all right," Brig said calmly. "I thought maybe you were having a farewell talk with James Morton before sending him on his way."

"I want to explain to you about that, Brigham," the President began confidentially, and with a sudden impatience Senator Anderson interrupted.

"Look, Mr. President," he said. "Let's skip the explanations, shall we? We're all grown up, so let's just skip it. I've had all I need in the way of explanations since yesterday afternoon."

There was a pause, and when the President resumed it was in a rather puzzled tone.

"I'm sorry it has upset you, Brigham," he said, "but I do feel in fairness to myself I should just say that it seemed to me best under the circumstances that he be sent away in order to clear the way for whatever might be necessary. I wanted to explain it to you yesterday, except, as I say, I got tied up."

"'Whatever may be necessary' is a delicate way to put it," Brig said. "Such as destroying me, for instance."

"Now, Brigham," the President said comfortably, "that's putting it much too dramatically, you know. I don't know exactly what you have in mind, but I'm sure it isn't as fierce as all that. I'll admit I did hope that a chance to think it over for a day or two might persuade you to change your mind, but as for destroying you, as you put it—how have I been doing that?"

"By turning Fred Van Ackerman loose on me," Brig said. The consummate actor, politician, student of human nature, leader of men, and global statesman to whom he was talking said, "No!" in a shocked voice.

"Brigham," he said solemnly, "believe me, I don't have any idea what Fred Van Ackerman has been doing. I haven't seen Fred Van Ackerman, I haven't called Fred Van Ackerman——"

"No, indeed," Senator Anderson said bluntly, "but he has called you, and not half an hour ago. Isn't that true?"

"He did call me, yes," the President admitted after a little silence. "But he didn't tell me what he had been doing to you, if anything. And I didn't ask him."

"Of course you didn't," Brig said bitterly. "You don't want to burden your conscience with knowing. But he told you he had me all softened up, didn't he? And your lying nominee for Secretary of State joined in and confirmed it, didn't he?"

"You seem determined to turn this into something hostile between us,

Brigham," the President said sorrowfully. "I really don't see what it gains you, honestly I don't. Fred suggested I might want to talk to you and see how you were feeling about it by now, and Bob said he thought it might be a good idea, too. I swear that's all."

"You've cleaned up their language a good bit," Brig said grimly, and the President responded more lightly.

"Well," he said, "they both did seem a little hot under the collar, but I suppose there's two sides to it. I gather they got you a little annoyed, too."

"Not annoyed, exactly," Senator Anderson said. "Just weary of lying, two-faced, deceitful people, that's all."

"Oh, well," the President said quickly, "lying and deceit can apply to many things and many people, you know, Brigham."

This time it was the Senator who paused, and when he spoke it was in a tired but still stubborn tone.

"That is very true," he said quietly. "Shall we compare notes?"

"Oh, I don't think that's necessary," the President said comfortably. "I think we understand each other, thoroughly. You really don't think you can see your way clear to changing your mind, then? It would make life so much simpler for us both."

"I really don't think I can, Mr. President," Brig said.

"And that is your final word?" the President inquired.

"Until it reaches the floor of the Senate," Brig said.

"Well," the President said regretfully, "I'm sorry, I really am. I don't like to see a young fellow with all your promise getting into a fight with a fellow like Fred Van Ackerman. You know," he remarked thoughtfully, "he seems to be completely unscrupulous."

"I assumed that was why you selected him to do your dirty work for you," Senator Anderson said evenly. The President sighed.

"I had hoped we could avoid this type of argument," he said. "I thought we could reach an understanding like reasonable men. Apparently we can't."

"We could have," Senator Anderson said, "if you had kept your word."

"I gave no word," the President said, "except to the country, to protect her interests."

"The country!" Brig said bitterly. "The country. You're always prating about the country and you want to give her a liar like that for Secretary of State."

"As well a liar like that for Secretary of State," the President said smoothly, "as for United States Senator."

"It isn't comparable," Brig said desperately. "How could people possibly be hurt, how could foreign policy possibly be affected, by what I—what I— It isn't comparable at all."

"I'll grant you that," the President said, "but try to tell Main Street."

"If society were honest——" Senator Anderson began bitterly, and stopped.

"It isn't," the President said practically. "It can't afford to be. Well, I'm sorry, as I say. Fred sounded quite determined, and I expect he has a very mean streak in him. If you won't change, that is."

"No, Mr. President," Brig said, "I won't change."

"He said something about shooting the works at this COMFORT rally of his tonight," the President said thoughtfully. "Of course I don't know what that means. He might do anything, I suppose, the type he is."

"No, Mr. President," Brig said again. "I won't change."

"Good-by, Brigham," the President said. "I'm sorry it's turned out this way. It's tough for a young fellow in your position. I hope it doesn't hurt too badly."

"I appreciate the thought," Senator Anderson said bitterly. "It's nice to have you thinking of me."

"Come and see me sometime after it's over," the President offered, "and we'll have a drink and bury the hatchet."

"Oh, sure," Brig said with a harsh, disbelieving laugh. "Oh, sure."

"Sometime . . ." the President said vaguely, let his voice trail away, and hung up.

After that there was just one thing he wanted, and that was to get home as fast as possible, to get away from the Capitol and out of the fetid air he suddenly felt surrounded by, to see his own yard and his own house and his own wife and daughter, and try to restore some semblance of rational sensibility to the world. But a couple of details remained. He picked up the phone and said, "The Vice President, please." A voice promptly said, "Hello," and because of the informality and the fact that it was Saturday afternoon he took it to be Harley's and began without preliminaries.

"Harley," he said, "how do you feel about Saturday afternoon press conferences? I think I'm going to take you up on that offer right away, if you're agreeable."

"Who is this?" the voice on the other end inquired.

"Isn't this the Vice President?" Brig said sharply.

"This is his assistant," the voice said. "Is this Senator Anderson?"

"Yes, it is," he said.

"I'm sorry he isn't here, sir," the voice said. "He had to catch a plane to go to Kansas City to make a speech tonight and another tomorrow afternoon. He mentioned you and said he wanted to wait as late as possible before leaving because you might be calling, but when he hadn't heard from you by three he felt he really must catch the plane. He said to tell you he will be back late tomorrow if you still care to call him."

"And you don't know where to reach him in Kansas City?" Brig said.

"At the Muehlbach tonight," the voice said, "but he won't be there until late. I'd suggest you wait and try him at home tomorrow night."

"I see," Brig said.

"He also said to tell you his promise still stands," the voice said encouragingly.

"Thanks," Brig said automatically. "You tell him I am very grateful for that, even if I have missed him now."

"He waited as long as he could, sir," the voice said, somewhat defensively.

"Of course," Brig said. "I understand that, and I appreciate it. Thank you very much."

"Thank you, Senator," the voice said.

And now it was with a rapidly rising worry that he might have waited until too late that he asked for outside and dialed the Knoxes' number; but even with all the evidence before him he had not been able to actually believe in the fearful dangers of his own position until he had heard them confirmed by the President himself. Now he could only hope quick action would bring him the help he obviously needed. Beth Knox came on the wire and he made no attempt to conceal the urgency in his voice.

"Bee," he said quickly, "there's something important I want to find out from you."

"Hi, Brig," she said carefully, and even in his haste he could sense a caution that wasn't like a member of the Knox family, "what's that?"

"I want to know where Orrin is," he said.

"Oh, that," she said, and the caution, curiously, was relaxed a little.

"Yes," he said, "that. It really is important, Bee. How do I reach him?"

"I don't exactly know," she said. "He sometimes gets rather mysterious about these things, presumably to keep me on my toes. Might be another woman, you know." She laughed. "Can't you see Orrin with a painted houri? I can. That's why I never worry. Brig," she said more seriously, "I really don't know. You might try his brother in Cairo, but I think he's only passing through there for an hour or two—it's one of those hop, skip, and a jump affairs all over Little Egypt, eating chicken à la king and Getting In Touch With The People. So I honestly wouldn't know. Is there anything I can do?"

"Well," he said, trying to keep the disappointment out of his voice but not succeeding very well, "no, I guess not, except that if he calls you, you might have him call me. I'd really like him to."

"I expect he won't," Beth said, "but if he does, where?"

"Why, home," Brig said in some surprise. "We aren't planning to go out tonight—unless you want to invite us over, that is."

"Love to," Beth said, and he could sense that the caution had returned again, "but it may not work out."

"That's an odd statement to make," he said, and she only laughed in a noncommittal way. "I tell you what, Bee," he said with a sudden inspiration, "you come over to see us. I'll get some steaks and fixings," he said, his voice quickening because for just a second he almost persuaded himself that this was just like any other happy night, that there wasn't any cloud over his world and that if he pretended hard enough that everything was all right it would be, "and we'll have the first cookout of the season. I'm sure the girls will be delighted. How about it, Bee?"

"Brig," Beth said, and she sounded tired and compassionate in a way that suddenly worried him very much, "you go home and see how things are and then if you want to call me again, you can."

"What's the matter?" he asked in genuine alarm. "Beth, what's happened?" A wave of fear crossed his heart. "Has anything happened to Mabel and Pidge? Have they done anything to them?"

"Oh, my dear, no," Beth said. "No. They're quite all right."

"They're with you, then," he said. "They must be. Why?"

"You go home," Beth said again, "and I think Mabel will be along presently."

"What's going on?" he asked despairingly. "Beth, what's happened?"

"She won't tell me," Beth said gently, "but I think perhaps she will want to tell you."

"All right," he said dully like a little boy obeying teacher, for he knew that something terrible must have happened and he did not know now whether he could handle it or not, "all right. I'll go home."

He did not know exactly how he managed to put his desk in order, dismiss the girls, go downstairs, get his car, safely negotiate Saturday afternoon traffic, and get home, for the well-trained mind has a way of functioning automatically in times of stress and he seemed to be out of touch with it just then: it had to get him home by itself. Presently he found himself in his own street approaching his own house, though he could not have told how he got there; the only thing that struck him at that moment was how peaceful and ordinary everything seemed, some kids playing down the block, guests gathering for a party across the street, a dog barking, the sound of birds, a warm wind stirring in the trees, a hazy golden peace on the world, a sense of happiness and well-being filling the neighborhood. Except for him, he thought dully; except for him.

Nor did he know, when he had parked the car and gone in and automatically taken a shower, changed from business suit to sports shirt, shorts, and sandals and come back down again, exactly what was expected of him or what he was supposed to do in the situation in which he found himself. His wife and daughter were gone, Mabel had packed a suitcase, Pooh and Piglet and Raggedy Anne had been included; and it was obvious that they intended to stay awhile, yet on the basis of what he could find upstairs he had no means of knowing why. Beth's cryptic remarks hadn't been much help, and though he had half expected a dramatic note in the bedroom—except that drama wasn't Mabel's forte—there had been none.

It was not until he wandered, bewildered, into the kitchen in search of a glass of milk that he found what he was looking for, propped up against a box of soap on the drainboard. "Thought it best to take Pidge to Beth's," it said. "Will be back to fix your dinner and talk later." Attached to it with a straight pin was an envelope with Mabel's name typed on it, apparently delivered by Western Union messenger.

He took it out on the sun porch, sat down in the glider, and removed the contents, which appeared at first blush to be the sort of ugly illiterate filth that comes to many an official desk, the snarl of the beast in the jungle that underlies the polite exchanges of society. Composed of pasted letters clipped from a newspaper, its message was quite explicit enough, even for Mabel, who was not very sophisticated about such matters, or indeed about much of anything.

His first impulse, a standard one in the capital in times of crisis, was to mix himself a drink; but he made himself reject the idea of liquor, concentrate upon the problem at hand and face up, however painful it might be, to the communication he held in his hand and the implications of his wife's abrupt departure upon receipt of it. He had never given her cause to believe it, yet in some way apparently almost instinctive she evidently did believe it, or at any rate she believed it enough to feel that it might be possible: and he realized now with a terrible clarity how badly he must have failed her down the years, not as a husband or a father or a provider, not sexually or socially or in any other of the ways that mattered together but did not matter so much one by one, but simply because in none of these relationships that went into the total structure of a good marriage had he given her enough of himself. Always, he could see now, there must have been some area where she felt herself barred and kept out, some inner kingdom of his being where she was forever alien. A heavy pity for them both touched his heart, for he had never meant it to be that way, he had done his best, he had always tried to be kind, and apparently it hadn't been enough; and he knew now that it was inevitable, he couldn't have helped it, it had to be so, for it was his nature to walk his way alone, and with the greatest and best and most sincere will in the world he could not have overcome it no matter how he tried. It went far beyond what a cleverer wife might have missed in the self-confusions brought on by more astute attempts to analyze it and reached into a region of instinctive understanding where someone like Mabel, not even knowing what she knew, would even so realize enough to suspect that her own exclusion might cover areas of his heart where others might conceivably be able to enter.

And now in this evil thing he held in his hand, this apparent crudity—which he suspected was probably a very clever parody of crudity—she had suddenly found it all spelled out with a brutal clarity that could not be evaded. Someone had entered those areas after all: it said so on this piece of paper, and though he knew she must have spent many anguished minutes trying not to believe it, she had ended by not being sure, for the one thing she did know for certain was that she never had. No wonder her first reaction had been to leave; the wonder was that she could possibly be brave enough to come back and face him. But he knew humbly that she would, for he understood, now that it was too late, a little of the depth of her love for him which, in her nervous, awkward, unhappily emotional way she had tried for so long, with so little success, to show.

When he heard her enter the house he touched a match to the carefully smudged paper and watched it burn down to ashes on the red-tile floor. Then he got up and went inside, closing the door to the sun porch behind him so that no word of their conversation could drift out into the gently golden afternoon. He felt a physical pain, as though he had run a great distance, climbed a great mountain, just escaped drowning—or, perhaps, was just about to drown. He squared his shoulders and held his head high, though he was so terribly tired and sick and unhappy that he did not know how long he could keep from collapsing. He heard her in the kitchen, and after a moment she came out and joined him in the living room.

"It was good of you to come back," he said.

"Oh," she said, not looking at him, "I couldn't let you get your own dinner. You probably wouldn't know how."

"I probably could have managed," he said, "but it's better with you here."

"Is it?" she said, looking at him from swollen eyes. "Is it really better with me here?" She gave a shaky little laugh and sat down in a chair across the room from him. "I've never really been sure."

He started to protest and then dropped it.

"Oh, beloved," he said instead, "I am so sorry you have had to be subjected to this."

"Well," she said with a forlorn attempt at bitter humor, "I guess that's politics."

"I guess it is," he said, "but I should have been able to protect you from it somehow."

"How could you have," she said, "once—once—it was done?"

"You believe it, then," he said. Mabel tried an ironic smile, but it didn't work.

"The note I got was—rather specific," she said.

"Yes," he said quietly. "Well, there's no need for anything but honesty between us now. It happened: it happened. Long before I ever met you, long before I ever entered public life, long ago when I was in the war. In Honolulu in the war, just like the man said. People go off the track sometimes, under pressures like the war. That's what happened to me. I went off the track. I hope you can believe that too."

"I do," Mabel said slowly. "I guess."

"Never before," he said, "and never since. You've got to believe it, if we're to come through this at all."

"I can't understand how you could—how you could do such a horrible thing," she said.

"It didn't seem horrible at the time," he said honestly, "and I am not going to say now that it did, even to you. But I have lived all my life since being as good a man as I could, to make up for it. I think," he said with a sudden bitterness, "that gives me the right to a little charity now."

"I'm trying to be charitable," she said brokenly, "except that——"

"Except what?" he asked in the same bitter way. "Charity isn't divisible. You have it or you don't. Except what?"

"Except that I don't know whether it was just the war, or whether—whether you might have done it anyway," she said, and began to cry, abrupt, racking sobs that hurt him terribly. "I don't—mean that—the way it sounds," she said between them. "But you've always seemed so—so closed-off from me, somehow, and I haven't been able to get through. *I just haven't been able to get through.*"

"Beloved, beloved," he said. "That hasn't been the reason. Oh, you must believe me. It hasn't been the reason, ever."

"Then it must be me," she said in a voice of utter desolation. "That's the only thing left, so it must be me."

"No, it hasn't been you," he said desperately. "You've been a wonderful wife and mother and helpmate and I don't know what I could have done without you. I don't know what I *will* do without you," he added in a tone as desolate as hers, "if this doesn't work out." He started to stand up to give his words greater emphasis, but he found that his legs weren't working very well just then, so he remained seated. "Whatever failure there has been," he said firmly through the gray haze of tiredness that filled the world, "has been my failure, and it hasn't been yours in any way at all. Nor has it had any relation to anything I did in the war. It's been my failure to be as good a husband and father as I should have been."

"You're wonderful with Pidge," she said, more quietly, and the name of their daughter seemed briefly to invoke a fragile calm upon their conversation.

"Well," he said, "all I can do is promise to do better, I guess. It seems a feeble foundation, but I suppose many a marriage before ours has been rebuilt upon it. I'm sorry, as I said, that you have been subjected to this, but I hope you can realize the pressures I'm under right now. I hope you will come back and—and help me. I need you to help me."

"I don't know," she said, beginning to sob again. "I just don't know what to do. If I could only believe that—that you really belonged to me, and that I—I really belonged to you, then maybe—— But I don't know," she said, and she gave him an anguished and searching look. *"How can I ever be sure again?"*

He felt then as though the world had ended, and that even if it weren't entirely official yet, they would notify him presently. Now he was dead inside, himself, and those who had wished to destroy him had achieved their purpose. He had never fainted, but he came as close to it as he ever would right now as the room seemed to spin and his wife with a sudden cry of despair and contrition said, "Oh, I didn't mean that," and ran to him.

"I didn't mean that," she said again through her sobs, "I didn't, I didn't, I didn't."

But her husband did not answer as he held her in his arms, staring out upon the gentle twilight and absently stroking her hair while she clung to him and cried as though her heart would break, as his already had.

After that time began to dissolve and the world no longer seemed to have much light or dimension. The golden day, the golden season, had vanished somewhere into night and he did not know whether it would ever return for them. Mabel did stay, and in a tremulous phone call to Beth she requested the return of Pidge, who was presently delivered troubled and upset but valiantly managing not to cry. Beth came in and kissed them both and deliberately stayed for a while, ignoring their ravaged expressions and chatting firmly about ordinaries until she began to perceive what seemed to be a relative calm returning. And somehow, so tenacious is the human animal and so capable when necessary of withstanding what seem at the moment to be the most completely devastating and destructive blows, calm actually did return and it actually was genuine —or genuine enough, at least, for Mabel to put together some kind of a meal for him, which he barely touched, and for them both to give Pidge her bath with a determined attempt at lightness that sent her to bed, though still troubled, not quite as uneasy as she had been. He said he wanted to watch the COMFORT rally and Mabel decided she would go up early to bed, trying not to cling to him too desperately again as she kissed him good night. He sat down before the television set to watch the junior of his two mortal enemies perform.

It was, for twenty-five minutes of it, a standard performance, notable principally because the Committee on Making Further Offers for a Russian Truce had managed to draw a surprisingly large crowd. The National Guard Armory was full to overflowing, an estimated 5,000 more were standing outside listening to the proceedings through loudspeakers, and had he been in a condition and a state of mind to appraise it with the political shrewdness he used to know before his world began to collapse, he would have considered this highly significant of the mood of worry and indecision in the country. Washington was not a town for big rallies or violent enthusiasms, everybody there had seen too much history parade by to get very excited about it, and the tides of national policy, evershifting, produced a lively interest but very rarely the type of fanatic concern that COMFORT fed on. Nonetheless, the crowd was there, the proof of it was fully visible on the little screen, and when Senator Van

Ackerman and the nominee entered together the mood was unmistakable. There was a roar of insensate sound that must have caused shivers in all rational men who heard it, and upon the man who knew he might be about to be offered up as victim it struck with a chilling impact that did not diminish even though he knew Fred was far too clever to make as crude an attack as he had threatened. He would be offered up, all right, but in this place and before a national audience, it would be smoothly done. The alley brutality that had shattered his home would not be visible here, for Americans, telling each other constantly that politics was a dirty business, did not dare let themselves realize that upon occasion it could actually be *that* dirty. That would really upset them; and while they liked to be clever about their own shortcomings, they did not like to be upset by them. Senator Van Ackerman would not upset them.

He introduced Bob Leffingwell, who got an enormous cheer; he spoke glowingly of the President, who got another; he dwelt for several minutes upon "the very real threat, yes, the very *real* threat that the Soviets may at this very moment be on their way to the moon, there to seize upon and establish over us a military advantage that could put this great Republic even more deeply in peril than she already is"; he gave them the line they were waiting for—"As for me, I had rather crawl on my knees to Moscow than die under an atom bomb!" and the roar without sense, without reason, without sanity, flooded forth again; and finally he turned to the Senate of the United States and the decision it would soon be called upon to render on the nomination of Robert A. Leffingwell. If, that is, the "inexplicable, inexcusable, unforgivable opposition of the senior Senator from Utah can be removed from the path of this great man!"

Once again this brought the savage, animal roar that came through the machine like a blow, and he went on in a slow and emphatic voice. Only now he held a white paper.

"I have here in my hand," he said, and he held it up for them all to see, "the means to do it." He waited for them to subside while the cameras swung back and forth across the hall, recording its excitement in a hundred straining faces.

"I will not tell you about it tonight, my friends," he said, and there was a sudden disappointed "Oh!" which he quickly caught up, "but I will say this: it is documented proof that this paragon of virtues who has set himself up to fight the nomination of Robert A. Leffingwell is not a paragon of virtues at all. Oh no, my friends, *not at all!*" He paused dramatically and in the house in Spring Valley a member of the national audience braced himself with a sort of sick defensiveness against what might come next. "He is not morally fit to lick Bob Leffingwell's boots!" Fred shouted with a sudden, explosive, fanatic vigor. "He is not morally fit, period! *And I have the proof!*" He held the paper aloft again as the crowd, somewhat hesitant, somewhat doubtful, but under the whiplash of his own obvious excitement, gave him growing applause. "I cannot tell you here,

my friends," he said, "much as I would like to do so. But I urge you to read
what I have to say in the Senate on Monday. There in that great forum
where this pretender of moral virtues presumes to sit"—and where, his
victim reflected bitterly, he would be protected by legislative immunity
and could not be sued or silenced, except by a claim of personal privilege
it would be an admission to make—"there, I will tell you exactly how
morally unfit he is. And I will show the Senate the proof and the country
the proof and the world the proof! And we will remove him from the path
of Robert A. Leffingwell!"

He waved the paper again triumphantly above his head as the crowd
burst into a last explosion of sound and the cameras panned again around
the Armory, and the wildly waving COMFORT banners, in one last inspired shot on somebody's part, filled the screen and faded out.

And that, he knew with an exhausted certainty, was a promise Fred
meant to keep.

He did not know exactly what became of time, except that it passed.
He sat alone in the living room and it got darker. He snapped on a light,
automatically thinking the neighbors might wonder if the house were still
too early. Sometime around ten the phone rang and AP said apologetically
out of old friendship, "Brig, I hate to bother you, but my office has asked
me to find out if you care to make any comment on——" He said shortly,
"I do not," and hung up. In rapid succession UPI and the major newspaper
bureaus did the same, and to them he said the same. There followed a
period when there were no calls, and during it he wandered into the
kitchen and, suddenly hungry, drank a glass of milk and ate several
pieces of bread and butter. He knew this was not enough to sustain him
after the day he had spent virtually without food, but as abruptly as he
had become hungry he could eat no more.

It was not so very long after that, probably around midnight, that the
phone rang insistently and he finally went to the downstairs extension
and picked it up. There came to him over long distance, from some point
he did not know, a voice he had never thought, and never wanted, to hear
again.

"Brig?" it said, and somehow he found the strength to answer it calmly.

"Yes," he said.

"Brig," the voice said, and he could tell that its owner was close to
crying, "Brig, did you see that television program?"

"Yes," he said, "I saw it."

"It's my fault," the voice said forlornly.

"*What?*" he said, and it seemed to him that there wasn't so very much
more that he could stand without going under.

"They looked me up," the voice said. "They traced me through the
service—I stayed in until about six months ago—and when they found me
I was—sort of down and out, and they offered me money—an awful lot of

money, Brig. I knew I shouldn't do it, but I needed it and so—so I told
them what they wanted to know. And then I signed it. And then they
paid me."

"Why didn't you come to me if you were hard up?" he asked, though it
didn't matter, for there was nothing to reverse what had been done, it was
done forever. "I would have helped you. All you had to do was ask."

"Well," the voice said, "you were married and settled and famous, and
I didn't think you would want me to—bother you."

"But I wouldn't have let you starve," he said. "Certainly I wouldn't. I
could have helped you get a job somewhere."

"Oh, Brig, I'm so sorry," the voice said in a rush. "I didn't mean—Brig,
I never meant to hurt you. Brig——"

He sighed. How old was he? How old had he been then? Eighteen,
hadn't he said? Somehow he had never thought of him as growing any
older, and apparently he never had.

"I know you didn't," he said slowly. "You did what you thought you had
to do. That's all I did, once. That's all anybody ever does. You aren't to
blame, I'm not to blame, nobody's to blame—except the war, maybe. And
there's nothing we can do about that now. Don't worry about it. I'll manage."

"Brig——" the voice said desperately.

"Don't worry about it," he said. "Try not to think about it. I forgive you,
and it's all right. I'm going to hang up now. Take care of yourself."

"But I don't want you to hang up," the voice said like a little child.

"I don't want to," he said, and he knew now at last in his loneliness and
despair that it was true, "but I must."

And he did, though an instant later he lifted the receiver again and
said, "Wait!" But the line was dead, the impersonally buzzing dial tone
was the only answer.

How far he had traveled, he thought, since first he had heard that
voice; how far, over land and over sea and through the forests of the
heart, to come at last to face himself.

He did not know how it was that he happened to be staring into the
open drawer of his desk in the study, and he did not know what time it
was, 2 A.M., or 3, or sometime thereabouts; but there was no doubt what he
was staring at. It lay before him sleek and black and gleaming, carrying
with it memories of boyhood days when it had first been given him by
his father, of days during and after college and the war when he had
taken it along as an auxiliary weapon for target practice on hunting trips.
He took it out now and balanced it with a practiced ease in his hand, and
suddenly he seemed to lose consciousness, the gray haze over the world
became even thicker, he remained there motionless, unfeeling, unthinking,
for he knew not how long. At last with an iron effort of the will he brought
himself back from wherever he had been, put it quickly back in the

drawer, and slammed it shut. "My God," he cried out despairingly to the empty room, "what am I thinking?" But he knew with an implacable certainty from which there was no escape what he was thinking. It had begun by reminding him of childhood and youth, but it had ended by saying something quite different. He realized with a sick horror for which there appeared to be no help that he was a long way now from hunting in the Uintas and fishing along the Green.

8

Sometime in the night, exhausted, he slept; sometime in the morning he awoke, exhausted. The day loomed before him an obstacle so vast and so filled with difficulty and anguish that he did not know whether he could surmount it or not. Somewhere in the depths of the midnight hours he had attained the fragile hope that Fred might not quite dare to go through with it after all; but it was a tenuous hope at best and one he had little faith in. If he could reach Orrin tomorrow morning, if he could ask Bob to help, if Lafe and Seab and Stanley and the rest of his friends would rally to him, there could be pressures brought to bear upon the junior Senator from Wyoming so powerful that he would think long and hard before he ventured to ignore them; but that he probably would ignore them when all was said and done seemed likely, for there was in him a streak of gambling that fed on opposition and knew no restraints. And he had the White House with him, and that was enough to cancel anything that decency and fairness might try to do.

So it seemed to the senior Senator from Utah as he rose with a dragging weariness and went about the business of getting ready to meet the day, that it was only by the most remote and slender thread that his reputation, and indeed his life, now hung. Somehow in spite of this, calling on the last reserves of a heart and mind and body driven close to their ultimate limits, he managed to get dressed and go downstairs, put a fair face on breakfast, though he ate very little of it, and talk to his wife almost as though it were any other day. His daughter mercifully was sleeping late for once, and so he had a little time to gather himself together and prepare himself to be casual before she began calling from upstairs. He was about to go up to her when a car stopped in the driveway and looking out in some puzzlement he saw the director of the Washington *Post* coming toward the house. He suggested to Mabel that she tend to Pidge, and with a heavy heart, for he knew this unprecedented call must mean more trouble, he went to the door.

"Come in, Ned," he said quietly, and the director of the *Post*, looking embarrassed and grave, complied.

"I won't stay long, Brig," he said, "but I thought you ought to know about this."

"Yes," he said absently, for his heart had begun to pound painfully. "Sit down and tell me about it."

The director of the *Post* sighed.

"This is a cruel town," he said, "when you get on the wrong side of it. A great town and a good town, and a petty town and a cruel town. And nobody ever knows from day to day which face it is going to put on."

"Write that down," Brig said with a last feeble attempt at humor, "you can use it in an editorial."

"Oh no," the director of the *Post* said with an answering wryness. "That would be telling the truth about it, and that would be much too upsetting. Brig," he said abruptly, "I have a column here that Henry Wilson has sent out for use in tomorrow morning's paper. Apparently he got it from Fred Van Ackerman, because it seems to tie in with what Fred was saying at the rally last night. I know how you must feel and how much it may hurt to read it, but I thought you should be forewarned, so I brought it to you."

"I don't want to read it," Brig said, and a sharp little ache seemed to be developing somewhere behind his eyes, "I just don't want to."

"Well, I don't blame you," the director of the *Post* said. "You know how he is. It isn't quite slander, it isn't quite libel, it's just enough to murder a man. He doesn't come right out with anything, he never does; he just skirts the edge of absolute evil, destroying people as he goes. I don't know why we continue to take his damned column, except that it's so entertaining and people want to read it."

"Oh, he backs some good causes," Brig said bitterly. "I believe he likes his grandchildren, and he helps the Red Cross."

"Yes," the director of the *Post* said. "Well. We're not going to use it, and I've destroyed the other copies of it that came to us. This is the only one left, and I'm tearing it up right now." And he proceeded to do so, in tiny, neat, savagely-ripped pieces that he put in the wastebasket by the desk. "We're against you on this, and as you know we haven't hesitated to say so, but there are limits. And there are limits for most of us. Nobody in this town, we or the *Star* or the *News* or the services or the bureaus or any one of a hundred others, will touch it with a ten-foot pole. Ninety-nine percent of the press won't touch it anywhere in the country. But somebody will, and I thought you should be warned. Some little paper someplace," he said with an expression of unhappy distaste, "will run it big as life, and then the wire services will feel they have to pick it up and send it across country, and then we'll be faced with the problem of whether to run it as a national wire-service story after refusing to run it as a column. And there we'll be, trapped in our own operation. Especially if Fred quotes from it tomorrow instead of attacking you direct, which would fit in with his usual slimy way of doing things."

The Senator from Utah managed a wan little smile.

"It's really—pretty brutal, isn't it?" he asked in an almost apologetic tone. "I guess if I weren't involved in it I'd find it quite interesting, the way you go about ruining a man. I've never done anything like that to anyone, myself. It's quite a revelation."

"I'm sorry," the director of the *Post* said. "I truly am. People start things—they take stands—pressures drive them farther and farther apart—before long it's completely out of hand. And I suppose we in the press are as much to blame as anybody. We don't mean to be cruel, but the prize begins to seem worth it, and before we know it we're being as bloodthirsty as everyone else." He shook his head in wonderment. "What a strange life we all lead in this town," he said, "and all because we think we're doing the right thing for the country."

"If all the people who talk about doing the right thing for the country only did the right thing for the country," Brig said with a weary dryness, "what a wonderful country it would be."

"It is a wonderful country," the director of the *Post* said. "It just gets a little mixed-up, sometimes."

"Yes," Brig said. He suddenly felt profoundly touched by his visitor's kindness, his genuine interest and friendliness even though they were on opposite sides of the nomination, the fact that he would take the trouble to come by personally on a Sunday morning. His voice was not very steady as he said, "Thank you for coming by, Ned. It was terribly decent of you. I appreciate it more than I can say."

"I hope it works out all right for you," the director of the *Post* said seriously. "We'll try to treat Fred's speech tomorrow with as much restraint as we can. We can't ignore it, but we won't go overboard. And we won't run the column."

"But somebody will," Brig said, and the director of the *Post* sighed. "Yes," he said. "Somebody will."

So there was no foundation for any hope that Fred would not go through with it, the thing was already in motion, Henry Wilson was already doing his dirty work for him, and in an alliance more cold-bloodedly ruthless than the President had perhaps conceived when he unleashed his forces, they were out to profit from his fall, each in his own characteristic way. For Fred it would be headlines and political advantage, and for Henry, possibly a few more clients on the strength of his latest sensation, and the standard accolade he always got from his readers: "Well, I don't know whether he always tells the truth or not, but at least he prints things about Washington you don't see anywhere else." The latest of these, it was now apparent, would provide the basis for the destruction of a Senator; and nothing he could see now could in any way stop it.

This knowledge, which meant the end of his reputation, his career, his marriage, all the great world and the fair things in it, all the things that made life worth living, the chance for public service, the chance to do good, the chance to achieve a little share of happiness for himself and his family, did not come to him as a shattering revelation, for he was past the

point for that. Rather it came into his being in a sort of subconscious
seepage, so that the tired dark eyes did not look more tired, the haggard
expression did not become more haggard, the desperate weariness did not
become more desperate. Instead a curious kind of numbness began to
envelope his heart and mind, the grayness over the world became more
gray; he did not seem to see so well, his hearing actually seemed to be
affected, his understanding appeared to fail a little, things did not penetrate
as they used to do. He moved around the house aimlessly, picked up
magazines and books and put them down again, leafed pointlessly through
the Sunday paper, spoke to Mabel with an absent air that frightened her.
With a great effort when Pidge wanted to play he managed to muster a
reasonable appearance of calm, took her out into the yard, pushed her in
the swing, tossed a ball back and forth, watched the fishes in the pond.
There began to come upon him, subtle, insistent, inexorable, inescapable,
the feeling that he was doing everything for the last time, that he was
looking his last upon things most lovely and most dear, that only a miracle
could prevent a culmination that had been growing in his mind ever since
he had come upon the gun last night. Once when his daughter asked him
worriedly, "Daddy, what's the matter?" it was all he could do to keep
from crying out in anguish, but in some way that was more instinct than
intent he managed to muster from somewhere something that passed for
a laugh, and by throwing the ball suddenly far down the lawn he diverted
her and by the time she came trotting back he was again in some sort of
control of himself and could go on a little longer.

Noon came and with it food he again could hardly touch. Looking
frightened and drawn, Mabel said she thought she would lie down and
take a nap and suggested that he do the same. He said he would put
Pidge down and then think about it. Possibly, he said, he might go on up
to the Hill to the office and try to get caught up a little, so if she woke and
found him gone she would know where he was. When she wanted to know
what there was to do there on Sunday, he said vaguely, "Oh, there are
letters and things." She started up the stairs and then turned back abruptly
and kissed him, hard. "I'm here," she said, as though it proved something.
It could have once, but it was too late now.

As soon as she had gone up and the door of the bedroom had closed he
put through a call to the proprietor of "Meet the Press." Eager and excited,
for in the wake of the COMFORT rally he was sure he had a sensation
on his hands, the little man greeted him. "I'm sorry to give you such short
notice," he said, "but I won't be able to appear this afternoon. "But,
Senator——" the little man cried in angry disbelief. "I'm sorry," he said,
and hung up.

When he put Pidge to bed there was some business, rather willful,
about wanting several special toys to take naps too; he got them for her
and bedded her down.

"Daddy," she said, "will you play with me when I get up?"

"If I'm here," he said in a muffled voice, and she looked at him in some alarm.

"Won't you be?" she asked. He shook his head.

"I don't know," he said finally.

"Where will you be?" she said.

"I'll—try to get back to you," he said.

"And then will we play?" she asked.

"Yes, my baby," he said. "Forever and ever."

"I do love you lots, Daddy," she said comfortably, snuggling down into the blankets.

"That's good," he said, and there was a terrible crying in his heart. "I love you too." He gave her a hurried kiss and went quickly to the door. "I'm going to go now," he managed to say.

"All right," she said sleepily. "Come back later."

"Yes, baby," he said as he closed the door. "Yes. I will. Sometime. Somewhere. Somehow."

He leaned his head against the wall and closed his eyes in agony.

Before the bedroom door he hesitated for a long moment and then went on.

I tried, he thought. I tried, my poor beloved who could never understand me. I wanted to make you happy, but God wouldn't let me. He had other plans. Go home to Utah and forget I ever lived. I wasn't worth it, after all.

He took the gun, got in the car and drove, guided by blind instinct and seven years of habit, through the golden afternoon to Capitol Hill.

A few cars passed, a few tourists meandered; a Sunday calm lay on the Hill. "Working, Senator?" the guard on the door said brightly. "Senator Hanson and Senator Cooley are too." He tried to enter his office quietly so that he would not arouse his upstairs neighbor, but his hands seemed to be trembling and the heavy door slipped shut with a thud. The phone promptly rang.

"Brigham?" the sleepy old voice said. "Is that you down there, Brigham?"

"Yes, Seab," he said, "I'm down here."

"Well, sir," Senator Cooley said, "I'm glad you are, Brigham, because I was intending to call you."

"Yes, Seab," he said automatically again. "What can I do for you?"

"I heard that evil little monster last night," Seab said, "and I have been thinking about him. Yes, sir, I have been thinking most carefully about him. I have decided to help you, Brig. I want you to know that I will be with you, and we will see what we can do about him. Yes, sir, we will surely see."

"Thank you, Seab," he said.

"That isn't all," Senator Cooley said.

"No?" he said, and braced himself for whatever might come. "What else?"

"Well, sir," Seab said, "I have decided that much as I despise Mr. Robert—A.—Leffingwell, and much as I despise that being in the White House, and much as I would dearly love to get them both, the pleasure is not sufficient if it is really going to mean harm to you. No, sir, it isn't sufficient if that's what it means. I am quite an old man, Brigham," he said, "and I know by now when a fine young man comes to the Senate, and I suspect that much as it might satisfy my ego to get them, an old man's ego isn't worth a young man's career and happiness. I truly suspect it isn't. I don't know what they have to fight you with, but I don't like the sound of it. I don't like the sound of it at all. I think you could be most severely hurt. I think this would be a real tragedy for you, and for the country, and for the Senate. I think you are worth a hundred times any satisfaction I might get from beating Mr. Leffingwell. I gen-u-inely do."

"Well, thank you, Seab," he said dully, for what was there to say? "I appreciate it."

"So," Senator Cooley said. "Therefore. You just do what you think best to save yourself, and if that means giving in to them, I want you to feel free to do so without any worries about me. As far as I am concerned, I have forgotten already that I ever knew about James Morton, and nobody will ever know that I did. No, sir. Nobody ever will."

"Thank you, Seab," he said again in the same dull voice. "I wish I could tell you how much I appreciate——"

"Now, then," Seab interrupted briskly. "I think the first thing we should do tomorrow morning is talk to Bob and Orrin and decide what to do about that twisted little man from Wyoming. I told Bob before the vote Wednesday that he ought to destroy him, and I suspect now he may agree with me. So you don't worry, Brig. We'll take care of him, and everything will be all right."

"That's good," he said weakly. "That's very good."

"Are you feeling poorly, Brigham?" Senator Cooley asked in some alarm. "You don't sound very well."

"I'm all right," he said. "I'm all right."

"I tell you," Seab said after a moment. "Are you planning to be down there awhile?"

"Yes," he said. "Awhile."

"I'll come down presently and we'll go eat something," Seab said. "Unless you are planning to go home?"

"No," he said. "I'm not planning to go home."

"Good," Senator Cooley said. "I'll see you later, then, hear?"

"Thank you so much for everything, Seab," he said.

"It wasn't worth it when I really realized how they meant to act," Seab said. "I'll see you later, Brigham."

"I'll be here," he said.

Two minutes later the phone rang again.

"Hi, buddy," Lafe said. "I tried you a couple of minutes ago, but the line was busy."

"I was talking to Seab," he said.

"Oh, is he working too?" Lafe asked. "The old war horse never stops, does he?"

"He's very kind," Brig said.

"I know he is, at heart," Lafe said, "even if it's hard to find the heart now and then. I just heard about your canceling out on 'Meet the Press.' What's wrong?"

"Maybe you could say Fred scared me out," he said. "Does it matter?"

"Of course it matters," Lafe said. "Do you want me to go and see him? Nothing would give me more pleasure than to mop up the floor with the slimy two-bit bastard."

"Thanks, Lafe," he said, and if it had been in another world he would have felt amusement, but there was no time for it now. "I don't think there'd be much point."

"Are you all right?" Lafe asked sharply. "You don't sound good at all."

"I'm O.K.," he said.

"Are you sure?" Lafe asked suspiciously.

"I'm O.K.," he said, trying to make it vigorous.

"I don't think you ought to be alone," Lafe said in a worried tone. "I can be up there in ten minutes if you need me."

"No, I wouldn't want you to do that," he said. "I'm all right, Lafe. Honestly I am."

"Well," Lafe said doubtfully. "I just think I might come up anyway. You don't sound good to me."

"No," he said hastily. "No, no."

"I think so," Lafe said firmly.

"Look," he said desperately. "Seab said something about coming down for a bite to eat later on. Why don't you come up in—say in a couple of hours."

"Well," Lafe said, still sounding doubtful, "if you really feel that would be better——"

"Yes," he said shortly.

"O.K.," Lafe said, not very convinced. "If that's the way you want it."

"I do," he said. He hesitated. "Lafe?" he said.

"Yes?" Lafe said.

"Thank you for everything too," he said.

"*Now* what the hell?" Lafe demanded in alarm. "I'm coming up there, buddy. I'm damned worried about you."

"A couple of hours," he repeated dully. There was a silence.

"All right," Lafe said slowly. "Unless I decide to come up earlier."

"I'd rather you didn't," he said. "Please, Lafe. I'll—I'll be here later."

"Is that a promise?" Lafe asked.

"That's a promise," he said.

"Well, all right," Lafe said doubtfully, "but I still don't like it."

Now there remained only the letter to Orrin, and slowly, trying to be as coherent as possible though not always succeeding, he typed it out: the call from James Morton, the negotiations with the President, the White House meeting, the developments of the past two days. With an absolute candor, for now there was no longer any need for false pretense and he was talking to an old friend for the last time, he told him also the basis of the President's ruthless action, Fred's speech to COMFORT and the speech he was threatening to make in the Senate tomorrow. If Orrin was to make the fight he would now have to make, he needed to know it all; and quite simply the Senator from Utah told him, wasting no time on apologies or justifications beyond the absolute minimum that would be fair to himself, trusting to Orrin's friendship to understand and forgive. When it was done he put it in an envelope, typed "SENATOR KNOX—PERSONAL" on it, and leaving his office quietly, walked down the deserted corridor, turned right down the connecting wing to Orrin's door, and slipped it underneath. No one was about as he went down, and no one was about as he returned. Apparently he and Seab and Powell Hanson up on the fourth floor were the only Senators in the whole vast building on this quiet Sunday afternoon.

Back in his office, he remained for some little time seated at his desk. Through his mind in a final mustering there passed the arguments for and against what he had done in Honolulu, for and against what he had done in the nomination. The one had appeared to be something over and beyond his own volition, the other had been a deliberate course of action. Knowing what he knew now, the terrible consequences of that course, he still could not tell himself that he could in any fundamental have done differently. He might have knuckled under to the President, he might have turned tail and run at the threat of blackmail, he might have been a coward to his political principles and betrayed what he conceived to be his duty to the country: but he would not have been Brigham Anderson if he had. Some people had the hard road to follow, if they would be true to themselves; and high and hard and lonely his had been, to bring to so tragic an ending a character of such great promise and such great worth, cast away like chaff on the wind.

Except that this was not how it had been cast away, of course. It had been cast away for a purpose and a cause which he deemed valid and which, being himself, he had had no choice but to follow where it might lead. Nor was he unaware of the cruel irony of it. Here was he, carrying a secret in his past, fighting the nominee, who carried a secret in his past; and what, essentially, except that his secret was purely personal and harmed no one else, while the nominee's went to his public philosophies and could conceivably be of great harm to his country, was the difference between them? Both were guilty of concealment, both were guilty of lying to the world, both had protected their reputations as best they could, and both had been discovered. The major difference then became that the nominee's was the popular cause, backed by all the combination of power and politics and press of Washington, while his was the unpopular, bitterly opposed by that combination; so that the nominee, if his luck held, might yet emerge unscathed, while he, driven to the wall by all the latent savagery of politics, must be a sacrifice. For he knew as surely as he knew Washington that if he had been a supporter of the nominee his past would never have been used against him; and by the same bitter token he knew that if it had been the nominee who had kept an inadvertent wartime rendezvous the fact would have been hushed up and covered over and hidden from the public, and under the protections of a bland, united conspiracy of silence his nomination would have been triumphantly confirmed. It had happened, and in the history that is not written but lives in the memories of the capital, there were examples men remembered very well.

As it was, he was the ideal sacrifice to ease the conscience of them all. The ruthless and the righteous could rejoice equally, for the one could say, "See? He stood in our way." And the other could say, "See? He broke our rules." And they could join hands together and dance around his bier.

And for that, was a man to stop judging when he had been chosen to judge? How could society continue if all whose hands were soiled with human living permitted themselves to be forever after paralyzed? It could not be. In any case, the distinctions were not clear enough. Who were the judges and who the judged, and who among them perfect enough to say, I am right and you are wrong? And what, essentially, did it matter?

Judge not that ye be not judged, the injunction said; let him who is without sin cast the first stone. But the practical needs of society had made the admonition impossible to affirm. First there came responsibility and then, if there were integrity enough and courage to face the consequences whatever they might be, there came the hard necessity to step forward and say, I will cast it, for someone must. And if the troops were with you, you succeeded in rendering judgment fairly or unfairly according to your lights, humbled as you might be, if you were lucky, by your own human failings: and if the troops were not with you, the stones were hurled back upon you, and the judgment was reversed.

But all of that was beside the point now, and in a dazed somnambulistic way he realized it. It was late, the time for philosophizing was over, there was little left to do and he did it with a dreamlike efficiency that was the only way it could be done. He closed the venetian blinds, turned off all the lamps but one, unlocked his outer door, so they would not have to break it in when Seab came by for him, got a towel from the washroom, returned to his desk, and sat down; saying to the Deity to whom he had been taught to pray as a very little boy, God, please help me.

Please let me be brave just a little while longer. Please. He wanted to cry and he tried to, but the agony was too deep, the tears would not come.

At the last he took a sheet of Foreign Relations Committee stationery bearing his name and wrote upon it in a large, irregular hand that was far from his usual careful script two words:

"I'm sorry."

And he was sorry, with a sorrow deeper than words could ever convey; sorry for himself, sorry for his family, sorry for the boy, sorry for all his friends and his country and the world and for all the things in human living for which there are no answers and from which there is no escape. And not the least of these, he knew now, were a man's weakness and a man's strength, for each in its time he had obeyed the commands of both, and together they had brought him down.

Somewhere in a crowded hall a loud voice was saying, "And so I present to you the man who——" On Bethany Beach a tiny figure was wetting the water, a lost boy was crying on the telephone, and on the floor of the Senate the senior Senator from Utah, that nice guy that everybody liked so much, was rising to seek recognition from the Chair.

Then it all ended, but not before, in one last moment of rigid and unflinching honesty, he realized that it was not only of his family that he was thinking as he died. It was of a beach in Honolulu on a long, hot, lazy afternoon.

The waves crashed and he heard for the last time the exultant cries of the surf riders, far out.

Above in his office Senator Cooley stopped reading abruptly. He had heard something, and with a sudden prickling of the hairs on the back of his neck he was almost sure he knew what it was. And he was almost sure it had come from the office directly beneath. He closed his book very carefully, got up very slowly and deliberately, and moving with great care, because he was beginning to tremble and knew if he didn't hold himself in he wouldn't be able to stop, he got up and left his office, locked the door neatly behind him, walked down the corridor to the stairs, down the stairs and back along the corridor until he stood before the door below.

"Brigham?" he called softly in the empty hallway. "This is Seab, Brigham. Are you in there, Brig?"

But there was no answer; and feeling suddenly very old and very tired and every bit of seventy-five, weighted down with the world's sorrow to which he now knew more was about to be added, the senior Senator from South Carolina took a deep breath, stepped forward, and opened the door; aware with a flash of thankfulness as he did so that he would not have to face it alone, the corridor was no longer empty, far down it the junior Senator from Ioway was hurrying, calling his name. He paused and waited, so that they could go in together.

Much later that night, after the news had babbled out over the airways and across the nation and around the globe, a tall young man with haunted eyes got drunk in a shabby café in a little town in Indiana and jumped off a bridge. There were no papers on his body and nobody knew who he was. No banner headlines heralded his demise, and far away in the beautiful city where ruthless men had used him ruthlessly for their purposes no one even knew that he was gone.

Four

Orrin Knox's Book

1

Now it is 4 A.M. and ghosts walk. See them as they march across the counterpane of the man who allows himself, as a small egotistical prerogative of his office, the privilege of sleeping in the Lincoln Bed: proud George and two tart Adamses, thoughtful Tom and angry Andy, careful Van the Used-up Man, Tippecanoe and Tyler too, patient Abe and steady Grover, bouncing Teddy and farseeing Woodrow, prickly-pickley Calvin, stolid-solid Herbert, dashing Franklin, headstrong Harry, General Don't-Tell-Me-Your-Troubles, and the rest. See them pass, calm, imperious, frozen into history, all passion spent, all battles over, defeats forgotten, victories recorded, everything neat and orderly and ruffled no more by the bitter passions and emotions that swirled about them in their time. Impassive and impervious, they stare back at him in the night, unable or unwilling to respond when he asks them, as he always does, the constantly recurring question for which there will never be an answer: "What would you have done? Just how would you have handled it?"

They never indicate by so much as a lifted eyebrow that they have heard, and of course they never deign to reply, now in this haunted hour or any other time, though when they ask him the same question he finds it easy enough to respond. He would have bought Louisiana, he would have broken the Bank of the United States, he would have put upon the South the moral burden of opening conflict, he would have taken Panama, he would have offered Fourteen Points and maneuvered the Japs into striking first and gone into Korea and sent the troops to Lebanon. He is willing enough to endorse what they have done, why can they never give him comfort, particularly when he needs it most?

But they never do, of course, nor will they now when he is confronted with a consequence of his actions so unexpected and so tragic that it imposes a sort of paralysis on his being when he contemplates it. He is not only a very powerful official, he is also a very powerful man, and it is not very often that he pauses to consider the non-political results of what he does. He is not, however, entirely without conscience even though conscience has been diminished over the years, and he knows that what he has done to the senior Senator from Utah has been deeply and fundamentally wrong in a way he will not easily exorcise. The knowledge is hammering against him everywhere, in his head, which is aching, his heart, which is beating with a painful rapidity, and his body, which feels tired and cramped and uncomfortable as he turns restlessly from side to side in the big old bed.

His error, he sees now, was in miscalculating the natures of both the Senator from Wyoming and the chairman of the subcommittee. He did not foresee, when he had his valet take the picture to Fred Van Ackerman three nights ago, that it would be used as fearsomely as it was; and this was because he did not realize the full extent of the irresponsible vicious-ness of that particular character, nor did he understand fully the bitter jealousy it felt toward Brigham Anderson. That there is something psycho-pathic there he is quite sure, now that it is too late; there have been such types in the Congress before, and this is one more in a tradition that goes back to the Founding. Every once in a while the electoral process tosses to the top someone smart and glib and evil, without basic principle, without basic character, and without restraints. Sometimes these are on the conservative side of the fence, sometimes on the liberal; but the essen-tial personality pattern is the same, the gambler, the sharpie, the thug in the blue-serge suit. Such men can be used for certain purposes, but there is always the risk that they will get out of hand. This had happened with the Senator from Wyoming, and he knows now that in using him he has not only done a terrible thing to a fine young man and the Senate he belonged to, but he has put himself in pawn. For Fred can come to him and demand favors, and it will not be so easy to refuse unless he wishes to embark upon the project of destroying Fred; and who will help him in it now? Assuming Fred can be destroyed, which is not so certain now that he has become the darling of COMFORT and is beginning to head up a growing movement in the country. He suspects that he has created a baby Moloch who will continue to demand sacrifices, and this too inhibits sleep.

As for the Senator from Utah, he realizes, again too late, that instead of being clever and devious—as his critics have so often, with some justice, bitterly charged—he should have been straightforward and forth-right, flung down the gauntlet and beaten him in fair fight on the Senate floor. It could have been done: the nominee's past could have been argued away by a party united behind himself and Bob Munson; but he is aware with a devastating bitterness that all hopes of party unity have been utterly destroyed by the death of Brigham Anderson. The Senate will regard this as a personal affront, the ancient instinctive antagonism be-tween the White House and the Hill will be rekindled a hundredfold. No pledge given yesterday to the Majority Leader, no promise conveyed to him in private telephone conversation or intimate White House chat, is worth anything tonight. He will be fantastically lucky if a handful of Senators is with him at this moment. All bets are off, the issue is wide open, and no one can predict the outcome now.

And because he is basically a decent man when he has the time to stand aside from his office and his responsibility and permit the kindlier side of his nature to come forward, he cannot help but be saddened and appalled by the human tragedy involved. He would give anything now to have the senior Senator from Utah alive just because he was a good man, and a fighter, and a stubborn battler with a tenacity of purpose that he could not help but admire even as he was moving most ruthlessly against him; in their brief clashes he had come to feel, almost in spite of himself, a real admiration and affection for him. It had been impossible to convey this, and the responsibility for friction had not been all on his side, by any means; but he had still genuinely hoped, in their last telephone conversation, that they could indeed sit down someday and have a drink and bury the hatchet. He had not known then, of course, how far Fred had carried it, and he had not known the fearful tensions that obviously must have been pressing in upon Brigham Anderson; and to that extent he might perhaps absolve himself and his conscience of a little of their burden for Brigham's death.

But even when that is said, he knows he cannot absolve himself very much. His was the basic motivating decision, his the act which placed the weapon in Senator Van Ackerman's hand, his the finger that touched the button that triggered the tragedy. His only consolation is that Tommy Davis too must be going through hell this night; and that is little enough consolation, for it is no help to him and it does nothing to solve the personal problem of finding serenity again that he faces himself.

This problem, in fact, he reflects as he rises restlessly from the bed and goes to the window to look down upon the silent streets, is becoming increasingly difficult, and it is not only the tragedy of the events surrounding the nomination—which has now become a somber thing that decent men, he knows, are beginning to curse—which are making it troublesome. Increasingly in recent weeks it has seemed to him that events have been moving too fast, that pressures of a global nature have been rising too rapidly. Now the Russians may be on their way to an actual landing on the moon, and even though he knows things about his own country's plans in this respect that very few men know, he is not overly comforted, even so. The evil machine that has pounded for almost half a century against the fabric of a reasonably secure and decent society in the world has never been more active everywhere; and it has seemed to him at times that it will be a miracle if he who carries so much of the burden of it can stand it much longer. No one outside his personal physician, one outside specialist, his wife, and his press secretary knows what happened to him two months ago; but the memory of that sudden blackout in his office never leaves him now. A warning, his physician said; a warning to be extra careful, and slow down.

But how slow down? In sixty-two years he has never really slowed down, and the insistent imperatives of his personal drive have taken him first to the House for four terms, then back home to the governorship of his native California, and then to the greatest office in the gift of his country. He has never slowed down; it is not his nature. Always there has been the steady drive, the voracious ambition, the ruthless achievement of goals which have left behind them a trail of thwarted opponents and blasted careers. And also, the party orators declare and he himself is certain, a trail of high achievements and sound contributions to his country and her place in the world.

"Our grrrrreatttt President!" his party colleagues always cry; and appraising himself with the scarifying candor which only those who have sat in 1600 Pennsylvania can appreciate, he is satisfied that it is not all partisan exaggeration. In many ways he has not been a bad President, and in some he has been an outstanding one. At least, he reflects grimly, he has understood that he was chosen to provide leadership, and provide leadership he has. From the day he set foot under the portico after coming down the wildly cheering Avenue from his inauguration at the Capitol there has never been any doubt who was boss; and for this, he knows, much can be forgiven and much can be overlooked. There are stresses in America which demand of a leader that he lead; and he who refuses to lead, he knows, betrays them and himself in a way so fundamental as to make himself a thing of pity in the history books. He himself will never be that; he will go down, in the neat little game of Categories that historians play, as one of the "strong Presidents"; quite possibly, also, as one of the great ones. It has been, in some ways, at a fearful price; but it is one he made up his mind to pay when he first began to perceive the possibility that he might someday achieve the office, and he has few regrets now.

But the doctor says slow down; and there is no slowing down. Far too often in recent weeks his heart has begun to beat too fast, there has been a sudden all-gone feeling for a split, terrifying moment, a sensation of going away that has caught him in Cabinet meetings, on public platforms, quite frequently right here in the historic bed in the middle of the night. Fortunately it is here that the most obvious and lengthy attacks have come. More and more often he has come awake gasping for air, has had to turn himself very carefully upon his back or his right side and begin the slow, delicate, deliberate process of breathing very slowly and carefully, trying not to panic, trying not to let it get out of hand, until he has managed to restore the normal rhythm of his heartbeat; and increasingly, he has noted, the rhythm has not seemed to return to quite what it was before. Inevitably, he supposes, the moment will come, a day from now, a month, a year, when this will occur full scale in public; and then, even if he recovers from it, men will know in truth that the hurrying gossip of the town is correct and a dying man sits in the White House.

This he is grimly determined to prevent if he can. He does not mind the thought of dying in office, for there is no surer guarantee of martyred greatness in the history books than to die at just the right moment when people will remember the good deeds and forget the bad ones and somebody else can clean up the mess you may have left behind; so in that sense he rather welcomes the idea of a dramatic demise with his hand on the helm, a great man sacrificing his life in the cause of peace, a gallant soldier giving his all for his country, a fearless, peerless leader taken from us at the very height of his—— And so forth and so forth and so forth. But he cannot contemplate without a shiver the possibility of being partially paralyzed, of lingering on too long while the government deteriorates and the country drifts and the enemy, ever vigilant, takes advantage of the national preoccupation to press forward wherever he can.

So it is that he has given some real thought to his condition in recent weeks; so it is that far more often than anyone outside suspects he is in bed and asleep by nine, that he takes two-hour naps in the afternoon and carefully husbands his energies for the great occasions on which he must appear in public and for the major legislation he must read and study. More and more he finds himself doing business on the telephone, requesting, suggesting, advising, cajoling, recommending, threatening, as he often must. Now the personal conference at the White House is becoming increasingly rare; and the press conference, for one excuse and another, always logical, always rational, always carefully calculated for reasonableness and acceptability, is more and more often put off so that the press is beginning to become accustomed to gaps of two weeks, three weeks, even four, between them. His entire thought now is to conserve himself for the major things and let the minor go by the board; for even though he would not mind dying in office and rather expects he will, there is one other reason why he wishes to remain alive: he has little respect for, and he is damned if he wants to turn the country over to, the well-meaning, goodhearted but unfortunately rather blundering, inept, and unimaginative man who occupies the office of Vice President.

Contemplating Harley Hudson in the White House, in fact, is one of those things that makes him extra determined to stay alive. He would be much more at ease about it all if things had gone differently at the convention seven years ago and his principal opponent then had been willing to take second place. But of course Orrin Knox never would, it was out of the question from the first, and even though he had requested his lieutenants to make some tentative soundings in the frantic turmoil of Chicago, nothing at all had come of it. He feels a great respect for Orrin, even though he knows the Senator despises him; and he wishes now in this lonesome hour as he looks out across the silent trees and lawns that things had worked out differently, that events had moved to bring Orrin into office as his running mate, so that together they could have worked for the country instead of being eternally at cross-purposes as they are now.

Thinking of their constant frictions over the years, he knows with a grim certainty that they will seem as nothing compared with the situation that has arisen as a result of Brigham Anderson's death. One thing he is quite aware of is the high regard held for the young Senator among his elders, and in particular he knows of the close family relationship between the Knoxes and the Andersons. Having studied Orrin very attentively, as a man will study the one who has been for many years his principal opponent in party affairs, he knows how fond the link has become, and he knows Orrin will fight him now with merciless intensity that will ask, and give, no quarter. And for the first time in many a day there comes into his mind the dismaying possibility that he may be beaten, and not only that he may be beaten but that all the shabby double-dealing behind Brigham Anderson's death may be displayed to the public which, after its first shock at the revelations concerning the Senator's private life, is quite likely then to turn with a bitter contempt upon the men who used it to kill him. There are many times, he knows, when politics violates fair play and decency, and as long as the public does not know it, little detriment results. But let it once break through the surface and an innate fairness in the country reasserts itself, and never after that do the people involved have quite the same stature that they had before. And since stature is very important to him, both presently and in the history books, it is not a prospect he regards lightly.

Nor, though he thinks party loyalty and their many years of working together will be sufficient to stand the strain, is he at all sure what the Majority Leader will do. He too was very fond of Brigham Anderson, and it was only by exerting the full strength of his personality and his office that he had been able to force him to play his part in weaving the web of circumstance that had entrapped his young friend. Again, he wishes bitterly now that he had not; but the event is over, there is nothing to do but try to pick up the pieces and recoup as best one can. If Bob draws away, the cause of Robert A. Leffingwell will be in jeopardy indeed, for then there will have to be a falling back upon such second-line defenses as Tom August and Powell Hanson and possibly George Hines and even Fred Van Ackerman; and without the Majority Leader it will not be the same. He does not think Senator Munson will oppose him openly, even though he too must be lying awake—in fact, he suspects, a good many men all over town must be wakeful this night, thinking of Brigham Anderson and searching their hearts for answers to things to which there may be no answers—but that the Majority Leader might abandon all attempts to help is a prospect he must consider. There will have to be a phone call in the morning, a sounding out to discover where he stands and what he will do, an appeal to all those ties of old friendship, mutual advantage, and the party which will convince him that he should continue to work actively for the nomination. He sighs, for he is very tired and he knows that before this is over he will be much tireder still; and he wonders whether a system already strained so near its limits can come through it as well as he would wish, or whether his martyrdom is going to come rather sooner than he had expected.

It is to Orrin that he keeps returning, however, for it is Orrin who holds the key. He wonders whether Orrin is thinking of him, and he is sure he must be. If hatred were a palpable thing he is quite sure he would feel it thudding against the walls of the historic old house right now, rising against his window ledge, threatening at any moment to flood into the room and swallow him up. But somewhere, if Orrin is the key, there must be a key to Orrin; and he sets himself now to considering practically what it can be, knowing that it does not lie in the methods used upon Brigham Anderson, for even if there were cause—which he long ago satisfied himself there is not, in any way—those methods have been destroyed by their own terror and cannot be used again upon anyone in the present controversy. He feels there must be some way to appeal to the senior Senator from Illinois, and much as he knows Orrin is despising him at this very moment, he would not be the powerful man he is, President of the United States and worthy to be, if he did not begin the slow, patient, stubborn process of trying to reason out for himself what it is.

If the President's astute mind could project itself but a little further in this tragic hour it would be ironically amused to know that in his own grief-filled house in Spring Valley the senior Senator from Illinois has anticipated him and is promising himself with a quiet implacability that no appeal of any kind from the man he dislikes so utterly will move him one iota. A long-standing contempt, the withering contempt of the honest for the dishonest, has always clouded his vision in that quarter; it has been replaced now by a hatred so deep and so cold that it lies upon his heart like a stone. Behind his brusque exterior there lives an emotional personality unsuspected by all but a few, and all of its force is concentrated now upon the objective of defeating Robert A. Leffingwell and making of the President's remaining months in office a frustrated hell as unpleasant as it can possibly be. He has rarely wished another man dead in his life, but right now, as violently as he once wished Hitler dead or Stalin dead or Khrushchev dead, he thinks he wishes the President dead. He believes now that nothing can sway him to change in this; and he is telling himself that not all the wiles of 1600 Pennsylvania Avenue will be sufficient this time to divert from the head of its occupant a justice he has often invited but almost always managed to escape.

This mood, which he is deliberately implanting in his being so deeply that he believes it can never be dislodged, is understandable enough, given the tragic events of the night and their profound impact upon him. Somewhere around six he had had a sudden hunch, inexplicable, elusive, but insistent, that it was important that he get in touch with Brig; there was no way to explain it, it had just come to him, and for some reason equally inexplicable he had put his call through to the Senator's office instead of his home. It was obvious at once that something was wrong, someone took up the phone but did not answer, there were shouts and movements in the background—he thought he heard someone cry "Hold the light over there so I can get a shot of his head!"—and for several moments he simply waited on the line until someone spoke. "This is Senator Knox," he said, "is Senator Anderson there?" "Just a minute, Senator," the voice said in a startled way, and he heard it call to someone, "Senator! Senator! This is Senator Knox." And then a voice he could hardly recognize came on the wire and said, sounding so old and so tired, "This is Seab, Orrin. We have lost our young friend, Orrin. He has shot himself." "But he didn't have to do that," he said foolishly, and Seab, seeming to understand the way a man could say something as stupid as that at a time like that, only said, "I think you had better come home right away, Orrin. We all need you here." "Yes, Seab," he managed to say. "Call Beth and tell her I'm on my way." And in a daze he had asked his administrative assistant, who was traveling with him, to cancel his three remaining speeches of the day, the local party people had rushed him to the nearest airport, and he had caught the next plane and come straight to Washington.

On the plane he had tried not to think about it too much, but it was of course impossible to shut out. Around and around and around his mind went, and over and over and over the same hopeless ground. The whys were never resolved, the futile protests went unanswered and only became more insistent. So too did his personal grief. At first he was in such a state of shock that he was unable to grasp it in terms of tragedy or even of human reality; but suddenly after about an hour it began to hit him very hard. He felt as though he might be about to cry, so he turned and stared earnestly out the window and pretended to be looking intently at the gradually dimming land below while his eyes filled with tears and the appalling finality of it struck him squarely with all its force. He remained so for quite some time until finally he put on a pair of dark glasses and leaned back, pretending to be asleep. He would allow himself an hour to cry, he thought grimly, because there would be no time to cry later. He had people to see and things to do, and he would do his mourning for Brig right now so that he could approach them unhampered by emotion and unclouded by a bitterness that could only interfere with efficiency.

At National Airport in Washington, still wearing his dark glasses but by now beginning to feel an iron inner calm, he found that the *Post* had put out an extra, filled with headlines, pictures, and political speculation. The photographers had done their jobs well, as befitted their experience and ability, which was great, and the taste and consideration of their editors, which was virtually non-existent. There was a picture of Mabel in tear-stained horror, a shot of Pidge looking sleepy, frightened, and totally lost. The cameras had been right there, stuck in their faces in keeping with human decency and the tragedy in which they were involved.

Most of the time Orrin found himself passably tolerant of this sort of thing, which was always excused on the ground that it was giving the public what it wanted to see at breakfast; but this time it only served to goad him even further into a harsh, black anger. It did not lighten his mood at all to be photographed himself as he stood studying the papers near the plane and to have some eager young television reporter ask brightly, "Senator Cooley says you are now the leader of the anti-Leffing-well forces, Senator, and he expects the nomination will now be defeated. Do you expect the nomination will now be defeated?"

The fellow was not one of the Capitol regulars, from whom Orrin might have taken such a question at such a time, and he had given him a look so full of distaste and disgust that the man involuntarily stepped back a pace.

"The nomination," he had replied with a tenuous self-control, "will be defeated."

"You think it will be defeated, Senator," the fellow had repeated automatically, as though he couldn't quite believe Orrin would want to be that positive.

"I said it will be defeated," he had said angrily. "It will be defeated. How many more times do I have to say it for you?"

"Thank you, Senator," the man had said hurriedly, and he had gotten quickly out of the way as Orrin brushed him aside and strode forward angrily into the terminal to get his luggage and catch a cab for home.

There he had found that the emotional storms of the evening were not yet over, for the Andersons of course were there, as were Hal and Crystal and Stanley Danta, and there had been an unhappy couple of hours getting everybody quieted down and off to bed. Pidge mercifully fell to sleep early, her mother went to bed in Beth's room about ten after breaking them all up by remarking wistfully, "I never really knew him, and now I never will," and after a time there remained only the immediate family to settle down and then he himself could get some rest. First, however, there had to be some fast planning for Hal and Crystal, who at first were determined to postpone the wedding on Wednesday afternoon, until their fathers talked them out of it. Brig, it was explained, wouldn't have wanted that at all, and while it was agreed that they should cancel most of the guest list and restrict it to just a few close friends, there was no reason to put it off altogether. Dolly was called and consulted; said she was canceling the reception but thought they should go ahead with the rest of it as Orrin and Stanley suggested; after a while Hal and Crystal agreed reluctantly and went off, much troubled, to bed, Hal to his room and

Crystal back to the Westchester, where she said she would make some coffee and sit up for her father. A call came from Brig's brother in Salt Lake City that he would be flying in in the morning, and Stanley volunteered to meet him and assist during the day Monday with the many details of liquidating the remnants of a life. It was decided that a memorial service would be held at National Cathedral at 2 P.M. Tuesday, with burial in Salt Lake on Wednesday. The Senate would devote itself to eulogies tomorrow, and because of the services on Tuesday and the fact that a recess for the wedding on Wednesday had been promised long ago, there was now no possibility of a vote on the nomination until Thursday. Orrin told Stanley bluntly that he was out to beat it and would use every means at his command; Senator Danta looked grave and unhappy and finally said he thought possibly he would go along with this. Shortly after he left the house Seab called to say he had already contacted fifteen of their colleagues, including Sam Eastwood of Colorado, Stuart Schoenfeldt of Pennsylvania, Ray Smith and Vic Ennis of California, Roy Mulholland of Michigan, and Powell Hanson. Of them all, he reported, only Powell Hanson and Victor Ennis had refused to abandon their commitments to vote for the nominee. Of the rest, ten were now opposed and three were leaning their way. Seab said he would go on telephoning until about 2 A.M. and then start in again at six-thirty in the morning. Senator Knox thanked him with satisfaction and suggested several others he might work on. Senator Cooley promised grimly to do his best. There was no word from the Majority Leader, and Orrin made no move to call him. He imagined Bob was having a rough time and he was damned glad of it. He will get to him tomorrow, he thinks now, and he will see then what remains of an old friendship and a close alliance in the face of these somber events. He does not know exactly what part Bob played in the tragedy of their young friend, but instinct tells him it was not helpful to Brig when the chips were down. If it was something really bad, he tells himself grimly, he may never forgive him.

It was not until two-thirty that he had finally gone to bed, by himself, on the sofa in the den, and between that time and this his mind has raced without let-up. Now at 4 A.M. he knows he should be asleep if he is to have the energy to be as busy tomorrow as he will have to be; but a sort of nervous tension, somewhat similar to that which sometimes follows sex, won't let him sleep, and the only comfort in it is that he expects it will probably carry him through whatever he has to face in the week ahead. Although he cannot now imagine the full extent of what this will be, for there are events of major and surprising import lying just ahead for his country, for him, and for the world, he does know that it will include the funeral of someone who was almost a son to him; the wedding of his own son; the settlement one way or the other of the fate of Robert A. Leffingwell —which in spite of his positive attitude at the airport he knows is still in some doubt, not much but enough so he will have to work hard at it—the breaking of Fred Van Ackerman, which is now inevitable; and perhaps some further point of development in his own long-standing ambition to reach a position where he can run the country as he thinks the country ought to be run.

"Why do you want to be President, Senator?" UPI had asked him candidly once.

"Because there are things I want to accomplish for the country that I can't accomplish in any other office," he had replied with an equal candor that had been greeted with that national mixture of approval, amusement, criticism, and scorn that seemed to greet everything he did. It is not, he thinks, that he particularly wants to be a controversial figure, or that he ever consciously set himself that goal; there is just something in him that makes him one, and every time he opens his mouth the legend of it grows.

And, he reflects grimly, there will be a lot for the legend to feed on this week, for he has no intention of softening either his words or his actions in any particular. Whatever the ultimate reasons behind the death of the senior Senator from Utah, he knows that they were directed and stage-managed, and made use of by two men, the junior Senator from Wyoming and the President of the United States, and both must be made to meet a reckoning. The first thing to do in the morning, he decides, is to call in Seab and Stanley and Lafe Smith, try to ascertain from their best guesses what the trouble was, and then plan strategy on what to do about it. Since Stanley has already shown a disposition to leave the Administration and the Majority Leader, there has already been a major gain, and the Senator from Illinois does not intend to let him back out on it. They are about to become members of the same family, in effect, and he intends to use every power of persuasion he has to assure that the highly respected Senator from Connecticut will not only give tacit support to the anti-Leffingwell cause but active support as well. If Bob Munson by any chance persists in standing by the nominee, Senator Danta's defection will be the first step in isolating him, and through him the President; it will spread like wildfire through the Senate, and before long the Majority Leader, if he does remain obdurate, will be leader of nothing but a rag, tag, and bobtail little army whose principal lieutenants will be people of no more stature than Tom August and Fred Van Ackerman.

There is not, in fact, any guarantee at all that Tom August will remain with him, for the chairman of Foreign Relations, while one of the fuzziest damned citizens Orrin thinks he has ever known in his entire life, is also at heart a very decent one. If it is true, as Senator Knox suspects, that Brig was driven to the wall by some sort of blackmail, Tom August will not condone it. Orrin does not yet know how this can be proved, if it should be the fact, but he decides he had better add Tom to the little caucus he is planning, for the next step after that of course is to call a meeting of the remaining members of the subcommittee; get a vote, which he is sure will be unfavorable to Bob Leffingwell; and then try to carry the same strategy through the full committee. Tomorrow afternoon, after the session ends and the memories of the eulogies and the full impact of Brigham Anderson's death are still sinking in, will be the time for that. In his own way, more blunt and obvious and often more emotional than the President's, Senator Knox too is fully as capable of seizing upon the tides of time and circumstance and the deeper feelings of men and making the most of them.

As for what will come next, he does not at the moment know with any exactitude, for almost thirty years in politics have told him that men can only build up to a certain point upon the thoughts and emotions of other men, and after that it has to be played by ear with a quick adaptation to whatever develops. If he can persuade the full Foreign Relations Committee to report out the nomination of Bob Leffingwell with the recommendation, in the traditional language, "that the Senate *do not* advise and consent to the nomination of Robert A. Leffingwell to be Secretary of State," it is quite likely that he can carry the day after that simply on the strength of the unfavorable recommendation and his own righteous anger at the treatment of Brigham Anderson. The Senate is a funny place, he knows, and sometimes a thoroughly righteous cause can win in ways that are completely unforeseen by those who think only in terms of votes pledged and favors conferred. Just when things seem at their most cynical, something comes along that appeals to idealism and fair play, and the forces of deceit go down before it like tenpins. He has seen it happen on many occasions, it is on just that basis that he has built his own reputation and influence, and this time he thinks it may happen again; particularly since this time there will be an alliance of himself and Seab and Stanley and Lafe and very likely several other commanding men to give idealism the boost it needs from years of experience, intimate knowledge of the Senate, and long exercise of the uses of power.

Then, he tells himself with a grim satisfaction, they will see what Mr. Big can pull out of the hat to salvage himself. It will not be very much, he believes, and it will not be enough to save Bob Leffingwell or his own prestige. Then there may come at last the time the Senate has long been waiting for, the long-cherished moment when it is he who will come to the Senate, hat-in-hand, instead of vice versa; and awaiting him on the door-step will be the man who couldn't enjoy it more, the senior Senator from Illinois, ready to impose the terms and indeed name the man whose substitution for Bob Leffingwell will finally provide the nation with its new Secretary of State.

And here he is again, he realizes with a wry smile in the silent night as the first birds begin to twitter outside and the first tiny graying begins to soften the blackness, with his thoughts where they are at least half the time, in the White House, revolving around its occupant. Yet he knows that he can say honestly that while they have had many differences in the past seven years, he has never opposed him just for the sake of opposing, and indeed in the careful statistics worked out by *Congressional Quarterly* has session after session ranked among those who have supported him better than eighty per cent of the time. Of course, as Arly Richardson once pointed out dryly, the remaining twenty per cent only involved most of the major legislation coming before the Congress, but even there he thinks he has been constructive in his stands. Frequently proposals have come up from the White House to the Hill, he has sniffed and snorted and damned them up and down in the first ten minutes, only to buckle down in due course and get to work patiently devising the compromises that have not only made it possible for them to pass but have substantially improved them as well. "The President is the best assistant Orrin Knox has in administering the country," somebody had put it in a crack at the Press Club bar that soon made the rounds of the capital; and there was enough truth in it to make them both smile, genuinely if a little grimly, when it came to them.

On this nomination, though, the situation is different, and, he knows, it has been different from the first. The President has obviously felt that his entire Administration, prestige, and standing in history were committed to the cause of Bob Leffingwell, and there has been an adamantine quality about it that has puzzled the Senator from Illinois. Under ordinary conditions the inevitable result would have been to harden his own opposition, except that in the case of a Cabinet appointment, and particularly the most important one of them all, he had felt like all Senators bound by the tradition that a President has a right to name his own official family and have around him the men he wants. If the incumbent had just left Brigham Anderson out of it, this would still in all probability be Senator Knox's position. But that is impossible now.

What defeat would do to the President's health, Orrin does not know, though it would not be accurate to say that he could not care less, for he does care, and seriously. Wishing the President dead in an angry reaction to Senator Anderson's death is of course an emotional extravagance that serves to satisfy pent-up tensions, but actually contemplating a situation in which he did die is something far more serious. As he had told Bob impatiently and more accurately on Thursday, nobody wants a President to die, it causes too much of an upset in everything. Yet there are sufficiently strong rumors, confirmed, it seems to him, by his own studies of the man on the rare occasions recently when they have attended something together, that this may not be beyond the realm of possibilities. Given what would appear to be the President's current condition, this is an event Orrin must consider, as he must consider also the possibility that by his own actions he may help to precipitate it. For this he feels no compunction, for did the President feel any compunction when he was setting in train the events that resulted in the death of Orrin's young friend? He did not, and by the same token, neither does Orrin.

Still and all, there are fundamental changes to contemplate if this should turn out to be the case. What Harley Hudson would be like in the White House, Senator Knox cannot exactly imagine; except that he is quite sure, with a unity of view with his opponent that would not particularly surprise either of them, that it would create a most bothersome and unhappy situation for the country. Men may differ on many things, but they all agree on Harley; and the possibility that he may just surprise them once the office and the power are his does not enter even minds as astute as the two most directly interested. What Orrin foresees is another John Tyler, or possibly even a Buchanan, presiding with an amiable inability over the continuing disintegration of his country's hopes. And he decides with an impatient movement of his head that they will just have to prop him up, they will all just have to stand by and give him advice and hold his hand and help him out, because, God knows, if they don't, things will be in a hell of a mess. The chance that Harley may have ideas of his own and be able to find in himself under the pressures of responsibility strengths they cannot imagine he has, does not occur to Orrin any more than it does to anyone else; which may eventually turn out to be just one more proof that you can't always judge people by appearances, that they are often unpredictable, and that those who happen to be dumped unexpectedly into the White House sometimes turn out to be most unpredictable of all.

In any event, on the basis of what he knows now, the Senator from Illinois wishes that things had turned out differently at the convention seven years ago, and that it had been possible for him to submerge his pride and his dislike—to say nothing, he thinks dryly, of his principles—and accept the Vice Presidency. He knows this would have been out of the question, so astringent is his honesty toward other people and so clearly had he made his personal opinion of his opponent known to all the world, and so deeply did he feel it; but it might have been better for the country, and for him, if he had. Now he suspects impatiently that Harley will want to run in his own right next year, and that just means one more bruising battle in the next convention and the possibility once again, even considering their respective qualifications, that the Senator from Illinois may find himself on the outside looking in when the final balloting is over. This is if Harley reacts normally to his new position and the possibilities for re-election that it opens before him; though here, too, Senator Knox, may be assuming too much.

And so here he is, he thinks with an impatient wryness, with the President dead and buried and Harley in the White House and his own hopes thwarted once more—and all on the basis of brooding too much at four o'clock in the morning. He tells himself with a stern annoyance to, damn it, stop thinking and go to sleep or he won't be worth a damn in the morning, nervous buoyance or no nervous buoyance. So for three short hours before the house begins to stir again with a day that will be filled with sorrow and conflict that will be fateful for them all, he does manage to doze off fitfully; knowing with a drowsy annoyance that, despite his firm intention each time he drifts partially awake again his thoughts are instantly in the great white house where his antagonist lies. For he realizes that they are approaching their final showdown, that everything which has gone before, both in their relationship and in his own life, has been but preparation for this.

2

For a man who had twice sought the presidency and was seriously considering another bid next year, his life seemed to him to have been in many ways a remarkably rounded preparation. It had provided him with about the right proportion of victories and defeats, about the right number of satisfactions and disappointments, to create the kind of balance that seemed capable of holding him steady through most things; and it had done so despite a basic personality that reacted far more sharply than most in politics to the shifting tides of circumstance and the triumph or betrayal of ideals. Growing up, as he came to understand after he had gotten safely through it, was essentially the process of learning not to care. The fact that he had never and entirely learned this, that there was at heart something incorrigibly innocent and direct and almost childlike about his reactions, that he was still at fifty-eight a man who deeply cared about many things and was not afraid to show it, gave him a certain distinction in a flaccid and flabby age. It strengthened his honesty, increased both his ideals and his prejudices, made him one of the people in public life about whom it was generally and truly said, "You may not agree with him, but at least you always know where he stands." This could not be said about too many in recent years, and it was perhaps the chief thing that gave him his difficult, prickly, controversial, and commanding eminence in the history of his times.

That this could not have been foreseen in his youth was one of life's little whimsies, for there was not much then to indicate that he was destined to be United States Senator and a leader of his land. His people had been moderately well-fixed, his father a kindly but mediocre lawyer in Alton, and they had enjoyed a modest middle-class standing in their modest little town.

None of the family had ever been in public life, none, in fact, had ever done very much of anything; back on both sides the genealogies disclosed some farmers, several handymen, a dry-goods clerk or two, one small storekeeper, a few lawyers, the vice president of a little bank. They were not the kind of people to stick their heads above water; a genteel capacity for being unnoticed was their principal characteristic, and while this had not brought much distinction, it also, of course, had not brought much trouble. His father carried on the pattern of his side of the family, and his mother, a quiet, pleasant little lady who seemed sunnily reconciled to the placid level of their existence in Alton, carried on the pattern of hers. Where this violently controversial son of theirs had come from they had never really been able to understand, though they had puzzled over it many times before going quietly off to their respective rewards. The bafflement was compounded because for quite a while it had seemed that Orrin would fit neatly into the family pattern, build up a quiet law practice of his own, have a quiet marriage, raise a quiet family, live a quiet life, and die a quiet death. In the early part of his life there were few indications of anything else.

This was so because he had started off, at least outwardly, to be one of the mildest and most timid twigs of a mild and timid tree. It is true that there had been noticeable in him from the first a profound capacity for feeling that jarred rather sharply with the family norm, but he soon learned to conceal it, for a long time most successfully; it was only later that he came to appreciate its public uses and make the most of them.

His was not a mind to treasure up slights and count them over in later years, but looking back he could remember that there had been a long, hazy period, now mercifully softened by time and distance, when he had not been a very happy boy. This had centered not only around slights and snubs at school but also in some inner fear and insecurity that for quite a while made a good many things an agony for him. Bit by bit as he grew older he managed to dissemble this with increasing skill until finally it seemed to go altogether; but the memory of it lingered on in his being, his own private remembrance of things past, so that sometimes, for instance, if he was out driving or walking and came suddenly upon a group of Boy Scouts, say, bicycling off to an overnight camp, he would know that somewhere among that laughing, confident group there would be one, there would always be at least one, tight and tense and worried and uncomfortable amid all the shouting and the fun. He knew, because he had always been that one. Even now, somewhere deep inside while the crowds roared and the voters turned out by the millions to return him time and again to office, he was still that one, always secretly girding himself to an effort just greater than necessary, to a pitch of endeavor that would permit him to fulfill expectations which were never quite as great as in his own mind he imagined them to be.

This, he supposed, was why he was so successful a politician, for he brought to everything a little extra. Indeed, that was what Warren Strickland called it, in his cloakroom philosophizings: "Orrin's little extra." "When Orrin adds that little extra," he would say, "then watch out." And the Senate did watch out, just as people had been watching out ever since a point along in his senior year in high school when, for some reason he had never been able to understand since, except that he was apparently just ready for it, he had begun to relax and get along with the world.

He sometimes thought, sardonically, how neatly it would fit into the psychological jargons of the present day if this had been brought about by some profound emotional or physical experience, some shattering event, an accident, a tragic first love or the overwhelming impact of some older teacher or mentor. But he had been in no accidents, his teachers, save for the average number of slightly-above-average exceptions, had not been the impact type, and he certainly hadn't had any tragic love affair. He hadn't loved anybody at all, in fact, until he went to college and met Elizabeth Henry, whom everybody called Beth, or Bee, or sometimes Hank for Henry, and then he loved her and after that he never loved anybody else. So there wasn't anything dramatic about it at all, which he thought dryly was undoubtedly a damned shame for all the people who liked to do profound analyses of public figures. You see old Orrin Knox there, boy? Well, you can turn in that leather couch and snap off that shuttered light, because old Orrin, there, he just grew up one day, in due course and in his own time and when he got good and ready; and after that he was free to use the very powerful capabilities that had been hidden away behind a personality that theretofore had seemed to be afraid the world was always after it. As soon as he discovered it wasn't, he began to move. He hadn't stopped since.

This emergence from the moted keep, coming as it did late in his high-school career, did not permit him to recoup much ground in his few remaining months, but he managed to make up for it at the university in Champaign. There he could acknowledge one profoundly important experience, and that was living in a fraternity house where he had to get along with other people and persuade them to get along with him, and where, having been taken in largely on his high-school grades and their potentials for the house's scholastic rating on the campus, he soon began to be accepted for a tartly humorous personality that asserted itself with increasing confidence as the months moved on. "Guess we have to have at least one grind," one of his older brethren, a football player, had remarked sarcastically to a pal as they passed the door of his room one night soon after he joined. Prompted by some impulse he had long since forgotten but which he knew now had marked a considerable turning point in his life, he had stuck his head out the door without a second's hesitation. "One grind," he had snapped, "and lots of grime. You can be damned glad you've got the one, because there's plenty of the other around here." For a moment he had thought he was about to be immolated by Saturday's hero, but the other had suddenly burst out laughing, reached out and mussed his hair in a friendly way, invited him to come down to the Student Union for a hamburger, and after that he was in. The next day he could tell that by the subtly implacable processes by which the young judge the young he had been appraised and found worthy of acceptance and approval, and from then on he could relax even more. For the first time he really began to enjoy life, and though he still had many broad areas of sensitivity, though he still cared much too much for his own peace of mind about the way things went, or the way people acted, there had begun the slow, insistent, inexorable development of a mature personality.

Aiding it were his grades, which continued to stay at a level that evoked stunned respect from his fraternity brothers; his participation in the politics of the house, largely at the insistence of his football buddy, which made him first secretary, then vice president, and in his senior year president; the debating society, where he began to learn the thrilling fact that emotion could be controlled and diverted into spoken channels that could move his listeners to reactions that surprised them both; and his meeting with Beth, or Bee, or Hank—"I suppose that's a sign of lots of friends, when you have three nicknames," he remarked wistfully once, soon after he first knew her; she had laughed in a way he couldn't quite analyze and it was not until long after that he realized that this had been one of the remarks which, added to some more insistent feelings suited to her youth and nature, had contributed to the protective emotions which eventually culminated in her decision to say yes, she would be very happy to be Mrs. Knox. It was a while coming, this decision, but he was quite sure from the first day he saw her in an English class that it would someday arrive, and patiently in that belief he had suffered—and there were a good many times when he really did suffer—through the years until it came about. These years had consisted of three more in college, at the end of which he had asked her to marry him and been told with a practicality as blunt as his own that he had better get his law degree first, and then the three years of law school. Seven years after they met, equipped with his B.A. from the University of Illinois and his LL.B. from Yale, he asked again, she said yes, and they were married in her home town of Galesburg amidst some mild, pleased Knoxes and some livelier but equally pleased Henrys.

By this time he had begun to discover in himself a driving ambition, something else that made him a sport in the Knox clan, and he was delighted to find that it had its complement in his bride. Hank, which continued to be his private name for her, was, in her humorous, friendly, and outgoing way, fully as intent upon his success as he was. To it she contributed her beauty, which was great, her brains, which were impressive, and her personality, which won everyone. "I've never known anybody who didn't like you," he had told her not six months ago; and even now with all his fame and power and prominence there had still been in his remark something of the same wistfulness of that other long ago, just as it had brought from her the same amused and affectionate response. "How do you account for your success, Governor?" a visiting high-school journalist had inquired gravely soon after he went to the Mansion in Springfield. "I married Elizabeth Henry," he said promptly, and the remark got picked up by the city papers and carried over the state and over the land and now was part of the legend.

He meant it, too, even though she knew, and always told him, that he possessed qualities that would have carried him high regardless of who went along with him. "But you must admit you've helped," he said, "surely you aren't going to deny it. I know you're modest, but you aren't *that* modest." This always made her chuckle, before she turned back to the list of bazaars she was supposed to open, or the church groups she was supposed to talk to, or the campaign schedule she was supposed to help him fulfill. One time in his first campaign for re-election to the Senate they had swung into a little town in the northwest part of the state; "VOTE FOR ORRIN AND BETH," a banner swinging over Main Street had admonished the citizenry. His managers had picked up the idea with delight, and ever since, in a very real sense, it had been the two of them that the voters endorsed. "I don't know about that," people would say on cool verandas along shady streets in sleepy towns, "but as long as we've got Orrin and Beth in the Senate, we don't have to worry."

The practice of law, in the mild way of his father, leading the mild life of his father for the mild purposes of his father, was not for him, and he had long known it. He tried not to hurt his parents when he told them of his decision to move to Springfield and go into practice there, but he knew it could not help but hurt them. Nonetheless they accepted it, as they had always accepted the things he wanted to do, and presently he was in the state capital, living in a pleasant little house in a pleasant little neighborhood and working with a rising law firm to which he had become attached through his father's intercession. "I guess your old man can do something for you," his father had said with a shy humor, and so he had, writing a letter to a schoolmate who had traveled high and far along ways that quiet Billy Knox had never known, and in two weeks' time Billy Knox's son had a job and a desk and was part of a growing practice.

For ten years this kept him occupied, and by the end of that time both he and Beth were beginning to perceive possibilities for him far beyond the practice of law. His oratorical abilities were not diminished by his employment, and before long he was beginning to receive requests to speak here and there, talks which he spent hours polishing and perfecting and then delivered with an easy power that inevitably brought standing ovations at the end. In the inner life of the capital he began to make his mark, his life and his work impinging more and more closely upon the operation of the legislature, his purpose increasingly magnetized toward government. One day on a visit home some family friend had remarked casually, "I guess you'll be running for the legislature, one of these days." The comment seemed to crystallize everything and he had replied quickly, "Yes, I guess I will . . . I think," he added thoughtfully, for it had just come to him that of course this was what he intended to do, "that I will run for the state Senate."

This, as it turned out, proved to be one of the first of the many blunt remarks which were to shock and startle and upset people in the course of his public life, for he had not really bothered to check the situation before his quick reply. If he had, he would of course have found out that the mayor of Alton intended to run for the state Senate himself, and that everybody had agreed that he should be allowed to do so, and that the whole thing was cut and dried. Into this peaceful scene Billy Knox's boy stepped with an impatient candor, an unyielding honesty, and a tart determination, fortified by his wife, to do as he damned pleased and let the chips fall where they might. It was quite a falling, what the chips did, and after they were all down the mayor of Alton had taken a shellacking, and Orrin Knox was a member of the Senate of the sovereign state of Illinois.

He got there, as he was to get to the governorship two years later and the Senate of the United States two years after that, by standing up on his hind legs and letting fly with the things he believed in with all the earnest vigor and oratorical ability at his command. He believed in Illinois and he believed in the United States and he believed in Abraham Lincoln; and he believed in them, and in all their implications and ramifications and refinements, with all the capacity of a powerfully determined, deeply emotional, and thoroughly decent heart. No ordinary opponent could stand against the passionate impact of his platform personality, any more than ordinary opponents could stand, in the arena of committee hearings and floor debate in Springfield, against the bluntly incisive tongue with which he cut them down to size. "If you do that you won't be liked," a fatherly fellow Senator had advised him on some controversial matter soon after he arrived. "I don't give a damn about being liked," he had retorted impatiently, "but I sure as hell intend to be respected." This remark, too, went winging around the corridors and out into the newspapers and over the state; and another cubit was added to his stature in the legend.

In one of those tragically fortuitous blendings of misfortune and opportunity—others' misfortune and his opportunity—by which many and many a public man has been lofted into his first national prominence, there occurred a mine disaster two months after he took office. It was followed for about a week, for reasons older hands cynically understood but he did not, by a vast silence in Springfield. During this the baby Senator from Alton went sniffing about in high dudgeon asking why nobody was doing anything about the mine laws; and after about four days, as he began to understand the answer, a terrific indignation started boiling inside. In another three days he had himself a speech written and on the eighth day after the disaster he blew the top off the capitol. When the pieces gradually settled into place again he was found to have introduced a resolution for an investigation, rammed it through by the sheer force of a towering indignation, and thereupon become the chairman of a special committee which consisted of one somnolent uncaring oldster, one terrified political hack, and himself.

For a period of six months—for as was often the case with him, violent indignations were succeeded by periods of calmly cold-blooded appraisal of where he had put himself and how to make the most of it—the investigation went on; not too fast, as the admiring capital press agreed, and not too slow, but at just the right pace to keep Orrin Knox constantly on the front pages and constantly in the public mind. Out of it he emerged with some powerful enemies but also with a solid and constructive mine-safety bill and a growing reputation, not only in Illinois but also nationally, where the gallant and dramatic fight of this youthful Galahad against the Interests was not overlooked. The fact that his bill was defeated in that immediate session didn't stop him at all. "Go to it, Orrin," some miner bellowed from the galleries as the tally was announced; "you can lick 'em next time!" "You bet I will!" he had shouted back exuberantly, and aided by a wave of public indignation which he fanned assiduously during the adjourned period of the legislature by a series of speeches all over the state, he did just that. His bill passed by the dramatic margin of two votes, went through the lower house by a tally almost as narrow, and was signed into law by a governor who was under pressure to balk at every step of the way and did so. The drama of this, too, was not lost upon anyone and when one of the reporters asked him, immediately after the signing ceremony in the governor's office, "What will you do now, Senator?" he gave the answer the state expected. "I think it would be nice to have somebody administering this law who really believes in it," he said with a scornful look at the angry executive. "I think I'll run for governor."

And so he did, in one of the wildest and bitterest campaigns in state history, out of which he rode angry but triumphant, having yielded not an inch to anyone on anything. "Honest Orrin," his more enthusiastic supporters dubbed him in their broadsides and banners; and beneath it, emphasized with heavy underlining, *I intend to be respected.*

"Senator Knox may have achieved this aim, now that he has bulldozed his way into the governor's chair," the Chicago *Tribune* remarked in cold disapproval on the morning after election, "but he has also achieved the other part of it too: he isn't liked."

The *Tribune* to the contrary, however—as, he found, and he came to welcome it, the *Tribune* always would be to the contrary where he was concerned—he was liked a great deal by a great many people. Although the public personality did not show too much of the warmth beneath, although he had already developed at thirty-seven a sort of tart, protective brusqueness, basically very shy, that kept people off, there was an instinctive affection for him among the great majority of his fellow citizens. He had an ability to phrase things in a bluntly sarcastic way that got to the heart of things, and he never hesitated to speak up. Nor did he hesitate to take on any and all comers who, in his opinion, planned things inimical to the best interests of the people and the state. In his basically conservative fashion he turned out to be a surprisingly liberal governor, just as he was later to be, in just the same way, a surprisingly liberal United States Senator. This could easily be forgotten by those who wished to forget it, because he usually approached things with a critical air and often a critical welcome, and it was easy to portray this as something close to reaction. When the record was totted up, however, it wasn't, and he often thought that he must have built a good foundation in his years in the Mansion in Springfield, because while his later record had a great deal to do with his continuing tenure in the Senate, much of the reason for it went back to the days when "Orrin was the best governor the state ever had."

In all of this his wife was his constant companion and his constant help. When his public personality got too tart, when the sarcasm got too cutting and the honesty approached arrogance, it was the Beth half of Orrin and Beth who stepped in and saved the day or lightened the atmosphere with an amiable wit which had its own edge, too, but managed to make its point without hurting. And in the deep hours of the night when honesty some- times did not seem sufficient to be its own reward, when it sometimes did seem that a dogged and invincible stubbornness, no matter how high its purposes, might not be enough to fend off the attacks of enemies and the opposition of the selfish, it was Hank beside him who gave him com- fort and encouragement and made it possible to return to battle the next day as independent and ornery as ever.

Along the way, out of their love and companionship, they produced Hal, and young Elizabeth, who died of rheumatic fever when she was five years old and left a void that nothing ever quite filled up again. On the remaining child they concentrated all the love of two powerful person- alities, and he was worthy of it. He was born sturdy, grew sturdy, thought sturdy, and walked sturdy: they never quite dared express, even to one another, their emotions now that he had safely negotiated childhood and adolescence and stood on the eve of marrying Crystal Danta. If anything ever happens to him—Orrin had thought when young Elizabeth died; but nothing ever had, except what was good and favoring. His parents felt most humbled.

During his time in Springfield he found that, like many an Illinois politician and many an American everywhere, he was, inevitably, affected and influenced by Springfield's most powerful ghost. It was impossible to escape that brooding presence, which here, of course, had not been brood- ing at all but rather had been just a crafty young politician on the make, possessed of too much guile and not enough prospects. Like most people, he found this character almost impossible to think into any kind of reality; he knew intellectually that it had existed, but the years of anguish and the years of glory kept blotting it out. When he went, as he sometimes did after tourist hours, to the house on Eighth Street to stand in the parlor among the horsehair chairs and sofas and think about his problems and those of its onetime owner, he told himself that this was the parlor of the man who jumped out the window of the old statehouse to avoid voting on a difficult bill; but somehow all he seemed to see standing in the doorway was the tall gaunt figure in the black cape and the stovepipe hat, saying farewell to all this and not knowing when, or whether ever, he might return. For Orrin as for the world, it was the patient, compassionate face, the tenacious, unbreakable purpose, the far-viewer of the centuries, knowing, as he demonstrated so clearly at Gettysburg, that he spoke not only to his own land but to all lands and all times into the unforeseeable future; knowing that it was not only the South that had been impaled upon the fatal fish hook of Culp's Hill, Cemetery Ridge, and Little Round Top, but all the forces everywhere in all ages that would defy free government and attempt to bring it down; and knowing that they must not be allowed to triumph in a future day any more than they had triumphed in his own stumbling, bumbling, tragic, bloody war.

To that purpose as he understood it the young Governor of Illinois too took a personal pledge, and when a Senate seat loomed up midway in his gubernatorial term he took the purpose with him into his campaign and with him to Washington after he had won. This came about by another of those fortuitous combinations of opportunity and enterprise that often characterized his career, for while he had fully intended to go to the Senate as soon as possible, the chance came early only because the incumbent suddenly dropped dead of a heart attack two years before the end of his term. Governor Knox, as somebody in the press corps put it dryly, took one fast look up and down the street to see if anybody was coming, and then grabbed for it—not that he need have bothered to look, as the wagster went on to admit, because nobody could have come between him and the voters at that stage in his career, anyway. He allowed one day to pass and then announced. This occurred early in the year, and he met the immediate cry that he was a governor with half his mind on Springfield and half on Washington by appointing a trusted old party regular to keep the seat warm for ten months, and then by announcing a program of social legislation that pretty well tidied up all the loose ends of his administration that he could still see lying around. In one of his abrupt tornadoes of energy he not only proposed the program but got out and stumped the state for it, fought the legislature for it, and wound up achieving just about all of it. So in November he won handily for the Senate, and with steadily growing pluralities he had won regularly since, until now he was into his fourth full term with the path open if he wished to try once more to follow in Father Abraham's footsteps and seek the lonely eminence of 1600 Pennsylvania.

To the Senate he contributed the honesty, the candor, the determination and drive and tart integrity that had brought him so much already in public life. On Capitol Hill it brought him much more. Because of his comparative youth on arrival, thirty-eight, because of his record as governor and his national reputation and because, unlike so many who come to the Senate with big statehouse build-ups only to fade quickly and quietly into the background, he did not let himself be inhibited by seniority but plunged vigorously into the life of the Senate, he soon achieved a position of prominence that was not accorded to many.

The Senate, generally not conducive to meteoric rises by widely heralded newcomers, bowed like so many before to his intelligence, unassailable purpose, and blunt, brusque ways. He began like many another freshman on District Committee and Public Works, but in three years' time he had wangled assignment to Foreign Relations and Appropriations, the real focal points of power in the Senate, adding Finance a year later during a period when he was educating himself in national monetary matters and the leadership thought it would be a good idea to encourage him in it. And always, along with the prodigious work he accomplished in committee and on the floor, the famed tongue kept right on going. There was always some tart comment to be had from Orrin, a colorful and forthright interview that usually had the self-propelling quality, dear to the hearts of the press, of arousing some colleague to a violent rejoinder. Reporters would come to his office on a dull day and get him to sound off on something, and then in their enterprising way they would go trotting off to somebody else's office and get him to sound off against Orrin's views. Next day, having laid the groundwork for a first-class newspaper row, they would trot back to Orrin. Fortunately everybody involved understood this game, and it was always played with a fair amount of good humor on both sides so that very few lasting animosities grew out of it; only Arly Richardson, snagged on the sharp point of some comment about, "Apparently the Arkansas Traveler hasn't traveled far enough yet to understand what's going on east of the Mississippi," developed a really lasting grudge. Mostly it just meant headlines, which he soon began to manage skillfully so that his cracks usually related themselves to the work he was doing, neatly calling it to public attention and, more often than not, commendation. It was not long before he was a big national name and highly respected by most of the Senate and a wide segment of the public. Then he made his first strategic error and decided to run for President. It was not, as his colleagues pointed out kindly but to no avail, Orrin's year.

This was something he had to learn for himself, and it also marked the occasion when he learned for the first time that national politics are a good deal different from state politics. The latter could carry a man up to the national level, particularly when aided by circumstances which he could see now had been largely sheer luck, but after that he was on his own and the going got much rougher. It wasn't enough, he realized after he had been trounced in several primaries and made a poor fourth-place showing at the Philadelphia convention, to decide that you wanted to be President, announce for it, and go after it; it demanded an approach much subtler than that. Enormous factors went into the selection of a nominee for President, an outgrowth of many conferrings by many people, a process of touching base with big labor, big business, big press, all the conglomeration and amalgam of wealth and influence and interest which, sometimes in united phalanx and sometimes by a sort of informal agreement to move in the same direction, runs the country. The only time a dark horse won, he found, was when the combination wasn't seeing eye to eye; and sometimes, for the combination was quite clever and had its own way of doing things that was not always apparent at first glance, it turned out later that the combination had seen eye to eye after all—on the dark horse.

To this interlocking directorate of interests he obviously had not yet found the key, and all his first try did, in effect, was to give him a reputation in some quarters that were important for being "too ambitious," "always running for President," "too anxious for the White House," and all the other easy sarcasms that have brought down many a white hope and high ambition. It did not, however, diminish his standing in the Senate or in the eyes of those of his countrymen who valued integrity, for he showed it on every occasion that could possibly destroy his chances.

On one big issue, for instance, an expansion of the draft, the press had asked the top contender, the clever young governor of a big eastern state, where he stood.

"In my opinion," he said with a winning, candid smile, "this is a matter of such gravity that it has to be considered in relation to all the relevant factors involved. If an examination of these factors should show it to be desirable to take this course, then it would perhaps be best to do so; if on the other hand such examination should show the better wisdom to lie in some other course, then it is possible that the other course would have to be followed. It will be my intention to study all the pertinent factors before determining whether it should be that course, or the other, which should be followed."

Asked the same question on the same subject Orrin Knox said:

"I'm against it."

So, for this and other reasons all tying in with the fact that he not only hadn't contacted the big boys but they also knew very well that they couldn't manage him if he did get into the White House, he lost the nomination and retreated to the Senate to fight again some other day.

It was not, however, an experience without its rewards, and he learned a great deal from it. Looking back upon his previous successes in the light of this defeat, he felt that in a sense he had just been playing at the game of government in Springfield. For all that he had been governor of one of the Union's biggest states, for all that he had done great things, made strong enemies and fierce friends, been a mover and a shaker in his own home country, those years, when matched against the realities of national politics, seemed in some way to be only a pale preparation for what he found in Washington. His defeat gave him several things, not least among them the beginnings of a wryly self-perceptive humility. "I think," he told Bob Munson humorously several months after that first convention, "that I probably let myself get sold a little too much on this 'out of the haunted prairies comes another Man for America' myth. It sounded good in the nominating speech, but Orrin ain't Abe." This ability to kid himself, which had heretofore been the more or less exclusive property of his wife, was a great step forward in itself.

Out of it also he acquired a love for and grasp of America that he had never known before. His preconvention campaign in the primaries, taking him back and forth across the country from one end to the other, putting him in touch with all the tides and trends and physical aspects of the great Republic, produced in him a profound emotional growth that he was never to forget. All this abundant, beautiful land, as moving to him in the early dawn of the Mojave Desert as in the high noon of a Michigan forest or a bare promontory in Maine, became something infinitely precious in a way it had never been before. He set his mind even more firmly on the goal of someday being its President; but he knew now that it must be carefully and patiently done, if it was to be done at all.

So for a while, though he did not in any way modify his basic ambition, he went about it in a way that for him was unusually patient. Two years in advance of the next convention he announced that he would not be a candidate; offered his services to the National Committee and at their behest made a total of sixty-three speeches over the country prior to the convention; agreed to place the leading candidate in nomination, and worked for him hard and faithfully up to the November which brought his defeat. That party obligation done, he began to work again for himself, and this time with most encouraging results. He devoted himself for the better part of three years to the assiduous cultivation of the sources of party power; not abandoning in any way his honesty or his candor or his vigorous statement of his views, but engaging rather upon what he thought of as his private educational campaign to make the party understand that these were qualities that could win a man election and make of him a good President once he was elected. He had gone about this carefully and with great thoroughness, for in addition to his tendency to be impatient and shoot from the hip he also possessed the ability to be both patient and thorough when he needed to be.

He had again traveled widely over the country, spoken in a great many places, taken the time to sit down for little private, friendly chats with state chairmen, national committeemen and women, big backers of the party, all the others of the combination who would see him, and many gladly did. Even though some, while professing great and sincere admiration, wound up with the feeling that was always to plague him—"He's a fine man, but he couldn't be elected"—he still went into Chicago with firm pledges of 473 votes, a scant 100 from victory. It seemed to him as he and Hank got off the train on that tense, hot, suffocating day and prepared to plunge into the maelstrom of the convention, that he had every right to consider the nomination almost as good as his.

Almost, but not quite; for although they entertained a steady stream of delegates and well-wishers in their lake-front apartment high in the Hilton, and although great crowds swarmed around him with wild excitement as he made his way through the lobbies of the Hilton and the Blackstone, and although the bands played in the corridors and the enthusiastic kids milled around everywhere with his banners and placards and out in the streets the throngs cheered happily as he passed, there was a disturbing sense of the presence of the Governor of California, who also got the bands and the crowds and the placards and the cheers, who also moved like a magnet through the masses of humanity that packed the lobbies and clogged the elevators and caroused and dickered and politicked all day long and all night too.

This was an opposition he had known since spring he must meet, for their paths had crossed in April at the Governors Conference at White Sulphur Springs, and sparks had flown at once, lending the conference an extra excitement for the public and the press. Orrin as a former governor and former chairman of the Conference, as a leading Senator and a leading candidate for the presidential nomination, had been invited to address the State Banquet that always climaxed the annual gathering of state executives. It was already clear by then that the Governor of California intended to make a try for it too, and the drama of their meeting was heightened still more when the conference chairman, the Governor of West Virginia, suddenly announced that he was ill and turned the gavel over to the Governor of California for the evening. This obvious political move, outcome of an obvious political arrangement, angered both the Senator from Illinois and those governors, and their number was sizable, who looked with favor upon his candidacy. For a tense and well-publicized hour or two he had let it get about that there was some serious question as to whether he would speak at all; when he did it was with an air of elaborate courtesy all around that managed to survive the Governor of California's graceful and politically pointed fifteen-minute introduction. "In the time remaining," Orrin began tartly; but he made his speech with a good humor nonetheless, knew it was one of his best, and had them on their feet applauding at the end. Then he and the Governor of California were photographed together and shook hands with a fair show of cordiality. It was a gesture not often repeated later.

Now in Chicago their preliminary battle was fought out for three days in the credentials committee, in the platform committee, in hotel suites and delegation headquarters and on the floor of the Stockyards Amphitheater. His delegation from Indiana was seated, the Governor's was thrown out, the Governor's delegation from New Jersey was seated, his was thrown out. Wisconsin caucused and came over to him; Pennsylvania caucused and split, with the Governor picking up almost half; Michigan, with Governor Harley Hudson at its head, and Ohio, with Governor Howard Sheppard in command, began to become more and more important to both headquarters. The convention, in the way of all national conventions, became a world unto itself, bounded by the hotels and the Amphitheater, in which there was no time, no outside world, nothing but the rising contest between two strong men vying for the greatest prize men could hope to achieve. There was no rest, little sleep, no surcease; five thousand increasingly tired delegates, reporters, and politicians—of whom two in particular, and their wives, had forgotten what it was to relax—began to brace themselves for the hour of balloting. At 3 P.M. on the fourth day the nominations were made and the wild demonstrations began, around and around and around the screaming, roaring hall, two hours and twelve minutes for him, two hours and fifteen minutes for the Governor of California; half an hour, until he withdrew, for Bob Munson, an hour for Harley Hudson and another for Howie Sheppard. There was a recess for dinner, eaten so hastily in the midst of last-minute conferences that nobody knew what was being consumed and nobody cared. At 9 P.M. the chairman of the convention banged the gavel and the proudest roll of names Americans know began to boom over the loudspeakers: "A—la—bama! . . . A—laska! . . . Ari—zona!" Destiny paused in the stockyards and the world settled down to watch. An hour later the hall went wild again: he and his opponent had finished neck-and-neck, but without a clear majority. Harley and Howie held the key.

There was a recess, then, for half an hour, and during it the great amphitheater buzzed and stirred; conventions are never still, humanity is always in motion, people milled and moved and crowded up and down the aisles, and in the galleries chants kept breaking out, first for him, then for the Governor, once in a while, rather feebly and ending in good-natured laughter, for Governor Hudson or Governor Sheppard. On its suspended platform at the far end of the hall the band played, "California Here I Come," the University of Illinois "Fight Song," and now and again "Dixie," with all its burden of poignancy and memory that do things to the American heart no other music can. The half hour passed, the roll began again. He had tried desperately to see Harley and Howie in the interval, had reached the latter for a noncommittal but fairly encouraging two minutes, but Harley was remaining aloof. When the roll began Harley was on the platform, as though wishing to speak, which caused great excitement in the Amphitheater; but he did not, the roll started; Michigan continued to stand firm for its Governor, Ohio did the same; Wisconsin broke and went to the Governor, but Minnesota came over to Senator Knox. Deadlock again. The chairman held a hasty conference with the managers of the two top contenders, a quick agreement was reached, the convention was adjourned until 10 A.M. next day. The supreme effort by both candidates began and lasted through the night.

Shortly after 3 A.M. Harley came to Orrin's suite, trailed by most of the press, who considered it highly significant that he was coming to see the Senator first. The Senator thought so too, and when they were finally alone he did his best to be persuasive. It was not an hour or a situation in which tired and exhausted and ambitious men could give much time to being circuitous with each other, so he tried to be frank but friendly. "Governor," he said, "I think I'm going to win, and I'd like to have you with me." Harley had given him a hesitant smile and Orrin had felt his good will, the kindly, rather bumbling, but essentially good personality. At the moment, however, it was a personality that knew it held strong cards. "I'd like to be with you, Senator," Harley said, "but I wonder if I should do it for nothing." "I said when I got off the train that I would make no deals for the nomination," Orrin replied. "Did you mean it?" Governor Hudson had inquired, rather dryly, and Orrin had given him a sudden smile. "Do you really think I didn't?" he asked, and he would say for Harley that he had stopped smiling and looked respectful. "I believe you did," he said, "but under the circumstances——" And his voice had trailed away. "*He* said the same thing," Orrin had said with just a trace of sarcasm. "Maybe there's better hunting there." Harley Hudson had smiled. "I'm going to see him after I leave here," he said, "and maybe there is. Still and all, I would like to do the right thing—if I can." Senator Knox had turned away, for this was a decision he had made months ago, and as far as he knew, none of his delegates had been bought with any pledge of Federal preferment. "I'm sorry," he said, staring out the window across almost-deserted Lake Shore Drive to the dim emptiness of Lake Michigan beyond. "Certain fundamentals a man has to stand by in this world. I'm standing by that. I hope you'll be with me tomorrow morning." The Governor of Michigan had given him a long look and a firm hand shake before they had gone back out to face the blinding flashbulbs and the television cameras and put off with bland and friendly wisecracks the eager questions of the press. "I hope I will be able to," Harley had said as they opened the door. "I hope everything works out."

Ten minutes later the television cameras outside the headquarters of the Governor of California had picked up Harley entering there; and half an hour later they had shown him again with Orrin's opponent, the same bland, friendly pose, the same innocuous, good-natured comments. Governor Sheppard's whereabouts were a mystery, as far as the press could discover he had not called on either candidate, and at four-thirty when Orrin went to bed, there was still no word of him. For two and a half hours the Senator slept as one dead, getting up bleary-eyed at seven to find that the banner headlines were screaming, "HUDSON OFFERED V.P. FOR SWITCH"; "REPORT SHEPPARD TO BE SECRETARY OF STATE IF OHIO BACKS GOVERNOR"; and "MICHIGAN SWINGS AS HUDSON GETS V.P. BID." Shortly after seven-thirty one of Harley's chief assistants arrived with a sealed envelope containing this third headline. The first two words had been underlined and above them was scribbled, "This is not true. H.H."

So, because he was a gambler and a brave man and in the grip of a great ambition, he took the chance—always resented by delegates, who, after being told in no uncertain terms by their leaders how they are to vote, like to maintain to themselves the fiction that they are exercising independent judgment—of going to the Amphitheater shortly before ten. There was a roar of boos from his opponent's supporters, swiftly drowned out in a roaring demonstration for him. Instantly apprised of this development in his room in the Stockyards Inn, the Governor of California five minutes later did the same, touching off an equally wild counter-demonstration that for a few moments threatened mayhem all around. By dint of energetic gaveling and a blaring assist from "Dixie" by the band, the chairman managed to restore order after ten minutes, directed the calling of the roll, and the secretary once more began, "A—la—bama!" Two minutes later Arizona yielded to Ohio, and Governor Sheppard blandly cast his entire delegation for the Governor of California. For a howling interval the contest seemed to be over; but abruptly there was an angry stir and fuss over by the California standard, a red-faced delegate grabbed the microphone and began bellowing for recognition. When it came he shouted something furiously unintelligible and profane, and then wound up, more slowly, loud and clear. He and thirty of his fellow delegates, he announced in high dudgeon, were tired of being bossed, and they were going to vote for Senator Knox, and they didn't give a damn what happened to them. A hall which had produced all the sound human lungs could make found that it could produce even more. Somehow the roll was completed, the secretary and the tally clerks went into a huddle, the room that had been filled with insane noise an instant before became so still only the hurrying, sibilant clatter of a thousand typewriters and the ringing of their little bells in the press section broke the silence. The secretary stepped forward and in a trembling voice once more announced a deadlock. Sound flowed back into the amphitheater, pounded and hammered and beat and roared.

At once there was a scramble of reporters and photographers toward the Michigan standard, for now, conceivably, there might in the wake of the California rebellion be one of those strange, frightening, mass stampedes that sometimes come when delegates finally do break loose and run wild. Harley Hudson at that moment probably stood closer to being President than at any moment until the present, when he perhaps stood even closer; but Orrin could see that he did not have the personality to make the most of it. Instead he could be observed, aided by a flying wedge of Michigan delegates and police, making his way slowly across the floor toward the podium as everybody stood up and watched in a screaming pandemonium that filled the universe.

It was then, impelled by some instinct he could not explain, his fighting heart, his stubbornness, his ambition, his fear that Harley would go for the Governor, that the Senator from Illinois in his turn jumped up and started for the platform. Above in her box he caught a fleeting glimpse of Hank waving and shouting, but he couldn't hear what it was—"No, no, no! Go back!"—and for once in his life it wouldn't have made any difference what she said anyway. All he could see was Harley Hudson, apparently about to declare for his opponent—for he didn't really believe the note; Harley wasn't strong enough to withstand that kind of offer, it wasn't human not to yield to a bribe of that magnitude—and the sight drove him forward oblivious of all else.

Halfway along the long ramp leading out over the press section to the podium, he caught up with the Governor of Michigan, grabbed his arm, and swung him about by main force. "What are you going to do?" he shouted into Harley's startled face, and for several seconds Harley was too stunned to speak. "Tell them"—he managed to shout back presently— "tell them what I——" "I suppose you've decided to take it," Orrin interrupted angrily, and although Harley's face suddenly became almost comically dismayed, he couldn't stop, he rushed on. "I suppose you're like all the rest," he cried, his mouth close to Harley's ear. "I thought I could count on your integrity, but I guess that wouldn't fix you up so well, would it?" "But——" Harley protested helplessly. "But—but——" "Go ahead then!" Orrin shouted. "Go ahead then!" And quite suddenly, out of nowhere, coldly shattering and inescapable, there rushed upon him the knowledge that he was being a fool, that he was offending Harley mortally, that he had said one of those things, hasty, horrible, not really meant but gone beyond retrieving, that break a heart, destroy a friendship, ruin a plan, or lose a nomination. He could see Harley's startled, changing expression, he tried to shout an apology, to change it, to retract it, but the noise in the Amphitheater was too overwhelming, he could not surmount it. They stood for a long moment staring at one another, suspended there on the platform above the hysterical sea, locked in a sort of embrace-of-the-eyes in the hissing, rustling, screaming, pounding uproar. Then Harley turned away, to go back to the floor, but not before an alert photographer had recorded the occasion for posterity. It was on the front page of the Chicago *Tribune* half an hour later. "Was A Nomination Lost In This Moment?" the caption asked. Possibly so, for when the fourth ballot started an hour later Alabama, Alaska, Arizona, Arkansas, and California held as before, but Colorado yielded to Michigan and across the hall as in a dream he heard Governor Hudson casting forty-seven votes for his opponent. After that he was out of the world for a while as all his hopes came crashing down.

For anyone else, to recover from so public a loss of self-control, to erase the memory of an action so hasty and ill-advised, would have been difficult if not completely impossible; but curiously his reputation for impulsiveness came to his rescue now. "Orrin usually comes out ahead when he shoots from the hip," people said; "so this time he didn't, so what?" There were a few thoughtful, critical editorials—the *Times*, in particular, was sternly disapproving concerning the light the episode cast upon his qualifications to be President—but it seemed to be generally felt that the loss of the nomination was both sufficient explanation and sufficient punishment. There was no doubt anywhere that his analysis of the situation, however flamboyant his reaction to it, had been entirely correct: Governor Hudson was about to do exactly what he did, and the Senator's intervention had only prevented a preliminary announcement that might have made the final stampede to the victorious candidate even more devastating than it was. And it was generally felt, too, that the Senator's request, toward the middle of the roll call, that the nomination be considered unanimous and by acclamation had shown a fine sportsmanship that largely excused his earlier action. Hardly anybody noticed that just before he made this final gracious gesture a floor messenger had handed him a folded note which he read and then destroyed after a quick glance and a reviving grin up at his wife, who grinned back. "Come on, Abe," the note said. "Simmer down."

On Labor Day, at the well-publicized request of the candidate, he appeared on the same platform with him at Gilmore Stadium in Los Angeles to open the campaign. His introduction—"Is it all right if I take fifteen minutes?" he had asked dryly, and the Governor had grinned and told him, sure—was a graceful and powerful endorsement that brought him a warm ovation and effectively canceled out any lingering reservations left from the convention. He made ten more major speeches before November and appeared again with the candidate on the final television presentation on Election Eve. After the triumphant result he issued a statement of support and returned to the Senate to tend to his knitting. The tenuous peace ended three weeks after election when the President-elect called him in and asked him to run against Bob Munson for Majority Leader; it wasn't that he had anything against Bob, he said, he just thought a new Administration perhaps could use new blood, and what better means of showing party unity than if Orrin——? The Senator told him tartly that this might suit the President's purposes, but it would not suit his or those of the Senate, and after a brief and frigid conversation in which their campaign-suppressed hostility broke out anew, he bade him farewell. Aside from an eight-word statement four years later—"I shall vote for the President for re-election,"—he had kept him at arm's length ever since.

Not that he considered him, on the whole, such a bad President, and not that he did not often vote in support of his proposals and help to ease their passage through the Senate; but there was a certain characteristic, which the President's supporters referred to admiringly as "real political know-how" and Orrin referred to as simple duplicity, which made it impossible for any genuine bond to grow between them. He had never told Bob of the President's suggestion about the leadership, and he doubted he ever would; it was all of a piece with a general pattern he did not like. There was too much cleverness, too much deviousness, too much going around by the back alley just for the sake of going around by the back alley, to suit him. Time and again he had brought the President up short by some blunt exposure of this process; many and many an elaborate scheme had run aground on the rock of his impatient integrity. And increasingly over the years his personal opinion of this had become more and more obvious to the public, and of course the President didn't appreciate that either. In their many battles he would say the honors had gone about fifty-fifty. He was too direct and honest to harbor the sort of grudge Seab had harbored for so long; that wasn't his way. Some men lived by being feudists and some lived by saying what they thought and getting it off their chests. He was the latter type, and the President had always known where he stood with him. He could trace it all the way back to White Sulphur Springs, if he liked, and he would damned well know why it had happened, every inch of the way.

Of the President's troubles overseas and his conduct of the nation's foreign policy, the senior Senator from Illinois had also been critical on many occasions, although here he modified his views somewhat because he understood from his own mail and speeches and journeyings over the country what the President was up against. It was a terrible and oftentimes disheartening thing to try to lead to safety a country that sometimes appeared not to care whether it got there or not. Coming to the full scope of their powers and influence after the war, as they both did, it was easy to feel a terrifying drag against efforts to move ahead, a frightening apathy that seemed to run through the entire structure of American life.

This was the era, domestically, when everything was half done; the era, in foreign affairs, when nothing was done right because nobody seemed to care enough to exercise the foresight and take the pains to see that it was done right. This was the time when the job on the car was always half finished, the suit came back from the cleaners half dirty, the yardwork was overpriced and underdone, the bright new gadget broke down a week after you got it home, the prices climbed higher and higher as the quality got less and less, and the old-fashioned rule of a fair bargain for a fair price was indeed old-fashioned, for it never applied to anything. The great Age of the Shoddy came upon America after the war, and Everybody Wants His became the guiding principle for far too many. With it came the Age of the Shrug, the time when it was too hard and too difficult and too bothersome to worry about tomorrow, or even very much about today, when the problems of world leadership were too large and too insistent and too frightening to be grasped and so everybody would rather sigh and shrug and concentrate instead on bigger and bigger cars and shinier and shinier appliances and longer and longer vacations in a sort of helpless blind seeking after Nirvana that soothed them but unfortunately only encouraged their enemies.

A dry rot had affected America in these recent years, and every sensitive American knew it. Being one of the most sensitive, and in a position where he felt it all as a personal challenge and a personal responsibility, he found it did not encourage restful nights or happy days.

"I fear for the country," he had said in a recent speech in Detroit, and he did, for her friends fell away, her enemies advanced, and in her heart a slow decay was working. She could have withstood anything if she had been strong inside; but somehow, with the war, she had lost her flying speed. It was as though, having been young, she had matured overnight, but not to middle age; instead it seemed at times that she had matured immediately into senescence, so that she was tired, infinitely tired, baffled and confused and either incapable of seeing the path to take or incapable of setting her feet firmly upon it if she did see it. Everywhere, in every phase of her life, there was a slowing down, an acceptance of second-best, an almost hopeless complacence and compliance with all the things that devious people wanted to do, an unwillingness to come to grips with anything unpleasant, a desire to lean back and sleep; and sleep . . .

And yet there were great strengths still in the land; she had all her great heritage, all her industrial vigor, her innate decency and good will which not all the vultures who preyed off her in business, in labor, in politics, and press and international affairs, could ever entirely destroy. She needed only to be lifted up again and shown the way, and all the shabby, flabby, drifting years would vanish as though they had never been.

To see this and to do it, however, were two different things; men of vigor and men of vision fought what often seemed a fruitless and fore-doomed battle. He would say for the President, Orrin often thought, that the drift-into-crisis-and-then-do-the-wrong-thing policies of the earlier postwar years had been replaced by a much more astute and careful leadership; but too often it moved no faster than the most vocal elements of the people wanted it to, and they often did not want it to move at all. He had seen the President many times embark upon some course of action that showed imagination and a real desire to settle some long-standing international issue; but it would mean risks, and after a few trial balloons, when he saw, or thought he saw, that the country did not want to take risks, he would let it quietly die. On such occasions Orrin said what he thought; the mocking rejoinder came back, just as it had from Bob Leffing-well in the hearings, "Do you want a war, Senator?" Of course he didn't want a war; he just wanted an end to this flabby damned mushy nothing-ness that his country had turned herself into. And he particularly wanted an end to the sort of flabby damned thinking that the nominee and his kind represented—the kind of thinking, growing out of the secret inner knowledge that a given plan of action is of course completely empty and completely futile, which forces those who embark upon it to tell them-selves brightly that maybe if the enemy will just be reasonable the world will become paradise overnight and everything will be hunky-dory. It was quite obvious to Senator Knox that the enemy would never be reasonable until the day he could dictate the terms of American surrender, and it was with an almost desperate determination that he returned again and again to the task of trying to make this clear to his countrymen. It was doubly frustrating because it was quite obvious that his countrymen knew it. They knew it, but they didn't want to admit they knew it, because that would impose upon them the obligation of doing something about it, and that might bother them, and they didn't want that. In the face of such willful blindness he came as close to a feeling of kinship and friendship for the President as it was possible for him to come; the problem in the Senate and the White House was essentially the same for men who did not wish to see their country cast herself away through sheer default.

And still and all, the President was capable of coming up with a nomination like that of Robert A. Leffingwell. Nothing would weaken the nation more, in Orrin's opinion, than to have that type of fuzzy thinking in charge of the State Department. It had only been with the greatest inner questioning and only because he respected the President's prerogative with regard to the Cabinet that he had been ready to go along. Now in the reassessment of everything that was following the death of the senior Senator from Utah, all his doubts were coming back and with them an inescapable feeling that he had been right the first time. On every count, he felt, he was justified now in opposing the nominee. Loyalty to Brig demanded it; his own instinct for what was right demanded it; and the welfare of the country demanded it.

It was in this mood, after a hurried breakfast with Beth before the rest of his troubled household began to stir, that he arrived at his office early on this Monday morning of the final week of the Leffingwell matter to find waiting for him on his desk an envelope bearing the typewritten notation, "Senator Knox—Private." And it was in this mood fifteen minutes later, compounded now by a heavy wave of returning sorrow and a savage renewal of bitterness against the President, that he placed it quietly aside and, taking up the telephone, called in rapid succession Senator Cooley, Senator Danta, Senator August, Senator Smith, and Senator Strickland to a private conference in his office.

3

On the terrace the sunlight fell warmly across the perfectly appointed table; a maid came out and left some toast with silent dispatch, in the distance a gardener went carefully about his work; there was a sense of everything in the right place, of being in the presence of an ancestral efficiency humming quietly along out of the far past and into the far future, incapable of being disturbed by the hurrying cares of the world. The master of the house chewed absently on a doughnut as he plowed determinedly through the Washington *Post*, the lady of the house swung out with a brisk busyness from her study. The British Ambassador and his Ambassadress were up at nine to face a busy day in the stately brick mansion on Massachusetts Avenue.

"Dolly just called," Kitty announced. "She's canceling the reception for Crystal."

"Oh?" her husband said politely. "The first but not the last of many rearrangements to be made in this intriguing city, I imagine."

"I am so sorry," Kitty said slowly, sitting down and glancing unhappily at the glaring headlines in the paper. "We saw him and Lafe Smith out at Normandy Farms on Thursday, you know. We thought he seemed worried. But who could have known?"

"You never know," Claude Maudulayne said. "Never, never . . . Well, I suppose now I must consult with my friend from the Commonwealth and my friend from La Belle Patrie and all my other friends. There is no end to the ramifications of a good man's death, particularly when it occurs in a political context."

"Will they defeat Mr. Leffingwell now?" Lady Maudulayne asked.

"I expect they may," her husband said.

"Will you like that?" she asked. He smiled at her over the paper.

"I don't know yet," he said. "London hasn't told me. I expect not."

"Why do you approve of him when he causes such terrible things?" his wife inquired. He shrugged.

"You've been a diplomat as long as I have," he said. "It's one of those things. Anyway, what do we know about this, actually? Maybe he isn't to blame. What else did Dolly say?"

"Not much," Kitty said, "except that she was terribly worried about Bob. She kept saying she didn't know what it would do to him."

"Oh, then," Lord Maudulayne said with interest, "if Bob was involved, the fat may very well be in the fire. Chilton came back from the Press Club last night with a rather ugly rumor——"

"Chilton!" Lady Maudulayne said scornfully, with a face for the press attaché. "He always picks up rumors, the uglier the better. The only man worse than he is, is K.K."

"Yes," Claude Maudulayne said. "Well, I don't know about that, although I expect I'll be hearing soon enough."

"Anyway," Kitty said, "it is not one of those things that is going to be talked about openly. I know this Washington. They can hound a man to death and then turn around and be as bland as you please. Just wait and listen to those speeches in the Senate this afternoon. Butter won't melt in their mouths. Wait and see."

"I was fond of him, too," Lord Maudulayne said mildly, "and I'm not happy about it, either. But I don't think we should be too rough on our hosts. After all, it's the same everywhere. *De mortuis nil nisi bonum,* and so on. They mean it, you know—mean it in spite of what they may have contributed. People aren't hypocritical when they say they're sorry; they rarely intend for things to happen as they do. They're always genuinely upset when they really go wrong."

"Well," Lady Maudulayne said tartly, "I think I'll be happy if they do defeat Mr. Leffingwell. It would serve him right." Quite abruptly she began to cry. "I'm really very sorry about it," she said through her hand-kerchief.

"I don't really know just what to make of it," her husband said thought-fully, putting the *Post* aside. "If I have them pegged right, this will defeat him and no mistake. They're as emotional as we are, underneath it all. We each have our ways of hiding it, but all hell is boiling around inside there ready to explode if the occasion calls. And this is it. I can't help feeling, though, that it would be better for the world if he were confirmed."

"Isn't there anybody else?" Kitty asked with some annoyance. "Must it always be the great Bob Leffingwell? Surely there are other Americans."

"He has the reputation abroad," Lord Maudulayne said. "We all more or less told the Administration that we wanted him, through Bob, that night at Dolly's party. He's been pretty well cleared, so to speak, with everybody. It would be difficult for the President to find anybody else with as much ready-made welcome overseas."

"Dolly thinks the President had a lot to do with—with that," Kitty said. Her husband's eyebrows lifted.

"Does she, now?" he said. "That's interesting. I wonder how much she knows?"

"More than she will tell," his wife said. "And," she added firmly, "more than I am going to ask her."

"All right," Lord Maudulayne said. "I'm not urging you . . . That," he said as a phone rang somewhere in the distance, "is either London or K.K."

"If it's that *Indian*," his wife said emphatically, "I hope you won't waste any time on *him*."

Her husband rose, kissed her forehead lightly as he passed, and then turned to give her a smile from the doorway.

"I think the Queen is very fortunate," he said gravely, "that she has me for her Ambassador and not you. I hate to think what would become of the Commonwealth if you were in charge here."

"And if it's London," Kitty said with equal firmness, "you tell them that you hate Bob Leffingwell and you strongly advise against any support for him now."

"Oh, they'll know how I feel about it," her husband said. "And I'll know how they feel. And the Senate, which at this point isn't giving a damn about anything or anyone outside the Senate, won't care less. Is this one of your rare days of not seeing Celestine, or have you got something planned?"

"We thought we'd go to the auction at Sloan's this morning," Lady Maudulayne said.

"Well, I'll let you be my diplomatic courier," the Ambassador said. "Tell her to tell Raoul that I said I am planning to set up an appointment with the Vice President sometime in the next couple of days. Tell her to tell him if he wants to come along I think it would be nice."

"Why?" Kitty asked. Her husband smiled.

"You guess," he said.

"I have," she said. "And I hope he does," she added with a vicious stab at a piece of butter. "It would serve him right for all the bad things he's done."

"I hope you won't say that to an American," Lord Maudulayne said, not entirely in jest. "You'll get us deported yet." A buzzer sounded three times. "London," he said. "See you at lunch."

In five years he had walked along this way on many a sparkling morning, but he knew today that the time had come when he would never walk it again; for he was walking it with a ghost, and that was not pleasant company. He moved forward automatically along Seventeenth Street past the Pan American Union to Constitution, along Constitution past the Monument and the White House. He wasn't quite aware of where he was going, or why, for instinct had taken over on this bright spring day as beautiful as those which had just preceded it. Instinct was walking him along; somehow he himself didn't quite seem to be there. Something seemed to be wrong inside, there was a desperate crying somewhere, a sort of terrible rending unhappiness unlike any he had ever experienced; he wondered, really, whether he could stand it or whether he would die as he walked blindly along. It would serve him right, he thought dully; it would undoubtedly serve him right. It would be justice rendered where justice was due. He was not a bad man, and he knew now beyond all recalling or redemption or peace of mind that he had been guilty of something from which he would never recover. "Hop in, Tommy," the ghost said cheerfully as he had so often, opening the door of his car and giving his quick, pleasant smile. "I'll leave you at the Court." But he wouldn't leave him, Mr. Justice Davis knew. He would never leave him again.

"Hal," the Indian Ambassador said cautiously, "I am sorry to awaken you if you are not awake. But I wished to know."

"I'm not awake," Senator Fry said tartly. "That's obvious. What did you wish to know?"

There was a sibilant sound at the other end of the line and the senior Senator from West Virginia made an impatient sound in return.

"What did you say?" Krishna Khaleel asked quickly.

"I grunted," Hal Fry said, "because I am old and tired and a dear friend of mine lies dead and I am sick at heart about it and I don't really want to be bothered with you. But don't mind, K.K. I'll feel better in a minute. Only, what in Christ is on your mind, anyway?"

"I wanted to know why it happened," the Ambassador said.

"You hear the same things I do," Senator Fry said shortly. "Is there any point in rehashing lurid details that may or may not be true? This is a real tragedy for us Americans, you know, however academic it may be to you objective observers from far away."

"He was my friend, too," K.K. said with dignity. "I do not like your tone, Hal. It is a very tragic event and I am truly sorry. I hope you will realize that, Hal. I did not call to create hostilities."

"All right," Senator Fry said, more mildly. "I don't mean it, I'm just unhappy, damn it. I may cry, after a while, when I finally realize what's happened. In the meantime, I have nothing to add to what you read in your daily newspaper or hear over your local radio or television station courtesy of somebody's pills to jack up your colon. By the way, how is your colon lately, Akbar?"

"Please," the Indian Ambassador said coldly. "Now, please, Hal. I must ask—I really must ask——"

"If you want to know what the Senate is going to do," Hal Fry said abruptly, "we're going to lick hell out of the Leffingwell nomination."

"Ah," Krishna Khaleel said softly. "That was what I wondered, among other things."

"That was what you wondered, period," Senator Fry said bluntly. "I suppose you aren't going to like it, either."

"I don't know yet what position my government——" The Indian Ambassador began, but his United Nations buddy cut him off with a snort.

"The hell you don't," he said. "You Asians work by radar, and the deeper the fog the quicker you get the message. They don't have to tell you they still want Leffingwell, you know it already."

"I would not assume that their position had changed in any great degree," the Ambassador admitted. "The Administration had gone quite far, you know, in checking it with all of us; quite far. It would be rather difficult now for the President to find someone else, I should think."

"He should have thought of that," Senator Fry said coldly. "I find myself greatly moved by his predicament. Touched, in fact."

"But after all, Hal," the Ambassador said reasonably. "Is there any evidence known to us which associates him directly with this unhappy occurrence?"

"My friend," Hal Fry said crisply, "after you've been around this town a while you don't need a road map to put together the things that go together."

"I see," K.K. said carefully. "You do not think, then, that he might still be able to bring sufficient pressure to bear on some of your more susceptible, shall we say, colleagues——"

"We shall say, Akbar," Senator Fry said, "and maybe he can. But I doubt it. Yes, I do doubt it. This is a family matter, you know, and you outsiders don't understand it. Not even many Americans understand it. But in Washington, we understand it. This is something between him and us, this is; it's one of those things they wrote into the Constitution, only they didn't quite know at the time they were doing it. There comes a day with some Presidents when they push the Senate just a little bit too far. And then, brother, there's blood on the pie."

"Blood?" K.K. asked in some alarm. "Whose blood, Hal?"

"His, I hope," Senator Fry said with relish.

"Surely you don't mean——" The Indian Ambassador said in a hushed voice. "Surely, Hal, you don't mean——"

"Oh, I wouldn't put it in the diplomatic pouch if I were you, K.K.," the Senator said airily. "It might get out before we're ready for him. But you just wait and see. Yes, sir, you just wait and see. There'll be blood on the pie, and no mistake."

"My goodness," K.K. said in the same hushed tone. "Oh, my goodness, Hal. I had no idea it could mean—I had *no* idea it could mean——"

"You'll be safe enough in the Embassy," Hal Fry said comfortably. "Don't worry about it. Nothing ever happens to the embassies. And now, good-by, K.K. I'll see you around. I'm going back to sleep for a little while. Or maybe I'm going to cry. I don't just know yet."

"Well, Hal," Krishna Khaleel said with a rather nervous laugh, "I know your love for a joke, so I shall not entirely believe what you have told me. At least not about—about blood."

"That's right," Senator Fry agreed. "You're right not to believe that. But you can believe what I said about Leffingwell. As sure as Shiva made little naked statues, you can believe that."

"I hope not, Hal," the Ambassador said. "I really think my government desires him very much to be in that position."

"It's a family matter," Senator Fry said. "Even in India you must know enough to stay out of family matters. Good-by again, K.K. I've just decided which it's going to be. I'm going to cry."

And rather to his surprise, after he hung up the phone and lay back against the pillows and contemplated the beautiful day and the black tragedy it held, he found that he came very close to doing exactly that.

"Let's skip this bastard," AP suggested as they walked down the corridor in the Office Building.

"Right," UPI agreed. "I prefer humans."

It was the second time this morning that he had been deliberately snubbed by the press. Fred Van Ackerman began to wonder angrily if they were so damned partisan they couldn't take a thing in stride. He could.

"I'm calling about the nomination," the President said directly, and Powell Hanson, who did not often receive communications from the White House, was suitably taken aback.

"Yes," he said cautiously, suppressing a desire to ask bluntly, "Why me?" It rapidly became clear.

"I am saddened and shocked about Senator Anderson's death," the President said, "and I have just issued a statement saying so."

Have you? Powell thought rather dryly. That's nice.

"Yes," he said again.

"So I won't waste time talking about that," the President told him. "I want to talk about the situation which now confronts me and Bob Leffingwell. What is it, in your estimation?"

The junior Senator from South Dakota paused for a moment before answering.

"Bad, hm?" the President suggested into the silence.

"Yes," Senator Hanson said.

"Hopeless?" the President inquired.

"No," Powell Hanson said slowly, "I don't think so. Not if you can find people who will stand by you and help."

"Will you?" the President asked bluntly.

"I might." Senator Hanson said carefully.

"I thought possibly you and Fred Van Ackerman——"

"Not with Fred Van Ackerman," Powell Hanson said, so sharply he forgot to be polite. "You leave him out of it, if you want to get anywhere."

"Well, you and Tom August, then——" The President offered. Senator Hanson snorted.

"I met Tom on his way to Orrin Knox's office a few minutes ago," he said. "They're having a council of war."

"Oh?" the President said sharply.

"Yes," said Senator Hanson.

"Is Bob Munson in it?" the President asked.

"I don't know," Powell said. "Tom didn't know who else was involved."

"Have you seen Bob?" the President asked.

"No, sir," Powell said.

"I would give a lot," the President said with a sudden flattering candor, "to know just what Bob is going to do about all this."

"Why don't you ask him, Mr. President?" Senator Hanson suggested.

"I tried to reach him at his apartment, but he had already left," the President said. "Then I tried to reach him there and Mary said he wasn't in yet. I'm not sure," he added with the same candor, "that she was telling the truth. Just between you and me, I think maybe Bob doesn't want to talk to me this morning."

Senator Hanson absorbed this confidence for a moment.

"If that's the case," he said, "you *are* in trouble, Mr. President."

"Oh, I'll keep trying," the President said cheerfully. "In the meantime, if you see him try to smooth him down for me a little, will you? I'd appreciate it."

"I will," Powell promised automatically, though it occurred to him a second later that this threw a startling light on the President's position at this moment, that he should appeal to a junior in the ranks to smooth down the Majority Leader for him. "In any event," he added, "you can count on me. I am very upset indeed about Brig's death, but I don't feel that it should have any effect on judging the nomination. I think we should be able to separate the two when we come to vote."

"Thank you," the President said. "I think you should too. I think that shows real statesmanship, which of course is exactly what I expected from you. It's why I called, in fact. Will you do some work on it for me, then? Talk to some of the others and try to hold them firm?"

"Well——" Powell Hanson said doubtfully.

"It could be a big opportunity for you in the Senate," the President suggested. "It could lead to many things."

"I know," Senator Hanson agreed, though he wasn't sure he did.

"After all," the President said, "Bob won't be Majority Leader forever." This so startled Powell that he exclaimed right out loud.

"Oh, I expect he will," he remarked. "At least in my lifetime. However," he said, "I do appreciate your confidence, Mr. President. I'll see what I can do."

"Maybe you can hold a council of war yourself," the President proposed. "Call in the press, and give them something to speculate about."

"A counterirritant, if nothing else," Powell remarked with just the faintest trace of sarcasm. The President chuckled.

"All you young fellows are too clever for me," he said. "You see through everything."

"Yes," Powell said on an impulse he couldn't explain except that it sprang from his own decency. "All of us but Brig."

There was an abrupt silence and for a second he thought he too had ruined himself forever with the President. But the stakes were obviously too high to let an unfortunate truth jeopardize them.

"I *can* count on you, then?" the President asked calmly, as though the other remark had never been made.

"Yes," Powell said. "I'll see who I can round up right away, and we'll do some planning."

"Don't forget the press conference," the President said.

"I'll take care of all aspects," Senator Hanson promised. "Just one thing, though, Mr. President—don't call Van Ackerman. He's finished in this place."

"I know that," the President said. "I was just testing to be sure."

"What sort of reaction are you getting?" the Miami *Herald* asked the Philadelphia *Inquirer* as they met shortly before ten in the corridor outside the silent and deserted Caucus Room. The *Inquirer* thumbed quickly through his notes.

"Jack McLaughlin of Georgia," he quoted rapidly, "'I believe in view of the event of last night that it will now be quite difficult to confirm Mr. Leffingwell.' Clement Johnson of Delaware, 'While there is no evidence on the record that Mr. Leffingwell was involved in this tragic development, it is inevitable that it will have some effect upon the Senate in passing judgment upon his nomination.' Courtney Robinson, that old stupe: 'There has been a grave turn of events in the nomination. I question now whether it can be confirmed.' Sam Eastwood of Colorado: 'I was for him. I'm not now.'"

"Well, good for Sam, a man who knows his own mind and isn't afraid to say so," the Miami *Herald* remarked dryly. "That's pretty much what I'm finding too. I've got Don Merrick, Lacey Pollard, Bill Kanaho and Dick Suvick, if you want them."

"I do," the *Inquirer* said, scribbling busily. "Same thing?"

"Pretty much," the Miami *Herald* said. "I expect we're going to find it pretty general all through the Senate."

"In spite of—Brig?" the *Inquirer* asked.

"A lot of them don't know the story yet," the Miami *Herald* said. "We didn't use it, and apparently nobody else did either. For once our great profession seems to have kept its mouth shut, all over the country."

"Didn't anybody anywhere have it this morning?" the *Inquirer* asked in some disbelief.

"Apparently not," the Miami *Herald* said. "Nothing on the wire services, and they would have picked it up if anybody had. We're really being very decent."

"That's nice of us," the *Inquirer* observed, "seeing as how we helped to hound him to death . . . Well, I still think there's *somebody* left who's for Leffingwell."

"I'll bet its dwindled to less than fifty overnight," the Miami *Herald* estimated. "Papa in the White House had better be talking fast, because he's got his work cut out for him."

"I'm still betting on Bob Munson," the *Inquirer* said. "He'll pull it through yet, wait and see."

"He might as well," the Miami *Herald* said indifferently. "He hasn't got anywhere else to go."

But this judgment, rendered out of the cold distaste for politics which occasionally sweeps the press in the wake of some particularly flagrant development—closely akin to the bitter annoyance which sometimes grips politicians following the latest bit of slanting by the press—was perhaps a little unjust. The Majority Leader was not in the position he was in by free choice, exactly, even though there had been a moment when the choice could have been his to make. Nor was he in a position anyone could envy, as he sat now at his desk, staring absently at his hands as they played idly and pointlessly with a letter opener. Like Justice Davis, he felt that he would carry a heavy burden for a long, long time, although there was a difference in that he was quite sure, too, that his own life was full enough and busy enough so the day would come when the burden would not weigh quite so heavily upon him as it did right now.

There was no minimizing it at the moment, however, any more than there had been in the long night when he had lain awake and reviewed without hope the bitter sequences of events that had ended in the Office Building yesterday afternoon. He had not spared himself in this review, and he was not sparing himself now. He had been grievously, terribly, unforgivably at fault; and finding some way to live with himself again was not his only problem. Knowing the Senate, he knew that perhaps the most serious and difficult challenge of all was the problem of somehow regaining the respect and approval of his colleagues. For his own peace of mind this far transcended anything else; and he was gradually coming to the conclusion that there was probably only one way to do it.

That it must be done he had known as soon as the news flash came over the radio. His instinctive appreciation of what it meant for him personally had been confirmed half an hour later when he had received a call from a voice he barely recognized, it sounded so muffled and heavy with pain. The junior Senator from Iowa, though he obviously could hardly talk from emotion, was straight to the point. "I just wanted you to know," he said with a slow determination more terrible than abuse, "that you and I aren't friends any more. You and your God damned Administration that you toady for can go to hell. Maybe you can count on me for a vote now and then, but inside here, where *I* live, there isn't anybody home to you, any more, Senator Munson. So just keep your distance and . . . leave . . . me . . . alone." And he had hung up abruptly, because he obviously couldn't trust his voice to hold steady any longer. The Majority Leader had braced himself for other calls of a similar nature, and when none had come he had understood that Senator Anderson's close friends were telling him their reaction in a way more crushing than words could ever have been.

And there was the nomination. There, too, he had known at once what the effect would be, and so he had made no attempt to call anyone and again no one had called him. His judgment had been confirmed on that when he reached the Capitol an hour ago. He had not planned to see anyone, but as he neared the restaurant he saw a small group of men bursting out, in their center a large, disheveled, disorganized figure, obviously the life of the party. He heard someone say something he didn't quite catch, gurgled on a burst of laughter, followed by a reference to "—good old Sam!"

How often, he could not help thinking wryly even as he suddenly decided to move forward and intercept the senior Senator from Colorado, had he witnessed just that scene, and in how many places. On the Hill, at the White House, downtown, in the Departments, on the Coast, down South, up North, at four national conventions, and once, very late at night, in a little town near the Continental Divide when he had been traveling with the President and Sam had come aboard to ride through the state. "—And that's what we think of Sam in Washington!" the President had said and clapped him on the back, and on a roar of laughter the train had pulled out and the little round white dots of faces split by eager grins had receded faster and faster and finally disappeared altogether, swallowed up in the cold night air of the high, lonely plains.

But now Sam had seen him coming, and the amused memories vanished at once as a veiled expression came into his eyes. He was a big fat man with a smile on his mouth, but it wasn't anywhere else.

"Oh, hi, Bob," he had said slowly, and the Majority Leader was aware of a wall between them as palpable as though it had been of stone.

"I was just wondering——" He began, and started over lamely. "That is, I was just wondering——"

"I wouldn't if I were you, Bob," Senator Eastwood said. "If you mean Leffingwell, the answer is no."

"But, Sam," Bob Munson protested, "you told me last week——"

"Last week and last night were two different times, Bob," Sam told him. "Isn't that right?" And suddenly he wasn't smiling any more at all anywhere.

"I suppose so," Senator Munson said slowly. "I suppose that's right, Sam."

"Yes, sir," Sam Eastwood said, "it is." And then he saw someone he knew off on the other side of the corridor, and, "Well, hi, *there!*" he shouted happily, and turning his back on the Majority Leader he was gone, apparently just a big jolly man bursting with friendliness and good will for the world. Only he wasn't.

And so it was with many of his colleagues now, Senator Munson knew; perhaps enough to defeat Bob Leffingwell. Certainly enough to make his own problem infinitely more difficult if he continued to fight for him.

Finally, there was the business of the Senate to be considered. Some way or other, the thing had to be cleaned up, and soon. It was true there had been the Fed bill and a couple of commercial treaties and fifty or sixty routine private-claims bills disposed of in the past few days, but there was no doubt the Senate was snagged on Bob Leffingwell. Half a dozen important things were piling up, a tax-revision bill, amendments to Taft-Hartley, the space-control bill, amendments to Euratom, and so on. Entirely aside from all the other aspects of it, he thought impatiently, it was time to get moving and get it out of the way; they had wasted enough time on it. His habit of mind as Majority Leader told him not much more could be tolerated. Eulogies today, services and Crystal's wedding tomorrow, burial on Wednesday and a delegation from the Senate attending so there could be no vote then; that meant that the first day to vote would be Thursday. Well, then, he would try to get a vote Thursday and finish it one way or the other. If, he caught himself short, it was still his decision to make by Thursday. The one he was in process of making right now might interfere, providing he went through with it. He was increasingly sure he would.

Aside from Lafe, only Dolly had called last night, to invite him to come over, but he had said with thanks that he would stay where he was. "You're all right?" she had demanded anxiously, and he had said, "Yes, as much as possible under the circumstances. I won't pretend I'm happy." This had made her start crying again, for him, and for Brig, and for all of them. But he had remained right where he was, ordering dinner from room service, tossing restlessly most of the night, eating again in his room in the morning and then going down a back elevator to catch a cab alone and go to the Hill. He didn't want to see anyone for a while yet. Sam Eastwood had been unexpected, and he had only forced a conversation with him because he wanted to prove to himself that his fears and assumptions about the effect on the nomination were correct.

So, now what? He didn't know, exactly. He had refused a call from the President at the hotel, and ten minutes after he reached the office Mary had informed him of another. "Tell him I'm not here," he said sharply, and she had. But there would be another call in a while, he supposed, and the President would keep it up until he answered. He might as well, next time, though he did not know right now whether he could manage to be civil or not. He would feel a lot better, he thought, if Orrin were the one trying to reach him; but Orrin, he knew, was busy on purposes of his own, and he knew they boded no good for Robert A. Leffingwell. At the moment he found it hard to care.

"I think something is going on in Orrin Knox's office," AP said, turning away from a phone in the press gallery. "They're awfully coy about his whereabouts over there."

"I haven't been able to raise Tom August," UPI offered.

"And I can't find Seab or Warren Strickland," the Wall Street *Journal* remarked.

"I don't suppose anybody would be in the mood for a stroll to the Office Building?" AP inquired.

"I'm with you," the *Times* said, throwing down a copy of his own paper. "I keep hoping that some morning I'm going to find enough time to read this thing, but it obviously isn't going to be today."

"It'll keep," the Wall Street *Journal* said. "It's history."

"*You* think you're kidding," the *Times* said with a grin, "but *we* know you're not."

And collecting the Birmingham *News*, the St. Louis *Post-Dispatch* and Paris *Soir*, who all happened to be in the gallery at the moment, they headed for the elevators and, they hoped, the news.

This was one of the times, Beth thought as she moved quietly about the big old house in Spring Valley, when she wondered how she had ever gotten mixed up in politics. But even if she hadn't, she decided, things probably wouldn't have been so very different. Sooner or later these moments came; it seemed to fall to men to create disasters and to women to come around and mop up after; and even in some other context there might well be a household of unhappy people depending upon her to keep things going while they gradually untangled themselves from the web of sorrow and despair in which they had become entrapped.

Politics, she had decided long ago, was neither as good nor as evil as people said; it was somewhere in between, with aspects of both, and on occasion one or the other predominated as it had now. Up to now the evil had been in control, but this, she knew, marked the turning point—a terrible turning point, but a turning point which for that very reason could not be evaded. From this point forward the good guys were going to triumph over the bad guys because in the curious development of the ever-changing American story there came a time when they always had to, and this was it. And leading the posse as it thundered toward the pass would be the volatile, stubborn, cantankerous, brusquely tender-hearted man she had married, his emotions rubbed raw, his feelings completely engaged, his whole being devoted with a grim single-mindedness to his purpose.

Thinking upon the number of times she had seen this happen, she could not refrain from a smile in which amusement and affection were inextricably mixed. From college right on through, she had always found it the most touching characteristic of the many she had discovered in her husband, and she had seen it take him from a modest beginning in the law straight to the top of his country without a pause along the way. The pauses had come after he had reached the top, when he had tried to go even higher and been stopped by factors composed about equally of organized political opposition and his own prickly character. It had been one of her own personal triumphs, which she never mentioned to anyone but which gave her much quiet satisfaction, that she had gradually over the years brought him to understand his own responsibility in this. And she had done it without conflict or tenseness or nagging—the note she had sent him at the convention had been only one of many such quietly humorous summons to sensibility that she had sounded—and without in any way jeopardizing their deep understanding and partnership. Indeed it had only become stronger all the time, so that she could not remember a period when their relationship had not been undergoing a process of growth. "I suppose that's a sign of lots of friends, when you have three nicknames," a wistful boy who didn't then have too many friends had remarked soon after they met; and at that moment, though he didn't know it at the time, Elizabeth Henry had decided irrevocably that helping him was what she wanted in life. And so she had, in the early years, the Springfield years, the Washington years, in all the triumphs and defeats of a gallant and controversial heart, knowing that because of her support the defeats were far less devastating than they might have been, and that because she was part of them the triumphs meant far more to him than they ever could have otherwise. "Orrin and Beth," the sign had said, and it had unknowingly paid tribute to far more than a shrewdly powerful political team; it had also paid tribute to a marriage as near perfect as any she knew.

All of it, she felt now as she went softly about the house while the Andersons still slept and the day's sorrow had not been fully taken up again to be carried until sleep could come once more, had in a sense been preparation for this supreme test arising out of the Leffingwell nomination. So much hung upon it: what would happen to the nominee himself, in the first instance; what would happen to the country, in the second; above all, from her standpoint, what would happen to her husband's future and to hopes and plans which she knew were temporarily dormant but still very much alive.

She had known at breakfast that he had been awake most of the night, for she had been too, although Mabel mercifully slept a druglike sleep in the other bed and did not disturb her. She had also known, without his telling her, what he planned to do. They had talked very little at breakfast, but she had seen him go out the door with the same air of implacable determination she had seen many times before. "Good luck," she had said as she kissed him good-by, and he had nodded rather absently. "I've got a lot to do," he said, "but if you need me here for anything, don't hesitate to call. I'll come home if necessary." "I'll manage," she said, and suddenly he had smiled and come back from the whirling storm of his own thoughts. "You always do, Hank," he said, rubbing his fist against her chin; "that's one of the reasons I like you." "It's mutual," she said lightly, and he had kissed her with a sudden warmth that showed he was paying attention to it. "Orrin and Beth," he said with a chuckle. "What makes anybody think he can lick *us*?" And he had driven off to the Hill comforted and fortified as always.

This had disposed of the first challenge of the day, and a few minutes later when Hal came down she had disposed of the second by giving him a quick breakfast and telling him firmly to go and get Crystal and get away somewhere and try to enjoy the beautiful weather and forget unpleasant things as much as possible. Her son's eyes still looked dark with pain and lack of sleep, and she could tell it was not going to be easy for him and his fiancée to escape the shadow hanging over them all; but she also knew that he grasped the wisdom of the advice, for he nodded quickly, gave her a quick kiss and hug and then hopped in his car and drove off. She said a little prayer as he left that the two of them would realize that the fact that life on occasion could be utterly tragic did not mean that it could not also on occasion be utterly happy. She would have to rely on youth and common sense to reassure them on that, and she guessed they would.

That left only Mabel and Pidge to be looked after and as she stepped out for a moment onto the porch to snap off some tulips and bring them in for the dining-room table she heard sounds of stirring upstairs. She knew this would not be an easy day for any of the Knoxes, but, she thought wryly, that was probably one reason the Lord had made them so tough, so that they could stand things. She stood quietly at the foot of the stairs for a moment, composing her thoughts and her person to their customary serenity, and then went up to say good morning to Brigham Anderson's widow and child.

"How are you, Mr. President? I thought I might come down sometime this morning and we could have a talk."

"Well, I'll tell you, Fred, I do appreciate your call and I would love to see you, but you know how it is. I'm just loaded down with work this morning and I don't quite see how——"

"Perhaps this afternoon, then?"

"This afternoon, too, I'm afraid. Why don't I try to square things away later in the week sometime and give you a call?"

"Well——"

"You needn't bother to call me, I'll call you."

"But it may be important for the nomination that I——"

"I'm sorry, Fred. We'll just have to wait and see how the week develops. Is that all right with you?"

"But——"

"It's good to hear your voice, Fred. We'll have that talk sometime, never you fear."

"But, God damn it——"

"Sorry I have to run, Fred, but I do. I'm sure you understand."

"I think you'd better see me, Mr. President. After all, I know certain things——"

"What do you know, Fred? How to murder a man?"

". . . I only did what you wanted me to."

"Oh? Who told you that? I don't remember that I did."

"But——"

"Don't do anything hasty you might regret, Fred. Now I really must say good-by. It's been grand talking to you."

"But, God damn it——"

"Good-by, Senator. Keep in touch."

Behind the locked doors of the Embassy on Sixteenth Street, Vasily Tashikov sat at his desk staring thoughtfully at the morning papers with their banner headlines and their skillful speculations. So far none of them had related the death of the Senator from Utah directly to the

Administration's drive to confirm Robert A. Leffingwell, but reading between the lines the Soviet Ambassador, who was an astute if humorless
man, could perceive that many of them felt there was some connection.
This, from what he had observed of all the personalities involved, led
him to believe that there might be something damaging to the nominee
which had been known to the chairman of the subcommittee, which in
turn had brought upon him such pressure that he had gone under. It was
the sort of equation a representative of Communism could understand,
for in one form or another it happened in his country all the time. He
decided he would advise Moscow that the nominee might fail of confirmation, necessitating some revision of plans that were already being
formulated on the basis that his reasonable approach to the ambitions
of the unfree world might soon be a dominant factor in American foreign
policy.

Not that it would matter in another day or two anyway, the Ambassador
thought with a vengeful satisfaction, for very shortly now his government
hoped to have an announcement that would put the arrogant capitalist
imperialists in their place once and for all. It wasn't quite certain yet,
but the cable the decoders had just given him indicated that only a matter
of hours, required by the necessity for complete scientific confirmation,
separated his way of life from a new and quite possibly crushing triumph
over the other.

If the President only knew, Harley Hudson thought, how far ahead of
him some people were, he might give up trying these indirect approaches
to things. The Vice President didn't suppose he ever would, for that was
his nature, but he for one wasn't fooled by the technique he had just
been subjected to.

It was all very well for him to call up and exchange commiserations
on the sad event that had befallen the Senate, but it had been all Harley
could do to refrain from a tart rejoinder—in fact, more than tart, for
he suspected the President knew considerably more about events leading
to the tragedy than had yet been revealed, or might ever be revealed.
Something about that White House conference hadn't quite rung true to
the Vice President. He had realized finally that it had been the President's sudden capitulation, which in spite of Brig's hopes, spurred by his
great relief at having the situation apparently so easily solved, had been
just a little too pat, seen in retrospect. It was this realization which had
prompted his offer of a joint press conference, unhappily sought too
late; and it was this which had turned to an iron indifference to the
President's wishes the sorrow and dismay he had felt when the news
came last night.

The President's calm show of regret now, in fact, had come close to
leaving the Vice President breathless; if what he suspected was true,
there had been a monumental nerve and gall about it that had both

"Stanley Danta came out early on his way over to the airport to meet Brig's brother," AP said, "but he wouldn't talk, either. He only said one thing—'You will find that nothing discussed in this office this morning will ever be divulged to the press'—which was strong language, for Stanley."

"And apparently," said UPI, "they mean it."

"Well, did they all seem to be in agreement on what they were going to do?" the *Commercial-Appeal* asked.

"That they did," the *Herald Tribune* said. "That they really did."

"So Knox, Cooley, Smith, Danta, Strickland, Tom August, and Harley are all agreed," the *Times* summed up. "And since we already knew how Knox and Smith and Cooley felt, that means bad news for somebody."

"I think we've got enough for a new lead," UPI said.

"Indubitably," said AP.

Calming down Walter Calloway of Utah, the Majority Leader decided, had been good for him. The habits of thought of many years began to function again, he found he was automatically studying, considering, weighing alternatives, making plans, even as his emotions tried to adjust to last night and its consequences. Minding the store was something he did instinctively, it was something outside emotions and he was very glad to be called upon to do it, for it was holding him steady to the course he had decided upon and giving him things to think about in the meantime. Brig's pedantic, fussy little colleague, showing a forcefulness no one could have imagined he possessed, wanted to introduce a resolution to censure Fred Van Ackerman.

"I want to get that little monsster," he had insisted angrily, his teeth whistling even more than usual in his anger and indignation. "He deservess it. He's committed murder just as ssurely as though he fired that sshot himsself. I want to get him, Bob, and I think the Senate will go along with me."

This estimate of truths and likelihoods had been difficult to refute, and before their talk was over Senator Munson had come to the conclusion that possibly Walter had the right idea—except, as he told him, he thought that the objective could be accomplished by indirection rather than directly. Senator Calloway had been doubtful—"Sseab thinks I should go right ahead with it," he said, and the Majority Leader said, "I'm sure"— but he came around before long.

"Suppose you call the Legislative Drafting Service and have them put it in shape for you right now," the Majority Leader suggested, "and then bring it over and let me handle it from there for a while. I think maybe we can achieve what you want without an open fight that might put a lot of unhappy things in the Record. I'd rather do it that way, if you agree."

Walter Calloway, who obviously had no inkling whatever that the Majority Leader had played a part in recent events and, pray God, never would know, said, "Well——" slowly. "If you agree," Bob Munson repeated firmly; and after a moment's hesitation Senator Calloway said he would do whatever Bob thought best.

"Good, Walter," the Majority Leader said quickly, "I appreciate your visit and your co-operation." And he meant it sincerely, for it opened the way to a solution for the problem of what to do about Fred Van Ackerman, and that was all to the good. One minor piece of house-cleaning would be taken care of; and not so minor, either, considering the possibilities inherent in an unchecked demagogue in the Senate. One piece of good fortune had come out of all this tragic muddle: one little demagogue had gone too far too fast and was going to be squashed once and for all; and for that the country, even though it might never hear about it, could be grateful.

Pondering the strangely confused and unexpected ways in which the destinies of America sometimes work themselves out, he found that his talk with the junior Senator from Utah—who was now, in fact, the senior Senator from Utah—had served in some measure to restore his energies for the day. They would be needed a little later on, he thought with a sigh, for the clock was moving toward noon and the toughest thing he had ever had to do as Majority Leader was steadily coming closer as the session neared. He was not entirely ungrateful or unhappy, difficult though he knew their talk would be, when Mary buzzed and told him that the minutes remaining before the session would be filled by a visit from the senior Senator from Illinois. At least it would pass the time, he thought wryly, and it was with the wry expression still in his eyes that he looked up to greet his visitor as he came quickly into the room.

"What's the matter?" Senator Knox asked shortly. "Do you find something funny in the world today?"

Senator Munson's face sobered abruptly, he started to protest but then dropped it.

"Sit down, Orrin," he said in a tired voice. "There isn't anything funny in the world today."

"I don't think so," Senator Knox said coldly. "You look like the devil," he added abruptly.

"I have things on my mind," Bob Munson said. Senator Knox nodded curtly.

"You should have," he said; and suddenly, having forced them tightly down inside him so that he could come and see Bob with reasonable calm, he found that all his anger and sorrow and resentment were abruptly boiling up again.

"God damn it," he said bitterly, "that was a hell of a thing you did. How can you stand yourself this morning?"

The Majority Leader looked at him with a weary thoughtfulness.

"You know," he said, "I wonder that too. However, here I am because I have to be. Who told you?"

"He did," Senator Knox said. "He wrote me a letter before he—before. It was under my door."

"Was it complete?" Senator Munson asked and then answered his own question. "But of course it would be," he said. "It wouldn't be characteristic of his honesty if it weren't."

"That's right," Orrin said, without mercy. "That was a fine young man you killed." He was pleased to see an expression of sudden pain come over the Majority Leader's face.

"Oh, please," Bob Munson said in the same weary way. "Orrin, please. How do you think I feel about it, for Christ's sake?" He turned away and stared out the window a moment before turning back. "Who else knows?" he asked.

"We had a meeting in my office," Senator Knox said. "Seab and Tom and Lafe and Warren and Stanley and Harley. I read it to them before I burned it. I thought they had a right to know it all before I asked them to help defeat the nomination."

"Did anybody back out?" Senator Munson asked. Senator Knox gave him a scornful look.

"Are you kidding?" he asked. Bob Munson shrugged and let his hands drop on the desk before him.

"So you've got a gallant little band together and you're out to beat him," he said.

"Yes," Senator Knox said coldly, "and if there were some way of getting back at you, too, I think I'd do it." Again he was satisfied to see the Majority Leader wince. "But I suppose I'll just have to be happy with making you take a licking on the vote. Which," he added positively, "I am going to do."

"Would it come as a great surprise to you," Senator Munson inquired, "if I said I no longer give a damn?"

Orrin laughed without amusement.

"It wouldn't surprise me at all," he said, "but it would sure as hell surprise me if you had the guts to do something about it."

"What would you recommend?" Senator Munson asked with a certain irony.

"I'll tell you what I'd recommend," the Senator from Illinois said bluntly, and he did so with a succinct directness. When he finished the Majority Leader gave him the first thing approaching a smile that he had managed in eighteen hours.

"Well, Orrin," he said softly, "Orrin, don't give me up as a lost cause forever, because I'm way ahead of you. That's exactly what I intend to do."

"Very well," Senator Knox said practically. "If you do you can count on me to see that things get straightened out later. It's the best way out for you, it seems to me."

"I think so," Senator Munson said. "It seems the least I can do for him.

And," he added quietly, "you don't have to see to anything for me, Orrin. Let it ride, if you want to. It would serve me right."

"Well," Orrin Knox said, and he found that he was feeling much better suddenly, for the future now was beginning to open up in a way that led straight to defeat for Mr. Robert A. Leffingwell, "we'll see about that."

"Don't promise anything," Bob Munson said with the faintest touch of humor, "that might tie you down." And for the first time, as he had hoped it might, the remark brought an answering glimmer of humor from Senator Knox.

"I won't, Bob," he said. "Don't worry." He got up abruptly. "I'll run along. I have things to do."

"You might like to talk to Walter Calloway," the Majority Leader suggested. "He wants to put in a censure resolution against Van Ackerman, and I told him I'd prefer it if he got it ready and then left it with me. Maybe you'd rather handle it. Since," he said wryly, "you're going to be running the Senate this week."

Senator Knox nodded matter-of-factly.

"I would," he said. "I'll talk to him."

"Talk to Lafe, too," the Majority Leader said. "He hates me."

"He'll get over it," Orrin said shortly.

"Will you?" Senator Munson asked. Senator Knox looked at him out of twenty years of friendship and close alliance and all the things that don't change overnight no matter what happens.

"I don't hate you," he said. "These things happen. It may be a while before I forgive you, but I don't hate you."

"I was on such a spot all around," the Majority Leader said, and he said it not as a plea for sympathy but as a statement of simple fact. "I never thought it would—would come to—to——" And he stopped because he was unable to continue.

"Of course you didn't," Orrin agreed in a tone that passed no judgment one way or the other. "I'll see you on the floor, Bob. I think everything will work out all right."

"I hope so," Senator Munson said.

But after the Senator from Illinois had gone swiftly out the door and on his way, he remained seated at his desk, staring before him without really seeing anything, knowing he would have the courage to do what he wanted to do but wondering what its consequences would be. Far-reaching and profound, he knew, for it was not something that happened often and it meant a political upheaval akin to a genuine constitutional crisis when it did.

While he was still wondering about it Mary buzzed again and he picked up the phone.

"The President is on the line again," she said. "Do you want to talk to him?"

The Majority Leader paused for a second, thought many things, and reached his decision.

"Oh, I don't think so," he said quietly. "I don't think so. But don't tell him I'm out. Tell him just what I said."

Just as the warning bell rang at eleven forty-five the senior Senator from Illinois got on the subway car with Dick McIntyre of Idaho, Victor Ennis of California, Marshall Seymour of Nebraska, and a dozen tourists and rode over to the Capitol. Marshall as usual was full of sharp comments that he liked to think were funny but weren't, particularly today, and Orrin found it hard not to take his head off. However, by a series of grunts and "Unh-hunhs" and a pretense of leafing through the papers in his briefcase he managed to complete the trip without an open breach with the insufferable old joker. And after all, he told himself ironically, he needed his vote. Inspired by this thought, he changed his attitude abruptly as they got off the car, linked his arm through Marshall's, and chatted away with him vigorously as they made their way to the Senators' elevator and up to the floor. "How to win friends and influence people," Victor Ennis murmured in some surprise. "I don't care what a fool you are, I need your lousy vote," Dick McIntyre murmured in return. "Well," Vic said with sudden seriousness, "he's got mine. How about you?" "I'm watching my mail," Senator McIntyre said candidly. "It's beginning to run two- and three-to-one against Leffingwell. He'll probably have mine, too." "He'll probably have a good many," Senator Ennis said. "Enough?" inquired Dick McIntyre. "We shall see," said Vic Ennis.

As for Orrin during this little exchange, he was telling himself dryly that it was talking to people like Marsh Seymour that fortified the soul and strengthened the character. He gave the old buffoon a final slap on the back and they parted the best of buddies.

And so far, he thought, as he came on the floor and observed that there was close to a full Senate already gathered, waiting to pay tribute to the Senator from Utah, everything was going very well from his standpoint. He had exacted a pledge of absolute secrecy from his colleagues at the meeting in his office, and even if they had not given it willingly to begin with, as they did, he could see it was no problem as soon as they heard Brig's letter. Their reactions had been exactly as his own, saddened and sobered and filled with a heightened anger against those responsible for the tragedy; plus, as he had been sure would be the case, a heightened respect for their unhappy young colleague whose integrity was affirmed for the last time in the straightforward honesty of his letter. After Orrin finished the reading he had burned it carefully in an ash tray and then sat back and surveyed them all.

"Now," he said. "Are you with me?" "I am," Harley said promptly, and for all but Tom August, that did it. In his heart the chairman of Foreign Relations reacted just as Senator Knox had expected; but his position, his love of feeling important in matters of high policy, coupled with his rare opportunities to do so, produced an uncertainty that was rather painful to see. He wanted to be with Orrin; but should he? He was not, however, reluctant to co-operate in Orrin's plans to speed a decision in the matter. When Orrin said that he would call a subcommittee meeting right after the session today, Senator August agreed promptly; and when Orrin suggested a full committee meeting tomorrow, he immediately proposed setting it for 9 A.M. "Two o'clock," Senator Knox said. "It might be better to wait until after the service at the Cathedral." "More strategic, too," Stanley Danta had remarked with the slightest trace of irony, and Orrin had made an impatient gesture. "I intend to use the materials at hand," he said bluntly, and Stanley had nodded. "I'm not criticizing," he said. "I think he would want you to."

As for Bob, that too was working out more smoothly than he had dared to hope; there also his luck was with him. Knowing his old friend, he had suspected that the course of action he proposed might already have occurred to the Majority Leader; but if it hadn't, he had been quite prepared to argue for it as passionately and forcefully as he knew how, not sparing in any way the feelings of the Senator from Michigan or holding back any of the emotion he felt about Bob's part in the tragedy. Fortunately Senator Munson's own decision had removed the necessity for much of this, so that it had been possible for them to discuss it on a reasonably calm basis, and to part with enough of their old closeness intact so that there had not had to be any irreparable breach. Orrin would not have wanted this to happen, but he was ready for it if it turned out to be necessary. That it hadn't was one small dividend for which he was grateful. So was Walter Calloway's censure resolution. He would get that resolution and then he and Bob would sit down in some quiet place with Fred Van Ackerman and have a little talk. And after that in logical progression would come the personal isolation, the political and legislative deep-freeze, the terrifying implacable ostracism that the Senate can impose upon a member when it so desires. It couldn't happen, Orrin thought with savage satisfaction, to a nicer guy.

Prompted by this to look about the chamber, he noted that for once the insufferable gall of the junior Senator from Wyoming had apparently failed him. He was not on the floor, and Senator Knox didn't think he would dare to come onto the floor. That meant that he was on the run already. He decided he must see Senator Calloway as soon as possible and get that resolution. Then he and Bob could have their conference with Fred this afternoon, another of the things that could be accomplished on the tide of emotion running in the wake of Senator Anderson's death.

At five minutes to twelve, he noted, the galleries were full, the space along the walls at the back of the chamber was jammed with clerks and secretaries, nearly every seat on the floor was filled. Many Senators were in black, voices were hushed, people moved about quietly with subdued and sober greetings. The press gallery was crowded, too, and there as everywhere in the room there was an atmosphere of somber expectation, as though people felt instinctively that today there was much more at stake, and much more to be expected, than on the usual day of eulogies for a dead Senator. Well, he thought grimly, they were going to get their money's worth. They didn't know it yet, but they were going to get their money's worth.

At one minute to the hour Bob Munson and the Vice President came onto the floor together and went to their respective chairs, followed by the chaplain of the senate, wearing the grave and preoccupied look he wore on such occasions. "Carney's buryin' face," Jack McLaughlin of Georgia called it; "Old Carney's got on his buryin' face." But this time, as with all the Senate, there was something deeper and more genuine about it; and when the opening bell rang at noon and the gavel fell and the galleries and the Senate stood with bowed heads, it was a more moved and genuine prayer than usual that he gave. When he finished Harley looked up quietly and said, "The Senator from Utah," as Walter Calloway arose to make the traditional announcement to the Senate of a colleague's passing.

"It iss my sad duty, Mr. President," he said in a voice that wasn't very steady, "to announce to the Senate the death of my dear colleague and beloved friend, the senior Ssenator from the Sstate of Utah, Brigham Anderson." He paused and slowly looked about the chamber. "I do not observe," he remarked quietly, "the junior Ssenator from Wyoming, who I should think would like to be here to see what he has accomplished." Good for you, Walter, Orrin told him silently; oh, by God, good for you. And on a sudden inspiration he looked quickly at the Majority Leader and they understood one another instantly. Bob returned a rather alarmed glance that said, "Not now," and Orrin said, "Why not?" as clearly as though he had said it aloud. The Majority Leader turned away, looking disturbed, but the mind of the Senator from Illinois was made up. Yes, why not now, now that Walter had opened the way?

"Therefore," Senator Calloway went on, "I shall not dwell on the tragic events with which we are all familiar. Rather I shall try, within my poor limitations, to pay ssome tribute, however feeble, to one who was one of the finest young men who ever held office in the Ssenate of the United States—one who, unlike some otherss, conducted himself with a decency befitting his high office."

"Wow," UPI whispered to AP in the Press Gallery above. "We're out for blood this afternoon."

"Why not?" AP retorted. "Why not?" And they scribbled sharp, busy, effective sentences as Walter Calloway droned on and concluded and then, one by one, Senator after Senator followed to pay tribute. It was noticed that soon after his own brief and emotion-filled remarks, which at one point were broken by absolute silence as he had to stop and struggle for control for a moment before going on, the senior Senator from Illinois went out to the cloakroom. It was noticed that presently the senior Senator from South Carolina casually followed him, and that after a few brief moments the two of them returned as casually as they had gone, Orrin sitting down as if by accident next to Senator Calloway, Seab resuming his seat beside the Majority Leader. There followed presently a short whispered conversation between the old man and the Senator from Michigan; a brief flare of argument, come and gone in a flash; then a sudden capitulation on the Majority Leader's part, a shrug and nod; something he apparently didn't favor much, but would go along with. The press, puzzled by his continuing silence as the eulogies went on, began to speculate.

"What's the matter with Bob?" the *Times* whispered. "Surely he's going to say something?"

"I don't know," the *Christian Science Monitor* whispered back. "Is something going on?"

And they all returned with heightened interest to their study of the sober-faced gentlemen arrayed before them in the brown leather seats. So it was that they noted that Orrin Knox and Walter Calloway were suddenly leaning forward tensely as Victor Ennis expressed his sorrow and Courtney Robinson rippled through the flowery little speech he had perfected for such occasions; and so it was that they were immediately aware when the Majority Leader turned slowly to catch the eye of the senior Senator from Illinois, who gave the slightest of nods; and that the Majority Leader gave a barely perceptible nod back. A moment later, it was noted, he got up and came to the Vice President's desk for a brief conversation. Then he returned to his seat.

A few minutes after that, when Allen Whiteside of Florida became the forty-fifth Senator to speak and a little silence had fallen, indicating that the point of redundancy had been reached and no one else wished to add to tributes that had already consumed more than three hours, the Majority Leader stood up and was recognized by the Vice President.

"Mr. President," he said quietly, "I too wish to pay my respects to my dear friend, and I should like to reserve to myself that privilege a little later on this afternoon. It is presently my intention to yield to the Senator from Utah, Mr. Calloway, for a privileged resolution, and I ask unanimous consent that it may be acted upon without referral to a committee."

There was a little stir through the Senate, followed immediately by the assumption that this must of course be the customary resolution of condolences to the family of the deceased; although such resolutions never were referred to committee, and it seemed rather odd to ask unanimous consent for it. But they decided that must be it, the stir ceased, and the Vice President said impassively, "The Senator from Utah."

"Mr. President," Walter Calloway said, and there was something in his voice that made the press gallery and many Senators lean forward quickly,

"I introduce a resolution for the censure of the junior Ssenator from Wyoming for the murder of my colleague, and I ask for its immediate consideration."

There was a gasp of surprise, followed by a stunned silence, and for just a moment it seemed the thing might be done before anybody could recover. The Vice President, in fact, got as far as, "Without objection, the resolution is——" before Powell Hanson and Arly Richardson were on their feet asking Senator Calloway to yield. The Senator from Utah hesitated for a second, then yielded to Powell; the junior Senator from North Dakota sighed as one recognizing the hopelessness of his task and then began to speak slowly, casting about for language sufficient to the event as the Senate and galleries exploded into a buzz of talk so loud he could hardly be heard.

"Well, Mr. President," he said, "reserving the right to object, there is one point I should like to get clarified at once. Is it actually the Senator's intention that this resolution should charge the junior Senator from Wyoming with the *murder* of his colleague? And if so, on what grounds does he base this fantastically serious charge?"

"Mr. President," Walter Calloway said, "I am afraid my paraphrase of the language of the resolution was more drastic than it should have been. I may have misspoken myself. Senators will undersstand that I am laboring under some emotional strain in this matter. Ssenators understand why. I ask permission for the clerk to read the resolution without my losing the floor."

"The Senator will send it to the desk and the clerk will read," the Vice President said. A pageboy darted up to Senator Calloway's desk, grabbed the resolution, and darted back. The clerk read:

"Whereas, the tragic death of the senior Senator from Utah, Mr. Anderson, was preceded by a vicious and unprincipled personal attack upon him by the junior Senator from Wyoming, Mr. Van Ackerman; and,

"Whereas, the junior Senator from Wyoming, Mr. Van Ackerman made diverse and sundry public threats against the senior Senator from Utah, Mr. Anderson, which apparently contributed directly to his death; and,

"Whereas, these threats and accusations were unbecoming the dignity of a United States Senator and the dignity of this Senate; now, therefore,

"Be it resolved, that the Senate deems the junior Senator from Wyoming, Mr. Van Ackerman, to be deserving of censure; and he is censured."

There was a flurry of noise from the press gallery as the first relay of wire-service reporters scrambled up the steps to file their opening bulletins, and a renewed buzz of talk from the floor. Powell Hanson waited until it died a little and then asked Walter Calloway to yield again.

"I wonder, Mr. President," he said, "if the Senator has any proof that the charges and allegations of the junior Senator from Wyoming in any way contributed to the—to the unfortunate tragedy of last night?"

"Well, Mr. President," Senator Calloway said sharply, "does the Ssenator from North Dakota require more proof than common sense and an intelligent appraisal of events would indicate?"

"In so grave a matter as this, Mr. President," Senator Hanson said quietly, "it would seem to me that perhaps we do. I do not say this in any derogation of the purposes of the Senator from Utah, which are clear enough and with which I agree, or of his personal grief, which is understandable and is shared by all of us. Nor do I say it in any spirit of endorsement of anything the junior Senator from Wyoming may have done, which I deplore as much as anyone. But I do think that in a matter as serious as this——"

"A United States Senator lies dead because of the actions of this worthless man," Walter Calloway said with a cold fury his colleagues had never seen before. "Does that strike the Senator from North Dakota as a serious matter?"

"Mr. President!" Arly Richardson said sharply. "Now, Mr. President; will the Senator yield? The Senator is violating the rules of this Senate when he refers to the junior Senator from Wyoming as 'this worthless man!'"

"I'm not violating the truth!" Walter Calloway exclaimed angrily, and from somewhere off on his left somebody said "Right!" in an approving voice that carried clearly to the galleries. Senator Richardson swung around.

"It is all very well for Senators to say 'Right!' when a Senator is attacked in violation of the rules of the Senate," he cried, "but there are decencies to be preserved here."

"Mr. President!" Orrin and Lafe Smith said together, and the press gallery leaned forward with a pleased, excited little wriggle. "Will the Senator yield?"

"I yield the floor, Mr. President," Walter Calloway said, and sat down white-faced and trembling. Lafe gestured to Orrin to go ahead. The Senator from Illinois waited until the chamber quieted again and then spoke in a driving, sarcastic tone.

"The Senator from Arkansas, Mr. President," he said, "is very touchy about the rules of the Senate. It is against the rules of the Senate to call a man worthless. It is against decency to tell the truth about him. Apparently it is consistent with the rules of the Senate to kill him, just so you do it politely. Very well, then—no, I shall not yield to the Senator from Arkansas until I have finished—on the theory he has just enunciated, does the Senator from Arkansas feel that the junior Senator from Wyoming did it politely? He heard his broadcast, I am sure; most of us heard it, or if we did not, we read it in the press. Was that a polite form of doing-to-death under the rules of the Senate, does the Senator think, or was it perhaps a little impolite? What is the Senator's opinion on that?"

"Now, Mr. President," Arly said angrily. "Now, Mr. President——"

"Just answer the question, Senator," Senator Knox said in an offhand manner, staring up without expression at the galleries. "The Senate is waiting."

"I will not answer that question, Mr. President, which the Senator knows is deliberately designed to force me into an unfair, ridiculous and cruel position before the Senate," Arly said sharply. "The Senator is attempting to twist this into something that——"

"Mr. President," Orrin said coldly, "can it be twisted into anything worse than it is?"

"By God, we *are* playing for blood," UPI whispered in some amazement. AP shrugged. "Orrin isn't about to give anybody time to think about anything but what a bastard Freddy is," he said. "That's the way he's going to carry this. Wait and see." Below the senior Senator from Illinois was neatly arranging some papers on his desk.

"Mr. President," Senator Richardson said, "the senior Senator from Illinois, with his usual debating skill and ruthless manner of proceeding, is attempting to force this through without giving the Senate time to consider either the merits of the resolution of censure or the degree of blame in this tragedy which may properly be placed upon the junior Senator from Wyoming. What does the Senate actually know about this, Mr. President? How decisive in bringing about the tragedy was the attack made upon the Senator from Utah by the Senator from Wyoming? What else lay behind it? What was actually involved here?"

"Now, Mr. President," Orrin said with a great show of patience and calm, for this was exactly what he had no intention of allowing the Senate to go into, "is the Senator from Arkansas, who is so meticulous about the rules of the Senate, purporting to conduct himself in accordance with those rules, or is he making a speech? Under the rules as I understand them, I have the floor and if the Senator wishes to speak he must do it in the form of a question to me, or be ruled out of order if I care to make a point of order against him. Am I correct in that understanding, Mr. President?"

"The Senator of course is correct," the Vice President said.

"Very well, Mr. President," Orrin said, "if the Senator has a question to ask me, why doesn't he do so?"

"All right," Arly said, suddenly getting angry, which proved to be his mistake. "I will ask the Senator what he wants me to do about this matter, since he is setting himself up, as usual, to be the fount of all wisdom for the Senate? Just what does he want me to do?"

"All I want you to do, Arly," Senator Knox said quietly, "is for once in your life to stop being a troublemaker and do what you know is right and what you intend to do anyway, without a lot of unnecessary fuss beforehand."

"Well," Senator Richardson said, and that was all he seemed able to say, so taken aback was he by this unexpectedly direct personal comment that produced a sudden titter from Senate and galleries despite the seriousness of the moment. "Well." And looking flushed and upset and for once out of words, he sat down abruptly.

Powell Hanson, however, was still on his feet, and almost as though they had planned it in advance the senior Senator from Illinois sat down and the junior Senator from Iowa stood up. "Second team," the Washington *Star* whispered to the Washington *Post*. "Fresh man from the same team, I'd say," the *Post* remarked. The Vice President again recognized the Senator from North Dakota.

"Mr. President," he said quietly, "it is not my purpose to delay the Senate, if it should be the Senate's desire to vote on this very serious resolution on such short notice and with so little discussion placed in the Record in support of it. But it does seem to me that we are about to do something—for I gather from the lack of support for a delay that we are about to do it—that is most unusual and extraordinary——"

"Mr. President," Lafe Smith said, "will the Senator yield?"

"If it is just to ask me if the tragedy which has occurred is not unusual and extraordinary, no, I will not," Senator Hanson said with some asperity. "We have had enough debating tricks of that nature this afternoon."

"I was about to ask, I will say to my courteous friend," Senator Smith said icily, "what he thinks might be achieved by delay? What can be gained by prolonged discussion? There was a vicious and unprincipled attack made, coupled with a threat to make disclosures"—and his voice suddenly became filled with a scornful disdain— "of some unknown nature, which would ruin a man's career; a death followed. Would the Senator from North Dakota have us believe that prolonged discussion could further clarify the glaring clarity of that sequence? Or is it his purpose, perhaps, that discussion should make it less clear?"

"I am not the one who has purposes here," Powell Hanson said gravely. "I think that is obvious to everyone. And if that fits the Senate's will, so be it. My only purpose is to have this done with at least a modicum of fairness to the Senator from Wyoming——"

"Now I *will* say," Senator Smith snapped, "how fair was he to the Senator from Utah? How fair was he to him?"

"Then at least the Senator from Wyoming should be here, Mr. President!" Powell Hanson said sharply. "We should give him that much, at least!"

"Where is he, Mr. President?" Lafe cried, his voice rising angrily. "Where is he, this brave man who is so cavalier about killing Senators? I don't see him, Mr. President! Nobody is keeping him away, Mr. President! Nothing but his own cowardice prevents him from facing us at this moment, Mr. President! Where is the little murderer?"

At this there was a sudden explosive release of breath through the chamber, a sudden excited buzz and stirring. The Vice President rapped vigorously for order.

"The Chair will say to the junior Senator from Iowa," he said firmly, "that he is now doing violence to the rules of the Senate indeed, and if he cannot proceed in order the Chair will entertain a motion that he be directed to take his seat."

"Very well, Mr. President," Lafe said more quietly. "Like some others I too am under some emotional strain today. I have lost a very dear friend and I—I am not too—calm about it, Mr. President. I apologize to the Chair and the Senate."

"How can they lose?" the Wall Street *Journal* asked the Denver *Post* in the gallery above. "You can't lick a dead man." "That's right," the Denver *Post* agreed. "Every time the other side speaks, they've got an opening."

As though he were only too aware of this, Senator Hanson spoke again doggedly.

"Mr. President, I deplore as much as anyone what has occurred," he said. "God knows I said so in my brief remarks a little while ago. I am not in any way condoning anything the junior Senator from Wyoming may have done. But I do think it is highly irregular procedure, one fraught with unwise precedents for the Senate, to use a solemn occasion such as this for the type of action that is contemplated here. It simply does not fit the time or the occasion, which is to pay tribute to a friend who is gone."

"Mr. President," Lafe said, "if the Senator will yield, what better time than now, while the Senate is vividly aware of the horror and vileness of this thing? And what better tribute can we pay, I ask the Senator and I ask the Senate, than to censure the man who more than any other was responsible for his death?"

"Every time," The Wall Street *Journal* murmured. "They can't lose."

"I still think——" Powell said wearily, but this time it was the Majority Leader who interrupted and the chamber quieted immediately.

"Mr. President," he said, "a parliamentary inquiry. Am I right in my belief that while it may have been customary in the past, at times, to refer resolutions of censure to a committee for hearings, that there is no requirement in the rules that we do so? And have there not been occasions of record on which such resolutions were taken up directly without hearings or delay?"

"The Senator is correct," Harley said.

"And am I not right," Senator Munson said, "in believing that this is a privileged resolution which need not be referred to committee?"

"The Majority Leader is correct," Harley said again. "It is true that a practice has grown up in the Senate of referring censure resolutions to committee, but it is also true that there is nothing binding the Senate to such a course. In this, as in most matters, the Senate can do anything it wants to do in any way it wants to do it." He paused and then went on in a thoughtful voice while they listened intently. "If the event warrants drastic and uncustomary action," he observed, "then there is nothing to prevent the Senate from taking it. The resolution is privileged."

"Even Harley's in on it!" the Philadelphia *Inquirer* blurted right out loud. There was a stir of amusement in the press gallery, but on the floor everybody looked dead serious.

"Then, Mr. President," Senator Hanson said, "if the distinguished Majority Leader will permit me, I should like to ask unanimous consent that the secretary of the Senate advise the junior Senator from Wyoming that this resolution is being considered and suggest to him that he might wish to be present in the Senate."

There was silence, and the Vice President took his time about his response.

"There is apparently no objection," he said finally, "and it is so ordered."

While the tension exploded and a babble of excited talk and comment filled the big brown room, the principal protagonists remained in their places, Orrin studying his papers thoughtfully, Powell leaning on his desk, Lafe exchanging some quick comment with Verne Cramer, the Majority Leader sitting back impassively, Senator Cooley looking straight ahead with a sleepy little smile on his face, his eyelids drooping. For ten minutes the Senate waited; then there was a sudden stir and excitement out in the hall, pageboys pulled open the doors quickly, Senator Van Ackerman entered. There was a burble of excitement, abruptly stilled.

"Mr. President!" Lafe Smith said, jumping up. "Do I have the floor?"

"No one else has it," the Vice President pointed out. "The Senator from Iowa has it."

"What does the Senator from Wyoming desire?" Lafe asked with a deadly courtesy. "Does he wish me to yield to him for anything? Does he have a statement to make before we vote? Is there anything he has to say which can explain his conduct? Can he give us any reasons why we should not censure him? I await the Senator's pleasure, Mr. President."

"To coin a phrase," Bell Syndicate whispered in the silence that followed while everyone looked at Senator Van Ackerman, "I'd say Fred's face was a study."

And so it was, and so, it appeared, it was going to remain, for after several moments in which he alternately paled and flushed, clenched his fists and unclenched them, looked about furiously and then looked about pleadingly, not seeming to know exactly what he wanted to do or even if he wanted to do anything, the junior Senator from Wyoming made his only contribution to the debate on the resolution.

"At least I will be here, I will say to the Senator from Iowa!" he shouted suddenly into the silent chamber. "At least I will be here!"

"All right," Lafe said indifferently, not even bothering to look at him, for it was all over and they all knew it, "be here. Mr. President, I ask for the Yeas and Nays."

"He's got 'em," AP said as more than forty hands went up.

"The Yeas and Nays are ordered, and the clerk will call the roll," Harley said, and the clerk did, slowly and portentously and rather like

God, as the Wall Street *Journal* murmured to the Denver *Post*. "The whole thing is rather like God," the Denver *Post* retorted. "It scares the hell out of me." "I hope it does the same," the *Journal* said cheerfully, "to Fred Van Ackerman."

And so it apparently did, for when the clerk reached his name he cleared his throat several times and then said in a low voice they could hardly hear, "I think—under the circumstances—I should vote 'Present.'" And did.

At the end of it, with ninety-four Senators having responded, the clerk ran through the roll of the absentees and then turned to the Chair to report the final tally. Into the profound silence that fell upon the chamber the Vice President spoke quietly to make official what they already knew.

"Ninety-three Senators having voted Yea and one Senator having voted 'Present,'" he said, "the resolution of censure against the junior Senator from Wyoming is agreed to."

In the wild flurry that followed Lafe Smith shouted for recognition again, and the Vice President, after hammering furiously for order and finally securing it, gave it to him.

"I just want to serve notice, Mr. President," he said, "that if the junior Senator from Wyoming ever again mentions the name of the late senior Senator from Utah, in this forum or any other, I shall introduce a resolution for his expulsion from the Senate. I think," he said dryly, "I may have the votes."

"Mr. President," Warren Strickland said, rising quickly at his desk across the aisle, "will the Senator yield?"

"Gladly," Lafe said.

"I just wish to say," the Minority Leader remarked softly, "that if the prohibition just uttered by the Senator from Iowa is ever violated, I shall do what I can, insofar as I am able, to assure him the united support of the Minority."

"And now, Mr. President," Senator Munson said quietly into the startled silence that followed, "if I may have the floor, I think I should like to make the remarks I mentioned earlier concerning the passing of our beloved colleague. If Senators wish to leave, they may do so," he said, knowing that not one would, "but since I also intend to discuss events leading up to his death and perhaps relate them to other matters pending before the Senate, I might suggest that they remain if they can. What I have to say may be of some interest to them."

"That's the understatement of the year," the *Times* murmured dryly above. "Somebody has to tie this can to Leffingwell's tail, and I guess Bob is going to do it."

Gravely and quietly, he did, while the Senate sat in intent silence to hear him. At first it seemed to them that this was to be basically just another eulogy; but as he proceeded, telling just enough of what he knew to bring the blame not only to Fred Van Ackerman but closer and closer to the nominee and finally to the President himself, some other purpose began to emerge. Before long the shrewder among them had begun to guess it—toward the back of the room Murfee Andrews of Kentucky took out a five-dollar bill, laid it on his desk, and said, "He will," to Alec Chabot of Louisiana, who took out another and laid it on his desk and said, "He won't," whereupon they shook hands with mock solemnity; and as he went on slowly and carefully to his conclusion, blending it all together with the skill of many years of speaking and many years of managing the minds of men, giving to it just the right mixture of sadness, regret, and righteous indignation, an extreme tension began to grip the Senate again. When he concluded, the press gallery burst into excited life as reporters swarmed to their typewriters to bat out the biggest sensation of a day of them, carrying to the country and the world the news that

MUNSON QUITS AS MAJORITY LEADER IN PROTEST AT ANDERSON DEATH
SAYS PRESIDENT 'HOUNDED' SENATOR FROM UTAH; DECLARES HANDS OFF ON LEFFINGWELL, REFUSES RE-ELECTION; RE-ELECTION SEEN CERTAIN

All in all, as everybody agreed later when there was time to stop and think, it was quite a day in the United States Senate.

There were three immediate results that made the Senator from Michigan feel much better and made him think that perhaps he was going to regain both his self-respect and his standing with his friends after all. The first was that Lafe went by his desk on his way out at adjournment and, without saying anything or looking at him, simply rested his hand, open palm down, firmly upon it for a moment as he passed; and the second was that Orrin overtook him in the hall and, without offering to stop, said shortly, "That's better!" as he swung on by.

The third consequence came as soon as he reached his office. "Mrs. Harrison is on the phone," Mary said. "She has been for ten minutes. She said she would wait until you came in."

"Darling," Dolly said without preliminaries, "I think that was just wonderful. I am so proud of you."

"Are you really?" he asked, and he must have sounded rather forlorn, for she seemed to be laughing and crying at the same time as she replied.

"Yes, you poor mixed-up ex-Majority Leader," she said. "I am. Damn it, darling," she added, "why don't you marry me?"

"Well," he said with a flash of returning humor, "why don't you ask me?"

"All right," she said. "I will. I am. I do."

"You don't have to make a Federal case out of it," he said with a chuckle. "I accept."

And so that, after so long a time, was that.

As for Fred Van Ackerman, he went down fighting, or what for him at that particular point in a suddenly eclipsed career passed for fighting. There was a hastily-called press conference, filled with peculiar incoherent, rambling statements, some vague references to the Senator from Utah which weren't explicit and which the press refused to take down, some bitter outcries against damned Knox and damned Smith, and finally a rather dazed prediction that the subcommittee would vote for Leffingwell and he would still win out. "Mark my words," he repeated automatically four or five times, "they'll confirm him. Mark my words."

But in this he proved at least partially mistaken, for at five-thirty in the afternoon it was announced that the subcommittee had met at the call of the acting chairman and voted three to one, Senator Richardson dissenting, to report the nomination to the full committee with an unfavorable recommendation. The subcommittee had the last word too, because when the press phoned Senator Van Ackerman's office to see if he had any further comment his administrative assistant said in a hostile voice that he had left for a month's vacation in Arizona.

"He won't be here to vote on the nomination, then?" the *Herald-Tribune* inquired politely.

"He won't be here," the administrative assistant said.

And that, after so long a time, was *that*. It would be a while yet before all the effects made themselves felt upon him, but for all practical purposes the junior Senator from Wyoming had had it.

4

Next morning, the senior Senator from Illinois noted cheerfully, the newspapers were giving him hell. The *Times* and the Washington *Post* in particular spoke with a combination of primness and severity concerning the events of Monday, and there was evident in their comments a growing alarm over the prospects of the man they favored as Secretary of State.

"This newspaper," the *Times* said, "deeply regrets the tragic event of Sunday night which removed from the American political scene one of its ablest and most promising young men. But we do not feel that this should be taken out of context and used as a club with which to beat down all support for Mr. Leffingwell and turn the battle over his nomination into a posthumous vindication of Senator Anderson. This is obviously what Senator Knox had in mind yesterday when he stage-managed the abrupt and extraordinary censure of Senator Van Ackerman, the sensational resignation of the Majority Leader (a little too much credit on that, Orrin thought), and the unfavorable vote of the Foreign Relations subcommittee.

"So far, the Senator from Illinois has succeeded brilliantly in what he has set out to do. We sincerely hope that today sanity will return to the Senate and that the full Foreign Relations Committee will remember that what is involved here is not a death, however tragic, but the future life of this great country and perhaps of the free world as well. Any other course, it seems to us, would be to make a mockery of the Upper House and its proper place in the American scheme of things."

The *Post* devoted to the subject an angry cartoon—which portrayed Orrin triumphant in a Senate chamber strewn with the bodies of the Senator from Wyoming, the Majority Leader, and the nominee, under the caption, "I Just Want People To Follow The Rules"—and a column and a half of editorial.

"It seems obvious," this concluded, "that Senator Knox is conducting a ghoulish and unprincipled campaign, using the corpse of his young friend as weapon, to turn the honest sadness all men feel at his death into an hysterical drive against Robert A. Leffingwell. Now that the Senator from Wyoming has been censured (No one, Orrin noted, paused to defend Fred) and the Majority Leader has resigned, few obstacles remain in the way of his success. It is our earnest hope that the Majority Leader will speedily reconsider his decision of yesterday, respond to the importunings of his many friends, and return to fight the good fight for Mr. Leffingwell. Only some such major event, it seems likely, can stem the tide now running against the nominee and deny the senior Senator from Illinois the grisly triumph he seeks."

Only a real alarm could prompt that kind of harshly personal attack, he knew; the *Post* must really feel that it was on the run. He only hoped it was right, though knowing the Senate he would not be prepared to rest easy until the final vote was held.

On the air much the same tune had been played; both the CBS and NBC news round-ups had contained strong intonations of disapproval and dismay concerning his activities. But his telegrams and mail, he saw with satisfaction as he went quickly through his office routine before leaving for the memorial service at the Cathedral, were beginning to turn decisively in his favor. By ten-thirty, when Lafe called to suggest they share a cab, he had received more than five hundred wires and almost one hundred special-delivery letters. Of these close to four hundred were approving; the remainder, with varying degrees of abuse and vituperation, were not. Lafe reported essentially the same. As his secretaries finished the count an ironic thought occurred to him and acting upon it at once, he put through a call to the director of the *Post*.

"Good morning, Ned," he said blandly. "I just wanted to call and thank you for all your many compliments to me this morning. I know they came from the heart, and I appreciate them."

"We didn't want you to feel neglected, Orrin," the director of the *Post* said cheerfully.

"I didn't feel that way at all," Senator Knox said with an equal cheerfulness. "By the way, I have a news item for you. Our mail up here is beginning to run about two to one in favor of what I'm doing and against Leffingwell."

"Oh?" the director of the *Post* said cautiously. "That's interesting if true."

"Yes, it is," Orrin agreed. "I thought inasmuch as you made a front-page story out of it last week when the State Department said its mail was running four to one for Leffingwell, maybe you'd want to publish another, now that it's running against him. Just as part of that fair, objective tradition of our great free press."

"We might," the director of the *Post* said slowly, "if that's general on the Hill."

"Would you really, Ned?" Senator Knox inquired. "Where would you put it, on page thirty-four?"

"I think we'd put it wherever we thought, in our best judgment, it ought to be," the director of the *Post* said coldly.

"I'm sure you would," Senator Knox said approvingly. "On page thirty-four. Well, you'd better check it, Ned. There might be a story in it. I'll see you at the Cathedral. I assume you'll be there. It would be fitting."

"I did what I could to prevent it," the director of the *Post* said angrily.

"I am aware you did," Orrin said in a friendly way. "And I imagine you'll be using that good deed to excuse a lot of things in the next few days, won't you?"

"This isn't winning you the friendship of the *Post*, you know," its director said. Senator Knox made an impatient sound.

"Do I give a damn?" he asked, "and does it matter? We decided that issue fifteen years ago. Anyway, he's licked and you know it. That's all that counts now."

"Thanks for calling, Orrin," the director of the *Post* said dryly. "I appreciate your advice about the news story."

"I thought·you might like to give it equal play with the one you ran last week," Orrin said. "Just for the hell of it."

"All I can say is," the director of the *Post* told him, "that our check had damned well better show what you say, because it's sure as hell going to be on page one."

"I'll take my chances," Orrin said. "See you in church."

And having accomplished one of his major objectives, for now he would receive a very self-consciously fair break in the news columns however bitterly he might be attacked on the editorial page, he went out to meet Lafe and go to the Cathedral.

On the way their conversation was desultory, mostly speculation about Moscow's sudden excited announcements that it would have "a statement of the greatest importance to humanity" sometime in the next forty-eight hours—"probably invented the Waring Blender," Lafe remarked, a rather puerile jest he was to recall shamefacedly later—and their talk did not touch upon what was uppermost in their minds, the sadness of the event in which they were about to participate. It was by just such deliberate concentration on other things that people got through such moments, and politicians, who must attend many farewells for many people, usually had the technique highly developed. At the Cathedral they found they didn't have to work at it, for the memorial service had been turned into a political battleground and there was quite diversion enough. He might have known, Orrin thought, for this was a contest between two men who did not intend to miss any tricks on either side. But it shocked Lafe, and he hoped it would shock a lot of others. So much the better for him, if that was the way his opponent wanted to play it.

"Well, by God," Lafe exclaimed in a disbelieving voice as they swung into the Cathedral yard past the long lines of parked cars and the little groups of black-clad men and women standing about talking soberly in the brilliant sunshine, "do you mean to tell me he's actually got the gall to come *here?*"

"Of course," Senator Knox said shortly as they paid the cabbie and got out. "What else did you expect him to do?"

"I didn't expect *this,*" Lafe said darkly.

Near the entrance several big black White House limousines were drawn up in impressive array and through the crowd the Secret Service men were already casually on guard. Standing together in a little group to one side of the door were the Assistant to the President, the Secretaries of State, Agriculture, Defense, Justice, and Labor, and some other White House staff people Orrin didn't know. Someone he couldn't quite see was in the center of the group, and when it parted a little and he caught a glimpse of him the Senator could hardly believe his luck.

"Leffingwell's here too," he said. "What a happy little party for us all."

"I think I'm going to vomit," Lafe said.

"It's all right," Orrin said. "It's all right. I never thought he'd make an error of judgment like this, but he has and it's all right."

And taking Lafe's arm firmly, he piloted him to another group near the other side of the door, the Vice President, Senator Cooley, Senator Danta, the ex-Majority Leader, the Speaker, and leaders of the House.

"Good morning," he said quietly. "I see we're to be honored with the presence."

"Both presences," the Vice President said. "How could they?"

"I'm glad they have," Senator Knox said savagely. "Nothing could be more fitting."

"They'll lose votes," Bob Munson said thoughtfully.

"Do you think I care?" Orrin asked shortly.

"Good Christ," Lafe said bitterly, "isn't anybody interested in just honoring Brig?"

"We are," Stanley Danta said quietly. And he repeated slowly, as if to himself. "*We* are."

"Bob," Orrin said, drawing him to one side, "when are we having the meeting?"

"What meeting?" Senator Munson asked.

"The meeting to re-elect you Majority Leader," Senator Knox said. Senator Munson smiled rather grimly.

"I haven't been accepting his phone calls," he said, "so he sent me this this morning."

URGE YOU WITH ALL MY HEART TO ACCEPT RE-ELECTION, the telegram said. CANNOT CONCEIVE OF THIS JOB WITHOUT YOUR STAUNCH AND LOYAL SUPPORT UP THERE. LEFFINGWELL DOESN'T MATTER ("Not much," Orrin interjected tartly), BUT OUR FRIENDSHIP DOES. SENATE WOULD NOT BE THE SAME WITHOUT YOU AT THE HELM. THEY NEED YOU, THE COUNTRY NEEDS YOU, AND I NEED YOU. PLEASE AGREE.

"Very touching," Orrin commented. "'Please,' too. That's unusual."

Bob Munson smiled again.

"Powell called me last night and told me he was after him yesterday morning to run against me," he said. "Of course that was before he knew I was going to resign, and maybe this is a more genuine expression of his feelings now. At least it hasn't been released to the press."

"It hasn't been released to the press, yet," Senator Knox said. "But it's the only thing he could do, isn't it? The Roosevelt-Barkley pattern is still the only one possible for a President, isn't it?"

"Under the circumstances," Senator Munson said.

"The meeting," Orrin reminded him.

"Why don't you set it up with Stanley?" Bob suggested. "He's acting Majority Leader now."

"All right," Orrin said, "we'll work it out. Not today, though," he added, thinking of the committee meeting at 2 P.M., his son's wedding at six here in this same great, gray, half-finished building dominating the Washington skyline. "Too much else on tap."

"Whatever you say," Bob Munson said.

There was a sound of sirens in the distance, a stirring among the many mourners standing about. With a dash and a flurry the final White House limousine drew up within its customary framework of motorcycle out-riders. The President, looking grim-faced and pale, got out and stood for a moment in the sunlight. Then he moved forward to his own people and together they started in, the crowd beginning to follow as the clock neared eleven. As he approached the door he recognized the congressional group and for a long second he and the senior Senator from Illinois looked one another straight in the eye. Orrin bowed without expression, he returned it gravely and went on in. It did not seem to them that he had seen any of the others, and it was quite possible that he had not.

And now, Orrin thought, bracing himself with a sudden intake of breath that hit his lungs like a knife, all I have to do is think about something else for forty-five minutes and maybe I can get through this without making a spectacle of myself. He found gratefully that this was not so difficult to do, for he made himself look forward with deliberate impatience to the committee meeting, and planning for it kept his mind pretty well occupied. As always when he had something in train he was eager to keep it moving and bring it to a conclusion as fast as possible. The Senate was going his way now and he didn't want to give it time to stop and catch its breath. He gradually became so intent upon his plans for keeping up the tempo that the service passed, mercifully, as in a dream.

"The Secretary of State," his administrative assistant said shortly after 1 P.M., and the Vice President said, "Hi, Howie," with a cordiality he did not altogether feel after the performance at the Cathedral. "How are we coming on those interviews with the Ambassadors?"

"That's what I'm calling about," Secretary Sheppard said. "I had hoped to be able to get a moment with you after the service, but it didn't work out."

"No, it didn't," Harley agreed. "We seemed to be in different camps, so to speak."

"Perhaps it was only seeming," Howie Sheppard said dryly. "He asked us to go with him, and there wasn't much we could do about it."

"I think it all made a very unfavorable impression on the Senate," the Vice President said. The Secretary of State sniffed.

"I expect so," he said. "Well, it was taken out of my hands long ago, so it's all quite academic as far as I'm concerned. I really couldn't care less."

"Does he seem discouraged?" Harley asked. Howie Sheppard made a sound of dry amusement.

"Does he ever?" he replied. "You know him. He may show the strain, and I thought he did, but he never admits it."

"He's a real fighter," the Vice President said. "Too bad he had to—— Well, it's too bad."

"Things work out for the country in odd ways," the Secretary of State observed. "Maybe it won't turn out to be too bad when it's all over. Let me ask you, is Orrin confident?"

"You know him, too," the Vice President said. "He fights just as hard. Only in his case I think he has more to base confidence on than the President has."

"I wonder what would have happened," the Secretary of State said thoughtfully, "if you and I had decided to go for him that night."

"He would have been President," Harley said. "It was in the cards that year. We couldn't lose."

"I know that," Howie Sheppard said. "I mean, I wonder what would really have happened. To the country. After he got there."

"It seems idle," the Vice President said. "He didn't."

"Do you ever wonder if we did the right thing?" the Secretary asked. There was a pause.

"I often wonder," Harley Hudson said. "How about you?"

"Yes," said Howie Sheppard. "I often wonder."

"Well," the Vice President said in a businesslike way, "about those Ambassadors, I've been thinking, Howie, that it might be better from my standpoint to see them together. I know it wouldn't from theirs, but there's safety in numbers and I'm not so sure I want to be involved in any confidential little tête-à-têtes with them individually."

"Why, Harley," the Secretary of State said dryly, "you sound just like a President."

"Maybe," the Vice President said with a matching dryness. "Maybe. In any event, I think I'd be willing to see them sometime Thursday afternoon. I'd rather not tomorrow, because I expect we'll be starting the session at ten to get started debating the nomination and I want to stick pretty close all day to see how it's going. I imagine we'll vote sometime Thursday night, so Thursday afternoon would be good. It would be too late to entertain any last-minute appeals that I exert my influence for Leffingwell. Not that I have any influence, of course."

"You're beginning to reach the point where you're just saying that," the Secretary of State observed shrewdly. "You don't really believe it any more. Anyway, they want to see you; that's indication enough. Incidentally Claude Maudulayne and Raoul Barre have asked for appointments too, so I'll just throw them all in together for you. How about three-thirty Thursday?"

"That will be fine," the Vice President said.

"Are you helping Orrin?" Howie asked bluntly. Harley paused.

"Are you?" he asked.

"Any way I can," Howie Sheppard replied.

"Maybe we did do the wrong thing that night," the Vice President remarked. The Secretary of State gave a dry little chuckle.

"I've thought so for quite some time," he said. "I'll tell the Ambassadors."

"In my office over by the chamber," Harley said. "You can come too, if you'd like."

"Gladly," Howie said. "It should be an interesting hour in which to visit the Senate. I'll see you then."

At the airport, he and Beth saw the Andersons off on their sad journey to Salt Lake City, where final rites would be held tomorrow. Mabel looked for a long moment at the gleaming white metropolis across the river before giving a little shudder and turning away to kiss them good-by. "I never want to see it again," she said. "Don't forget to visit us when you get to Utah." They promised they would, Brig's brother lifted a sad-eyed little girl into his arms and the three of them entered the plane which bore in its rear compartment the Senator's coffin. "I'm not sure I do either," Orrin said grimly as they got in the car.

But by the time Beth dropped him off at the Office Building his mood had changed. The committee would meet in half an hour and he felt ready for it. So much so, in fact, that his wife thought a cautionary note was in order. "Good luck," she said casually. "Don't do anything I wouldn't do." He gave her a quick kiss and a sudden grin. "How many years ago did I stop taking that advice?" he asked, and she chuckled. "Very well, my boy," she said, "but just don't mess it up. It's going your way, so keep it like that." "I'll try," he promised more seriously. "I really will try. I'll get home as soon as possible after the meeting breaks up." "Yes," she said. "We do have a son getting married tonight, after all." "I wish him luck," he said gravely, and tears came into her eyes. "Too much emotion, these days," she remarked. "I hope we can get away for a while after the nomination is settled. I need a vacation." "So do I," he said. "I'll try to get things squared away so we can. Maybe we can take a real trip to Europe this time." "Famous last words," she said with a smile as she started the car. "How many years ago did I first hear that?" "I'll *try*," he shouted as she drove off, but she only shook her head ironically and gave him a rueful wave.

The television cameras were in place, the bright lights were on, reporters milled about, and the usual tourists stood in little gaping groups as the members of Foreign Relations arrived for their final date with the matter of Robert A. Leffingwell. Except for the one absence caused by death, the press noted that the full committee was present this afternoon, brought to its full complement by Hal Fry and Clarence Wannamaker, who had passed up the UN session to be on hand. Despite the combined efforts of the news industry, there was a polite and consistent refusal to say anything of any moment for the busy pencils and the voracious cameras.

"How do you think the committee will vote, Mr. Chairman?" they asked Tom August, and the senior Senator from Minnesota said softly, "Oh, I wouldn't want to predict at this moment. I just wouldn't want to predict." "And you, Senator?" they said to Orrin Knox. "My job is to report to the full committee what the subcommittee did," he observed; "after that, we'll see." "And what's your guess, Senator?" they pressed Arly Richardson, who gave them a skeptical look. "I don't guess," he said, "particularly about this committee."

Altogether, they agreed as they settled back to wait outside the slatted door in the ornate old corridor, the pickings were rather sparse. Some had a hunch the committee would probably support the subcommittee by a small margin, but there were some who saw it otherwise and some who wouldn't guess. The only certainty was the significance of the occasion to the world at large, for at least a hundred reporters stood about, and everyone from Tass to the Bangor *Daily News* was on hand to speculate about what was going on around the green-baize table under the mammoth cut-glass chandelier, and to report it to the far reaches of the globe once it had been formally announced.

"The committee will be in order," Tom August said, and, "Mr. Chairman!" Senators Knox and Richardson said.

"If the committee will be patient," the chairman said gently, "I should like to ask if the committee wishes to make this a formal meeting with an official reporter present, or shall we discuss the matter informally?"

"Let's take our hair down," Verne Cramer said. "After all, we're among friends. Only half a dozen of us will tell the press what went on."

"That was my thought," Senator August said with a wistful regret. "I should like an informal discussion if we could all agree that it would be truly confidential, because it seems to me there are matters involved here that . . ."

"Mr. Chairman," Orrin said, "I move that we have a discussion off the record and formalize only the final vote and our recommendation."

"I second that, Mr. Chairman," Senator Richardson said. Tom August looked hesitantly about the table. Everyone nodded.

"Without objection, then," he said. "Orrin, did you care to say something further?"

"Not a great deal, Mr. Chairman," the Senator from Illinois said, making his characteristic gesture of straightening the papers before him as he began to speak, "because the events of the past two days speak for themselves. As the result of a deliberate decision on the part of the President of the United States, made as a part of his campaign to confirm this nominee, the senior Senator from Utah was driven to his death. Accessories before the fact were the junior Senator from Wyoming and the nominee himself. Proof of these facts is known to at least six members of this committee, who I think will vouch for them, without going into details, to the other members. Am I right in that, Mr. Chairman?"

Senator August looked uncomfortable.

"You state it rather harshly," he said, "but in essence I would say you are correct, yes."

"The proof of this is known to six members of this committee?" Senator Richardson asked. "What about the rest of us?"

"Well, Mr. Chairman," Orrin said tartly, "maybe I am a liar. Maybe you are. Maybe Bob and Stanley and Warren and Lafe are. Are we? Arly? You may think I am, but are the other five? How about it?"

"You don't have to fly off the handle," Arly Richardson said quietly. "You're riding high, after yesterday, and I'll grant you have a right to feel triumphant, but you don't have to overdo it. If you say it's so, we'll accept it. I wonder if the Senate will."

"I would hope the Senate would not be called upon to go into that phase of it at all," Senator Knox said. "I'm only mentioning it for our own background right here."

"Somebody may bring it up," Senator Richardson said.

"If you encourage it, yes," Orrin said shortly. "I have some hopes you'll be decent enough not to . . . In any event, that is what lies behind the tragedy. But there are other aspects of it, and these are more important, and I believe they should be placed in full detail before the Senate."

"And they are damaging to Leffingwell," Arly said dryly.

"They are damaging to Leffingwell," Orrin said crisply. "You will remember he denied the testimony of Herbert Gelman that they had been copartners in some sort of Communist cell in Chicago. According to Gelman there were two other members, one dead, the other a man known as James Morton. He denied knowing Morton, too. Last week the Assistant Secretary of Commerce for International Economic Affairs, now traveling at the specific direction of the President, after the President was advised of his true identity, called Seab Cooley and disclosed that he was James Morton, that there was such a cell, and that Bob Leffingwell was a member. Seab told him to call Brig, which he did, and it was because of this knowledge that Brig wanted to reopen the hearings and tried, without success, to get the President to withdraw the nomination. For that," he said bleakly, "he died."

"Why wasn't all this brought out in the subcommittee meeting?" Senator Richardson demanded. "It was all put on an emotional basis of Brig being hounded to death by the Administration because he got in the way and nobody said why he got in the way. I might have voted differently had I known all this. One reason I voted the way I did was because I thought you were just stampeding Johnny and Win."

"Thanks so much for that vote of confidence, old man," John DeWilton said sharply.

"Very touching tribute," John Winthrop agreed. Senator Richardson looked impatient.

"Well, damn it," he demanded, "did we have all the facts yesterday or did we not? Did you vote emotionally because you were upset about Brig or did you not?"

"Well," Senator DeWilton said angrily, "I am not about to account to you for my motives when I vote. I'm damned if I am."

"Whatever the reason," Senator Winthrop pointed out quietly, "it apparently was a sound decision, wasn't it?"

"I'm not so sure," Arly Richardson said.

"Not so sure?" Lafe Smith demanded. "What more do you need, for God's sake?"

"I need something to prove to me that because Bob Leffingwell did something stupid years ago he is unfit to be Secretary of State now," Arly said sharply. "That's what I need."

"I should think," Warren Strickland said quietly, "that lying like a trooper under oath ought to be some indication of that."

"Oh, hell," Senator Richardson said shortly. "Anybody will lie to protect himself."

"But the validity of the protection is what we are supposed to judge," the Minority Leader said reasonably. "Whether it was justifiable and forgivable or whether an honest avowal of his mistake would be more in keeping with the integrity we have a right to expect in the Secretary of State. It's not a minor office, you know."

"I am fully aware of its importance," Arly said. "More so than ever right now. Have you seen this?" And unfolding an early edition of the Washington *Star* that he had been holding carefully under his arm, he displayed its headlines to them:

ARE REDS ON MOON? MOSCOW HINTS IT
WORLD-SHAKING ANNOUNCEMENT
PLEDGED SOON

"I say we have delayed this thing long enough," he said soberly. "I don't know whether the bastards are ahead of us again or not, but I do know we need a strong Secretary of State to deal with them if they are." He turned suddenly on Hal Fry and Clarence Wannamaker, sitting quietly together at one end of the table. "How about you boys?" he demanded. "You're at the UN. Aren't we being hurt by this in the eyes of everybody all over the world?"

Hal Fry shrugged.

"If there's anything I'm tired of," he said calmly, "it's being told how something looks in the eyes of the rest of the world. Nothing we do ever looks good in the eyes of the rest of the world; if the Russians don't have the knife out for us, some one of our old pals like the British do. We can't win no matter what we do. My feeling is this is our problem and we shouldn't be stampeded in deciding it."

"Let's just do what we feel is right," Clarence Wannamaker remarked. "All the rag, tag, and bobtail in the world will come trailing along after us if we do that. Subconsciously that's what they want, for us to make up our own minds, no matter how hard they try to talk us out of it."

"Well, what about this?" Arly demanded, hitting the newspaper. Hal Fry nodded.

"That's the talk up there," he said.

"All right, then," Senator Richardson said. "I think we should forget this stupid youthful error——"

"He was thirty-four," Orrin said stubbornly.

"—and judge this man on his merits now, as the man we need in the crisis that faces us. Or may face us," he amended. "It doesn't yet . . . Doesn't anybody else think I have any point at all?"

"I do," George Hines said cheerfully. "I think you do, Arly boy."

"Thanks, George boy," Senator Richardson said dryly. "Does anybody else?"

"I think perhaps you do," Stanley Danta said slowly, and the Senator from Illinois gave him a sharp look. "I'm sorry, Orrin," he said quietly, "but I've been thinking it over and I'm not so sure you're right."

"Call off the wedding," Verne Cramer said brightly, but his seniors were not amused and his happy little chuckle trailed away into silence.

"How can you defend him?" Orrin asked passionately. "How can you possibly defend him?"

"I'm not trying to defend him," Senator Danta said. "I'm just trying to understand him and judge him objectively without letting it get all cluttered up with Brig's death."

"All cluttered up with Brig's death!" Senator Knox echoed bitterly. "Do you have any realization of what Brig's death means? There was a human life involved here, you know."

"That's completely unfair," Stanley Danta said quietly, "and you know it. I've been in your house for most of the past two days. I know what Brig's death means, I will thank you to recognize."

"I apologize," Senator Knox said more quietly. "I do apologize, Stanley, and you know I do. But I just don't see how you can take Leffingwell's side when——"

"I'm not taking his side, exactly," the Senator from Connecticut said. "It's more objective than that. At least, I hope it is."

"Well, I'm not sorry I voted the way I did," John DeWilton said abruptly, "and I'm prepared to vote that way again today. And the sooner the better."

"How about you, Bob?" Senator Richardson asked, and the ex-Majority Leader looked at him thoughtfully.

"I told the President I would vote for him," he said, "and so I will. That's all I care to say about it. I don't quite understand your excessive loyalty all of a sudden, though."

"Something of the same," Arly Richardson said. "I told Leffingwell I'd vote for him if the record didn't disclose anything damaging. It doesn't, so I'm sticking by my promise."

"Who gives a damn what the record discloses?" Orrin Knox demanded angrily. "I'm telling you what the truth of the matter is, and that's what's going to be put before the Senate."

"Then it seems to me," Senator Richardson said indifferently, "that if part of the truth is going to be put on public display, it should all be put on public display. That would only be fair."

"If you're indecent enough to kick a corpse," Senator Knox shot back furiously, "go ahead and be damned to you."

Arly Richardson flushed and half started from his chair. The Senator from Michigan spoke in a tone that took no back talk.

"Now, Mr. Chairman," he said, "I want Senators to sit down and keep their tempers and act like gentlemen and Senators of the United States. We've had enough of this childish bickering. God damn it, I want it to stop. I ask you to impose order on the committee, Mr. Chairman."

"The Majority Leader is entirely right," Tom August said with an indignant show of firmness. "We will proceed in order here or I shall call in the official reporter and we'll go back on the record. Does anyone else wish to express an opinion before we vote?"

"I don't want to express an opinion," John Winthrop said quietly, "but I want to get a guarantee from Arly that he isn't going to make a spectacle of himself and of the Senate by bringing to the floor matters that could only add to a burden of tragedy that God knows is heavy enough for all of us."

Senator Richardson made an impatient movement.

"Oh," he said, "I probably won't. I probably won't. But I get so damned sick and fed up with his domineering ways"—and he gestured angrily at Orrin—"that I just thought I'd make him stop and think for once in his life."

"That strikes me as no basis at all for what you've done," Senator Winthrop said politely, "but of course you know what satisfies your own feelings better than we do."

"I want to serve notice right now," Senator DeWilton said firmly, "that if no one else brings up James Morton on the floor, I will, because I agree with Orrin that this has a direct and fundamental bearing on the character of the man we are asked to entrust with our foreign policy. How about that, Arly?" And he looked belligerently at the Senator from Arkansas, who again gave an impatient nod.

"All right," he said. "All right. Of course it has a bearing, though I don't think, myself, that it's as vital as you make out. Of course we'll debate it."

"And without mentioning Brig," Ed Parrish of Nevada offered suddenly out of the brown study he had appeared to be in all afternoon.

"Probably without mentioning Brig," Senator Richardson said.

"Is that the best you can do, 'probably?'" Senator Parrish inquired. Arly shrugged.

"That's the best," he said.

"I think perhaps we had better vote," Senator August suggested, "if we are ready."

"Mr. Chairman," Orrin said quickly, "I move that the committee send the nomination of Robert A. Leffingwell to the Senate with an unfavorable recommendation."

Lafe Smith, who had been quietly studying his colleagues' faces and putting together scraps of previous conversation with each of them, spoke up hastily.

"Wait a minute, Mr. Chairman," he said. "Wouldn't it be better for someone who favors the nominee to make a positive motion that we do recommend him, and then we can vote it up or down?"

"Why?" Orrin asked. "Isn't my motion clear enough?"

"It is perfectly clear," Lafe said, carefully avoiding Bob Munson's eye, though he knew from a sudden little motion that Bob understood exactly what he was driving at. "It just seems a more orderly way to do it, that's all," he added lamely.

"Of course it is, Mr. Chairman," Senator Munson said firmly. "Arly, why don't you put the motion?"

"I wouldn't want to pre-empt Orrin's right," Senator Richardson said
blandly, and it was obvious he got it too.

"I'm sure Orrin wouldn't mind," Lafe said rather nervously, and Senator
Knox suddenly smiled.

"Are you absolutely certain?" he asked. "Very well, I withdraw it. Go
ahead, Arly."

"O.K.," Senator Richardson said indifferently. "I move that the Foreign
Relations Committee report the nomination of Robert A. Leffingwell to
the Senate with a recommendation that it do pass."

"I'll call the official reporter," Tom August said, "and we'll poll the
committee."

Ten minutes later as they began to come out into the corridor, the press
and television reporters swarmed around them asking eager questions
which were shunted aside with amiable wisecracks and the assurance that
the chairman would fill them in. George Hines and Ed Parrish, walking
out arm in arm, intrigued them considerably because George just grinned
and said, "Oh, boy, oh, boy," and Ed smiled a little and commented,
"You'll be surprised."

And this, they were frank to confess to one another, they were, for they
had not expected the result to be quite what it was or to come in quite
the way it did when Tom August, flanked by Arly and Orrin, took his
place before the waiting circle of cameras and reporters.

"The Foreign Relations Committee," he said, looking pale and in a
voice that trembled—"But, then," the Philadelphia *Inquirer* reminded the
Los Angeles *Times*, "he always looks pale and his voice always trembles"—
"having had before it the question of the nomination of Robert A. Leffingwell to be Secretary of State, and whether to recommend to the Senate
that it be confirmed or to recommend that it not be confirmed"—"For
Christ's sake," AP whispered savagely, "get on with it!"—"has voted
seven to seven on a motion by Senator Richardson to report the nomination
favorably to the Senate. Under the rules of the Senate a motion receiving
a tie vote fails of passage, and accordingly the nomination will be reported
to the Senate unfavorably."

"You will note, however," Senator Richardson said quickly, "that the
failure of my motion was only on the basis of parliamentary custom. A
majority of the committee did not vote against the nominee."

"Or for him, either," Senator Knox remarked.

"Can you tell us how the committee members did vote, Mr. Chairman?"
someone asked. Tom August hesitated, looked at his two colleagues, who
nodded, and made up his mind.

"It isn't the usual practice," he said gently, "but in view of the great
interest in the nomination, perhaps I can tell you. Voting for Senator
Richardson's motion, to report favorably, were its author, Senator Munson,
Senator Danta, Senator Cramer, Senator Parrish, Senator Hines, and the
chairman. Voting against the resolution, in other words to disapprove,

were Senator Knox, Senator Smith, Senator Fry, Senator Strickland, Senator Winthrop, Senator DeWilton, and Senator Wannamaker."

"Any predictions on what the Senate will do?" the Detroit *News* asked Arly and Orrin, and they looked at one another and smiled grimly.

"After you," Arly said.

"The nomination will be defeated," Orrin said flatly.

"And you, Senator Richardson?"

"If it is," Arly said, "it will be by a narrow margin."

"But you won't say positively that it won't be?" the press pinned him down quickly. The Senator from Arkansas looked unamused.

"No," he agreed. "I won't say positively."

5

"Well," his son said, looking up with a grin from his struggles with a dress shirt, "I didn't know whether you'd be able to stop being a world statesman long enough to come to my wedding or not. How did the committee meeting go?"

"So-so," Orrin said. Hal paused a second and looked at him closely.

"Did you get licked?" he asked. His father smiled.

"Not exactly," he said. "It was a seven-to-seven tie vote on Arly's motion for a favorable recommendation, so the motion lost, and the recommendation will be unfavorable. But it's only a parliamentary device, as Arly pointed out. The significant thing is that I couldn't muster a majority against him. And I almost ruined it by trying to make my own motion for an unfavorable recommendation, which would have had just the opposite result."

"What stopped you?" Hal asked with a smile. "I didn't know anything could."

"Well, yes," Senator Knox said with an answering smile. "I'm not as bullheaded as all that. Lafe stopped me. He apparently checked the committee a little closer than I did and knew what might happen."

"I like Lafe," Hal said. "He chases around too much, but his heart's in the right place."

"He's going to stop chasing," the Senator said, and his son gave him a look of surprised interest.

"Don't tell me he's going to get married too?" he said in some disbelief.

"So he tells me."

"Well, well," Hal said. "All of us old rakes are retiring from the competition. But I guess it's time to leave the field to younger and fresher men. God *damn* it," he said suddenly. "Will you fix this stud for me?"

"Gladly," Orrin said. "Where's your mother? I was sure she'd be here, hovering around."

"She's at the Cathedral checking on things," Hal said. "She kissed me, and started to cry, and ran." He smiled. "I like the old girl," he said.

"So do I," Orrin said. "I only hope you're as lucky as I am."

"Oh, I think so," Hal said with a new note in his voice suddenly. "Yes, I think so."

"I think so, too," his father said. "She's a wonderful girl."

"She is that," his son agreed softly. A little twinkle came into his eyes. "Isn't there anything you want to tell me?" he asked.

The Senator from Illinois tried to look surprised, and that failed, and tried to look dignified, and that failed. He wound up laughing rather self-consciously.

"I do believe you're blushing," Hal said.

"I'm not blushing," Orrin said flatly. "I was just wondering what a man of my generation could possibly have to tell one of yours that you don't know already, and that a long, long time ago."

"I remember you tried to tell me once," his son remarked, with the same little twinkle.

"Well, did you understand it?" the Senator asked.

"I understood it," Hal said, "but it hardly seemed logical." He grinned. "Doesn't yet, as far as that goes, only now it doesn't matter whether it's logical or not. That's the least of the things that matter."

"I thought it was a clear and objective discussion," Orrin observed. "Factual, straightforward, and to the point."

"It was," Hal agreed. "It certainly was. It was a good basic presentation. I felt I was well-launched."

"When did you get your pilot's license?" his father asked dryly, and was pleased to see that it was his son who was blushing.

"That's all right," Hal said. "That's all right, now. What time is it?"

"It's five thirty-one," his father said.

"How do I look?" Hal asked, and for a moment the Senator couldn't see him at all, except he knew that somewhere through the haze there was a little boy and a tall young man, both of whom apparently belonged to him, fantastic though it suddenly seemed.

"You look wonderful," he said, not too steadily, and then his eye lighted on something that brought the world back to perspective. "Except that you're wearing your bedroom slippers."

"Well, by God, so I am," Hal said, and suddenly he started laughing in a way that was tense but happy.

"Nobody can say I'm nervous!" he exclaimed. "Ohhhhhh, no!"

I've done the best I could, Stanley Danta said in the private conversation he often carried on, and I've tried to do all the things I think you would have done if you hadn't—if you had been here. I doubt if I've done everything, because I never did think of everything, and without you to remind me I've probably forgotten some things; but on balance

I am well pleased and I think you would be too. She's a nice girl and she's marrying a nice boy and they're getting a good start in life, and that's about all one can hope, or guarantee, for anybody. I don't think she'll let him down or let us down. So having managed that, I guess it's time for us to wish them well and retire gracefully from the premises, isn't it? I just wish you could be here to see her . . . I just wish you could be here.

It would be thirteen years in November since she had been, and never a day had passed without that same futile wish, which the passage of time, though easing its pain, could not erase from his heart or mind or being.

"How are you coming?" his daughter called from her room, and he realized with a start that the hour was moving on and he had consumed precious minutes daydreaming. He tied his tie hastily and gave himself a critical look in the mirror.

"Fine, thank you," he called back. "How about you?"

"There will be some tucking and tugging and buttoning and zippering for you to do here in a minute," she said, "but I'm making progress. In a way—it sounds awful, but you know how I mean it—I'm kind of glad things worked out so the wedding would be small and quiet and I could be here with you alone these last few minutes without a lot of fussy females running around the place."

"I'm flattered," he said.

"Well, after all," she said, "you're the only daddy I ever expect to have, you know. Do you want to come in now?"

"You look beautiful," he said gravely, and so she did, young and earnest and flushed with excitement. "What do I tuck and tug and button and zipper?"

"Look back there," she said, pointing over her shoulder. "There are various infernal devices you'll see that I can't reach very well."

"Yes," he said. "I think—that—ought—to do it. Jump up and down and run around the room ten times and we'll see if anything falls off."

She kissed him suddenly.

"I'm going to miss you," she said.

"And I you," he said quietly, and for the first time they both realized just how alone he was going to be from now on.

"No, you aren't," she said fiercely. "We'll be here for a while, and while we are you're going to be in and out all the time . . . As a matter of fact," she added firmly, "what you ought to do is get married again."

"Do you really think so?" he asked in some surprise, for this was a topic they had never discussed. She had been nine when her mother died, and that made the memory strong enough to inhibit other talk; even if the possibility had arisen, which it had not.

"Uncle Bob's going to marry Dolly," she said, "and you ought to make it a double ceremony."

"Well," he said reasonably, "I can't just go out on Connecticut Avenue and say, 'Hey, marry me,' to the first woman I see."

"You *could*," she said with a smile. "You know perfectly well you *could*. But anyway, you ought to give it some thought."

"You think I never have," he remarked with a touch of irony, and she smiled again.

"I know," she said. "But you just haven't found anyone to match Mother."

"That's the exact truth," he said quietly. She kissed him again.

"O.K.," she said, "forget I ever suggested Connecticut Avenue. Anyway, Illinois is only minutes away, and we'll expect you every weekend. I hope to provide you with several extra inducements before long, too, Gramps."

"Oh, you do?" he said with a chuckle, and she blushed.

"I'm determined upon it," she said.

"I'll bet Hal is, too," he observed, and she blushed again.

"I understand he has some interest," she said.

"I expect he wants to go back to Illinois," he said, "and follow his father into politics, doesn't he?"

"Yes," she said, "he does. And I guess I want him to, when all is said and done."

"It's a rough life."

"But capable of honor," she said.

"Yes," he repeated softly, "capable of honor." And seeing her there, so bright and young and sure, he was moved to ask what struck him later as probably the bravest question he had ever asked anybody.

"What do you think of me?" he said. "Really."

"I think you're a wonderful father and an excellent Senator," she answered promptly. Then her eyes narrowed in the thoughtful manner of her mother.

"I think," she said slowly—and he could see she really was thinking, because her face got the concentrated, dead-earnest look he could remember through all the years from long ago when she was a little girl, "I think you're a good servant."

"Then I've succeeded," he said.

"Yes, you have. And now, Senator," she said lightly, "before you get too misty-eyed to be able to see to do it, you can help me on with my veil and we'll go. My groom awaits."

"He's a lucky man," said Senator Danta.

"It's mutual," his daughter said.

An honest mind, a candid intelligence, a loyal spirit, and an understanding heart. Yes, he said, you would like our daughter.

And there the years went, Beth thought, hurry, hurry, hurry, and away with you. Where did they go, and what had you accomplished when they were over? Well for one thing, she brought herself up tartly, you had accomplished this good-looking young male up there at the altar, and that was quite enough to have accomplished. And more than that, you had also helped in a very major way to accomplish this vigorous public servant beside you, and that wasn't such a small achievement either. And you had also, not to be too modest about it, accomplished your own place in the world as distinct and recognized, almost, as his, and that was a fair triumph too. So why should you do something as stock and standard and un-imaginative as cry at a wedding? It hardly made sense in the face of so many accomplishments, except that the sense of loss and the sense of gain got so muddled up and confused at a wedding that tears seemed to be the only possible comment to make upon them. Lose a son and gain a daughter, people always said; but they said "lose" first. Everybody lost somebody at a wedding, even up there at the altar where they were losing the boy and girl they were yesterday.

And the gain? Well, if you were lucky, enough to balance; and she honestly felt, even allowing for a mother's prejudice, that the balance was sufficient here. She was well satisfied with her son, and she knew—she hoped—that Crystal would be too. Marrying a Knox had its difficult mo-ments, but it also had great triumphs, and she suspected that Stanley Danta's daughter possessed the character to survive the difficulties and aid in the triumphs. The last thing Elizabeth Henry had thought to do on that long-ago day in college was assist in the establishment of a politi-cal dynasty, yet it appeared that might be what she had done. The pattern seemed to be repeating. Thinking of what it had meant for them, with all its excitements and satisfactions, its hits and near misses in a tale that was not yet done, she wished them well with all her heart. To seek, to strive, to serve—above all, to serve; tend to the serving, and the seeking and the striving took care of themselves. Whether their son knew this or would have to learn it like his father, she did not know; whether his father had learned it entirely even now, she was not sure. Anyway, Hal was no longer her problem; Crystal, daughter of a Senator, daughter-in-law of another, wife someday, no doubt, of still another, would have to worry about that from now on. Her own problem was the same as always: here it sat beside her, blowing its nose, sentimental as ever underneath the prickly exterior the world knew. She began to chuckle, a muted sound that no one heard but transmitted by contact through her arm to his. He turned toward her with a startled expression and then winked gravely before beginning to smile. Something suddenly seemed awfully funny to her, but it was unlikely that she would have been able to say exactly what if anyone had asked. It was something, she thought, that her daughter-in-law would understand someday; not yet, probably, but some-day.

"I think," he said in the motel, "that was the nicest wedding I ever expect to be in."

"I liked it," she said, unpacking busily and bustling about.

"Why is it," he asked suddenly, "that a bedside radio always sounds so furtive and sexy?"

She laughed.

"Because that's often just what it is, I suppose," she said, hanging up dresses, smoothing out blouses, whisking shoes swiftly out of sight.

"Speaking of sexy," he said, and she laughed again, inspecting drawers, checking linen, looking for dust.

"Were we?" she said.

"Well, in a manner of speaking, yes," he said. "Why don't you stop being so industrious and come over here?"

"Do you think I should?" she asked.

"You've no idea how I'm counting on it," he said.

"Well," she said, pausing abruptly. "Well—O.K."

"I should hope, well, O.K.," he said a few minutes later. "How are you, Mrs. Knox?"

"I'm very fine, thank you, Mr. Knox," she said. "You know," she added a moment later against his ear, "I'm glad we were old-fashioned and waited."

But on that Mr. Knox had no comment, because by then Mr. Knox was beyond conversation.

6

"Orrin," the senior Senator from Michigan said next morning, "this is Bob. I just got a phone call I thought you might be interested in."

The senior Senator from Illinois laughed shortly.

"I don't think I could ever guess who it was from," he said. "Anyway, I didn't know you two were going steady again already. You haven't even been re-elected."

"He seems to assume I will be," Bob Munson said. "And—he asked me to talk to you. And—old loyalties are hard to shake, in spite of everything. And—and. So I'm passing it along. He wants you to come down and see him."

"One more traveler into that distant bourne from which some travelers do not return," Senator Knox said.

"Oh, don't be too bitter," Bob said. "He's really very upset too, I think."

"Well, I don't know," Orrin said. "I just don't know. I can't see what earthly good it would do, in the first place, and it would only be unpleasant for both of us, in the second. We haven't had a real talk for five or six years."

"Maybe that's been the trouble," Senator Munson said. "You've held each other at arm's length too long."

"I doubt if it would have made any difference," Orrin said. "Did you get your complimentary copy of Leffingwell's book this morning?"

"Personally autographed," Bob Munson said.

"Mine, too," Senator Knox said. *"Do We Really Want Peace? A Program for America,* by Robert A. Leffingwell. To my friend and fellow patriot, Senator Knox, in admiration and respect. Rather modest, I thought."

"I notice the papers treated it as a news story rather than a book," Senator Munson said.

"That was the only way to get it out front," Senator Knox said. "I see in the *Post* he's going to be down at Brentano's this noon for an autographing party. Well," he said grimly, "let him have his little hour. It'll be something to remember during those long winter nights at the ODM."

"About the White House," Bob said. "What shall I tell him?"

"You let me think about it a little bit," Orrin said. "The first item of business this morning is to get you re-elected."

"That shouldn't be too difficult, he said immodestly," Senator Munson observed.

"Well," Senator Knox said, "I just hope it isn't going to mean that everything will be just as it was. I've seen one Majority Leader throw away his advantage by crawling back to be patted on the head and called nice puppy, and I hope you learned something from that."

"I did," Bob Munson said. "I made one promise I can't abandon, but aside from that I don't think you'll be too disappointed by what I have to say."

"Good," Orrin said. "If I were you, I think I'd——"

"Just relax," Senator Munson said. "I said you wouldn't be disappointed."

And when the members of the Majority met an hour later after running the usual gauntlet of reporters and cameramen, the Senator from Illinois had to admit that he wasn't disappointed. By prearrangement with Stanley, he was recognized to make the motion that the Majority Leader be re-elected unanimously, it was seconded by Arly and Powell Hanson, and there was a burst of applause and cheering, duly noted by the newsmen hovering outside the closed door. The wire services promptly filed a new lead: "Senator Robert D. Munson of Michigan was re-elected Majority Leader of the Senate by acclamation today. The decision climaxed a dramatic battle with the White House which——"

Inside the room, however, once the enthusiasm had died away, it was not as a battler that the Majority Leader resumed his duties. Instead he spoke gravely and without animus as they listened intently.

"I want you to know," he said, "that it is with a profound humility and gratitude that I accept your decision that I again be Majority Leader. There is no need to go again into the considerations which prompted me to resign. Suffice it to say that your reaffirmation of loyalty and support heartens me more than I can say, and it will be a constant source of strength to me as we go forward together in these difficult times which confront our beloved country.

"We will begin final debate today, in about half an hour's time, on one of the most controversial and disruptive matters to come before the Senate in many years. It has been for all of us a matter of soul-searching and, I am quite sure, prayer. It is not an easy thing to vote against a Cabinet appointment; it is no easier to support it when it involves a man whose ability to arouse impassioned loyalties is as great as his ability to encourage implacable enmities.

"You will want to know," he said, and they became if possible more attentive, for this was exactly what they did want to know, "where I stand." He paused reflectively and there was absolute silence in the room. "Let me state it for you very simply.

"I have given my word to the President of the United States that I will vote for his nominee for Secretary of State.

"I will keep my word."

There was a little release of pent-up breath and for a brief second the senior Senator from Illinois felt the stirrings of an impatient dismay. But the Majority Leader sought his eye as he resumed, and he knew then that it would be all right.

"You will want to know," he went on," "where I think others should stand.

"In determining that, the fact of my resignation and subsequent re-election to the office of Majority Leader will have to be taken into account. I do not know how others regard it," he said quietly, "but for me these two events are not a continuum. They bridge a definite break in my approach, both to my office and to the matter in hand."

He paused and there was a murmur of approval.

"In the past, perhaps, as is often the case when the Congress and the Presidency are controlled by the same party, I have spoken too much for the White House—to you. From now on," he said firmly, "I shall speak for you—to the White House."

There was a hearty and renewed burst of applause that puzzled the reporters outside. "Must be a hell of a speech," AP said. "Yes," the *Times* agreed. "Do you suppose he's scuttling Leffingwell?"

"On that principle," said the Majority Leader, who was doing exactly that, "I do not consider that pledges and promises made to me prior to my resignation are valid or binding, except insofar as individual Senators may wish them to be, now that I have been re-elected."

Again there was applause, led by Sam Eastwood and some others who had been wondering how they could vote as they now wanted to vote without antagonizing Bob too much.

"As of Monday morning," Senator Munson went on, revealing a figure he had disclosed to no one heretofore, "I had received assurances, on this side of the aisle and on the other, of a total of sixty-eight votes to confirm the nominee. A number of these Senators in the past forty-eight hours have signified to me their desire that they be released from this obligation.

"I herewith release them all, and I shall so advise the Minority Leader with the suggestion that he transmit the information at once to the interested members of his party."

More applause, led this time by Senator Knox and Senator Smith, both of whom looked triumphant. Senator Richardson looked disgruntled but finally shrugged and joined in, there being little else he could do under the circumstances.

"As far as I am concerned," the Majority Leader concluded, "I am out of it. I shall vote for Bob Leffingwell, because I promised I would. I release from their promise all those who promised me the same. I shall neither assist, nor will I attempt to hinder, the efforts of those who favor, and those who oppose, the nominee. For once in my life in this old place," he said with a chuckle, "I'm going to be a spectator and enjoy the show. Have fun!

"This conference is now concluded."

It took approximately fifteen minutes for the inside story of the meeting to get out, and about fifteen minutes after that for it to get all over town. After that it took about five minutes for an urgent call to be placed to the senior Senator from Illinois. A familiar voice spoke without any pretext of small talk or any attempt to conceal its deep concern.

"Orrin," it said, "I want you to come down and see me."

"Why?" Senator Knox asked bluntly.

"I want to make clear the importance of this nomination," the President said.

"It seems to me you have already made it amply clear," the Senator said. "In a number of unfortunate ways," he added coldly.

"It is imperative for the country that I see you," the President said. There was a pause.

"All right," Senator Knox said finally. "I don't see what good it will do, but all right."

"We won't set a definite time, because I know you're busy," the President said. "But come down as soon as convenient and I'll drop every thing else when you get here."

"It will probably be early afternoon sometime," Senator Knox said.

"That will be fine," the President said. "Better come in the East Gate, so the press won't see you."

"Yes," the Senator said.

"Thank you, Orrin," the President said. "I appreciate it."

"Do you?" Senator Knox asked dryly.

"Yes, I do," the President said, ignoring his tone.

"All right. I'll see you later."

And thus the turning points of one's life arrived, at least for him, as directly and simply as that, met head on and without equivocation. He supposed there would be some sort of bribe offered—what could there be, he wondered sardonically, Illinois had all the dams and military installations she could possibly use—and there would be tart words and he would turn it down and that would be that. Or would it? In spite of his initial impulse to be completely skeptical, he could not help but be intrigued by this direct appeal. Maybe his opponent had one more rabbit left in the hat; he had pulled out some surprising ones, over the years. Well, it would do him no good this time. They had passed the point of accommodation long ago, and it would do him no good.

There followed an intensive two hours of activity as he went to lunch, went to the floor and helped to launch the debate on Robert A. Leffingwell. No sooner had he put down the phone than it began ringing again; when an interval came a few minutes later he picked up his briefcase and fled; otherwise he would have been trapped at his desk for hours. In that time, however, he had picked up votes from seven of Bob's defectors, including Lacey Pollard of Texas, who was no mean addition, and Lloyd B. Cavanaugh of Rhode Island, who with his air of dignified melancholy and rigid personal integrity was a good prestige factor to have on your side. In addition Carroll Allen of South Dakota; Powell Hanson's blandly insipid colleague, Charley McKee of North Dakota; the two North Carolinians, Rhett Jackson, and Douglas Brady Bliss; and stodgy George Carroll Townsend of Maryland—"He may be stupid," Blair Sykes of Texas put it succinctly once, "but at least he's honest, and that's saying something, in Maryland politics"—pledged their support.

In the hall on his way to the Capitol he ran into Roy Mulholland of Michigan, and the Majority Leader's colleague said without preliminaries, "Count me in, Orrin. Let me know what I can do," which he appreciated. He also took occasion to stop by the office of his own colleague, Nelson Lloyd, a quiet little auto dealer who had been appointed Senator from Illinois to fill out an unexpired term. Nelson went around in perpetual awe of the Senate and the vigorous senior Senator who so monumentally overshadowed him. "I assume you're with me," Senator Knox said, and it was virtually an order. "Oh, yes, Orrin," Senator Lloyd said fervently, "I'm with you."

On the subway car going over, he rode with George Keating of Nebraska, already in his customary midmorning state of well-oiled exuberance; Grady T. Lincoln of Massachusetts, enacting his customary Cautious Yankee, ay-yah, ay-yah, ay-yah; the two New Yorkers, Taylor Ryan and Irving Steinman, and Luis Valdez of New Mexico. Of these only Irv Steinman refused to join in the growing chorus of adherence; and even he, Orrin thought, showed some signs of weakening in their brief private chat on the way to the elevator. "I hope this isn't your final position," the senior Senator from Illinois had said, and the senior Senator from New

York had given him a characteristic bland, noncommittal, it's-your-move-Mister glance. "A lot can happen by tomorrow night," he said; "we'll see how it shapes up by then." "By then, Irv," Senator Knox said quickly, "I don't think one vote more or less will matter one little damn to me." "Said with characteristic modesty," Senator Steinman said with a laugh, clapping him on the back. "In the State of New York, however, it may matter to me. That is what I shall have to determine in my own mind."

For the most part, however, he found as he came on the floor and joined in the routine of listening to Carney's prayer—which backslid a little into a renewed type of arch admonition to the Senate, he just couldn't seem to resist the importance of the occasion—it all appeared to be quite simple. As the morning hour dragged on and various Senators put editorials, clippings, and contributions from constituents into the Record—"Oh, help dear America in her hour of need/We are blessed with our great Senator Hugh B. Root indeed," began one characteristic entry from New Mexico, modestly offered by the Senator of the same name—there was a steady procession of Senators to his desk. He was the logical man to fall heir to the Majority Leader's abandoned pledges, and by 1 P.M. when the routine business was at last concluded he could count a solid total of forty-seven votes, four votes short of the fifty-one vote majority necessary in the one hundred-man Senate. This was a gain of fourteen over the thirty-three votes in opposition noted in Bob's calculations as of Monday, and he had no doubt at all that he could pick up the other four. What he wanted to do, of course, was pick up many more than that and make it a really devastating repudiation of the President. He had no doubts on that score either, for following Senator Munson's withdrawal from the fray the supporters of the nominee appeared to have pretty well lost heart. Powell was much too junior to rally the necessary strength, Arly was finding himself trapped in his own reputation for erratic cussedness, and elsewhere on the floor his own lieutenants, Seab and Lafe and Warren Strickland chief among them, were at work with an organized zeal that was picking up adherents hourly. Years of experience in the Senate told him that he was in good shape, and it was quite obvious when Tom August arose to start the debate that he knew it too.

Perhaps because of this, the chairman's remarks were nervous, hurried, and very brief. He presented the nominee's biography and record of public service, he described the parliamentary situation under which the committee had been constrained to bring in an unfavorable recommendation, he stressed the fact that half the committee favored confirmation, he urged the Senate to follow suit, and then, after looking about vaguely as though he expected to be violently challenged, he sat down. From his seat beside the Majority Leader a tousled old figure in a crumpled gray suit rose slowly to his feet and said, "Mister—President."

"The senior Senator from South Carolina," Harley Hudson said, and all across the crowded floor and the galleries filled to overflowing there was a stir of anticipation. Seab surveyed the chamber with a look of sleepy amusement and then with an air of sardonic courtliness he turned and bowed gravely to Senator August, who looked upset and responded with an uneasy nod.

"Mister—President," Senator Cooley said. "Now, Mr. President, that was a mighty fine statement just made by the distinguished chairman of the great Foreign Relations Committee, Mr. President. Yes, sir, it was filled with his typical wisdom, his typical candor on all subjects, his typical determination to e-lu-ci-date. If there ever was an e-lu-ci-datin' man, Mr. President, it is the chairman of the Foreign Relations Committee. Then *why*, Mr. President," he roared suddenly, raising his left arm high above his head and crashing it down on the desk in his typical gesture, "does he not tell the Senate the truth about this evil man who wishes to be Secretary of State? Why does he not tell the Senate *all* the truth about this man? *Why are we denied a total e-lu-ci-dation, Mr. President?*"

"Mr. President," Tom August said nervously, "will the distinguished Senator yield?"

"Oh, pshaw, Mr. President," Seab said with a comfortable chuckle. "Now the Senator has been here long enough to know I'm not asking these questions of him, Mr. President. I'm asking them of myself," he said, as the official reporters dutifully noted [Laughter] in the Record. "And," he said with a menacing softness, "I intend to answer them, Mr. President. Yes, sir, I surely intend to answer them. I shall tell you first," he went on with the same gentle menace, "about a man named James Morton."

It was then almost one-thirty, Senator Knox noted, Seab was well-launched and it would probably be a couple of hours before he finished. It seemed a good time to leave. He paused at Warren Strickland's desk and said, loud enough for Bob to hear, "I'm going to 1600, be back soon. Take care of things." They nodded and he started out. At the door he met Lafe just as he turned away from a confidential chat with Bessie Adams of Kansas. "I'm going to the White House," he said, and the junior Senator from Iowa grinned. "Give him hell," he said. "We'll mind the store." "Thanks," Senator Knox said. "I shouldn't be long."

Just outside the door he stopped briefly once more to use the door-keeper's phone. "I've been summoned," he said. "Good luck," his wife said. "Wish *him* luck," he said grimly. "He's the one who needs it now." She started to protest and then dropped it. There were moments when her husband was on his own, and she recognized from long experience that this was one of them.

Yet for all that he departed the Senate with such a cavalier air of confidence, it was in a brown study that he caught a cab and sat through the ten-minute run to the East Gate. Many, many things were going through his mind; many things. Seven years—more than seven, eight or nine, actually—of contention and mutual mistrust were about to culminate in this confrontation which he knew instinctively would be final. He never intended to talk to the President again. The only reason he had agreed to now was that appeal to the country's interests, and the knowledge that he was the only man left for the President to treat with. There was literally no one else for him to approach. The Majority Leader had removed himself, no one else had the stature; Senator Knox at this moment stood supreme in the Senate, and if there was any hope of an accommodation left for the President in the matter of Bob Leffingwell, it lay between these two men who had fought one another so long and so bitterly and always, basically, over so great a prize as the office which was held by the one and desired so strongly by the other.

Thinking of this, with all its aspects and ramifications, so deep, so serious, so full of emotion and at the same time so interlaced with ironies only the two of them could appreciate, he arrived at the East Gate and was shown in quickly and taken down the long glassed-in corridor past the Rose Garden to the President's office. But in Washington few sparrows, let alone a United States Senator of his prominence, fall without being noticed by the press, and by sheer happenstance the AP White House man was returning from a leisurely luncheon at the Press Club just as Orrin alighted from his cab. Surprised and excited, he went at once to the press room and sounded the tocsin. Within seconds the wire services had sent out a note on the wire: "Correspondents: Senator Knox has just arrived secretly to see the President. We are watching." This immediately stirred up the Press Club bar, the congressional press galleries, and all the newspaper bureaus in town. Within minutes there was a sudden flurry of cabs arriving at the West Gate to discharge hurrying reporters. The press secretary was annoyed but helpless. "God damn it, you guys," he said in response to their clamorings, "I don't know anything." "Do you intend to find out?" somebody asked. "I may or I may not," he said coldly in his friendly way. "We'll wait," the press promised coldly in theirs. The big lobby with the brown-leather sofas and the round bull-legged mahogany table in the center filled up with gossiping, smoking, arguing reporters. Half an hour later a late edition of the Washington *Daily News* told the town what was going on in its customary carefree fashion:

AT THE SUMMIT!
THE BOSS (1600 PA.) CALLS IN THE BOSS (U.S.S.)
IN LAST-DITCH MOVE TO SAVE LEFFINGWELL.

Inside, they knew nothing of this. The hallways were deserted except for a clerk or two, there seemed to be only the minimum of guards about, and when he was shown into the oval office with its thick carpet, its pale green walls, and its flat surfaces cluttered with the hodgepodge of trinkets most Presidents seem to collect, he had not as far as he knew been seen by anyone of any importance. He had half expected he would be made to wait, but the President was cleverer than that. He was there, and as the door closed behind the Senator he arose and stepped forward around his desk with hand outstretched. He looked, Senator Knox thought, pale and tired and not at all well.

"Orrin," he said, "it's been a long time."

"It has," Senator Knox agreed calmly. His host waved him to a chair. "Don't stand on ceremony," he said. "Make yourself comfortable and we'll talk."

"Thank you," Orrin said. "How are you feeling, Mr. President?"

The President gave him a quick glance from eyes that looked bloodshot and poorly rested.

"Not too well," he admitted.

"I'm sorry to hear that," the Senator said. The President smiled.

"Are you?" he asked.

"I am now," Orrin said. "I wouldn't have been on Sunday."

"Yes," the President said gravely. "Well, I want you to know that nothing turned out the way I wanted it to. No one regrets more than I what happened. That's often the way, though, have you noticed? You set men and events in motion and before you know it they've gotten out of hand and things you never contemplated have occurred."

"Maybe you shouldn't try to play God so often," Senator Knox suggested bluntly. The President started to look angry, then shrugged and let it pass.

"You can't just sit still, in this office," he said. "You've got to do *something*. Surely you can appreciate that, if no one else can."

Senator Knox nodded. "I do," he said.

"Good," the President said. "Incidentally," he said with more animation, "I want to congratulate you on one thing, and that's knocking COMFORT in the head. That thing was getting to be a real menace and I didn't quite know how to handle it, myself. I'm certainly glad you did."

"Oh?" Orrin said. "How was that?" The President looked surprised.

"Why, getting Fred Van Ackerman," he said. "That knocked the props right out from under them. They were building him up to be their front man and he was all set to go—and then you came along and put a stop to it with that censure motion. I think it was a fine service to the country."

Senator Knox laughed without much amusement.

"I didn't think of that at all," he said. "My only interest was in avenging Brig and ridding the Senate of a demagogic nuisance."

The President gave him a whimsical smile, half-rueful, half-affectionate.

"Orrin, Orrin!" he exclaimed. "Why will you never foresee the consequences of your actions and make the most of them?"

Senator Knox, with an angry look, rejected the whimsy, the rue, and the affection.

"Well," he said tartly, "I am as I am. Maybe I don't calculate the things I do in some slick and clever fashion the way you do, but at least I do them honestly and because that's how I feel, without worrying how they'll come out. That's exactly the difference between you and me and it always has been, illustrated right here in this conversation. I for one am damned glad there is a difference, I can tell you that. Damned glad!"

And for a long moment he and the President surveyed one another in extreme annoyance.

"Well," the President said at length, "I suppose we'll have to leave it to the history books to record which of us was right."

"As long as they record which of us won this fight," Senator Knox said crisply, "I don't give a damn what else they record."

"You think you have, don't you?" the President asked.

"Yes," Orrin snapped. "Don't you?"

"As of this moment," the President said slowly, "perhaps. Perhaps. If you persist in it."

"I see no reason why I shouldn't," Orrin said shortly. "But," he added with a note of sarcasm, "I suppose that's why I'm here. To be shown a reason."

"I would hope so," the President said quietly. He turned away for a moment and stared out at the Rose Garden glistening greenly in the spring. "How can I best explain it you?" he asked rhetorically, and his visitor brought him off it promptly.

"Well," he said, "don't give me the dramatic tale of how hard it is to be President, because I *know* how hard it is to be President." He gave an ironic laugh. "I ought to," he said. "I've thought about it enough."

The President laughed too and swung back quickly.

"Well, then," he said, "if we can't put it on a basis of friendship, maybe we can put it on a basis of being honest about ourselves and about each other and about this office you wanted and I won. How's that?"

"I'm willing," Senator Knox said matter-of-factly.

"All right," the President said slowly, and suddenly, in a quite unguarded way, he put up a right hand that trembled very noticeably and rubbed it across his eyes with a hard, digging motion as though he might thus drive out the devils of foreign pressure and domestic difficulty that tormented him. "I suppose you wonder," he said, "why I have let myself get committed to Bob Leffingwell to the point where I can't afford to back out?"

"I can understand it," the Senator said. "These things come on step by step. I think you've had plenty of opportunities when you could have backed out, however. You didn't take them and," he said coldly, "that's your worry."

"Well," his host said, "it began as a genuine judgment that this man, an excellent and experienced public servant with a broad view of world problems—incidentally," he said, picking up a copy from his desk, "have you seen his book?"

"I intend to quote from it extensively before the debate is over," Orrin assured him.

"An excellent and experienced public servant," the President went on calmly, "was far and away the most qualified man, in my opinion, to name to the post about to be left vacant by the Secretary's resignation."

"Why are you forcing Howie out?" Senator Knox asked curiously. "Everybody knows he isn't sick, and he seems to have done a pretty good job for you."

"Well," the President said, "I'm not saying anything to derogate Howie. He's done a good job and I have no complaints as far as it goes. It's just that he's associated a little too much with inflexibility, that maybe we need someone younger and more forceful and dynamic, in view of what faces us. Particularly now." He paused, considered something, reached a decision.

"They probably are on the moon, you know," he said.

"Oh?" Orrin said.

"Yes," the President said. "If everything went right for them, we think they probably landed sometime Saturday. I expect this thing tomorrow will be some sort of broadcast."

"From there?" Senator Knox asked.

"From there," the President said.

"Why in the *hell*," Senator Knox demanded in sheer exasperation, "didn't we get there first? Time after time after time after time. What *is* the matter with us, anyway?"

"I know," the President said, and sighed. "We're creatures of plan, you see. We always talk about how adaptable we are and how rigid they are, but scientifically we're always the ones who get trapped in our own timetables. Our expedition was planned to go tomorrow morning, so that's when it's going to go, in spite of the fact that I gave the Pentagon an absolute order Thursday morning that it was to go not later than Thursday night. You can't imagine all the sound reasons I've been given why it wasn't possible. Anyway, it goes tomorrow, and if we're lucky, as there's every reason to think we will be, it should arrive in roughly three days and we'll have our own broadcast."

"But not before we've taken another hell of a licking in the eyes of the world," Orrin said bitterly.

"Not before we've taken another hell of a licking in the eyes of the world," the President agreed gravely. Then he said with a sudden sharp defensiveness. "How do you think I feel about it? You feel bad, but how do you think I feel?"

"Yes, I suppose so," Senator Knox said, more sympathetically. "Well, what do we do then, go to war with them up there?"

"Maybe," the President said grimly. "Nobody knows. It isn't a situation that has precedents."

"What is going to happen to us?" the Senator asked, and from anyone else it might have sounded despairing. From Orrin it just sounded intensely annoyed, and it brought an answering smile from the President.

"I expect we're going to get along all right," he said, "if it makes the country as mad as it does you and me."

"Do you think the country is capable of getting mad about anything any more?" Senator Knox asked angrily. "They'll give another shrug and roll over and go back to sleep again."

"That makes it all the more imperative that those of us who have the responsibility and the imagination to get excited about it should stand together as much as we can," the President said; and again he raised a hand that betrayed him and moved it jerkily across his eyes. "It is against that background," he said quietly, "that I must ask you to permit Bob Leffingwell to be confirmed."

Senator Knox stared at him thoughtfully.

"How do I know you're telling me the truth?" he asked calmly, and the President looked at him in some disbelief.

"Do you think I would fabricate something as lurid as that?" he inquired dryly.

"You might," Orrin said. "But," he added quickly, "I don't think you are. I fail to see, however, why it should change my attitude about your nominee. If anything, I should think it would make me even more determined that he not be confirmed."

"I feel he is what we need in this situation," the President said with a quiet insistence. "It is inconceivable to me that you would stand in his way under the circumstances. I am asking you as a patriotic American to permit him to assume the office."

"Well, by God," Senator Knox said sharply, "so now it's patriotism, is it? Well, let me tell you, Mr. President. To me it's patriotic to do what I deem best in my own judgment for the country; it isn't to give in to you and let you ride roughshod over everything decent just because you claim it's patriotic and imply that those who oppose you are unpatriotic. What kind of a damned slippery argument is that?"

"Senator," the President said, "do you have any conception of what I have just been telling you?"

"I have a conception," Senator Knox said shortly. "I also have a conception of what is decent and honorable and best for the country which I think is just as good on the moon as it is on earth or Venus or Mars or any other place we're going to go to. And my conception has no room for Bob Leffingwell and his wishy-washy attitudes toward the mortal enemies of the United States. Why, good Lord. You know as well as I do exactly what they're going to start doing tomorrow. They're going to start pressuring us as they never have before. And you want an obliging stooge like Bob Leffingwell to deal with *that?* What kind of a concept do *you* have, for Christ's sake?"

At this language, which only a most senior and most powerful United States Senator would dare to use to the President of the United States, and then only because he was carried along on a tide of anger and indignation, the President did not, as Orrin half expected, flare up. Instead his whole aspect said: this is too grave to quarrel. And his answer was couched in the same serious mood.

"I cannot abandon him," he said. "I have gone too far. I have presented him to our allies as the next Secretary of State, they like him, they have accepted him. Furthermore, other things have gone too far. There has been a death because of this, not my desire and not my conscious doing, but it too has helped to commit me further. I have gone so far that it is impossible for me to turn and go back. The nation's prestige, my own prestige, are at stake. I will defend them both"—he paused and concluded quietly—"as long as I live." And when the Senator from Illinois smiled in a cold and wintry way he did not flinch.

"How long," asked Orrin Knox, "do you think that will be?"

This the President did not answer, but turned again to the Rose Garden and sat for several minutes staring out. His face had grown more drawn and more haggard as they talked, and if he had not been under the whip of so furious a current of dislike and distaste the Senator from Illinois might have been genuinely alarmed when he turned his white face back. As it was Orrin just thought impatiently that it served him right, he deserved no charity.

"What must I do to persuade you?" the President asked. The Senator made an impatient movement.

"There is nothing," he said. "This talk was pointless from the first. I knew it would be, I told Bob so and I told you so. But he wanted me to come, and you asked me to, so I agreed. It was useless." He started to rise. "I might as well go," he said. The President raised again a hand that shook off his control in a way that was painful to see.

"Please sit down, Orrin," he said quietly. "There is one more thing. We said we would discuss it on the basis of this office. Will you listen to what I have to say on that?"

"What are you going to do," Senator Knox asked scornfully, "offer to make me President?"

"Yes," the President said quietly, "I am."

Senator Knox snorted right out loud.

"That's ridiculous," he said flatly.

"Is it?" the President asked slowly. "Do you really think it is?" And he noted that his impatient visitor, a second before on his way out the door, was sitting slowly back down in his chair. But the stubborn, skeptical expression remained, and it was obvious he was in no way convinced. The President spoke in complete earnest.

"It isn't ridiculous at all," he said, "and you know it. There are lame-duck Presidents and lame-duck Presidents; the two-term amendment is what you make of it, and I don't think you'll deny I've made a great deal. You may not like me, but a hell of a lot of other people still do. Right at this minute there isn't a stronger man in the party or the country. Isn't that true?"

He paused challengingly and the Senator nodded, though with some reluctance.

"You're still very dominant," he admitted.

"All right," the President said. "I am. And there isn't anybody else who is going to have more to say about who the next nominee will be, either. Isn't that right?"

"I expect you will be listened to," Orrin said grudgingly.

"You're damned right I'll be listened to," the President said. "Nobody more so. So I think you will have to concede that my support is not something to be tossed off with a sniff and a snort and a go-to-hell. Correct?"

"I'm not so sure you could make the convention take your choice," Senator Knox said slowly, "but I think you could make it rather difficult for anyone you opposed."

"Well," the President said, "that fits in with your way of thinking about me, but it doesn't fit the facts. Why, do you know how many members of the National Committee have already asked me who I favored? And asked because they don't dare make their own choices known until I make mine? You'd be surprised."

"Where's the National Committee been, by the way?" Orrin asked. "It seems to me they've been lying awfully low on Leffingwell."

"It's a very controversial issue," the President said. "I haven't asked too many of them to help, although I have asked some. I didn't feel they should take a formal stand as a group and they didn't either. Maybe they will when they meet here next week, if it isn't settled by then."

"It will be," Senator Knox promised grimly.

"Yes," the President said. "So we have established that I am still very strong and that for all practical purposes I will hand-pick my successor, which I fully intend to do."

"And I'm it," Senator Knox said ironically.

"You can be," the President said.

"You think it's an office to bargain with," Orrin said. "That's your idea of it." The President smiled.

"Men have," he said blandly. Then he looked more serious. "Actually, I would like to co-operate with the inevitable."

"Me?" Orrin asked. "Me, inevitable? Don't make me laugh."

"Inevitable if I support you, yes," the President said. "And possibly, since we're being completely honest with each other——"

"For once," Orrin interjected tartly.

"—for once," the President agreed calmly, "inevitable anyway. After all," he said seriously, "who else is there? Bob doesn't want it, Stanley knows he couldn't make it, Harley's headed for pasture as soon as I go, and we have, to be candid about it, a rather undistinguished lot of governors at the moment. So who else is there? I could pick somebody out of the governors and he could be transformed into a great leader by publicity; but why should I, when a real President is available?"

Senator Knox smiled skeptically.

"Mr. President," he said, "you've no idea how touched and flattered I am by all this, but who are you kidding? Not me, certainly."

"I'm not trying to kid anyone," the President said. "I repeat, who is there? You go over the list and tell me."

"Oh, well," Orrin said sardonically, "when *I* go over the list, of course, there's only one answer. But that doesn't mean there's only one answer for the convention or the country. After all, I've made many enemies, I'm not smooth, I'm not tricky, I'm not much of an operator——"

This time it was the President's turn to interject.

"Not much," he said dryly.

"Well, I'm not," Senator Knox said. "I'm a bull in a china shop. Everybody says so. I do everything wrong. I stumble and blunder and make mistakes. I'd probably have us in a war in ten minutes. Furthermore," and this time a little of the real bitterness he felt about the egregious slogan that had dogged him for so long crept into his voice in spite of himself, "you know Orrin Knox. He can't be elected."

"I think he can be," the President said quietly, "for he has three great qualifications. He is strong and he is honest and he is able to learn. And that to me seems sufficient."

"It would be like Vulcan succeeding Zeus," Orrin said with a smile. "The supple breezes would be followed by a great wind."

"Well," the President said, "don't talk yourself down too much. The country needs variation in the office. Maybe it's time for the supple to be succeeded by the direct. Maybe we can stand that for a while. Maybe the Commies need a dose of it too. Maybe you can accomplish by a head-on approach some of the things I haven't been able to accomplish by a more subtle one. Maybe," he said, and the remark above all others convinced the Senator from Illinois suddenly that he was absolutely sincere, "maybe I've been too clever for my own good sometimes . . . At any rate," he said with a chuckle of genuine amusement, "I'd like to sit back in my rocking chair and watch you try."

At this Senator Knox had to laugh, quite genuinely too, and for a rare and tenuous moment a feeling of real friendship linked them together. Then he shook his head.

"It won't work," he said. "It probably wouldn't work under any conditions, and it certainly won't if you make it subject to my support for Bob Leffingwell, because that I won't give."

"Let me ask you," the President said, "were you intending, before you came in here today, to run next year?"

"I was," Orrin said without hesitation.

"And do you still intend to, now that we have talked?" the President asked.

"I do," Orrin said with equal emphasis.

"Do you think you can win over my opposition?" the President asked, and this time the answer came more slowly.

"I don't know," the Senator said honestly.

"But you know you can win with my support," the President said.

"Yes," Orrin said. "I know that."

"Then why make it difficult for yourself?" the President said. "Why not accept a certainty when you have it given you on a silver platter?"

"Because the price is Bob Leffingwell, that's why," Orrin said tartly.

"There's a price for everything, in this world," the President said rather bleakly. "You're no less immune to paying it than any other ambitious man. Are you?"

"Perhaps," Senator Knox said, "and perhaps not."

"Don't make the gamble again, Orrin," the President said. "You've lost twice already. It won't be easy at best to win the third time. But with me on your side you can and you know it."

"Yes," the Senator from Illinois agreed, "I know it." And suddenly he thought he saw the way out of this conversation in which the great wind was finding itself met at every turn by the supple breeze. He would make a suggestion so extremely absurd that it would end the fantastic discussion at once and bring everything back down to earth once and for all.

"Will you give me that in writing?" he asked, and for a second he thought he had the President on the run. But like many another, he had underestimated his man.

"I will," his host said without hesitation. And calmly and matter-of-factly, taking a ball-point pen from his vest pocket and a sheet of White House stationery from his desk drawer, he leaned forward and proceeded to write slowly and carefully and almost as though he had expected this. Which, Orrin thought with a respect he had never quite felt before, he probably had. When he was done he put the pen back in his pocket and tossed over the sheet of paper.

"Will that do it?" he asked quietly. Senator Knox read it through slowly twice and then stared at him. He stared at him for quite a long time. Finally he spoke.

"Yes," he said, "that will do it."

"Fine," the President said. "I can count on you, then?"

"I didn't mean that will do it as far as Leffingwell is concerned," Senator Knox said sharply. "I meant that will do it as far as my wanting the offer in writing is concerned. I don't know what I will decide. I'll have to think it over."

"Surely," the President said with a wave of his hand, and suddenly he appeared to be reinvigorated, refreshed, not so haggard, not so tired, once more in control of himself and the situation. "I know you'll want to discuss it with Beth."

"Beth and several others," Senator Knox said.

"Of course," the President said, and as he leaned back with an approving air the telephone rang.

"Yes?" he said and listened. "Yes," he said again. "I think that would be fine. Yes. Yes, I will. Thank you . . . That was Pete," he said. "He says somebody saw you come in and the lobby is full of reporters and photographers who want to catch us together. I told him to send them right on in."

Senator Knox looked alarmed and displeased and started to rise angrily, but the President went smoothly on.

"While we're waiting," he said, "there is one thing I would like you to do for me and the country, completely aside from this business, and that's make a speech tomorrow afternoon after the Russian broadcast to reassure the Senate and the Congress. I'm going on the air myself at 8 P.M. to talk to the country, but it will mean a lot more if you have already spoken up there to rally the Congress behind me. Will you do that?"

And in spite of his annoyance at being euchered into an appearance of cordiality on the Leffingwell issue that the facts did not support, the Senator from Illinois on this other matter nodded without hesitation.

"Of course," he said. "Of course I will. I don't suppose you want me to mention our own expedition, do you?"

"I'd rather you didn't," the President said. "I was thinking that would be a little more suitable coming from me, don't you agree?"

"Of course," Orrin said again. "Of course."

"You know what to say," the President said. "Don't try to pretend it's a phony, because it isn't. Give them something to stiffen their backbones. That's what you're good at. Here we are in the jaws of hell, so let's get a move on—that sort of thing." He smiled. "O.K.?"

The Senator from Illinois nodded in a way that had to display, despite his personal feelings, a grudging admiration.

"O.K.," he said.

And then the press was upon them, reporters were crowding up close around the desk, television cameras were being wheeled in, the still photographers were suddenly everywhere shouting urgent requests that they smile and shake hands.

"Might as well," the President said with a show of long-suffering compliance, and Senator Knox, who knew his host was secretly delighted at thus being forced into a show of apparent good-fellowship, complied with an expression that he tried to make not too disapproving.

"Have you reached an agreement on Mr. Leffingwell, Mr. President?" someone asked eagerly and the President looked at the Senator with a little bow.

"I expect Orrin should answer that," he said. Senator Knox smiled with as much blandness as he could muster.

"We have had a most interesting discussion of the subject," he said. He paused. "I think that's about as far as I intend to go," he said.

"Was it an *agree*able discussion, Senator?" a voice called, and there was laughter in the room.

"Oh," he said, "my talks with the President—such as they are—are always agreeable. He's an agreeable man."

"Was the conclusion *agree*able?" someone else inquired and again they laughed.

"The talk was agreeable," Senator Knox said, and a slight note of irritation came into his voice. "That really is as far as I'm going to go."

"You mean we'll have to report the news as it happens, Senator?" the AP spoke up, and once again they laughed, Orrin and the President this time with them.

"I'm afraid so," he said, and after insisting on a few more smiles and handshakes they let him go. But he noted as he finally shook hands in farewell that they were, as usual, after the President for still more of their countless thousands of shots of him sitting at his desk.

So it was that the last thing he saw of him as he left the room—the last thing, although he did not know it then, that he was ever to see of him— was an upright figure and a confident face, no longer looking drawn and white but somehow in the stimulation of the moment miraculously restored to its customary vigor, appearing calm and confident, glowing and strong amid the glare of the lights and the hectic confusions of the room.

With a final wondering shake of his head for one of the phenomena of the age, the senior Senator from Illinois turned and walked all alone back down the long corridor past the Rose Garden to the East Gate, a conveniently passing cab and a very thoughtful ride to Capitol Hill.

"There comes Orrin," the Washington *Post* said in the gallery above.

"Looks awfully sober," UPI observed.

"Yes," the *Herald Tribune* said. "I guess we'd better try to get him off the floor and talk to him."

"He wouldn't say anything at the White House," AP said.

"And he won't say anything here," predicted the *Times*.

Accurately.

At three fifty-nine the senior Senator from South Carolina concluded an address which, they all agreed, had been one of his most dramatic, and sat down, looking scarcely a whit more tousled and rumpled than he had when he stood up; though he had banged his desk twenty-six times, upset two glasses of water, startled Courtney Robinson of New Hampshire out of a sound sleep on three different occasions, and caused exactly thirty-nine notations of [Laughter] to be made in the Congressional Record. In between the [Laughter] there had been a most damaging speech against Robert A. Leffingwell, and it was in full awareness that he had his work cut out for him that the senior Senator from Arkansas thoughtfully sought recognition from the Chair. He was not experienced in the ways of politics for nothing, however, and without a moment's hesitation he went straight to the question that was exciting them all, on the floor and in the galleries.

"Mr. President," he said, "the distinguished senior Senator from Illinois has just come from a conference with the President on this matter now before us. I wonder if the Senator cares to tell us what word the President had for him to convey to the Senate at this time?"

For a moment the Senator from Illinois, who appeared to be in a deep dark study, seemed not to have heard; but just as Rob Cunningham of Arizona leaned over to jog his arm and catch his attention he stood up with a sudden impatience.

"I will say to the Senator, Mr. President," he said, "that my conversation with the President was a private affair. It did not involve any 'word for the Senate,' as he so cleverly puts it."

"Perhaps the Senator can tell us then, Mr. President," Arly said smoothly, "since there is great interest in this body about it, what word did he have for the Senator?"

"I don't think it's any of the Senator's business, Mr. President," Orrin said, "but since he asks so politely I will tell him that the President's word for the Senator from Illinois was just exactly what it is for all Senators: Confirm Bob Leffingwell."

"And how did the Senator respond to that, Mr. President?" Arly pursued blandly. "With his customary violent indignation? Is there a roof still on the White House? Are the grounds intact? Does brick still stand on brick? More importantly, is the President still alive after broaching so naughty a suggestion?"

"The President is still alive," Orrin said shortly. "And again I have to commend the Senator on his cleverness. He positively scintillates this afternoon. I wonder if it will do his cause any good?"

"Let me ask the Senator, Mr. President," Senator Richardson said calmly, "following his talk with the President is he still one hundred per cent, absolutely, irrevocably, and forever opposed to this nominee?"

And at this, dismaying his friends and sending a sudden stir of interest through the Senate, the senior Senator from Illinois hesitated. It was not a very long hesitation, perhaps three seconds, but it was long enough to give Arly Richardson his advantage.

"I see the Senator pause, Mr. President," he said softly. "Are we to take it, then, that the Senator is modifying his views in the wake of his talk with the President?"

"I didn't say that," Orrin objected rather lamely.

"No, Mr. President," Senator Richardson said. "The Senator did not have to say it. His hesitation said it for him. And now, Mr. President," he said, dropping it abruptly with bland skill and going smoothly on, "let us examine this famous episode of the witness Gelman, the cell in Chicago, and the duplicity of the nominee. What does this interesting tale really mean, and how much weight should we attach to it? It seems to me, Mr. President——" And he was off, while Senator Knox sat slowly back in his seat and Lafe and Seab exchanged a puzzled glance and across the room a little buzz of whispers and talk began to drift.

And that was what you got, he thought bitterly, for agreeing to talk to that seducer in the White House. You couldn't come near him without being corrupted by his cleverness, without having your own will and determination sapped in some subtle degree, without yielding at least a little to what he wanted. Now they all thought, he knew, that he was beginning to give in. He could see Paul Hendershot of Indiana buzzing like an old woman with Walter Turnbull of Louisiana; Ed Parrish of Nevada, Porter Owens of Montana, and Shelton Monroe of Virginia were in an excited huddle casting glances his way, and above in the press gallery he could see the hurried little conferrings, the brisk scurrying up the steps to send stories, the rumors, and the speculation flowing like a visible tide. Damn him, damn him, he thought just before honesty reasserted itself, for doing this to me.

But then honesty returned and he told himself with a wry anger that of course it was his own damned fault for even hesitating when Arly challenged him. That was where the fault lay, not with the President who in his customary fashion had simply dangled temptation and left it to the tempted to make the decision whether or not to accept it. He should have fired back something tart and pointed and firm to his friend from Arkansas, and the seeping doubt about his intentions that now pervaded the atmosphere of the chamber would not have developed. And yet if he had done that—not that he intended in the slightest to yield to the President's persuasions, but supposing he did—if he had done that, it might have foreclosed too abruptly and finally the possibility that he might—that he might——

That he might what? Give in to him? Take his evil offer? Did he really intend to do that? And if he was so sure he did not then why had he hesitated? Why had he not made the quick reply that would have been characteristic? Why had he not acted like Orrin Knox? Why had he betrayed himself?

Well, he knew why; because he wanted to be President, and this was the surest way to do it, as sure as anything in life and politics could be. The President had been entirely correct in his analysis of his own position; he was still the strongest man in the party and the country, he was indeed in a position to dictate the next candidate; and the party was in good shape, the candidacy would be no futile project or empty honor, they were good for another four to eight years before the tide turned again.

Accepting this bargain, the handwritten voucher he held in his pocket, a piece of paper before which even his most determined enemies would bow, would put him in the White House; of that he was as sure as the President was. And that was why Orrin Knox had not acted like Orrin Knox, if truth were known; because there came a point, even with him, at which the imperatives of ambition gained triumph over the dictates of conscience, no matter how strong that conscience might be.

Or did they? Did they really? He looked again about the room where many people were looking at him, and he thought for a moment of what Orrin Knox had been and what Orrin Knox was supposed to be; and there came to him with a fearful clarity the question: Is it really worth it? Is it worth it to give up the image of Orrin Knox, ambitious but no trimmer, for the image of Orrin Knox, ambitious and a trimmer? Is even the White House worth that kind of bargain?

For several more minutes he thought about this, staring down at the papers on his desk, no longer listening to Arly, no longer conscious of the staring eyes, the whispering tongues, the speculation flickering over the surface of the Senate. He was still thinking about it when a page placed under his eyes a card bearing the name of the National Chairman and the scrawled message, "Orrin: Can I see you? Urgent."

He realized then that this time the President wasn't going to let temptation do its own work but was going to help it along as much as he could; and since this made his own decision even harder, for it indicated that this was not an empty gesture but something his opponent sincerely intended to go through with, he sighed heavily and nodded at the boy.

"I'll be out," he said.

In the big reception room off the back lobby near the Vice President's office he worked his way through the crowd of constituents, government officials, and other visitors who wait for Senators each day and walked toward the National Chairman, who had thoughtfully appropriated two isolated chairs in a corner by the window.

"Jim," he said directly, "what's on your mind?" The National Chairman smiled with an expansive joviality.

"I just had an invitation to convey to you, Orrin," he said, "and I thought I'd be formal about it and deliver it in person."

"Well, that's nice," Senator Knox said. "I appreciate that. I hope it lives up to its build-up."

The National Chairman laughed heartily.

"Old prickly Orrin," he said affectionately. Then he sobered a little and added thoughtfully, as though he were seeing it on a campaign poster in mind's eye, "Honest Orrin."

"O.K.," Senator Knox said with an impatience he managed to keep good-natured, "stop being coy and let's have it."

The National Chairman grinned and slapped him familiarly on the

knee, a gesture he managed to sustain without flinching. A long past of knee slaps, back claps, easy jokes, and loud-mouthed, facile laughter stretched back down the years for the National Chairman. He had never, you might say, known anything else.

"Well, Orrin," he said, "the situation is this. We're having a two-day meeting here next week, as you know, and we were all set to have the President give us a speech at our final banquet and wind it up with a bang. But he just called me a little while ago and said he didn't think he'd be able to make it. He's going to Key West on Sunday, he said, and so he suggested we get a substitute. In fact," the National Chairman said in a rather puzzled voice, "he suggested you."

"You sound delighted," Senator Knox said, and the National Chairman had the grace to laugh.

"Well, we are," he said. "I'm just a little surprised, that's all. I didn't know you two were that close."

Senator Knox laughed too.

"You've no idea," he said.

"Will you do it?" the National Chairman asked. "We'd really be very glad to have you. It's a good opportunity, as you know."

"Yes, Jim," Orrin said dryly, "I know. Did he say anything to you about Leffingwell?"

The National Chairman smiled knowingly.

"Oh, no," he said. "He wouldn't."

"That's right," Senator Knox agreed. "He wouldn't. Well, I tell you what, Jim. Suppose we wait until this thing is finished and then I'll call you on Friday and let you know what I decide. That would still be time for you to get somebody else if I should bow out, wouldn't it?"

"It would," the National Chairman agreed, "but I don't think I'd pass it up if I were you, Orrin, and had any—any plans. He was quite emphatic about wishing you to do it, and that might indicate—something—quite—interesting, don't you think?"

"Who knows?" Senator Knox said. "Who knows? Thanks for coming up, Jim. I'll let you know Friday."

"Right, Orrin," the National Chairman said. "We'll be hoping you can make it. I know it would please him, too."

"And that's important," Orrin Knox said in a tone the National Chairman couldn't interpret.

"Oh, it is, Orrin," he said heartily. "Yes, it is."

At five-thirty, Senator Richardson having completed his speech after three sharp brushes with Lafe Smith, two with Seab, and one with Bessie Adams, the Majority Leader obtained the floor briefly.

"Mr. President," he said, "if Senators will give me their attention, it is my purpose to hold the Senate in session rather late tonight in order that we may dispose of as many speeches as possible in the hope that we

can get a final vote on this nomination by sometime tomorrow night. I want to put Senators on notice that we will probably run as late as eleven or eleven-thirty tonight, so I hope they will adjust their programs for the evening accordingly."

"Mr. President," Powell Hanson said, "if I might address a question to the distinguished senior Senator from Illinois, does he plan to make an address tonight?"

There was a sudden attentiveness to hear the answer as Orrin stood up slowly and looked about the chamber. The question was forcing him toward a decision, and he welcomed it for that.

"I will say to the Senator that it is my intention," he said, although it really hadn't been until he said it. "I expect to state my position in this matter briefly sometime shortly before we adjourn tonight. I would expect this would be sometime around ten o'clock according to the Majority Leader's tentative schedule."

"I thank the Senator," Powell Hanson said. "Then we can plan to be here, for I know many Senators are very anxious to hear what the Senator has to say."

So am I, thought Orrin dryly, though he didn't say it aloud. Instead he nodded, said, "I thank the Senator," and sat down.

And thus he had committed himself to a deadline in making up his mind, and that, he knew, was a good thing. It would serve to clear away a lot of wasted thoughts and wasted time and force him to reach a decision in reasonable order. He could see as he looked about the floor that Lafe and Seab were watching him questioningly, and he shook his head in a way that baffled them both. It must have baffled the Majority Leader too, for in a moment he came casually over.

"I think I'll have the restaurant send dinner to my office upstairs," he said. "Why don't you and Lafe and Seab join me?"

"Yes," he said gratefully, for this too was forcing his hand, and he understood what the invitation conveyed, that Bob understood, possibly half guessed, the exact problem confronting him and thought a quiet dinner with old friends might help. And so it would, for he honestly wanted their views.

"Ask Stanley and Warren, too, will you?" he said, and the Majority Leader nodded.

"About six-fifteen," he said.

"Right," Senator Knox said, and went to make the telephone call he had been putting off until the pattern of events shaped itself a little more clearly for him. It was clear now, and he said, "I suppose you've been wondering why I didn't call earlier."

"I wondered," she said, "but I thought you'd probably let me know when you got around to it. What did he offer you?"

"The White House," he said. She gave a startled little laugh.

"He *is* desperate, isn't he?" she said. "Are you going to take it?"

"Shall I?" Orrin asked simply, and there was silence again.

"Can you?" Warren Strickland inquired quietly, and the senior Senator from Illinois, for the first time any of them could remember in all their years of public life together, looked puzzled and driven and unhappy.

"I don't know," he said slowly. "That's what scares me. I don't know." And again he glanced around the circle.

"Should I?" he said.

"Well, sir," Seab said finally, "Lafe and Warren and I, now, of course our judgment is colored by our feelings about Mr. Leffingwell. And Bob and Stanley, they feel the other way and that affects their judgment, too. But leaving aside all of that and speaking just for myself, Orrin, it has been my observation that when a man deserts something he basically and fundamentally believes in, he loses something inside. Yes, sir, he loses something inside. Not," he added ironically, "that I haven't seen it happen many a time in this old Senate. No, sir, not that I haven't seen it happen. But a man pays for it. Yes, sir, he pays. And sometimes," he said softly, "sometimes what he gets for it doesn't quite make up for what he pays for it. Sometimes it truly doesn't."

"Maybe I should ask you this," Senator Knox said. "Have I got any right to want to be President? Isn't it terribly presumptuous of me to even think about it at all? Have I got any right to bargain on that basis to begin with? Maybe you should tell me that first."

Senator Cooley smiled a little in his heavy-lidded way.

"Now you are seeking the easy way out, Orrin," he said. "That's what you are doing, you are seeking the easy way out. I don't think," he said, and he too looked slowly from face to face, "that there is any man here, or any man out there on the floor—including your dear friend from Arkansas—who doesn't think that you're fully qualified to be President of the United States, or wouldn't feel perfectly comfortable to have the government in your hands. Am I correct in that, Senators?"

"You're correct in that, Seab," the Majority Leader said. "You have to match yourself against what's available now and what's been available in the past. After all, Presidents are only men. Some of them weren't much when they were trying to get it and some of them weren't much after they got it. Surveying the lot, I wouldn't say you had anything to worry about on that score."

"In other words," Orrin said with a sudden smile, "I'm no worse than the worst of them."

"Let's say you're as good as the best of them," Bob Munson said with an answering smile. "I agree with Seab, false modesty doesn't enter into the problem right now."

"I think it comes back," Senator Danta said thoughtfully, "to the kind of man Orrin Knox has been and the kind of man you want him to be from now on."

"Spoken like the father of my daughter-in-law," Senator Knox said, again with a smile.

"And to be solved, I have no doubt, like the father of my son-in-law," Stanley said. "I'm not worried about that. I don't think, really, that it has any bearing on Bob Leffingwell, or that Bob Leffingwell, actually, really has much to do with it. He's the issue on which it turns, but the fundamental decision is something involving your own being, and it goes far deeper than this nomination."

"Yes," Senator Knox said, "and that's what I'm not yet sure of. You all know," he went on quietly, looking down at the paper lying open before him on the table, "that I have wanted for a long time to be President. I've failed twice. I want to try again. With this piece of paper and the support it represents and guarantees, there is very little doubt in my mind that I can have the nomination and, in all probability, the election. This piece of paper represents the Presidency of the United States . . ." He sighed and looked up with a strangely beseeching smile. "It isn't easy," he said.

"Of course it isn't," Lafe said sympathetically. "And," he added, "it isn't really something that we can help you on, either, is it? It's something that only one man can decide, really, and that's you. I don't know about the rest of the fellows, but I wouldn't presume to try to advise you." He smiled. "I wouldn't want the responsibility, frankly."

Again there was a little silence, and finally the Senator from Illinois looked up and spoke in a way that moved them all.

"Well," he said quietly, "my friends—my dear friends, of so many years' standing and so many battles together . . . Of course Lafe is entirely right. He doesn't want the responsibility, and neither do any of you, and I haven't the right to ask you to help me shoulder it. So I won't, any more. It's something I've got to solve, and solve alone, I guess . . . Although," he added in a more hopeful voice, "maybe Hank can help me."

"I'm sure she will do all she can," Senator Cooley said softly, "but I'll wager even she won't be able to finally do it for you, Orrin. Something like this, only one person in all the world can do for you. You know that, Orrin."

"Probably," Senator Knox said in a desolate voice. "Probably . . ."

"Well," Bob Munson said with a sudden briskness, "I think I'd better get back to the floor and see what's going on."

"I'm with you," Lafe said with a grin. "I feel like saying a few things to make a few people mad."

"So do I," Stanley said, and Warren Strickland laughed as they left the table.

"I might join in, too," he said. "I think this debate needs a little livening up."

"Thank you all," Orrin said in a voice that wasn't quite steady. "Thank you all so much."

"What are friends for?" Lafe asked simply. "Come on, Bob, last one out is something I might say if it weren't for the N.A.A.C.P."

And thus they emerged laughing together from the Majority Leader's office and, still laughing, brushed aside the queries of the eager band of reporters who had inevitably found their place of meeting. No cautionary word of secrecy had been uttered by any of them, nor was it necessary, for the thought of revealing anything of so intimate a conversation did not even cross the minds of these old friends.

A few minutes after they reached the floor, however, the junior Senator from Iowa just happened to have occasion to wander into the cloakroom just behind the senior Senator from South Carolina.

"I don't know about you," he murmured, "but I'm going to keep right on rounding up votes as though there weren't any doubt at all."

Senator Cooley nodded.

"I don't think there is," he said. "No, sir, I don't think he quite knows it yet, but I don't think there is, at all."

Despite this calm assurance on the part of his friends, however, it was still with the inner turmoil that couldn't quite keep from showing that he sat through another hour of debate as the floor and the galleries which had emptied for dinner, began to fill up again as they always do for a night session. The press sent in three different times to try to get him to come out for an interview, and each time he refused; some of them even tried, humorously, to mouth questions silently to him from the gallery, but he only smiled firmly and shook his head. Let them guess and keep guessing; he wasn't going to complicate his own difficulties by getting himself in a false position answering questions. There still faced him the promise he had given Powell Hanson of a statement before the Senate recessed for the night, but he was not even sure now that he would do that. It might be better to sleep on it. He would have to talk to Hank and see what she thought. Then it might be clearer.

"We just tried to corner Orrin," the AP and UPI reported breathlessly to their colleagues a little later, "but he outran us."

"Where's he going?" the *Times* asked, and his colleagues shook their heads.

"I don't know," AP said, "but he's sure hell-bent for something."

"We paced him through the Rotunda," UPI said, "but he gained on us going down the British Stairway. By the time we reached the bottom he had doubled back toward the Senate and gone to ground in one of the back elevators. The door slammed in our faces just as we got there. It went up."

"I haven't had such a problem in pursuit since I was at O.C.S. during the war," AP said. "You never saw such a neat piece of evasive action in your life."

Behind him as he waited in the archway under the great stone steps of the deserted House side he heard the revolving door go around, and then a friendly hand gave his elbow a firm squeeze.

"Orrin," the Speaker said, "this is a nice surprise for us lowly characters of the House. To what do we owe the honor?"

"It isn't an honor, Bill," he said with a smile. "I'm just hiding out."

The Speaker smiled in his fatherly fashion.

"Good place," he said. "We've got lots of room over here. A man can get lost faster in the House, I say, than he can anywhere else." He chuckled suddenly. "That's what I tell my freshmen when they come here. Yes, sir, I say: 'You know, a man who doesn't co-operate can get lost faster in this House than he can anyplace else on earth.' " The chuckle grew to a laugh. "Scares hell out of 'em," he said.

Senator Knox laughed too.

"You're an old reprobate, Bill," he said. "I'm glad I'm not under your thumb."

"You're not under anybody's thumb, Orrin," the Speaker said. "Except I hear this afternoon maybe you're under *his* thumb. Is that true?"

And he looked at the Senator from shrewd old eyes that over the decades had seen thousands of ambitious men come and go, each seeking his particular place in the sun, some making it, some failing, almost all in one way or another dependent upon his favor or enmity for it. But the Senator from Illinois never had been, and he questioned him now not in the sense of wanting to interfere but with a respectful curiosity, because he liked Orrin Knox and wanted to know how things were with him.

"No," Orrin said slowly, "it isn't true, Bill." He paused. "Just between us——" He began and then stopped to give the Speaker a quick glance. The Speaker nodded gravely.

"How else?" he asked simply.

"He's offered to back me next year if I'll go along on Leffingwell," the Senator said. "What shall I do, Bill?"

The Speaker was silent for a while, and then he too rejected, kindly but firmly, the opportunity to give advice.

"Seems to me that's your problem, Orrin," he said. "I don't honestly know what I'd say. Appears to me you'll have a good chance next year. Whether you can do it without him—whether you can do it over his opposition—that's another matter . . . On the other hand," he said slowly, "whether you'd want to keep on living with Orrin Knox if you got it on a bargain of that kind, that, too, I don't know . . . It's been a bad business," he said with a sigh. "Messing the party up like this. Killing people. I was awfully sad about Brig. Awfully sad. He was a fine boy."

"That's one reason," Senator Knox said, "that I just don't see how I can make a deal with him."

"Mmm," the Speaker said. "I reckon he was a little upset about that himself."

"Oh, he was," Orrin said shortly. "After the fact." They fell silent again.

"Well," the Speaker said, "it's a hard problem, Orrin, but I guess I'm no different from everyone else you've asked, if you have asked anyone. I imagine everyone's turned you down. Nobody wants to give advice on a thing like that."

"That's right," Orrin said, rather forlornly, "nobody does."

"Who are you waiting for?" the Speaker asked, and, being a shrewd and wise old man, guessed. "Bee?"

"Yes," the Senator said.

"A fine woman," the Speaker said. "A fine, fine woman. I hope she'll be able to help you, Orrin . . . But in any event," he said, "one thing, anyway: I think maybe you can count on me for next year. I don't know what you'll decide or what he'll do, but I have a pretty good idea what I'm going to do. I'm going to be for you, if it's any help."

"Any help?" Senator Knox demanded. "Any *help?* My God, Bill, you know it's all the help in the world. I appreciate it more than I can say. I'll never forget it. Never."

The Speaker smiled.

"Oh, you might," he said. "Men have a way of forgetting things, in this town."

"Well," Orrin Knox said tartly, "I don't."

"I know you don't, Orrin," the Speaker said. "I expect that's one of the reasons I'm for you. You're not a forgetter. It's all of a piece with the rest of you. I know where I stand with you. That's more than I can say," he added with a dry little smile, "about our mutual friend."

There came a flash of headlights, a car swung into the archway.

"Here she comes," the Speaker said, and then as he saw the long, black limousine, "Nope, it's mine." He held out his hand. "Orrin, my friend," he said. "Good traveling, whatever your road."

"Thank you, Bill," the Senator said. "You're a true friend."

"You have more than you think," the Speaker said as he got in. "Never think you don't."

He waved in a kindly fashion and his chauffeur took him off, a figure grown old and wise in the ways of men and politics, brought successfully by the years to a position where all his ambitions were achieved, all inner storms were over, he could look with a firm but friendly eye upon those of other men; and where his word, once given, could not be swayed by anyone.

"Well," she said, turning the car down Independence Avenue, "what shall we do, go to Hains Point and neck?"

This general irreverence and insouciance, which had done so much over the years to help him keep his balance, provoked the chuckle it always did.

"I'm afraid not," he said, making it sound regretful. "The boys in the house tell me you're a hell of a hot number, but——"

"Orrin Knox!" she exclaimed. "Nobody ever told you I was a hot number!"

"I wish they had," he said. "Then I would have been prepared for it." She laughed and, he noticed, blushed a little.

"Now, cut it out," she said. "You win. I'm sorry I even mentioned it."

"I'm not," he said. "It evokes many pleasant memories. It holds out promise of many future——"

"So are you going to be President of the United States?" she interrupted firmly, and his mood sobered at once.

"I don't know," he said as they came to Agriculture and passed under the covered bridge between the North and South buildings. "Do you think I should?"

"I've always thought you should," she said. "Whether you should in this context is another question. What do the others think?"

"They wouldn't say," he remarked glumly. "They said, and rightly, that it was too important a thing for them to take responsibility. They told me I was on my own. So did the Speaker."

"Oh?" she said. "When did you see the Speaker?"

"Just now," he said. "He was just going home. He said one thing that in a way makes it even more complicated. He said he'd be for me regardless of what the President does."

"That's nice," she said. "He's a good friend."

"He's great," he said. "But he wouldn't advise me either. And you know something? Nobody thinks you will, either."

"Really?" she said as they came to a turnout along the Tidal Basin and she drew off and parked. "How did they guess?"

"What do you mean by that?" he asked in genuine alarm. She leaned back and gave him the long, straight look he had often received in their life together.

"What did it sound like?" she asked.

"It sounded as though you weren't going to help me," he said in dismay. "That's just what it sounded like."

"Of course I'll help you," she said. "I always have, haven't I?"

"Then tell me what to do," he said.

"My dear," she said quietly, "do you really want me to?"

At this he paused and thought for a long, long time, staring out across the water while she watched him with the same appraising, waiting look. Finally he spoke slowly.

"You know," he said thoughtfully, "I don't know. In a way——"

"Go on," she said.

"In a way I'm not so sure I do."

"Good," she said. "That's the first step in really coming to grips with it."

"But you've always given me your advice——" he began.

"Yes, but this is really it. This is It with a capital I. This is the Presidency. What right have I got to put in my two-bits' worth?"

"I'd give you the right," he said, still protesting but knowing in his heart that he was already accepting her decision and beginning to be glad of it, it had come like a dash of cold water, but of course it was the only thing and he knew it, "if you wanted the right."

She shook her head.

"My dear," she said again, "nobody could want that right. The others were wise. It's too big. Much as I want to help you, and much as I am prepared to help you in whatever you decide, the decision has got to be yours. About all I can say is what I expect Bill said and what I expect the others said: Orrin Knox has lived in a certain way and come to mean certain things to his country and his time. He has to decide now whether he wants to mean something else. It's as simple as that."

"Simple!" he said with a groan. "My God, what a word. Look at this," he said, remembering the paper and giving it to her. "Does this make it simple?"

She glanced at it quickly and handed it back.

"Why don't you give it to the Smithsonian?" she suggested with a smile. "They have everything else."

"Oh, Hank," he said, reaching for her hand in a last dependent gesture, "what am I going to do? What am I ever going to do?"

"I suppose," she said, squeezing it firmly, "that you're going to do what's right for you to do. I've never known you—with a few exceptions," she added with a chuckle, "to do anything else."

"But if I decide the wrong way——" He said. She shook her head.

"Who's to determine that?" she asked. "You, or the Lord? Have a little faith, Senator. It will all work out for the best."

He thought for a moment and spoke in a much lighter tone.

"All I can say is," he said, "you're a hell of a lot of help."

"I think," she said as she started the car, "I have been. Where do you want to work this out?" she asked humorously. "Staring at Abe or brooding by the Capitol?"

"Abe may be a little tired of me by now," he said with an answering, returning humor. "Why don't you drop me at the foot of the Hill and I'll do a little walking and thinking before I go back to the floor?"

"That's fine," she said. Five minutes later she stopped the car at the bottom of the long lane of slate steps leading up to the West Front of the Capitol and leaned over and kissed him firmly.

"I love you very much, Senator," she said. "I'm not worried about you."

"That's good," he said wryly. "You're about the only one."

Above him the great Capitol loomed against a sky still tinged faintly with a lingering, lemon light; a few cars passed, most of them bound up the Hill to discharge the visitors who were converging upon the Senate to hear his speech; a lone cop stood sentry in the distance, a few tourists wandered; there was a peaceful stillness under the trees and along the walks and over the vast expanses of the lawn.

Here between the Capitol and the town he stood suspended between the two parts of his life, the great floodlit building above, and below, when he turned to stare down the Mall, the imperial needle of the Washington Monument, the lower mass of the Lincoln Memorial, the glow of the city, the dim hills of Virginia . . . and the White House, distant and almost lost amid the haze of lights and the soft concealment of the trees.

Almost lost . . . Almost lost. Why did he not be honest with himself and say, completely? For it was, he knew it now, there had never really been the slightest doubt in his heart of hearts what he was going to do. He had gone through the hours since receiving the President's offer as though he were sleepwalking; and each new rebuff he had received from those he had counted on to help him in his time of greatest need had simply confirmed his strange impression that somehow it was all something in a dream, that he was wandering out of bounds on the edge of destiny and sooner or later would have to wake up.

Well: they had made him wake up, and that, apparently, was what they had all intended to do, from his old friends, each of whom had contemplated at one time or another the goal that now lay within his grasp and so could understand the turmoil of his indecision, to the Speaker, who understood the ways of ambition as few men did, to his wife, who not only understood the ways of ambition but understood him. Make up your own mind, they had said, making it up for him in their own calculated refusals; make up your own mind, and act like Orrin Knox.

And yet—and yet. Here within his reach lay all that he had dreamed of for thirty years, the chance to be President, the chance to run the country as *he* believed best, the chance to do the great things for America that he knew, he *knew*, he could do if he had the power. With all the vigor of his passionate heart he was convinced that he could serve the country in a way that would be to her great and ultimate good. He knew he could be a good President, quite possibly a great one; he had thought so often about what he would do, how he would handle it, the goals he would set and the ways he would achieve them, the clear direction he would chart and the strong leadership he would provide. Here it all lay, in the palm of his hand, needing only the bargain to be completed, the deal to be struck, for the hand to close tightly at last upon the prize it had reached for so long.

The Lord will judge, his wife had said; but who was to know for sure but what the Lord wanted him to have the prize? Maybe, in the way things had of working themselves out in fashions men did not expect and could not foresee, that was the decision he was supposed to make.

Possibly God wanted him to be President . . . or possibly, of course, He did not.

It seemed to him then, as the final moments of indecision gripped his heart and roused anew the turmoil in his mind, that somewhere, somehow, in all this great universe, there must be some sign that would tell him what to do. But it did not come, he could not find it anywhere. All he saw was the clear spring evening, the great Capitol, the town where Power and Ambition lived and worked and had their way with men. All that came to him in that time of ultimate clarification of his life were voices: a wistful boy said, "I suppose that's a sign of lots of friends, when you have three nicknames"; another, brash and confident, said, "I think I'll run for the state Senate;" yet another said, "Governor, I hope you will be with me," and a little later, in that horrible hour, "I suppose you're like all the rest! I thought I could count on your integrity, but I guess that wouldn't fix you up so well, would it?" And more immediately, other voices said: "It has been my observation that when a man deserts something he basically and fundamentally believes in, he loses something inside. Yes, sir, he loses something inside." And, "Whether you'd want to keep on living with Orrin Knox if you got it on a bargain of that kind, that, too, I don't know." And, "Orrin Knox has lived in a certain way and come to mean certain things to his country and his time. He has to decide now whether he wants to mean something else. It's as simple as that."

But I want to be President, his heart cried out in bitterness. I have such great things in me for my people and my country; I want the chance to do them, I want to save this blundering, helpless, goodhearted nation that is fundamentally too decent to know how to deal with the ring of sharpies who encircle her, some with the face of enemies, and some with the face of friends. I want to do what I know I can for her. I want to help her find the way.

He realized with a start that he must have spoken half aloud, for a pair of tourists whose approach he had not even heard had paused and were watching him curiously nearby. He managed a smile and a firm, "Good evening," and after a moment they said, "Good evening, Senator," in a reserved and curious tone and walked slowly away, murmuring to one another. Don't you see, he felt like crying out, I am deciding whether or not to be President and you must not wonder about my strange noises. This is an agony not many know, and you must forgive me if I do not keep it entirely under control.

But he must, he realized; he must. It would soon be ten o'clock, and he had promised Powell Hanson, knowing even as he did so that he was also promising himself, to have an answer by that time. It was not something that had to be prolonged, after all: an offer like this came like a thunderclap and like a thunderclap it would go away, and only the echo would rumble a little in his own heart, and then in the passage of time the heart would come to rest and even the echo would at last be gone. He

did not need hours to decide about the Presidency, when he had contemplated it so long; nor, in truth, did he need hours to decide about
Orrin Knox, with whom he had lived for fifty-eight years, and with whom
he must continue to live until it pleased Providence to call him home.

But oh, he did not want to do what he was about to do. Knowing as he
did that he had no real choice, still he was not ready for the rending
pain that struck his heart as he prepared to turn and go up the long
steps and back to the forum where the whole world watched his actions.
Now he would never be President, for his opponent would never forgive
him, he would do everything he could, and it was quite enough, to defeat
him in the convention. Never again would Orrin Knox come even close
to the goal he had always sought. All the things he might have done,
vanished; all the contributions he might have made, possible in that office
as in no other, lost beyond recovery; all his hopes and plans and dreams,
forever at an end.

And why? Because two men, equally strong, equally ambitious, had
come to their final meeting over an issue that both regarded as fearfully
vital to the country; and because both, he was finally charitable enough
to perceive, were completely sincere in their approaches to it. The President, this time, was being completely honest in his attitude toward the
nomination, and also, strange as it might seem, toward the Senator's
potential candidacy. He was offering a bargain, but Orrin did not think
so little of him but what he knew that the bargain would not have been
offered if the President did not feel in his own mind that the result of it
would be good for the country. For he, too, in the ironic way of Washington, which so easily turned the dreams and plans and basic convictions of
men back upon themselves, carried in his heart a vision of the country and
what he could do for it every bit as sincere and all-dominating and all-
consuming as the Senator's own.

But this could not weigh with the Senator. He could not change his
own views, nor could he modify himself, however great the personal
advantage might be, when the consequence the President sought was
something he so greatly disapproved. There was no possible compromise
left for him and his opponent, and actually there never had been. They
were met upon a ground where all men in government ultimately stood
to be judged, the ground of what was best for the nation, and no more
than the President could he retreat an inch from his own position. The
President had not been without precedent in trying to persuade him,
for some men might yield; but Orrin was not some men. "Well," he had
said tartly: "I am as I am." And so he was, and that concluded the argument.

He turned away from the city below in a slow and reluctant and painful
fashion as though he were giving up the whole meaning of his life, as he
thought in a very real sense he was, and faced the Capitol.

The great dome loomed above him against the deepening sky, shimmering, perfect, white and pure, over the city, over the nation, over the world. On the Senate side the flag slapped lazily in a gentle breeze. Utter peace, utter serenity, lay upon the Hill.

Surprising and sudden, tears came into his eyes.

O America, he thought, and it was like a crying in his heart: *O America!* Why do you suffer us your people, who are such fools, and what have we done to deserve you?

Then he shook his head with a quick, impatient movement and strode firmly up the long flight of steps to keep his date with Robert A. Leffingwell.

7

On the morning of the day of Bob Leffingwell's defeat the major supporters of his cause went all out in one last hysterical insistence to the Senate that it overlook his shortcomings, uphold his general record, and confirm him. Although there was some falling-away, there were still quite a few vigorous editorials demanding his approval; several early-morning television programs managed to work in several plugs for him; there were statements by prominent citizens issued over the radio, special commentaries were put on the air, full-page ads by something known as "Citizens for Leffingwell" appeared in major cities over the land; and lending the inevitable final touch, a noisy line of picketers marched back and forth in front of the Capitol until the cops hustled them away shouting sarcastic comments to the passersby and carrying placards reading, "We Need Leffingwell, The Man of Peace!" and "You Talk Peace—*Vote* Peace!" and, "What Now, Little Men? Leffingwell and Peace? Or WAR?"

In the office buildings of the Senate, too, the final drive was on, telegrams, special-delivery letters, and last-minute telephone calls were flooding in, final talks and conferences were being held. An air of excitement pervaded the Hill, made greater by the news that Moscow, quite possibly with an eye to the Senate's scheduled meeting at noon, had now confirmed that its broadcast would be received in the United States at twelve-thirty Eastern standard time. REDS SAY MESSAGE MAY DECIDE FATE OF WORLD, the headlines read; SENATE TO VOTE TONIGHT ON LEFFINGWELL. It was a combination of dramatic tensions to rank with the best to be found in the history of a capital that had known many of them.

Busy at his desk, reading the angry analyses of his speech last night, impatiently scanning the concluding personal attacks and the last spiteful smears, the senior Senator from Illinois paused long enough to tend to two personal matters before going to Seab's office for a final strategy conference. The first was to call the National Chairman and say to that embarrassed and uneasy gentleman, who now thought himself to be caught in a bind between two imperious personalities, that he wasn't. Orrin had found he would be tied up next week, he said, it would be impossible for him to speak to the National Committee, much as he appreciated the invitation, so many thanks and perhaps some other time. The National Chairman's relief was so fervent as to be almost maudlin, for most of his night had been spent amongst uneasy visions of an angry President breathing fire on one side and an angry Senator breathing fire on the other. "Thank you, Orrin," he said earnestly as their brief conversation concluded. "Thanks a million. You're a real prince, boy." "Just call me Prince, Jim," Orrin suggested dryly. "As in, 'Sick-'em, Prince!'" But this was too deep for the National Chairman and he said good-by with an uncertain laugh and reiterated fervent thanks.

That done, the Senator called the White House, and when the operator, who was politically hep as anybody, had put him through to his objective with a surprised and knowing, "Why, yes, Senator!" he spoke without preliminaries of protocol.

"I have a message for you," he said. "In writing. I'll have my administrative assistant deliver it in fifteen minutes if you will arrange to have him admitted at the West Gate."

"I will," the President said in an expressionless voice.

"Thank you," the Senator said in the same tone, and hung up.

He picked up the handwritten statement on White House stationery and looked at it for a long time; for it was indeed, as they had all assured him, a most historic document and neither he nor any other man, in all probability, would ever see its like again. He thought of his wife's suggestion that he give it to the Smithsonian, and suddenly he grinned. Then without adding an enclosure to it or commenting upon it in any way, he refolded it neatly, slipped it into an envelope, sealed it, and wrote, "The President" in a firm hand which he underscored with a heavy black line that looked as emphatic as he felt.

"Art," he said into the intercom, "I have something here I want you to deliver personally to the President for me. Right now."

And with a shiver of his shoulders as though he were finally freeing them of the last of a heavy burden, he rose and carried the envelope to the outer office and his waiting messenger.

"I wonder," AP said thoughtfully at the press table in the restaurant where the usual ten o'clock coffee crowd was gathered, "whether this would have worked out any differently if Leffingwell had been honest with the committee at the start."

"Oh, I think so," the Newark News said. "I think so. I don't think he would have had any trouble."

"With Cooley and Knox on his trail?" UPI asked skeptically.

"Knox wasn't, at first," the Times pointed out, "and Seab could have been overcome, easy enough."

"Well, not so easy, maybe," the Philadelphia *Inquirer* said, "but it could have been done."

"There comes a time for most clever men in this town when they get too clever, particularly when they deal with the Senate," the *Herald Tribune* remarked philosophically. "The Senate doesn't like it."

"I see some of the boys aren't giving up, though," the Chicago *Tribune* observed. "There are still some editorials for him, regardless."

"Well, maybe the Russians will have a diversion for us," the Detroit *News* suggested.

"Apparently," UPI said. "We got off a moon shot ourselves this morning, didn't we? The Cape's been closed off completely since yesterday afternoon, and something awfully big went up this morning."

"Yes," AP said. "I understand from the office everybody's under a strict ban of secrecy, and we're supposed to expect big things."

"Everything's big these days," the Atlanta *Constitution* said humorously. "How do we all stand the gaff?"

"By not having time to stop and wonder how we do it, I imagine," *Newsweek* said.

"I know," AP agreed. "We shouldn't be here right now, as a matter of fact. We ought to be over at Seab's office, where they're deciding how many pieces to cut Leffingwell into."

"If I thought there was news in it, I'd go," UPI said, "but it was all decided last night, really."

"I just can't quite believe they'll completely ignore the President's wishes," the Newark *News* said. "I still can't feel it's really over."

"If I may quote from the not-so-honorable Douglas Brady Bliss of North Carolina," UPI said, flipping through his notes, "'The only question now is the size of the vote.'"

"I wonder who he'll appoint instead?" the Philadelphia *Inquirer* remarked.

The AP grinned.

"Let's not worry about that now," he said. "That's tomorrow's story."

In Senator Cooley's office they heard their last from the principal backer of the nominee shortly before noon when the White House switchboard tracked down the Majority Leader there.

"Bob," the President said, "who else is at your meeting?"

"Several people," Senator Munson said.

"Will you tell them for me," the President said, "that I shall make no further communication to the Senate on this nomination, but I want them to know that I regard it, in absolute seriousness, as being absolutely vital to the welfare of the nation. I have never been more serious about anything. I would regard it as a calamity for the world if he were not confirmed."

"I'll tell them," the Majority Leader said, "but I don't think they'll listen."

"But, God damn it, I may be beaten on this!" the President said angrily, and Senator Munson smiled with a certain grimness as he answered.

"Yes, Mr. President," he said, "*this* time, something may happen to you . . . You know," he remarked thoughtfully as he turned away from the phone, "I expect this is the first time in his life that he's actually been able to grasp that idea."

"It's just about the first time he's ever had to," Stanley Danta said. And he added, half in jest but half-seriously, too, "I hope it doesn't kill him."

"Standing by itself, I don't think it would," the Majority Leader said soberly. "Combined with the Russians, I don't know—"

"I'm going to help him with the Russians," Senator Knox remarked and they all looked surprised. He shrugged.

"It's a different matter," he said.

And half an hour later on the floor, when a nearly full Senate had met in sober concern, not only about the nomination but about the impending Soviet announcement, he began to keep his word.

After Carney Birch's somber prayer, filled with foreboding and exhortations to stand steadfast, and after the Majority Leader had announced that because of the great interest in the Russian broadcast the Senate would stand in informal recess until 1:15 so that they all might listen, the Senator from Illinois obtained the floor.

"Mr. President," he said, "before the Senate recesses I should like to announce, for the information of Senators if they are interested, that immediately after we reconvene I shall make a statement in response to the broadcast, whatever it may be.

"I do this," he said, while they all listened attentively, "at the express request of the President of the United States, who asked me to do so at our meeting yesterday." And to their startled looks he said firmly, "He feels, and I agree with him, that this event will be of such a nature that there should be an immediate reply from the Congress to go with his own reply, which will be made at eight o'clock tonight. I shall of course not wish to pre-empt the right of anyone else to make a statement too, but since he asked me and I promised I would, I thought I should inform the Senate."

"Now, what the hell does that mean?" the *Christian Science Monitor* asked the Houston *Press* in the press gallery above. The Houston *Press* shook his head. "Damned if I know," he said. "It looks to me as though Orrin is patting him on the head at the same time he's kicking him in the tail." "That's known as statesmanship," the *Times* remarked with a grin. "Right now," the Washington *Evening Star* said as the chamber began to empty, "I'm not interested. All I want to do is listen to that broadcast." "Bob told me they have a couple of radios set up in the Senators' lobby and we're welcome to come down if we want to." "We want to," the Providence *Journal* said. "Let's go."

And so it was that the Senate gathered, and the press gathered, and the government gathered, and out across the land the country gathered, and around the globe the world gathered, to a turning point in time that most of them knew, instinctively, had always been destined to come. If it had not come over this, it would have come over something else, for sooner or later it had to come. The game of leapfrog played for so long by the United States and the Soviet Union inevitably had to reach a point where one party or the other would grow impatient; and since the Russians were better equipped, by temperament, by government, and by ambition, to be impatient, it was only natural that they, having made a great new leap, should finally move to bring things to a head and take advantage of it if they could.

But in few places of the world at that hour were sane men truly glad of this, and for most it was a thing of great foreboding. They were silent and grim in the Senators' lobby, in the House, in all the government departments downtown, in homes and drugstores and bars and public places over the land, on all the great continents and all the broad seas where those who had some regard for human kindness and human decency contemplated the possibilities lying in the latest triumph of those who did not. A hush held the world as Moscow Radio came on the air promptly at twelve-thirty EST and an announcer said, in a strong voice:

"Peoples of the nations, we take you to the moon."

This was followed seriatim by translations into Chinese, French, Spanish, and, finally and deliberately last, English.

This in turn was followed by a silence that lasted for several minutes while the tension rose everywhere and in Moscow somebody suddenly gave an exclamation, obviously of impatience, that echoed harshly around the world. But then the silence began to be punctuated by uneasy cracklings and weird howlings—sounding rather, some thought with shivers, like all the demons of time let loose—and again in Moscow someone said, "*Da!*" in a tone of great excitement and satisfaction.

And distant, lonely, broken, and interrupted frequently by terrific static and the darting atoms of the cosmic winds, yet still bearing resemblance to human sound, there came over 245,000 miles the first words spoken by man to man across the depths of space. They were not, characteristically, loving.

"We wish to report," they said, while the winds rushed and the furies howled, "that representatives of the Union of Soviet Socialist Republics have established a successful permanent base on the moon, which we claim for the Union of Soviet Socialist Republics and for all the peace-loving peoples associated with the U.S.S.R.

"Everything went well on our journey. We are in good health and preparations are now under way for a return of part of our party to Earth.

"A base party has been established and will remain, equipped to repel capitalist imperialist invaders should any be so foolhardy as to attempt a landing on the moon.

"All hail the peoples' peace!"

The words stopped and for several more minutes only the crackling static from the void was heard on Earth before the Moscow signal abruptly cut off, and excited announcers, some coherent, some babbling, some on the verge of tears, told the nations that the first communication from the skies was over.

What was needed most after that was a strong dash of cold water, and that, as he arose to speak in the tense chamber ten minutes later, was what the senior Senator from Illinois proposed to provide.

"Mr. President," he began slowly, looking thoughtfully about the room, "I see before me Senators of the United States, seated in the Senate of the United States, here in this great Capitol of the United States, with our sister house of the Congress just across the way and all around us the great symbols of our heritage and our purpose and our future. And I ask myself, and I put to you these questions:

"Are these things suddenly turned to nothing in half an hour's time?

"Are a few words from the moon sufficient to erase all we have stood for and all we are?

"Should we who have done so much, and have so much, and have yet before us such great tasks for ourselves and for all humankind, be struck dumb and paralyzed because we have been temporarily bested in our continuing contest with the Soviet Union?

"Does this suddenly cancel everything that America is?

"Mr. President," he said quietly, "I cannot believe it. I know not how others feel, but I know how I feel.

"There are certain things in this life that are still valid, and will always be.

"There are ways of dealing with other people which are just and honest and honorable and decent; and these have not been changed.

"There are standards of character and of integrity which honorable men, while they may not always achieve them, at least have before them for their goal; and these have not been changed.

"There is human good will and loving-kindness and tolerance towards one's fellow man in all his shortcomings, whatever they may be and bearing in mind one's own; and these have not been changed.

"There is a great nation and a great people and a great mission of liberty and freedom and justice for all, coming out of the past and moving on gloriously into the future, insofar as God helps us to achieve it; and neither have these been changed.

"Nothing of the essentials of the human heart or the human character or the human story as good men see it have been changed.

"Senators," he said softly, and in the utter silence there was a powerful emotion in his voice that powerfully moved them all, "I commend to you your country: a very great nation, which has a job to do.

"Let us get on with it!"

And he sat down, and for a moment the silence continued. Then the chamber burst into a roar of approving sound, and Senators began hurrying from all sides to his desk to shake his hand, and the press rushed out to file their stories, and in the mind of the Vice President as he blew his nose and then tried rather futilely to gavel for order an idea began to grow.

A little later, as Senator Knox passed his desk, he took the first step toward putting it in operation.

"Orrin," he said, shaking hands, "that was wonderful. Just wonderful."

"Well, thank you, Harley," Orrin said with a pleased smile. "I meant every word of it."

"That was part of what made it wonderful," the Vice President said. "I was just wondering if you would like to join me in my office at three-thirty? Howie has an appointment set up with me for Tashikov and Khaleel and Claude and Raoul, and I thought possibly you would like to sit in on it with me."

Senator Knox looked very pleased.

"Why, Harley," he said, "I'd be delighted to." He chuckled. "Maybe we can set friend Vasily back on his heels a little."

"I hope so," the Vice President said, "because I'm quite sure he'll be insufferable."

But how insufferable they did not at that moment know, though a little later they could begin to suspect. For at 3 P.M. sharp further word came from Moscow. It was addressed to the President of the United States and broadcast in all languages; and so cold and forbidding was its tone that men lifted up a little by Orrin's speech were once again cast down.

To the President it said tersely:

Excellency:

I have the honor to inform you that the premier of the Union of Soviet Socialist Republics and the chairman of the central presidium of the Communist Party, U.S.S.R., together with other peoples' representatives of the U.S.S.R., will arrive in Geneva at 1200 hours Saturday to confer with you and such representatives of the United States of America as you may wish to have with you.

We are sure you will understand the vital importance of this meeting to the future of the United States.

Varanov

They were not, as the *Times* remarked with a sigh to the *Herald Tribune*, out of the woods yet.

In the Vice President's office just off the floor half an hour later, however, one would never have known it, for neither he nor the Secretary of State nor the senior Senator from Illinois seemed anything but calm and unperturbed when their distinguished visitors were shown in. If anything it was the Ambassadors whose feelings were apparent, for Vasily Tashikov could not conceal an obvious air of triumph, K.K. looked white and worried, and even the British and French Ambassadors were in the grip of a concern they could not quite conceal. In this situation, Senator Knox and Secretary Sheppard noted with surprise and a growing respect neither had believed possible, that the Vice President acted as though he had been meeting crises all his life; either that, or perhaps had made up his mind finally that he was going to have to be meeting them from now on.

Whatever the reason, he stepped forward with a bland air and a firm handshake to greet each of them in turn, ignoring the Soviet Ambassador's triumphant aspect and the worried looks of the others, gesturing them easily to chairs and then taking his own behind the big desk on which he had caused to be placed several manila folders bulging with papers. Through these he went for a last look while they waited, riffling through them slowly, shaking his head a little here, nodding it a little there, exclaiming softly once or twice to himself, while the silence lengthened and his visitors began to look decidedly fidgety. Finally with a deliberation that both Orrin and Howie applauded silently inside, he put the folders by and leaned forward with a cordial but appraising air.

"Now, gentlemen," he said calmly, "what can I do for you? The Secretary tells me you wanted to see me." He looked at them pleasantly and suddenly focused on the Soviet Ambassador. "Why?"

The abrupt challenge seemed to take Vasily Tashikov aback for a brief second, and he permitted himself an expression of surprise. Then he shrugged.

"It seemed a necessary courtesy," he said. "We had not met and I thought it would be helpful to my country to know you."

"I think that is nice," the Vice President said, and his tone was so noncommittal that they could not tell what it held. "I wish," he added gravely, "to congratulate your country upon its latest scientific achievement. It is a great triumph and a great inspiration to us."

"How is that?" the Ambassador asked quickly. "As I understand your use of the expression 'inspiration to us,' it means that one is inspired to do the same thing."

"That is very true," Harley said.

"But did you not hear our broadcast?" the Ambassador asked sharply.

"I am sure everyone on earth, more or less, heard your broadcast," the Vice President said.

"We said we would repel any invaders who attempted to land on the moon," Tashikov said flatly. Senator Knox snorted.

"Did you hear about my speech?" he asked. The Ambassador shook his head, though they all knew he must have.

"I said go to hell," Orrin said. "And," he added, "you understand my use of the expression."

The Russian Ambassador lost for a moment his air of careful calm and seemed about to make some sharp rejoinder. The Indian Ambassador held up a hand in nervous placation.

"Well, now," he said quickly, "I do think that gentlemen should try to remain courteous and pleasant with one another when things are on this—this high level. My government does hope everyone will continue to deal with one another kindly and with a full awareness of all those things which—which hang in the balance."

"Thank you, K.K.," Senator Knox said dryly. "It is always good to have you around to keep everybody well mannered."

"We have found," Krishna Khaleel said with the same nervous politeness, "that sometimes good manners are a barrier against—other things."

"They are," Lord Maudulayne agreed, "if they are based upon good will. Whether they are in this instance, my government is not sure. Indeed, on the basis of the evidence we have received so far today, they are not."

"What do you propose to do about it?" the Soviet Ambassador asked bluntly, and Claude Maudulayne shrugged.

"We propose to wait just a little longer, and see," he said. "Although your kind invitation to Geneva did not include Her Majesty's Government, I feel Her Majesty's Government will not be entirely unconcerned with what may go on there."

"If anything does," Raoul Barre suggested. "If the Americans accept."

"They will accept," Vasily Tashikov said coldly. "They will accept if they are not utter fools."

"Mr. Ambassador," Harley said quietly, "you will speak with proper respect for the United States or you will leave my office at once."

The Soviet Ambassador turned on his sudden smile that the press made so much of, the smile that hovered around the lips and never reached the eyes.

"Well, Excellency," he said, "you know how it is when one has just won a great victory. One is sometimes a little ruthless toward the delicacies of diplomatic conduct. I would not wish to indicate that I did not respect the United States as a second-cla—— As a power occupying the international status which she does occupy."

"What would you people do," Harley Hudson asked suddenly, "if I became President, recognized Red China, gave them a billion-dollar loan and started doing everything I could to divide the two of you?"

For just a second an expression of quite genuine alarm crossed the Soviet Ambassador's face. It was followed quickly by another smile.

"Such precipitous action," he said smoothly, "would hardly be character-istic of the great democracy which controls the free world."

"Who knows?" the Vice President demanded, and he smiled too, look-ing like the amiable, easygoing Harley they had always known but with a sudden edge to him that was new to his friends. "Who knows," he repeated softly, "what I would do if I were President of the United States? There isn't a man in this entire world—perhaps I should say, now, entire universe—who knows what I would do, except the man who sits right here. So watch out, Mr. Ambassador. Watch out! The future might not be as simple as you think."

Vasily Tashikov stared at him for several minutes until Harley, staring impassively back, made him lower his eyes.

"Yes," he agreed. "We do not know. That is why my government wanted me to meet you, so that we might perhaps find out."

"Well," Harley said in a pleasant voice, "now that you've been given a little taste, I trust you will enjoy analyzing it."

"You cannot bluff us!" Tashikov said in sudden anger, and Krishna Khaleel sucked in his breath with a sharp sound. The Secretary of State sat forward calmly.

"Nor you us, Mr. Tashikov," he said quietly. "So there we are."

"There you have always been!" the Indian Ambassador remarked brightly "Is it not so?"

The French Ambassador made a little gesture, one of those things that made people say, "So French!" because, of course, it was French.

"How many times," he said, "has our dear colleague from the great subcontinent restored amicability and reason to heated discussions. How many times has that significant and commanding hisssss (and he pro-longed it for a moment) brought us up short when passions were running away! . . . As for my government," he said dryly, "we are impressed by the achievement of the Soviet Government, but we are no more afraid of her, and no more inclined to submit ourselves to her blackmail, than we were before. And that was not at all."

"We are losing the subject of the visit," the Soviet Ambassador said harshly. "We came here to talk to the President."

"I'm not the President," Harley Hudson said pleasantly, "but I know he feels the same way, and will tell the world so when he speaks tonight."

"Do you not think, Mr. Vice President," the Soviet Ambassador asked softly, "of the enormous and fearsome responsibilities which some fluke of fate or nature might put suddenly in your hands? Do you not wonder how you would deal with all these vast problems that confront your country as she tries without success to match the progress of the U.S.S.R.? Do you not feel some doubts about your abilities to handle them?"

"I certainly do," Harley Hudson said with an agreeable laugh. "But," he added, "many a man has become President feeling doubts about his ability to handle his problems. They've all managed somehow, some

better than others but they've all done it, and we've gotten along. I dare
say we would get along under me. What was your suggestion, Mr. Ambassador," he asked suddenly, "that you be allowed to appoint a regent
for me if the situation should arise?"

The Soviet Ambassador looked slightly off balance—in fact, Orrin
thought with some admiration, Harley seemed to have kept him there
pretty much all through the conversation—and made a gesture of protest
and denial.

"Oh, of course, Mr. Vice President," he said, "of course I do not suggest
anything so fantastic. But these are serious times for your country. And
now that the U.S.S.R. has achieved this great victory, they are even more
serious."

"Victories can be matched," Harley said bluntly, and Senator Knox
decided the President must have told him too, an unusual sign of confidence that made him wonder for a sharp second about the President's
own judgment of his health on this climactic day.

"Not always," Vasily Tashikov said quietly. "No, Mr. Vice President,
not always."

"Well," Harley said. "In any event. Obviously the United States is not
frightened, so if that was the initial aim, it has failed."

"Lack of fright can sometimes come from ignorance as well as bravery,"
the Soviet Ambassador said sharply, and the three Americans started to
react in unison so angrily that Lord Maudulayne decided it was time to
speak up in his best drawl.

"I *say*, old boy!" he said, sounding as though the whole Commonwealth
and Empire were suddenly looking down its collective nose at this little
urchin before him. Raoul Barre came in on cue with a laugh to ease the
tension.

"Good old Claude," he said affectionately. "You know, I sometimes think
that on the Day of Judgment, when the last bomb has fallen and the
last trump has sounded, and our gracious friends in the Kremlin have
finally had their way with civilization, and there are ten people left living
on the earth—that suddenly one of them will speak up and he will say,
'I *say*, old boy!' in just that tone of voice. And automatically all the rest
will feel inferior."

The others laughed, but the Soviet Ambassador suddenly looked terribly angry.

"That is ridiculous!" he said. "There will be no such day. There will
be no bombs falling. There will not be ten people left. And certainly,"
he concluded spitefully, "one of them will not be English!"

Lord Maudulayne smiled blandly.

"I should hope, old boy," he said, "that they all were."

"Well," the Vice President said with a businesslike air, "I feel that we
all have much to do, and must not prolong this conversation too long.
I hope Mr. Tashikov may have received the idea that the Vice President

of the United States is not inhibited by the Soviet Union's latest achievement. And the rest of you, too, if that was why you came here."

"We wished," Krishna Khaleel said politely, "to talk to your Excellency, whom we had not seen intimately in Washington——"

"I'm modest," Harley Hudson said dryly. "I'm the kind they list under the statement, 'His Vice President was——'"

"Well," K.K. said uncertainly, "we wished to know you and have you know us, in case—in case events developed as—as there is some thought they might."

"I thank you, Mr. Ambassador," the Vice President said calmly. "Let us all hope these events do not develop. As for those events which have developed, the events which the Soviet Union has precipitated and is trying to precipitate, let me make my position clear once more to take back to your governments.

"I am fully in accord with the policies of the President. If I were unhappily to succeed him, a possibility that cannot entirely be ignored in all our plans, my only change, if any, would be to strengthen them insofar as the Soviet Union is concerned. In this," he said, looking questioningly at Senator Knox, "I believe I would have the support of the Senate——?"

"You would, Mr. Vice President," Orrin said firmly. "The Senate has been impatient for a long time that the leadership wasn't strong enough, I believe. We would back you in everything you wanted to do. I think I can give that assurance."

"Even in China?" Lord Maudulayne asked, and the Vice President took back the conversation with a friendly smile.

"I would not be entirely sure where I stand on China, if I were you," he said. "As I said earlier, it is just something for Mr. Tashikov to consider. I might do that or I might not. I will let Mr. Tashikov and his government find out, if it should come to that. But even there," he said, and he looked challengingly at the Senator from Illinois, "I should expect to have the support of the Senate. Would I?"

Orrin hesitated for a moment, because quite suddenly they all realized that the Vice President was not fooling, that this was a fundamental and calculated step he was taking to fortify himself in case events moved toward his accession. This was, should it turn out to be so, the start of a new Administration, right here and now.

And because under the circumstances as Harley had arranged them there was only one answer he could give, the Senator from Illinois decided to give it decisively and without quibble.

"The Senate will support you in whatever you deem best," he said firmly. "And that includes China and anything else you may wish to do."

"Well, then," Harley said comfortably, "I guess I don't need to worry, whatever the future may bring."

There was a little pause while they digested the implications of this, and then the Indian Ambassador spoke abruptly.

"If I may ask," he said, "what is the fate of Mr. Leffingwell to be?"

"The fate of Mr. Leffingwell," Orrin said shortly, "is to be defeated."

"This is your final decision?" the Soviet Ambassador asked, and the Senator from Illinois looked at him with distaste.

"You don't know much about us, do you?" he said. "This isn't my decision. It's the Senate's decision."

"I know enough about you," Vasily Tashikov said dryly, "to know that at this moment you *are* the Senate."

"Must he be defeated?" Krishna Khaleel asked regretfully. "My government was so hoping—we had so counted——"

"Yes," Senator Knox said. "Well. Your government, I regret to say, will have to make other plans. Mr. Leffingwell will be defeated."

"It is not wise," Tashikov said thoughtfully. "He is our friend. You will need a friend of ours in that office. It is not wise."

The Secretary of State made an impatient movement.

"Mr. Ambassador," he asked, "haven't you learned that you really can't name the American Secretary of State, no matter how hard you try? Surely you've discovered that with me."

"At least," the Soviet Ambassador said spitefully, "it will no longer be you. At least we can be happy about that much!"

"I don't regret a single thing I've done to stop you," Secretary Sheppard said flatly. "I'd do it all again tomorrow, and I hope my successor, whoever he may be, will do the same."

"It will not be possible," the Soviet Ambassador said smugly, "for this is no longer the world in which you were Secretary of State. This is a new world which began at 12:30 P.M. Eastern standard time."

The Vice President smiled.

"Just possibly the world will not agree with you on that, Mr. Ambassador," he said. "Maybe our clocks are still running on the old time. We shall have to see." He stood and they perforce did the same. He held out his hand.

"Mr. Tashikov," he said, "an enlightening visit. My congratulations again to your country on her marvelous accomplishment which we hope," he said with a little twinkle, "to be inspired to equal. You can tell your government, I think, that whatever happens the United States will still have a President." He smiled in a kindly way. "That was what you came here to find out, wasn't it?"

"I shall tell my government of our interesting conversation," the Soviet Ambassador said without replying to the question.

"All of it," the Vice President suggested, and the Ambassador scowled.

"Of course, all of it," he said. The automatic smile broke forth about the lips.

"I shall tell them," he said, almost waggishly, "that we must watch you closely."

The Vice President gave a perfectly relaxed and untroubled laugh.

"Everybody will!" he said, and it struck them that he didn't sound in the least worried by the prospect.

"Mr. Khaleel," he said, "it was nice to see you. Stop up again, when you have the chance, and we will talk some more. I am sure your ancient country has much to give this new and growing one of ours."

"Yes," K.K. said, sounding flattered. "I should like that."

"Claude and Raoul," Harley said, holding out a hand to each, "it is always good to see old friends. Perhaps you too will make a habit of coming round."

"Thank you, Mr. Vice President," Raoul said, and with a sudden disdain he looked at his colleague from the U.S.S.R. "If you need assistance at Geneva—or anywhere—I think my government will be quite disposed to provide it. And this," he added, "in spite of men in the moon and other hobgoblins of our happy and enlightened century."

The Vice President laughed.

"Now you are making Mr. Tashikov unhappy," he said. "He has stopped smiling."

The Soviet Ambassador turned back at the door.

"You are fools," he said in sudden anger. "All you westerners are fools. You are dead, but you do not know it."

Lord Maudulayne smiled.

"My dear fellow," he said with a note of impatience, "my country has been dead innumerable times in the past thousand years and hasn't known it. That's why we're here today." And suddenly he didn't sound diplomatic at all, but angry in his turn with an emotion they had never seen him display. "And now get along," he said, spitting the words out. "Just get along. I for one am sick to death of the sight and the sound of you. So get on, and be quick about it!"

And before the Soviet Ambassador, suddenly livid, could speak, he had turned his back upon him and held out his hand a final time to Harley.

"Mr. Vice President," he said quietly, "God bless you." The diplomat's mask came back and he smiled at the French Ambassador. "Come along, Raoul," he said. "I think Celestine and Kitty want to attend the session tonight, and I expect we'd better get on home and see about getting some dinner first."

And taking his colleague firmly by the arm he brushed past the Soviet Ambassador without a glance; and after a moment, while the Indian Ambassador fluttered and twittered nervously about him, Tashikov too with some obvious struggle regained his professional composure and trailed by his worried colleague stomped out through the reception room to the elevator, and his waiting limousine.

After they had gone there was silence for a little while as the Vice President and his friends looked at one another. Presently the Vice President began to laugh and they joined him, not sure why, at first, but after a moment quite genuinely amused.

"I thought the Crimean War was going to start all over again," Harley said finally. Howie Sheppard smiled.

"I don't think we need to worry about our friends supporting us, whatever befalls," he said. The Vice President nodded.

"It's good to know," he said thoughtfully. He paused and shot a look at the Senator from Illinois.

"Well, Orrin," he said. "How did I do?"

Orrin smiled, started to answer lightly, and then found that he was suddenly quite serious.

"I'm proud of you," he said; and because he was surprised to find that he really was, he repeated it slowly; "I'm proud of you."

"Thank you," Harley said, and he looked rather proud of himself.

"I've got to get back to the floor," Orrin said, standing up abruptly. "Why don't you stick around, Howie? It ought to be interesting to see the windup."

Secretary Sheppard smiled in a tight-lipped way.

"Considering my personal feelings in the matter," he said, "I doubt if that would be seemly, would it? Anyway, the President wants me at the White House for his speech. What time are you planning the vote?"

The Senator from Illinois looked at the Vice President speculatively.

"I think it might be better, don't you," Harley said, "to wait until after he speaks?"

Orrin nodded.

"Yes, we ought to give him that much," he said. "It wouldn't look good to have to go on the air right after taking a licking from the Senate."

"You're quite sure under all the circumstances that it's right to make him take a licking?" Harley asked, and the Senator's jaw set.

"Yes," he said, "I am."

The Vice President nodded.

"All right," he said. "I just wanted to be sure you were sure."

Orrin Knox smiled without amusement.

"I'm sure," he said.

It was quite possible that when the President of the United States spoke at 8 P.M. his worldwide audience was even greater than that which had attended the Soviet broadcast earlier in the day. The world wanted to know how the United States intended to meet this challenge, and although the Voice of America had carried the full text of the speech by the Senator from Illinois on all wave lengths all afternoon, the final and definitive word of course had to come from the head of state. Promptly at eight the announcers said, "We take you now to the White House for a

special address by the President of the United States," on the screens the
presidential seal appeared, and in the lobbies and cloakrooms of the Senate, once more in temporary recess, as in all other places reachable by
air or channel around the world, men and women prepared to listen.
For the second time in eight hours a hush quite literally fell upon the
globe. Into it a man who looked so tired and strained that his countrymen
gasped in dismay spoke in a voice that sounded muffled and heavy in
the beginning but presently began to gather vigor as it continued.

"My countrymen:" he said, "peoples of the earth:

"I should tell you first that there departed Earth at 2:01 A.M. our time
a United States expedition to the moon. This launching was completely
successful, and all information received by our scientists indicates that
the expedition should reach objective sometime on Sunday.

"When it does," he said, and his voice began to pick up sarcasm and
strength, "there will be no pompous and pretentious claim that the United
States owns the moon. There will be a broadcast which will, we hope, give
some information on the fascinating new world now opening up to humanity, and there will be a sane recognition of the facts of life as they apply
to it.

"No nation owns the moon. And," he added coldly, "no nation ever
will own the moon. If mere man can be so arrogant as to say he 'owns'
that distant sphere, all nations will 'own' it, and they will own it jointly,
for the United States expedition is instructed to claim the moon for the
United Nations and to plant thereon the flag of the United Nations.

"I shall go to New York to formally certify this hegemony to the General Assembly of the United Nations."

"When?" the Majority Leader asked in the lobby, and somebody said,
"Shh!" tensely.

"So much," the President said, and he said it with scorn, "for the arrogant assertions of little men that they have 'claimed' the moon. And so
much for their hopes that they can intimidate the United States from
doing its duty for mankind.

"It will take more," he said, and by now his marvelous recuperative
powers were coming to his aid, he was looking much more vigorous and
much less strained, "than little men shouting in the vastness of the universe to block the forward progress of humanity.

"Our expedition will do what it has been instructed to do. In the unlikely event that it lands near the Soviet expedition, or has any contact
with it, it will continue to do as it has been instructed to do. I do not
anticipate that it will be interfered with. If it is," he said calmly, "it will
know how to deal with the situation.

"And now," he said, "let me turn to the courteous note which I received
this afternoon from the Soviet Government. This communication, couched
in typical friendly language, full of that genial co-operative attitude that
has long distinguished the Soviet Government in its dealings with other

governments which, unlike the Soviet Government, strive sincerely for the welfare of the world, invites me—indeed, it commands me—to be in Geneva on Saturday for a conference of unspecified nature with the Soviet Government.

"My own instinct is the same as that of the great Senator from Illinois, the Honorable Orrin Knox——"

"Flattery will get you nowhere," UPI whispered to the Cleveland *News*, "look at that face." The Cleveland *News* glanced across the lobby at Senator Knox and nodded with a grim little smile.

"—who," the President said, "in his great speech in the Senate this afternoon following the Soviet broadcast stated the unchangeable fact that the United States is not, and cannot be, frightened with such blatant threats. I hereby reaffirm that magnificent statement of American principle. It bespeaks my own views exactly."

He paused and reached for a glass of water. His hand trembled hardly at all, and Senator Knox paid silent tribute once more to the awesome will power of the man.

"Under ordinary circumstances," the President went on, "I should reject out of hand any such arrogant, discourteous, dastardly, and unprincipled message as that sent me by the Soviet Government." He paused and looked squarely into the cameras.

"I have given very serious consideration to such a course," he said. He paused again, long enough to raise the tension all over the world. When he deemed it sufficiently high he resumed.

"I have decided," he said, "insulting and unprincipled and despicable though this message is, to take another course. Even though the leaders of the war-mongering ruling clique of the Soviet Union——"

"Good for you!" Hal Fry said happily. "Give the bastards their own medicine!"

"—ignore their responsibilities to mankind, the President of the United States cannot. The President of the United States knows that his country wishes him to strive unceasingly for peace, and that all decent peoples everywhere wish him to do so. He knows that he will be judged by God, by humanity, and by history if he does not.

"Therefore," he said, "I shall go to Geneva. Not because the war-mongering ruling clique of the Soviet Union demands it, but because humanity and conscience and the cause of peace demand it. Because I feel a duty to mankind even if the war-mongering ruling clique of the Soviet Union does not. Because I desire, and my people desire, true peace even if the war-mongering ruling clique of the Soviet Union does not desire it.

"I shall not, however," he said, "be there on Saturday, for it will be impossible to complete preparations in so short a time. I, and my delegation, will be there on Monday.

"I wish to tell you that we will be bound by no rules of secrecy. This will be an open conference in which the United States will make everything known to the world. The Soviet Union pretends that in some way this conference will be decisive in world events. Very well, we shall see. We shall *all* see. The world will judge who is the war-monger and who the servant of peace.

"I pledge to humanity," he said, and in conclusion his head came up and his eyes gave their old, challenging look and he suddenly seemed to dominate the world, "the heart and mind, and if need be the blood and treasure, of the United States in the cause of peace.

"We shall see who profits from this childish exercise in arrogance put forth to us by Moscow!"

His face, strong and powerful and no longer looking tired, faded from the screen, the great seal of the Presidency came on again, and heavy and insistent the strains of "The Star-Spangled Banner" crashed around the globe.

The world did not see, and did not know that even before he rose from the desk he had paled suddenly again, and, looking around desperately for his doctor, had been helped from the room. But all the reporters and the visitors and the television newsmen and technicians saw, and in ten minutes' time the news was racing like wildfire over the town, in the Press Club, the newspaper bureaus, the press gallery and the Senate as its members streamed back to the floor for statements of approbation and support and the concluding hours of the matter of Robert A. Leffingwell.

And now they came at last, the Majority Leader thought, to that final, almost anti-climactic time when the final arguments were offered and the last words were said and the Senate could dispose of its pending business and get on to something else. Thirteen Senators had spoken yesterday afternoon and last night, another fifteen had spoken today; many others had interrupted with questions and comments clarifying their own positions. Raymond Robert Smith of California had made his views known in his indefinably willowy way; he was for the nominee. Tom Trummel of Indiana in his ponderous fashion had been against; Murfee Andrews and John Baker of Kentucky had openly joined Orrin's forces, Alec Chabot of Louisiana and Billy Canfield of Mississippi had fallen away. Magnus Hollingsworth of Wisconsin, small, neat, and precise, and Dick McIntyre of Idaho, small, loud, and bouncy, had had their say, and many another had spoken in the past forty-eight hours while other events moved on outside the Senate.

The debate had finally entered that rather sporadic, desultory, uninteresting last few hours which always preceded the concluding, climactic drive to the finish.

This was always the way with Senate debate: there were hours, days, sometimes weeks of preliminary skirmishing, formal statements of position, speeches for the record; the pace slackened, the Senate jogged along, members got caught up on other matters, tended to office routine, kept speaking engagements across the country, were busy on other things. Then the agreed time came and in a last flurry of controversy, sometimes very pointed and very sharp, the end came and the Senate moved on to something else and the process started all over again.

Not that this debate had been cut quite to the pattern of others; there had been factors that lifted it above them, made it more tense and more bitter, gave it a character of direct association with the fate of the country that only the most major Senate controversies had. This debate had acquired its own extraordinary character, compounded of the clash of great principles and great personalities. It would be a long time before the Senate, and the country too, forgot the nomination of Robert A. Leffingwell; many and many a future day's decisions, a future day's triumphs or failures, would go back to the complex of men, motives, and events that had swirled around this brilliant and ill-starred character.

What sort of Secretary of State he would have made, no one now would ever know; whether his rejection in the long unfolding of history would prove to be good or bad for his country, no one could ever say, for it would be only speculation what he might or might not have done, whether his actions would have affected in any way the fundamental course of events, whether he would have been help or hindrance to America. Now, the Majority Leader reflected, he would be completely removed from the direction of the nation's foreign policy; and for this his friends would be aggrieved and his enemies would be happy, and who could say, in the ultimate assessment of the record, which would have the more cause for their emotion?

He looked around the chamber, almost filled now, as the clerk moved toward the end of a quorum call, and at his desk Orrin impatiently waited for recognition. His eye fell on Orrin himself, looking firm and determined as always, victor at last in his long contest with the President, and on an issue that would hurt the President as few things could; he wondered if Orrin were really satisfied with his triumph, in his heart, and knowing Orrin he expected he probably was. He saw Seab, just entering down the main aisle, gesturing to the clerk to record his name on the tally, a lock of hair falling over one eye, a sleepy, satisfied expression on his face like a great old cat that was about to dine well: and so he would. And he saw, too, Stanley Danta, quiet and kind, Powell Hanson, who had earnestly tried to stem a tide he did not entirely in his inexperience understand; Arly Richardson, sardonic and shrewd, jaunty as ever even in the defeat of a cause for which he had not really, in his heart, fought so very hard; and Warren Strickland, neat and pleasant across the aisle, piloting the Minority smoothly into line behind the vigorous lead of the Senator from Illinois. And finally he saw, sitting uneasily in his seat far at the back, the symbol of the steady, inexorable continuance of the American Government, the new Senator from Utah, a doctor from Logan hastily appointed by the Governor yesterday immediately after Brig's interment in Salt Lake

City and rushed to Washington to be sworn in; one more vote against Leffingwell and a reminder of the grimness of this issue to help Orrin sap the President's powerful address of its effect insofar as it might be used by the nominee's few remaining supporters to bolster his cause.

And surveying all these men, and thinking about them and about this old Senate which he had known so long and loved so much, the senior Senator from Michigan could not find it in his heart to be so concerned about his country, when all was said and done. The system had its problems, and it wasn't exactly perfect, and there was at times much to be desired, and yet—on balance, admitting all its bad points and assessing all the good, there was a vigor and a vitality and a strength that nothing, he suspected, could ever quite overcome, however evil and crafty it might be. There was in this system the enormous vitality of free men, running their own government in their own way. If they were weak, at times, it was because they had the freedom to be weak; if they were strong, upon occasion, it was because they had the freedom to be strong; if they were indomitable, when the chips were down, it was because freedom made them so. He said a little prayer of thankfulness, sitting there at his desk in the United States Senate, to all the men and women back over the centuries who by their dreaming and their striving and their working and their dying had made it possible for their heirs to take with them into so dark and fearful a future so great and wonderful a gift and so strong and invincible an armor.

But now the quorum call was almost over, the clerk said, "Mr. Wannamaker! . . . Mr. Welch! . . . Mr. Whiteside! . . . Mr. Wilson!" with an air of finality. The Vice President declared the presence of a quorum, and Orrin Knox said, "Mr. President!" in a commanding voice.

"The Senator from Illinois," Harley said quietly, and on the floor and in the galleries silence descended as his countrymen gave him their sober and undivided attention.

"Mr. President," he said gravely, "let me say first that I associate myself, as in effect I did earlier, with the speech of the President. It was a magnificent speech, and one to which I know every American subscribes. We are not to be intimidated, Mr. President; no more are we to be beaten. We must all hope the men in the Kremlin will realize this fact once and for all; it will save the world a lot of time and save them from errors which well might be fatal for them."

His tone changed and became more businesslike.

"And so we return, Mr. President, to the pending business before the Senate. On this matter, many Senators have already spoken; all yesterday afternoon and evening, all day today except for the interruptions to hear the Soviet broadcast and the President's address, members have been stating their positions and their sentiments. Rarely in the history of the Senate, I think, has there been a matter to concern us so deeply; and though he comes here under tragic circumstances, the distinguished

junior Senator from Utah—successor," he said quietly, "to another who but
lately was in this body—I think will someday realize that he has been
privileged to join us in a truly historic moment. This will be looked back
upon as a major event, one of the few times when the Senate has rejected
a nominee to the Cabinet of the President of the United States; probably
the only time that it has ever rejected a nominee for Secretary of State.
History will wonder why, and the importance of the event will increase
from our reasons."

"Mr. President," Senator Richardson said, "will the Senator yield to me?
Does the Senator not think that——"

Senator Knox shook his head with an emphatic motion.

"Mr. President," he said, "virtually everything that can be said on this
subject has been said; virtually everything that can be thought has been
thought. I should like to make this brief summation of the position of
those of us who oppose the nominee, then let the distinguished Senator
from Arkansas summarize the position of those who favor him, and then
vote. It hardly seems to me that prolonged personal controversy now
would help the Senate or the country, and so I must respectfully decline
to yield at this time.

"Our reasons," he went on, "briefly, are these. There is, first, the personal
integrity of the nominee, which has shown itself in a lie direct to a subcommittee of the Foreign Relations Committee. There are those who
would attempt to dismiss this as a mere youthful peccadillo; so the event
itself may have been. The concealment of it under oath, however, was a
deliberate decision of maturity, and it is on that, I submit, that judgment
must be rendered. To me it casts a light upon the character of the nominee
so intense and so merciless that I do not see how any man could trust
him further; certainly not, it seems to me, with the foreign affairs of this
nation, beset as she has never been.

"There is, second, the philosophy of the nominee, entirely aside from
the episode in his past; his attitude toward the Soviet Union, toward the
world in which we live, toward the future we must try to achieve." He
paused and thoughtfully, rather absently, held up a copy of the nominee's
newly published book. "I do not know, Mr. President," he said, "whether
all Senators have yet read this interesting volume, but it merits perusal.
It is all of a piece with his testimony before the subcommittee. It is all of a
piece with the speeches he has been making around the country.

"It is the philosophy of a man who would, in effect, turn tail and run if
the defense of principle and policy created the risk of war with the Soviet
Union. Rather than stand firm, he would retreat; rather than pursue firm
policies that would ward off long-run defeat, he would compromise them
so severely that defeat would eventually be inevitable.

"This book," he said, "sets forth a program of flexibility so flexible as to
be flaccid. There is nowhere in it to be found the strength that was
apparent in the President's speech. There is nowhere in it the strength

which was apparent in mine. The President and I, I submit without false modesty——"

"No one," Jack McLaughlin of Georgia murmured to Bob Johnson of Connecticut with a chuckle, "could ever accuse Orrin of that."

"—draw our strength directly from the basic mood and the basic spirit of the American people. This book, and this man, do not.

"Accommodation here is projected to the point where it would come, I think it is fair to state, dangerously close to surrender. Compromise is carried to the point of capitulation. He does not say where he would stop this process. It can be argued, with ample evidence which he himself has provided, that he would not attempt to stop it, or would attempt to stop it so late that it very likely could not be stopped. This is a blueprint for adjustment which verges directly upon appeasement.

"I submit to you, Mr. President," he said, "that America cannot afford it. Only firmness will save us now. Only a steadfast adherence to principles we know to be sound, and an absolute and unhesitating willingness to die for them if need be, will rescue America from the plight which confronts her.

"Senators will say," he said, and his voice grew sarcastic, "as the press says and as the nominee himself said, 'Oh, then you want a war, Senator!' By God," he said, "I do not! But I know something that too many Americans, including this nominee, forget, and that is that unless we are prepared to accept the possibility of war and act fearlessly in defense of our principles in spite of it, then war will come as certainly as that clock above the Chair will presently strike the hour of twelve midnight.

"Either we are fearless and firm, or we will be nibbled away, paralyzed by our own fears which this man so suavely and smoothly reflects and expresses.

"Mr. President," he said quietly, "I am done. There are many reasons of my own why I oppose this nominee, and many of them are known to you. The overriding reasons, and the one I think the Senate should endorse, is the one I have just discussed. He is weak in a time when we need strength. We simply cannot afford him."

There was a burst of applause from the galleries as he sat down, instantly met by a wave of hisses, and the Vice President used the gavel vigorously.

"The Chair will advise visitors," he said sharply, "that they are here as guests of the Senate. They will be silent, or they will be removed."

"What's with Harley?" the St. Louis Post-Dispatch whispered to the Chicago Tribune. "He sounds almost presidential." "Maybe he's heard the word," the Chicago Tribune said with a rather grim chuckle. "Lord, I hope not!" the Post-Dispatch exclaimed.

"Mr. President," Arly Richardson said thoughtfully, "I shall not consume much time in stating the case for those who favor this nominee. And I shall begin by conceding one of the Senator's main points.

"It is hard to condone, and I do not condone, Mr. Leffingwell's handling of this episode in his past. But I think that without condoning it, and without in any way defending his decision to resort to evasion before the subcommittee, that it is possible to find in it certain strengths of character that are far from the weakling the Senator from Illinois would have you see.

"Who but a strong man, Mr. President, would defend himself so vigorously? Who but a man of positive and unyielding personality would be so adamant and so serene in his own protection? I ask you if this is the act of a weakling?"

"Mr. President," Senator Knox said quickly, "will the Senator yield?"

"The Senator would not yield to me," Senator Richardson said. "I will not yield to the Senator."

"It was the act of a moral weakling, anyway!" Senator Knox shot out angrily, and the Senator from Arkansas said furiously, "Now, Mr. President, I have refused to yield!"

"The Senator is entirely correct," the Vice President said firmly. "The Senator from Illinois will be still. Proceed, Senator."

"I repeat, Mr. President," Arly said, breathing hard and looking flushed, "that this is not the act of a weakling. It is the act of a strong man. It is the act of a man who can be expected to bring to the defense of his country's interests the same unyielding firmness that he has brought to the defense of himself. It is the act of a man we can trust with the protection of the foreign policy of America."

"It won't wash," Rob Cunningham of Arizona murmured to Rowlett Clark of Alabama, and Rowlett, who up to that very moment hadn't known what he was going to do, nodded suddenly and agreed, "You're right, it won't wash."

"Furthermore, Mr. President," Senator Richardson said, "it seems to me we have rather lost sight of this man's long record of public service and his many fine qualifications for this job. I hope this will not be wiped out entirely in the minds of Senators by one unfortunate foible of his youth. This, after all, is a great public servant, one of the greatest the American system has produced; and that I think is recognized even by his most hostile critics. Let us not forget that.

"Finally," he said, "let us turn to one other basic fact that the Senator from Illinois has overlooked, and that is that this man has been chosen by the President of the United States because he feels he needs his assistance in these parlous times. This is not some junior clerk we are discussing here. This is the man the President has chosen to be his principal assistant in foreign affairs.

"Is it the purpose, is it the duty, is it even, really, the right, of the Senate to set itself up to pass judgment upon the President's choice of this principal assistant? Mr. President," he said hastily, for Senator Cooley was on his feet, holding aloft a copy of the Constitution to which he pointed elaborately as he turned slowly about to all points of the chamber before grinning sleepily and sitting down, "of course we have a constitutional right to advise and consent to this nomination. But I mean, do we have a personal right, so to speak, to interpose ourselves between the President and a man he wants to sit beside him and work with him in these matters of such fearful import to our country? This," he said rather lamely, "is something I think Senators should consider.

"A final word," he said, "as to the personal views of the nominee, of which the Senator from Illinois makes such a point. I too heard his testimony. I too have read his book. The record of the hearing will show that I was as sharp in my arguments with his philosophy as any other Senator on the subcommittee. I cannot conceive, however, that he would carry this philosophy so far as to endanger the country. I simply do not believe it, for I do not believe any patriotic American would do so, and I believe he is a very patriotic American.

"And so, Mr. President," he said, "I urge the Senate to confirm this nomination. We are in an extraordinarily dangerous hour for America. The President wants him, the President needs him, the President is asking us to give him this man's help. I believe it is our patriotic duty to do it."

"Mr. President," Orrin Knox said, "is the Senator finished with the main burden of his remarks, and will he yield to me now?"

"Briefly," Arly Richardson said.

"I'll be brief," Orrin promised grimly. "Mr. President," he said angrily, "I will simply not stand for this to be put on a sentimental, emotional basis of helping the President! He has conducted a cold-blooded, calculated, unprincipled campaign to confirm this man, a campaign which has brought many evils in its train including a death in this Senate. I will not permit the Senate to be confused with this touching picture of the President in need. The President has brought this on himself. He has his responsibility, and he has chosen to exercise it in a way that has defeated his purpose and caused much controversy and unhappiness. We have our responsibility, and it is time we exercised it and put an end to this shabby, unfortunate business. I ask for the Yeas and Nays, Mr. President!"

"Mr. President," Senator Richardson said calmly, for there was no point in further talk, he might lose such votes as he had if the debate continued, "I join the Senator in that request."

Hands went up all across the chamber, and the Vice President said, "Evidently a sufficient number."

"I suggest the absence of a quorum, Mr. President," the Majority Leader said, and while the clerk droned once again through the roster the tension rose rapidly in the big brown room. Suddenly this was it, at last, after almost two weeks of bitterness and trouble and tragedy and strain, and the excitement suddenly flared as it always does before a final roll call. Members of the House, Senate staff members, and aides came in and crowded six and seven deep along the back wall; every seat in the public

galleries was filled; in the diplomatic gallery the Barres and the Maudulaynes, sitting together, leaned forward intently while near them Vasily
Tashikov looked impassive and K.K. looked nervous; out in the hall a line
of waiting visitors who had no chance of getting in wound four abreast
along the corridor, down the stairs, and along the hall below; the press
gallery buzzed with reporters sitting, standing, filling every seat, and
crowding in the aisles. With the exception of Fred Van Ackerman, absent
in Arizona, and Reverdy Johnson of Alabama, lying in his living death at
the Mayflower, every Senator was present. Ninety-seven men and one
woman were about to pass judgment upon Robert A. Leffingwell, and
even though it was a foregone conclusion now what that judgment was
going to be, the moment could not be robbed of its fearful tension and
high, paralyzing excitement.

"A quorum is present," the Vice President announced to a chamber
that was suddenly absolutely silent. "The pending business is the nomination of Robert A. Leffingwell to be Secretary of State. The question is,
Will the Senate advise and consent to this nomination? The Yeas and
Nays have been ordered, and the clerk will call the roll."

"Mr. Abbott!" the clerk said solemnly, and the junior Senator from New
Hampshire, who had not gotten his hoped-for aid for the Portland Navy
Yard, shot the Majority Leader a spiteful look and said:

"No!"

"Mrs. Adams!" the clerk said, and the senior Senator from Kansas, not
looking up from her desk, spoke quietly.

"No," she said.

"Mr. Andrews!" the clerk said, Murfee Andrews hesitated a moment and
said, "Yes!" in a firm voice, and there was an excited intake of breath
across the galleries.

"Mr. Albertson!" the clerk said, and the junior Senator from West
Virginia said in a loud voice, "No!"

"Mr. Allen!" the clerk said, the bustling little professor from South
Dakota said, "Yes!" in a chirpy voice, and again there was the sudden
tense inhalation.

But as the Clerk moved slowly and deliberately on, through the rest of
the A's, John Baker of Kentucky and the B's, on through the C's and
the two D's—"Yes," said Stanley Danta quietly, and, "No," said John
DeWilton loudly after—the E's and the lone F, Hal Fry, who said, "No!"
emphatically, on down the alphabet to the M's and O's and P's and Arly
Richardson, whose "Yes!" came with a certain spiteful air, it was obvious
that nothing could stem the tide. The press gallery began to stir with a
great restlessness, and long before the clerk came at last to "Mr. Wilson!"
and the tension suddenly burst in a roar of excitement, the wire-service
reporters were already long gone with their

FLASH. SENATE DEFEATS LEFFINGWELL.

There remained then only the quick tally by the clerk, the whispered consultation with the Vice President, the bang of his gavel, and in Harley's voice, trembling just a little with excitement, the official result:

"On this vote the Yeas are twenty-four, the Nays are seventy-four, and the Senate does *not* advise and consent to the nomination of Robert A. Leffingwell."

After that for a while order was unknown in the Senate as the tension exploded, voices rose, and in a sort of restless migration many Senators got up and moved about the floor talking to one another while in the galleries prolonged applause met boos and hisses and there was actually one brief fist fight, hastily quelled by the guards, between a triumphant opponent of the nominee and one of his frustrated adherents.

Five minutes later, a reasonable semblance of decorum restored, the Majority Leader, thinking again how simple and yet how marvelous the free deciding of free men was, said quietly,

"Mr. President, I move that the Senate stand in adjournment until noon on Monday."

"Without objection," the Vice President said with equal quietness, "it is so ordered."

And so, thus peaceably and in the traditional, continuing way, at eleven o'clock and twenty-four minutes P.M., the process was completed and the deed was done.

But if the Senate and the press and the diplomatic corps and the whole wide world thought that this was the last FLASH out of Washington that night, they were most profoundly mistaken and it was not very long before they knew it.

It was only a very little while after the story of the vote had gone out upon the wire and begun its repeated circlings and recirclings of the troubled globe that there occurred within the heart and mind and body of a certain famous man in a certain famous house a most sudden and surprising—at least that was his expression, surprise, in the brief second he had in which to feel it—and fearful spasm of his system. He had no time to even make a sound as it hit him. One hand flew to his chest, the other struck some books spread open upon the counterpane of the Lincoln bed; a piece of wire-service copy with NEW LEAD LEFFINGWELL on it, disturbed by his final convulsive movements, fell off upon the floor; and he slumped over and lay still.

Very shortly thereafter his secretary, entering at his orders but against his doctors' advice to take some late dictation, ran screaming from the room, and within twenty minutes after that his press secretary was announcing the news in a shaking voice to reporters hastily summoned.

Within minutes after that men all around the globe were stopping thunderstruck, sobered and shaken and knowing that in that fateful moment the world had changed forever, so great is the power that resides in that one heart in that one house.

Five

Advise and Consent

For a day and a night, as tradition dictated, the dead President lay in state in the White House, and then on Saturday morning he left it for the last time and began the long, slow procession through the city to Union Station and the black-draped train that would carry him home to the great valley in California, now bright with poppies and strewn with spring, where he had been born. By order of his successor the Mansion was thrown open to the public on Friday, and all day long, in an endless line two abreast, shuffling and slow, native and foreign and black and white, they moved patiently up the curving drive, under the portico, into the East Room and around the candle-lit catafalque and slowly, slowly, out the door and down the other drive and out the East Gate. It was estimated by the press, which kept round-the-clock vigil as the day passed and the night came on and the city went fitfully to sleep and the dawn came again, that more than 200,000 people passed through 1600 Pennsylvania on this last farewell; and when the coffin on its horse-drawn caisson moved out the West Gate at 10 A.M., turned and started along Pennsylvania Avenue with its procession of sleek black limousines following behind, it was estimated that more than a million more lined the route.

On this day the weather was beautiful, the sun bright, the sky clear, a soft wind rising, a delicate felicity upon the world; and in the somber hush that held the city only the clop-clop of horses' hooves, the jingling of accoutrements, a sudden sob or outcry from some overcome citizen, and now and then the high, silver sound of birds disturbed the awesome solemnity of the hour. America buries her Presidents well, and this one, greatly loved and greatly hated, was no exception.

In the second car back, following the late President's widow, his daughter and son-in-law and twin grandsons, the figure of the new President and First Lady could be glimpsed by the crowds; a rather portly, kindly-looking couple, the man not very handsome, not very commanding, but friendly—they could all sense that. "He looks nice," they said to one another, and it pleased them, and he felt their pleasure. A warmth flowed out to him from his countrymen, compounded of their good will, their innate friendliness, their appreciation of his great burden, and their desperate hope that for all their sakes he might carry it well; and feeling this, he was comforted as he passed by, good-hearted and decent and well-meaning, shaken by the events of the past thirty-six hours but not shattered by them. He was not shattered at all, in fact, now that the event was actually here, and somehow this knowledge passed back to them, and they were comforted in turn.

In succeeding cars there came the members of the Cabinet, the leaders of the Congress and the Supreme Court (save for Mr. Justice Davis, who had gone three days ago to Jamaica, for his health), the Chief Justice riding with the Speaker of the House and the President Pro Tempore of the Senate, the senior Senator from South Carolina; behind them the Majority and Minority Leaders of the Senate and the Majority and Minority Leaders of the House; other Justices, senior members of both chambers including the senior Senator from Illinois and the senior Senator from Arkansas, and then a commingling of House and Senate, sub-Cabinet members and members of the late President's official family. One hundred and seven limousines were in the procession, and according to the AP, which clocked it at Treasury Corner, it took half an hour to pass a given point. It was fitting and proper that it should be so, for this was a man who had dreamed great dreams and done great things, and persuaded his country to dream and do them too, and it was right that he should be so honored.

So the cortege passed slowly along the silent Avenue under the bright blue sky, and as it did the thoughts of the men who had known him well, as the thoughts of those who had known him hardly at all, rode in the caisson up ahead with its trimmings and its trappings and its even-stepping grays with their slow-measured, jingling tread. The senior Senator from South Carolina, author of the severest and perhaps the only truly honest expression of opinion the press had received on that hectic midnight— "He was an evil man, and the Lord has rendered judgment upon him"— sat silent, bland, and unblinking as they rode along, his face impassive; men did not dare imagine what he might be thinking in that shrewd, unforgiving old mind. The Speaker too was silent, lost in thoughts of his own, not sad, not happy, simply accepting what time and politics had brought and planning how best he might adjust to the new personality in the White House. In their car following, the Majority Leader of the Senate caught from time to time the eye of the Minority Leader of the Senate, and between them there passed on several occasions a look of mingled regret, relief, and concern, regret as one regrets the passing of any major force of nature terrible and magnificent in its ability for good and its capacities for evil, relief that they no longer had to deal with him, concern for the pleasantly undistinguished man who had taken his place and now bore all their hopes.

And coming next in a car which he shared with Senator August and Senator Richardson, an ironic little expression in his eyes and around his mouth, the senior Senator from Illinois too was thinking of the figure who was gone. Their long, curious duet of affection and hate was over now, and aided by the blow of Providence, the Senator had won. Or had he been the instrument of Providence, forcing upon an overburdened heart the final pressure which had crushed it? And if he had been, had that too been Providence's purpose, or had he done something forever unforgivable to a fellow being?

He did not know, nor, as the cortege slowly turned off Pennsylvania into Constitution and then into Louisiana Avenue, moving on through the silent, massed spectators, did he know whether he should even bother to wonder. Things happened. Sometimes you controlled them, sometimes you forced them, sometimes they ran away with you or left you behind or suddenly did something you had not intended. If God has asked him, "Do you wish to kill the President?" he would have said no, like any decent man. But if God made him so act in a way that had in all probability helped to bring about that result, who was he to question the wisdom or the mystery of it? Being himself, he could have done no other. It did not seem to him profitable, in that hushed and solemn hour, to worry himself with doubts about it now.

In the final analysis, he knew honestly, he was glad his opponent was dead. He had regarded him for so long as both a personal obstacle and as the author of policies that were in some ways gravely detrimental to the country, that he could not help but be relieved in the private candor of his heart. Even he had not had the courage to say what Seab had said—only a years-long anger and the impregnable citadel of age permitted such shocking honesty—but he too felt a certain Old Testament judgment by Jehovah in the recent course of events. An eye for an eye, a tooth for a tooth—and a death for a death. He could not be too sorry.

As for what the man had accomplished, the lasting record he would leave in the history he was always so concerned about, that too the senior Senator from Illinois could not accurately discern. It took a long time to assess so dominant a personality and so forceful a career. Many men would be born and live and die before, looking back, their children could say with certainty, This was a good man, or, This was a bad.

The cortege reached the station, the caisson went slowly in, the limousines began to park in ordered ranks, their occupants got out and began walking soberly forward. There would be brief trainside ceremonies, the casket would be placed aboard the train, the mourners and the crowds would disperse; the long journey home across a sorrowing continent would begin.

Going in gravely with the Senator from Minnesota and the Senator from Arkansas, the eye of the Senator from Illinois fell suddenly upon an inscription carved high on the face of the great gateway building.

He that would bring home the wealth of the Indies, it said, *must carry the wealth of the Indies with him.*

And he thought of his opponent as he had seen him last on television, the commanding presence, the magnificent defiance, and as he had seen him in their last talk together, laying the Presidency itself on the line in one supreme gamble to save his political reputation and his political power; and he thought with a grim, inescapable admiration that he had indeed brought home the wealth of the Indies, and indeed had carried the wealth of the Indies with him; and what it had all meant for his country, of good or ill, what man in this hour could truly say?

2

"Bob," the President said, and the Majority Leader, scarcely back in his office from the ceremonies at the station, was startled by the vigor in that heretofore hesitantly amiable voice, "I would like you to have Seab and the Speaker call both houses into session this afternoon—not jointly, but so they can transact business. Will you do that for me?"

"Harl——" Senator Munson started to say reassuringly, and then stopped and started over again. "Mr. President," he said, "I'm sure we can do that. It's eleven-thirty now, nearly everybody is still in town, we can round them up without much trouble. Suppose we go in at one o'clock."

"Fine," the President said. "I want you to pass a joint resolution for me, if you will, expressing the support of Congress for me when I go to Geneva."

"Oh, you are going?" Bob Munson asked, for the silence on this since the late Chief Executive's death had caused great speculation and two arrogantly petulant calls at the State Department by the Soviet Ambassador. "You can probably duck it if you want to, you know. It was his obligation, not yours."

"It was the obligation of the President of the United States," the President said, rather tartly. "Certainly I'm going. Furthermore, I want you to go with me. Also Tom. Also Warren. Also——" He stopped abruptly. "Also somebody else you'll find out about later."

"The Secretary of State," the Majority Leader suggested. "I suppose you'll keep Howie on now and not make any change for a while, won't you?"

"No, indeed," The President said. He chuckled. "Now figure that one out," he said. Senator Munson chuckled too.

"I think you're beginning to like the job," he said.

"It's growing on me," the President admitted, and he didn't sound at all displeased. "I want to talk to the Senate about the State Department later in the afternoon."

"How do you mean, talk?" Senator Munson said.

"What I said, talk," the President told him. "After you've got the resolution out of the way, just stand by and I'll be coming along to tell you about your new Secretary of State. Some time around three P.M., I imagine—it shouldn't take you long on the resolution, should it?"

"Ten minutes," the Majority Leader said.

"Good," the President said.

"What's the news from outer space?" Bob Munson asked.

"All good," the President said. "We're on our way, high, wide, and handsome. We'll be there by Sunday, just as the Pres—just as my predecessor said. Not that it will solve very much."

"Nothing ever solves anything, very much," Senator Munson said, "particularly these days. But at least it will give us a little more equal standing."

"On the edge of hell," the President said. "I'll expect the three of you to go with me, then."

"Right," the Majority Leader said. "And, Harley," he added, "—Mr. President: don't be afraid."

"I'm not afraid," the President said firmly, and it was quite apparent that he wasn't. "I just want my old friends with me."

"Nothing," Bob Munson said, "could honor your old friends more."

"By the way," the President added casually, "where is the senior Senator from Illinois at this moment?"

"We're meeting for lunch in fifteen minutes," Senator Munson said.

"No, you're not," the President said. "I'm going to appropriate him to have lunch with me. Send him on down, will you?"

"Are you sure you can handle him alone?" Senator Munson asked dryly. "He'll be bursting with ideas on how you ought to run the government, you know."

"I can handle him," the President said.

The Majority Leader chuckled.

"All right, Mr. President," he said. "You're the boss."

"I aim to be," the President said cheerfully.

3

He didn't know why Harley wanted to see him, Senator Knox thought as he caught a cab once more for the East Gate, but it was a good thing he had asked to, it would save a lot of time, they would have a good chance to talk about the government and get things squared away for the new Administration. He felt that at the moment Harley needed plenty of good advice, for all his outward calm in the cortege this morning. Orrin could not forget the daze in which he had taken the oath, white and stunned, shortly after midnight in the oval office at the White House. The Chief Justice, hastily routed out of bed, had administered the awesome words in the presence of everyone who could possibly crowd into the room, and Harley's response had been barely audible. Many people had cried, and the new Chief Executive had looked as though he might, too. He had started to say something and then stopped, overcome; finally, "I want you all to know I shall do my best" was all he could manage. It had hardly seemed enough at the moment, but the press had made a great thing out of it on Friday morning, its sincerity, its humility, its simple goodness.

And those, the Senator reflected, were qualities that Harley could genuinely claim, and they were not by any means such inadequate qualities to have. In fact, they were about what he needed to meet this new situation; they and a little starch in his backbone which Orrin and his other friends might be able to give him. Certainly they had a duty to try, at any rate, for everyone who knew the President intimately must come to his assistance in this fearsome hour.

Thinking these thoughts, which brought a look of frowning concentration to his face, he walked past the Rose Garden and came again to the door he had entered two days ago. Curiously, it seemed to have changed with the change in personality that sat behind it. It no longer looked ten feet tall; there was no longer the sense of an imperial personality on the other side, looming over the nation. It was only Harley. He knocked briskly, was invited to enter, and walked in, still frowning in deep thought.

"My goodness," the President said mildly, "what have I done?"

"What?" Orrin asked, startled, and then smiled. "Nothing, Harley," he said. "I was just thinking."

"About the President, I suppose," his host said, and the Senator said, "No, about you."

"I am the President," his host pointed out gently, and before Orrin had time to really digest the kindly but ironic way in which he had said it, he gestured him politely to a chair. "Do sit down, Orrin," he said. "I'm awfully glad you could come. I've told them to send lunch for two in here. What would you like?"

"What are you having, Harl——" Senator Knox said and stopped. "Mr. President," he amended with a smile, and the President smiled too.

"I thought," he said, "that I would have some soup and a sandwich and coffee."

"That would be fine for me—Mr. President," Orrin said. He grinned. "You'll have to give me a little time, Harley. I'm not quite used to it yet."

"Me, either," the President admitted, "but I'm getting more so by the minute." He looked more serious. "I asked you down, Orrin, because I wanted to talk to you about the government. I wanted your advice."

"Why, Harley," the Senator said, looking pleased. "I think that's very nice of you, Mr. President."

"Oh, I expect you thought I should," the President said lightly. "Now, didn't you? I'll bet when you walked in here you were thinking, Well, I'm damned glad Harley had the sense to call on *me*. Isn't that right?"

Senator Knox had the grace to laugh. In fact he laughed quite hard, in honest amusement.

"You know me too well," he said.

"That's what I thought," the President said. "I told myself, if anybody thinks he ought to be advising me, it's Orrin Knox. And," he added seriously, "I told myself that if there was anybody I wanted advising me, it was Orrin Knox."

The Senator from Illinois gave him a sudden smile.

"Watch it, now," he said. "You're in danger of becoming as crafty as he was."

"Oh, I mean it," the President said honestly. "Of course," he added with a chuckle, "I didn't say to myself that I had to *take* Orrin's advice, you understand. I just felt I ought to have it."

Senator Knox smiled again.

"I swear," he said, "I think you're going to be good. I really do."

"I'm going to try," the President said. "I'm certainly going to try. Excuse me, and I'll order." He lifted the phone, did so, and turned back.

"What changes do you think I ought to make in domestic policy, Orrin?" he asked. Senator Knox answered promptly.

"Not too much," he said. "Maybe a little more liberalizing of things here and there. And a great deal more tightening up all along the line. He wasn't a very good administrator, for all his brilliance."

"No," the President agreed gravely. "He wasn't. I'd like to appoint a committee, mostly Cabinet but a few others, to go into that for me. Would you like to serve?"

"Anything you say," Orrin said. "Any way I can help."

"Good," the President said. "And in foreign policy, I think you've made your views pretty clear in recent days."

"I think so," the Senator said with a frown. "I've tried to do what I thought necessary and still explain it so people wouldn't think I was just being obstructionist."

"I think you've succeeded quite well," the President said. "I noticed the papers conceded you your sincerity yesterday morning after it was all over, even while deploring your actions."

"That's a pet trick of theirs," Orrin said dryly. "You'll find out."

"I expect," the President said as lunch arrived, "I'll find out a lot of things before I'm through here."

They were silent for a little. Presently the Senator from Illinois looked up.

"You know, Harley," he said and added with a smile, "I won't call you anything but 'Mr. President' after this, but just for a minute be Harley for me again—there's one thing I've always regretted, and one thing I've always wanted to do. And that's what I said at the convention. I want to apologize to you for it."

The President looked surprised, touched, and pleased.

"Why, thank you, Orrin," he said warmly. "You needn't. I knew you were under terrific strain, so I tried to forget it right away. I've never held it against you."

"Well, I appreciate that," Senator Knox said, feeling quite emotional. "It really has disturbed me many times, over the years."

"It's gone," the President said, and they shook hands solemnly. Then a little twinkle came into the President's eyes.

"By the way," he asked curiously, "what made you so sure that night that I was going to announce for him? The delegation voted unanimously to leave it to me and back whatever I decided to do. I was on my way up there to announce for you."

And having by this piece of true and hitherto undisclosed history silenced, for once, his volatile and determined friend, he proceeded to tell him what he had in mind; finding that Senator Knox, as he gradually revived from the appalled silence into which he had fallen, had many arguments and objections to offer; but finding also that as he went on further to outline his idea and explain its advantages the practical politician and responsible citizen before him began the grasp its possibilities and find them good. And so he should, the President thought with a tartness to match Orrin's own, for they were certainly hand-tailored for him.

When the Senator from Illinois returned to his own office he called his wife. She laughed as he related the conversation and a curiously light and relieved note came into her voice.

"You see?" she said. "Patience does it, Senator. Patience does it."

He gave a rueful laugh.

"Maybe I'm beginning to learn that," he said. "At last."

4

The joint resolution of support for the President, as the Majority Leader had predicted, went through the Senate in jig time, was sent promptly to the House, and by two-thirty had been passed there. A brief period of tense waiting ensued, while the galleries and chamber stirred restlessly expecting the Chief Executive's arrival. Then there was a sudden stir in the hall, the sergeant-at-arms came in and announced to Senator Cooley in the Chair, "Mr. President, the President of the United States!" And looking a little nervous but smiling about him in a friendly way, the President returned to the friends he knew so well, who thought they knew him so well.

Just before he began to speak, while they were all standing and applauding wildly, he took a pencil from his vest pocket, scratched out the word "peril" in the first line of his text and wrote in firmly "concern." Then he began.

"Mr. President," he said, "my dear friends of the Senate:

"I come before you in this hour of our beloved country's concern to make a brief statement of my plans and purposes for the government. I expect when I return from Geneva to appear before both houses in joint session and talk more fully about what I have in mind. I appear in the Senate this afternoon because here rests the most immediately pressing problem that faces"—and he said the next two words with a little air of pride that they found quite touching—"my Administration: namely, the selection of a Secretary of State.

"I think," he said, and he spoke with a deliberate slowness that held them absolutely silent, these men who thought they knew Harley Hudson and were suddenly beginning to wonder if they did, "that before I give you my nomination for that office, I should make a clear, unequivocal, and final statement of my own plans."

He paused and there was a tensing through the room, on the floor, along the walls, in the public galleries and in the press gallery, where reporters stood poised to dash up the steps and file their bulletins.

"I did not," he said quietly, "wish to be President of the United States. There was a time when I did, but that had long since passed. But now that the burden has been laid upon me in this tragic fashion, I expect to bear it to the best of my ability. I expect to bear it to the end of the present term. Then," he said, "I shall lay it down."

At this there was an excited stirring through the chamber, quickly stilled. Oh, Harley, the Majority Leader told him silently in his mind, my boy, I expect you are about to be very clever, very, very clever indeed.

"I shall not, in other words," the President said, "be a candidate for election to the Presidency next year. This announcement is final. I make it now so that you may act upon what I shall now ask you to act upon with no thought of partisan politics whatever, but only in the thought of what is best for our dear country. For it is in that spirit that I stand before you now."

He stopped and slowly took a sip of water as the first relays of wire-service reporters rushed out to file their FLASH. PRESIDENT WON'T RUN NEXT YEAR.

"I am well aware," the President went on quietly, "as are all of us in this Senate—more aware than anyone outside could be, for this has been our testing and our travail and our unhappiness here in this chamber, in a way no one who has not been directly involved in it could understand— of all the somber aspects surrounding the nomination upon which you voted Thursday night.

"On that nomination you rendered your final decision. You decided, by an irreversible vote, that you did not wish Robert A. Leffingwell to be Secretary of State. In that decision I concur. "Yet"—and he looked slowly and directly across all the chamber, all the tensely waiting faces of the colleagues he knew so well—"I must tell you that I do not wish to lose the abilities of Robert A. Leffingwell, which are great, or the services of Robert A. Leffingwell, which are many and worthy. I must tell you that I wish him to be a part of my Administration."

Again there was a stirring, uneasy and almost hostile, but he went firmly on.

"I say this because he is a valuable man within the sphere of his own competence. The reasons for his defeat yesterday were complex, and not all of them bore directly upon his abilities. I hope that having done what, under the circumstances, it had to do, the Senate will now reappraise this man, understanding that he has great support in many sections of the national community, understanding that national unity at this time is imperative, understanding that he, too, perhaps, may have paid in full, in his way, for his errors; and trusting"—and his voice became solemn with a note they had never heard from him before—"that you will have faith in your President, a man whose integrity as well as his frailties I hope you have all had occasion to note over the years, when he asks you to give this man another chance.

"I have decided," he said, "to create a special commission, somewhat similar to the Hoover Commission, to study and overhaul the administrative side of the government, something which has not been done for some years and which I think badly needs doing. To the post of executive director of this commission, a post for which I think his administrative abilities amply qualify him, I should like to appoint Robert A. Leffingwell. It is not a post which requires Senate confirmation, and I shall not submit his name to you for confirmation; neither is it a policy post, for I take it the Senate does not want him in such a post. But it is a post where I think he can be of real assistance to the country, and I should like to think that you will understand my reasons and will not criticize them too harshly.

"I feel that I can use him. I feel the country can use him. I had a long talk with him yesterday afternoon, after he had submitted to me his resignation from the government, which he felt he should do in the light of your vote, and I am satisfied that he will justify your confidence if you will give it to him. I will say to you, too," he added thoughtfully, "that I have the assurances of the man I have decided to nominate for Secretary of State that he too is willing to give him a second chance in this post which will in no way impinge upon policy, foreign or domestic. I would hope, now that the heat of controversy has died a little, that you would understand and support this particular solution for this particular problem."

He paused, and in the little private conversation Bob Munson was carrying on in his mind he paid tribute to the unexpected and surprising shrewdness of the man before them. For this of course was by no means an ideal solution for anything, but rather an astute and practical move to both mollify and win the active support of the many vocal and powerful elements that had backed the nominee. In this it was both politically perceptive and quite symbolic of the government in which it occurred. In a way, he thought sardonically, this was a perfect democratic solution, not wholly satisfying anybody, not wholly antagonizing anybody, not white, not black, not good, not bad; pragmatic, realistic, sensible within the context and climate in which the President, any President, must operate if he would lead his widely diverse land; and gratifying completely neither the idealistic who had opposed Robert A. Leffingwell nor the idealistic who had supported him.

At these thoughts, wry and half-amused and filled with the wisdom of many years experience with the government of his country, the Majority Leader glanced at Orrin Knox with a quizzical grin and shook his head in mock wonderment; but the senior Senator from Illinois did not seem amused. Instead he looked back with a strange expression Senator Munson did not understand, and nodded absently. The Majority Leader wondered in some alarm if Orrin were going to raise more hell at this late date. He hoped not. Surely he wouldn't if Harley asked him not to. Harley, after all, was the President.

"I come now," the President said, "to the nomination for Secretary of State. I shall say little on this score, because I do not need to. I shall say only that I hope you will speedily confirm his nomination, for I must leave tomorrow morning for Geneva and the time is short."

He paused and slowly gathered up the sheets of his speech, looking down upon them thoughtfully and placing them neatly back in their folder before he spoke. Then he looked up again, directly and strongly out across the room, once again meeting their eyes squarely all around the Senate.

"I nominate," he said quietly, "for the high office of Secretary of State my old colleague and dear friend, the senior Senator from the State of Illinois."

Into the pandemonium that followed UPI looked dazedly at AP.

"But—but—but——" He said.

"God damn it, man," AP shouted, clapping him on the back, "don't stand there and gibber. Get up there and *write!*"

And so they did.

5

Long before the presidential party started at 9 A.M. Sunday from the White House out across Fourteenth Street Bridge and over the Potomac, the crowds had begun to gather at National Airport, coming up from Maryland, over from the District, in from nearby Virginia. By eight-thirty, when the presidential plane and the accompanying plane for the State Department delegation to the conference were wheeled slowly out on the apron, there were an estimated 175,000 people massed about the field entrance to the MATS terminal; and shortly before nine-twenty, when amid screaming sirens and the usual accompaniment of motorcycle out-riders the President's limousine and the four cars following arrived at the field and drove out on the apron with a flourish, police and press estimated that the figure had grown close to 300,000.

To this great gathering, covered by every means of press, television, and radio, carried throughout the nation and overseas, the President's words were brief as he stood on a platform facing them in the bright blue day. Flanked by the leaders of the Senate, the new Secretary of State, the Speaker, and the President Pro Tempore of the Senate, he looked wind-blown, kindly, earnest, and unperturbed.

"My countrymen," he said in a clear voice that boomed across the field in the waiting hush, "I am leaving now for Geneva. I go on your behalf, and I think," he said, "that I go with your love."

At this there was a great roar from the crowd and he paused, obviously touched.

"Apparently," he said, "I do. I hope this will be noted in certain places where it will do the most good."

There was a burst of laughter and applause.

"I cannot promise you," he said soberly, "that the United States will emerge from this conference with all her objectives in the cause of peace achieved." A deep silence suddenly fell. "But I can promise you," he said, and his voice rang out firmly and emphatically, "that she will not come home with any of her objectives abandoned, or any of her principles yielded, or any of her courage diminished." And a great roar came again.

"The United States and her President," he said, "are unafraid. We go in good faith, pledged to do our honest best, striving always for a decent and lasting peace. From this purpose we cannot be intimidated or diverted. Humanity knows it can trust us. We will not let humanity down." And the roar came again.

"Now," he said, almost conversationally, "it is time to say good-by—or, rather, *au revoir*. In these brief hours that I have been your President, you have been more than kind to me. Your love has sustained me in all I have done for you so far. I know it will sustain me until I return, bringing safely home to you the dignity, the future, *and the honor* of the United States of America—intact.

"God bless you all. Thank you so much for coming out to see me off."

He waved and turned, and while the roar of shouts and applause grew and swelled again, the members of his party also waved and began to enter the planes.

He held out both hands, one to the Speaker and one to the President Pro Tempore, and gripped them firmly.

"Take care of things," he said, and they both smiled in a fatherly fashion.

"Don't you worry, Mr. President," the Speaker said. "Old Seab and I, we'll mind the store."

"Yes, sir," Senator Cooley said, and he gave the President's hand an extra squeeze. "Now just you don't worry about a thing, Harley. Just you don't worry. After all," he grinned sleepily and poked the Speaker, "Bill and I, here, we've wanted to be President too, you know, from time to time. Now's our chance to show our stuff." He chuckled. "Yes, sir, now's our chance to show our stuff."

"God bless you both," the President said seriously. "I only wish you could be with me."

"Keep us advised," the Speaker suggested, and the President nodded. "Daily," he said.

And then with one last wave to the crowd he entered his plane, the door closed, the great silver machines began to taxi slowly down the runway, turned at the far end and came back, faster and faster and faster until suddenly they were airborne and on their way.

The crowd followed them intently, in utter silence, until they were no more than little silver dots. Then suddenly they were lost, and over all the great field a curious, profoundly moving sigh went up before the throng began to disperse and go home.

Sitting silently in the forward plane as it passed over Balitmore and moved up the spring-green Maryland countryside, the presidential party was lost in its thoughts. There seemed little need for conversation and for a while there was none.

Senator August read a magazine or stared out the window. The President, appearing perfectly calm, leaned back in his seat and closed his eyes. The Majority Leader, feeling comforted by this homely sight, tossed a quick, kindly glance of amusement at the Minority Leader, and did the same. Only the new Secretary of State seemed wide awake and unable to doze.

He that would bring home the wealth of the Indies, it had said, *must carry the wealth of the Indies with him.*

Well, he had gone forth—the country had gone forth—now they in this plane were going forth, hoping to bring home, not the wealth of the Indies, perhaps, but only, if they possibly could, a little pinch of accommodation with this enemy so hostile to every human decency in the world; and not necessarily carrying the wealth of the Indies with them, but only a few scraps of things, the memory of a meeting in Philadelphia, a speech at Gettysburg, a few fragments of valor still echoing down the American wind from distant battles and far-off things, Chancellorsville and The Wilderness, the Alamo and San Juan Hill, Belleau Wood and the Argonne, Bataan and Corregidor, Omaha Beach and Salerno, Midway, Iwo Jima, Guadalcanal; a certain way of looking at things, a certain way of living, a form of government that might or might not turn out to be all it was cracked up to be, when all was said and done: on that the final judgment had not yet been rendered.

And what of his own pilgrimage stretching back down the years to Springfield and ahead to—what? He couldn't say—he would have to wait and see—time would have to tell. It would be just his luck, he thought with a wry inward smile, for the President to stumble in his good-hearted innocent way upon some utterly unexpected triumph that would bring him home a hero, cancel out his determination not to run next year, and so once more foreclose his own chances . . . And if he did, so what? He would not fret over that, Orrin thought. It would probably be for the best in a greater design than his.

Who knew? Who could tell? At least he was no longer so restless, at least he was beginning to find a reasonable equanimity, at least in the rushing events of the past three days, beginning with the shattering revelation of what he had done to himself at the convention and culminating in his appointment as Secretary of State, he had begun to take things as they came, without too much impatience and too much anguish and too much regret. And that, perhaps, was wealth enough of the Indies for him.

So they rode on, old friends from the Senate together carrying their country's hopes, while below America sped away, the kindly, pleasant, greening land about to learn whether history still had a place for a nation so strangely composed of great ideals and uneasy compromise as she.

Washington–Orlando–Sanibel
October, 1957–November, 1958